THE WIDOW QUEEN

THE WIDOW QUEEN

ELŻBIETA CHEREZIŃSKA

Translated by Maya Zakrzewska-Pim

A TOM DOHERTY ASSOCIATES BOOK
New York

THE WIDOW QUEEN

Copyright © 2016 by Elżbieta Cherezińska

English translation © 2020 by Tor

Translation by Maya Zakrzewska-Pim

Originally published as *Harda* in 2016 by Zysk i S-ka Wydawnictwo s.j. in Poznań.

All rights reserved.

A Forge Book
Published by Tom Doherty Associates
120 Broadway
New York, NY 10271

www.tor-forge.com

Forge® is a registered trademark of Macmillan Publishing Group, LLC.

The Library of Congress Cataloging-in-Publication Data is available upon request.

ISBN 978-1-250-21800-1 (hardcover)
ISBN 978-1-250-21798-1 (ebook)

Our books may be purchased in bulk for promotional, educational, or business use.
Please contact your local bookseller or the Macmillan Corporate and
Premium Sales Department at 1-800-221-7945, extension 5442,
or by email at MacmillanSpecialMarkets@macmillan.com.

First Edition: April 2021

Printed in the United States of America

0 9 8 7 6 5 4 3 2 1

To all the anonymous, forgotten princesses
The nuns, wives, mothers, and rulers about whom history is silent
The girls marked in biographies of dynasties with a sad "N.N."

The Aesti

Veliky Novgorod

The Livonians

NOVGORODIAN
RUŚ

The Novgorod Slavs

The Lithuanians

Połock

The Yotvingians

The
Krivichs

...ans

...ians

Drohiczyn

The
Radimichs

...sovia

Brześć

...zersk

...OLAND

Lublin

KIEVAN
RUŚ

Wołyń

Kiev

Sandomierz

THE CHERVEN CITIES
(UNDER POLISH RULE
UNTIL 981)

...aków

Przemyśl

...Sącz

The Volhynians

Halicz

...NDS

...UNGARY

POLAND
in the 10th century

THE BRITISH ISLES
in the 10th century

NO[RTH]
SEA

ALBA

Bamburgh

NORTHUMBRIA

IRELAND

ISLE OF
MAN

Slane

York

GWYNEDD

Nottingham

POWYS

MERCIA

EAST
ANGLIA

ANGLIA

Ipswich

DYFED

ESSEX

Oxford

GWENT

Maldon

London

WESSEX

Andover

Canterbury

Sandw[ich]

Winchester

KENT

Folkesto[ne]

HAMPSHIRE

SUSSEX

Southampton

CORNWALL

Exeter

THE SOLENT

ISLE OF
WIGHT

ISLES OF
SCILLY

SCANDINAVIA
in the 10th century

FINNMARK

LAPLAND

LOFOTEN

HÁLOGALAND

NORWAY

JAMTLAND

SWEDEN

Agdanes
Lade
Nidaros
Trondheim
TRØNDELAG

SUNNMØRE
Hjorungavagr

SOGN   OPPLAND

SOGNEFJORD

HORDALAND   DALARNA

THE ÅLAND ISLANDS

The Finns

ROGALAND   VIKEN

AGDER

Fyrisvellir
Birka   Uppsala
Sigtuna
LAKE MÄLAR

GULF OF FINLAND

The Aesti

Sola

HAFRSFJORD

RANRIKE

HALLAND

SKAGERRAK

SWEDEN

GOTLAND

NORTH SEA

Hobro
Viborg
DENMARK
Jelling   Roskilde
Leire
DENMARK

BLEKINGE
DENMARK
SKANIA
Lund

Ribe

Trelleborg
Arkona

BORNHOLM

Gdańsk
RÜGEN   Kołobrzeg   Truso
Jomsborg
Wolin   POLAND

The Lithuanians

The Prussians

Hedeby

Lübeka
Hamburg
THE CONFEDERACY OF THE VELETI

A.D. 960

The Prince of the Forest Glades

Duke Mieszko I of Poland was the fourth son of the Piast line and the strongest of them yet; a ruthless leader who expanded Poland's borders through cunning and strength. For the good of his growing young nation, he married a Czech princess, Dobrawa, and brought her father's armies and her religion to Poland. For her, Mieszko betrayed the old gods and slayed the old priests. The duke had many children with many wives, but Dobrawa was his true love. The two children she gave him bore the weight of the dynasty on their shoulders: their son, Bolesław, and their daughter, who came into the world under dark omens. And so, like a spell for happiness and strength, they gave her a holy name—Świętosława, she was called. The bold one.

PART I
LAMBS TO
THE SLAUGHTER

⚜

The Piast House
984–985

1

##

POLAND

The island in the middle of the frozen lake, the home of the great Polish duke, was lit by cold moonlight.

Like every winter, the ice connected the island to the surrounding banks, but the stronghold could not be reached by crossing the frozen waters. The bridges were the only way to reach the duke's dwelling, which was guarded by double ramparts, high as ash trees. Two bridges, like mooring ropes holding boats in place. West and East. Two arms, like a mother's, nursing her child. The western bridge led to the road to Poznań. The eastern—to Gniezno. Between them was the isle of Ostrów Lednicki, hidden like a treasure. After all, it was a treasure hold. The dynasty's hidden nest. The place where the duke's children were raised. And the bridges, like umbilical cords, could lead those children into the world. Two bridges, two children who had almost reached adulthood, and ice all around them, on a night lit up by a winter's full moon.

Świętosława let her eyelids fall shut. She was sitting on a wide bench with her legs tucked beneath her, a servant combing her long hair. Small clouds of mist escaped with her every breath. She was breathing deeper and deeper, until she finally rested her head on the soft fox fur that covered the bench. Her hair fluttered as it fell below the backrest. The hand holding the comb froze in midair.

"Is she asleep?" the servant asked, looking to the corner of the chamber, where a girl in a simple woolen dress sat on an iron-clad chest. She sat in the same position as Świętosława, with her legs tucked under her, head cocked to one side. Her face revealed nothing.

Bolesław moved his shoulders to settle his chain mail over his leather caftan. He buckled his belt. He checked that his knife slid smoothly from its sheath.

Sweeping hair away from his face, he glanced at his waiting comrades. Dark-eyed Zarad, ginger Bjornar, and fair-haired, skinny Jaksa stood at the chamber's door watching him tensely. Two dogs lay at Bolesław's feet.

"Ready?" he asked.

"Your cloak," Jaksa said, throwing him the wolf-fur-lined wool.

"Gloves," Bjornar added as he passed them over.

"And your sword." Zarad's eyes flashed in the chamber's darkness.

One of the dogs raised its head, alert.

"No," Bolesław said, pulling on his gloves. A barely discernible shadow flickered across his face. "That wasn't Father's order."

The other three nodded as if on command, and Zarad whistled quietly with admiration for the absent man.

"The duke," he added.

They left the room, leaving the door open. Bolesław called back over his shoulder:

"Duszan, guard the dogs!"

Their footsteps echoed on the stone floor of the palatium, then—nothing. A young man emerged from the shadows. Slender and tall, dressed inconspicuously, unarmed. The dogs whined. Duszan walked over and patted their heads. He poured water into their bowls and began to pick up the items strewn around the room. He placed the sword carefully back on its stand.

Świętosława lay draped over the bench.

"Is the princess asleep?" The servant repeated the question insistently.

The girl rose from the chest silently and walked over to the princess's still form. She crouched next to Świętosława and, gently sweeping away her hair, looked in the princess's face. The silent girl raised her eyes to the servant and nodded in confirmation.

The servant sighed with relief. She covered Świętosława with a blanket and picked up the objects scattered around them. Two bone combs, a hairband decorated with silver, silk hair ribbons for plaits. She closed it all in a box and glanced nervously around the room. A cup of now-cold tea stood on the edge of the table. The servant poured it into the fire, and the remnants evaporated quickly. She dried her fingers on the edge of her dress.

"Take off her shoes when she wakes up. Help her get into bed, cover her, and wait by the fire. Anyway, you know what to do," she said to the girl, and left without waiting for a response.

The door closed behind her with a hollow clunk.

Świętosława was a master at faking sleep. Now, she opened her eyes, which were dark with anger.

"What a bitch," she whispered to the girl crouched in front of her.

The girl placed a finger on her lips and gestured toward the door. Świętosława remained on the bench, but pushed away the covers. They could hear footsteps approaching the other side of the door. The two looked at each other, keeping still. Then the silent girl took the blanket and laid it on the stone floor. The princess was wearing tall, hobnailed boots, but they made no sound as the girls walked carefully across the soft fabric.

Bolesław listened to the rhythm of footsteps on the bridge. Counting the steady footfalls helped to steady his own thoughts. One, two. One, two. One, two. After another moment, he stepped onto the bridge, too, Bjornar and Zarad by his side, Jaksa bringing up the rear.

The East Bridge. As a boy, it had taken him four hundred steps to cross it. Then, three hundred. Every year, he would check, until now, at sixteen, it took him the same number of steps as it took a grown man. Two hundred and fifty.

Father took only strong, fit, well-built men into his personal squad. Those who needed only two hundred and fifty steps to cross the East Bridge. Father. The duke. Bestowed by their people with love and fear in equal measure. A master of politics, who switched alliances faster than the wind changes direction. A warrior at the head of a boundlessly loyal army. A father with an iron hand on the back of his son's neck. Bolesław did only what his father wanted. So, what did he want tonight? The night before the winter festival? Why had his father ordered him to come, unarmed, to the harbor by the East Bridge? One, two, one, two. Bolesław tried again to let the rhythm of their steps in the night's silence calm his racing thoughts.

For sixteen years, Bolesław had been the duke's only son. Until a few months ago, when Father's wife—whose reign had begun after the death of Bolesław's mother, Dobrawa—had given birth to a son. A son to whom the duke had given his own name, Mieszko the Second.

It hurt, like a slap in the face. Until then, Dobrawa's two children, like the island's two bridges, had been the only ones that mattered. They would secure their father's legacy as the first ruler of a united Poland.

Father had more daughters, from the olden days, the old wives, but that was a different story. None of them could threaten his sister's position, the daughter of Dobrawa, the woman Mieszko had given up the old religion for, had taken the baptism and forsaken all other gods and wives for. Świętosława would be okay. Daughters were the seals of peace, alliances, ceasefires. But the heir is always the son. The son!

A few days earlier, there had been a feast to celebrate Duchess Oda, as beautiful as a dancing flame but as cold as ice, and her newborn son. Oda wearing new golden earrings, the child—the wedge between Bolesław and his father—on her lap.

"My Mieszko!" Father had toasted and laughed, Bolesław gritting his teeth and Oda listening to a monk read the story of Abraham and Isaac. When Abraham was building the altar on top of the mountain, Oda blushed and interrupted the monk with a swish of her slender, ringed hand.

"Enough. Mieszko is too young to listen to these horrors." But the duke had protested: "If he wants to be a duke, he should listen, just like Abraham listened to the commands of his god. Unconditionally." He had ordered more mead brought out then, as if this word—*unconditionally*—gave him pleasure. He drank with his squad and didn't see how Oda's expression brightened the closer the firstborn son was to being sacrificed in the monk's tale. Bolesław, though, couldn't take his eyes off her. He watched as she stroked her son's blond head, hugging him to her breast; how she raised her chin commandingly.

And that was why, now, as he walked the East Bridge at his father's orders, he felt fear. Fear which he tried to dispel with the confident rhythm of his footsteps. One, two. One, two. Was there an altar awaiting him at the docks? One, two. He touched the knife at his belt absentmindedly. He had another in his boot. One, two.

Whatever happened next, he wasn't going to be a lamb led to slaughter.

Świętosława listened by the door. She heard the clang of weaponry against a belt's metal fittings. It sounded like two, maybe three men, accompanied by the click of a woman's shoes.

"Is she asleep?" The haughty voice could belong only to Oda. Świętosława could have sworn she smelled the cloying scent of the rose oil the duchess dabbed on her temples and heard the musical chime of her new, prized golden earrings.

"As you commanded, my lady," replied Juta, the servant who had been combing her hair only moments before. "She's asleep, and won't wake up anytime soon."

Świętosława gritted her teeth. She should have guessed whose orders the servant had been following.

"Good. Is she alone?"

"Yes. That is, only Dusza is with her, the clod."

"Good. You can retire for the evening, too." The hint of a German accent, Oda's mother tongue, coloring her command. Then the click of the servant's shoes retreated and grew faint, along with the metallic clang of the duchess's guard.

Silence fell behind the door. Świętosława turned and looked into the silent girl's gray eyes. They gave away nothing. Świętosława climbed nimbly onto the bench by the wall and pulled herself up to reach the high window. She pushed the wooden window frame, and an icy breeze swept into the chamber. Two lines of torches were visible in the night, gliding toward land over the East Bridge.

One, two . . . she counted in her head. . . . nine, ten . . . Father is leading a whole squad out of Ostrów. On the night before Koliada? Her heart beat faster. Maybe it was time? For what other reason would a squad have to leave the stronghold at night, if not to greet an important guest?

She jumped off the bench. She forgot to close the window, so Dusza, wordlessly, climbed up and did it for her.

A guest, Świętosława thought frantically. The most important one of all. The one whose name they are still keeping from me . . .

"Come on, Dusza," she whispered. "Take your dress off. Tonight, we switch. I knew that . . ." Świętosława thought snake, but instead spat out: "Juta! She's in the duchess's service. I asked Father to let me make my own decisions about the servants, but no. 'My wife,' he says. 'Yes,' I tell him, 'she's your wife, but not my mother!' What was in the cup?" she looked at Dusza.

The girl stood in front of her in a white linen shift, her dress in hand, shivering in the cold room.

"Poison?" Świętosława asked.

Dusza shook her head and passed her dress to Świętosława, who turned and lifted her hair from her back. Dusza unlaced her mistress's dress with deft fingers. She helped Świętosława undress and replace the princess's fine garment with the rough wool one.

"So it wasn't poison?" Świętosława repeated, taking a breath with difficulty. "It's too tight. Your breasts are growing slower than mine."

She touched her own, held in by the fabric.

"Or perhaps mine grow too fast, since Father has been talking about marriage so much? My marriage, to God knows who!"

She reached out a hand for Dusza's cloak and hood.

"I'll ask for new ones to be made for you in a larger size. Ones that will fit us both. But, you know, it's a secret." She winked at Dusza as she pulled her hood over her head. "Do I look like a respectable servant? One who must run across the bridge on important business at night?" She spun around, laughing.

Dusza looked at the princess, not answering.

"Come on, get into bed and cover yourself up. Sleep, my Dusza!" Świętosława whispered. "Tonight, you are the Piast princess. Just don't get your hopes up for any sweet dreams."

She closed the door behind her and, with the hood covering her head, she walked boldly through the narrow corridors of the palatium. This wasn't the first time she and Dusza had done this. Escape, disguise, a small trick. Anything that would give her more information. "When will the delegates arrive?" she asked Father often, but he'd just laugh. "What tongue will I use with my husband?" she'd surprise him at the end of a feast, when his head would be swimming from drink, and in response he'd stick his tongue out at her. When he'd return from the hunt, she'd accost him with the question: "Where will I go? South, west, or east?"

"The East Bridge . . ." she whispered now, the chill from the frozen lake embracing her. "My husband will come from the east!"

She pulled the cloak tighter and, running across the bridge, looked for the flicker of torches. She wanted to know. Which of her father's alliances was she to guarantee? Kiev? Would it be Kiev? Duke Mieszko hadn't declared war on Rus yet, and he was already planning peace? *Ah!* she thought, *maybe the price of my hand is the return of the Red Cities* that were stolen from us last summer?*

Whatever awaited her this Koliada, she wasn't going to be a lamb led to slaughter.

Bolesław waited at the docks, as Father had commanded.

Zarad, Bjornar, and Jaksa stood beside him, as they always did. The four of them had trained together in a squad since they were children. Fights with wooden swords, archery, horse riding, wrestling, hand-to-hand combat from dawn until dusk. Bolesław could rely on these three as he could on himself. They were his brothers, not of birth and blood, but of bruises, shared sweat-inducing effort, sprained ankles, dislocated wrists, broken fingers.

Father treated him as if he were any other boy on the training ground. Except he expected even more of him. And when Bolesław asked: "When

---

* An area of dispute between the Kingdom of Poland and Kievan Rus at the turn of the tenth and eleventh centuries.

will I get my own squad?" Mieszko laughed instead of answering. While he still needed three hundred steps to cross the East Bridge, Bolesław could convince himself it was only a matter of his youth. But when he crossed it like a man, in two hundred and fifty steps, without any tricks or exaggerated strides, and Father still only laughed, he thought perhaps there was something more hidden behind the merriment. Was it his stepmother's second pregnancy? With another son potentially on the way? Bolesław hadn't slept through the night since Mieszko had given his name to Oda's firstborn. He waited, not knowing what his father had planned for him. He shared his doubts with no one, not even the three brothers-in-arms standing with him tonight. If their bond was as deep as Bolesław thought it was, they should know. And if not, it wasn't as if they could help him anyway.

"I'm freezing," Zarad moaned. "The servants are probably still serving mulled mead in the hall."

"Are you cold, or do you want a drink?" Bjornar questioned him.

"It might get warm here in a minute," Jaksa whispered, pointing at the bridge.

Bolesław's heart raced again at the sight. Now the East Bridge echoed with the sound of marching soldiers, lit by fiery torches.

"Bloody hell," Zarad hissed. "What's going on?"

"I don't know," Jaksa replied. "But the duke is leading them."

"Bolesław." Bjornar nudged his side. "You . . ."

The young prince didn't reply. Father and his squad were walking off the bridge now, and turning toward them and the docks. Another dozen steps and they'd be on solid ground. Bolesław flexed his fingers, stiff from the cold even in his gloves. He stood straighter, a reflex at the sight of his father, and his comrades followed suit. The duke was in front of them now. Bolesław bowed.

He lifted his head slowly. First, he saw the high hobnailed boots. The chain mail that reached Mieszko's knees, and the sword hanging at his side. The studded sheath for his knife. The gloved hand resting on his belt. A royal red cloak lined with white dormouse fur. His father's dark beard, with a single white stripe, and a mustache stiff from the cold. Narrowed eyes. And a fighter's undecorated helm on his head.

"Son," Mieszko said in a voice that gave no hint at his intentions for the evening.

Twenty armed men stood behind him. Not twelve. Twenty.

"Father," Bolesław replied, struggling to keep his voice from breaking. "I'm here, as you commanded."

His father's men walked onto the dock, placed the torches in their holders, then stood still. Bolesław realized he and his friends were surrounded. He looked into his father's eyes.

"Start the fire," Mieszko ordered.

Bolesław thought of the monk's reading for Duchess Oda, how Abraham commanded Isaac to carry the logs to the top of Mount Moriah and build the sacrificial pyre with his own hands. He regretted the thought as Mieszko smiled sternly and said, "No, wait. Let my son and his companions do it."

Bolesław moved forward. He held his father's gaze as he passed him, until the last moment. He didn't turn around but he heard Bjornar, Jaksa, and Zarad's footsteps behind him. They walked to the boat shed, where logs waited in a neatly arranged stack. He looked at the naked tree trunks of the sparse wood behind the shed. He could . . . no, he couldn't. Escape was not an option. *I am the firstborn son, a prince, and not a coward who runs into the night.*

As he bent to pick up the wood, Bolesław slipped a hand into his boot. The knife was exactly where he'd placed it. His father was stronger, but not faster. His mates indicated they'd seen him. Zarad touched his own boot with a finger as well.

I'm not alone, Bolesław thought. *At least for a moment more, I'm not alone.*

They arranged the logs for the fire, all four of them crouching down to start it. Bjornar took the flint from Bolesław's shaking fingers so nimbly that Mieszko couldn't have noticed. He started the fire, and flames climbed up the dry wood.

"Son," Mieszko called. "Come here."

Bolesław went, forcing his back straight so that his father wouldn't notice how weak his knees were.

"Tonight is the last of the long nights," Mieszko said.

"It's Christmas tomorrow," Bolesław replied, not knowing whether there would be a tomorrow.

"Are you ready?" Mieszko asked.

"For what?" Bolesław replied, more aggressively than he'd intended.

His father laughed and took off his gloves.

"To face the cold!" He raised his hands to the fastenings of his cloak and dropped it to the ground. "What are you waiting for? Undress, young prince!"

The cold? Bolesław thought fervently, taking off his own gloves and cloak. *Not fire?*

His father threw the rest of his clothes off with ease, as if undressing in front of the army on a freezing winter night was a perfectly ordinary thing to do. Bolesław pulled off his shoes with cold fingers. He caught Zarad's eye. It was too late now. The hidden knife lay on the snow along with his boot. Bolesław slipped off his trousers, tossed them aside, then stood and stared straight ahead. In front of him, Mieszko was entirely naked. His thick hair fell to his shoulders. A golden cross gleamed on a chain around his neck, resting on his muscular chest, and he held an axe in one hand. The moon had sunk lower in the sky and now hung behind his father's back like a silver shield. Mieszko's skin steamed in the cold night air.

"Come with me, son." The duke touched Bolesław's bare shoulder, and it was as if he'd been burned. His father stepped out onto the ice. "Where do the shallows end?"

"There." Bolesław pointed automatically, used to following orders. He heard his voice in his own head and thought he sounded hoarse. There was only one thought at the forefront of his mind: *Father has an axe, and I have nothing.*

"Here," Mieszko stopped at the point where the water should have reached a grown man's shoulders, and handed the axe over. "Break the ice."

Does he want to drown me? Bolesław wondered, sinking the axe into the frozen lake. *Why did he undress too? Why did he bring eyewitnesses? The entire squad is watching . . .*

"Be careful," Mieszko said. "Listen as it breaks, so that it doesn't pull us under."

At that moment, a dry creak reached their ears, and bubbles of water appeared in the crack on the ice's surface.

"Cut out a hole," Mieszko commanded.

Bolesław swung the axe once, twice. He threw away chunks of ice. The water shone, reflecting the moon's silver shield.

"Carefully!" his father said. "Don't disturb the ice around the hole, or we won't have a way back."

"Way back?" Bolesław raised his head and looked at Mieszko.

"The duke and his firstborn," Mieszko replied, laughing. "The dynasty's future can't lose its footing on unstable ice. Give me the axe, that's enough."

Bolesław straightened and handed over the weapon.

"You're taller than me," Mieszko said, eyeing him, and for a moment Bolesław thought he heard pride in his voice. "We're going in!"

Father placed the axe on the ice and jumped into the water. He disappeared beneath the surface for less than a breath, and snorted as he emerged, shouting:

"What are you waiting for?!"

Bolesław crouched down, leaned on the edge of the ice, and slipped into the water with his eyes closed. The cold stabbed through him, robbing him of breath. The water covered his head. Then he felt his father's hands grasp him under the arms and pull him back to the surface. Bolesław broke through the water, catching his breath with difficulty.

"Can you stand?" his father asked.

"No!" He coughed, the icy water in his mouth and nose. "Can you?"

"I'm not as tall as you!" Father splashed water into his face, as if this was nothing but a game. "We have to keep moving, otherwise we'll freeze." Mieszko's eyes were bright as frost settled on his dark mustache.

"It's bloody cold, but let me tell you, when my father gave me my first squad, it was even colder." Mieszko's lips were blue. He leaned back his head and shouted into the night: "The trees were cracking open!"

"Squad?" Bolesław sputtered, his teeth chattering.

"Yes! It's Koliada tomorrow. I have a present for you, and I wanted to see whether you were ready to receive it. Get out, that's enough! And? Have you frozen yet?"

"No," Bolesław answered, pulling himself onto the ice. The surface creaked under his weight. "Shit, it's breaking!"

"No," Mieszko replied, pulling himself up from the water as well. "It's only . . ."

Mieszko didn't have a chance to finish. The section of ice he was climbing onto broke away and he was plunged back into the water. Bolesław grabbed the axe lying on the ice, and when his father emerged again, Mieszko was able to grasp the axe's handle and stay above the surface as he gasped for air. In that moment, they looked in each other's eyes, father and son, the edge of an axe between them, ready to dole out life or death. The silver-blue moonlight shone on on their blue lips.

"I'm getting you out!" Bolesław said, and carefully, but with all his strength, pulled the axe. Soon Mieszko was kneeling on the ice beside him. Bolesław offered him a hand. His father stood up and reached for the axe with his other arm.

"No, don't let go," he ordered Bolesław. "Grab onto the handle and pull up, on three."

They picked it up together, and the squad gathered on the bank responded with a cheerful shout, beating their weapons on their shields.

"And now we walk."

They turned toward the bank and took a step, then another. They heard the ice creak under their feet.

"Stand up straight. We must walk confidently," Mieszko said quietly, without turning his head, "as if the ice isn't breaking underneath us. Remember, son, you can be a duke, or even a king, but if your soldiers don't admire you, you will never be a leader. Every one of my father's gods was a tyrant. Perun, Trzygłów, black Weles, bright Swaróg—every one of them. My men are baptized. They believe in Christ, like I do. But their Slavic souls want to worship strength, and if you want to lead them, that is what you must give them."

"Is that not blasphemy?" Bolesław choked, placing step after step on solid water.

"No. It's a ruler's reality."

"Father, we might not have come out of that hole alive. Did we risk our lives to impress our people?"

"Yes," Mieszko replied. "And thanks to that they won't hesitate to give their own for us."

2

⚛

POLAND

Świętosława was hiding behind the boat shed, watching as her father and brother's men stood around a fire and the two of them bathed in an ice hole.

Damn it! she swore silently. The squad hadn't been marching out to meet a guest. East, west. The question of her marriage would remain unanswered for another night, it seemed. She had no intention of moving from her hiding spot, though. She had come out into the cold night to see something meant to be hidden from her, and she had no intention of missing that opportunity, even if the scene before her was not the one she had been expecting.

The men were chanting now, "Duke Mieszko! Duke Mieszko!" Two silhouettes emerged from the frozen lake, the figures obscured by the wall of soldiers surrounding them.

What were they doing here? Why had they undressed on such a cold night and jumped into the water? Was this some sort of royal ritual? Was it not a sin? Her heart beat quickly. She had already forgotten that moments before it had beat like this because she'd thought she'd learn who her husband would be.

Her father and brother had stepped onto the bank confidently, the warriors chanting both their names. They formed a circle around the fire, and made such a racket banging on their shields that she was sure they were trying to wake up all the saints in heaven. *Was it heaven?* The thought crossed her mind, because what she was seeing did not look very holy. It was more like . . .

"What are you doing here?" She heard a voice colder than the winter air behind her. Duchess Oda. "This is not meant for your eyes, Princess!"

Świętosława turned around slowly.

"It's not meant for yours either, if we are both hiding in the bushes."

Świętosława saw three armed guards behind Oda. The duchess pursed her lips and snorted. "Will you step out from behind that boat shed yourself or should I have you escorted?"

"You may command Juta or other servants, but you do not command me." An angry flush colored Świętosława's cheeks. Everything she had wanted to say since the duchess had arrived at the Piast court, almost three years earlier, finally spilled out. "You're a marchioness, *my lady.* You have no royal blood in your veins. Father married you because he needed you, and when you stop being useful he'll send you back to the abbey he took you from. My father had only one beloved wife, and that was my mother, Dobrawa. Do you know how many wives he had before her? Seven! And he sent them all away when Dobrawa came to Gniezno. He might have another seven after you, and he can send them away just like he did the first ones. Remember that, Oda von Haldensleben. The truth may not be pleasant, but it's easier to live with it than without it."

By now, Świętosława was shouting, but Oda's face remained as still as an ice sculpture.

"You aren't controlling yourself, Mieszko's daughter," she said, when Świętosława finally fell silent. *She still avoids saying my name,* Świętosława thought, wanting to feel smug despite being the one caught in the bushes. *Her fat German tongue trips on it.* "My S-vento-schwava," she could hear her mother whispering, *"you were born a half devil, so we had to give you a blessed name,"* she would always say, smiling.

Oda's angry voice pulled her back to the present. "You don't control the words you say. A sign that you aren't ready for your father to send you out into the world." She turned to the guards accompanying her and added carelessly: "Help the lady out of the bushes."

Then, not sparing Świętosława another glance, the duchess made her way to the fire burning on the dock.

"Don't touch me!" Świętosława snarled at the armed man reaching a hand toward her.

He pulled back as if scalded, and she hissed at him again as she stepped out from behind the boat shed. A blush was now flooding the soldier's cheeks. *Good. Shame on you,* she thought vengefully. *You should be serving me, not her.*

A twig caught the hem of her dress and Świętosława briefly faltered. She pulled and heard the rip of wool. Oda was at the fire now. Her father's men stepped aside for her and bowed.

I cannot run like a child, Świętosława reminded herself, and only lengthened her step, pretending not to have noticed the tearing fabric.

Mieszko and Bolesław were dressed. Only the curls of their wet hair suggested they had been in the freezing water minutes before. She caught her brother's surprised gaze.

"My wife and daughter," Mieszko said. It wasn't a greeting.

"Forgive us, my lord." Oda bowed slightly to him. "We should not be here . . ."

"True," Mieszko replied, his voice hard.

". . . but you left your daughter in my care, and your word is my command. I couldn't leave her alone, and since she decided to take an evening stroll and slipped out of the palatium . . ."

Świętosława cursed the duchess vehemently in her thoughts.

"What are you doing here, Świętosława?" Mieszko asked, casting an eye over her dress.

"I was spying on you," she said loudly, meeting her father's gaze directly.

"And what did you see?"

"Your men's backs are so broad that I could only see them." She raised a hand and, pointing at each man in turn, counted: "Czcibór, Bogowit, Siemir, Czabor, Świelub . . ." the ones whose names she called bowed their heads to her. ". . . Czedrog, Derwan, Dalebor . . ."

Dalebor sent her a bright smile. Świętosława continued naming them in a single breath:

". . . Gardomir, Kalmir, Jaromił, Tasław, Miłosz, Warcisław, Lutom, Mścibor, Ostrowod, Radomir, Unimir . . ."

She pointed then at the last one of the surrounding men, shook her head, and said with a hint of accusation in her voice:

"This one I don't know."

The one she'd picked out was very young to be part of Father's squad. He looked askance at her.

"That's Wilkomir," Mieszko said.

"Oh, right," she sighed, pretending to be surprised.

Wilkomir looked at her wildly. A few of the warriors laughed, Mieszko among them. Świętosława felt more sure of herself. She stuck out three fingers, pointing to her left at the same time.

"Bjornar, Jaksa, and Zarad are over there, too. And, of course, the two men of my life." She bowed with a wide smile. "My father and brother . . ."

"That's enough, daughter. You saw everyone, but you're mistaken when you say these are my men. From this night forth, they are your brother's."

So that's what this was about! she thought, but when she spoke she sounded as innocent as a child.

"All of them? Father, have you given them all to Bolesław?"

"It's time for you to return to the house, child," her father interrupted. "And for you, my lady." He bowed to Oda. "Thank you for keeping an eye on our . . ." He stopped, searching for the best words. ". . . most treasured daughter. I expect you will both retire to rest now."

"As you wish, my prince," Oda replied obediently, and grabbed Świętosława's elbow.

Once they were out of the men's view, past the first line of trees which rose in the direction of the East Bridge, Oda let her go.

"As I'd thought. You still aren't ready. But if you want to see what your father is capable of, come on the night of the hunt."

"Where to?" Świętosława asked.

Oda didn't reply, only shrugged lightly.

Bolesław wanted to be alone. He wanted to ride, or to run through the woods and yell, *The world is mine!* He felt as if he were being struck by lightning, electrified, energized, time and time again. Instead of burning on the sacrificial pyre, he had a squad of his own from his father. A squad! The old aurochs had picked out his heir and announced it to the herd. The memory of the freezing water, instead of being cold, burned and warmed him like the sweetest mead, which was poured from jugs into goblets, cups, and horns that were passed between the benches at the feast the following night.

It was time for Koliada, for celebrating the birth of God's Son, and he felt as if he himself were that son. As if he'd been reborn the previous night. Once again the firstborn, and the only one that mattered. Mieszko, in his eyes, was the war-god father, and the golden cross on his chest swung in Bolesław's memories as it had that night, half paganly, blasphemously. But that didn't matter. The memory of the freezing water was almost holy itself, so he hadn't mentioned comparing his father to God in his confession.

Everything tasted stronger, deeper, clearer, as if his previously dormant senses had been awakened. His heart beat faster day and night, his blood coursed more swiftly through his veins.

On the second day of the winter celebrations, there was a hunt. The court gathered in the yard in front of the palatium, and the duke's priest blessed them all before they left. Oda, with young Mieszko at her breast, now seemed to him as gentle and caring as a mother.

"Take care of yourselves." She made the sign of the cross over them. "Fruitful hunting!"

The child in her arms no longer bothered Bolesław. He could even accept him, adorable and clumsy as he was, like a small, helpless pup.

Świętosława had a pearl-studded diadem on her head, and her hair was down, bright and shining like pale amber. She was biting her lip, as she always did when she was trying to stop herself from speaking her mind. He walked over to her.

"You're beautiful," he said, stroking her hair.

"You too," she replied, and he was certain she was being earnest.

His sister either kept her mouth shut, or said exactly what she thought. Now, she stood on her toes and said quietly,

"Oda told me to come to her the night of the hunt."

"Why?"

"She said I'd find out what Father is capable of."

"You're bold, sister," he said with pride. "Back there, on the docks, you didn't let her walk over you. But don't go to her alone. Wait for me."

She placed a hand on his shoulder and pulled him into an unexpectedly fierce hug.

"And if you don't come back?"

He pulled away, looking down at her unusually solemn face.

"I'll come back," he promised.

The horns sounded in farewell.

The canter, the wind in his face, wet snow at midday, freezing air flooding his nostrils—all this swept away the memory of his sister's question, *What if you don't come back?* It had pierced him from ear to gut. He shook it off, focusing on their prey. A festive hunt! The herds of deer didn't interest him; Bolesław was seeking only the rarest prize, the great royal stags. Their group split into two, Mieszko with his squad and hunters, and Bolesław with his own. Bjornar, Zarad, and Jaksa rode beside him. Wilkomir and Dalebor were excellent trackers. Lutom chased the young stags out of the forests with unparalleled precision. But Bolesław wanted something more.

"Dalebor," he shouted. "Can you get the old one out of the thickets?"

They tracked it for two days. They found the giant marks its hooves left in the snow. But each time they came near, the stag heard them and disappeared farther into the forest. They found it in the end though. The old royal stag had the largest antlers that Bolesław had ever seen. Its dark, almost black fur formed an elegant mane around its neck. But of course, Mieszko was the one to kill it. He was walking along with the hawk on his shoulder.

"It wasn't easy," he said, stretching and drinking from the horn with mead. The hawk on his shoulder cawed and beat its wings.

After the kill, Mieszko had knelt by the stag and looked in its milky eyes for a long moment. He'd slid a twig into its mouth, saying:

"A last bite, my friend."

Lutom, who had chased the animal for Bolesław, and Wilkomir and Dalebor, who had tracked it. Derwan, Czcibór, Tasław, Miłosz, Warcisław, Mścibor, Ostrowod, who had hunted it with Bolesław for two days; none of his father's old squad said a word. None mentioned that the trophy his father had won had been pursued by the son.

There was a fire burning in the clearing, a doe was crackling over the flames, and the servants carried mead. The squads mingled once again, the hunters drank to the soldiers, and vice versa. Bolesław kept to the side with Jaksa. He stared into the stag's dead eyes. Father's prize. Dalebor came over to them with a jug, and Bolesław offered him his horn. Dalebor could have ten years on him, no more.

"A young stag, while he's a calf, sticks to the swarm," Dalebor said, when Bolesław had taken a sip of mead. "Once he has grown some, and the mating season approaches, he mounts his does as if he were an adult. When a stag fights for them, the young one runs, and returns only when it's safe. He tries to fight for the does himself the following year—and usually, he fails. The grown stag will chase him off easily with a roar or two, and antlers if necessary." Dalebor laughed, then continued: "The exiled ones will band together for a year or two into their own herds. When they finish their fourth, fifth years, they approach the does more boldly when the mating season comes around. If they're successful, they get braver. And eventually, the strongest one will defeat the old stag and take his place."

"What happens to his companions?" Bolesław asked. "With the herd of young ones?"

"It scatters." Dalebor shrugged. "Each one wants his own herd."

Is the squad that Father gave me mine, or still his? Bolesław wondered as they made their way back to Ostrów Lednicki.

Before they crossed the East Bridge, Mieszko called Bolesław over, so the two could ride in together. Side by side. Guards sounded horns over the gate as they entered. Torches were lit. There was chaos in the yard. Musicians. Iron baskets with burning wood. Snow, freshly covered with sand. And the chants:

"Miesz-ko! Bo-le-sław!"

The duke's priest was intoning a psalm, but this was drowned out by the noise. Oda emerged to greet her husband, but the duke didn't dismount until the last cart of prey clattered into the yard. Then, he raised his arm and shouted:

"God has blessed us! The forest's gifts are many!"

Bolesław dismounted in time with his father. He saw his sister, who raced past Oda to their father. As she threw her arms around his neck, Bolesław heard the question she had put to their father countless times:

"What tongue am I to learn before I marry?"

"It would be enough if you learned how to hold it," he answered, but Świętosława was already gone from Mieszko's side.

She says what she wants, and listens only to what she chooses, Bolesław had time to think before she was by his own side, murmuring,

"Remember? The night of the hunt. That's tonight."

Świętosława knew where to go. Oda's bedchamber had belonged to their mother, Dobrawa, only five years ago. After her death, Świętosława slept in her mother's bed as long as she could smell her scent. When that too was gone, she left the room.

A year later, Father and his armies had caused the emperor so much trouble that the emperor was forced to negotiate a peace with the Polish duke to protect the empire's borderlands. The emperor summoned a nun from an abbey, one of the daughters of Margrave von Haldensleben, who had already taken her vows, to be wed to Mieszko: Oda.

Because of their marriage, the Polish were united with the noble families of the Reich, and Father, as a wedding gift, had freed a thousand Saxon prisoners and ceased fighting in the west. Everyone knew that this peace wouldn't last. Świętosława nurtured that certainty in her heart, that any day now Mieszko would gather his forces and attack, as he had done so many times before, and that would be the end of Oda's reign.

"Here." She showed Bolesław the way.

A broad, beautiful marble shaft lay adjacent to the bedchamber, which Father had intended to use to direct smoke out of the chambers. Unfortunately, he had accidentally, in a surge of fury, killed the Carinthian building master who had been working on it, and so the chimney had stood empty for years, and the chambers remained cold. There was a small wooden door in the shaft, built so the interior could be cleaned. It was no larger than a window, and Świętosława knew where it was.

"Get in," she whispered to Bolesław. "There are steel spikes in the wall you can use to climb down. What?" she asked, surprised by his startled expression. "You didn't think we'd walk into the bedchamber, say 'Good evening,' and sit down by the wall to find out what's happening, did you? Fine. I'll go first."

She lifted her skirts to avoid getting tangled in them, and disappeared into the depths of the unused chimney. She climbed down the metal spikes with practiced ease. When darkness fell, she knew he had followed.

They stood side by side at the bottom of the shaft. They looked at the duchess's bedchamber from above, through a narrow crack in the wall, and heard every word.

Oda was waiting for Mieszko. She must have been cold, because she had wrapped herself in fur. A servant was brushing her long hair. She then slipped the rings off her mistress's fingers. Oda sent her away. When she was alone, she put the rings back on. She stood up and walked over to a small box. She rummaged through the golden chains inside and picked one, fastening it around her neck. She pulled the fur more tightly around her. Mieszko entered, the hawk that stayed with him at all times perched on his shoulder. Oda opened her arms.

"My duke's favorite bird," she said in a voice Świętosława had never heard her use before. It was lower, throatier.

Mieszko moved the hawk over to an empty torch holder, threw off his cloak, and walked to her. "He flew from the hunt straight to a warm nest . . ."

He grabbed Oda's shoulders and pulled her toward him. She slipped out of his grasp, laughing.

"So he came only to rest? Oh, no, my lord! You don't sleep in my nest."

Father unbuckled his belt and, for a single moment, Świętosława hoped he would use it to hit Oda. She held her breath. No. She was fooling herself. Mieszko undressed and stood naked in front of Oda, who was still draped in fur. It crossed Świętosława's mind that she shouldn't be seeing this, but there was no choice anymore. She and Bolesław couldn't move until Mieszko and his wife fell asleep; any sound from the chimney would draw attention.

Father lay down and looked up at the duchess. "Do you want me to beg?"

Oda walked around the bed with a light, almost dancing step. She stood at the foot and let the fur fall open.

"Please," Mieszko moaned.

What is he asking her to do? Świętosława thought frantically. *Oda said I'd see what Father is capable of. Is this what I was meant to hear?*

"Oda, don't tease me, give me what I'm waiting for . . ." Father's voice, always commanding, was suddenly soft.

The duchess laughed, a sound long and low. She threw her head back, cocked it to one side. Her hair spread over her fur-covered back. Suddenly, she turned her back to the bed and walked over to a small bench that stood right beneath the crack in the wall they were watching through. She reached for a jug and cup.

Świętosława looked at her brother. She could see only his eyes, nose, and mouth in the darkness. His lips were parted.

Does Oda know we're here? Did she expect this? Does she think we're eavesdropping by the door? Nonsense. There are guards by the door.

"Wine?" Oda asked melodically from below. "Golden Riesling . . ."

"I don't want wine! I want you."

"How much?" She cocked her head, placing the jug by the bed. She drank some.

"I want you more than anyone in the world," Mieszko murmured.

Świętosława pressed her fingers into her brother's hand. She looked at him. Yes, he also had fury shining in his eyes. How could Father talk like that? What about their mother?

Oda handed her cup to him, and he drank greedily. She was slipping the fur off her shoulders slowly, languidly. Mieszko choked on the wine and threw the cup into a corner.

She's poisoned him! Świętosława thought, but Bolesław squeezed her hand to still any reaction.

The duchess was completely naked under the fur, decorated only by jewels. She still hadn't gotten into the bed, she was still walking around it, stretching like a cat, and Mieszko's eyes followed her every move as he sighed.

"Come here, please . . ."

She couldn't believe that Father, the great duke, would beg like this.

Oda moved smoothly onto the bed. She sat on top of Mieszko. He groaned.

"Please . . ."

Oda moved her hips up and down in an even rhythm. Świętosława heard her brother's quickened breath. He leaned toward her and whispered:

"Close your eyes."

"No," she said just as quietly. "No."

"You shouldn't . . ."

"Should you?" She placed a finger on his lips to silence him.

Oda leaned over their father and whispered something to him. Mieszko laughed throatily and flipped her onto her back.

"Your wish is my command," he said as he climbed on top of her.

Świętosława felt as if Oda had slapped her. With that white, ringed hand. *"Your word is my command"*—that's what Oda had said to Mieszko when he'd asked them both to leave the docks. Then, she had been the picture of obedience. So, this is how it was? Their love game? She gives the orders in the bedchamber, and he at court?

And I fooled myself into believing that Oda was just the guarantee of peace on the border, Świętosława thought desperately. *Nothing more. I hoped that Father still loved Mother. He always remembers her with such respect. But clearly, an absent woman cannot rule a man's heart.* She felt tears streaming down her cheeks.

"We're leaving," Bolesław whispered and pulled her hand.

He climbed first. He opened the little door carefully, checking that they'd be able to leave unnoticed. Then, he offered her a hand and helped her out of the chimney. Saying nothing, they walked through empty corridors until they finally reached the palatium doors, pushing them open. The cold from the yard surrounded them. Wet, melting snow was falling. Świętosława lifted her face to the sky.

"Do you still want to get married so badly?" Bolesław asked after a moment.

"I never wanted to," she replied calmly.

"But you keep asking about it, as if . . ."

"As if what?" she asked sharply, feeling anger rise at his words. "As if I had any other choice? Father has been talking about it ever since I was born! Rus. Meissen. Bohemia. Hungary. What else did he name?" she grabbed his caftan.

"North March."

"Yes! North March." She let go of Bolesław's tunic, pushing him away. "He doesn't need me for that, because he's married a daughter of the North March himself. I know what role he intends me for, and the only thing I wanted to know was where I'd be playing it. And do you know why? Because I still had some stupid hope that he might let me rule here! That he'd start a war with the Reich and win it, he'd place you on the emperor's throne, and me . . ." Świętosława felt dizzy and sick.

Bolesław caught her to stop her from falling. She took a deep breath and freed herself from his arms.

"But now I know that this land is ruled by another," she said quietly. "And there is no place for a daughter here."

"There isn't even enough for a son," Bolesław said soberly. "Father may have given me a squad, but he has no intention of sharing his power. He'll keep a close eye on me. He wants to rule by himself. Świętosława." He pulled her to face him. "Our father is the great duke Mieszko. That was never going to make our lives easy."

3

⚜

Sven hated his father so much that if the old man weren't surrounded by a horde of soldiers day and night, he'd probably sink a dagger into his heart right up to the hilt. A king with a young son capable of ruling had no right to live this long!

The great hall at the royal manor in Roskilde echoed with shouts and laughter of hundreds of soldiers. The tired servants made their rounds more and more slowly, carrying bowls of meats and jugs of mead. His father, King Harald, couldn't seem to get enough. His red cheeks shone with grease as he puffed in anger. He slammed his fist on the bench and shouted until saliva dripped from his mouth, shining on teeth that had been whittled and scarred to look like blue-gray fangs.

"If you don't have enough space in Denmark, sail off to raid!" he roared at his son. "Conquer your own land, because while I live, this one is mine! Mine!"

Sven stood at the head of the bench and felt the blood surging to his face.

"What? Are you sad at the thought?" the drunken Harald screamed. "Did you hear that? My son is sad at the thought of leaving his home!"

King Harald got to his feet shakily and Sven thought for a moment that his father would keel over. Someone's hands held him upright, though. The old man leaned on the bench and lifted his chin defiantly.

"If you aren't brave enough to go out into the world, then be quiet and do as I say. And I say that we won't join the Slavic revolt. No, and that's that. Let the Veleti fight the emperor themselves, it's got nothing to do with us."

The loud hall was falling quiet. Noblemen and warriors were turning to listen to their exchange.

Good, thought Sven, scanning their faces. *You'll hear every word that's uttered tonight.*

He took a breath to make sure his voice sounded clear, and said,

"It's got nothing to do with us? Have the baptism and company of priests dulled your brain, Father, or are you just getting old? Oh, yes! When Emperor Otto stole the port in Hedeby from you ten years ago, you preferred to slink away with your tail curled under you. You gave it to him like a child gives up his bowl to a bully, didn't you?"

"Silence!" Harald snarled. "You understand nothing, so be silent!"

"What is there to understand?" Sven asked, spreading his arms wide, and turning left and right to the listening nobles. "You were baptized, and you allowed priests into Denmark, the emperor's spies. You let them baptize us with water and you've weakened, as if you were drinking that water rather than mead!"

His father's eyes narrowed. He was sobering up, and Sven didn't want for him to be sober right now. He wanted the old man to lose control. He couldn't give him mead himself, not in the middle of an argument. He glanced discreetly at Adla, who was serving his father at the feast. She stood behind Harald with a jug.

"I won't be risking myself for the Veleti," his father said loudly. "They've started a war and they can die in it. It's nothing to do with us!"

"You've grown blind with age," Sven said calmly, "but I can still see clearly. And I see that the emperor and his Saxons are busy putting out the Slavic fire, and I won't help them."

"I never said I want to help the emperor," the old man hissed through his teeth.

"And I'm saying that I want to be the wind that spreads the flames!" Sven shouted.

"What are you talking about?" Confusion showed on Harald's face. "What fire?"

"Saxony is burning, Father. The Veleti have taken Połabie. They've chased the Christian bishop out of Havelberg; his palace and church are up in smoke, and they used the altar for a feast."

"The Saxons will gather their armies and attack." Harald shrugged and collapsed carelessly on the bench. "Mead!"

Adla leaped over with the jug. Sven hoped that it was the same jug he had given her before the feast. The girl poured some for Harald and looked at Sven. She blinked slowly.

"I'll drink to the bishop's escape, why not! I'll drink to the short victory of the Veleti, and I'll drink more than once! But before my hangover is over, the Saxons will humble them and dip them in blood." Harald chuckled and took a swig from his horn.

The mead from the chosen jug did its work; sooner or later even the

strongest heads would be conquered. Harald drank, and Sven knew that he
was already gone. He heard the whispers behind him of at least three of his
father's military leaders. He would strike the iron while it was still hot. He
just had to hold his tongue for the moment. Say only the right amount and
not a single word more. He spoke calmly.

"I have no intention of letting this occasion slip by, Father. The Saxons
are busy with the Veleti and have taken their eye off our southern lands. Yes,
I say ours, because even though you humbly allowed the emperor to take it,
I still consider it to be our land. And I will go there with armies. I will take
back the great Hedeby from Saxon hands. Who's with me?" he called louder,
looking at his father stretched out in his large chair.

Harald glanced with a dull eye at the guests who had gathered around the
benches. His head was wobbling again.

"Son." He waved a hand carelessly. "How old are you to . . ."

"Twenty-three, Father," Sven announced loudly. "Twenty-three. And I
swear that before I've lived another year, Hedeby will belong to the Danish
once more!"

"Eee . . ." Harald burped. "Eee . . ."

"Do you want to bet?" Sven said quickly. "If I lose, I promise I will shut
my mouth and never question you again. But if I win, you'll give the throne
to me yourself! You'll go to your wintry sleep willingly."

Adla poured more mead into Harald's cup. The horn was endlessly full.

The king swallowed and shrugged. He muttered something. His eyes
were falling shut.

"Did you hear that?" Sven shouted. "The king agreed. Who will come to
Hedeby with me? Who will attack the Saxons with me? Which one of you
leaders wants to sail under Odin's sign once more?"

A roar broke out over the hall. "We sail with the young king!"

Sven walked between the benches, grasping their right hands.

"To the boats!" he called as he neared the door.

On his way, he pressed a silver brooch into Adla's hand. She deserved
it. The door of the manor was thrown open, and a river of Danes surged
through it, thirsty for Saxon blood.

The old king slept.

Palnatoki waited for Sven by the smaller stable, the one housing the farming
horses and the servants' mounts. If it hadn't been for the previously decided
upon place and signal, Sven wouldn't have recognized him. The great jarl of

Jomsborg, the Viking stronghold, home to the infamous Jomsviking mercenaries, was dressed in a simple gray cloak, and looked more like a poor wan-
derer than the wise warrior he was. Sven and the jarl entered the stable and
closed the door. Once inside, Sven embraced his teacher. Palnatoki had been
like a father to him all these years, while Harald had been doing everything
he could to avoid acknowledging Sven as his son and heir.

"I don't want to be seen here." Palnatoki pulled the old sailor's hood back
from his face. "Even if half your father's men have followed you tonight, the
other half has remained loyal to him. Remember them, boy."

Sven smiled. Palnatoki was the only man who had the right to call him
"boy."

"Won't you sail with me?" he asked, but his old friend shook his head.

"You know I can't openly stand by you yet. Besides, I'm needed in
Jomsborg. Someone has given us a job worth pure silver, and you know that
we haven't had too much of that recently." He smiled a crooked smile. "But
I've brought you two young men to fight in my stead. Sigvald and Thorkel.
They'll be happy to sail to Hedeby."

"Are they yours? Jomsvikings?"

"Not yet, boy, they're still too young. Reckless, like you. Let's say that I'm
keeping an eye on them."

"They'll be welcome in our fight," Sven said, clasping Palnatoki's shoulder.
In truth, he would welcome anyone who might help him achieve his goal.

"You haven't told anyone?" Palnatoki asked after a moment.

"No. I said only as much as you suggested. About the Slavs spreading
flames. Not a word about how the Veleti have sent Brenna up in smoke as well.
Or about how the margrave of the North March, noble Ditrich what's-his-
name, ran so fast that all he left behind him was a cloud of dust. Father is sure
that the Saxons are able and will certainly take their bloody revenge on the
Veleti still this summer."

"Good. Let him believe that, it will keep him in Roskilde." The old man
patted his mount's neck and gave Sven a smile. "So you managed to hold
your tongue. That's something to be proud of."

"Yes. Father doesn't know that the Saxons have more to worry about than
the bloody Slavic revolt. He has no idea that the emperor has been taught
an expensive lesson by the Saracens in Italy or that he has trouble gathering
any kind of army."

"Yes, the emperor is as short of breath as an old goat," Palnatoki agreed.
"Today, your father has no idea what a difficult situation the Saxons are
in, but when he sobers up tomorrow, and hears from his spies the day after

that, he'll know what's what. It's in your interest to be at least a step ahead of him. To show everyone that you are young, bright, and quick. Time for me to go, boy. For you, too. Your new army is loading the boats with weapons. You have to rein them in to sail through the Great Belt."

"I'll split up my men," Sven said, watching Palnatoki's reactions carefully. "I'll send half through the Little Belt."

His teacher's gray eyes were calm. He nodded as he said,

"It's not a bad idea. No one should see how many boats you have. It's not a bad idea at all. I'll give you another one. If you run into trouble, go to your grandfather, in Hamburg. Mściwój loved his daughter, your mother, very much. If you only knew how much."

"He also loved Harald Bluetooth, his son-in-law," Sven snorted. "I remember how they drank together when Mother died."

The memory of his mother's funeral was a thorn in his heart. Mściwój, the Obotrite leader, a Christian like his father Harald, allowed for her to be buried in the earth rather than burned. Damn it! He had been haunted for years by a dream in which Tove showed him how she was rotting underground. They hadn't budged from the idea that, since she had been christened, she must also have a Christian funeral to allow for her resurrection, but then they had drunk and cried, their grief the strongest evidence of the frailty of their faith in the resurrection of the dead.

Palnatoki led his horse from the stable. Sven followed.

"Think what you will, boy, but remember: in the allegiance with the Obotrites, with your mother's people, you'll be twice as strong. And if you aren't the one to reach out to Mściwój, your father will. You must be the first to do it, Sven, because to Mściwój, you are his blood. He'll accept you."

Then he clasped Sven's hand and slipped a foot into a stirrup. Palnatoki wasn't one for sentimental goodbyes. Pulling himself up, he added:

"When you take back the south from the Saxons, when you open the beautiful port in Hedeby to the Danish once more, and you stand here, in Roskilde, before old Harald and all the nobles . . ."

"What then?" Sven smiled. "Am I supposed to also say: 'Father, the Obotrites stand with me today like they once did with you. I have taken one of their beautiful daughters for my wife, and when she bears my son, you can jump into the Roskilde fjord with a stone around your neck, because there is nothing more for you here?' Should I say something like that?"

Palnatoki nodded, his eyes on the royal Roskilde manor. The servants were cleaning up after the feast, putting out the torches. The great carved doors had already been closed.

"Don't start a war with Harald until you have Mściwój on your side. And don't think about whether he has been baptized, that has nothing to do with it when you are fighting on the same side. Who cares about some Christ! Besides, if my spies aren't mistaken, when Mściwój led the Obotrites in burning Hamburg, I don't think that he was particularly careful in avoiding the abbey and church there. You have to know who to side with and when, that's what I'll leave you with."

The next day, thirty armed ships pushed off from the port in Roskilde, and at Sven's command, set sail west. When he felt the wind from the Kattegat, wind that smelled of the wide North Sea, he gave a signal to the helmsmen to bring the ships closer together. He greeted Jarl Haakon from Funen, whose ship carried a dragon's head at its bow. And Thorgils from Jelling, who brought five ships, and sailed on the sixteen-benched *Vengeful Dog*. And Gunar from Limfiord, the one who gained fame by his daring attacks on Frisian shores. And the two new companions, Sigvald and Thorkel, the brothers Palnatoki had sent.

"Comrades! We're sailing to feed our hungry swords with blood! The Saxons are dead. We'll take our revenge on them as we would on a knife through the gut of one we loved. Because Hedeby is our family, kidnapped in youth." He lifted his sword, and a shout answered him from the decks. Waves rocked the ship. Sven spread his legs to catch his balance. He lifted an arm and shouted,

"When I was a child, my father, Harald Bluetooth, baptized me. He allowed for the emperor to become my godfather and to give me the Christian name Otto—his name. Otto! Was that a name given to our forefathers? No!" Sven took a deep breath and roared with all of his might: "I'm sailing to kill my godfather, whose power I refuse to acknowledge! I sail with Odin's name on my lips. Odin!"

"Odin! Odin! Odin!" a hundred throats replied to him, and the water amplified the shout.

"Odin! Accept from us a sacrifice of Saxon blood!" Sven leaned his head back and let his long red hair fly in the wind.

POLAND

Świętosława was a summer child. Dobrawa had given birth to her on Kupała, the shortest night of the year. She said later that while she fed her, the milk in her breast smelled of flowers. So, every year when the days grew longer, when the sun lay on cheeks in golden spots, Świętosława came back to life. The clearings brightened by cornflowers, sky-blue fields of flax, the blushes of poppies and golden freckles of chrysanthemums, this was her time.

When her mother was alive, they would spend the warm summers in a small village by the Warta River. Away from the raucous courtly life. They would have a dozen ladies with them.

Bolesław had stopped coming with them as he got older, when Świętosława had been about four years old, so she had no memories of summers with her brother. Only with Astrid and Geira, her half sisters. Mieszko's daughters from his marriages before Dobrawa. From the dark times before the baptism. Świętosława adored Astrid, who was only a few years older. Świętosława loved her sister's hair, the color of dark amber. And Astrid's strong hands, which always saved her at the last minute. They pulled her from hollows which were too deep, confidently lifted her down from trees, pulled her from the water when she suddenly lost her footing. Dobrawa also liked Astrid, calling her "Bogumiła," *dear to God,* as that's what her northern name meant. Maybe that's why Astrid clung to Dobrawa so? Perhaps she longed for the maternal warmth which Dobrawa had in seemingly endless supply. The rest of the year, Astrid lived with her grandfather Dalwin, the master of Wolin's port.

Geira was older. Her mother, Gunn, a northern woman, had come to Mieszko's country as a slave, but Mieszko, spellbound (or so the story went) by her beauty, bought her out of slavery and settled her somewhere by the Vistula. Świętosława liked her sister's sharp chin, her straight, heavy hair which fell below her waist. She had the cold, northern beauty of her mother, and Mieszko married Geira off when she was still young, to Gudbrod, one of Bornholm's jarls. Apparently, her marriage had made it easier for him to build his human fleet. A human fleet consisted of ships used to carry slaves, which made their father large sums of money. And so Geira, the daughter of a woman sold into slavery, became a lever in the slave market. The winds of fate can be cruel and strange at times. But now, that was in the past, as Gudbrod, Geira's husband, had died. A widow sister, how odd that sounded when Świętosława herself was still treated like a young girl.

Apart from the sisters, Dusza always accompanied them. This was father's will, not mother's. Mieszko, driven by a half-forgotten tradition, had found children who'd been born on the same day as Świętosława and Bolesław. A girl and a boy. He paid their families with pure silver, and he didn't stint. He paid them the weight of the children. He ordered for the children to be raised together, so both of Mieszko's royal heirs had human shadows. They were called Dusza and Duszan, names meaning *soul* or *spirit*. Neither Dusza nor Duszan looked like her or Bolesław. Nobody kept a record of their parents' names. Duszan raised no doubts. He was a skillful, if quiet, boy. But it was different with Dusza. After a few years, it became clear that she was mute. She could hear, but she couldn't make a sound. Mieszko was furious. Dobrawa cried that it was a bad sign for her daughter. But Świętosława wouldn't allow anyone to tear Dusza away from her. She spoke enough for them both anyway.

Dusza was like a mirror to her. She could see herself in those gray eyes. They understood each other through a language of gestures, blinks, and grimaces. Świętosława could share the full depth of herself, of her anger, in front of Dusza. Everything that stewed within her from dawn until dusk, everything that boiled inside. Everything that she had to hide from the world and keep silent about; all that came of being the only legitimate daughter of a great Piast duke. Of being the one with the holy name.

4

❋

RUS

Olav left his crew on board and ordered Geivar to replenish their supplies.

"As if we were planning to leave today," he whispered to his friend. "But do it discreetly, so the news doesn't spread around the port."

"The water carries, and the Dnieper is wide." Geivar gave a crooked smile.

"Narrow it to the crevice of your lips." Olav winked at him and made his way on horseback to Kiev. He had gifts for the royal couple in his saddlebags, and only one thought in his mind: *This is the last time.*

Olav Tryggvason was paying off his debt.

His memory was divided into two: the time of slavery, starvation, abuse, and the time after, of endlessly proving his gratitude to his saviors.

He'd been only three when the ship he and his mother had been escaping on had sailed straight into a slave ship. He hadn't seen his mother since. He could hear her piercing scream, though, as clearly as if it had been yesterday, and he could see her fair hair grabbed by a bearded bald man who placed a slave's collar around her neck. Olav, along with twenty others like him, found himself on the market in Loksa, in the country of Estonians. His first owner had paid for him with a bunch of dead ducks. A year later, he'd been sold on, and he was worth a pretty goat by then. When he turned five, a man called Eres had to exchange a cloak embroidered with a silk thread for him. Then when Olav was eight, a man came to visit Eres's home to collect taxes on behalf of Prince Vladimir, the ruler of Rus. The tax collector was tall, had fair hair, and bore the name Sivrit. He took one look at Olav and seemed to recognize him.

"What's your name?" the tax collector had asked Olav, looking at him carefully. "Olav, son of Tryggve." The newcomer's eyes had widened. He'd grabbed Olav by the shirt and picked him up as if he were no heavier than a baby. "Your mother's name?" Sivrit had whispered. "Astrid, Eric's daughter,"

Olav had replied. "Eric?" the newcomer had repeated after him, and suddenly his voice had caught in his throat. He put Olav back on the ground. "Eric from where?" he asked after a moment. "From Ofrustadir, my lord. That's where my grandfather is from. But I'm . . ." Sivrit had put a hand to Olav's mouth and whispered: "Don't say it. If you value your life, don't say it, because in the best case you'd never leave slavery. I know who you are. The same blood runs in our veins. My name is Sivrit Ericsson, and I'm your mother, Astrid's, brother. She was running to me when you were intercepted by the slave ship. Remember her name, but for your own good, forget your father's name today." And Olav, obedient to his kin, forgot.

Sivrit bought Olav from Eres, though the latter insisted on being paid in gold.

"I'll take you to the court of Vladimir in Holmgard," he said. "There are many of our people there, merchants and warriors alike. The king surrounds himself only with Varangians*. His ancestor was Rurik himself, who traveled here from the north."

Holmgard, known by those who lived there as Novgorod, turned out to be a city pulsing with life and riches, a center of culture within the spreading Rus empire, which had recently conquered Kiev. How was it that in this lively crowd he was spotted by Duchess Allogia? Olav hadn't asked any questions, not then. Allogia held the title of duchess, and she was one of Vladimir's many wives.

She had welcomed Olav with open arms, cried over the story of his separation from his mother, and gave Sivrit silver to search for his sister, Olav's mother, Astrid. Then, she kissed Olav's forehead, and with that one kiss, he felt that the years of pain might have finally come to an end.

Olav became a ward of the royal couple. Vladimir allowed him to train with his Varangian squad, and he rejoiced at Olav's strength. Olav himself had no trouble gathering people in his corner. Perhaps it was because he had a good ear; he learned languages quickly and perfectly. He had a talent for the spear and bow, and was patient when learning the sword.

When he turned twelve, he sailed out on a ship full of warriors for the first time. He was honed in the waters of the Volga, sailing with the prince's convoys. Young and skillful, he caught the helmsman's attention, and the man taught him the mysteries of steering a ship and how to set the drift for the night. This crew's mission was to protect the ships which sailed the Volga,

* Name given to the Vikings who ruled the state of Kievan Rus. They first settled there under Rurik, who was of Scandinavian descent.

and to ensure the safe passage of Arabian merchants into Novgorod. Ships full of expensive furs and leather, wax, honey, valuable weapons, trained hunting falcons, and the bark of white birches. And the barges, heavy with human cargo. The slaves on their way east. Olav boarded each barge and he searched. But among the thousands of women, there wasn't one who had a face as pale as his mother's. And so, the Slavic river Volga felt as useless to him as water with no fish might be to a fisherman.

He still hadn't heard from Sivrit. Duchess Allogia sensed Olav's growing impatience, or perhaps she just noticed the deepening grimace of his lips. She begged her husband to send Olav to sail the Dnieper, to give him a new searching ground. "Aren't you afraid, my lady, that the boy will sail over the Dnieper to Byzantium? To serve the emperor of the east, Basil, for gold?" Prince Vladimir would ask, and the duchess would whisper: "Husband, husband, not him! Our Olav is unconditionally loyal to us. He won't betray us, because Sivrit is using our silver to find his mother. Husband, he won't betray us, because we gave him his freedom."

Vladimir gave in, and Olav understood from his first day on board the new ship that the duchess was unconsciously testing that loyalty. No, he wasn't thinking about escaping to the wealthy Byzantium. Serving the emperor of the east for gold was not a lifestyle that appealed to him. But the waters of the Dnieper had stolen his soul. These weren't the wide and lazy waters of the Volga; they were a force to be reckoned with. There were treacherous rapids which announced their presence with barely a threatening murmur, rapids which swiftly turned to furious surges of water. He loved all of them: Rykuna, Horse's Head, Scythian Throat, Sharp Muzzle, Cursed, Insatiable, and, above all, the Thundering One. He was the first to jump from the boat to direct it across the stony thresholds.

He was enchanted by the Dnieper's banks, overgrown with alders and birches. The wetlands and swamps which stretched along them. Hunting catfish as large as sea monsters. The Dnieper tamed Olav's wild soul; it ruled him. The swish of the water helped drown out his yearning for the mother out of whose arms he'd been snatched so many years before. He still dreamed of her sometimes, but he no longer heard her piercing screams. Now, she moved her dry lips soundlessly. The thick fog that lay on the Dnieper helped obscure Olav's bloody memories.

Then spring came, with a violence here like nowhere else; spring which burst from a single sun ray, vanquishing snows from the vast fields by the river, only to cover them with the white of blossoming blackthorns in a matter of days. A spring that seduced him like a lover. He dreamed of nothing else; he wanted to sail all year, to experience once more this grand show of awakening nature. To feel his blood course through his veins, ever faster, bringing him back to life.

When a messenger reached them from Duchess Allogia, between one spring and the next, in a port near Smoleńsk, Olav felt as if someone were once again tightening the slave collar around his neck.

"Come back to Kiev. The prince has a new mission for you. You will attack the Radimichs."

So Olav went, leaving the Dnieper behind. He had to pay back his debt, after all. Allogia and Vladimir showered him with gifts, as if to fill the gap left by the lack of news of his mother. He accepted them, to avoid offending the royal couple. For two more years, he fought in the east, forcing the Radimichs, then the Vyatichi, to concede defeat. He didn't care who he was forcing to bow down. The only sweetness in his life was sailing across his beloved Dnieper on his way east.

Until recently, when, during an insignificant skirmish with the already defeated Vyatichi, Olav was unable to dodge a flying arrow. When it grazed his forehead, just over his eyebrow, he heard a piercing scream. It was Astrid, his mother, screaming in his head. Blood ran into his eyes from the arrow wound, and he fell from the saddle onto the hoof-churned ground. He lost consciousness, though he could still hear his mother's voice.

He was awoken by an aged whisper: "No, no, no! I won't heal him! I won't place herbs on his wound! I want him to die . . . for the bloody king to die . . . he is the ruler who walks in a river of blood." He opened his eyes with difficulty. He saw an old woman leaning over him, held by the back of the neck in the iron grip of his comrade Geivar.

"Let her go," Olav ordered.

"You're alive!" Geivar said happily.

Yes, he was alive. And his past had caught up with him at last. He could no longer stay lost in the beauty of the Dnieper or the violence of spring.

And now, he had returned to Kiev with his crew. He was carrying presents for the royal couple. And carrying the conviction that this was the last time he would fulfill someone else's desires before his own.

"Ole! My Ole!" He heard the young voice as soon as he entered the prince's courtyard. "You've returned! You've finally returned!" The prince's five-year-old son, Jarisleif, was running toward him, tripping over the long coattails of his fur cloak.

"He's not your Ole, he's mine!" a larger boy shouted and stuck out his leg, tripping Jarisleif.

The youngster slid in the mud. Olav jumped off his horse and picked him up, swinging him high.

"Jarisleif! How you've grown! I wouldn't have recognized you." He kissed the youngster's forehead.

The larger boy pushed through toward them and shouted up at them,

"Would you have recognized me, Ole? Have I also grown?"

"Is this our Rus prince who has grown so young?" Olav scrutinized him carefully and, seeing the boy's cheeks redden with pleasure, he added: "Oh, no, it's his brave son, Świiatopołk, as like his father as two peas in a pod."

"I look like him too!" the younger one burst out. The older one snorted and pushed him.

"That's enough, enough," Olav tried to hush the royal sons. "Is your father home?"

"No," Świiatopołk grumbled. "He went down to the river to make sacrifices."

"And he didn't take us." Jarisleif sniffed mournfully.

"Jarisleif, come here!" a voice sounded from above.

"Świiatopołk, time to go home!" They heard another from the opposite direction.

Olav straightened and lifted his head. Two women stood on the wooden cloisters of the Kiev manor. They faced each other: one in the right wing, one in the left; two of Vladimir's wives. Olav bowed to them both.

"Run to your mothers," Olav whispered to the boys. "We'll see each other again."

Jarisleif grudgingly moved off in the direction of the steps. Świiatopołk pulled Olav's sleeve and whispered into his ear:

"Father said that Jarisleif's older brother will receive the Polotsk* kingdom. But that's impossible, because Izjasław is stupid."

"You gossip too much." Olav laughed and tousled his hair. "Run along."

They heard the creak of shutters being opened. Duchess Allogia appeared in a window at the center of the manor. She wore a tall fur hat, and golden chains framed her face.

"Olav! You are a joyful sight!" she said when she saw him, lifting both her hands.

"And *she* gave birth to another daughter," Świiatopołk had time to whisper before scampering off.

Allogia received him in her private rooms, sending away her maids and

---

* City in modern-day Belarus, on the Dvina River.

the wet nurse with her baby girl, who was wrapped in gold-threaded cloth. He sensed an unfamiliar anxiety hidden beneath the duchess's blushing cheeks.

"Daughters serve you well, my lady. You are more beautiful with each one. What have you named the newborn?"

"Predsława," she replied carelessly. "What's happening with the Vyatichi?"

"They will pay the prince a tribute for every plow they own."

She nodded. Allogia's slender fingers moved constantly, as if they were conducting their own private dance. Olav found himself staring at them for a moment.

"Olav, don't leave me," she said, so unexpectedly that he shivered.

How could she know what he had come to discuss? He'd heard the whispers, of her abilities, of the things she knew that she had no right knowing. He had never paid them any heed. Until now.

Olav said nothing. The duchess stepped toward him, graceful as a forest cat.

"Not now, when . . ." She hesitated, biting her lip. "Vladimir has too many sons . . ."

And none from your womb, Olav thought soberly. One must be blunt with a witch.

". . . too many to be tied to just one." She spoke with barely hidden fury. "He's getting older, he's finding it harder to mount his horse, do you understand?" She peered into his eyes, cocking her head to one side.

But he can still father children. The thought crossed Olav's mind, even if it didn't cross his lips.

Allogia was looking at him with beautiful, dark eyes.

"None of his sons," she began after a moment, "has impressed their father with anything yet. And death . . ." She uttered the word worshipfully, as if speaking words of love. "Death could come at any time."

She was so close that he felt her warm breath. She was slight, and had to lift her head to look at him.

"Vladimir used to be the gallant Vladimir, when, flanked by his Varangians, he conquered Novgorod. Ah, he could have fought across all of Rus, as far as the Dnieper's outlet, as far as the lands of the Pechenegs, if . . ." Allogia lowered her voice and suddenly spread out the fingers of both her hands, wiggling them.

"If what?" he whispered throatily.

"If he didn't spend all his energy on new love conquests. Olav, he's not a gallant Viking anymore. He's moldered, he's as quarrelsome as a Slav. Ah!

He conquers new lands not for power and fame, but for women. Do you know what he prides himself on? That he's bedded eight hundred women. And that's supposed to be an exploit for a ruler? I'd prefer it if he bragged about winning eight kingdoms."

"I don't think I'm the one you should be talking to about this, my lady," Olav said.

"Don't you understand?" she continued. "You could be his heir."

"Me?"

"Yes! He must be thinking about who to name as his successor, and he can't rely on his own sons. He'll adopt you if you ask him."

"I don't . . ." Olav took a step back, but Allogia grabbed his wrist.

"Yes, you! His sons will accept you as a leader sooner than they will accept any of their brothers. You'd be the guarantee needed to ensure the kingdom won't dissolve after Vladimir's death."

Her hand on his wrist was like the iron bracelet of a slave's chain. And he felt himself giving in, his will bending to hers.

"Don't be afraid, Olav, it might be mad, but it's not impossible. All you have to do is ask him to adopt you. He has been saying for a long time that you remind him of the Vladimir who conquered Novgorod with fire. It's a sign! That, and the fact that the royal blood of the Ynglings runs through your veins."

Olav snatched his hand back.

"You knew, my lady?"

"I knew," she replied. "I've known since your first day in Novgorod. I couldn't sleep for the bright light I saw in the middle of the night. It was your fate, your happiness, your hamingia." Whatever *hamingia* was, Olav didn't know, and he wasn't sure he wanted to. "When Sivrit brought you here, I knew who had shone over Rus."

Olav felt now as if he were choking, while Allogia spoke more fervently with every word.

"You're the one the northern songs speak of. The boy with shining white hair, clear, pale eyes, a glance as sharp as a young snake's . . . the son of a god wandering the earth . . ."

"Stop!" he shouted. And for the first time, he said aloud what his mother's voice had awoken in his skull: "I am Olav Tryggvason, son of King Tryggve. The last living heir of the Norwegian kings. Kiss me."

Allogia reached out with slender fingers, fastening them around his neck and sealing her lips to his. He pulled free, wiping his mouth.

"Not like that, you madwoman!" He heard the deep anger in his own voice. "Kiss my forehead, like you did when you welcomed me under your roof. With that kiss, you took my memories. Now I want them back."

Allogia inhaled, the air whistling in her chest. Olav lowered his head. She placed her lips on it, as cold as steel. Then she pulled him up by his hair, studying his face. He broke free and, without a backward glance, walked to the door. When he reached the threshold, he heard her whisper:

"You've been marked by death."

Olav found Prince Vladimir on a hill overlooking the Dnieper. The prince's silk tent glinted golden and purple in the sunlight. Servants were preparing a feast in front of it in silence. The statues of Vladimir's gods stood nearby, beside ancient oaks. Dadźbóg, Perun, Mokosz, Strzybóg, Simargł, Chors. Olav knew their names, though they were only empty words to him. Vladimir was walking slowly in their shadows, a hand tucked into his belt.

"It occurred to me," the prince said, after they greeted one another, "that Odin and Thor's likenesses should also be here. Or perhaps the golden Freya, hmm? Tell me, what do you think, young Viking?"

Vladimir laughed then. "I used to have only Perun's statue, but when I took the lands of the Drevlians, Severians, Kryvichs, I began to worship their gods too. But perhaps, to adequately honor the country that my kin come from, we need Thor, too? Well, boy, cat got your tongue? You bring me a victory over the Veleti and yet you say nothing?"

"Do you know who I am?" Olav asked bluntly.

Vladimir sighed and answered with a question. "Who told you?"

Olav stayed silent, looking into the bearded face of Kiev's prince. Into the puffy eyes amid folds of loose skin. A nose which had lost its falcon's sharpness a long time ago.

"Allogia, was it? You went to see her! She swore she wouldn't say anything. That's what I get for sharing secrets with a woman."

"How did you know?" Olav interrupted him.

Vladimir's features twisted in misery.

"My mother told me. It's silly, isn't it? One might think I am ruled by women. But no, a mother is different, and anyway, she died that winter. She'd been a fortune teller. She was never wrong, though who knows really? She also told me I would be the murderer of gods before she died. I think that's an exaggeration, don't you?"

Olav said nothing, watching the prince with unease.

"Right, you'd like me to tell you what happened." Vladimir pulled at the dark tangles of his beard. "She told me my fortunes every year before Yuletide—here, we called it Koliada. They carried her in on a tall chair, and I wasn't allowed to take a drink before she arrived. If I had, she wouldn't say a single word, to punish me. That winter, ten years before you arrived, she said that a royal son had been born in Norway, in secret. That he was in exile, hunted by an old queen. And that I would be lucky enough to raise him. When Sivrit brought you to Novgorod, she was dead, but Allogia saw your soul or whatever she calls it—hamingia—and she begged me to bring you to court. I'll be honest with you; if it weren't for her, I wouldn't have remembered those old fortunes. I don't have the head for such things. But Allogia had made up her mind, and you know the rest . . ." Vladimir guided him by the elbow to the food-laden tables.

"Why did you keep my heritage a secret from me?" Olav asked, sitting next to the prince.

"A secret? No!" He poured wine for them both, filling their cups to the brim. "We just didn't talk about it, for your own good, my boy." The prince took a large swallow of wine while Olav bit his tongue, trying to ignore that word, "boy." "You have no chance of regaining your throne at present, so I didn't want to confuse you."

"Is that what your mother said, Vladimir?" Olav pronounced the prince's name with the clearest Nordic accent and watched the other man's face change.

"More or less," the prince replied. "Why don't you drink? Are you trying to insult me?"

"No. I want to keep a clear head. What did your mother say about my kingdom?"

Vladimir drank in silence. He put down his cup for the servant to refill. He wiped his mouth on the back of his hand and sighed heavily.

"She said that one day, you would win back the power you were born to wield."

Olav's heart beat faster, and his head reeled as if he'd already drunk the wine in front of him. He looked into the silver cup, still full to the brim. The purple surface of the wine seemed to shimmer. He picked it up suddenly and downed it in one gulp. He felt a warmth in his stomach, calming him. The prince laughed and nudged his shoulder.

"You drink as if you were mine! So, boy, let's get to the matter at hand. If old Mother was right about your kingdom, she must have been right about mine."

"What are you talking about, Prince?" The peace that had only just settled on him began to disintegrate. A note in Vladimir's voice was reminiscent of his conversation with Allogia.

"About my mother, the fortune teller, the witch. Wine!" He paused to take a drink. "She said that before you win back your throne, you'd bring fame and glory to mine. That's a sign that you cannot leave me yet."

Olav felt his temper rising.

"I forced the Radimichs and Veleti to bend a knee, isn't that enough?"

"It is not enough, my boy. If you only knew how keen my appetite is." As if to make his point, he reached for the roast. He turned a piece in his fingers, searching for the best place to bite into. "I have a mighty neighbor in the West, Duke Mieszko. He has a well-trained army and a young daughter. I'd take some of his settlements on the border, but . . ." He turned, sending the servant a chilling glare. "Wine! I sent messengers asking about her, but Mieszko told me she's a Christian and will not marry a pagan who already has wives. An old pagan, that's what he told them to say. He humiliated me!" Vladimir buried his teeth in the meat furiously. "Rogneda didn't want me either, she preferred my brother, that traitor, so I took her by force, and then killed her father, I did that!"

"Prince," Olav interrupted him calmly. "You have many wives."

"What, do you begrudge me wives? Ah, you young one, you don't yet know that it's easier to satisfy someone else's wives than your own."

"Do you want me to go to Duke Mieszko and ask for his daughter's hand for you?"

"I would"—Vladimir took a swig—"but he won't listen to pleas, he's already denied me. So, I would prefer if you went to him with my Varangians and burned him. A proper fire, so that . . ."

"I won't go," Olav said calmly. "It's time for me to return to where I come from."

"Not yet," the prince pleaded, surprisingly softly. "Stay, we have done so much for you, Allogia and I . . ."

Olav rose from the table, though he knew he shouldn't, since the prince was still seated. Their eyes met.

"Have I paid my debt of gratitude with my services yet, Prince Vladimir?" he asked firmly.

"Yes," the prince replied, breaking eye contact. "Don't look at me like that, it stings."

5

⚮

POLAND

Świętosława loved the moments when her father, with his hawk on his shoulder, paused in the doorway of the common room and said, without a shadow of a smile: "My daughter and son, I'm kidnapping you." When she'd been small, she would squeal at the sight of him as loudly as she could, trying to make her father's hawk respond with its angry, high-pitched scream. "I'm kidnapping you" meant they would go somewhere alone, together. She, her father, and her brother.

Mieszko had returned from Quedlinburg a few weeks earlier, but he hadn't settled back at home. He'd ordered the western boroughs to be supplied with more guards, he'd sent troops of scouts into the north, west, and south. Even the grumbling Jaksa, who followed Bolesław like a dog, had been sent on a secret mission. Her brother was furious, because another of his companions, Bjornar, had been similarly issued with a secret task and, saying nothing to Bolesław, Bjornar had mounted his horse and left.

"And we're kept in Ostrów Lednicki, with Oda and the court, like children! As if he wanted to tie me in swaddling clothes, for God's sake!" Bolesław raged, banging his hand against a wall before disappearing to exhaust himself riding his horse around the woods by the lake.

"He's shut us in here like chicks in a wicker cage. He'll fatten us up with golden seeds before we are served," Świętosława would laugh, and then Bolesław, incensed to breaking point, would burst out: "Can't you help me calm down, you little witch?" "No," she'd reply seriously. "But I know how to taunt you. Am I doing well?" Yes, she was doing quite well.

Then, on a hot evening two weeks before Midsummer's Night, Mieszko stood on the threshold of the communal chamber and said: "My daughter and son, I'm kidnapping you."

Just the three of them. Father, daughter, and son, like in the old days.

They rode out of Ostrów by the East Bridge.

Gniezno, then, she thought, counting the horse's steps. The even click of its hooves calmed her. Click, clack, four, eight, twelve . . . the last thing she wanted to do was ruin this day with a preemptive question. She breathed deeply. Click, clack, one hundred. Her father's squad was with them, but not the rest of the court, and they had little luggage. A hundred and fifty, click clack. If they were going to Gniezno, they would arrive in the middle of the night along the dry summer roads. Why at night? Had something happened? Though she tried to stay calm, her heart was still beating faster than the rhythm of her mount's steps. Click clack, a hundred and eighty; they dragged themselves over the bridge, one after another . . . only once they reached the road would they speed up to a trot, though if it had been up to her she'd make it a canter . . .

"Over two hundred steps!" she shouted suddenly, when her mare's hooves touched dry land. "Dear Father, why is the East Bridge so long?"

"Are you asking God or me?" Mieszko sent her a sidelong glance.

"You, God," she sighed. "Come on then, let's go."

"Where to?" Mieszko asked calmly.

She caught herself. "Wherever you want to take us, Father."

"Right then, let's go." Mieszko laughed and led the way.

It was after midnight, and the sickle-shaped moon barely lit their way as Mieszko turned off the path that led up the main hill of Gniezno. He went left, into thick bushes.

She wanted to ask where exactly they were going, but her brother's warning glance kept her silent. They were going slowly again, down a path which was clearly meant to be traveled on foot. Young birch branches grabbed at her face. After a while, the horses stepped out of the woods into a glade.

"Get down," Mieszko said to them, and to his men: "Light it up."

Small fires, one after another, were lit around the glade. Świętosława narrowed her eyes, letting them adjust to the sudden brightness. She blinked, then froze. An enormous oak grew in the middle of the glade, between four grass-covered mounds, each one as large and high as the royal manor. She looked to her father. He stood with his arms crossed and his eyes fixed on the tree. Bolesław walked over to her and took her hand. They walked toward the oak. Before they reached the mounds, though, they heard their father's voice.

"Stop."

They paused obediently, like children, like royal subjects. Her brother's hand was sweaty in hers. Mieszko stepped between them and grabbed their hands, turning them to face away from the mounds.

"We enter backward," he said, and pulled them gently along.

After a few dozen steps, they were under the oak. Her father didn't stop, but led them along by the mounds, saying:

"Siemomysł, Lestek, Siemowit, Piast."

"Your father, grandfather, great-grandfather . . ." Bolesław counted.

". . . and the first of the dynasty," his father finished for him. "Their ashes rest under the mounds, like royal heads under warm hats."

"Do you have to hold our hands?" her brother asked nervously.

"No, not anymore." He let go.

Bolesław made his way to Siemomysł's mound, knelt by it, and looked for something in the grass. He turned around after a moment, surprised.

"Someone made a sacrifice here recently."

"People still come here," their father said. "Less frequently, but they still remember."

Świętosława walked around the mounds slowly. She lifted her head, marveling at how high they were. She imagined all those who had made them, what the glade would have looked like full of people. Her mother's funeral appeared in front of her eyes. A crowd with lit candles. Dobrawa's body carried to the palace chapel. Then, the never-ending procession, a human river bidding goodbye to the duchess's remains. And the stone slab enclosing what was left of her in the cold depths of a grave.

Mieszko took out a jug and four small dishes from a hole in the tree. He placed one in front of each of the mounds, and poured out the contents of the jug. The scent of mead drifted on the night air.

"There used to be celebrations held on the mounds to call on the spirits of the dead," he said.

He stood still for a moment, then replaced the jug and, as if there was nothing strange about it, took their hands again. Her father's palms were covered in sweat now, too.

"We leave facing forward," he said. "Don't turn back. I brought you here so that you could meet your ancestors, but not to reminisce. Some things should remain in the past."

When they found themselves by the fires again, the squad members brought them their horses. Świętosława stroked her mare's neck.

"You're quiet." Mieszko stood behind her. "You didn't say a word under the oak."

"Where are their wives' mounds?" she asked. "My grandmothers, great-grandmothers . . . where are they?"

"There," he nodded toward the place they'd just come from. "They went to the pyre with their husbands."

"I see." Her voice was hard as flint.

Bolesław couldn't free himself from the vision of the mounds. Siemomysł, Lestek, Siemowit, Piast. Yes, for a moment, when the fires were lit and his father had grabbed both their hands and pulled them with him, he'd thought again about Abraham's sacrifice, but he'd quickly pushed the thought away. He knew Mieszko had shown them this place for a reason, and now he waited to find out why, but their father was silent.

They left Gniezno for Poznań. On the way, Mieszko pointed out the young trees which were growing to replace those cut down by their forefathers. Thousands of oaks used to build the unconquered might of the Piast boroughs. They passed Ostrów Lednicki and, not stopping, they rode on.

"What's that?" Bolesław asked, pointing at an oval mound covered with long grass on the right side of the road.

Świętosława, not waiting for her father's response, rode off the path and onto the wide, flat-topped hill.

"It looks like ashes!" she shouted from the top. "Like the ashes of a borough! Father?"

"Come back!" Mieszko called angrily. "Come back this instant!"

His sister returned reluctantly, looking over her shoulder as she did. Bolesław noticed his father's displeasure, but asked anyway,

"What did that place used to be?"

"Nothing worth remembering," the duke said, his tone making it clear there would be no further discussion of the matter. "Daughter, come here."

Bolesław slowed his horse until he was alongside Wolrad. His father's companion leaned out of his saddle and whispered as he nodded toward the grass-covered mound, "The borough of Moira. Never mention it to the duke again."

When they rode into Poznań, which was tightly surrounded by the defensive ribbons of the Warta and Cybina Rivers, the noise of the city felt louder than usual after the silence of the forest paths. Merchant carts crowded the bridge; children shouted in front of the gates as they tried to sell fish caught in the Warta; fishwives with baskets of barley cakes called out: "With honey!

With nuts! With salt from Kołobrzeg!" Young girls sang the praises of rasp-
berries and wild strawberries that had been collected into bowls of plaited
green leaves. The royal squad was visible from afar, towering over the people. Dogs slipped between the pedestrians, butchers' boys chasing them away
from their fathers' stalls; someone was playing a pipe, drawing passersby into
their pottery stall. The rhythmic clang of hammers sounded from the forge.
Weavers spread their works out on benches, from paintings to colorful circles
of rolled-up ribbons. A gray-bearded old man in a fraying dress leaned on
the wall nearby, but the snot-nosed children running around gave him no
chance of a doze.

"Tell us a story! Grandfather, the one about the snake and the eagle and
the girl!"

"No, I want the one about the fern!"

Piglets squealed in a makeshift enclosure, while chickens, geese, and ducks
beat their wings against the walls of their wicker cages. Finally, they passed
through the final gate, entering the palatium's calm yard.

"Oh, Maria!" one of the round housewives cried when she saw them. "My
lord is here, with master and mistress!"

A shout answered her from inside the walled kitchen,

"What about the duchess Oda with the little devils?"

The housewife said nothing, bowing low and blushing in embarrassment
at such familiarity.

When the stable boys had taken their horses, Świętosława whispered to
Bolesław, "I want to go to Mother."

So brother and sister went together to the chapel that adjoined the palatium. The light looked like hundreds of dancing fireflies when reflected
through the glass panes. Bolesław prayed for Dobrawa silently, then stood.
His sister remained with her head bowed.

"Go away now. I want to stay alone with Mother."

Bolesław nodded and left for the common room in search of food.
Świętosława could spend hours praying by their mother's grave.

But not long after he left, his father and sister appeared in the doorway.
Even more surprising, Jaksa and Bjornar stood behind them.

Mieszko sat down on a high chair, Świętosława on one side, Bolesław on
the other. Jaksa and Bjornar remained standing.

"Speak, our Redarian wolf. What news of your kin?" Mieszko said.

Bolesław gritted his teeth at his father's thoughtlessness, but Świętosława
burst out laughing.

"And you say that I'm the one who speaks without thought!" she said.

"What?" Mieszko glared at them both, not understanding.

"Jaksa has more than enough reasons to despise the Redarians. Have you forgotten what they did to him?"

"I said, '*our* Redarian wolf,'" Mieszko protested.

"You said, 'what news of your kin,'" Świętosława fired back. "What kin? The Redarians chased him away, unable to forgive his baptism, even though . . ."

"That's why I said ours!" Mieszko repeated stubbornly.

"Yours," Jaksa spoke up. "I am yours."

"Speak, then," their father said, ending the disagreement.

"The Veleti are gathering their tribes again," Jaksa began. "They're all arming themselves. A year ago, they managed to prepare for war in such secrecy that their attack surprised the empire. They don't seem overly cautious now, though. The Veleti have summoned the tribe leaders to a temple in Radogoszczy. After days of heated debate, it was agreed that the Redarian tribe would take leadership of the joined forces."

"Who leads them now?" Mieszko interrupted Jaksa.

"Wojbor."

"Wojbor? I don't know him. Must be a younger one."

"He's thirty. He gained fame in last year's attack on Brenna. He's the one who dragged Dodilon's body from his grave and took his clothes. And he set fire to the cathedral altar once they finished using it for their feast."

"Do you know him?" the duke asked.

"Yes. Wojbor was my brother, once."

Silence followed his words. Bolesław knew better than anyone that, for Jaksa, talking about his family was like walking on a hot sheet of metal. The boy hadn't even been five when his father, the Redarian chief at the time, was forced to give him up as a hostage to the emperor. The Saxons treated Jaksa brutally, like a wild Slavic pup. They forced baptism on him, then returned him to his father. But the Redarians cast him out as well, like a bitch does her pups when she smells a foreign scent on them. Since that day, Jaksa had been fueled by anger. He hated both the Redarians and the Saxons for what they had done to him. He referred to himself as "Swaróg's bastard" and "Christ's stepson." Pain was the foundation for his self-image, as the former had denied him, and the latter had taken him by force. After so many years of feeling he belonged nowhere, he now followed Mieszko and Bolesław with a loyalty like none other.

"Swaróg's priests consulted the oracles," Jaksa continued in a colorless voice. "And declared the signs favorable. The men clamored as Wojbor swore he would lead them to victory over the Saxons and all their allies."

"Did he name those allies?"

"Only one, my lord. You."

"He didn't mention my brother-in-law? The prince of the Czechs?"

"No, my lord, not a word. He said, though, that their first target should be Meissen."

Bolesław saw his father's anger building. The Czechs had likely betrayed them.

"Bjornar!" Mieszko called out, thanking Jaksa with a nod. "What have you found out about the Danes and Obotrites?"

"Sven, Harald Bluetooth's son, used the rebellions in Połabie not only to win back Hedeby from the Saxons, but more importantly, to move against his father. Sven, the hungry son, proved his swiftness and deadliness to the Danes with his campaign. Harald also moved against the Saxons, but he did it with more caution, and Sven used this as proof the old king is lethargic and unfit to rule."

Bolesław didn't even flinch as he listened to the story of the son's rebellion.

"And to ensure that no one could forget who won back Hedeby, Sven has ordered his name be carved into a giant stone he placed in the port."

"Sven, Harald's son," Mieszko said, placing a hand on Świętosława's shoulder.

Bolesław heard something in his father's voice, something that could be admiration or mockery. Świętosława sent their father such a glare that he withdrew his hand.

"Battles between father and son aside, an alliance between the Danes and Obotrites is certain. The Obotrite leader Mściwój's daughter was married to Harald in Denmark; she was Sven's mother," Bjornar finished.

"What news of Jomsborg? Have the Vikings been dragged into the game?"

Jomsborg was a constant topic of interest for their father. The Danish king Harald had built the Viking stronghold in Jom, and though Mieszko had succeeded in gaining influence in Wolin's port, next door to Jom, Jomsborg itself remained firmly under Harald's control.

The Jomsvikings proclaimed that they were independent from any external influences, and their willingness to work as hired mercenaries supported this, but their loyalty to Harald was widely known.

"I didn't sail into Jomsborg itself," Bjornar admitted. "The iron gates of the sea stronghold are open only to their own. But there is an inn on an island nearby, in which all paths cross, and it churns with gossip. That's where I learned the Jomsvikings won't be joining the fight for the empire, on Otto or Henry's side. They have been summoned to fight a different war."

"For what?" Mieszko cut in, and Bolesław thought how hypocritical it was for his father to scold Świętosława for her impatience.

"For the north, my lord," Bjornar replied. "Harald wants to prove to the Danes, especially to his own son, that he is still the ruler of the north. Norway, which is under his authority, is slipping between his fingers. Jarl Haakon, the leader of the northern Norwegian lords, who Harald named his viceroy in Norway, has declared independence. He isn't paying taxes or sending his troops when Harald calls for them, he reigns as if he were a ruler in his own right. Harald has summoned the Jomsvikings to attack Norway and defeat Jarl Haakon."

"If the Jomsvikings succeed and the Norwegian armies come under Harald's command again, his forces will be doubled. He'll be able to send them to face the Saxons." Mieszko pounded his fist on the carved armrest. That would make Harald far too strong a ruler to be so close to his borders. "Have you confirmed this, Bjornar? Or perhaps the war for the north is merely drunken Viking brags?"

"I've confirmed it, my lord."

Mieszko stood up. "I'm unhappy to hear the news you've brought. But you, my young scouts, satisfy me greatly."

Bjornar and Jaksa walked out with their heads held high. Praise from the duke was rare. Bolesław bit his lip as he tried to recall when he had last received any himself.

Once he'd sent Jaksa and Bjornar away, Mieszko paced the chamber of the palatium. When it seemed he'd gained control of his anger, he turned back to Bolesław and Świętosława.

"We're surrounded."

They looked at him calmly. The seventeen-year-old son and fifteen-year-old daughter. He'd never lied to them, but he had never been so open with the truth, either. He went on,

"The ring of enemies on our western borders is tightening. The Danes have joined the Obotrites in the north. And the Obotrites, though they have been trying to break free of the Veleti fellowship for years, will now march beside them. The Czechs will join the Veleti in the south."

"The scouts didn't say that," Bolesław observed.

"Your uncle Boleslav, my brother-in-law, the Czech prince, has sent me a separate invitation to cooperate," Mieszko replied bitterly. "In his invasion of Meissen."

"The Christian Czechs with the pagan Veleti?" Świętosława raised her eyebrows in disgust.

"Not for the first time, daughter. The Czechs make you think of your mother, whose faith ran deep, but if you want to understand what fighting wars is all about, you must be able put that image aside."

"No, I don't," Świętosława said. "It's enough that I must remember we're not bound by any alliance since her death."

Mieszko wanted to strangle his daughter sometimes, but it was usually when she reminded him too much of himself. She was his child, through and through.

"In spring, after the emperor's death, the Czech, Obotrite, and Miessen leaders all supported Henry of Bavaria's claim to the imperial throne."

"So did you," Świętosława added.

"Do you want to hear more, or do you already know everything?" Mieszko snapped.

"I'm listening, Father," she said, and put on such an innocent face that Bolesław would have believed she was being sincere if he didn't know her so well.

"Some of the Reich lords also supported Henry, but in recent days they've been abandoning him, leaving him for the emperor's widow, one by one. Henry will be forced to work with the pagans, because by reaching for Czech and Obotrite help he will, in reality, be allying himself with the entire Veleti fellowship."

"From what I understand, Father," Bolesław spoke up, "you want to push these alliances off the course they are currently on."

"I'll withdraw my support for Henry in favor of Theophanu, the emperor's widow. I won't aid the Czechs against Meissen, but I'll help Meissen against the Czechs. And I'll stand by Denmark's enemies to weaken it and destroy its unity with the Obotrites."

"Oh!" Świętosława couldn't stifle the exclamation.

"What now?"

"I was worried that you'd decided Sven would make a good son-in-law."

"Don't you like Vikings?" Mieszko asked, his voice deceptively casual.

"I don't like sons who stand against their fathers," she replied, the humblest of daughters.

"Will the empress accept you?" Bolesław asked. "You backed Henry twice. She's sharp enough not to trust you."

"She'll accept every Christian ally, although you're right, son. Women in power are particularly vengeful. Theophanu is unforgiving, and she can be cruel."

"Do my ears deceive me?" his daughter asked. "When you spoke of Mściwój, Boleslav, or Sven, you didn't utter a single insult, but for Theophanu you have so many! 'Vengeful, unforgiving, cruel.' Perhaps she is too bold for you?"

"You're the bold one, daughter," Mieszko said, visibly straining to keep his anger in check. "And the empress isn't playing fair. Haven't you noticed that no new bishop has arrived here since Bishop Jordan's death two years ago? An abbot has been ordained as bishop to come here. I've been waiting for him for two years, but the Greek tyrant won't let him leave his abbey."

"Vengeful, unforgiving, and cruel, yet she holds so much power," Świętosława said sweetly. "I like hearing about Empress Theophanu."

Mieszko felt a surge of anger, but couldn't help laughing at this. She was too much like him indeed. *My bold one,* he thought, and replied, "You'd be even worse in her place, Świętosława."

"I'd love to be in her place, Father."

"Then learn!" He slammed his fist on the table so suddenly that his hawk startled and leapt from his shoulder to the back of a chair. "A woman dons a crown only as the wife of a ruler. And a ruler's wife must be smart enough not to be dismissed and replaced by another. And, above all, she must give birth to an heir."

Świętosława reached out. Not to him, but to the hawk. The predator cocked its head and looked at her with a golden eye. It stepped cautiously onto her arm.

"And I think that, above all, she must be strong," she replied, looking at him. "To not die in childbirth. To survive her husband in good health, as Theophanu has survived Otto. And to rule as a widow and regent. Have I learned today's lesson well, Father?"

He stared at her. Her hair was like amber, her skin pale, her eyebrows dark. Her eyes were green or gray, like Dobrawa's. She was ugly, because she resembled them both. And beautiful, because she was like no one else in the world.

Mieszko took Bolesław and Świętosława to the banks of the Warta before sunset. A group of young people were gathered on the opposite shore, driving stakes in the ground and carrying over firewood. Midsummer was approaching.

"You'll give the blessing to the newlyweds this year," he said to Bolesław.

"Why can't I come with you to the Hoftag?" Bolesław asked, his annoyance clear.

"It would be incredibly foolish to send out a ruler and his heir together. In case something were to happen."

The hawk on his shoulder shifted its weight. It was hungry.

"Are you expecting something to happen?" Świętosława asked.

"Are you naming me your heir?" Bolesław inquired simultaneously.

"Yes."

"Yes what? Danger or heir?" His daughter laughed.

Sometimes it's one and the same, he thought, but aloud he said,

"Bolesław, you'll be my heir when I die. I don't think anyone has ever doubted this."

Even if my Oda won't like it, he added to himself.

He shrugged and let the hawk fly off to hunt. The bird pushed itself from his glove with strong legs. Mieszko lifted his head and followed its flight, curious to see what the bird would hunt. Crows were clustered nearby, and he could hear their warning caws. The hawk must have seen them, too, because it was hurtling toward them, gaining speed. It wasted no time scouting and circling its prey. It dove suddenly, scattering the crows, then flew back with one of the dark birds clutched in its talons.

"Victory is beautiful." Mieszko stretched and looked at his children. The hawk landed near them and tore into its prey with a sharp beak. "You asked me if I expected danger. Yes, always. I expect it at every meeting with the Reich leaders, when I set out to every war, hunt, feast, even when I bed my wife and, to anticipate your question, let me clarify; it doesn't matter whether it was Dobrawa or Oda. I'd be a fool if I wasn't always prepared. But . . ." He laughed and spread his arms. "I'm not afraid of it. Fear takes away a person's freedom, it's more crippling than any wound."

The hawk finished eating and took off once more. The youngsters on Warta's opposite bank were practicing the pipe, and uneven sounds interrupted by laughter drifted toward them across the water.

"Four mounds, like the four cardinal directions," Mieszko said, and though he was rarely moved, he felt something nearly overwhelming now. "Four generations ago, Piast won the people over at a rally. My great-grandfather, Siemowit, Poland's first duke, inherited his power and fought war after war. He was focused on pushing back enemies. His son, Lestek, understood that if he attacked an enemy after successfully defending against them, he would double his gains. By the time he passed on power to my own father, Siemomysł, no one dared attack our boroughs and villages. Your grandfather was free to pour all his energy into strengthening the country."

The young people across the river lit a fire. One of them notched an arrow and lit its head. They aimed at the straw wreath on one of the poles.

"I received beautiful lands from my father, but it wasn't enough."

He stopped. Should he tell them about the endless hunger? That he had been born with it and couldn't satisfy it, even now? That he felt constant discontent, that when he looked at a forest he didn't care about the trees, only what was beyond them? That watching a sunset, he already wondered about the sunrise? How could he explain?

The wreath on the pole now burned brightly across the Warta. The kids began to dance around it.

"My grandfather and father achieved much, but they were still only tribal chieftains. They had to stand in front of crowds and listen to the endless talk of the people. And the people, once they gain a voice, will hold on to it. They can judge a ruler, punish or reward them. The people see only what's in front of them: the harvest, a full breadbasket, the neighbor who stole a cow, a horse with laminitis, a sick child. It's life, of course, but a ruler must see more."

Dusk was falling. The hawk squawked as it returned to them. Mieszko pulled on his leather glove and raised his arm.

"Because if an enemy comes, there will be no harvest. If neighbors sense a weakness in our lands, they will invade and steal our horses, cows, homes."

The wreath had burned out, and the young people on the other side were stamping out the remains of their fire.

A narrow boat arrived on the Warta's current, with a white sail and a single rower.

"Your mother and her religion were a revelation for me. I'd waited for a sign, a lesson like that for my whole life, something to show me the path on which I'd succeed. For a god who gives a ruler the right to rule."

A few of the youths now walked into the river, but only one got into the boat and sailed away with the rower. The bright sail fluttered in the wind as the others watched them go.

"Now, the people believe only God can anoint a leader. Not factions or priests or the people."

The others began to play their pipes again.

"Not the gods of fire, sun, water, war, peace, life, death, harvest, different ones for each tribe. The one God. One Lord and one ruler. Him and me. Since the day of my baptism, God has given me the right to rule, and I have opened the borders of my country to him."

The hawk began to clean its feathers, which interrupted Mieszko's musings. He stretched out an arm and let the bird walk over to Bolesław's shoulder.

"I built an army, trained and armed by me. Always ready to attack or defend. And I doubled the lands I inherited from my father."

He watched his son with the hawk on his shoulder. He saw himself, not in the past, but in the future. He said, slowly:

"I'm a predator, but I don't hunt alone." He looked in the eyes of his children, and emotion threatened to choke him. "You, my children, are now grown, and strong. But I have only two heirs, and I must reach for all four corners of the earth. Try to understand. That's why I can't stop with you. I have to reach for your half brothers, Oda's sons, as well."

He pulled his children to him then, embracing them. He felt the warmth emanating from their bodies. They were bone of his bone, blood of his blood. And he was about to rob them of their childhoods.

6

POLAND
JOMSBORG, WOLIN ISLAND

After reclaiming Hedeby from the Saxons, Sven, the future king of Denmark, had sailed to Jomsborg, home to the Jomsvikings—mercenaries of legend who had been steadfast in their loyalty to his father. He would need their support before standing openly against Harald.

Sigvald's ship was the one leading them into the Viking stronghold. Since the victory in Hedeby, Sven had come to greatly respect the brothers Palnatoki had sent to him, Sigvald and Thorkel.

As their ships slipped forward, Sven stared around him. This was his first time in the legendary port, and without a guide, Jomsborg was nearly impossible to find.

The old king, his father, had picked this place perfectly, Sven thought. A massive wooden gate blocked their path into the channel, flanked by a stone wall, and a stone bridge with a manned watchtower. Sigvald stopped his ship and gestured for the others to do the same.

"Your ship and captain?" a soldier shouted, though he had to have seen the emblems on their sails.

"Jarl Sigvald's *Zealand Falcon* and young king Sven Haraldsson's *Bloody Fox*."

A horn sounded from beyond the gates, and hinges creaked as the giant doors swung inward. Sigvald didn't signal their men onward, and after a moment Sven realized why. There was another gate beyond the wooden one, this one made of iron. The head of a wolf was emblazoned on each door, the sign of the Jomsvikings. The second gate now opened too, and as they sailed through both gates, Sven understood why Jom was said to be unconquerable. The iron gates clanked shut behind them.

They sailed into a port that could have easily fit a hundred longboats. Fifty were anchored there now. Sven disembarked, following Sigvald's lead, and studied the Jomsvikings who greeted them. They stood in a silent line, stretching all the way to the manor entrance. Sven couldn't help but feel as though they were trying to hide the inside of the stronghold from him. And that, as they silently watched him approach, they were comparing him to his father.

My hair is just as red, and I'm taller by a head, he thought with a vengeance.

The chiefs of the three houses of Jom awaited him before the manor, alongside the jarl of the Jomsvikings, his tutor and old friend, Palnatoki.

"Young king," Palnatoki greeted Sven formally.

"Jarl!" Sven opened his arms. "It's good to see you again!"

They embraced, and Sven felt his throat go dry. Palnatoki felt fragile in his arms, the skin on his cheeks loose, marking his face with two deep lines.

"You look good," Sven lied. His tutor looked at him meaningfully, but didn't challenge Sven's comment in front of the others.

"Come, join us for a feast, young king. A traveler from afar awaits you."

Fires burned in the long hall. Shields of fallen enemies decorated the walls. Sheepskins were draped across the benches. The bowls and chalices were plain and unornamented. There was nothing excessive or luxurious about the hall. And there was not a single woman present, as Jomsborg's laws denied them access to the stronghold. Before arriving, Sven had dismissed this as a mere story, but now he saw that not only were there no women, but there were also no servants. Jugs of mead stood on the tables, inviting guests to pour for themselves. All places at the chiefs' table were equal, and Sven sat on Palnatoki's right, with Sigvald and Thorkel next to him. The Zealand brothers were leaders of two of the houses of Jomsborg and had once studied here under Palnatoki themselves. They had been crucial in the fight to reclaim Hedeby from the Saxons, and Sven was grateful his tutor had brought them to his side.

A young, dark-haired man in a rich caftan threaded with silver walked into the hall and bowed his head toward Sven. "Styrbjorn, Olof Björnsson's son."

"I didn't know your father," Sven said, "but I know some who fought by his side, and I know he deserves a place in Valhalla."

"True," Styrbjorn agreed. "My father ruled our country justly when he was alive. But when he died, his brother refused to acknowledge my right of inheritance. Eric disinherited me and decided to rule Sweden himself."

A father and a son, a nephew and an uncle, thought Sven. *Each fighting for power.*

"What do you expect from me?" Sven asked aloud, realizing that the arrangement of the chiefs' table wasn't accidental. They sat in a line on one side, not looking at each other when talking to a guest or interrogating the accused.

"Support in my fight against Eric," Styrbjorn replied.

"How old is your uncle? He was older than your father, if I remember correctly. Would it not cost you less to wait for him to die?"

"My father didn't die in his bed," the newcomer said indignantly. "Eric may have seen more than forty years, but he's still as strong as a wild boar. I don't want to wait for his death, I want to deliver it!"

Mine's older, Sven thought, *and I also would prefer to be rid of him by my own hand.*

"If I help you, what will I get in return?" he asked bluntly.

"I will share Eric's treasure."

"That's not enough," Sven replied. "The Jomsvikings fight for silver, but you asked for a meeting with a king. You must offer more than silver to a king."

He reached for a jug, not because he was thirsty, but because he needed an excuse to look at Jom's chieftains. What effect did his words have on them? He couldn't tell. They sat, leaning back, their faces visible only to the newcomer.

"What do you mean, my lord?" Styrbjorn looked unsettled.

"Power, guest," Sven replied. "If I won the Swedish throne for you, that would mean I'd be strong enough to sit on it myself. So, I ask again: What's in it for me if I give it to you?"

"The young king is thinking of a viceroyship," Palnatoki interjected.

"I don't understand." Styrbjorn studied Sven nervously, then his gaze slid sideways, first to the right, then to the left, over the faces of the other chieftains.

"If I won Eric's throne, I'd give it to you as my viceroy, you would be Denmark's ruler in Sweden. Is that clear enough?"

Styrbjorn reddened. Yes, he understood it now. He rose from the table.

"I cannot agree to this, my lord. Allow me to bid you goodbye."

Sven nodded to him and the young Swede left.

"I want to speak to you alone," he told Palnatoki quietly, as Sigvald walked their guest out.

The jarl made a gesture for the other two chiefs to leave them.

"You have made an enemy, boy," Palnatoki said when they were alone.

"Not by accident," Sven replied, turning his chair so he faced his aging mentor. "I'm in trouble myself, Palnatoki, and I can't help Styrbjorn stand against his uncle. But I'd prefer him to think that I'm choosing not to because he won't pay me as I wish."

"Ah. Cunning," his mentor said. "If I didn't know you, I'd have believed it. I'd have thought you arrogant and demanding."

"I did it for them, too." Sven nodded toward the empty chairs at the table. "The houses of sailors, scouts, warriors, and hosts. The four chiefs of mighty Jom. Each one is comparing me to Harald, each one is wondering which of us is better, the father or the son?" He reached out and gripped the old man's shoulder. "Palnatoki, I may trust you, but not them. They, and each one of the Jomsvikings, is loyal to my father. Do you know what I fear? That when I face him, your Zealand boys who fought by my side at Hedeby will move against me at one whistle from Harald."

"As long as I'm alive, that won't happen. But look at me. Skin and bone." Palnatoki spat onto the ground and ran his boot over the saliva. "I wrap a belt around me like . . ."

"Are you ill? What the devil is wrong with you?" Sven watched him, unsettled, noticing again the old man's hollow cheeks.

Palnatoki shrugged. "My time is coming to an end."

"Stop. A codfish drying in the wind grows skinny, but it's still strong when placed back in the water. Palnatoki, you must sail out, don't rot in a stronghold, go somewhere. Even if it were with that boy, Styrbjorn. Set a high price, get your arse on a longship, and sail. It'll do you a world of good!"

"If life is a jug of mead, then I, my little one, am at the last sip. But perhaps you're right. Death with a sword in my hand, death at sea . . . a good ending."

Sven didn't want to hear this. He grabbed his mead, then let it go just as quickly, as if it burned him. The jug was empty. He stood up and brought over a new one. He filled their cups, and they drank. But instead of sweetness, Sven tasted salt.

Sven, don't cry like a child! He bit his tongue. "What will happen after you've . . ." He hesitated at the word. ". . . left?"

"Ragnarök, perhaps?" Palnatoki joked.

"Stop!" Sven slammed his fist on the table. Palnatoki spoke so calmly, and Sven didn't want to make peace with the old man's imminent passing.

"The Jomsvikings will choose a new jarl," Palnatoki continued, "voting for one of the leaders of the four houses. If Vagn or Fat Bue is chosen, Jomsborg will remain loyal to your father. Those two belong to him like nuns to Christ. But if they choose Sigvald or his brother Thorkel, you have a chance. Unless you follow the advice you gave the young Swede." He grinned, showing un-even teeth. "You wait for Harald's death. But then, you'd have to arrive at Jom immediately, the day after."

"Why?"

"Because Mieszko, the Polish duke, is increasingly interested in Jom. He is the sole ruler of Wolin now, and that's so very close. Your father used to dream that, thanks to Jomsborg, he could take Wolin; some even said that was why he built it in the first place, but that was just a story. Wolin stands on gold, silver, and slaves. They pay us to protect the port and merchant ships, so robbing Wolin would be like chopping off the branch you're sitting on, and wetting your whole arse. The merchants would stop coming, and the robbed silver would eventually finish. Jomsborg and Wolin both gain by working together. We protect them, and they pay us handsomely for our services. Our people go there for better food, whores, and jewels. They sell their plunder. We're good neighbors. Except that Wolin works with Mieszko just as closely, and if the new jarl is closer to the Polish prince than to you—well, you can see what I'm getting at, boy. If I were you, I'd drop in to Wolin tonight or tomorrow, see it for yourself. Only leave the *Bloody Fox* in Jomsborg, you don't need to announce your presence. Sigvald's sailors can give you a boat that won't attract attention."

"Mściwój was asking Mieszko about a wife for me." Sven swept his red hair from his shoulders.

"Very good."

"Not so good." Sven pulled a face and poured himself more mead. "Mieszko doesn't like the fact that I prefer the old gods."

"You're as greedy as you are ginger, boy." Palnatoki laughed. "Why did you ask for Dobrawa's daughter when she's even been given a saint's name? Mieszko has two other daughters to marry off, and neither of those has been baptized. One is Astrid, Dalwin's granddaughter, Wolin's own jarl. She makes quite the impression, and I know this for a fact, I've seen her more than once. She'd seem to be made for you, right? But that's exactly why old Mieszko won't give her to you, because he's as smart as we are. Think about Geira, the young widow."

"Geira?"

"Gudbrod's widow. Would that suit you?"

Sven's expression clouded over. It would suit him, perfectly, if it wasn't for the war with the Saxons he had stepped into. Empress Theophanu, the Saxon leader, had regrouped her troops and her armies were beginning to win back the lands they'd lost. Geira of Bornholm wouldn't help him defend himself or Danish borders from Theophanu. But the empress's armies would follow the youngest princess, Świętosława, who his grandfather Mściwój was suggesting he marry. The one with the name of a saint.

"I'll think about it, old rogue," Sven answered eventually, and changed the subject. "Is it true that you sail to my father's summons? Will you rob Norway?"

"Not rob, only discipline. The lords of the north and Jarl Haakon need reminding that they are Danish subjects. My boys are as eager for this war as if it were their wedding nights."

"When do you raise the war shields?"

"Any day."

Sven thought for a moment that this was also in his favor. It would be good to inherit not only Denmark, but also Norway from Harald. Just like his father had ruled in his best days. But he reined his thoughts in quickly, recalling that for the time being he had the Saxons on his back; if he didn't defend what he had gained, he would lose his people's respect and then his chance of inheriting anything at all.

"'Any day' means you don't have fighters to spare, do you? I need a few good crews," he finally said, what he'd come here to ask in the first place, forcing his tone to remain light.

"I don't, my boy. All my troops will sail to face the lords of the north. You picked your time poorly." Palnatoki met his eye with a sad expression.

Sven felt as if he were choking as he met his gaze. "See you soon then, my friend."

"In Valhalla, son," the old jarl replied.

7

POLAND
WOLIN, WOLIN ISLAND

Świętosława embraced Astrid and Geira. She couldn't have been happier to see them.

"Three sisters! Together again, just like in the good old days. Do you remember when we went fishing for trout in Moscow? Oh, that was something!"

"I remember when you tore your dress, and 'that was something' Duchess Dobrawa wasn't too pleased about," Geira teased.

"And I remember the largest trout I'd ever seen getting away because you were yelling so loudly to reel it in faster." Astrid pinched her arm. "You have grown, though, Świętosława. I can tell, and it's so nice to see."

"It's nice to see? As if I wasn't lovely all along!"

Astrid laughed. "You were a troublesome little girl. Your mother's ladies-in-waiting prayed to the graceful Mary when Dobrawa ordered them to fetch you."

"Not to the graceful Mary, you pagan." Świętosława wagged a finger at Astrid. "You're twisting the story on purpose to annoy me."

"That's what they whispered! Do you want to know what they called you when nobody was listening?" Astrid lowered her voice conspiratorially.

"I do," Świętosława replied just as quietly, and stared at her sister's lips as if bewitched.

"Little Satan, Lucifer's child, a half devil!" Astrid declared, while Geira stifled a laugh beside them.

"You lie," Świętosława jumped up. "Dusza, Dusza! Come here. True or false?"

Dusza nodded three times.

"Oh, damn you, the whole lot of you are plotting against me!"

Astrid, laughing, cupped Świętosława's face in her hands. She looked in
her eyes and kissed each cheek.

"It's so good to see you!" Świętosława couldn't stop herself from embracing her sisters again. "Kind souls. Finally, I have someone to talk to. Dusza
has so much to say that she says nothing at all."

"All right, that's enough of all these affections," Astrid said. "Why has
Duke Mieszko brought you to Wolin?"

Neither Astrid nor Geira ever referred to him as father.

"To learn," Świętosława replied, not meeting their eyes.

Astrid's grandfather, Dalwin, Wolin's viceroy, showed them around. What
Świętosława saw surpassed her expectations. Two hundred ships were
moored by a massive embankment that was reinforced by logs. There were
modest dugout canoes and small, nimble sculls, but these were barely visible, since the rest of the port was overwhelmed with Slavic corabias and
Scandinavian snekkes and knarrs. A flock of sheep would have fit on the
medium-sized ones, and a few cows could be added to the largest, along with
thirty men and countless barrels of cargo. Shallow and wide, bow and stern
identical, with a large free deck. Their stem and stern were elegantly arched,
as if inviting travelers aboard. Dalwin pointed out different ships in turn.

"These have come from the east, from Rus, Vladimir's dukedom. That's
where the rich Holmgard lies, known by the Slavs as Novgorod. They
brought marten skins, beaver furs, sables, and dormice. And plenty of wax
for the Saxon churches and their candles. These two have come from as far
as Miklagard, the large Greek city that they call Constantinople, after an old
emperor. They look like mere shells next to the northern knorrs, but their
main job is to get across the long River Dnieper, and believe me, Princess,
many a brave man has lost his life on her stone threshold."

"What have they brought?"

"Something that doesn't require a large hold." Dalwin laughed. "Silver
coin for your father, and rose oil for Duchess Oda. These two ships will
take sable furs to the khalifs in Baghdad. Look, if you will, at these powerful knarrs. The treasures of the north have arrived on them. Long narwhal
horns, morse fangs, whale skins, seal furs and fat, by far the best at sealing
out water."

"Incredibly valuable," Astrid interjected with a laugh. "If you get as much
as a drop on you, you'll stink until you're shrunken with age."

Geira brought her head close and whispered innocently, "Would you like some for the duchess stepmother?"

"And these sea monsters?" Świętosława asked, barely controlling her laughter and pointing at heavy ships with high gunwales. "They look like floating houses."

Dalwin nodded. "Geira can tell you about those. She knows more about it than anyone."

"Not anymore," Geira said sharply. "I've not taken part in it since I've been widowed."

"Oh," Świętosława realized. "Those are slave ships?"

"Yes, sister. Floating prisons. Many on board don't last long enough to reach port."

"Don't say that," Dalwin interjected. "The Arabs take good care of their cargo. If they are paid with pure silver, they make sure the slaves reach the khalifs alive."

"I don't know how the Arabs take care of their human cargo. But I know how headhunters do, before they put people up for sale, and believe me, the fate of the lowest servant seems better than what happens on those ships."

"Enough!" Astrid interrupted, knowing how painful this conversation was for Geira. "Let's show Świętosława the stalls. Perhaps our beautiful princess will pick out something for herself?"

"Wait!" Świętosława said. "Dalwin, where will I find the famous warships?"

"Do they interest you more than gems?" Astrid asked impatiently.

"And rightly so," her grandfather added. "But I'm sorry, Princess. They aren't here. This is merely a trading port. I have space in my harbor for merchants and sailors, the working people of the seas, but not for the ocean's armies. War ruins trade, and in the long term trade is stronger than war."

"And Jomsborg?" Świętosława asked.

"The opposite. If need be, they provide the escort. We pay them for protection."

"I'd like to see this famous Jomsborg."

"Women aren't allowed there," Astrid pointed out, and pulled Świętosława toward the borough.

There was plenty of space on the embankment to unload the ships, and cargo was carried along wooden bridges into the borough. The palisade that protected the hidden city inside stretched as far as the waterfront itself. And there was much to protect. Piles of cargo, merchant homes, workshops

altering the goods brought to Wolin. Crowds of people of every nation. The
dark faces of the Arabs, wind-hardened sailors, fair-haired Normans, and
dark-haired Finns.

"And who is that beauty?" Świętosława asked, looking at a tall woman
with a gold scarf wound around her head.

"Her, I don't know. Perhaps she's come from Miklagard? I've heard the
Greeks wear scarves like that."

"No, Astrid, Greek women veil their faces," Geira said.

"A true tower of Babel," Świętosława whispered, amazed at the bustling
scene around her.

"What?" Geira and Astrid asked together. *Of course,* Świętosława thought,
they don't know the story of that magnificent tower.

"Nothing," she replied, feeling suddenly alone among the crowd.

They meandered between piles of eastern silks that shimmered like drag-
onfly wings. They touched thin, almost transparent fabrics from Flanders,
and thick spools of Icelandic wool, arguing over which fine material was the
prettiest, until Dusza found the clear winner, which Świętosława bought her
as a prize. Then there were ear cuffs, rings, bracelets, necklaces, chains . . .
the stalls seemed endless as the sisters strolled through them.

"I like all of it," Geira sighed, "so much so that I don't want any of it
anymore."

"Then look here, sister," Świętosława called out to her, studying a fur coat
spread over one of the benches. "Oh, my!" She grasped the soft hair, touching her face to the red, mottled fur. "Lynx? Is this a lynx? I want it! Whose is
it?" Świętosława looked around, searching fervently for the seller.

"It belongs to you, holy lady," a slender older woman said, emerging from
the stall.

"I'll pay whatever you want for it. And for any others you have!"

"I have only this one, holy lady. And since I've been selling furs I've had
no other. A lynx is a quarry that by far outsmarts man, and is a prize rarely
won by hunters."

As her excitement over the fur settled, Świętosława picked up on the title
the woman had used. "Why do you call me that?"

"That's your name, isn't it?" The woman bowed to her humbly.

Świętosława felt a flush creep into her cheeks. She had embarrassed herself again, acting like the impulsive girl her sisters saw her as. She paid for the
fur and, clutching it to her chest, quickly left the stall.

Astrid pulled her toward the cottages of purse-makers, tailors, wood-carvers, but Świętosława was no longer interested in the market's treasures. Though at a blacksmith's forge she found herself examining the daggers on display.

"You'll see some real treasures there," Dalwin praised. "Blades from every corner of the world."

Świętosława liked the intricate pattern on the blade of Damascene steel. She chose two, one for herself and one for Bolesław, then her eyes fell on a row of idols, gleaming, each with four gloomy faces. *"Not the gods of fire, sun, water, war, peace, life, death, harvest, different ones for each tribe. One Almighty God,"* her father's voice from their day by the Warta echoed in her head.

"The beautiful princess has bought the best blades, let her take a whetstone for them too." The merchant passed her a whetstone decorated with the four faces.

"This princess could sharpen knives with nothing but her tongue, Gunnar." Astrid stepped between them and firmly moved the merchant aside.

"I'm not a child," Świętosława said, once they'd left the stall. "You don't have to protect me all the time."

"It's a reflex, I'm sorry." Astrid took her hand and kissed it. "Tell us again about why Mieszko has sent you here," she said, clearly trying to take Świętosława's mind off the incident. "For learning, you said. For learning what?"

Geira, Dalwin, and Dusza were walking ahead of them.

"You want to talk here? In the crowds?" Świętosława threw the lynx fur over her shoulder.

"No one can eavesdrop in a place where everyone can hear you," Astrid replied, helping Świętosława fasten the fur with a golden clip.

"Father has sent me for you and Geira. He wants us all with him."

"Oh!" Astrid's eyebrows rose. "So what I've seen in my dreams is coming true?"

"You have seen this in your dreams?"

Astrid placed a finger on her lips.

"Maybe you can dream something for me?"

"Perhaps, my sister. If you really need it. Tell me, what's wrong? I can see that something's bothering you."

"Duchess Oda," Świętosława said, unable to keep the anger from her voice.

"Oh, Świętosława. Leave her alone, or I really will believe that you're still a spoilt young princess. I loved your mother like my own, but you can't stand Oda? Mieszko has had many wives. None of them are alive today, and you begrudge him the newest one? Don't be so possessive, sister."

"That's not it, Astrid. Father is planning my marriage, but he won't tell me who it is. He speaks of it only in riddles."

"Perhaps he hasn't chosen yet? Perhaps he hasn't decided? The duke is known for his ever-nimble alliances."

"He says I'm important, his valuable daughter, a precious heir, but then it turns out to be no more than a lie, just another story. He doesn't share what's truly important with me. He took me and Bolesław to see the ancestral mounds, and to Poznań, and he talked to us about . . ." She hesitated. No, she wouldn't reveal what he'd spoken of. ". . . his visions and plans. And then, the day after that, Oda arrived. If you'd just seen her! Draped in riches, pale, proud. She grabbed me and hissed into my ear: *Learn the tongue of the Vikings.* As if I would believe a word she says. She's wretched, Astrid, truly."

They were interrupted as a tall, red-haired man collided with them.

"Tilgiv mig!" he said, as surprised as they were.

"Hold øje på hvem du rører!" Astrid replied sharply.

"Nej, du skal holde øje!" he snarled.

The crowd around them had stopped, as if it could scent a fight brewing. Dalwin was already pushing his way back toward them. The angered man had long, fiery hair, with a beard just as bright and red. His eyes darted between Astrid, Świętosława, and the lynx fur over her shoulder. Then, as quickly as he had appeared, he turned and disappeared among the crowd.

"What happened?" Dalwin asked, worried.

"Nothing, grandfather. A red-haired Viking tried to walk over us, but as you can see, he's run away. See, my dear?" Astrid turned cheerfully to Świętosława again. "Perhaps it will be useful to learn the Viking tongue after all."

"Tilgiv mig! Hold øje på hvem du rører! Nej, du skal holde øje!" Though she hadn't understood the exchange, Świętosława repeated what she'd heard, her pronunciation matching Astrid's almost perfectly. *Learn the tongue of the Vikings,* she thought with disdain, though the phrases she could not understand echoed in her mind the rest of the afternoon.

POZNAŃ

Bolesław mounted his horse and set out with no particular destination in mind, only a determination to ride as long as it took for his anger to evaporate.

Mieszko had told him what he'd brought back with him from Rohr's Hoftag. It was early afternoon, and he was out of Poznań in a matter of moments, taking the East Bridge toward Gniezno. Sharp birch branches hit his face when he moved off the path, which he soon left behind completely. His horse slowed, finding other faint trails instinctively, ones probably used by wild animals, or children in search of berries. He could hear a second horse behind him and knew that Duszan had followed, like a ghost. He didn't know how much time had passed, but he still couldn't shake his anger. The horse was slowing, worn from the long journey. Only when it stopped and resisted his urging to carry on did Bolesław realize that the sun was flitting through the leaves with the purple glow of the sunset.

"My lord." Duszan rode up beside him. "The horses need water . . ."

"Where are we?" Bolesław swiveled in his saddle.

"I can't honestly say, but let go of the reins, the horse will find water."

Duszan was being sensible, as always. And patient, which drove Bolesław mad. He let it go, though, ashamed he'd ridden the animals this long without stopping. He released the reins and his mount snorted and picked a direction. They stepped onward slowly but with purpose, while mist rose between the trees.

"Water is near," Duszan said happily from behind him.

He was right. When they reached the edge of the forest, the horse's hooves sank in soft moss, which soon turned to pale wet sand. There was a small lake in front of them, and the bloodred shield of the sun was drowning on its surface.

They dismounted and let the horses carry on as they wanted. Bolesław crouched down and cupped water in his hands, splashing it on his face. Thirst was hitting him now, too. He pulled off his caftan, shirt, and trousers, tossing them carelessly aside. Duszan caught them before they could hit the wet sand, and Bolesław was already running into the water, throwing himself forward, diving.

He opened his eyes underwater. He swam hard, surrounded by opaque green waters, and emerged only when his lungs burned from lack of air. He gasped as he broke the surface, then froze. Smoke and flames surrounded the lake. Had he woken up in a nightmare? No, there was Duszan on the bank, and the horses, too. The fires weren't surrounding them. Midsummer, he remembered. It was tonight. He was supposed to bless the newlyweds by the Warta River. Everything had been ruined, though, when Mieszko arrived from Rohr early and announced who he'd brought with him. Damn it, with the memory all his anger returned, and again he dove furiously into the water. If he couldn't shake the rage while riding, perhaps he could drown it? When he finally turned back toward the bank, his shoulders were aching. He rolled to his back and allowed the water to carry him briefly. A thin crescent of a moon shone in the sky, like a mocking smile.

"I have only two heirs, but I must reach for all four corners of the earth." Damn Mieszko! That night by the Warta had been priceless to Bolesław, just him, Świętosława, and Father. He would give his life for his father, their family, their legacy, and he . . . how easy it was to tarnish someone's pride, blast it!

Floating in the water wasn't doing him any good, though. He made another lap around the lake, watching the fires that burned on its banks. There was singing and laughter. Boys and girls, women and men, dancing together or sneaking off into the forest, choosing partners as they wished. Damn it all!

He reached the edge and walked out of the water, shaking himself like a dog.

"Have you washed away your anger?" Duszan asked hesitantly. "I think if you remain ruled by your temper like this, you will soon be the strongest on the duke's squad. I've seen you almost bend horseshoes before in your fury."

"Be quiet," Bolesław whispered. "Can you hear that?"

Duszan cocked his head. "The water carries the songs to us."

"Someone is coming." Bolesław listened.

"I'll check."

"No, guard the horses. I'll go."

He walked forward, Duszan mumbling something as he did. He stepped into the forest. Someone was sneaking toward them. Bolesław hid behind the trunk of an alder tree. The person coming nearer was breaking twigs as they walked; they weren't expecting to find anyone.

They're not sneaking, just walking, Bolesław thought.

Water dripped from his hair and down his back. He hadn't taken any weapons with him, everything was still by the horses. The specter moved quickly, as if it were almost leaping in his direction. *It's a woman,* he realized.

He moved, and the specter stopped.

"Is someone there?" He heard the fear in her voice.

"Don't be afraid," Bolesław said, stepping from behind the alder tree.

They stood close to each other; a horse would have cleared the distance in one leap. She was naked, completely naked. She had a flower chain in her dark hair.

"You're . . ." she whispered.

"Yes, I am . . ." he said.

". . . You're naked!"

He held his tongue. *How stupid, I thought she'd recognized the prince.*

"You are, too," he replied. "What are you doing here?"

"Looking for a fern flower," she said, as if this were the most obvious thing in the world.

"Why?"

"Are you a fool? To gain a lifetime of riches!"

It was difficult to see her face in the darkness. He walked closer.

"And I thought it was love that folks searched for on Midsummer's Eve," he said.

"Only the ugly ones. I can find love in broad daylight," she said.

Bolesław laughed. If he didn't know better, he might have thought he was speaking to his sister.

"Do you want me to help you look?" he asked, though he wasn't sure he could tell a fern from other plants.

"I don't know." She hesitated. "The old wives all say you have to search in solitude."

"Do you know anyone who's found such a flower?"

"No."

"And you think you could be the first?"

She didn't reply. She lowered her head.

"And what are *you* doing here?" she asked, sweeping hair from her face.

"Me?"

"Admit it, you were looking for it, too, yes? You'd also want to find riches, because you don't look like one who is searching for love."

"Why not?" he asked, feeling warmth spread through him.

"Well, you know . . ." She jutted out her chin.

"Are you saying I'm handsome?"

"I don't know . . ." She sounded embarrassed. "I'm not a phantom, I can't see in the dark."

He stepped closer, close enough that he could smell the flowers in her hair.

"And now?" he asked.

They studied each other. She had full lips. Large, slightly slanted eyes. Narrow eyebrows, lifted and bent like a swallow's wing. Dark hair covered her shoulders, and it was long enough to cover the tips of her breasts.

"Yes," she said quietly, lifting a hand and placing it on his chest.

"Me, too," he whispered, his hand on her waist.

Her skin was cool to the touch, and smooth. He pulled her toward him, and she moaned quietly, sweetly. *My god,* he thought when her soft chest touched his ribs. She embraced him and stood on her toes, her face nearing his. He lowered his head, clumsily bumping her nose with his own, touching his lips to hers. He opened his mouth and felt her warm tongue on his lips. He shivered. This was what it was like? He'd wondered hundreds of times what it felt like to be with a woman, but he had never thought it might be like this. As violent as anger, as hot as a flame, as sweet as honey. He held her, picked her up; he lay her down on the moss, and she gasped, "It stings!"

But she spread her legs, and he sank down on top of her. It crossed his mind that she knew what to do better than he did. She lifted her hips and gripped his shaft, guiding it inside her.

God! When I sheath my sword, it means rest, but now it's the opposite, the sheath is an attack, a push, a battle!

She moaned.

Mist obscured his vision. The girl beneath him raised her hips and they met so fiercely that he felt pain.

He rose and fell in her depths. He felt bliss and knew it was her. He smelled the damp moss, forest, mist, and her. Everything mixed together into one scent he knew he would never let go of, like a hunting dog. He was hunting. He was the javelin thrown by a sure hand. The taut string of a bow. A loose arrow. A knife that cut.

"Ah!" he snarled, though he wanted to be a silent hunter.

When they were finished, though, he felt as if he were the prey. He fell beside her onto damp moss.

"Ah," she sighed quietly. "You're my fern flower . . ."

It took him a moment to catch his breath. He hadn't realized he'd been holding it, as if he had had forgotten how to breathe.

"Who are you?"

"They call me Jaga. And you?" she asked with a languid and sleepy voice.

"Duszan," he lied smoothly. "I'm from far away."

"That's a shame. I'm from the nearest village. What a find you are for Midsummer's Eve, Duszan."

On Saint John's head, he thought, *which he lost for the pagan Salome's desire.*

"Will you wait for me a moment, Jaga?" he asked, heaving himself up with difficulty.

"I will. But hurry, my sisters will be searching for me." She rolled onto her stomach.

After taking a moment to figure out in which direction the lake lay, he headed back the way he'd come.

Duszan was waiting on the sand, throwing pebbles into the water.

"Has my master finished?" he asked when Bolesław emerged, swaying slightly, from between the trees.

"Not yet," he said, and walked over to his horse.

He took a few Arabian silver coins from the pouch at the saddle.

"I'll be right back," he said over his shoulder and walked back into the forest.

Jaga was sleeping on her side, an arm cushioning her head. He placed the coins quietly into its curve.

"I'll be your fern flower," he whispered, and lowered his head to breathe her in one last time.

He returned to Duszan, dressed, and let the stallion find its way back. His anger at Mieszko was gone.

They rode at a walk, the noise of hoofbeats lost in the moss, the sound disappearing like his anger at his father, who had brought with him from Rohr a pale, fair-haired girl and announced, "This is Gertrude Rikdag, the margrave of Meissen's daughter. She'll be your wife. You can call her Gerd." Gerd wasn't a woman. She was a child, pale and terrified. "Her father has the Veleti on his borders. Fires, smoke," Mieszko said, as if this would gain Bolesław's sympathy. "You should be proud, it's an excellent alliance," he added, noticing Gertrude's slouch and gritting his teeth. "But we won't have a wedding just yet, and you won't bed her, because although we plan to win back Meissen from the Veleti, if they are faster, it might not be worth it."

Yes, his father was a master of alliances. But he didn't care at all for the feelings of his allies. Even those closest to him, those of his own blood and bone.

8

⊗

GULF OF FINLAND

Olav held the helm of the ship firmly. *Kanugård. Kiev,* that's what Allogia called it, so that he would always remember who his fairy godmother was once he'd left Rus. A living witch for a godmother.

It wasn't a war drakkar, a longboat fit only to be sailed alongside land and down rivers. *Kanugård* was a snekke that could be thrown onto open waters, that could leap and cut with ease. "A beautiful vessel," Prince Vladimir had said, when they were looking at it in port. "Sixteen benches, ho, ho! The duchess has given you a ship, and I will give you a crew, I can afford it."

Vladimir gave Olav thirty-two men, Varangians experienced in sailing along the Volga and Dnieper, bored with Rus's rivers, longing for the open seas. Vladimir bartered only for Geivar, the only man he didn't want Olav to take. But as rumor spread through Kiev that Olav was a Tryggvason, and that the blood of the Ynglings ran in his veins, Geivar left Vladimir's service of his own volition and threw his leather bag on board.

They had good winds in Finland's bay. The crew studied Olav curiously, and Geivar called to him, "Olav, what's the course?"

"I know you dream of northern seas, but I need to settle some debts in Estonia," he said, setting the course of *Kanugård.*

"That suits me, but I don't know if the same can be said about them . . ." Geivar glanced toward the crew. "They watch you, following your every step."

"I know." Olav nodded. "I can feel their eyes on my back."

Olav had been one of them while they sailed along the Dnieper and Volga Rivers. "Young Olav," the royal couple's favorite. But since his heritage had been revealed, much had changed. People used to offer him friendship with ease, saying there was something about him that called to them. Now, he felt the weight of expectation in their gazes. It was easy to steal a lover's heart— many had fawned over him, whispering to him how beautiful they thought he was. But how to win the loyalty of thirty men who had been sailing their entire lives?

At night, when he the let *Kanugård* drift and Geivar stood at the helm, the crew stretched out on deck for the night. This evening, one of the men, Omold, began to sing, tapping a rhythm on his knife handle.

Silent and thoughtful
Should be a king's son,
Brave in battle,
Swift in command . . .

He sang quietly, as if just for himself, but Olav heard every word.

Fortunate is he
Who will win for himself
A good name and fame . . .

Olav pulled the leather blanket over his head. His life, so far, had been divided between slavery and paying his debts; he didn't remember his escape with his mother. He had heard endlessly of how he owed Vladimir and Allogia his freedom, while he paid and paid his debt to them. He had never felt free in Rus. Only the time he spent on the Dnieper was happy. The ship, the overhangs, and the fight with a wild river. Now, he sailed toward his future, and the land that belonged to him by right of blood. He knew that no one would give him anything, that he would have to win it all for himself, and pay for it with his own blood.

But before he reached the usurpers, he'd have to prove to these thirty men that he was worth fighting for.

Olav didn't sleep. In summer, night fell for only a moment, and before the sun had even risen, he took the helm back from Geivar and set the course for Cape Loksa in Estonia. By late afternoon, they were so close to port that he could distinguish the colors of women's skirts. The people on land raised their hands to shield their eyes from the sun as they watched the *Kanugård* float closer on the waves.

"We're turning around!" he shouted to the crew, once he'd spotted what he'd been looking for. "We'll sail into the bay!"

It had all come back to him now. For so many years, when Sivrit had forbidden him from speaking his father's name, and Allogia had taken his memories, this had been struck from his mind. He'd needed to feel the deck sway beneath his feet again, in this place, on this water, and now the memories returned to him, down to the smallest detail.

The bay was exactly where Olav had thought it would be. His crew moored the ship and he allowed them to disembark, though he forbade them from lighting any fires. He climbed onto the high, stony embankment and watched the sea. At dawn on the second day, the ship he had been waiting for came into view. He recognized both the ship and sail. He even recalled its name—*Wolverine*. Was it possible this very ship was still sailing, after all these years? If not, the ship currently rocking in the waters before them was the *Wolverine*'s twin. Olav watched it sail into the port at Cape Loksa. If his newfound memories were true, the ship would stay for three days. That's how long it would take to sell its human cargo to the slave traders. The crew would then spend a day drinking in the port's tavern, and return to the ship for another hunt. They would hurry to gather their harvest before the summer ended. Autumn storms made the risks higher than the potential gains.

Olav had calculated this moment endlessly. And now, when the time had come, as the *Wolverine* made its way for its next journey, Olav went down to his men and said, "Shields on deck. Prepare your weapons. I promised you a hard fight, and I vow to you it will be worth it. On deck. We go without a sail, only oars."

The slave hunters had set a straight course east. Olav waited until the other sail was as small as a flower petal on the horizon, then he ordered his men to raise their own sail.

"*Kanugård*, leap!" he shouted. "Let's see how much you're worth."

The wind hit the massive square sail, and the chase began. He knew he needed to strike his target on the open sea, so no help could come to them from land. He risked losing them, but the risk made the blood course through his veins all the faster. The *Wolverine* was heavy and hard to steer; it had been built to take thirty or forty slaves on board. The distance between the two ships grew smaller with every breathless moment; they were gaining. Two, three long breaths of wind and they'd be sitting on the *Wolverine*'s stern. He checked how smoothly his sword slid out of its sheath. Geivar appeared at his side.

"What are you doing? Do you want to batter them?" he exclaimed. "*Kanugård* won't survive that, we have an unarmored bow."

"No, I want to kill their crew and take their ship, my friend."

"Boarding? Have you done that before?" Drops of water shone in Geivar's beard.

"Not yet. This will be my first time!" Olav laughed.

"Fuck! Friend, either we will all die, or . . ."

"Or what?" Olav asked, and suddenly he could smell the filthy sail in front of them. Only the *Wolverine* could stink like that.

"Or you truly are a king," Geivar shouted over the roar of the waves.

"You'll find out today," Olav said. Then he called to the crew, "Hooks! Prepare the hooks, we're boarding that ship!"

The Wolverine has gunwales higher than half the height of a man. We're going to have to jump up, not down, he thought.

They could see *Wolverine*'s crew searching frantically for weapons. Their helmsman was asking "What's happening?" because he could see the ship of thirty armed men coming toward them. Olav moved the helm at the last minute so the gunwales ground together.

"Throw the hooks!" he roared.

And he heard the metallic crunch. Five of the six thrown hooks had found their marks. He let go of the helm and threw himself at a rope, not taking a shield with him. Then he was jumping over onto their deck. He heard his men behind him. He slipped on the wet boards, but he didn't fall, just knelt. The perfect time to draw his sword. He scanned the deck as he stood: three groups of six men. That was all right. For a moment shorter than a breath, he saw their fear and hesitation. He lifted his sword and shouted:

"Kill the headhunters!"

He didn't wait for his men, but moved ahead and cut down the first slaver in his path. It wasn't the first drop of blood that he'd spilled, but none had been so satisfying. For the first time, he was doing something just for himself. He wasn't paying off a debt. He was fighting for himself, for his family.

The fight was short. They had the slavers outnumbered.

"That's everyone," Thorolf soon shouted, searching the deck. "Everyone."

"Search for anyone who might be alive," he shouted, before pulling back the heads of those on their bellies, searching the faces of those on their backs. Five were bald with beards. None of these had taken his mother; they'd have to have been fifty years old today.

"I have one," Thorolf called, lifting a small, lean man by his long, dirty hair.

Olav crossed to them, stepping over corpses.

"What's this ship called?"

"*Wolverine*," the prisoner mumbled, sputtering with blood.

"How many years on the water?"

"Five, maybe si . . ." His eyes were already closing.

"Did you know any other ship that bore the same name?" Olav asked, needing answers before it was too late.

"Every one of ours . . ." the other said, and died.

"Throw the scum overboard, and the others too," Olav snarled, pointing at the corpses. "Search the ship."

There were two iron-clad chests on the front deck. Two more in the back. Nothing else.

"The helmsman probably had the keys." Geivar spat overboard, where they had thrown the bodies moments before.

"It doesn't matter. Every one of you has an axe. We're going back to the *Kanugård,* and we'll open the chests on land."

"Olav, if you don't want the families of these wolverines to search for you, we should sink this barge," Geivar said.

Olav Tryggvason looked him in the eye and replied:

"I want their sons to know that their fathers have been punished. This wasn't banditry. It was revenge."

They reached land the following evening. On Olav's orders, the men chopped open the chests. Four were filled with silver. Grzywnas, Arabian coins, even some ore chunks.

"Blood silver," Olav said. "The output of but a few ventures. This is what the lives of two hundred people are worth."

"For this silver, thirty modest people could live quite nobly," Geivar laughed.

"What's in the fifth chest?" Olav asked Ingvar, pointing to a smaller case he hadn't noticed on board.

"See for yourself," Ingvar said, throwing aside the splintered lid.

There was a weather vane inside. Olav took it out. It had the triangular shape of a flag, forged in sheet metal, with a meager snakelike ornament. It was plated with gold. Olav lifted it so the men could see, and the setting sun lit it with a red glow.

"The silver is yours," he shouted. "Let the thirty men who have come here with me live richly for it. I took my revenge, and now I take this, for me and for *Kanugård.*"

They stood motionless, surprised, among the heavy chests, hardly believing what they'd heard. Their leader wanted none of the coin they had claimed? But Olav left them there and walked back to the deck alone. He climbed the mast, the first time since he'd been a boy in the fleet on the Dnieper. He fastened the weather vane.

There was a fire burning when he returned to land. His crew were gathered around it with their swords bared. Geivar stepped out, showing teeth filed to a point and painted a gray-blue.

"My sword and I belong to you, Olav Tryggvason," he said.

Ingvar followed. "You are my leader. I will sail wherever you steer."

And Eyvind, Thorolf, Ottar, Orm, Vikarr, Torfi, Lodver, Rafn.

"Whatever you say will be our command."

All of them stepped forward, until Varin was the last one left, the second one, apart from Geivar, to have his canines painted.

"I've been waiting for you, my king," he said. "My father fought beside yours, in Viken, before the widow Gunhild condemned King Tryggve to death. After his death, we were forced to leave our home and go into exile, as did all of the king's men. A whisper passed from one mouth to another, though; that your mother escaped the trap set for her and was running east, but no one ever learned what became of her. I had lost hope that it was true."

"Today, you fought for Queen Astrid, Varin," Olav said. "I know that she is still alive, and I will find her."

"We'll find her together, King," Varin replied, and knelt before him.

They sailed the Baltic, moving west, stopping at ports and harbors. They asked after slave traders, pretending to be interested customers. One name was repeated: "Gudbrod from Bornholm." They weren't that far away now, one or two days at most. At night, Olav sat on deck and stared into the murky waters.

"The *Kanugård* didn't escape the fight completely unscathed," Geivar said, joining him.

"I know, a board on deck broke. I told you it was my first time."

"Will you drink, chief?" He offered Olav a cup.

"No."

"We need to change those boards soon. And we need a proper port for that." Geivar took a few sips and asked, "Why didn't you look behind you when you jumped onto the *Wolverine?*"

"I heard you."

Omold sat by the mast and hummed,

Silent and thoughtful
Should be a king's son,
Brave in battle,
Ruthless in command . . .

Varin joined Olav and Geivar on the deck.

"Tell me about the widow Gunhild," Olav asked him.

"The last of the Ynglings, the great Norwegian kings, Harald Fairhaired, had many sons from many wives. One of these was Eric, who killed his own brothers in his thirst for power, and so won himself the name 'Bloodaxe.'

"He took Gunhild as his wife, the daughter of the Danish king, a woman just as hungry for power and not afraid of using witchcraft. Bloodaxe committed many a murder with her at his side, and the people began to hate him. After Eric's death, Norway was ruled by his sons, one after another, but it was Gunhild who stood behind each of them.

"The people cursed the reigns of her and her sons, so much so that she felt the threat of their anger, and worried they might rise against them. So, she rid herself of detractors, one by one, until only one remained: Tryggve Olavsson, your father, a grandson of Harald Fairhaired and one of Eric the Bloodaxe's nephews. Through plots, betrayals, and lies, she brought about the battle in which Tryggve Olavsson died. Then, she sent her armies to find your mother, who was pregnant with you. You can tell us the rest, my king."

"Don't call me 'king,' I haven't won my kingdom back yet. I haven't even found my mother, who risked her life by leaving Norway with me in her belly. She gave birth to me during her escape, hidden in the reeds of Lake Rond, when the widow Gunhild's men were searching the banks. Only after dusk, once they'd left, did she come onto land with me and rest in an old boathouse."

"You can command me not to call you king," Varin said, "but one day you'll return, and they will name you one, because royal blood is priceless, and today it runs only in you, Olav. Norway has had no king since the death of the last of Gunhild's sons. It has the northern lords, the jarls of the land, but it doesn't have a king."

"But there is Jarl Haakon. He leads the other jarls, does he not? And was named viceroy to the Danish king," Olav said.

"Exactly, my lord. He's the viceroy of a foreign ruler, in whose name he rules our country."

"Jarl Haakon," Omold the bard interrupted, "is strong and beloved by the people, but he doesn't have a drop of Yngling blood in his veins. The country is ruled by foreign leaders, and no man gains honor from that. But before you sail to reclaim the Norwegian throne, you must have allies and a fleet, to defeat both Jarl Haakon and the Danes who rule him from afar."

"And I will have it," Olav said.

"Like the weather vane with a snake, the sigil of the Yngling dynasty," Varin nodded.

"Fortunate is he who will win for himself a good name and fame . . ." Olav sang under his breath. Then he stopped suddenly and rose to his feet.

"Can you hear that?"

"What?"

Olav lifted his head. The night was moonless and cloudy, but he hadn't been mistaken; the weather vane was spinning in the wind.

"A storm is coming."

The wind was indeed picking up, and after several warm gusts, the *Kanugård* was thrown over a wave. Lightning ripped across the sky.

"King," Varin called out, holding on to the gunwale. "Allow me to take the helm. I've lived through many a storm."

Olav gave it to him without a second thought. Baring his painted teeth, Varin maneuvered the ship so it faced the waves, steering into them rather than under. It worked with the first, but the second wave broke over the deck.

Geivar and Olav threw themselves toward the sails, but Ingvar and Omold were already there.

"Olav, with me on 'two'!" Geivar ordered. "You go to the ropes."

They pulled the heavy ropes, their muscles straining. The sail was already soaked and heavy with water. If another wave broke over the ship, the sail would be heavy enough to break the mast. They pulled again, with the last of their strength, a final violent tug, and Olav thought his spine would shatter. It didn't. Omold was already placing the sail on trestles and Ingvar was tying it up. Olav and Geivar, red from the effort, collapsed on deck, hearing Varin's order:

"To the oars! Now! We need to maintain speed."

A sailless ship was easy prey for the increasingly strong waves. Eyvind, Ottar, Orm, and Thorolf were already rowing. Olav and Geivar made their way to the benches on all fours. They grabbed the wooden blades.

"Maintain speed!" Varin shouted, maneuvering the *Kanugård* onto the crest of a furious, mercurial wave.

For a moment, their oars cut through air, because they had risen too high for the paddles to catch water, until the ship slid along the surface again. One, two. They moved, keeping rhythm. One, two. Olav lost track of time, only coming to when he realized the wind was weakening.

At dawn, they found themselves drifting. The men began scooping water overboard. A sail was shredded, a cover was damaged, but the mast remained upright. The weather vane stood atop it still, as if the night and storm had been merely a bad dream. The horizon was a green line. There was land ahead.

"To the oars," Olav called, collapsing beside his crew.

"You're lucky, Olav Tryggvason," Varin called with a grin. "We have survived."

"Not yet, Varin. Call me 'lucky' once our feet are on dry land, and we've found shipwrights and a good port."

"And a hot dinner! Then I'll call you a god, my king." Varin bared his painted teeth.

They rowed until the sun was directly overhead. The beach before them had golden sands, and a forest stood on a high dune. Then they saw the small boat making its way toward them from land.

9

⨯

POLAND

Astrid stood on the bow of her boat and shielded her eyes from the sun, watching the ship with no sail approach. She hoped it was . . . well, it was strange, but she was hoping it carried a person who she wasn't even certain was real. And she had the horrible feeling that the storm had changed everything. Last night's dream had been a dark one, and she had many reasons to believe in her dreams.

This was the first and only time Mieszko had given her a task, and she desperately wanted to fulfill it. To earn the happy flash of green in the eye of the duke she loved as a father but wasn't bold enough to call by that name.

"Leszko," she said to her helmsman. "Do you think that's them?"

"I'm not here to do the thinking, my lady. I'm just here to ensure your ship sails wherever you command."

"Damn you."

Mieszko was waiting for messengers from the king of Sweden, Eric. And he sent her as his daughter and, as he called her, his "eye in Wolin," to intercept them when they reached the edge of the Baltic. The storm that had hit last night had come about quickly and unexpectedly, and was so strong that even Dalwin, as experienced as he was with rough waters, had said, "Bloody hell! Perun has fucking smashed the Baltic." And her grandfather swore so rarely.

They were sending patrol boats from Wolin to search the nearby coasts for the messengers, and she had stepped onto one of them because she couldn't sit still. She was terrified of disappointing Mieszko. And she was one of the few to know what the great Eric's messengers would be sailing with. She knew more than little Świętosława, her sharp and beloved sister.

"Leszko, can you see anything? Are they pulling a white flag up the mast?"

"Your eyes do not deceive you, my lady."

"Snekke. Twelve . . . no, sixteen benches. Without a sail. What's shining on the mast like that?"

"If that's a weather vane, then it must be pure gold, my Wolin lady."

"Gold? Perhaps these are royal men. Why don't they have Eric's sigil on their mast?"

"Maybe the storm stole it?"

The storm, the storm. The god of the seas. The god of life. The one who gives death in waves. A beautiful death.

"Leszko, how would you choose to die?"

"Diving into the waves, my lady. Or between the legs of a woman."

"Oh, hush!" she admonished, but he had managed to ease her anxiety some.

The ships were approaching each other now. She could see the silhouettes of the oarsmen. Yes, it was a weather vane that shone on the mast. The sail must have been ripped to shreds in the wild winds of the storm. No sigils. Eric, the king of Sweden, should have a golden boar on the mast, but the storm might have claimed it.

There was a short, dark-haired man in a leather caftan standing at the bow.

"Who am I welcoming?" she shouted into the sea.

"Who's asking?" was the reply.

"Astrid, daughter of Duke Mieszko," she called, the wind tugging her hair.

"Our ship is called the *Kanugård,* and it needs a shipwright. The storm has taken a bite out of us," the helmsman shouted to her.

It's not them, she thought with a wave of disappointment, but then she saw him.

A tall young man stepped onto the deck, approaching them. He had long hair, blond and shining, and pale, bright eyes. He wore chain mail over his leather caftan, with belts over his shoulders and across his chest. Yes, this was the man from her dream.

"My name is Olav Tryggvason," he said in a voice that carried over the water. "I need a safe harbor."

That's what I am, Astrid thought, following with her dream. Aloud she said:

"My father, the lord of this land, welcomes you as his guest," and she offered him an open palm.

Mieszko sat on the raised platform in the audience hall and looked at his guests. His hawk was perched on his shoulder. St. Peter's sword was displayed on the wall behind him. Jarl Birger, the messenger from Sweden's king, stood before him, a stately, thirty-something-year-old man. His long, fair hair was held back with silver rings. He was dressed richly, his wide shoulders covered with a cloak stitched with a golden thread; after all, here, in Poznań, Jarl Birger represented his king.

The duke stared into his guest's eyes, trying to read from them what King Eric was truly like. Much depended on his decision. He might gain a son-in-law, or lose a daughter.

"Let us rejoice," Mieszko shouted, clapping his hands. "God has allowed our guests to arrive unharmed across the seas. Jarl Birger, your place at this feast is beside me."

Mieszko beckoned for the messenger to join the table on the raised platform, where the duke sat with Bolesław. Mieszko had ordered that the tables be arranged differently than usual, to ensure an easier conversation with his guest. The women sat at another table nearby. Oda looked particularly beautiful tonight. She wore a purple dress and green cloak, a royal diadem resting proudly on her raised head. Since the day many years ago when her nunnery had been attacked by Redarians, Oda had been afraid, but with that fear came a fierce determination that suited her. Beside her sat small, quiet Gertrude, Bolesław's Saxon fiancée, a child who didn't draw one's eye but was very high-born. Margrave Rikdag had sent many messengers, asking "When is the wedding?" Mieszko had assured them all it would be soon, that very year, but still he'd ordered his son not to touch the girl, though Bolesław would not have done so regardless. Świętosława and Geira sat next to Oda, his two daughters, as different from each other as fire and water. Astrid's place was empty. The tables and benches beside them were filled by his best men, the squad chieftains.

"Father John," Mieszko called over his chaplain. "Bless the dishes we will be eating."

Everyone stood up. John made the sign of a cross and said a prayer, ending it with the words:

"Praise be to God and to Duke Mieszko. Amen."

They sat back down. He signaled to the musicians to begin playing. Servants circulated through the room with jugs full of mead.

"You crossed yourself, Jarl Birger," Mieszko observed.

"Yes, my lord. I've been baptized."

"And you know our language quite well."

"My king respects you enough, my lord, not to send a person who cannot speak with you to your court."

"Two of my daughters also know the language of the north, from their mothers," Mieszko laughed. "Women can teach us many things, don't you think, Jarl?"

"Indeed, my duke. My mother was a Slav." Birger raised a goblet.

"Women connect us." Mieszko took a sip of mead. "Over there sits my wife, my future daughter-in-law, and my two daughters." He looked at them and met Oda's gaze. "Each one is an alliance, a truce, peace, or even a ceasefire. If we only had sons, we would have nothing but wars." He lifted the goblet again, smiling at his wife from afar.

She responded with a bright smile, one he knew so well. For a moment, he thought of putting down his goblet, disappearing with Oda into the bed-chamber for a while, then returning to the feast. The hawk on his shoulder screeched then, bringing Mieszko back to the situation at hand.

"Explain to me, Jarl," Bolesław spoke up, "how is it that you, a believer in Christ, serve a pagan king?"

"King Eric respects his countrymen's attachment to the old gods," he an-swered, and Mieszko sensed Birger was choosing his words with care. "And at the same time, he understands that the world is great and varied."

"Does he accept Christians at his court?" Bolesław asked. "Or does he merely tolerate them, thinking them harmless to his position?"

"If he chose me to represent him in a matter as important as an alliance with Duke Mieszko, then what would you say, young prince?"

"Is he prepared to be baptized?" Mieszko asked bluntly.

"That's not a condition of our alliance," Birger answered. "But if you're asking me privately, Duke, then I will respond with your words: women can teach us many things." He lifted his goblet to his lips as he spoke and took a sip without breaking eye contact with Mieszko, then nodded toward the table where the duke's wife and daughters sat.

"If Eric wants an alliance as badly as I do, and if he doesn't care, for ob-vious reasons, for a sacramental marriage, then I can offer him the hand of one of my older daughters," Mieszko said, setting down his goblet.

Birger frowned, and said after a moment, "My king promises you that he will attack Denmark. When he destroys it, the ring of enemies around your western borders will be broken. Mściwój and the Obotrites are nothing alone. You will defeat the Veleti and the Czechs yourself, great Duke. You'll be free from worry. But Eric, king of Sweden, will only give you such a pre-cious gift for the price of your most valuable daughter's hand. We speak only of her, and have been from the very beginning, my lord."

"Can you even tell which one she is?" Mieszko asked, his tone harsh and mocking.

"The one with hair like amber, eyes like a wildcat, and a tongue as sharp as a knife," Birger said. "Those are the stories the bards tell Eric in the great manor at Uppsala."

"Can you pronounce my sister's name, messenger?" Bolesław asked, rising slightly in his seat.

"Women change their names after marriage," Jarl Birger said calmly. "So it may be more easily pronounced by their new subjects."

Świętosława took a sip of mead and nudged her sister.

"Geira, father is looking at you."

"More likely at Astrid's empty seat. Can you see that frown? He's picturing how best to punish her, I'm almost certain."

They clinked their goblets, laughing. From a distance, it was easier to joke about their father's stern look.

"Why so merry, my dears?" Oda asked, leaning across Gertrude to speak to them.

"We're wondering which convent Mieszko will send you to, since your one in Kalbe has been destroyed," Świętosława answered with the sweetest of smiles.

Geira kicked her under the table, but Świętosława continued to smile over at her stepmother. The sip of mead had given her courage.

"Your father, Duchess Stepmother, has already been forced to visit Rikdag, Bolesław's future father-in-law, isn't that right, Gerd?" She lifted her goblet to her brother's fiancée.

Oda puffed out her cheeks and jutted out her chin. The girl flinched when she heard her name.

"Don't be afraid, little Gerd." Świętosława placed a hand on the girl's shoulder. "You're safe here, like a chick in its nest. I won't let anyone hurt you, and you'll soon grow out of your flat chest and those pimples, I promise. My sister Astrid will know how to help. She's gotten many a girl out of trouble, and she's attracted the attentions of a cold husband for quite a few, too."

"The insolence!" Oda interrupted, but fell silent as the hall doors opened and Astrid walked into the room.

She was wearing a dark cloak, the hood dripping with rain. She looked frightened, Świętosława thought, as if she had come to tell them that the

Final Judgment had begun. She watched her sister open her mouth, as if to speak, but then glance carefully around the hall instead, her eyes resting for a moment on their father, then on her own empty place.

Astrid bowed to Mieszko and the guests. She gave her cloak and hood to the servants. And, refusing to meet her sisters' eyes, she took her place beside them at the table.

Bolesław studied Gertrude from afar. Next to his sisters, she looked even more plain. Geira, with her height and long, fair hair that fell in waves across her broad shoulders. Astrid, who had only just arrived, with hair like dark tree sap and unsettlingly blue eyes. Świętosława, with her gleaming amber plaits and her beloved lynx fur draped over her shoulder. Next to his royal siblings, his fiancée seemed pale, ordinary, almost transparent. Jaga's image rose to his mind, the girl from Midsummer's Eve. She would have outshone any princess, Bolesław thought.

But his betrothed was the frail daughter of the great margrave. Gerd the pale. Gerd the shy. Gerd the ordinary. He couldn't even find it in himself to pity her, though he knew she was likely as unhappy in their home as he was to have her there. But Bolesław felt nothing, only indifference toward her. These were not, however, his feelings about the conversation Mieszko was currently having with Jarl Birger.

"Remind me, guest, what do they call your king's troublesome nephew?" The boy who hoped to stand against his uncle for the Swedish throne.

"Styrbjorn Olafsson, prince."

On the table next to his father's own plate was a golden bowl with raw meat, for his hawk, who no one save Mieszko was permitted to feed. Now, the duke chose a piece of the bloody meat and placed it in the bird's open beak.

"Styrbjorn," he repeated after Birger. "He was seen in Jomsborg."

"We know that Styrbjorn has asked the Jomsvikings for help against his uncle, King Eric," the Jarl replied. "And we also know that he wasn't successful."

"He was second." Bolesław's father clicked his fingers.

"What do you mean by that, Duke?" Birger asked, unsettled.

That the first in line to gain help from the Jomsvikings is always the Danish king, *Harald,* Bolesław answered silently. Of course, he wouldn't voice this thought, because Mieszko was the one to decide what knowledge they shared with their guests and what they would keep for themselves.

"After Jomsvikings carry out King Harald's command and have returned

Norway to him, they'll be free," Mieszko answered. "They might find some time for Styrbjorn then."

For a long moment, there was silence. Mieszko spoke again:

"I have no interest in giving my daughter to a king who expects trouble, Jarl Birger. I want a strong son-in-law, who will give my daughter and her children a stable throne. I don't want her to have to worry that Styrbjorn will appear and demand his power back after her husband's death."

"You talk of widowhood before the wedding?" Birger asked.

"Look at my wife, Jarl," Mieszko answered, pointing at Oda. "Beautiful, isn't she? And twenty years younger than me. Which is, more or less, the age difference between Eric and any one of my daughters."

Bolesław had to bite his lip to stop himself from laughing. Father was still baiting Birger, acting as if he might offer Eric not Świętosława, but Astrid or Geira.

"My wish, Jarl Birger, is to give my daughter a good future."

"If the guarantee of that is Styrbjorn's head, then I can promise you that can be arranged. But not before the wedding. That would create unnecessary unrest. King Eric will not be like the widow Gunhild, chasing usurpers to his crown halfway across the world, because he doesn't see it as a worthy occupation. However, if his nephew ever does declare war on him, then Eric will be ready, and he will defeat Styrbjorn, with or without the help of the Jomsvikings."

"Good." Mieszko slapped a hand on the table. "Then we have that point discussed. I will give you men who will accompany you to my viceroy in Wolin. Dalwin knows how to reach men who have Styrbjorn's ear, and it will be up to you to convince the arrogant nephew to declare war. Because neither you nor I doubt Eric's victory." He signaled the servant to pour him more mead.

Bolesław looked at Świętosława from afar. Did she suspect that Father, at that very moment, was toasting her future? That he was proposing to start a war, and that she would soon be the queen of Sweden? Her future husband's crown came not from the pope or the emperor, because Eric, as a pagan, did not desire the former, and, as a leader of a country with no ties to the empire, had no need of the latter. Nevertheless, the independent Swedish Viking hoped to enter Europe through marriage. Did Eric know that apart from the splendor, this would be mean endless trouble? And Świętosława, how would she navigate the far north? What would she say when she learned her husband was almost their father's age? And that he hadn't been baptized?

Imagining her reaction, Bolesław felt, for the first time in his life, that there was nothing in the world that would have convinced him to trade places with his father.

Astrid went through the motions as the feast carried on around her, though the smell of roasted meat was making her feel faint, and the music was grating. She could feel a headache building behind her eyes. But every time she closed them, she saw Olav's pale eyes. They were reflected back at her in every goblet, every bowl. She had left him and his crew in the guesthouse behind the manor, but she felt his presence beside her everywhere she turned.

She knew what Mieszko and King Eric's jarl were talking about. Mieszko had told her what he intended to do when he'd sent Astrid to intercept the royal messengers. But instead of Jarl Birger, she had welcomed Olav in from the sea. Instead of the king of Sweden, she had brought them the future king of Norway. Astrid bit her lip and clasped her hands tightly under the table, trying to remain calm, to seem unworried, normal, as those around her laughed and drank deeply from their goblets. But she knew the news of Olav's arrival would interrupt the negotiations between Mieszko and Eric. And she didn't need to ask anyone to know which of the two kings her sister would prefer.

Several times, she almost rose, wanting to make her way to the duke, to bow and whisper to him who she had brought with her from Poznań. But she didn't stand. Her hands shook as she repeated to herself: *Mieszko wants all three of us together with him, which means that Świętosława isn't the only one he's trying to marry off. If she gets King Eric, as the duke has planned, then perhaps I can have the one I fished from the sea. The unplanned one.*

There was nothing she wanted more.

"Astrid, what's wrong?" A laughing Świętosława grabbed her elbow.

"Nothing," she lied, avoiding her sister's eyes. "I'm just tired after the journey."

She knew Mieszko would be angry if she interrupted his conversation with the jarl, but feared his anger would be even greater later, when he learned Astrid had kept the news of their guests to herself. Could she claim ignorance, she wondered, that she hadn't appreciated the importance of Olav's potential status? It's only a man with a claim to the throne, she kept telling herself, and there are many of those in the world. Mieszko wouldn't exchange an established ruler like Eric for the unsecured Olav. The duke did not change his plans.

But even as she thought it, Astrid knew that it wasn't true; no one changed plans as swiftly and shrewdly as Mieszko. Was that why she was still sitting at the table instead of standing up and passing her information on to the duke? Yes, she thought, that was precisely why.

But as she watched the duke signal for more mead for himself and the jarl, a new horror came to her mind. She had been so focused on her dream, on the reality of the man who'd come ashore, on his pale, pale eyes, that she had neglected to consider the most important thing; whatever happened next, Jarl Birger's people could not know the young Tryggvason, the rightful heir to the Norwegian throne, was currently at Mieszko's court. She allowed herself one more moment in which to imagine that she said nothing; that the feast ended and her wild younger sister was wed to the Swedish king, and she and Olav . . . Well, the time of dreaming for herself was over now. She stood and approached Mieszko, bowing as she stepped before him.

"My duke . . ."

She met his gaze, which held surprise and irritation in equal measure.

"My daughter Astrid," he introduced her to the jarl. "She'll be your guide on your way to Wolin. She is Dalwin's granddaughter."

Astrid felt dizzy. She spoke before the jarl could reply.

"My duke . . . I'm afraid that . . ." she stuttered. What was she supposed to say? Would he object? "I wanted to say, that I brought a guest . . . someone who very much wants to speak with you . . ."

"Now?" Mieszko looked as if he wanted to hit her. "Now, we are going to make the happy announcement! The guest must wait."

"As you wish, my lord." She bowed and, though terrified, she felt a surge of relief.

Returning to her place, she called Bjornar over and whispered into his ear:

"In the guesthouse, there are thirty-two men, survivors from a ship that was sailing from Rus and nearly drowned in last night's storm. It's up to you to ensure that they don't meet the Swedish jarl and his men. Treat them as you would royalty. Do you understand?"

"No," he replied, just as quietly. "But I'll do as you command."

As he walked away, Astrid sank slowly into her chair. Her hands were trembling, so she clasped them once more under the table.

"What secrets were you just exchanging with Father, hmm?" Świętosława pinched her affectionately. "And with the ginger Bjornar, too. Whose side are you on? Your father's or your sisters'?"

But Astrid didn't have time to answer, because Mieszko called Świętosława over to him.

It's happening. Astrid held her breath. *Let it happen.*

Świętosława knew more about what was happening this evening than most people suspected. She only pretended not to have guessed anything. Dusza, reliable and silent, had sped over to her the previous evening, covered her hair with a hood, and led her to the servants' quarters which adjoined the main hall. There, hidden between the chests full of polished cups, goblets, and bowls, Świętosława had heard her father's conversation with his chaplain.

"Sven, though baptized as a child, openly rejects Christianity, and is building his power on promises of returning to the old gods. Eric is merely unbaptized," Father John was saying.

"What's worse in God's eyes?" Mieszko asked.

"God's child denying the Church and the holy water that has washed him is committing a deadly sin. Saxon bishops call them the cursed children of the Church. God awaits pagans with the Word. Maybe your daughter is fated to the same destiny as her mother?" the chaplain replied. Mieszko laughed nervously at this.

"Yes, Dobrawa also married a pagan."

Father and the chaplain left the hall, and Świętosława sat in the maintenance room, waiting for Dusza to lead her out when it was safe. She considered what she'd heard, unconsciously lifting a large silver goblet out of a chest and placing it on the empty table. Since Oda had angrily whispered to her: *"Learn the tongue of the Vikings,"* she'd known there was a grain of truth in the duchess's words. Oda had wanted to hurt her, had wanted to say: *"You'll marry a barbarian, because you're just as wild as they are,"* as if the duchess had forgotten that Margrave Ditrich, her own father, just ten years earlier had been calling Mieszko a barbarian. And after that he wanted him for a son-in-law.

And she'd promised herself, kneeling in the servant's room before the empty goblet on the table, that she would accept this fate her father had chosen for her, not with humility, but with pride.

And that's exactly how she walked toward him now. Chin up and unafraid.

"Daughter." Mieszko stood, and everyone in the hall followed his lead. "This is Jarl Birger, the messenger from Sweden's king, Eric . . ."

Father's hawk leaped from the backrest of the duke's high chair to his shoulder.

Standing before them, Świętosława could see that Birger was not an old man. He was strong and stately. She liked his long fair hair, held back by silver rings. Did he look like his king?

". . . the king of Sweden, the great country beyond the seas. A country in which the sun doesn't come up in winter, and in summer it never sets." Świętosława greeted the jarl, meeting his eye. He seemed embarrassed, damn it. "The jarl has brought noble gifts from his master. Northern jewels, beautiful reindeer and polar bear furs, chests full of . . ." Mieszko broke off here, and Świętosława was amused by how transparently he was avoiding having to tell her he had just chosen her a husband.

"Thank you," she replied, and smiled to Birger. "I agree."

Mieszko froze, his mouth hanging open. Birger blushed. Bolesław choked on his mead.

"Daughter," Mieszko cleared his throat. "I am trying to say that King Eric is asking for your hand in marriage."

"I hope, Father, that you haven't accepted mere reindeer and polar bear furs and chests full of something for the hand of your most valuable daughter, though we want for nothing. Tell me, really, how much I'm worth."

"You're the guarantee of our alliance with Sweden, Daughter," her father managed to answer through his surprise.

Jarl Birger knelt and said:

"My king promises to defeat Denmark."

"Is he strong enough to do that?" Świętosława asked.

"Yes, Princess. He'll do it for you."

"What'll happen if he fails?"

"I swear that he won't."

"Then let us celebrate," she said.

10

⚔

POLAND

Olav had taken the weather vane from the mast when they left *Kanugård* in Wolin's port. He felt attached to it, as if the snake sigil snatched from the *Wolverine* was an extension of his body.

Since Astrid had guided their ship into Wolin's port, Varin had declared him a god three times already. For the place to moor their ship, for the shipwrights who had immediately begun the repairs of *Kanugård,* and for the dinner that Dalwin had given them. Now, in Poznań, preparing to meet Mieszko, he thought of how fickle fate was, leading his ship to the lands of the very duke whom Prince Vladimir had ordered him to burn.

Astrid came to fetch him at noon.

"The duke is waiting," she said.

Walking through the courtyard, he took in the white stone palatium silhouetted against the heavens, so different from Vladimir's wooden palatium in Kiev. It was pure, like runes etched in an impossibly blue sky.

"Here," his savior said, leading him down a stone corridor.

They entered a small, bright audience chamber. Purple-red silks hung from the ceiling. Warriors stood along the walls in silver chain mail, and a strange, ancient sword hung on the main wall, next to an enormous golden cross.

Oh, yes. He remembered his conversation with Vladimir. *Mieszko was baptized.*

The main seat on the raised platform was occupied by a dark-haired man with a beard that ended in a sharp point. He had a hawk on his shoulder. A young man sat on his right; he looked like an eagle dressed in a purple tunic. *Bolesław,* Olav recalled the duke's son's name.

"My lord, here's your guest." Astrid bowed and took her place on one of the slightly lower seats.

The bearded duke waved a hand at him, and the bird on his shoulder opened its beak, but it made no sound. As he approached, Olav noticed a gray streak in Mieszko's beard.

"My name is Olav Tryggvason," he said. "My ship was damaged off your coast during the storm, my lord."

"What's the name of your ship?" the duke asked.

"*Kanugård*, my lord."

"Kiev has splintered against my shores." Mieszko laughed. "Why have you chosen such a name for your ship?"

"I did not. Duchess Allogia did, Prince Vladimir's wife," Olav replied.

"So you are her servant?" the duke asked mockingly.

"No, my lord. *Kanugård* was a gift from the duchess for me, and so she chose its name."

"Who are you, then?"

"I am Tryggve's son, the last of the Norwegian kings. My mother, when on the run from the widow Gunhild, gave birth to me in exile. I spent my youth in Rus. Now I return to win back the Norwegian throne."

The hawk on the duke's shoulder took off. Olav raised an arm, offering it as a landing place for the bird. The predator hesitated, then flew on. Olav turned sharply, following the hawk's flight. The bird perched on the shoulder of a girl who stood in the hall's doorway.

He looked at her and felt his knees go weak. She was dressed in a rich, royal red dress, and wore a speckled lynx fur on her shoulders instead of a cloak. She gave the impression of being tall and proud, but as she passed him he realized she barely reached his shoulder. She looked at him carefully, and he bowed under the weight of her gaze, feeling as if he should have done so the moment he saw her.

Is she the wife or daughter? he wondered. *Confident and commanding like a queen, but young, very young.*

"It's the season for Scandinavian kings," she said, walking up onto the platform and sitting at the duke's left hand.

The hawk immediately leapt from her shoulder to Mieszko's chair.

"Were you eavesdropping?" the duke asked, and kissed the girl's proferred cheek.

"No, my sister told me. I decided to skip hunting and come meet our guest instead."

"Olav," Mieszko spoke to him, "meet my most treasured daughter, Świętosława."

So, a daughter—the thought crossed his mind and was followed by an unexpected flood of relief. And then he remembered that this was the one Prince Vladimir wanted to marry.

The girl was studying him with curiosity.

"The last of the Norwegian kings has crashed against our shores on his way from Kiev, and my sister has fished him from the Baltic," she said in one breath, a cheerful gleam in her eyes. "Astrid, if I recall the sea laws correctly, then what the ocean throws out belongs to the finder. Has father given you this treasure yet?" She nodded toward him.

Astrid blushed, and Mieszko reprimanded his daughter. "Świętosława, your jests are inappropriate. Astrid, it's time for you to go. Take the Swedish messengers to Dalwin."

Astrid rose, bowed, and said, "As you wish, my lord," then hurried from the hall, studiously not looking at Olav as she went.

Mieszko turned back to his guest.

"My apologies, Olav. Daughters are truly a father's joy," he said, though his expression suggested the opposite. "So you say that you haven't been in your country since birth. Is anyone from your family still alive?"

"Sivrit, my mother's brother, is a servant of Prince Vladimir's, he collects taxes in Estonia. He's been searching for his sister, my mother, for the last few years. Fruitlessly, so far, but I believe that Astrid is alive."

"Your mother is named Astrid, like my sister? What happened to her?" Świętosława asked questions quickly, and Olav wasn't sure if he should address her or the duke.

"She was taken by slavers," he said, finding it difficult to form sentences when he looked at her.

"Someone should call Geira," she shouted. "My sister is the widow of Gudbrod of Bornholm, the most famous . . ."

"Świętosława," her father interrupted. "You can reign as you wish in a few weeks, in Uppsala."

The reprimand had absolutely no effect on the girl.

"It was to Gudbrod that we were sailing, to his home on the island of Bornholm in the Baltic Sea, when the storm caught us," Olav said. "Am I to understand that he is dead?"

"For a year now," Mieszko said. "But Geira, my daughter and Gudbord's widow, is well-versed in her husband's business. You're lucky, Olav, since Geira is currently here with us, in Poznań. We'll call for her."

Świętosława made a face as if to say, "I told you," and was opening her mouth when the duke's son spoke.

"Do you intend to sail straight to your country?"

"Jarl Haakon rules Norway," Olav replied. "I am sure he won't hand power over to me simply at the news that I have arrived. I must first gather people loyal to my cause."

"Do you know that Jomsborg's fleet has set out to face Haakon? The Danish king intends to remind the Norwegian vassal who is the real master," Bolesław said.

"No. I come from the east, I didn't know that," Olav replied, frowning. "But it grates on my ear to hear you say 'Norwegian vassal,' prince."

"That's not necessary," Świętosława piped up cheerfully. "Jarl Haakon is the Danish vassal, and you as the true king who sheds the Danish yoke—it sounds like a good start, Olav."

"I agree with you, royal daughter," he spoke to Świętosława, though he felt like a mere cabin boy when he looked at her again, "because I intend to throw off both Haakon's and the Danish reign in my country. I meant only the word. I don't want anyone thinking of my great country under the thumb of another. 'Norwegian vassal,' it pains me."

Her eyes were green and gray at the same time. Her hair gleamed like amber shot through with sunlight. He had never met such a woman before. Girl? She wasn't a witch, but her gaze made him feel like a bigger man than he had been only moments earlier. She seemed simultaneously as beautiful as the northern lights, and as old and wise as a sorceress. Tall, like when she stood in the hall's doorway, and as fragile as a child when she passed him. He was sure of one thing, though: he wanted her to stay, because her presence gave him a strength he hadn't felt before.

He knew that he should look away from her, and turn his eyes to the duke. And in that same instant he heard a horn sound from beyond the audience chamber. A horn at the sound of which the warriors lining the chamber all hit their swords against their shields.

"The terror," Mieszko said calmly.

Świętosława's eyes didn't leave Olav's face when the horn sounded. She didn't care what unhappiness it was announcing. If it was Judgment Day, she'd run to Olav, baptize him herself, and they'd walk to heaven's gates hand in hand. Because if today, now, the world ended, she wanted to cross the border with this white-haired man. *What is it like to kiss someone?* she wondered, and only then recalled that she had willingly given her hand in marriage to King Eric through Jarl Birger just the previous afternoon.

A messenger ran into the audience chamber.

"Duke." He fell to his knees in front of Mieszko. "The Czechs have killed your father-in-law, Margrave Ditrich, in Meissen, along with Lady Gertrude's father, Margrave Rikdag."

He'll send Oda away, she thought vengefully.

"How did it happen?" her father asked calmly.

"Your brother-in-law, Boleslav, the prince of the Czechs, has no scruples. He arrived in Meissen with pagans who ride under Trzygłów as their patron. The margraves weren't prepared for an army that has no respect for holy ground. They sought protection in the church, but the nonbelievers set fire to it and the last of Meissen's masters burned to the sound of bells ringing out the alarm . . . Boleslav gave the bodies to the Veleti, who had a feast worshipping idols at the temple's altar, ripping apart the remnants of the bodies . . ."

"Nonsense," Mieszko exclaimed. "The Veleti may be pagans, but they do not eat human flesh. Tell me what you know, but don't repeat lies."

"They are both dead. Meissen is in the hands of the Czechs," the messenger said, embarrassed by the reprimand.

And Oda is done for, Świętosława thought, looking in Olav's pale irises, which told her a story about something else entirely. *God, thank you for hearing my prayers . . .*

"Bolesław," Mieszko said harshly. "Meissen's daughter is of no use to us now that her country has been invaded by Czechs and the Veleti."

"Father." Świętosława dragged her eyes away from Olav's pale ones. "Have you no pity for the child? Where will you send Gerd? To a burned land?"

"I will send her wherever I please, daughter," Mieszko answered coldly. "Your brother will not remain in the fetters of an alliance that no longer makes sense. Fickleness is a privilege of rulers."

"And Oda?" she asked. "Will you send her away, too?"

"Be silent!" Mieszko shouted back. "This time, you have gone too far."

The horn sounded again, now announcing a guest rather than danger. A disheveled Geira ran into the audience chamber. She opened her mouth, her eyes shifting between her father and her sister. Father stopped her with a gesture, looking back at Świętosława angrily.

"Daughter?" he said in a voice that sent a shiver down her back.

"Forgive me, Father." She spoke the words with difficulty. "It wasn't about the duchess, I meant to speak only of Gerd."

She preferred to lie than to speak the truth once again.

"Don't fear for her. Not a single hair on her head will be harmed. She still has a powerful family in Saxony." Then he turned his head away from her with a look of such disdain that for the first time in her life she felt as if he'd hit her.

"Geira, my daughter," he called her sister gently, reaching out a hand to her. "Meet our guest, Olav Tryggvason. Olav." He reached out another hand to the white-haired man. "This is my eldest daughter, Geira. I would like for the two of you to get acquainted."

Świętosława bit her lip so hard it bled.

Sigvald, one of the Zealand brothers the great Jomsviking Palnatoki had introduced to Sven, walked into the audience chamber. Though they had only met once before, Sigvald recognized the duke immediately. He guessed that the young man on Mieszko's right was his firstborn son and heir. He knew Geira, Gudbrod's widow, from Bornholm, and besides, she had just greeted him in the palatium's yard. The girl on the duke's left must have been his youngest daughter. But who was the fair-haired man standing before the duke? Sigvald's heart beat faster; it seemed his future might depend on this one moment, and he felt, with a dark certainty, that if he had accepted Mieszko's invitation six months earlier, this would not have been the case.

"Jarl Sigvald has finally found his way to Poznań," the duke greeted him, confirming his horrible gut feeling. "What brings you here, Jomsviking?"

Fear, my lord, Sigvald thought. *I'm sitting on board a ship that burns from bow to stern.* Aloud, he said:

"It's not hard to find friends in times of glory, my lord."

Mieszko studied him carefully. "I don't know anyone who makes a living at war and hasn't tasted the bitterness of defeat," he replied.

Sigvald's heart beat faster. He had to say it, now.

"The Jomsvikings haven't brought back victory from the far-off fjord in Trondheim. It remains with Jarl Haakon, who has unworthily summoned the powers of evil to aid him."'

"What does that mean?"

Sigvald took a deep breath. He knew that horror should color the words he was about to utter.

"He paid the price of his youngest son's life, sacrificing him to their hungry goddesses."

"Nonsense." Mieszko shrugged. "Superstitions."

"The power of the old gods, my lord. Haakon's men weren't the only ones fighting against us. I saw a black cloud with my own eyes, which appeared in the clear sky out of nowhere. It spat arrowheads and blades at us. I had to turn the fleet around."

"I have already heard of pagans who consume human flesh today." Mieszko waved a hand. "One must separate the grain from the husk. The grain is the fact that you lost."

"The grain is the fact that we fought and won no victory. We remained true to Jomsborg's laws, my lord. Our men, captured by Haakon, accepted death, laughing in its face. By doing so, they won the admiration of his eldest son, Eric. He released Vagn, leader of the house of warriors, and everyone who was still with him."

"Interesting." Mieszko narrowed his eyes. "Besides, I never said you lacked courage."

"We had it until the end. That's how Vagn managed to save a few dozen warriors. They are fit and healthy in Jomsborg, and can confirm my words," he added defiantly.

"If I didn't want to believe you, I wouldn't welcome you, Sigvald," Mieszko said, without a hint of a smile. "How is Palnatoki?"

"Palnatoki is dead. I led the charge against Haakon."

"Have the Jomsvikings chosen a new jarl from the house leaders?" The duke cocked his head at the same angle as that of his hawk, which was perched on the back of his chair.

"No, my lord. We will be choosing one any day now."

The two men stared at each other, taking in the weight and opportunities of the moment. Sigvald managed to avoid blinking.

"We'll come back to this conversation." Mieszko waved a hand and stood.

11

⚜

POLAND

Olav walked toward the stables, thinking over the events of the last day. He knew he had not ended up here by accident. He just wasn't sure whether it was Thor, Odin, or the master of lust, Frey, who had guided his ship through the storm. The Ynglings traced their heritage back to Frey, so perhaps he had guided Olav's ship? It didn't really matter, so long as the trickster Loki wasn't involved.

He had been sailing to gain a throne, for a royal inheritance, for news of his missing mother. He found Świętosława and had been touched by a fire he had not known before. A fire that wasn't dampened by Mieszko's carefully articulated implication that she was already betrothed to the Swedish king. Quite the opposite; he was prepared to stand before the duke and ask for her hand regardless. And Sigvald's arrival was like throwing a hot stone into boiling water, a torch onto a burning pyre. Taking his throne from Jarl Haakon would be more difficult than anticipated. After a victory like the one Haakon had just had over the Danish king and his Jomsvikings, the Norwegian people wouldn't abandon their jarl, not even for the rightful king.

"Olav." He heard a voice behind him and turned.

It was Bolesław.

"My father will spend the evening talking with Sigvald. He's asked Świętosława and me to take care of you. You won't deny us your company?"

"A great feast, royal clothes, golden goblets, and a chaplain singing psalms?" Olav asked.

"No. A quick escape on horseback to the other side of the Warta. A hunting lodge and a barrel of mead. Does that suit you?"

"Is Świętosława allowed out of her father's house?" he asked, recalling the argument she'd had with the duke earlier.

Bolesław laughed and walked into the stable.

"Do you see that empty stall?" he pointed in the gloom. "That's where her mare should be. They have both crossed the river already. Don't worry, Olav, she's far too precious to father for him to hurt her in any way. She'll be sailing for Sweden any day now. Let's go!"

Bolesław was a far better rider. He held himself in the saddle as confidently as a vagrant, and Olav had seen many of those along the southern end of the Dnieper. The road was short, and they turned left off the path on the other side of the river, entering a thick forest. There they found a small lodge, not unlike the one Astrid had placed him and his people in. It was built from oak logs, covered with a neatly laid thatch, and guarded by lookout points hidden in the trees. He saw Bolesław's men giving their master a sign that they were vigilant.

"Do you always have so many people with you?" Olav asked.

"Usually, there are more." Bolesław laughed. "Get used to it. When you take the throne, you won't go anywhere without them either. It's one of the more questionable charms of being a ruler. You're never alone."

A tall young boy ran into the yard, a girl with him. The girl took his horse and the boy took Bolesław's.

"That's Duszan and Dusza," Bolesław said, nodding toward them. "Our shadows."

"They don't look like you," Olav said.

"They were born on the same days my sister and I were. Father bought them from their families and they've been raised with us."

"He's spying on you through their eyes?" Olav tried to understand.

Bolesław shook his head.

"They are loyal to us. And Dusza is mute, anyway."

"The opposite of your sister."

Świętosława appeared in the doorway of the lodge, still wearing the bloodred dress with the lynx fur across her shoulders.

"Olav, you've been in the palatium—now, welcome to our more humble abode," she called, and he couldn't help but imagine this was his wife greeting him as he returned from a long journey.

"Sven-to-schwa-va," he pronounced her name slowly, syllable by syllable. For all its difficulty, it was the most beautiful name he'd ever heard. "With you, I could feast even in a tent on a ship in the middle of a storm."

"Oooh." Bolesław patted his shoulder. "You may know more than me about storms, but you know little about life with my sister, so don't be so eager. The Swedes will be the ones sharing meals with her, anyway. Speaking of, do we have anything to eat here?" The young prince entered the cabin first, and Olav paused to let Świętosława walk in ahead of him. "Today's been like the Apocalypse, hasn't it, sister? It began with Olav, and was more difficult with every rider," he said, walking the length of a long table and picking roasted meat from a bowl.

"Why didn't you speak up for Gerd?" Świętosława asked her brother.

Bolesław grabbed a deer rib and laughed as he buried his teeth in the meat. He looked like an eagle tearing apart its prey.

"Why didn't you bite your tongue?" he said to Świętosława. "Father knows now that you hate his wife; before that, he could only have suspected. Yes, bold one, it's all the same to you, you'll board a ship and sail away to Uppsala."

"Don't you pity Gertrude? She's still a child!"

"It's Saxon blood, sister. Sooner or later the poison would leak out of her, like Oda."

"Oh, stop," Świętosława hissed at her brother and clapped her hands. "Dusza, bring us some meat. Olav, you must be hungry."

"You don't ask," Olav laughed. "You're ordering me to eat."

"I'll eat with you," she said, looking in his eyes, and his knees wobbled again. "And I'll drink!" she shouted to hurry her Dusza along.

"Yes," Bolesław said, taking a swig from his goblet. "Let's get drunk. I'll drink to forget the loss of my Saxon fiancée and the war with the Czechs, which my heart rejoices at . . ."

"Even if it is war with our mother's brother?" Świętosława asked sharply.

"We've already talked about this." Bolesław sighed. "He's no longer our uncle, he's our enemy. And I'll drink to a new wife."

"Are you joking?" she exclaimed. "Has Mieszko already . . . ?"

"Yes, already." Bolesław nodded. "He plans to hit the Czechs from two sides, so I'll wed the daughter of the Hungarian prince. Damn him! . . . Old Hawk! He doesn't ask, he just acts." He emptied his goblet and called out: "Olav, do you mourn your father?"

"I didn't know him. On sleepless nights, I try to imagine what he was like," he answered honestly.

"Imagine your father, then, but don't regret not knowing him. Ours rules us as if we were his property, an extension of the arms he uses to play his games . . ."

"Stop it," Świętosława said. "Maybe Olav's father was different?"

"All rulers are the same." Bolesław shrugged.

"I'll remind you of that when you become one." She threw an apple at his head.

Bolesław ducked.

Olav began to laugh. And he reached a hand to Świętosława across the table.

"I've never met a girl like you before."

And she took his hand, holding it tightly.

"It's the first time I've ever seen someone like you, too."

Olav shivered at her words.

"Be careful, friend," Bolesław interjected. "My sister . . ." He fell silent. "We call her 'the bold.' It stuck, like a second name."

"What does it sound like in your tongue?" she asked Olav.

"Storråda," he said, looking in her eyes.

Świętosława, not breaking eye contact, squeezed his hand. She called Dusza over and offered her goblet.

"What will you do now?" Bolesław asked, more somber now, studying Olav with narrowed eyes. "Will you set out to face Jarl Haakon?"

"I'm not a fool," Olav said. "After a victorious battle the jarl will have much respect in the country, and my appearance in Norway won't change that. Royal blood must wait for the fame of glory to cool. I'll set out as a Viking."

"To plunder, rape, and burn?" Świętosława asked sweetly.

"No. To find silver and men with whom I can sail back to win my country."

"Smart." Bolesław nodded. "Providing you avoid our shores."

"I swear it," Olav said seriously.

"Will you come to Sweden?" Świętosława glanced at him.

"Yes, if you'll agree. I'll defeat your husband and ask for the dowager queen's hand in marriage. Would that suit you?"

They looked in each other's eyes.

"At the moment, you have no one to stand at your side to defeat him with," Bolesław reminded him. "Although I'd have nothing against you being my brother-in-law."

Olav felt dizzy, from the mead, he told himself.

"If I had a sister, I'd ask you to marry her, Bolesław."

"Everyone wants to marry me off!" Bolesław laughed. "Duszan, bring the mushrooms."

"You eat the ones that give you visions?"

"No. What are you on about? We have porcini mushrooms casseroled in butter," Bolesław replied.

"What were you talking about?" Świętosława asked Olav, curious.

"There are mushrooms that can bring visions."

"I've heard of these." Bolesław slapped his hand against the bench. "But I thought they weren't visions so much as bloodthirst, or so they said."

"There are different kinds. Some offer visions of the future, others turn warriors into beasts that feel neither fear nor pain. Although my compatriots place a higher value on bloodthirst evoked without the aid of mushrooms."

"Have you tried them?" the duke's son asked.

"No," Olav replied honestly. "But . . . I have some in my saddlebag. Duchess Allogia gave me a handful and told me I should eat them if I wanted to find out what the future had in store for me."

Świętosława stood up and went to the grill which hung in the corner, over the fire. She reached out her hands, as if trying to warm them. Then she turned to him.

"Well, go get them. We'll do it together."

Świętosława picked up one of the dry, tawny mushrooms. Her brother held another, and Olav was left with the third.

"Dusza," she called sensibly. "Guard us, you and Duszan, because we don't know what will happen next."

Olav bit into the dry mushroom, chewing and washing it down with mead. Świętosława did the same, watching her brother. He swallowed, too. Then she looked up at Olav. His pale blue eyes seemed to sting her. She breathed in. She smelled the salty scent of his skin. Fresh sweat on his brow. The sweetness in the knot of silk on his tunic. She shuddered when she realized she could distinguish between the smell of warp and weft. And the scent of the selvage which decorated the edge of the tunic at his neck. *Dnieper*, she heard in her head, and saw Olav on a ship sailing across this river, the Dnieper.

"God, save me!" she whispered, and the Almighty Father, instead of holding her in his arms, pushed her with a long finger straight into Olav's.

Bolesław tasted the dry mushroom in his mouth, and after that a sting, as if a knife had cut his tongue in half. In his mind, he saw himself jumping onto his horse's back. He felt the coolness of the wind on his chest, and warmth on his stomach from the horse's steaming back. He rode naked, heading east. The sun was a huge, golden-red shield rising over a great river. He stretched out an arm and the river turned to blood. He rode into it. Human insides bubbled under the horse's hooves. It slowed from a canter to a walk. Step after step, Bolesław felt his body aging. He saw gray tangles of hair falling from his shoulders down to his chest. The skin on his hands was covered in liver spots. He leaned down to wash them off, but instead just gathered blood under his nails. The hooves of his mount clanked loudly against the stony bank. It shook its head. Bolesław stretched out an arm and pointed in the direction he wanted to go with his scepter. A moment later, he rode under a golden gate and stopped, yanking dangerously at the reins. A beautiful, golden-haired girl appeared in front of his horse, and she spread her arms wide like a cross. He reached out a hand to her, and she jumped into the saddle lightly. He felt the warmth of her back on his stomach. "What's your name?" he asked. "Predsława," she replied, letting him kiss her rose-petal lips.

Olav was sailing on a ship twice the length of *Kanugård*. Geivar was at the helm, but he didn't recognize anyone else in the crew. A stony island appeared in the mist. They reached a hastily built harbor. A white dog with a long neck sat on the shore. It didn't bark. It turned around, and Olav followed it across the dry lichen that covered the rocks. Scented smoke hung in the cool, humid air. He crossed through a stone archway. He unbuckled his belt and threw down his weapons. He tore the cloak from his shoulders. He stripped off all of his clothes, and faced the dim entrance to the stone building. He walked into it naked. He felt the coolness of old stones under his feet. A spring of water ran inside. He walked into it, and was filled with brightness.

The white dog howled and leapt onto his back in a single fluid movement. "I will be your dog," Olav whispered, and shivered. Strong, warm hands held him. He opened his eyes; it was her.

Świętosława grabbed the burning torch which flew toward her. She howled with pain. It wasn't a torch, but the burning end of a spear which buried itself in her chest. Her fingers tightened around the shaft. It didn't burn her, but sent waves of pleasure through her body. It was stuck fast in her, like a thorn. She held on to it, even though it gave her pain which she felt deep in her bones. Pleasure and pain. She stood in water. Ocean waves brought her two royal crowns. There were high baskets behind them, from which she could hear the cooing of babies. The baskets stopped in the shallows, one after another. A dark-haired boy emerged from the first one. Two clumsy ones from the next one. Girls crawled after them. The children's hair was covered with frost. The ocean wave hit viciously. Two more crowns floated out from the sea's frothy lips. Arterial blood pulsed from one of them. The spear head rusted inside her heart. The pleasure turned into salty pain.

Duszan caught Bolesław around the shoulders and shook him from his dark visions.

"Let's drink to the future," Bolesław exclaimed, pulling his sister by the hand.

She fell into him hard, with a face warmed by the fire, pulling Olav with her. They collided, chest to chest. Olav had white, absent irises, but he sobered momentarily.

"I love Świętosława," he said.

"As do I," Bolesław replied honestly. "But she doesn't love us."

"I'll go to your father and ask for her." A drop of blood fell from Olav's lips.

"Go, then. But if I know him at all, he won't give her to you."

Świętosława had collapsed across Bolesław's chest. Shivers racked her body. Olav's blood fell onto her shoulder. She opened her eyes. They weren't green, as they were in ordinary life. They looked like molten gold.

"I change my mind," she murmured. "I want him instead of those crowns." She pulled herself from Bolesław's arms, leaning into Olav's instead. She covered her face with her hands.

Świętosława freed her eyes from the cover of her fingers. Olav's chin was over her forehead, smelling of the sea. The skin of a seal, the scent of a wet cotton sail. Blood? She thought for a moment that she was standing in the door of a manor, and he was returning from a long journey. She reached out to him and whispered:

"I knew you'd come back. I love you."

And then she saw her brother's face, which morphed into Mieszko's stern features.

Jarl Birger stood behind him. She bowed to Birger, as she had during the engagement, and she allowed him to hold her hand in his when they made their marriage vows. "Yes, Eric," she heard her voice say.

She shook herself. Olav and her brother both looked sober. Now she too sobered up.

"Dusza, mead! Let's wash away the sharp taste of these visions. Yes,

Bolesław and Olav." She tightened her grip on their hands. "Let's drink to all the crowns we will wear."

Astrid returned from Wolin as quickly as she could. She was haunted by the feeling that every day she was away from Poznań would lead to damages difficult to recover from. She hadn't even had time to change after her journey when Mieszko summoned her to him. He was alone.

"Daughter," he greeted her softly, and it was enough to awaken hope in her breast. "Did Birger sort out everything he needed to in Wolin?"

"Yes, my lord."

"Good. I'm so happy that I can rely on you." He spoke slowly, as if sifting his words. "Possibly more so than on any other of my daughters . . ."

She should have felt proud, but instead fear clutched her heart.

"Astrid, I have another task for you. One which may seem obvious, but those are only appearances." He cocked his head and studied her, with more attention than ever before. "The fate of daughters is to marry . . ."

Her mouth went dry. Hope leaped to her throat. Olav's pale eyes gleamed in her memory, as if he were standing in front of her now.

"Yes," she said, her voice trembling.

"The fate of my daughters is to marry as well as they possibly can."

Świętosława to Sweden, and I to Norway, she repeated silently, again and again, as if that could make it so.

"You'll make my dream of a powerful fleet come true."

"Yes!" The word escaped her, because he couldn't have spoken any clearer.

Mieszko laughed, and added,

"My daughters surprise me. Do you mean to say that, like Świętosława, you have seen through my designs? I know they say you can see the future, but to this extent? Unless you heard of Sigvald's arrival while you were in Wolin, hmm?"

"Sigvald?" The fear was back in a single heartbeat. "You want me to marry the Jomsviking?"

"Who else did you think I meant, child?"

"Olav Tryggvason," she said, honestly and helplessly.

Mieszko laughed lightly. "Much time will pass before Olav wins back the Norwegian throne. I like him, I won't deny it, but Sigvald is a far better choice. By joining you with him, we'll end the Danish influence in Jomsborg, and we'll gain the iron boys, an ocean army. You, my daughter, Dalwin's granddaughter, Wolin's viceroy, as the wife of the jarl of Jomsborg—it's the perfect solution. See it, my clever Astrid."

"My prince, Sigvald lost to Jarl Haakon. He has no chance of being chosen as the chieftains' leader. After such a defeat? The reputation of coward and bad luck will stick fast to him. Someone like that will not become the jarl of Jom . . ."

"They will choose him," Mieszko interrupted her firmly. "When they see that I have supported him by giving him my daughter."

"No." Astrid disagreed with the duke for the first time in her life. She didn't believe she could sway him, but she had to try.

"Yes. Listen to me, and learn. Sometimes it pays to back a loser, because by winning their eternal gratitude you can gain even more. Sigvald's fate will depend on me and you, remember that. And he'll do everything to make the most of this opportunity. He'll snatch Jomsborg from Danish influences and give it to us, do you understand? The dreams I have dreamt for so many years will finally become reality. What I fought Count Wichman and Hodo for. No one will threaten my reign at Odra's estuary. Do you know what that means for the entire country? Just think!"

She gathered all the strength she still had left and for the first time called him "Father."

"Father, please, I'm begging you as I have never begged you before. Marry Sigvald to Geira. Please, so long as it isn't me."

"Why?"

"Because I cannot find a shred of respect for him inside of me. To me, he is nothing but a coward."

"Even better," he replied coldly. "Instead of loving him, you can control him."

"Father . . ."

"I have made up my mind. Geira will marry Olav."

Astrid felt those words like a kick in the gut. She didn't think the next ones could hurt her even more.

"The young Tryggvason is worth backing. I'll wait until he has a son with your sister, then I'll let him sail to get the riches and men that he cannot win his throne without. I'll ensure he and Sigvald are friends, too, loyal to one another. The Jomsvikings will aid Olav in his fight against Norway in a few years. Eric, Świętosława's husband, will also be useful in that battle. All this to smother Denmark, my daughter. You must understand this. The faraway Sweden and even more distant Norway pose no threat to me, to us. Only Denmark, and that's precisely why I am solving that problem. Even if

Sven, after his father Harald's imminent death, claims power in an expansive Denmark, he will end up in a country as small as a fishing village."

Astrid began to shake. At first, she thought she would burst into tears, like a child. Then, she felt something strange happening to her entire body. Her fingers went numb, as if she'd shoved them into ice.

"You're mistaken . . ."

"Stop it, don't be childish. It doesn't suit you, Astrid. Wisdom, strength, the gift of foresight, those things suit you."

"You're mistaken . . ."

"I know what I'm saying. I've watched you for so many years, my child. Get Olav out of your head. You wouldn't be happy at the side of a man who dreams of another. Świętosława has stolen Olav's heart. He has asked me for her, and I denied him. Can't you see? She asked me for him, too, and I denied her as well. I'm not such a tyrant as you might think. I have to deny all my children what they want, to give them what they need instead."

"You're mistaken, Father . . ." The words slipped from her lips for the third time, and she knew that though her voice was speaking them, the words were not hers. She flinched. She moved her hands. She grabbed Mieszko's hand and bowed to him.

"I will do as you command, my lord. I feel that you are wrong, but I don't know what about."

PART II

TO ALL THE CROWNS
WE WILL WEAR

The First Crown
986–995

12

⊗

SWEDEN

Spring trilled, like birds in their nests. It gleamed with the bloody glow of cold sunsets, cool sunrises, and the warm breezes which arrived in daytime. Flowers bloomed wildly, and grasses rose from dead, strawlike stems with green, arrogant offshoots. The snow had melted and the gray of winter gave way to the boldly arriving spring. Spring walked between the islands in Mälaren Bay with a confident step, the pale-eyed ruler of the sun, so sure of herself that, busy commanding Nature, she misses the moment that she turns into summer.

Świętosława held the child in her arms. The red, wrinkled baby had finally fallen asleep. She hadn't been able to get a good look at him while he'd screamed, all she'd seen were toothless gums and the open abyss of his mouth. He was all shout, as if he were furious he'd been born at all.

"What a wonderful child!" Thora, Jarl Birger's wife, had praised a moment earlier. She'd delivered the baby. "Beautiful and strong, like our king."

"You think Eric is beautiful?" Świętosława had asked, forced to raise her voice to be heard over the boy's cries.

Thora moved away from the pail where she'd been washing blood from her hands. Servants handed her a towel. Drying her palms, she stared at Świętosława as if she'd never seen her before.

"Don't you think so, my lady?"

Świętosława swept sweaty tendrils of hair from her forehead and lost herself in her thoughts. While sailing aboard the *Haughty Giantess* to Uppsala, she'd seen Olav every time she'd closed her eyes, white-haired and bright-eyed. Young and beautiful. His image was with her in every moment, in every breath and heartbeat. But the journey didn't last forever, even if she'd secretly hoped it would. They sailed into Mälaren Bay to the sound of horns echoing off the water. Three ships led them in, moving together in a row. A golden wild boar shone on the sail of the middle one, and Eric stood at the bow. Broad-shouldered, bearded, and bald. Completely bald. The sun bounced off his smooth skull. He was terrifying, but she was meant to be his wife, so she couldn't fear him.

"I think that he's strong, but it would never have occurred to me to think of him as beautiful."

"That's what a man's beauty is though, my lady! Strength! And you hold the evidence of his prowess in your arms. He will bring you another when he returns from the expedition. He promised he will be victorious when he faces Styrbjorn, and he will give it to you!" Thora let out a clear laugh.

She wasn't Christian like her husband, Birger, and everything she said about Eric was laced with a pagan devotion to the king.

Pagan? Świętosława thought. *The people adore Mieszko just as much.*

A few of her ladies from her family home had made the journey with her, but Świętosława had known the first thing she'd have to do in her husband's land was to befriend the powerful and wealthy who surrounded Eric. She had to build her own alliances in this new country. If her primary concern when choosing allies was faith, all she'd be left with was Jarl Birger and a few servants. She'd decided to start with Thora. And Thora, at least when it came to the birth, had done marvelously.

"Rest now, my lady. I'll come back when I hear your son has woken."

"Son," Świętosława whispered after the other woman left, and she took another look at the child.

A purple-red body, long and thin. Fists no larger than plums, in which, in just a few years, he would want to hold his first wooden sword. He breathed strongly and deeply. She rolled him carefully over onto his stomach. He had a patch of soft hair on his lower back.

"Just like your father," she muttered, tracing it with a finger. "And you're bald like him, too. God, I hope you grow hair on your head and not just on your back!"

She touched his elongated skull and let her thumb pause on the back of his head.

"What do you have here? A birthmark? I need to have a look at you in the sun. It's dark in here." She swaddled him as she spoke.

She hated the old royal manor in Uppsala as much as Eric loved it. It was large and vast, that was undeniable. Comfortable, too, with an enormous hall that could hold a hundred guests, and private chambers in both wings. Nothing, however, could change the fact that it was eternally dark. The smoke holes in the high ceilings were sunlight's only way in, and gloom fell on the entire mansion as soon as the fires or lamp flames dimmed. "You'll appreciate it in winter, my lady," Eric laughed when she shared her feelings with him. "You'll be as warm as a vixen in her den." She was, but that wasn't enough. Not for her.

The gloom of the royal manor was found even beyond its walls, in something far more dangerous and powerful—in the shade of the giant royal cairns, the sacrificial trees, and the enormous temple. Jarl Birger had tried to prepare her for what awaited them during their journey, but her imagination hadn't been able to match the reality of what she found on the Swedish shore.

Yes, Eric's residence lay in a fertile valley, whose vibrant green was a joy to see. But this was the illusion of the north. A ridge of burial mounds stretched out to the south. The tall, green hills weren't a part of nature, but the creation of human hands. The cairns of long-dead kings.

"Imagine green hills when you look at them, and don't think about the fact that they hide the remains of burned rulers, the ashes of their boats, horses, dogs, and wives," Jarl Birger told her, trying to reassure her. Yes, that wasn't too difficult. It got harder to keep his words in mind, though, when she let her gaze drop from the peaks of the hills to their bases. Because between the range of mounds and the royal manor stood an enormous pagan temple, surrounded by sacrificial trees.

Each of the nine trees was as large as the oak that grew in the cemetery of her forefathers in Gniezno. But there, the oak was the green lord of the forest, while here it played the part of the somber gallows. The remains of horses and people, sacrifices to Odin, hung from its branches. The crows wouldn't leave the crumbling corpses alone, and Świętosława heard their calls every time she stepped outside her husband's manor. Even now, as she gazed at her son's face, born just that dawn, she heard a flock of the sinister birds. They flew over the manor, ever hungry for more of their cadaverous banquet. She wrapped her arms around the child instinctively, protectively. It didn't matter that he was as bald as Eric, red and ugly. He had come from her womb.

"My son." Świętosława kissed him for the first time.

He opened his eyes. Small and dark blue. He wrinkled his nose, as if trying to catch her scent.

"I'm your mother," she told him. "I'll teach you my language. I'll teach you my faith. I'll teach you my true name. Your father cannot pronounce it. He's a bald king, headstrong, and with a stiff tongue, that's why he named me Sigrid Storråda."

At the sound of this, the child began to cry. Świętosława covered its mouth with her hand. She wanted to be with her son alone, she didn't want Thora and the servants to come running. Dusza appeared beside Świętosława then and parted the nightshirt on her chest. She delicately pulled Świętosława's hand from the child's mouth and moved him to her mistress's breast. He bit and began to suck without closing his eyes. Dusza stepped quietly back to the chair beside the bed.

"I'll tell you everything, my son. I come from a beautiful country beyond the sea. My mother was born even farther south, and though only rivers run through her country, she knew this curse, *From another side of the sea!* She taught it to me when I was small, and when I lost her, I swore at the ocean frequently, never knowing that that's how I would reach my husband. Perhaps that's why I have met such evil here? Maybe I have cursed it for myself? I took with me, as a wedding gift, the lightning steel from my father, your grandfather, the sword made of metal which fell straight from the heavens. His name is Mieszko. He has a dark, pointy beard with a single gray stripe. There is a hawk on his shoulder that cannot be fed by anyone other than Father. Not even his wife, the evil duchess Oda. I have a brother, Bolesław, who will inherit our great kingdom from Father, and two half sisters, Astrid and Geira. I used to love them both, but now I only love Astrid. For Geira, I now feel a hatred so strong that if I confessed it to Father John, he'd never forgive me this loathing, because there is no desire in me to be rid of it. But Father John has remained in Poznań, and the chaplain I've been given didn't survive the journey; the poor man died on board the *Haughty Giantess* and now there is no one at my side who could save my soul. There are only the corpses of sacrifices hanging from oaks and the temple of your fathers' gods. I won't tell you anything about them. You won't suck out Eric's dark faith with your mother's milk. Am I strong enough to change him? I don't know, my son. Old people don't change, and your father carries the weight of four decades on his shoulders. He has gone south now to hunt his nephew, Styrbjorn. *I'll give him a beautiful battle,* he boasted as he sailed to the sound of horns. He promised a few things when he asked for my hand. Firstly, that he would kill Styrbjorn." She tickled her son's nose.

"He's doing it for you, my little one, so that no one dare take away the power you have a right to. Secondly, he promised to annihilate Denmark's strength. It's a gift for my lord father. He promised me that he'd never stand between me and Christ. And that I would never want for anything. But he demanded just as much in return." The boy let go of her nipple and looked at her as if he was about to start crying. She quickly gave him her other breast. "Listen, I'm not done yet." He began to suck, his eyes never leaving her face.

"He took me to bed and believe me, little one, I had no desire to laugh

then. I didn't moan like Oda with Mieszko. I howled, and bit into the polar bear fur he had lain me down on. I can still taste it. Your father is an
axe in bed, like the axe he never parts with. Heavy, sharp, fat, and never
rusty. Don't worry, this isn't your problem and never will be, my little one.
Listen to what happened next. He brought me morgengold in the morning,
in payment for my virginity. He valued me highly. Thora says that I could
have bought three boats with armed crews for the treasures in that chest.
It's good to know that, isn't it? But then he announced during the feast that
he is changing my name, and from that moment everyone was to call me
Queen Sigrid.

"I told him, *I have learned your tongue, husband. You learn my name.* True, perhaps I shouldn't then have added, *What, will the holy name not pass your pagan
throat? Wash it down with water, not mead—come on, try it.* And he choked at this,
and his people began to laugh and shout, 'Sigrid! Sigrid Storråda!' and so it
has remained. Your father, by calling me Sigrid Storråda, thought to irritate
me, to prove I was now his, and Sweden's, but you know what? He's a fool.
Because he doesn't know someone has called me Storråda before him." She
gave the child a warning look.

"This will be our secret, remember! Only you and I know about this, son.
And Dusza. Dusza doesn't speak any language, so it's as if she spoke all of
them. Isn't that right, Dusza? Take him from me. I've told him enough for a
first time. I hope the child's smart enough to remember."

Dusza rose swiftly and reached her arms out for the child. Świętosława
gave her the boy and stretched her stiff body.

"Do you think I can get out of bed yet? Thora says I should lie down, but
I gave birth in the morning and it's probably noon now, I'm tired of lying
down . . . Can you hear that?"

Dusza rose and walked to the bedchamber door with the child in her
arms.

"No." Świętosława shook her head. "I thought it came from outside, a
commotion or . . ." She trailed off, and Dusza's face gave nothing away.

The servant shook her head.

"Strange." Świętosława shrugged. "I do hear something, though, you don't?
Maybe I just thought I heard it . . . Thora!" she called out. "Thoraaaaa!" she
shouted, louder.

Dusza opened her mouth warningly, and the child began to wail.

"Oh, I need to learn to be quiet around him," Świętosława observed un-
happily. "Do something with him, Dusza. Children have wet nurses . . ."

A moment later, Thora appeared.

"My lady." She curtsied and glanced at Dusza, who was calming the baby. "Maybe he needs to be fed?"

"No. He's been feeding this whole time. Dusza will manage. I want to get up, wash, and change."

"You should rest . . ." Thora began hesitantly.

"Perhaps I should, but I don't want to," Świętosława said firmly.

"I'll order water to be boiled." Thora turned to give the command, but Świętosława stopped her before she could leave again.

"Any news from the king? Can a battle last so long?"

"One battle, no, my lady, but we don't know if it will end with just one fight, and how long the negotiations may take . . ."

"There was no talk of any negotiations," Świętosława interrupted. "I should send word to my brother and father. I want to share the joyous news of my son's birth."

Servants brought basins with hot water and poured it into the bath, which was laid out with a clean sheet. The bedchamber was soon humid and stifling with steam, and the servants helped Świętosława undress. As the warm water enveloped her body, she felt very, very tired. The girls washed her hair and gently wiped the blood and mucus from her skin. She closed her eyes. The gloomy royal manor in Uppsala disappeared, as did Thora and the strange maidservants, and the child. There was only Dusza and her. They were both five. They splashed in the warm waters of Lake Lednica. The sun warmed them, and Dobrawa hummed softly, stroking Świętosława's hair.

Świętosława longed to stay lost in the memory, in that moment of bliss. It crossed her mind that since Dobrawa's death no one had shown her love like this. Father had never spoiled any of them. Her brother hugged her often, but then would tousle her hair as if she were a clumsy puppy. Perhaps Astrid had stroked her hair once or twice, but her sister's affection was often harsh. And so she, the most valuable of daughters, the most carefully guarded, the best fed and dressed, showered with jewels, grew up without that one thing. The one you can't see with the naked eye, that she herself didn't recognize until this very moment.

She didn't open her eyes, but felt the tears streaming down her face, hoping they would be mistaken for drops of water falling from her wet hair. The child began to cry suddenly. Świętosława felt a sharp pain in the bottom of her belly and sore nipples. Without opening her eyes, she said:

"Dusza, hand me the child."

"My lady," Thora said, her voice filled with concern, "you shouldn't bathe the child before the father has seen it with the blood of birth on his body."

"Thora, neither you nor I know when the king will return," she replied gently, still not opening her eyes. She reached her arms out for the boy.

"You're right. Ah, we can always smear him with fresh blood." Thora laughed and sniffed. "Women have been doing that for generations . . ."

"Are you crying?" Świętosława asked.

"No . . . of course not . . . I'm happy, Sigrid . . ."

Dusza placed the child in her arms gently, and supported him while Świętosława made them both comfortable. She held the boy's head to make sure it stayed above water.

"Why are you crying?" she asked Thora quietly.

"My womb is dry and infertile," Thora whispered. "And you have allowed me to witness the miracle of birth today."

"How old are you, Thora?"

"Almost thirty, my lady."

"Sarah was ninety when God gave her a son. I will tell you of it one day."

The child on her breast stopped crying. She held him in the warm water and stroked his bald head. Yes, if Thora did have a child in her old age, like the biblical Sarah, it really would be a miracle. But Thora was right. The miracle before them was her son's birth, a mere ten months after the wedding. A healthy boy whose presence in this world ensured she was a full-fledged queen. Even if Eric died in battle, she, Świętosława, Sigrid Storråda, was a ruler in the name of her son from this moment on. She opened her eyes and kissed her miracle on the forehead.

The next evening, Świętosława again heard the noise that no one else seemed to. She couldn't name it; it was as if something were making the air around her tremble. But when the horns sounded a welcome for Eric at the gates a moment later, she thought she understood. She and Eric were connected now, as if by an invisible thread, whether she loved him or not. Her mother Dobrawa had always sensed her father's returns.

There was time to prepare for her husband's return even after the horns had sounded. Eric was riding from the south, and he stopped at the temple and grove to make sacrifices to his bloodthirsty gods before coming to her. Sacrifices of thanks, Świętosława knew, since the messengers carrying the good news had arrived before him.

There is a price for everything, she thought. *He fulfilled the first condition of our marriage, and I bore him a son.*

She donned her richest dress, made of thick, red silk bordered with a wide golden band. A servant braided her hair into crowns, pinning them high around her head. A band threaded with gold held them in place, and the servants put rings on her fingers.

"Dusza, the lynx." Świętosława reached out for the fur, then she was ready to greet her husband.

"And the child," Thora reminded her.

A servant offered a cup with fresh blood, and Świętosława marked her son's cheeks.

She stood on a raised platform in the great hall, with the lynx fur on her back and the child in her arms. In the torchlight, accompanied by the victorious sound of horns, she watched from above as her lord husband approached, King Eric. Bald, bearded, with powerful shoulders. Great and heavy, but still nimble. The embodiment of strength, like the boar whose image was displayed on his shield. With polar bear skin thrown over his back, he seemed twice his normal size. His dark eyes shone. His belt clanked against the chain mail's metal. His eyes never left her as he walked. Her, or the bundle in her arms. His noblemen walked behind him, then the helmsmen of his ships and his squad leaders. Jarl Birger walked on his right, smiling reassuringly to her.

"Queen Sigrid," her lord husband said loudly when he reached her.

"King Eric," she replied.

"What awaits me at home?" he asked.

"A royal son. And what have you brought the queen?"

"Victory, my lady. Fyrisvellir's fields drowned in the blood of our enemies. My nephew Styrbjorn is dead. We took no prisoners."

Shouts of triumph rang out.

What does he value more? she asked herself. *His son, or victory over his nephew?*

She handed him the child. He unwrapped the blanket and looked at his son, taking in every inch of him. He even counted all his toes and fingers.

"He has hair on his back, like you, my lord," she told him.

He checked that, too. He liked it. He lifted the boy high in the air and showed his people.

"My son!" the king roared. "My son and heir!"

The child burst into tears, but this only made the guests happier.

"He has some voice."

"A strong boy."

"He's greeting us."

"My king, do you have a name for him yet?" Świętosława asked, taking the child back.

He held her hands and pulled her toward him.

"This is our firstborn. You've made me happy, my lady." His eyes gleamed the way they did when he took her to bed.

"The noise here is terrible." She smiled to him. "Repeat that, please, because I didn't hear you."

"You've made me happy by bearing me a son!" he shouted, so loudly that the hall went quiet.

"As you have with your victory," she replied.

They drank to her health, his health, and the child's. They drank to the victory, a safe return home, and a quick healing of wounds. The servants couldn't carry the jugs in fast enough. Laughter, roars, the cheerfulness of women greeting their husbands drowning the sobs of those whose loved ones had remained on Fyrisvellir's fields.

Eric invited Thora, Birger's wife, to sit at the honored place at his side, as the first of the noblewomen and as the one who had brought his son safely into the world. Świętosława asked Jarl Birger to join her, as an acknowledgment of his bravery in battle.

The bard sung verses of Styrbjorn's defeat. He rhymed Fyrisvellir's green fields with the blue of a river running nearby, which turned red with the blood of the dead.

In the moments when the bard paused for breath, Birger summed up battle in his own way, saying only, "Three days of killing."

He left the description of the dancing swords, whir of lethal arrows, murderous flight of spears, and walls of shields to the poet. The bard praised the courage of the Jomsvikings who had supported Styrbjorn:

Their courage gleamed
But they served the wrong cause
They fell valiantly
Never begging for mercy . . .

The poet called Styrbjorn an "undeserving nephew," and acknowledged his death with a single couplet, dedicating his talents to praising "Eric the Victorious" instead:

Segersäll. That's the name which now belongs
To the bravest of kings!

"And what name will you give your son?" Świętosława heard Thora's question between the song's verses.

"Perhaps Bjorn, after my father?" Eric said, taking another drink from a huge, silver-coated horn. "Maybe not . . ."

"Was Styrbjorn's father, and my husband's brother, well-liked in the country? Are any of his supporters still alive?" Świętosława could use her own tongue when speaking with Birger.

"There are always some, my lady. Your husband risked much when he announced that his heir would be the son you carried in your womb. It was a challenge. If you'd given birth to a daughter, many would have wondered in the logic of Styrbjorn's death. But you, my lady, bring good fortune. You are a true queen."

"Was it difficult to convince Styrbjorn to declare war on Eric?"

"No." Birger laughed. "Young men are like dry kindling. A single spark is enough to set them on fire."

She gave him a sign with her hand to stop him from talking, because the bard was singing of something she didn't understand.

"What royal wedding is he singing about?"

Birger shifted uncomfortably.

"Ask your husband, my lady. He can tell you himself. I . . ." He checked that Eric was busy talking to Thora, and finished quickly: "My lady, there will be an official ritual of naming your son, and his father will sprinkle him with water. I wouldn't suggest this to anyone else, but we are joined by faith. Pray over the water so that the king doesn't know it, and let it be at least in part a baptism for your son . . . someday you are bound to be able to fulfil the sacrament, but . . ."

"Thank you, Jarl," she said, not looking at him, and everything inside her trembled.

Only Birger would understand how much she feared her child dying without being baptized. Children often die.

The bard finished his song about the battle and began a new one, one unknown to the crowd:

Silent and thoughtful
Should be the royal son,
Brave in battle,
Unswayed in his commands . . .

"My king." She turned to Eric. "If you haven't decided on a name for your son, allow me to advise you."

"Cold is the advice of women," Eric hummed cheerfully, but this was a line from his favorite bard performance, and Świętosława had heard it often.

"Name your son Olav, husband."

"What?" His eyes gleamed dangerously.

"Your dead brother was called Olav. Styrbjorn was his son. You denied Styrbjorn his right to power, but if you name your firstborn Olav, you'll show that you respect your brother's memory, and that you defeated your nephew in a just cause. Those who supported them in hiding won't be able to accuse you of any ill will."

"Cold is the advice of women," Eric repeated. He grabbed her hand and squeezed. "Cold advice is good advice, my lady. I wouldn't have thought of that."

She smiled at him, sensing she had won.

"But first ask your heart, my king, if you'll be able to call your son 'Olav' and not see your brother in him, the one you disagreed with in the past."

"I won't call him 'Olav' but 'Olof,' that's what it sounds like in our tongue." Eric laughed. "And I assure you, my queen, that every time I call him by name I will be worshipping your sharp mind. Mead!" he called out. "We can fulfill the naming ritual even today."

No, she thought, then *I'm sorry, my son,* and pinched the child as hard as she could. He began to scream.

"I need to feed him," she said apologetically. "He's lasted a long time anyway."

"Then we will do it tomorrow," Eric agreed and rose. "Bid good night to my son and Queen Sigrid," he ordered his guests.

They put so much heart into their good nights that the old beams supporting the hall trembled. They shouted that "Segersäll and Storråda go well together." She heard them when Dusza was undressing her in the bedchamber. Naked, she lay in bed with the child and held him close.

"It's all right, my Olav-Olof. You're mine now."

Before she fell asleep, the depth of her triumph reached her. From now on, she could say the name she longed to hear as often as she desired. Aloud, whispering, shouting—however she wanted. Holding her son while the cheers faded below, Świętosława finally felt the full extent of her love for him.

13

GERMANY

Bolesław wasn't present at the birth of his first son, because Mieszko had decided to give him another lesson in political alliances. They journeyed together to Połabie.

Mere days after Gertrude's procession left Poznań, Bolesław had married Karolda, the Hungarian prince's daughter, at Mieszko's bidding. The Hungarian woman was unlike his previous fiancée in almost every way. Passionate and bold, loud and wild. She learned his language slowly, but her desire in bed was insatiable. They didn't talk much, but they made love passionately, often from dusk till dawn. During the day, they stayed away from each other, because in the morning light Karolda seemed, at best, strange to him. Her dark eyes unsettled Bolesław. He caught her staring at him sometimes, but when he smiled and spoke to her, she'd turn her head and pretend not to have heard.

"Hungarian witch," Zarad called her when they were alone. "Be careful, Prince, that she doesn't enchant you."

"She has another name," Jaksa teased. "Her servants call her 'Lady Emese.'"

"More proof that she's a witch," Zarad said, laughing.

"Or that you're an idiot." Bolesław slapped him on the back. "Women change their names after marriage."

"Indeed, but she was introduced to you as Karolda." Zarad wouldn't let it go. He despised Bolesław's wife. "Emese is her secret name, I'm telling you, my friend. But I understand that these are matters of state." He spread his arms wide as if he were surrendering. "A witch in exchange for Hungarian support in our attack against the Czechs. What one wouldn't do for power."

"Is there any news of your sister from Uppsala?" Bjornar said, changing the topic in hopes of shutting Zarad up.

"Not yet," Bolesław said. "Although I can guess what I'd hear if I asked Eric's closest friends: 'The Piast witch doesn't know when to bite her tongue and endangers our king and the whole kingdom with spells only she knows.'"

"No, no, no. Świętosława is something else entirely. I'll cut off the head of anyone who speaks of our sister like that," Zarad chimed in angrily.

"Don't flatter yourself. She's not your sister, but Bolesław's." Jaksa took Zarad's goblet.

"My comrade's sister is my sister, and what will you do about it, huh, you gloomy beanstalk?" Zarad threw himself at his friend.

"All right, that's enough." Bolesław waved a hand. "Tomorrow, we head to Połabie, so save your energy to use against the Veleti."

He stood and whistled for the dogs. They heaved themselves up reluctantly. Duszan chased them to make them walk by the prince. They took a few steps and whined.

"Come on, we're going," Bolesław scolded.

They ran in the opposite direction to the door and hid behind a bench. Zarad burst out laughing.

"Every night. Smart dogs, they don't like Mistress Karolda."

Bolesław rolled his eyes.

"Go on, go on, don't abandon your master," Zarad said to the dogs, fake concern in his voice. "The dog may not want to, but the prince must."

Their journey to Połabie was reviving. Bolesław rode at the head of the Polish armies with Mieszko, with a squad of heavy infantry behind them, mounted scouts in front, and light infantry and shield-bearers on either side. Father was a declared enemy of armies cobbled together from commoners.

"Heavy infantry is expensive, but every coin spent on their training and living will come back to you tenfold," he'd advised repeatedly. Mieszko had three thousand armored infantrymen and ten thousand light infantrymen, waiting at his beck and call. He took far fewer than that to Połabie, though.

"Three hundred heavy and six hundred light, that's enough to show the Empress Theophanu how loyal our allies are," he said as they crossed the Elbe River.

"Does the old doe with a calf at her side lead the Saxon herds?" Witosz, one of Mieszko's commanders, asked, when they set off west again after a brief break.

Mieszko laughed.

"Theophanu won't miss a chance like this. She wants to show off her son to all the swords of the empire, the son she had to snatch from Henry the Bavarian's claws. She'll be there to bless us before we face the pagans, with all her imperial widow glory. Besides, she must see for herself which of the dukes make an appearance, and who has ignored a command from the lady of the Reich. And I assure you, she will not miscount. Heavy infantry, light infantry, horses, swords, spears, shields. Even the carts. After she removed the imperial grandmother Adelaide from power in spring, she needs a swift success. If the courtly rules didn't forbid women from donning armor, she would lead the armies herself."

"Behind a wall of shields, of course," Witosz threw in, and they laughed at Theophanu.

Bolesław didn't participate in the mockery; the conversation about the empress reminded him of Świętosława. Suddenly, he missed his slight, bold sister. There was no news from beyond the seas, but was that good or bad? He spurred his horse on and separated from the column.

His father had been right, Theophanu was stationed on the sprawling commons on the Elbe's banks where the armies were to meet. Her golden tent was the center of the war camp, on a small raised hill, as impressive as a manor. The Reich lords settled around it. The archbishop of Magdeburg, Giselher, with his allies; Ezykon and Binizon, the counts of Merseburg. Then Godfrey, count of Lorraine, with his son and son-in-law. Count Dudo of Brunswick. Archbishop Willigis of Mainz, a great supporter of the Ottos and empress, and Bishop Folcold of Meissen, under Willigis's protection. And finally, Count Herman of Angeron, a Westphalian nobleman who had gained Theophanu's respect when he participated in the negotiations with Henry of Bavaria that led to the rebellious prince's finally swearing fealty to the empress.

The space intended for Mieszko's camp was directly opposite the entrance to Theophanu's.

"Damn her." Mieszko whistled through his teeth. "The old doe wants to show that she's watching us. Witosz, find out who's responsible for arranging the quarters and tell them they didn't give us enough space. Ask if that means I'm to send half my forces across the Oder."

Bolesław chuckled to himself. This was an interesting start to his political lesson. Of course, they could have fit within the space designated by the small wooden posts if they wanted to, but a glance at the largest camps, Giselher's and Willigis's, was enough for Mieszko and Bolesław to know that the archbishops had arrived to the banks of Elbe with forces that equaled their own, so Mieszko intended to emphasize this. It wasn't long before Theophanu's administrators arrived and hurried to enlarge their camp space, glancing curiously at the carts.

"Bolesław!" Mieszko called him over when he was satisfied with the space he was given. "Go back for our gift. Just make sure you're not seen."

Bolesław went with Zarad, Jaksa, Bjornar, and his team. The animal was under the care of the grooms, and it awaited them calmly in a grove.

"The 'bull' has eaten all the leaves off the young birches," one of them informed him. "We had to take him further into the trees because he was roaring like a mad thing."

"Just make sure you're not seen," Bolesław echoed his father.

Before him stood an enormous, two-humped camel.

"We'll throw a small tent over it and . . ."

". . . it will be fine," Zarad reassured his prince.

They rode in after dusk, covering the animal with a tent, leaving only its muzzle free, because it roared nervously every time they tried to cover that too, and that roar could be mistaken for anything but the bull they were pretending it was. Bolesław gave the order to a dozen of his men to surround the camel tightly, and led them with Jaksa, Bjornar, and Zarad.

"Who's there?" the guards at the camp's outskirts called out, waving their torches around.

"Prince Bolesław, son of Duke Mieszko."

They rode through without incident. Huge fires burned next to the second line of guards, and they had to cover the animal's muzzle for just a moment as they went past. It roared wildly.

"Who's there?"

"Prince Bolesław, son of Duke Mieszko, with his squad."

"What are you bringing with you?"

"An auroch for dinner for my father and his army," Bolesław replied calmly in Old Saxon.

"Aaaah. . . ."

They passed without stopping. The camel squealed under the cover of the tent.

"Why is it making such strange sounds?" The guard ran after them.

"It's learning Latin for its meeting with the empress," Zarad whispered.

"It's afraid. So many soldiers here, and it's straight from the wilderness," Bolesław answered without slowing or even turning around in his saddle.

The camel was meant to be presented the next day. The groom had combed its thick fur for the occasion, and given it reins with bells and a silk throw. Mieszko came to inspect the gift and ordered the throw be taken off.

"It covers the humps. Decorate it differently. Flowers perhaps?"

"It's eaten those, my lord. It eats everything. It ate its blanket during the night, and it seemed to enjoy even that."

"Then add more bells to the reins. It won't touch those, will it?"

"I don't think so, my lord."

"Damn it," Mieszko said, because at that moment the camel raised its tail and excreted everything it had eaten since morning. Which was a lot.

"It can't behave like this at the audience," he said furiously.

"It's an animal, my lord," the groom defended the camel. "Nobody bats an eyelid when horses . . ."

"It's a gift, you fool. A gift cannot shit the moment it's changing hands. I don't care what it does when Theophanu has it. But as long as my son and I are there, it is not to raise its tail."

"We could withhold its food, Father," Bolesław suggested. "If it doesn't eat, it won't shit."

Mieszko looked at his son with appreciation, though Bolesław would have preferred to receive such fatherly pride for less shitty business.

The next day, all the Reich lords and allies who'd answered Theophanu's call for aid in the war against the pagans were invited to gather for an audience with the empress and her son. Hordes of noblemen gathered around her tent at noon, awaiting the empress and her son, the young king of the Reich. Two thrones stood on a specially constructed platform. The empress exited the tent to the accompaniment of trumpets, with Otto in front of her. The six-year-old king had a white tunic and small golden breastplate to underscore that his meeting with his people was occurring during a war. He had a silver-plated helmet on his head, which seemed to have come straight from the Rheinland, a region known for producing weapons of unmatched quality. There was a golden crown attached to the helmet. All of this, though made to fit a six-year-old child, must have weighed a lot, and Bolesław could see that the boy walked carefully, only just managing to keep his back straight. When he began to step onto the carpeted steps of the platform, everyone held their breaths. The little one almost fell over.

"A truly Byzantian gesture on the part of our lady," Archbishop Giselher whispered to one side, and his voice contained everything except admiration.

"These are not Germanian traditions," Count Ezykon agreed, pursing his lips. "These are Greek excesses. Raising yourself above all others."

Mieszko smiled lightly and whispered quietly to Bolesław so that no one else could hear:

"May God stop you from ever donning golden armor. And if the Lord ever blesses you with a royal crown, don't wear it to war. Those are not Piast traditions."

"They say that gold begets gold," Bolesław whispered without moving his head, "but from what I can tell it finds no admirers among warriors. It's almost strange they accept it so readily as the price for fighting."

"Those aren't warriors," his father replied just as quietly. "These are the ones who don't like to have a Greek woman ruling them. The warriors are over there." He nodded his head at Eckard.

Bolesław studied him carefully. Theophanu had proclaimed Eckard the new margrave of Meissen, after the dramatic death of Rikdag, the father of his would-be wife, Gertrude. Though the flag bearers behind them displayed the black lion of Meissen, the margrave didn't resemble a lion at all. He was barely ten years older than Bolesław, and with his lithe body he looked more like a wildcat preparing to pounce.

Too young to have a daughter old enough to wed, Bolesław thought, then remembered he was already married. Karolda had remained in Poznań. How was she doing there, by herself, heavily pregnant? He hoped that Duchess Oda was taking good care of her.

One by one, the empress and her son accepted gifts from their noblemen. Mieszko, knowing their time was about to come, discreetly gave Witosz the sign to bring out the camel.

"Misico Dux Sclavorum et Bolislaus, filius eius," the herald announced them.

They walked in front of the thrones of mother and son. They bowed to the majesties, but they didn't kneel like tributaries. Theophanu barely hid the disapproval that flitted across her face.

"King Otto, Empress," Mieszko said, "I have come with an army to prove that we are connected by a joint purpose, which is to establish peace in

Połabie. Like everyone else here, we want to return to Christ the destroyed temples and dioceses that the pagans claimed for themselves with such violence."

The bishop from Meissen sighed loudly.

"God bless," Otto said in a melodic voice, his eyes never leaving Bolesław.

"We have brought gifts for Your Grace," Mieszko continued, "as proof of our friendship."

Theophanu nodded, and the duke's men began to arrange chests with presents in front of the thrones.

"My son, Bolesław, has a special gift for King Otto."

The sound of bells on the reins told them the camel must be near.

"What kind of gift?" Otto couldn't restrain himself.

"One which you won't find in any of the beautiful cities of Germania," Bolesław replied.

A rustle and occasional shouts ran through the crowd.

Ah, Bolesław thought, *the camel is very near.* Then the animal's squeal sounded right behind them.

Bolesław took the reins from Witosz and led the animal toward the thrones. Little Otto clapped his hands, his cheeks red with excitement.

"Is it an elephant, Mother? An elephant like the ones you told me about?"

Theophanu's eyes shone with tears. She wiped them with the back of her hand and answered the child, emotion coloring every syllable:

"No, my king, it's a camel."

"Like the one you rode when you were little?"

"Yes," she replied with a sad smile. "We had many of them in Constantinople."

Bolesław had to bite his tongue to stop himself from voicing his thoughts. *Cunning hawk,* he thought of his father. When they had led the two-humped camel here, he had thought the old man wanted to make an impression on the empress, the young king, and the Reich lords with the wonderfully rich and rare animal. Only now did he understand that the gift had another motivation behind it, appealing directly to Theophanu's memories of her childhood.

"Can I touch it?" Otto asked.

Theophanu hesitated.

"They can be unruly," she said, unsure.

"This one is tame, my lady," Bolesław assured her. "Without a special saddle, I wouldn't recommend riding it, but touching, why not? I will guarantee the young king's safety."

Otto glanced at his mother once more and, when she nodded, he rose from his throne and walked over to them. Only now did Bolesław remember how unbalanced the boy was in the heavy helmet on his head. He quickly gave the reins back to Witosz and ran over to the blanket-covered steps. He sensed that he should not climb them, that they were reserved only for those two, but he didn't want the little one to slip on the carpeted steps and diminish the gift and the moment with a royal fall. He reached out a hand to help the boy balance himself. Otto shook his head with childish stubbornness to indicate that he would manage on his own. But that very moment caused the boy to sway. Bolesław decided not to wait for a catastrophe; he grabbed the child around the waist and carried him down the last few steps.

"What a funny nose," Otto squeaked. "And he moves it so . . ."

"He's hungry," Bolesław said, hoping the camel's bowels were empty. "You can stroke its neck, here."

"We thank you, Duke, for a present worthy of a future emperor," Theophanu said, moved. "King, we still have meetings to attend." Her voice left no doubt that Otto should return to her.

"May I have the honor of walking the king back to his throne?" Bolesław asked.

The empress nodded. Otto was reluctant. The camel interested him far more than this gathering. Bolesław didn't want to insist. He reached out a hand. The royal child sighed and leaned on his arm as he walked up the steps and sat back down on the throne next to his mother.

"Thank you, Duke Misico and Prince Bolislaus," he said. "It's the nicest gift I have ever received."

Bolesław bowed and walked back down the steps. Only Giselher and Willigis's indignant stares made him realize he shouldn't have turned his back on the empress and young king. It was too late now. Witosz took the camel to Theophanu's camp administrator, and he, unsure what he should do, tied the camel to a wooden post next to the gold tent, where all the day's gifts had been taken so far.

The audience continued. Theophanu spoke of how she accepted Henry of Bavaria back despite his having blemished his honor when he rebelled against her and her son. She didn't say a word about Mieszko's role in the rebellion.

"To end the disagreement and give him proof of our infinite imperial forgiveness, we have made him viceroy of Bavaria once more."

Bolesław listened, watching the expressions of those around him. He watched and remembered. The empress thundered, criticizing his uncle,

Boleslav, the prince of Czechs, who fought hand in hand with the Veleti against the faith, against common human decency, and against the Reich. He knew that this part of the speech was of the utmost importance to him and his father. He listened, trying not to lose a single word of it. But his attention was stolen by the golden tent, which swayed a little behind Theophanu. Another sway, and he knew what was happening.

Bloody hell, he swore silently. *That camel must have been ravenous.*

"My most serene empress," Mieszko spoke, and there was a note of humility in his voice Bolesław had never heard there before. "Could Your Highness, or one of the lords gathered here today, explain to me why Prince Boleslav didn't lay down his arms when his protector, Prince Henry, humbled himself before Your Imperial Majesty?"

Unease settled over the Greek's handsome face.

"He was summoned to join an excursion which offers him the chance for redemption. But he's a defiant, willful prince," she said with emphasis.

"I agree, my lady, but even so I cannot understand why he fights. Even the most defiant prince must have some common sense."

"You, Duke Mieszko, are the best example of that," Archbishop Giselher pointed out.

"Of fighting or common sense?" Mieszko asked, most innocently.

"Both," Theophanu settled the matter, seeing that Giselher was opening his mouth to say something likely very different.

"My lady," Eckard said in a calm, hoarse voice, "we need to consider the doubt that Duke Mieszko draws our attentions to. We cannot forget that it was the Czech armies that attacked Meissen and led to Margrave Rikdag's death. The Czech prince still hasn't left Meissen. You have made me Meissen's margrave while it's still under Czech occupation."

"A margrave with no domain?" Ezykon scoffed. "A warrior like yourself, Eckard, should chop his way to a title with a sword."

"I have received the right to Meissen from our lady," Eckard replied calmly. "And I assure all of you gathered here today that I will win it back from the Czechs. It's not hard to see that when our armies gather here to move against the Veleti, the Czech leader benefits. I'd say that this is his trap; he ties Saxon powers up to win back land occupied by the Veleti, strengthening his own position in Meissen."

A murmur rustled through the crowd.

"Are you questioning the sense in our cause?" Willigis asked carefully.

"No, Archbishop. I'm suggesting a division of our troops. Part of the army should move to face the Veleti, and the other half should march against the Czechs."

"Attacking Boleslav from both sides will be expensive," Mieszko observed with concern. "But harassing him where he least expects it might have the desired effect."

"The prince of Prague has placed his troops all along the western border and Meissen," Eckard said.

"But he isn't anticipating an attack on Silesia," Mieszko replied.

Only now did Bolesław fully understand the plot his father had concocted. He could now watch with appreciation as the Old Hawk put the finishing touches on another of his strategic masterpieces. The gathered nobles decided that, with Empress Theophanu's support, Mieszko's troops would cross the Oder between Głogów and Niemcza and begin a systematic hit-and-run war, while the main Saxon armies would be winning back lands the Veleti had taken during the great rebellion, and Margrave Eckard would haunt the Czechs occupying Meissen. The most magnificent part came at the end, when Giselher tried to discredit Mieszko with a final sting and said he came to the Elbe, gave a camel, and in return would take back his armies to fight his own war against the Czechs. Father, without so much as a flinch, replied:

"Everything stays. The camel, my three hundred heavy-armed soldiers, and the six hundred light-armed ones. My son Bolesław will be the only one to leave camp, and he'll lead the attack on the Czechs without taking any of my men."

Triumphant trumpets sounded in Bolesław's soul. It was time to end the audience.

"Let's retreat before our gift eats the entire imperial tent and shits into the chests bearing gifts from the Reich lords," Father whispered soundlessly. The Old Hawk was as content as if he himself had shat on the margraves' treasures.

Bolesław left that same day. Not entirely alone, of course, but with a dozen members of his squad, and Zarad, Bjornar, and Duszan. Father kept Jaksa with him, wanting his experience of Połabie, forgetting once more not to call him a "Redarian wolf," but it didn't seem to bother Jaksa anymore. Bolesław went to Poznań first, where he learned that Karolda had given birth to a son.

"My firstborn!" he shouted, running from the stables to the palatium.

"Be careful, witches can have children, too," Zarad whispered to him.

Bolesław didn't listen. His heart beat as hard as a hammer. His first independent journey, first chance to be a leader without his father watching his every move. And his first son!

He swept into Karolda's rooms like a summer storm. He found her with her hair tousled and her nightdress creased. Though it was the height of summer, she was crouched by the fire.

"My lady . . ." He stood in the doorway. "Are you unwell?"

She looked at him absently. One of her maids, or rather Oda's maid, there to help Karolda, spoke up quickly:

"But the child is well, my lord. We're making sure that your wife feeds him."

"Where is he?" he asked, looking around the chamber.

The servant pointed at a cradle. He ran to it. Inside, on clean white sheets, lay a boy. He was asleep. He was small, his ribs clearly visible through his skin. He had dark fluff covering his head. Bolesław touched him.

"You can pick him up, my lord," the maid whispered.

He didn't know how. The child seemed so small and fragile, weighing less than a quiver of arrows. He picked it up and laid it across his shoulder.

"Is he healthy?" he asked the servant.

"Yes, my lord. Healthy. Your wife . . . well, she isn't feeling her best, but the child is healthy."

"What's wrong with her?"

"I . . . I can't say, my lord. It would be best to speak with Duchess Oda."

Bolesław laid the child back in the cradle. He didn't wake, but Bolesław could see the tiny chest rising and falling. He went to approach his wife, but Karolda hissed and waved a hand to scratch him.

"Karolda? Do you recognize me?"

She watched him distrustfully. Then, suddenly, she threw herself at him, grabbing his hand and sniffing it.

"It's me, Bolesław," he said quietly.

She pushed his hand away and covered her face with her arms.

"She can sit like that for hours," the servant said condescendingly. "When we give her the child to feed, she sniffs him first, too."

Bolesław knelt by her and brought his face close to hers, whispering:

"Karolda, my girl, my brave, Magyar warrior. Can you hear me?"

She cocked her head, and her hair, stuck in long dark tangles, fell onto her face. He could see her watching him.

"Wife, Duchess," he said, talking gently, as if to a child. "We'll ride horses together yet. You, our boy, and I."

She covered her ears with her hands. He rose and felt as if a great weight had settled on his shoulders.

"Look after my son," he said hollowly to the servants, and left.

He went straight to Oda. Could he trust her? The duchess had enough reasons to spite him, but from what he could see, no harm was being done to his son. He called Bjornar and Zarad. He needed Zarad, his oldest friend, beside him more than anyone right now.

"Come with me, but don't say a word," he ordered.

Oda was in the common room with her two sons. Father John was reading psalms to them. He stopped when they entered.

"My lady," the prince said, bowing respectfully to her.

"Bolesław." She looked at him carefully and nodded. "So, you've been to see Karolda and your son?"

"What is this?"

"Your wife's birth was violent and difficult. Karolda was behaving as if she didn't know what was happening, as if she didn't know she was pregnant and about to give birth. Your royal child. In the last few days beforehand, she wanted to go riding somewhere. She couldn't understand why we wouldn't let her mount a horse. My most experienced midwives were with her. You know that they brought my two sons into this world, your half brothers, Mieszko and Świętopełk. These women know what they're doing. Karolda wouldn't let them do what they could to ease the birth. She tossed and turned, tried to break free, biting at them . . ."

She does the same in bed, he thought. *What if I mistook insanity for passion?*

"The most important thing is that your son is healthy. As for Karolda? I don't know." Oda spread her arms. "I'm afraid she might refuse to feed him in this state. She does it reluctantly enough as it is."

"Find my son a wet nurse, Duchess," he said firmly. "And take Karolda out of the child's room. Let the servants take care of her. Look after her, feed her, wash her, do her hair. Bring our son to her once a day so that she may remember she has one. If you decide her condition is improving, let her hold him, but only with servants present. Father John, Zarad, Bjornar, I take you as my witnesses that I have asked Duchess Oda to take care of my wife and son until my return. And that I'm immeasurably grateful to her for having looked over them as she has until now."

He went to see his son one more time before departing. Karolda was no longer in the chamber. A wet nurse held the baby. A dark-haired girl who reminded him of Jaga and the Midsummer they'd spent among the trees.

Bolesław shook the thought from his head and waited until the child had finished feeding, then reached for him.

"Duszan," Bolesław called, then handed him his son. "You aren't coming with me. You're staying with him."

The child lifted his eyelids and looked up at his father with dark, wet eyes—his mother's eyes.

Bjornar and Zarad didn't mention "the witch" again. They fell silent, as if no bad word had ever been spoken of her. They didn't ask about his son either, probably trying to avoid evoking painful thoughts of the mother. Bolesław let himself think of Karolda, think of their time together and the happiness he had felt, only until they reached Silesia.

Bolesław had summoned one hundred armed soldiers from Głogów, and ordered another hundred to join him from Wrocław and Opole. A hundred came with him from Giecz. He had as many men with him as Mieszko had taken to Połabie. The locals brought scouts. They crossed the river in three places simultaneously and set out to defeat the Czechs.

14

⚯

DENMARK

Sven knew it worked in his favor that the widow empress had tied up her Saxon troops in Połabie; that war gave him time to fight his own battle against his father, for control of the Danish throne. But he also knew he had to hurry. The Reich lords tended to fight only in summer. Autumn rains turned roads into mud and swamps, making them impassable for heavy warhorses and carts. The thought of fighting on land had repulsed him since he'd been a child. Water was his element, his ship was his steed whose sharp beak could squeeze into the estuary of any bay or river. He loved the punch of the wind in a square sail, the leap with which the drakkar began its journey. The roar of the waves in his ears when the wind snatched at his long red hair.

Over a year ago, before the Jomsvikings had even set out against Jarl Haakon in Norway, Sven had come to Jomsborg to bid Palnatoki goodbye. He'd stood in the harbor as the greatest of Jom's leaders had sailed to Valhalla to the sound of a black horn. Sven had hoped to shoot the burning arrow which would light the pyre on Palnatoki's boat himself, but the Jomsvikings wouldn't allow it.

"Jomsviking laws," they said curtly. "Even kings and their sons don't stand above them." And the four house chieftains shot the arrows instead. The Zealand brothers, Thorkel and Sigvald, along with Vagn and Bue. Bue, who left the land of the living barely a month later; he'd died fighting Haakon, and what had it all been for?

Perhaps his father, Harald Bluetooth, had been a berserker in the past, a warrior who turned into an animal, a warrior who felt no pain and ripped apart anyone or anything standing in his way, but since his father had allowed Otto to baptize him, he had been a shell of himself. A single blue tooth was all he had left of his painted canines, that he'd scarred and inked blue to seem even more frightening to his enemies. That's what they had called him; "Bluetooth." But only behind Bluetooth's back, from afar, preferably from another island and against the wind. People were afraid of him, and Sven couldn't understand what caused this fear.

No one, not even Sven, could say a bad word about Harald Bluetooth in Jomsborg without the Jomsvikings reaching for their weapons. Not even him, the strong young son.

The Jomsvikings were still chewing over their recent defeat, and if mulling over defeats could fill one's belly, they would undoubtedly have been sated. First, Jarl Haakon in Norway had dispersed the Jomsvikings led by Sigvald, then the Swedish king Eric had destroyed his nephew Styrbjorn's troops in the decisive battle on Fyrisvellir's fields. Out of all those who had accompanied Styrbjorn, only one in twenty Jomsvikings had returned home.

And, though King Harald Bluetooth was the one to push the iron boys into every one of these conflicts, making him directly responsible for the losses they had suffered, they still didn't dare curse him, led by a loyalty Sven couldn't comprehend.

Palnatoki had been right in saying he should only have come to Jom the day after his father's death, and not before. Let the gods make that day come swiftly.

Yes, he had bid Palnatoki goodbye over a year ago. Palnatoki, his teacher, the one he considered his real father deep in his heart. Afterward, Sven sailed out of the Viking stronghold knowing he wouldn't return until he'd torn the life out of that son of a bitch Harald's breast.

The old king hid himself in Roskilde. He surrounded himself with lookouts, a cordon of armed men who didn't sleep, guarding the Bluetoothed Bull. Sven bided his time in Jutland, in the south of Denmark, at the beautiful manor in Jelling.

This is where our family is from, he told himself over mead every night. *We are the Skjoldungs of Jelling.*

His grandfather's home had been uninhabited for years, but it hadn't lost any of its grandeur. It was guarded by two cairns. Huge hills poured over the funeral pyres of Gorm and his wife Tyra. Beyond that were two runestones. Gorm had placed the first one there for his wife. The second one . . . this was the one which made Sven's blood boil in anger. Harald had etched his name into it, so the world would remember he'd been the one to baptize Denmark. As if that was a thing to boast of. And he had built the church, too. A small wooden doghouse in which no mass had been said in years, but still it was guarded by royal men, as if it hid God-knows-what kinds of treasures. Sven had been there more than once. A cross plated with silver, a couple of tin chalices, some books—nothing more. What was there to guard? The sight of the great bell tower irked him daily, standing boldly against the horizon, until he realized it might very well be an opportunity for him. Sven went to the church once more, and the soldiers let him pass after he set his weapons down outside. No one searched him. When he emerged, he went straight to Karli the Dwarf and made his request.

Then, he invited the chieftains for Yule. The ones who had fought for Hedeby alongside him, and the ones he knew were dissatisfied with Harald's rule. He even invited his half sister Tyra, named after their grandmother, Gorm's wife. Their relationship had never been strong, but in a play for the throne it was wise to have all the board pieces within reach. Sven spared no expense in his preparations. The manor in Jelling was restored to its full splendor. The benches in the main hall were covered with fresh reindeer skins. The servants scrubbed the soot from the shields hanging along the walls, and polished the weapons that decorated the hall. The squeaks of strangled geese, the roars of butchered rams and pigs, and the clank of mead barrels rolled across the ground resounded in the yard for days.

Sven gave equal care to his own appearance. Little Siggi washed his long red hair. Kalle trimmed his beard. He donned a woolen tunic the shade of blood, and a cloak trimmed with white fur from an arctic wolf. Red and white was a good start. Silver bracelets adorned his wrists, and Mjolnir, the god Thor's holy hammer, The One Which Crushes, hung around his neck. It hadn't been forged by ancient dwarves, as the old songs described, but by Karli the Dwarf, the blacksmith from Jelling. Karli also studded the belt Sven buckled around his waist before his guests arrived, and he covered Sven's gloves with iron plates.

As he greeted his guests, his betrothed stood beside him. Mojmira, the daughter of an Obotrite chieftain, who his grandfather Mściwój had ordered him to marry for more support against the Empress Theophanu's armies. It was a wise decision; Sven's own mother had been an Obotrite, after all, and a continued alliance with the Obotrites would secure Denmark's southern border. Forging ties with the empire's enemies was a necessity. But though Mojmira was here and Sven had paid her dowry, he hadn't officially made her his wife. News of Mściwój's failing health—the old man seemed to have finally succumbed to the pressures that leadership had placed upon him—held him back. Sven kept Mojmira as his intended, but was not yet certain if she would be the one he tied his fate to. Nevertheless, she was well cared for in his home.

When the chieftains had arrived and taken their seats in the hall, Sven greeted them all, celebrating the presence of each one of them with a toast. He toasted his half sister, Tyra, Harald Bluetooth's daughter, who could rally around her those who did not approve of Sven's open disdain for Christianity. He toasted Jarl Stenkil from Hobro, who controlled much of the land north of Jelling. Uddorm from Viborg, the land rat who shouldn't be underestimated, because, thanks to his fertility, half of Jutland was related to him. Ragnfrid, known as Ragn of the Islands, because he had over a hundred stony strait islets, and though many of them were little more than rocks shat on by seagulls, each could become a port and hiding place during a sea war. Ragn, then, was welcomed with special affection. Jarl Haakon of Funen, Gunar of Limfiord, and his neighbor Thorgils of Jelling he greeted with a double toast, because they had fought alongside him against the Saxons in Hedeby. He knew none of his guests had truly accepted the new faith. The only one he couldn't be sure of was Tyra, his sister. There were too many years between them.

Sven fed them and quenched their thirst during the first day. He did the same on the second, and added in his gifts. He had planned carefully, plotting the surest way to gain each guest's support for when he challenged his father. The time of Harald Bluetooth and Christianity in Denmark was nearing its end, Sven would see to that.

On the third day of the Yule, a hailstorm hit the roof of Jelling's manor.

"Hail is the coldest grain," Sven shouted, raising a toast, his horn full with an endless supply of mead. He drank a long, sweet gulp, and passed the horn along.

"Voice carries over ice," Thorgils of Jelling said, passing it to Gunar.

"Reindeer run across hard snow," the lord of Limfiord passed it to Haakon of Funen.

"The hawk's grip is strong," Haakon called out.

"The naked freeze on ice." Ragn drank gloomily and passed the horn to Uddorm.

"Loki's luck is deceptive," the land rat announced.

"Gold is an expensive decoration," Stenkil of Hobro recited.

The horn reached his sister, sitting beside him.

"If you light a fire, expect the smoke to char you," she said, and drank a sip from the horn.

He listened to her sentiment warily, but thanked her for the toast with a smile.

"Since my sister has evoked fire, I invite you all to the burning."

"Logs have been burning in the yard since our arrival," Uddorm protested sleepily, his desire to remain seated clear in his voice.

"Logs burn through an ordinary Yule, Uddorm of Viborg," Sven said. "But I have invited my guests to an extraordinary one. Come, the mead will accompany us. Servants!" He clapped his hands, and attendants already dressed in cloaks displayed the jugs they hid beneath the fabric. "Come."

He led them onto the flat square in front of the church. His squad had killed the guards of Christ's church before the feast had begun, and their bodies were nowhere to be seen. Dry straw surrounded the small block of a church. His servants poured mead into his guests' horns. They made another toast, and Sven started the fire.

"Let's bring back the time of the Skjoldungs of Jelling. An end to the foreign faith. And end to the cold, dead god my father raised houses for. A new time is coming . . ."

"Sven's time!" Haakon of Funen poured his mead into the flames, sending up sparks.

"The undefeated leader!" Gunar of Limfiord shouted.

"Sven, under whose rule we will fight and conquer!" Thorgils drank and poured out the rest, feeding the flames.

Tyra's voice pierced the air then. "Brother, you are a sight! Your red hair, the flames! It's as if Thor himself stands before us!"

Sven swept back his cloak and walked to her.

"This terrifies you, sister? Thor was a victor. Don't be afraid."

But she was clutching her head, shielding her face from him, twisting in all directions.

"You have Mjolnir on your breast, iron-clad gloves, a triple belt."

Sven laughed loudly.

"The cross which had been left in this miserable tabernacle was forged by the blacksmith into The One Which Crushes, Thor's hammer. The iron bars which guarded the hideouts of the chalices were remade to decorate my gloves. And the leather binding of the book is now the belt on my hips. Look, Tyra. The church burns to celebrate the old gods. There is nothing to be afraid of."

Laughter rang out from the crowd, and Gunar called out:

"Mead! To Sven, the god of our war."

Tyra shook her head, still hidden in tightly enclosed arms, and turned away from the church, never once looking over her shoulder as she vanished between the trees.

"Who listens to women ends up in fog," a drunk Ragn of the Isles announced, looking at the tower of sparks and the burning roof. "Sven Haraldsson. You have my sword in your fight against your father, Harald Bluetooth."

They sailed a week later, once the hammering cold had receded and left their heads clear. The Kattegat's waters were covered in a thin sheet of ice, like fat on a cooled lamb dish, and spring cut through this weak shell like a knife. When they caught the wind beyond the straits, the ships leaped forward. No one in Roskilde was expecting guests, in Denmark's capital and Harald Bluetooth's lair. Especially not armed ones. Sven and his followers felled the first defenses, three rows of soldiers, with barely a shout uttered. They cut down the defenders surrounding the royal manor and found Harald feasting. Those feasting with the old king were defenseless, as no one was permitted to enter the hall with a sword.

When Sven was nearly face-to-face with his father, the king's comrades stood and called in unison, "A wolf's anger!" And only then did Sven recall that berserkers were just as dangerous without weapons as they were when armed.

Their painted canines gleamed and the huge bodies of Harald's closest companions blocked Sven's path. He cut down the first one with a blow to the shoulder, a blow that should have been deadly, but the bearded giant merely shook himself. Not a drop of blood appeared from under the leather caftan. He roared and swung his arms, catching Sven across the face. Blood streamed into his eyes. Nearly blinded and trying to escape, Sven threw himself forward wildly, and, ducking under the berserker's outstretched arm, the tip of his sword touched Harald's chest. It was a shallow cut, but Harald howled and clutched his heart. Blood poured from between his fingers.

Is this it? Sven thought. *That's how one kills a father, as if he were an enemy?*

Harald paled, baring his blue teeth; they used to be proud, painted canines. As a young man, he'd had patterns etched into the enamel, then had the teeth rubbed with black dye and filed into sharp points; painted fangs marked only the bravest warriors—the berserkers. Bearing those teeth in battle, with a wild grin and guttling snarl, was known to strike terror in the hearts of even the bravest of opponents.

But, now, they had no effect on Sven. Harald swayed. He was as gray and swollen as an old man. Sven wanted to say something, but he heard Stenkil's moan, and Ragn of the Islands' howl. He glanced behind him and saw them both writhing on the ground. This split second was enough for the berserkers to carry their bleeding king out of the hall.

"After them!" Sven shouted to his people. "Even if they are beasts, we can't let them go."

They spilled out into the yard, but the king and his men had disappeared.

"My lord." Adla, a servant Sven paid to spy for him, clutched at his sleeve. "The king has a secret harbor in a grove north from here. He's been expecting you for days, and had time to build it. Look for it by the rock that's as sharp as a spear."

"To the harbor," Sven yelled.

But they didn't go to the sharp rock, because the harbor was useless to them without their own ships. They went back to these and sailed out into the waters of the Roskilde fjord. Waves and wind were not elements friendly to human beasts. It wasn't long before Sven saw his father's sail in the north.

"After them," he shouted to the oarsmen, grabbing the helm. He didn't like sailing in shallow waters, between islands, but he had no choice until they reached open sea. He chased his prey and was determined not to let it escape.

A cold wind from the Kattegat blew into their sails in the early morning.

"Set the course east," he shouted, because although he couldn't see Harald's sail in the thick, milky fog, he knew only one place his father could run to now.

15

⚛

HUNGARY

Bolesław accompanied Karolda's embalmed body in its oak casket. A procession of his squad and a small number of camp servants joined him. If not for the casket and their slow and somber pace, they would have looked like a fighting troop. They rode through the Moravian Gate quickly; after all, merchant caravans had taken this road from south to north for centuries. As soon as they entered Magyar territories, where his wife was from, a troop rode out to meet them.

Bolesław's Hungarian guide, named Lajos, whispered to him in broken Polish,

"Boleszláv fejedelem, Gejza has sent his younger son. Sign anger."

And it's my job, Bolesław thought, *to turn this anger around.*

He knew it wouldn't be easy. His deceased wife had been the younger sister of Sarolt, Prince Gejza's wife. Sarolt had helped raise Karolda and cared for her as if she had been her own child rather than younger sibling. Upon hearing the news of Karolda's death, Sarolt had been inconsolable, they'd been told. She wouldn't forgive the loss, she had screamed, and reminded everyone that she had been against her sister's marriage to Bolesław from the outset—and, not least, Sarolt had demanded that Karolda's son, Bezprym, be sent to her court.

"The girl didn't pick a good time to die," Mieszko had commented when he heard the news, not pausing in feeding meat to his hawk. "We need the Magyars' friendship now more than ever."

Father was referring to Moravia, south of their lands, which was currently under Czech rule. This was Mieszko's next target, now that he controlled Silesia. The next of Bolesław's tasks.

Young Honta, the prince's son who stood before them now, couldn't have been more than sixteen. He was short and stocky, and a silver-plated headband held back his thick, dark hair. He nodded to Bolesław in greeting and raised a hand.

"I bring the remains of my beloved wife, your and my lady, Karolda," Bolesław said.

"Duchess Sarolt awaits her sister in Veszprém," Honta replied as they continued moving.

"And Prince Gejza?" Bolesław asked.

"He might be there, he might not," Honta replied, and Lajos translated.

They are playing games, Bolesław thought, *testing my patience.*

They crossed the wide Danube River on barges. Bolesław dismounted and stood next to Karolda's coffin. The barge swayed from side to side. Zarad stood next to him. "A daunting river," he observed.

"Mmm," Bolesław replied, narrowing his eyes against the sun.

"Are you looking for places to cross?" his friend asked. "This is the strangest scouting expedition I have ever been a part of."

"I'm accompanying my dead wife," Bolesław said firmly, gently patting the lid of the coffin resting on the cart.

His friends hadn't understood his love for Karolda, from the first day of their marriage until the last of her life.

She only showed her true face when we were alone. Or when we went riding together, he thought. *My beautiful, wild warrior.*

The ferrymen checked the depth of the river with poles. Helpers awaited them on the opposite bank. Ropes were thrown out and the barges were pulled onto the gently sloping sandy shore. Bolesław's squad led their horses onto land carefully, while Bolesław personally watched over the cart that carried his wife's body.

"We will reach Veszprém in two days," Honta said when the full procession was finally on the Danube's bank. "Let's go."

Bolesław was fascinated by Honta's Hungarian riders. He couldn't keep from staring. Bolesław had ridden since he was five, and it was said that he held himself in the saddle like a nomad, but it was only when he watched the young Hungarian prince and his men that he understood that the blood of steppe riders still ran through Magyar veins, those who had arrived with their small, resilient horses decades ago from the steppes by the Volga. Karolda had been the same. She'd felt smothered in Poznań's palatium. She didn't feel well at the feasts with Oda and Father John; she found courtly celebrations dull and often seemed absent at them, but she became herself the moment she mounted a horse. Her eyes shone, and her red, wide lips stretched into a smile. If he hadn't gone with Father to Połabie when she'd had their son, would she still be alive today? Bolesław had asked himself this question many times, and he wasn't certain of the answer.

Before he'd set out with Mieszko, every morning, after nights filled with laughter and love, Bolesław had hoped this would be the day. That they had reached a turning point. When Karolda would begin to learn his tongue, when she would stop turning away from the courtly life a duchess and wife must lead. But this day didn't come, their nights together the only sign of their love. The only thing the Hungarian princess and Polish prince shared.

The landscape changed on the second day, from rich green flatlands to a gentle plateau. Prince Honta was silent as ever, but Lajos, Bolesław's Hungarian guide, said they would reach Veszprém before dusk.

"Do you hear that, Karolda?" the prince asked, standing beside the coffin. "Our journey won't last much longer."

He caught Zarad's unsettled look and the dark glance Honta cast. They set off once more; Hungarian riders didn't need long breaks.

The wide road led between gentle hills. Then a mountain appeared in front of them, looming over the path as if to say, your journey ends here. It seemed so strange in this place, as if it wasn't nature's creation at all, but the work of an insane giant who simply placed it in the middle of the road.

"That's Veszprém, my lord," Lajos said.

The approach was very steep; Honta's men's horses climbed easily, but the Polish mounts stepped timidly. As they made their way up the incline, Bolesław watched the casket, afraid Karolda's coffin would slide off on the steep journey. He jumped from his saddle to walk beside the cart, the solemnest of sentinels. Several times the wheels bounced dangerously on stones, and after a moment, Zarad joined Bolesław at the coffin's side. They had to push the cart up themselves over the last part of the ride.

"It would be difficult to seize Veszprém," his comrade panted, when they had finally reached the top.

"This climb is a better defense than any rampart I've seen," Bolesław agreed, wiping the sweat from his forehead and looking around.

Something between a royal encampment and a village stretched out over the flat plateau before them. It was surrounded by a waist-high wall, built from the stones that were plentiful in the area. They rode through gates mounted not in the wall, as it was too low, but in a sturdy-looking wooden frame.

The yurts on the edge of the plateau were small and modest, covered with horse skin. Horses grazed between the tents, and children ran around them.

Women cooked food in carefully arranged stone fireplaces. Tufts of thick grasses dried in places, the kind used for making baskets. The encampment was organized into quarters which were separated by intersecting roads

Honta gave a sign for them to follow. Bolesław didn't mount his horse again, preferring to stay close to Karolda. They made their way between the tents for Gejza's squad. Richly decorated Magyar saddles were arranged on trestles in front of these. There were fewer horses here; most grazed on the other side, while one or two stood near every tent, kept nearby for times of urgency.

"Red and yellow are the colors of Gejza's squad," Lajos said as they passed between the tents, pointing out the homes of the individual squads, whose tents and flags differed in color. "Blue belongs to Sarolt. There are more blue here because we are in Veszprém, which belongs to my lady."

They finally reached the square in the middle of the encampment, where a few low buildings stood, built from wood on foundations of local stone. One of them might have been a church; it was small and round, and the sloping roof was marked by an equal-armed cross. Three huge yurts stood behind it, covered in colorful fabric, with a sigil at each entrance—a black bird standing on a flag. Two of the yurts had small wooden doors; the central one's entrance was wide open.

"We're here," Lajos announced, dismounting. "This yurt with the blue flag belongs to my lady Sarolt, the other to her husband, the Grand Prince Gejza. The middle one is for guests, feasts, and the meetings of leaders."

Servants and those curious about the newcomers filled the square, standing in small groups, pointing at the cart with the coffin and at Bolesław. Honta disappeared into his mother's yurt without looking around at him, and didn't emerge again for a long time.

Bolesław once again felt that they were intentionally trying his patience, but he had come this far, such a long way, and he would wait as long as he had to now. Finally, the door to Prince Gejza's yurt opened and a short, broad-shouldered man, with legs bent from horse riding, appeared. He was dressed in trousers of soft leather, tall riding boots and a leather caftan over which he'd thrown a richly decorated cloak. A long, dark beard covered his tanned face. His graying hair fell loose down his back, with two braids framing his face. A boy stood behind him, almost a man, only slightly younger than Bolesław.

"Grand Prince Gejza and his eldest son, Prince Wajk," Lajos said.

They studied each other without a hint of a smile. Then the door to the princess's yurt swung open, and Honta stepped out, followed by a woman. It was hard to determine her age. Though she was undoubtedly over thirty, he couldn't tell by how much. Her dark hair had been plaited into four braids, each one heavy with decoration. The hat she wore came to a sharp point and was richly embroidered with silver thread and lined with fur; gemstones hung from golden chains that framed her face, visible under the edges of her cloak.

"Grand Princess Sarolt," Lajos said, though it couldn't have been anyone else.

The resemblance between her and Bolesław's wife was astounding. The same dark eyes, the same sharp cheekbones covered by a blush, the same pale complexion and black, black hair. A determined set to her lips.

Would my Karolda have looked like this in a few years? he wondered with a sharp pang of emotion.

"Boleszláv fejedelem," Lajos introduced him. *Fejedelem* meaning prince.

Bolesław nodded to Gejza, Sarolt, and their son. They responded with shallow bows, nothing more. They stared at one another in silence, until Sarolt noticed the cart and coffin; she ran to them, crying out as she did.

"My lady says: 'My little girl, my love, my poor girl,'" Lajos translated.

Sarolt tore around the cart, sobbing, hands pressed to the coffin lid.

"My lady says: 'What have you come to, my little one? Where is your son, our son?' And also . . ." Lajos hesitated, listening to Sarolta's sobs. "'We must give you a funeral . . . a mountain of fire . . . a pyre.'"

Christ! Bolesław thought. *Do they intend to take her body out of the coffin? It was embalmed, but as to what condition it'll be in after the journey . . .*

Still, he maintained a stony expression. Sarolt quieted in time, then began issuing instructions to her servants.

"Yes," Lajos confirmed. "The princess wants a funeral pyre to be prepared. But not to burn your lady, just traditional gifts."

Bolesław sighed with relief. Prince Gejza then spoke him to in a loud voice, and Lajos translated.

"Why do you come, Boleszláv fejedelem?"

"To bring back my beloved wife Karolda's remains to her kin. To return her to the land of her ancestors," Bolesław replied.

The prince exchanged words with the princess and their son, then Lajos translated:

"You and your squad will receive your own yurt. You can rest there after your long journey. At dusk, the funeral rituals will commence, and afterward, a feast that you are invited to."

"And none of the usual 'Welcome, dearest guests, it's an honor'?" Zarad grumbled as they walked into their assigned yurt. "A man bruises his arse in the saddle, drags a coffin over thousands of miles of mountains and rivers, and this is all they can do?"

"A man didn't drag the coffin, horses did," Bolesław corrected him sharply. "Have some respect for their culture."

"I don't know what kind of culture it is when the royal couple lives in tents," his friend snorted, but after entering their own yurt, he had a change of heart. "The beds are comfortable," he admitted, lying on a blanket-covered bed. "Quite something."

"The princess has plans to build a great borough in Veszprém," Lajos explained. "But her lord husband is constantly busy with one war or another, and they haven't had time and, as you might expect, building on this plateau is difficult even with their full attention. They live in yurts while they travel, but they have beautiful royal accommodations in Esztergom and Białogród."

"Tell me, Lajos, what will my wife's funeral look like?" Bolesław asked, a note of concern in his voice.

"Well, I don't know, exactly, my lord," the Magyar spread his hands help-lessly before bowing and leaving the yurt.

There would be trouble tonight, Bolesław sensed. Prince Gejza had been baptized, but Sarolt, before she'd married Gejza, had accepted the Eastern Orthodox faith. The faith of Constantinople, which had been spreading among the Eastern Slavs, reaching as far as Rus. What's more, even when Bolesław had married Karolda, it was said that Christianity in these parts was a mixture of influences from the West and East, with the local nomad cults dominating. Hungary, then, the country of barely baptized and barely settled nomads, where the governing rules of the faith were known only to royal families, could become the host to the strangest of cults, where cross and horse head fought for equal rights.

Whatever happens, I'll accept it, he thought, when Lajos returned at dusk to take him to the funeral. Bolesław had changed into fresh clothes, a golden tunic and a navy cloak. He placed his royal diadem on his head, the golden eagle protecting his forehead.

"You must leave your weapons, Prince," Lajos warned, so Bolesław un-buckled his sword.

He had a dagger inside his boot, like every one of his squad members. He'd never walk entirely unarmed among people he still considered poten-tially hostile.

Karolda's coffin had been carried to the round building, and it was placed in front of a low altar. Lajos just had time to explain that this small church had been funded by the princess and that she'd named St. George its patron. Sarolt, Gejza, and their two sons were already standing in front of the coffin. When Bolesław walked in, they made space for him between them. Even a priest appeared and said a short mass, mixing Greek with Latin. Bolesław pretended not to notice the strange lithurgy.

Magyar riders wearing the princess's colors filed in after the prayers and pulled open the wooden door set into the round building's stone wall. They slid Karolda's coffin into the opening. Sarolt stopped them as they moved to enclose her in the wall. She slipped her arms into the darkness and bade her sister goodbye, crying quietly. When she stepped back, Bolesław walked over to the coffin. He knelt, his hand resting on the coffin for a quiet moment, then he stood. The soldiers closed his wife in the church wall.

The priest had vanished. Prince Gejza exited the building next, followed by his sons and the princess. Bolesław hurried after them, nearly blind as he stepped out into the church square. After the dim light in the chapel, the blaze from the enormous fire was almost too much to bear. The pyre had been arranged when they entered the church, but he hadn't realized it would be lit during the mass. The royal family were gathered around the flames, once again making space for him.

Sarolt lifted her hands, and servants slid rings off her fingers. The princess said something in a choked voice, and they threw the rings onto the fire. Sarolt looked at him with wet, sad eyes. He could offer something to his wife as a gift too, he sensed. He took off his heavy cloak, folded it neatly, and, unafraid of the leaping flames, placed it gently onto the fire, careful so as not to smother it. Music began. Three brightly dressed musicians plucked dulcimer strings. The notes were wild, and ringing out faster and faster. Sarolt's servants whirled around the fire, and their long braids raced the flames. The girls danced, shouting, each one holding a clay vessel. When the dance was finished, one by one, they placed the vessels at the pyre. More fires were lit around them; ordinary, small ones. Riders appeared and jumped over the fires with long whips flying.

"Don't be offended, Prince," Zarad whispered into his ear, "but I prefer the fires on Midsummer's Eve."

Bolesław said nothing; he watched. The servants took Sarolt's cloak from her shoulders, and she let herself be swept into the dance around the pyre, which was slowly burning down. She'd lift her arms and cover her face, bowing, but she never stopped dancing. She never stopped speaking throughout it all. Bolesław summoned Lajos.

"My beloved, ride, fly, let the angel winds run through your hair, let the

Holy Mother take you into her arms . . ." the Magyar translated what he heard.

When the pyre was little more than embers, Prince Gejza signaled it was time for the feast. They went toward the central yurt, where a fire burned in an iron basket, the smoke escaping through the hole in the top of the yurt. Low seats had been placed along the curved walls, laid out with horse skins and blankets. Bolesław was asked to take the seat of honor between Sarolt and Gejza. Both sons sat at either side of their parents. Lajos, as his interpreter, took his place behind Bolesław. He had time to whisper before the feast began:

"A good place. There's none better."

The servants carried in trays of food, first approaching Gejza, who picked out meat with his fingers and placed it in his bowl. Then they offered it to Sarolt, who selected the largest piece and placed it on Bolesław's plate. He understood the gesture and thanked her. Jugs of wine were brought in and poured into expensive cups. Gejza raised a toast.

"To our dear guest, Boleszláv," Lajos translated.

The wine was strong, and thicker than he was used to.

"How did my little one die?" the princess asked through Lajos, taking a sip of her wine.

Bolesław told her of the difficult labor, about the apathy and insanity which haunted Karolda after it. About the wounds from the birth that had refused to heal.

Sarolt focused on Bolesław's words as he spoke them, even before Lajos translated them for her. She was so like her sister. Karolda hadn't wanted to learn the tongue, but she loved listening to the tone of voice. He called out words of devotion to her when they made love, and she could repeat them afterward. He never knew if she'd understood them.

"My lady is asking abut the child. Why haven't you brought Bezprym to her?" Lajos translated.

"Tell her that my wife rejected her son. She didn't want to see him or feed him."

"My lady is still asking why you haven't brought him."

Was I meant to take a baby and a procession of wet nurses through mountains? Bolesław thought, but replied calmly.

"He is my firstborn son. A little Piast. Children belong to the dynasty."

His words were discussed between Sarolt and Gejza, though Lajos didn't translate what was said. Eventually, he repeated Prince Gejza's thoughts for Bolesław.

"The lengths you've gone to in returning your wife's body are unheard of, even for a princess. They want to know why you, my lord, have undertaken this difficult journey."

"Tell them that my wife was born a Magyar and died one as well. If she is to ever find peace, I felt her soul must rest in the land to which she was born."

Silence fell when Lajos translated his words. Then Sarolt stood up, leaned over him and, taking his face between her hands, kissed his forehead. She whispered something to him which sounded like "Lana." He remembered this word.

"The prince and princess thank you for your efforts, and they appreciate what you've done for Princess Karolda. Prince Gejza considers the peace between our two countries to continue despite the princess's death."

The feast went on. Thick, red wine flowed in streams. When Bolesław left the guest yurt at dawn, he had Prince Gejza's and his heir Wajk's assurances that the Magyars had nothing against the planned Polish invasion of Moravia. Bolesław's goal had been achieved. He walked out into the cool air and summoned Lajos.

"A huge success," the Magyar said. "Young Honta related the story of how you cared for the deceased during your journey three times. How you guarded her on the barge to ensure she didn't fall into the water. Here, to drown is the worst way to die. It's a good thing you knew that, my lord."

I didn't, he thought, and asked Lajos:

"What does 'Lana' mean?"

"Lana? It's a . . ."

"No. What was the princess whispering about?"

"Possibly she was saying 'lánya'?" Lajos asked. "'Lánya' means 'daughter.'"

Daughter. Karolda had been so much younger than Sarolt. Could she have actually been her daughter, not her sister? *Why would they have hidden that from us? Unless she wasn't Gejza's child, but a pre-marriage secret, a daughter whose existence Sarolt hid under the guise of a sister?*

Whatever the answer was, he wouldn't ask about it tonight. The riddle wasn't worth risking the alliance that had been so difficult to ensure. As he walked to his yurt, he saw servants gathered at the burnt-out pyre. Girls were picking melted decorations from the embers, and placing them with the ashes in colorful ceramic pots, scooping them out with small shovels. When they finished, the servants bowed to the remains of the pyre and made their way to the church. Bolesław followed and, standing in the church entrance, watched as they opened the wooden door in the wall and placed the pots next to the coffin. They smiled in greeting as they exited.

"Boleszláv fejedelem."

Two days later, a troop of Princess Sarolt's Magyar riders and another, Prince Gejza's, under the command of his son Wajk accompanied Bolesław out of Veszprém. When they reached the bottom of the hill, he turned around and memorized the shape of the steep ridge.

I will tell Bezprym about this place when he is grown, he thought. *And about his mother, the fierce Magyar princess, who has given me so much joy and passion. Who lived violently, with fire, and not for long enough, burning fast but bright, like a pyre.*

16

⚘

POLAND: JOMSBORG AND WOLIN

Astrid, at the duke's command, had indeed married Jarl Sigvald, the man who been defeated by Jarl Haakon but was voted the new jarl of Jomsborg anyway, thanks to Mieszko's show of support.

Theirs was not an ordinary marriage. For one thing, they didn't live together. Jomsviking law forbade women from entering the stronghold. Though the first thing Sigvald had done as jarl of Jomsborg was announce that his wife, the daughter of the great Mieszko, was more than a mere woman. He took her to Jom and arranged a feast in her honor. Though none dared defy Sigvald, Astrid could see the warriors whispering their unhappiness throughout the feast, and was content to decline when Sigvald tried to invite her to the stronghold more regularly.

Dalwin, Astrid's grandfather, had given her the manor in Wolin as a wedding gift and had moved to smaller quarters. "Jom and Wolin are so close together," she'd told Sigvald, "that if you come here for dinner you can be back in your stronghold just after midnight."

Mieszko's support had positioned Sigvald as a leader, but acting like one didn't come naturally to her husband, and Astrid worried that he placed too much faith in his father-in-law. He didn't yet understand about Mieszko and the kind of help he gave.

At the time of their wedding, Sigvald had just lost a battle and was a step away from being named a coward by his men—a loss of honor that would have been no different than death for a Jomsviking. Mieszko, having given him his daughter's hand, restored Sigvald's reputation, and he expected much in return. Astrid, whether she liked it or not, was a part of this, the reluctant guardian of the arrangement. She knew just how far the duke's plans reached and committed herself to helping Geivar—a close friend to Olav, the Norwegian heir—gain the Jomsvikings' trust in Jomsborg.

"Fat Bue died during the fight with Haakon, and a new chief is needed for his house. Make Geivar a chieftain," she advised her husband.

"Why would I do that?" Sigvald cocked his head, his long, dark hair streaming down his back. If she were to name one beautiful thing about her husband, she would choose his hair.

"He is an excellent sailor, he knows Rus like no one else, and who knows where he might lead the Jomsvikings in the future?"

"He can be one of us," Sigvald said, shrugging, "but that's no reason for him to be a chieftain."

And what have you done to deserve it, my sweet one? she thought spitefully, but aloud she said, "You need new blood in the council. Someone who isn't connected to the Danish king. Is that enough, or should I speak more plainly?"

Sigvald laughed and reached out to touch her. She slipped away.

"You are beautiful when you're angry, Astrid."

"Even so, that's no reason to look for ways to frustrate me, husband."

"Why not?" he shook his head. "Will you complain to your father? He's not here. Or maybe you'll summon old Dalwin? You'll say, 'Grandfather, my husband angers me'?"

"No. It would be enough for me to tell your men about our wedding night."

"You can't say you didn't like it. You were moaning like a she-cat in heat," he laughed.

"I was admiring your skin, Sigvald," she snapped. "I'd never have thought that a warrior might have such smooth and silky skin. Without a scratch or scar to be seen."

"Silence!" he yelled, no longer laughing.

"Why?" she echoed him. "Will you go and complain to the Jomsvikings?"

Astrid held his honor in her hand, but she knew there were limits to his patience. Even if Sigvald had run from that battle, he was still dangerous.

"I will accept Olav Tryggvason as one of us, not Geivar," he said firmly.

"Tryggvason's destiny is to win back his throne."

"Invite your sister and her husband. We can talk then." He ended the conversation and left for the port.

These were the moments she sighed with relief at the fact that they didn't live together. No, she wasn't afraid that he would strike her. The fear was slippery, something she couldn't quite pin down, and she couldn't figure out the reason behind it. Her feelings for Sigvald danced on the thin line between the superiority she felt toward him and the fear he made her feel.

He fights for himself, she thought. *To avoid feeling as if he owes Mieszko and me everything.*

Astrid fought with herself as well as with her husband. After the vision she'd had during her conversation with her father, that deep and terrifying feeling that a wrong choice was somehow being made, she'd sworn not to touch the herbs, spells, or runes which spoke of the future. Never again. She'd had a talent for seeing what others could not since she was a child. She had dreamed of things that eventually came to pass for as long as she could remember. But in one of them she'd seen Olav, and had loved him before she awoke. When Mieszko had taken that future away—the duke was a force stronger than even fate, she had learned—she no longer wanted to know what lay ahead. Every night, she drank a brew that gave her a deep sleep, one black and free of dreams. It was better this way.

Mieszko, the true lord and ruler of dreams, had given her a task. To fulfill it, she must remain focused on Sigvald and help guide his decisions.

Eventually, he gave in and accepted Geivar, though she found out only by accident that Tryggvason's friend had become a house chieftain; Sigvald never mentioned it to her. This was when she learned her husband was not a man who liked to fight on open ground.

As Sigvald had suggested, Astrid sent a letter to Geira, inviting her and Olav to Wolin. It had been a year since Mieszko had thrown a joint wedding celebration for his two eldest daughters, Astrid and Sigvald, Geira and Olav marrying on the same day. The sisters had not seen each other since, and Astrid knew that, however happy she would be to see Geira again, meeting with her and Olav as husband and wife would be painful. Though she lived day to day in relative contentment with her own husband, Astrid was under no illusions that her feelings for Olav had disappeared. Geira, though, had blossomed in their time apart.

"Did you know that my beloved has found his mother?" Geira was saying. She and Olav had arrived that morning, and now the sisters were exchanging news before the evening meal. "She bears the same name as yours, sister. Astrid. She is now Lodin's wife, and has three children with him, daughters Ingireda and Ingigerda and a son, Torkil. They live in the south of Norway, in Viken."

Astrid had never seen her sister so lively. Geira had never been talkative, but now she spoke easily and with pride, like a baker praising the morning's fresh crumpets. Her cheeks were pink. Her fair hair was plaited in shining braids, and her dress was as snug as if . . .

"You've noticed?" She smiled. "Yes, Olav and I are expecting a baby." She stroked her stomach. "It's wonderful, isn't it?"

"Yes," Astrid agreed, trying to summon a smile. She heard her father's voice in her head, *"I'll wait until he has a son with your sister, then I'll let him sail to win the riches and men."*

"I'd like you to be with me when the time comes. Your herbs can fight off the pain and stop bleeding . . ."

"I don't do that," Astrid replied harshly. "It wouldn't suit a jarl's wife . . ."

"What about you and Sigvald?" Geira asked, not picking up on Astrid's tone and embracing her sister warmly. "Will something come of it?"

Astrid gritted her teeth.

"I don't know," she said shortly as they entered the main hall where Olav and Sigvald sat, speaking comfortably.

Olav was just as she remembered, though the strange, unsettling spark Astrid had seen on their first meeting no longer burned in his eyes. *He's found his mother and is more at peace,* she sensed. She no longer had dreams, but she could still see into the hearts of others at times. She looked away from him, not wanting to stare.

"What a meeting." Geira couldn't hide her joy. "Only a shame that Świętosława and Eric aren't here, too."

A smile crossed Sigvald's lips, and he held back a laugh.

"Apologies, sister, but I don't regret that at all."

"Of course," Geira said quickly, realizing her error. "I'm sorry, Sigvald, I forgot that Eric . . . and the defeat . . ." Geira trailed off, hoping the subject would pass.

"He didn't defeat us, but his nephew Styrbjorn. Call it a battle with 'our modest participation,' and it will sound as it should," Sigvald said amicably.

"A shame, though," Geira sighed. "I'd prefer there be peace in our family."

"There's nothing preventing Mieszko's sons-in-law being allies in the future," Astrid said lightly. "Even the Jomsvikings can learn from their mistakes. Especially if favorable breezes blow."

"Some mistakes lie at the source," Sigvald replied mysteriously. "And drag on for years."

"King Harald Bluetooth of Denmark won't live forever, and after his death . . ." Astrid began.

"Sven's time will come. He's an excellent chief, I fought alongside him when he was fighting for Hedeby," Sigvald said.

"Sven did not make you a Jomsviking, and you have no ties to him, husband." She wanted this conversation to take place in front of witnesses so that Sigvald wouldn't be able to deny it happened. "With Harald Bluetooth's death, the ropes connecting Jomsborg to Denmark will break."

Harald may have built the fortress, but Jomsborg's laws were clear: the Jomsvikings need only answer to their leader. Not to any king or country. They remained loyal to Harald because of their shared history, but there was no cause for this loyalty to surpass death.

"You talk like a bard, wife. I won't deny that the vision is a tempting one, but you're wrong to say that I have no ties to Sven."

Astrid felt uneasy at this. "I don't understand . . ."

Sigvald didn't immediately reply. He called a servant over to pour more mead, then turned to Olav.

"Does your wife also think she knows everything about you?" he asked.

"Ask her yourself, Sigvald," Olav replied.

Geira didn't need more encouragement to speak.

"We are happy, brother! I don't need to know anything more."

As if to show the truth of her words, she kissed Olav's cheek. He smiled, but Astrid's keen eye caught the flinch of impatience that flitted across his face like a shadow.

"And what do you mean by that?" she asked her own husband, perhaps a little too harshly, but she needed to distract from the flicker of hope she'd felt as she realized that the "happy couple" were perhaps not as happy as Geira said. It was an ugly sort of hope, and Astrid wanted desperately to push it away.

"My brother, Thorkel the Tall, would allow himself be drawn and quartered for Sven." Sigvald smiled, as if waiting to see what effect his words had on Astrid. "What do you think, my wife who loves her sisters so? Should it come easy for me to work against my own brother?"

"Thorkel is a house chieftain, and you are the leader of Jomsborg," Astrid said sweetly. "I'm sure that you will make the right decision, husband."

Astrid turned back to her sister then, changing the conversation, understanding that saying anything more on the subject risked pressing her husband down a path opposite to the one Mieszko would want for him. Sigvald was both hot-tempered and cunning. Violent and mysterious. Astrid was learning him as one learns to weave a colorful yarn.

"Oh!" Geira exclaimed, happy for the shift in conversation. "Have you heard that Świętosława gave birth to a son?"

"No," Astrid and Olav said in unison.

"One can understand that I haven't heard," Astrid said, forcing her tone to sound lighthearted, "but that you don't know, Olav, when your wife does?"

"I only heard the news the moment we were leaving." Geira reddened. "I wanted it to be a surprise . . ."

I'm horrible, Astrid thought. *I'm being cruel to my own sister. After all, this blush shows that her joy hides more than she's saying.*

"It is indeed a surprise," Olav said. "So tell us about this boy, then."

"Messengers from Uppsala came to Mieszko to give him the happy news. He has a healthy and strong grandson." Geira sounded suddenly hesitant.

"What name did they choose?" Astrid asked.

"Olav," she said quietly.

Tryggvason was unable to control his reaction. He pressed up from the bench, as if about to run from the room, as if there were somewhere else he needed to be. He gathered himself quickly though, realizing what he had done, and now stood awkwardly in the silence that followed. In that moment, Astrid felt her sister's sorrow.

"Or rather Olof," Sigvald said with the strangest of smiles. "They named him after Styrbjorn's father, the nephew Eric sent to Valhalla."

Geira gave Sigvald a look of such gratitude that Astrid felt her heart squeeze.

"Your sister," Sigvald said, "has strengthened her position at her husband's side. By giving him an heir she has made herself untouchable. They say that Eric adores Sigrid Storråda."

At least one of us has been lucky, Astrid thought.

Tryggvason sat back down. His expression was unreadable. He lifted a horn with mead to his lips and put an arm around Geira's shoulders.

"If we have a son, we will name him Sivrit, after my uncle. And if a daughter, we will call her after my mother, Astrid."

"They are beautiful names." Geira's cheerfulness had returned.

"Although I won't hide," Olav said, turning to Astrid, "that by naming my daughter Astrid I will also be thinking of you. I have never ceased to be grateful to you for bringing *Kanugård* safely to shore. A toast to you!"

Astrid feared she was blushing stupidly. She felt hot and flustered, and could feel Sigvald's eyes on her. Blessedly, Olav now steered the conversation to a new topic.

"You haven't filled all the empty houses yet?" He turned to Sigvald, asking after the chieftains of Jomsborg.

"No. The house of sailors has had no leader since I became the head jarl. The house of warriors is currently empty, as Vagn has gone to see his wife.

The house of hosts has been taken by your comrade, Geivar Painted Fangs, since Fat Bue's death."

"Is that what you call him?" Olav asked.

"They're difficult to miss." Sigvald smiled, baring his own white teeth. "To be honest, warriors with their teeth painted and filed are a dying breed. I don't speak of your Geivar, but I mean to say there is no need any more. Their old traditions, charms, the biting of shields . . ." Sigvald shook his hair as he spoke, as if unconsciously trying to assert his dominance. "Now any-one, with the aid of mushrooms, can be a berserker."

"Mushrooms," Olav repeated. "One should be careful, Sigvald. Their juice can give strength, but it can also poison the soul. Do you know what happens to old berserkers who have strengthened their bloodthirst with mushrooms too frequently?"

"Yes, yes, I've heard." Sigvald fiddled with his ring. "They fall victim to wraiths of insanity in old age, so they say. But why do we speak of this, Olav? It doesn't affect us, does it? Young, strong, beautiful, we don't need mush-rooms to go boldly into battle."

"It's true." Olav raised his horn to Sigvald now. "Those who don't need the herbs to embrace the bloodthirst and immunity to pain are far more valued."

I'll ensure he and Sigvald are friends, too. The Jomsvikings will aid him in his fight for Norway in a few years. Mieszko spoke again in Astrid's memory, but as she watched them today, she found herself thinking that a friendship between Olav and Sigvald was impossible. Olav was fire, even if his flame was less visible today than it had been at their first meeting. He was fire, she could feel it. And Sigvald, with his volatility and elusiveness, was like smoke.

She gave the servants the sign to bring more dishes. Perch-pikes baked with onions and garlic. Smoked and fried mackerels. A dish of eels. Peas with fresh butter.

"The riches of the sea," she said, inviting her guests to feast.

At that very moment, the doors of the hall flung open, and her grandfa-ther, the master of Wolin, entered. His tangled hair and wet hood told Astrid he had come straight from the port.

"Child . . ." he said, as if he wanted to spare her. "I am forced to interrupt your dinner."

"Speak, Dalwin." Sigvald stood up from the steaming dishes, as if sensing his dinner was ending as well.

"Jarl, your people will come for you in a moment. You should go to Jom without delay; you have an unexpected guest."

"Who?" Astrid asked, knowing the answer would not be a good one.

"King Harald," Dalwin said in a strangled voice. "He is running from his son."

"Sven has declared war on his father?" Sigvald flinched.

"Yes, Jarl. The old king's ship has sailed through the iron gates of Jomsborg already, but I suspect that Sven's ship and his men will be arriving at the stronghold any minute. Jom will defend itself, but I'm afraid that the Danes might plunder Wolin." Wolin, the defenseless market town, where strength of trade was valued over strength in battle.

Sigvald was already reaching for his belt. He remained poised as he spoke.

"Dalwin, I won't allow Wolin to be touched. I'll defend it as I would my wife." He kissed Astrid on the lips, perhaps a little too theatrically. "Keep the merchants in the city until we can guarantee that the seas are calm. Olav, would you take charge of defending Wolin? If Dalwin has nothing against it, of course." Sigvald bowed to both Dalwin and Olav, which seemed to Astrid to be another act.

"I will," Olav said.

"Thank you," Dalwin said.

Sigvald leaned over her suddenly, as if he wanted to kiss her again, but he moved his lips away from hers at the last moment and whispered:

"Don't tell me what to do, wife. The decisions I make will be the right ones."

Sigvald listened to the guard captain's report at the stronghold's gate.

"One ship, Jarl, and not Harald's royal vessel, but something fit more for his berserkers than a king, with a plated bow. None of the king's men have uttered the word 'escape,' but it's obvious. There was no luggage on deck and the wounded king was wrapped in nothing more than blankets."

"Will the old one make it?" Sigvald asked, making sure that concern for the king's well-being could be heard in his voice.

"I don't know, Jarl." The captain shook his head. "I only saw him briefly when he was being carried to the Sacred Site."

"Increase the guards and order your men to be ready to defend Wolin if the need arises," Sigvald ordered. "It won't matter how many ships Sven has brought with him. We won't let him into Jom, and if he attempts to enter Wolin we'll close off the Dziwna's estuary."

"As you command, Jarl," the captain straightened his back. "We've also sent a ship to your brother, my lord."

"Is Thorkel not in the stronghold?" He grimaced.

"The chieftain of scouts must often be outside these walls," the captain replied evasively.

Sigvald didn't bother commenting on this. If his brother had sailed to scout, he would have told him himself, at once, and they wouldn't have been caught off guard by Harald's visit. He had sailed to one of his women. Sigvald bit back a retort; what was done was done. Harald was already here.

He made his way to the Sacred Site, the great hut which served as a tavern. Jomsborg was divided into four camps, known as houses. The house of sailors, which he had previously led; the house of scouts, under his brother's command, Thorkel the Tall; the house of hunters, or hosts, which he had given to Geivar; and the house of warriors, currently without a leader while Vagn was away. Each of the four camps consisted of four long houses, three of which were intended as living quarters, and one meant for common use, with a hall, kitchen and cellar. In their spare time, the soldiers of different houses met in the Sacred Site, which stood in the center of the four camp-bases. It was governed by the House of Hunters but served as a common space among the four camps, a place for socializing or respite for any soldier. Those whose days were spent working at their posts for the separate houses came there in the evenings to share gossip and mead. The scouts drank with the hunters, the sailors with the warriors. Sometimes fights broke out, but no weapons were allowed in the inn, and most disagreements fizzled quickly. The house of chiefs, near the Sacred Site in the center of Jomsborg, was where war meetings took place, and where important guests were received.

Why was the wounded Harald taken to the Sacred Site instead of there? Sigvald wondered as he walked toward the inn, but when he saw the lookout, a boy from the house of hunters, he understood. Since he, the head jarl, and his brother Thorkel had both been out of Jom when Harald arrived, Geivar was the chieftain effectively in charge. And he, leader of the house of hunters, had decided the inn was the better place than the more respected house of chiefs for the wounded king. *Good,* he thought, *that was wise.*

Torches burned at the entrance and the guard reported, "King of Denmark, Harald, with twenty men, including twelve berserkers. Some with minor wounds. The chief of the hunters and his guards."

"Thank you." Sigvald nodded to him and walked inside.

The large chamber had been hastily arranged, a bed for the king brought in, and sleeping places made for his men. Geivar came to greet the head jarl, stepping quietly so as not to disturb those resting around them.

"How is he?" Sigvald asked, nodding toward the bed.

"Not good," the chief of the hunters replied. "Sven got a cut in, on the king's chest with his sword. The wound is shallow but infected, and isn't healing."

"He didn't protest when you brought him to the Sacred Site rather than the house of chiefs?" Sigvald watched Geivar carefully as he asked the question, wondering if he had guessed the chief's motivations correctly.

"He was unconscious," Geivar replied, meeting the jarl's eyes.

"You did well."

He might have added that this was a clear signal they were removing Harald from power at Jom, but he remained silent. Geivar, as Olav Tryggvason's man, was also loyal to Mieszko. Better to speak carefully now, because where the night might lead was yet to be seen.

A moan, and then an audible voice reached them. The king was waking. The two Jomsvikings approached him.

This was Sigvald's first meeting with Harald; the king of Danes had not visited Jom since Sigvald had lived there, though apparently, Harald been a frequent guest in the past, and the older Jomsvikings fondly recalled feasts held in his company. Harald was shirtless now, a wide dressing crossing his torso. The king's face was pale and covered in sweat; wet, gray hairs stuck to his skin. His eyes were open and he tried to sit up as they approached, leaning on the arms of two strong men.

"King, I am Sigvald, the jarl of Jomsborg."

"I don't know you," Harald murmured. "Where's Palnatoki?"

"Palnatoki has been dead for over a year, my lord," Sigvald explained, though he knew that news of the old jarl's death had been delivered to Roskilde.

Harald collapsed back onto his pillow. He wiped sweat from his forehead and groaned, reaching to the dressing on his chest. Blood and pus seeped from between his fingers.

"Get a cloak," he croaked to one of the giants serving him. "I'm a king, it's not appropriate for me to sit naked in front of the jarl of Jomsborg." These last words were said with a hint of mockery. The king looked at Sigvald, a challenge in his eyes. "What, pretty one? So you're saying that you've been chosen to lead my iron boys?" Spittle glistened on his bluing lips, and his voice dripped with disdain.

They are my iron boys, Sigvald thought coldly.

"Yes, my lord," he said calmly.

"All the young ones think they made the world themselves. You're Sven's age." Harald glared at him. "Where's Palnatoki?"

"He's dead," Sigvald repeated.

"Why? Was he injured?"

"No, King. It's normal that people die at a certain age." The edge of politeness in his voice was as sharp as a knife.

"You're a fool, like my redhead son," Harald hissed. "Palnatoki was younger than me."

"I'm sorry, my lord. We'll take good care of you, and I'm sure you'll regain your health soon. That wound doesn't look dangerous, though I can see it isn't healing."

"What do you know of wounds, whelp?" the old man snarled.

The men beside the king hissed then, in unison, which apparently was meant to calm the old man. It seemed the old comrades had a right to discipline their master, if not in so many words. And just in time. Though this exchange worked in Sigvald's favor, he wished there were more to witness it than just Geivar and a few of his men.

"Yes, yes, you're a young chief," the king corrected and laughed. "No one should mock a Jomsviking, especially behind the iron gates." The laughter turned to coughing.

"It's true that the boundaries of my politeness are dictated by my respect for you, my lord," Sigvald said, watching Harald spit blood. "I assure you that you and your men have sanctuary here."

He waited for a moment before adding, "Your son's ships sail for Jom."

"Are you afraid . . . what's your name, young chief?" the king cocked his head.

"My name's Sigvald, and I'm not afraid of Sven, my lord."

"Come closer, Sigvald. Closer. Lean down, because I want to tell you . . ."

Sigvald leaned over Harald, though he knew what the other would do. As he expected, the wounded old man grabbed his caftan and pulled him nearer.

"Jomsborg owes me protection. I created the stronghold, and it must serve me. The final fight, to the death."

They stared into each other's eyes. Sigvald could smell the other's sour breath, and he could see the mist beginning to creep into his eyes. This presence of death made it easy for him to know what he must do. When Harald released him, Sigvald straightened and said loudly:

"For so long as you live, King, you're under our care. Allow me to leave you, I must give my orders."

He nodded to Geivar as he left. They finished their conversation in the house of chiefs, not in the Sacred Site.

"Send men to Duke Mieszko. Harald won't survive three days," he said.

"Jarl, your brother, Thorkel the Tall, might stand alongside Sven," Geivar observed bluntly.

"I do not intend to break my brother's love for the young king. Quite the opposite; I want to give him a chance to demonstrate it."

"What do you mean, Jarl?" Geivar's eyes narrowed to slits.

"Leave Thorkel to me. He's not the one who might meddle in our plans, but Harald taking too long to die might be a problem. It would give Sven time to arrive at Jom's gates. Let's make sure the old one helps us and bids this life goodbye swiftly."

"That can be arranged, Jarl," Geivar smiled slightly. "All it will take is for the dressing my men will soon be changing to have a drop of . . ."

"Shh." Sigvald put a finger to his lips. "Let it happen."

Harald began to die in the morning, and whatever the songs may proclaim, he did not die with a smile on his lips. He shouted for drink, and they gave him as much mead as he wanted. He cursed his son Sven's sword, arrogance, ambition, thirst for power, and eventually even the loins which created him, in his final confused state of mind.

"And so he dies a cursed man," Geivar said, quietly, almost to himself.

Thorkel had managed to return in time and now stood off to the side, watching the dying king with disgust. Twelve berserkers, no longer young but younger than Harald, his loyal comrades, surrounded the king's bed. The thought had crossed Sigvald's mind that these men might start a fight once the king died. He didn't want to find out how many Jomsvikings it would take to defeat just one of the human beasts. He watched them. Their eyes swung between expressing emptiness and despair. They stood like a wall of shields.

"Palnatoki," the king called out. "Palnatoki, come here . . ."

Sigvald, Geivar, and Thorkel all approached the bed.

"I am Sigvald, the jarl of Jomsborg. These are Geivar and Thorkel, house chieftains. Palnatoki is dead."

"Don't lie, pretty one, I can see him more clearly than I see you. He's here. And you dare call yourself a jarl in his presence? You're all mad, to even claim such a thing. Pups who bark in their mother's wombs."

Harald was so exhausted by his own anger that when he finished speaking, he only had strength left for a small moan. The final breath. He walked into the darkness with an insult on his lips.

"The king has died like a true warrior," Sigvald announced ceremoniously. "From wounds he sustained in battle. Each one of us desires such a death."

The twelve berserkers howled. This was the moment Sigvald had feared. That morning he had given the order—outside, the Sacred Site was surrounded by fifty armed men. The berserkers ended their farewell call and fell silent. They looked from the dead Harald to one another.

"The king has a right to a royal funeral," Sigvald said calmly. "My brother Thorkel, the chieftain of the house of scouts, will take Harald's body to Roskilde with the Jomsvikings' honors. I hope that you, the dead one's closest companions, will not abandon him on his final journey."

"I'm the helmsman of his ship," one of them said.

"I'm his shield on the battlefield," another announced hollowly.

"We are all his blood brothers," the others said. "We sail with him."

"Thorkel? Are the ships ready?" Sigvald asked, as if it was obvious they must leave without delay.

"Yes, brother," the scout chieftain replied, with some surprise.

"Then the blood brothers will take his body to the ship. To the sound of the black horn, the one that bids farewell to all our brothers. You will all sail to Roskilde," Sigvald announced, and noted with relief that the berserkers were already lifting Harald's body. He let them lead the way. As he made his way behind, he grabbed Thorkel's elbow and whispered, "Don't board their ship. Who knows what they're capable of. Let them sail with the body alone. You sail first, with an unfurled sail of Jomsborg. You should encounter Sven and his men tonight, or tomorrow at the latest. Tell the young king what he likely already knows: that nothing aids the taking of power in a country better than a funeral. Maybe you'll be able to calm Sven's feverish ambitions. Even if he fought with his father when the king was alive, he should now play the part of a son and heir who leads the ceremony of his burial. He should give feasts, invite his nobles and chieftains, and celebrate Harald's memory as much as he secretly rejoices at the old man's death."

"Should Harald Bluetooth not have his funeral in Jom?" a surprised Thorkel asked.

"No, my brother. He wasn't one of us. He was no more than a king."

17

∞

SWEDEN

Świętosława was teaching Olof to walk. She felt her son should be able to do everything sooner, and better, than other children. Dusza shielded the boy from falls.

"My lady." A servant entered her bedchamber. "Messengers from your country have arrived."

Świętosława leapt up. Eric wouldn't return until the evening, so she would have to greet the guests herself, which suited her just fine.

"Bring them to the great hall," she commanded. "And prepare food."

As the servant exited, happy squeals rose from the other side of the room. The handmaids who had come with her from Poznań.

"My lady," they cried, one over the other. "We will finally hear news from home!"

"Your home is here," she reminded them strictly. "If I hear any one of you complain about your life in Uppsala, I'll marry you off to the berserker with a missing front tooth. You know which one I mean."

"We know," they cried, their happiness undampened.

She always scared them with Great Ulf. He was Eric's trusted man and was responsible for her safety. He was as bald as her husband and had as powerful a frame. His face was marked by scars, running along his cheekbones and across his chin. A broken tooth made his smile as fearsome as his anger.

They helped her change and pinned her hair. They slid rings and armbands on her, gifts from Eric. They draped the lynx fur across her back. She wanted Father's messengers to see the queen of Sweden, Sigrid Storråda.

"Dusza, give me my son. I will greet our guests with him."

There were four messengers, and she knew them all. Litobor, one of Mieszko's chieftains. Bjornar, her brother's friend, and Wilkomir, one of Bolesław's squad members. And Geivar, Olav's companion. She was happy to see them all, and she trembled at the sight of the fourth, because she couldn't help but think of Tryggvason when she saw him.

Two tall chairs stood at the head of the great hall, hers and Eric's. When she had settled into hers, she motioned for them to approach.

"This is my son, Olof, Eric's heir." She lifted the child. "Bjornar, come closer and hold him. He's been looking at horrible warrior mugs since birth, so your face shouldn't scare him. I want you all to hold him and tell everyone at my father's court what a beautiful grandson he has."

Bjornar took the child and lifted him up.

"He's bigger than Bezprym, Bolesław's son," he observed.

"Bolesław has a son?" This was wonderful news! "Tell me everything," she said.

Bjornar stroked Olof's bald head and studied the birthmark he found there.

"They have the same mark, my lady. Just here." He showed her the dark round mark on the back of Olof's head. The birthmark she was so fond of.

"Piast blood." She laughed. "Tell me, what goes on in the country? My brother has married, as I understand it?"

"For the second time, my lady. Bolesław has recently taken Karolda, Bezprym's mother, back to Hungary . . ."

"Let me guess," she interjected. "Mieszko has switched alliances again? Well, at least he didn't send her back while she was still pregnant. He let her give birth, such a princely gesture! What of the child?"

The messengers exchanged glances.

"Bolesław didn't send his wife away. He took her body to her family in an oaken casket. Karolda died."

"Oh."

"But if you ask me, my lady, I was relieved. Karolda was a strange one. Your brother loved her, but everyone else . . ." He looked at Świętosława meaningfully. "Even Bolesław's dogs couldn't stand her."

"Even his dogs," she repeated after him. "And, I suspect, his concubines, his closest friends, Duchess Oda, and eventually the duke, my father, himself. You could speak openly, Bjornar, instead of blaming the dogs. Poor girl, she died right on time."

Bjornar reddened to match his hair, which confirmed her suspicions.

"We have brought you gifts, my lady. Presents from your loved ones, and much news we hope to share with both you and your husband," Litobor said, trying to introduce some order into the meeting.

"Then let us begin with the presents." Świętosława felt giddy at the prospect. "Dusza, take Olof."

Geivar excused himself from the hall while the others stepped forward with their offerings. First was a cross with a silver engraving of Christ from her father, so like the one which decorated the royal chapel in Poznań. Then riding boots from her brother, of the highest quality, and beautiful ear cuffs from Astrid. Geivar returned with his men, who carried something covered by a dark fabric.

"This is a gift from Olav," he said. "And your sister Geira," he added, after a pause.

He pulled off the covering to reveal a cage, with two young lynxes sleeping inside.

In that moment, Świętosława forgot that she was a queen. A Swedish ruler, Sigrid Storråda. She jumped from the throne and knelt by the cage.

"My master caught the lynxes in the forest and commanded me to say when they had been given to you, 'The queen once loved a fur snatched from a lynx's back. She will undoubtedly want to see what it's like to love a live animal.'"

The creatures awoke, slowly opening their green and golden eyes. One stood up and gave her a disdainful snort. The other followed her with its eyes, never lifting its head. They were no bigger than large puppies, their fur a mottled red, with paler areas around their throats and underbellies. She could see dark speckles on their skin, barely discernible through their thick fur.

"Open the cage," she told Geivar. "I want to hold them."

"My lady," Wilkomir spoke up. "I wouldn't. They will be irritable after the journey."

"I wasn't asking," Świętosława said coldly. "I gave an order."

Wilkomir gave her a look of surprise at this but didn't back down.

"Their appearance is the only thing they have in common with cats, my lady. They are predators."

Świętosława stood and walked away from the cage, not looking at Wilkomir, and turned to the eldest man present.

"Litobor, I have awaited your arrival for a long time, and the presence of my father's messengers gives me more joy than any gifts. My king will celebrate your arrival with a great feast and wonderful presents. I expect to have long conversations with you, Bjornar, and master Geivar. But I cannot understand why this man feels it is appropriate to disagree with a queen at her own court."

"My lady." Litobor bowed. She could remember him calling her "little princess" when she was young. "Wilkomir may lack manners, but he does not lack courage. He is doing what your father has ordered him to do: protecting you."

"My husband's men are responsible for my safety now. Have you seen Great Ulf? He's enormous, and I think his scars speak to his bravery."

"Where is he now?" Wilkomir spoke up. "If he protects you, my queen, where is he when you intend to let wild animals out of a cage with a newborn present?"

She sucked in a breath. Yes, she'd forgotten that Olof was also in the hall. And that was when she fully understood Litobor's words.

"Are you saying that Wilkomir is to stay?"

"Yes, my lady. Duke Mieszko, apart from jewels and presents, has sent you a squad of a dozen men under Wilkomir's leadership. They are to be your personal guard."

"What will my husband say to this?" She cocked her head. "Won't he interpret such a gift as a slight to his honor? And, I feel obliged to warn you, my husband loves his honor as much as his battle-axe."

"I am no gift," Wilkomir growled.

She heard him but bit back a reply.

"Leave it to us to convince Eric to accept the squad," Litobor said.

Świętosława placed her hands on the cage. She heard a warning growl.

"If Olav can capture lynxes, I can tame them," she said, then pulled her hand back quickly, as the animal that had been lying down seconds before sprang up, trying to catch her fingers. She was faster. She snapped her unbitten fingers. "Take the cage to my rooms. They should get used to their mistress's scent."

The feast was a proper celebration: noisy, rich with mead, and heavy with food. Eric, who had arrived that afternoon, invited the four guests to sit with him at the raised table at the end of the hall. Jarl Birger and two other chieftains in Eric's army joined them. The king boasted of his victory over Styrbjorn at Fyrisvellir's fields, and about his son.

Almost as if he gave birth to him himself. Świętosława sighed inwardly as she pasted on a smile. But of the two subjects, she preferred he talk of Olof.

"My lady will give me many sons yet," Eric thundered happily, and his dark eyes gleamed. "Many strong bald boys will leap from this wondrous womb."

"My king knows much about war and ruling a country, but the mystery of birth remains." She lifted a goblet.

"If I jump in . . ." Eric began.

"Don't finish that thought, husband, not unless you intend to bed me in front of your guests."

He gave an uncomfortable chuckle. Even Eric could be embarrassed.

"We've brought important news, King," Litobor said, finally bringing them to the reason for their journey. "The king of Denmark, Harald Bluetooth, is dead."

"Ah, news indeed!" Eric exclaimed. "I cannot say that I'll mourn his journey to Valhalla. Has his son Sven taken over yet?"

"He's trying. Half of Denmark is on his side, and the other half, Harald Bluetooth's supporters included, are against him. The latter have gained an influential ally in his half sister, Tyra. Sven's open attack on his father the king has not done him any favors."

"The rich don't like strong kings." Eric wiped his mouth. "And the people don't like it when sons kill their fathers."

"Princess Tyra is a Christian, and thanks to that, those who oppose Sven can easily use religious disagreements to their advantage. They're prepared to use Tyra in their negotiations for support with the Saxon courts, though from what I know they have not yet resorted to doing so, knowing that calling the Saxons in to face Sven will likely be a double-edged sword."

Świętosława had had time to talk to her father's men in private before the feast, and she spoke up now.

"Geivar is one of the new chieftains of Jomsborg, husband."

Eric studied Geivar carefully. "I bear no grudges against the defeated," he said finally, referring to the Jomsvikings who'd fought against him on his nephew's behalf.

"And I wasn't a Jomsviking when you vanquished Styrbjorn," Geivar replied. "Much has changed in Jom."

"Have the iron boys gained some sense and stopped leaping to be at the beck and call of Danish kings?" Eric asked, smiling.

How easy it is to converse as a victor, Świętosława thought.

"The Jomsvikings are prepared to support Duke Mieszko," Geivar said calmly.

"Excellent." Świętosława clapped her hands and signaled for the servants to refill their goblets. "You, my king, by marrying your queen, promised to break apart Denmark. Is this not the perfect time?"

"With Sven precariously perched on his throne, unrest in the country, and Jomsvikings for allies?'" her husband growled, lifting his horn. He drank, wiped his lips, and summoned the Icelandic bard. "Cold is the advice of women," he repeated the words from his favorite song.

"Cold advice is good advice, my king." She smiled brightly at him.

"Thorvald! Entertain us with the 'Song of the Mighty.' My guests can listen while I think."

The Icelandic bard had won Eric's favor for his song about the king's defeat of Styrbjorn. His voice was clear and strong, and as the verses swept him along, he spread his arms and his body seemed to pulse with the song. Świętosława liked listening to the bard's words, his voice, the pictures he would paint. Dark, fluttering stories that took her out of herself. She closed her eyes and saw the dark Baltic waves, the lively depths of the ocean she'd sailed across. She missed Father John reading the Bible and the clerics singing bright psalms. But that was on the other side of the ocean. They weren't here. There was an Icelandic bard and his 'Song of the Mighty,' praising Odin. And her lord husband, who had let his eyelids droop, listening as she stared into the flames.

Fortunate is he who gains for himself
wisdom and fame during this life;
because a man received wrong advice
too frequently
from the breast of another.

She opened her eyes. She noticed Bjornar studying the king, worried. Yes, perhaps Eric wouldn't make up his mind today. Then, once night fell, it would be her time.

"It's good to make decisions about war once the mind has had some rest," Eric announced, confirming her suspicions. "Be my guests and feast beside my chieftains."

He stood up and looked to his wife. Świętosława rose, and the two left the hall together.

18

⚅

SWEDEN

Świętosława hadn't come to Eric's bed since Olof's birth, citing wounds that needed time to heal and the discomfort of breastfeeding. She knew both of these excuses had long lost their sway with Eric, though. Jarl Birger had warned her that if she didn't return to the king's bed soon, he would take a mistress. "I'm afraid he might sire bastards, my queen, and then what fate might meet your son?" That image was enough for her to decide it was time to enter Eric's chambers, but just as she'd made her mind up to do so, Eric left for an endless hunt and had only returned today. During the feast, when he'd mentioned her wondrous womb out of which more sons would leap, she was under no illusions about what she must do. Dusza helped her change into a nightshirt embroidered with silver thread, as fine as a spider's web. Świętosława let down her hair, brushing it.

"Give me the armbands I received from my king. And my rings," she commanded, though Dusza received this with raised eyebrows. "And cover me with the fur of white foxes. And take care of Olof," she said at the end. "I don't want the boar to hear the child's crying."

A throaty snort came from a dark corner of the bedchamber. The lynxes. She walked to the cage and held a strip of raw meat out to each of them. The starved cats sniffed her distrustfully. She stood patiently, holding the meat between the bars.

"Don't you want to eat? Okay, then. Dusza, don't feed them until I get back."

Great Ulf, with a torch in his hand, led her and her procession of servants. One had to walk across the entire manor to get to the king's chambers from the queen's rooms. March through the hall full of guests. She hadn't forgotten her walks through it before Olof's birth. Each one caused her great discomfort, but from the very first night, when a group of thirty men had escorted them to the bedchamber, along with a few noblewomen, Świętosława had vowed to turn her embarrassment into a weapon.

No one will respect a frightened queen, she'd told herself that night, and walked with her head high, smiling to those watching the bedroom march. She even stopped once or twice on her way to the king's room, accepting toasts from guests who raised their glasses to her. She drank a goblet of mead and discovered that it lessened the pain Eric caused her in the bedchamber.

"Queen Sigrid Storråda," Great Ulf shouted, his broken tooth on display.

"To the health of the queen," the guests responded, raising their horns and cups.

Jarl Birger stepped off the platform and handed her a full goblet. She caught Bjornar and Litobor's surprised glance. At the courts in Ostrów Lednicki and Poznań, matters of the marriage bed were handled with discretion. Wilkomir wouldn't meet her eyes, and Geivar's face was hidden in shadows.

"A toast, to all the swords under my husband's command," she said, and took a drink of the mead. Strong and thick.

"Beautiful are Freya and our lady," the slightly drunk Icelandic bard was shouting. "Golden-eyed, golden-haired, golden-fingered! . . ."

"Silvertongue, if you start a song about his wife's beauty without your king present, my husband will rhyme you with the clang of his blade," she responded cheerfully. "You'll know with your own skin why they call him Eric the Victorious." She took another sip of the mead and handed the goblet back to Birger. She gave Ulf a sign that they were walking on. Shouts of flattery followed her.

She needed the noise they made, to give her courage. Great Ulf closed the doors of the bedchamber behind her. Silence fell.

Eric was waiting in bed.

Be like Oda tonight, she commanded herself. *Like Oda.*

"Will you drink, my lord?" she asked, making her voice sound gentle.

"From you," he murmured, and his eyes gleamed in the dark.

She poured some mead for herself and walked to the bed. She leaned against its sculpted frame and, drinking, looked at Eric. Light reflected off his bald skull.

"Come to me," he demanded.

"What's the hurry, husband?"

"I want you."

Eloquent, she thought, sneering internally.

"Are you already prepared?" she cocked her head, trying to remember what else Oda had done that night.

"Why don't you check, my lady," he said, sitting up.

She'd walked. She'd walked all around the bed like a cat. Oda's image came to her just in time.

Świętosława set the goblet down and let the fur slip from one shoulder, revealing the bare skin under her nightdress. She walked toward the bed with slow, languid steps. The king's eyes followed her, his breath quickening. When she was within reach, he began to take his shirt off.

"No, my lord," she whispered. "Allow me."

This took her husband by surprise, and she stepped onto the bed as if she were climbing a stair. She leaned over Eric so her hair brushed gently against his bare head. She took off his shirt slowly. She smelled the sharp tang of his sweat and for a moment, she felt faint. She wanted more mead, but the goblet was too far now. She knelt opposite her husband. She stroked his chest.

"Sigrid . . ." he whispered fervently. "I want . . ."

She kissed his broad chest lightly, then lightly jumped off the bed. She leaned down to pick up her goblet.

"Here." She gave it to him.

"Not mead. I want you."

"How much?" She drank some herself, greedily.

"Like I've never wanted anyone before."

With the mead, the memories continued to flow; she was in the unused vent with Bolesław, watching Oda and Mieszko through a crack in the wall.

"Say it again," she demanded with a slow smile.

"Like I've never wanted anyone before. Come here. Do you want me to beg?"

"Yes," she said, shaking out her hair. "Beg, my king."

"Please." A note of impatience crept into his voice.

Świętosława knew not to play with fire. She came back to bed and sat down on top of him.

"What are you doing?" he asked, surprised.

In all their times together, Eric had been the one to take her, never the other way around. She untied his trousers now with nimble fingers. She laughed without raising her head.

"I see you are indeed ready, my king."

She held him in her hand. Eric's powerful sword. Then she realized, in a moment of panic, that she didn't know what to do next. She had no idea how Oda had sat down on her father, she'd only seen them from behind. Thankfully, Eric seemed to know what to do. He grabbed her by the waist and pulled her on top of himself. She cried out and trembled. It felt as if he'd pierced her straight through. He held her hips and rocked her forward. But no—in the palatium, Oda had ridden her father, not he her. Świętosława pulled his hands from her hips, leaned over him and, overcoming the piercing pain, she began to move herself. As if she were in a saddle. Up and down. Eric writhed and moaned under her. She was sweating. Without stopping, she let the fur slip from her shoulders. When she lowered her head, her hair stroked Eric's chest. The scent of his sweat was sharp, but it no longer disgusted her. Quite the opposite; she breathed him in, and it made her dance faster on top of him. And that was when she realized she no longer felt pain. She could feel him inside her, but not that piercing pain.

Don't lean forward in the saddle. Sit up straight! the lessons from when she first learned to ride came to her now. *You must lead the horse, not the other way around.*

She straightened. Eric was a hurtling stallion, bucking underneath her. She leaned on his chest to regain her balance. Canter, canter, gallop.

Her mount shivered, reared up, and threw her from the saddle. She landed softly on the bed. There was a buzzing sound in her head, but she could hear his ragged breathing. The smell of sweat surrounded them. His and hers.

"Sigrid," he said, catching his breath with difficulty. "I sang the 'Song of the Mighty' in your arms. I should pay you morgengold a second time after a night like this."

"There's nothing you should do, husband," she replied quietly. "But you can do everything," she added after a long pause.

"And what shall I start with?" he asked.

"Mead." The honest answer slipped out of her.

Eric rose and handed her the goblet. Only when she took it from him did she realize something had changed between them. She took a swallow of the mead and handed the goblet to Eric.

"You know that I'll ride out against Sven," he said. "I'll keep my word to your lord father."

A wave of relief rushed through her, but she only raised her eyebrows, feigning surprise.

"I was never going to ask that of you, husband. It never occurred to me you might break your word and mar your honor."

"So what do you want, then?"

"You," she lied, and embraced him with a smile. The scent of his sweat didn't push her away anymore. Instead, it seemed to draw her closer, with a dark, dangerous note. "You," she repeated, meaning it this time.

He laughed throatily and put an arm around her, bringing her close. He stroked her breasts, kissed her lips, then her forehead.

"I never thought I would say this," he said, still holding her to him, "but what you've done with me is enough for one night, Sigrid."

"We have many nights before us, Eric."

"Just enough to make sure I don't turn into a moldering old man." He laughed.

"And even if you do, I'll nurse you."

"Never. A man must die when he's in full strength. A death should be like life."

"What do you mean?" she asked, sensing there was more to his words.

"No more than I've said," he replied shortly, unwilling to give her the true answer. "I ask again, what did you want to ask me for, Sigrid?"

"To fulfill one of your other wedding promises. You said you would never stand between me and Christ."

"I did promise that." His rough fingers played with the softness of her skin.

"There is a temple at the bottom of the mounds that I must pass every day on my way to prayer. This stands between me and the God I worship. And the sacrificial grove, where the trees grow corpses instead of fruit."

"I won't burn the temple," he said calmly.

"And I wouldn't ask you to, my lord. Build me a new manor, in a different place. Somewhere I can breathe clean air, close to water. Where I can awake to sounds other than that of the crows pecking at the sacrifices to your gods."

"Doesn't your god accept sacrifices?" he asked, his finger tracing her nipple.

"Quite the opposite, Eric. My god sacrificed his son for all sinners. He saved our souls from endless darkness."

"And he wants nothing in return?"

"He wants love and loyalty. He doesn't accept sacrifices where one takes a life, but by giving life."

"A strange god, though I doubt he's harmful." Eric's powerful shoulders rose and fell as he shrugged. "Perhaps I could accept him, but it wouldn't be to my people's liking, or that of the priests of Odin."

"When my father was baptized, there was a sacred grove with priests near every village. The priests rose up against him. They threatened him with godly anger and retribution, shouting that the people wouldn't forget. But Mieszko was afraid of nothing. First, the statues of the gods disappeared, and then, so did the priests. Quietly, with no shouting. He left the groves where they stood. What harm could trees do? So, people came to empty groves and brought their sacrifices. They saw that birds pecked the peas and grits they left under the trees. Deer ate their apples. Mead attracted only wasps. They understood that since the statues were gone, so were the gods who accepted sacrifices. They came less and less frequently, until they finally stopped coming at all."

"An interesting story," he whispered into her ear. "Where did the priests disappear to?"

She laughed and bit his shoulder playfully.

"So big and yet so childish! Mieszko killed them. But he made sure it wasn't a public butchery, to ensure the people didn't rise against him. They simply disappeared, one by one. A rumor began that the god known as Almighty had defeated them. And that my father is the almighty one in his country is, I think, quite clear."

"And the statues?"

"Old wood burns easily." She caressed his back.

"What did your father get in return? What has this new god given him?"

"So much that it's hard to name it all in one breath. My mother, the duchess Dobrawa. Bolesław and me . . ."

"Do not mock me. You know what I'm asking."

"He gave him unbridled power over his people. One god, one ruler. The Almighty blessed the dynasty. Since the day of his baptism, my father has won every battle he's fought."

Eric laughed.

"Do you see, Sigrid? Everything always comes back to victory in the end. Odin aids me, Christ supports Mieszko. Maybe your god doesn't need payment in the form of life from kings, but . . ."

She grabbed his shoulder and squeezed.

"Husband, tell me the truth. What did you promise your Odin in return for victory in the fields of Fyrisvellir? I heard your bard."

They looked into each other's eyes. She could see that he wasn't going to answer, and a cold fear took root in her belly.

"None of your concern, Sigrid. I couldn't promise him something that wasn't already his. Odin is not your god, my sacrifices aren't yours."

And yet he's told me much, she thought, her eyes not leaving his.

"I will summon the army in a few days. We will sail for Denmark and defeat Sven, son of Harald Bluetooth. When I return, I'll take you to a place by Mälaren Bay, known as Sigtuna. If you decide there is enough fresh air and water there, I'll have a new royal manor built for you."

"And a chapel," she added. "I'll await your return, Eric."

The hall was silent as Great Ulf walked Świętosława back to her bedchamber. Her father's messengers had fallen asleep on the benches and the platforms next to walls. Bjornar, her brother's friend, rose as she approached.

"May I have a word, my queen?" he asked.

She glanced around the hall.

"We can speak here," she said. "Apart from us and the ones you came with, there is no one who speaks our tongue." Birger could, of course, but he was likely sleeping peacefully this time of night.

She gave Ulf a sign to sit down and have some mead.

"Your husband will move against . . ."

"Don't speak any names of people or places. They sound the same in every tongue," she warned.

"Like your son's name and . . ."

"Does he know?" she asked. "Is that why he sends me lynxes? For remembering him when I named my son?"

"I don't know the language of love, my lady."

"Is he happy with my sister?"

"She miscarried."

Świętosława wanted to feel pity at this news, but she felt none.

"And my other sister?"

"Astrid is ensuring her husband is a good jarl of the ocean stronghold."

"Tell her I miss her. If she can ever leave her grandfather's port, I would happily welcome her here. Tell me about my brother. A third wife!"

"A second wife," he corrected. "The small Bavarian one, as you may recall, was sent home before the wedding. The Hungarian one died, and her son has remained at court. He has beautiful wet nurses, your brother picks each one himself. And his new wife is a Slav from the Sorbian March. A good Christian and a lady as beautiful as a sunrise."

"Do her husband's dogs like her?" she asked, teasing.

"Dogs, cats, horses, the servants, the old duke, and even his hawk."

"Oh, that must be a great love! And the duchess Icicle?"

"She has shown no malice toward the new princess."

"Maybe she's ill? I'm beginning to worry about the poor thing. Perhaps she's beginning to lose form?"

"Quite the opposite. I know you won't be concerned to hear she lost her younger son to a fever."

"You guessed right, I won't mourn her cubs."

"You wouldn't have had time, because she's already given the Hawk another son. Let's say that motherhood and working on the lord duke to avenge her father's death are keeping her occupied."

"Is she successful?"

Bjornar laughed so openly that she felt for a moment as if they were young again, back home in her own country and on a hunt in the Notecka Wilderness.

"Your lord father has decided to make the most of favorable winds and your brother's unfailing strength. The duke is marching south, claiming the richest lands step by step, pushing back the Czechs and his old brother-in-law. Taking over mines of silver, ore, and the trade route as he goes."

"Śląsk beyond the Oder?" she squealed happily.

"You lost," Bjornar laughed. "You said a name first."

"Forget it. 'Śląsk' sounds to my scar-decorated guard the same as every other rustling sound in our language. Oh, the Old Hawk! I've missed his greed. It won't be long and, thanks to my husband, my father's dream of destroying the power of . . ." she struggled to find another word for "Denmark."

"The redbeard's country," Bjornar suggested, enjoying their game. "The young king has redder hair than I do."

"I don't believe that. He'd have to be a squirrel's son, and I don't know a people who would bow to a redtail."

"Your husband won't fail?" Bjornar asked, bringing them back to the real reason they were having this discussion.

"No. For him, a word once given is a gift you don't take back," Świętosława said solemnly.

Bjornar sighed with relief.

"What do you want me to tell your father and brother?" he asked softly, warmly, as if he himself was a brother to her. "What is life at this court truly like for you, at this manor that can only be reached on paths between the burial mounds of pagan kings? Under an oak laden with the corpses of humans and animals alike? In the shadow of the temple of the One-Eyed?"

Świętosława took a deep breath, answering with a question of her own.

"What have your eyes seen? What have your ears heard?"

"My eyes have seen a Viking queen, decorated with jewels, silks, and expensive furs. More beautiful than the girl who boarded the *Haughty Giantess*, the ship with a golden boar on its mast. They saw her son, treated with the respect a future king deserves. My ears heard the toasts given in her name, with honest love and fervent admiration."

"Tell them that."

He nodded. "Your father will be proud of you, my lady." Then he winked at her, not like a messenger, but like a childhood friend. "I know of no other country in which a sharp tongue and untempered character would be a queen's strengths. You are fortunate."

"Is that what you truly believe?" she asked, the smile slipping from her face.

She signaled to Ulf then. His scarred head had been swaying from side to side as he fought sleep. It was nearly morning now. The scarred man walked Świętosława to her bedchamber, which she entered alone. She stood with her back to the door, eyes closed in relief.

Dusza rubbed sleep from her eyes. Little Olof was in her arms, they'd fallen asleep in the big bed. Świętosława stopped her from rising with a gesture.

Świętosława took off the polar fox fur and approached the cage with the lynxes. They watched her with mistrustful green and gold eyes. She picked up a bowl with meat. It had dried since the evening before. She licked a strip of raw lamb, then slid it between the bars of the cage. They threw themselves at the meat, ripping it from her fingers. She picked up another piece. She licked it and fed her cats. They ate hungrily. She fed them piece by piece until her knees had gone numb from kneeling on the hard floor. Finally, fed and sated, they began to purr and close their eyes. She opened the cage and slid a hand inside. She touched the soft fur on one head, then the other. They meowed, and Olof began to cry at the noise. She closed the cage and walked over to the bed. She lay down beside her son and gave him a breast. He sucked hungrily. She caressed his bald head and listened to the lynxes settling once more in their cage.

"He wants me to know what it's like to love a live animal," she said, repeating what Olav had said through Geivar.

She felt a stab in her belly. As she drifted toward sleep, she thought of her family. About Geira, who had miscarried. Bolesław's wild and dead wife. His firstborn, who would grow up without a mother. Eric, whose secret she was afraid to uncover. Olav, who had lost a child in her sister's womb and who hunted dangerous cats for her to tame.

A few hours later, she rose quietly, trying not to wake her son. She walked to the lynx fur which was draped over a bench. The one she'd worn so often. The one which made her feel stronger. She folded it gently and placed it in a chest. She couldn't wear the skin of an animal she wanted to tame.

19

POLAND

Olav felt relief every time he got the chance to ride away from his home.

He was the viceroy of Pomerelia now, with a home on the Baltic shore, so he could no longer complain that he felt like a fish out of water. But he was. His days were spent overseeing the construction of the port and guarding the shoreline from potential attacks. Olav didn't neglect either task, but day after day felt the same. His life was a continuous cycle of grayness and ennui.

There was no danger from the north; an alliance with Eric was ensured by Świętosława's marriage. Pirates from the east had visited once, but, hungry for battle, Olav had chased them as far as Truso, catching them in the Vistula Lagoon. A cloud of burning arrows, let loose by his men, had turned them into floating torches, which sank, leaving behind nothing but trails of black smoke. Dozens of fishermen watched from the shore.

After this, Olav became known as "The One Who Burns Ships," and the attacks on his shore ended. Now, he was left with only fantasies—imagining the great duke Mieszko breaking his alliance with Eric, calling on Olav to lead a fleet to vanquish Świętosława's husband and bring her back. Dreams. Mieszko had no fleet. He had married Astrid to Sigvald, and the old Danish king had died, so Mieszko had the iron boys of Jomsborg, and that was enough for him.

Bolesław and Świętosława's words came back to him, like the steadying sound of oars cutting through water: *"Imagine your father, then, but don't regret not knowing him. Ours rules us as if we were an extension of the arms he uses to play his games."* Yes, Mieszko had placed them on the game board like troops before a battle. Astrid and Sigvald watched over the unsettled western shores. He and Geira were responsible for the eastern one, which was as spitefully calm as a calf near its mother. Świętosława guaranteed peace in the north. Bolesław, an extension of his father's strength, conquered the south.

It wasn't enough for Olav. He had his crew still. Vikarr, Torfi, Lodver, Ingvar, Orm, Ottar, Eyvind, Rafn, Thorolf, and Omold the bard had stayed with him. Varin was his right hand. Geivar had gone to be a chieftain in Jom.

Kanugård had regained mobility a long time ago. Olav built new ships, like the *Kanugård*, though this wasn't easy at first, due to the lack of experienced shipwrights. Only once Astrid had sent some of her grandfather's masters from Wolin did the hulls of the ships begin to take shape. Olav had twelve now, and this was only the beginning. He trained sailors, looking for good crews, and he never stopped thinking of Norway, of his exiled mother and his rightful throne, not even for a day. He wanted to be ready. He sailed to Wolin and Truso, he talked to sailors, sought out information. He knew that Jarl Haakon in Lade still had a strong hold on the Norwegian people. Love for a victorious ruler was strong.

"Your time will come," Geira kept telling him, seeing his frown whenever news like this was delivered from Norway. He felt gratitude toward her; she had helped him find his mother. Geira was the one who'd made it possible for him to take his mother in his arms, to find out what a son should know of the father who had been killed before he'd even been born. Killed by the widow Gunhild, from whom his mother Astrid had escaped and saved his life. Geira was sweet. As sweet as honey eaten by the spoonful. But her efforts to gain his love only pushed him further away. Too much gratitude has a bitter aftertaste, but Geira was oblivious to this. When she miscarried, she had cried and apologized to him. Inside, Olav had felt quietly relieved, though he never shared this with his wife. She was soon pregnant again, and like a child whose moods change rapidly, the tears were replaced with unbridled joy. Thankfully, this was the moment Thorolf arrived, bringing news that was like water in a drought to Olav's ears.

"War, my lord," Thorolf shouted, as soon as he walked into the hall of Gdańsk's manor.

Geira trembled and placed a hand on her still-flat belly.

"Don't scare my wife, Thorolf," Olav said, but his eyes shone. "Geira, don't be afraid. War is like a breath of fresh air for a man."

"You're my fresh air. If you sail out, how will I breathe?"

Thorolf glanced at Olav, surprised, murmured an apology, and withdrew.

"Don't say that," Olav said, hoping to calm her. "Most of your life was lived without me by your side."

"I don't remember anything that was before you. I beg you, don't leave me . . ."

"Geira, I have pledged my loyalty to your father," Olav said, using the argument he knew she could not deny.

"And you pledged your love to me!" she shouted through tears.

Not love, but care, he thought, though he kept that to himself, too.

"War is not women's business, wife. Duke Mieszko summons me. Forgive me." He ended the conversation and left.

Thorolf was waiting at the port.

"I envied you your wife, my lord, but I don't anymore," he said bluntly.

"I don't think I'm made for a quiet life," Olav said, unwilling to say anything against Geira. The wife he didn't love but to whom he owed so much. "Tell me what you know."

"King Eric has answered Duke Mieszko's summons. He is gathering a fleet and will strike Denmark any day. We are to join forces with him in Bornholm, then the Jomsvikings will join us."

"Then it is time for us to put these new ships to the test."

It was good to feel wind in the sails again. *Kanugård* leapt over the waves as if it had never been touched by a storm. The storm that had led Olav to Świętosława. Everything reminded him of her. And now, damn him, her husband stood at his side as an ally.

Meanwhile, Mieszko was fighting his old brother-in-law in the south, the prince of the Czechs, and had placed Olav in charge of the northern excursion. Mieszko trusted Eric, but a massive fleet of foreign ships at your shores is never a safe thing, especially when their forces differed so much in number. Olav had twenty ships. The Jomsvikings promised fifty. Eric sent two hundred. He knew how to make a statement.

"He knows how to make a statement." Varin had echoed Olav's thoughts and clicked his tongue with admiration when the majestic *Golden Boar* came into view, leading the huge fleet behind it.

During their midday chieftains' meeting, Olav's eyes never left Eric, who, as a king and main supplier of ships and men, hosted the meeting in his tent, sheltered from the winds by the rocks on Bornholm's shores.

"You keep an eye on the king," Varin had whispered to him, "and I'll keep one on you, my lord. Forgive me, but I won't let you do anything you might regret later."

"How do you know I'd regret it?" Olav asked just as quietly.

"Because I am older and wiser than you, my lord."

Varin and Geivar knew of his feelings for Świętosława. How? Olav had never spoken of them to anyone. Geivar claimed it was enough to see the way they had looked at each other the day the duke's daughter had sailed from Wolin with Jarl Birger. Now, as Olav stood opposite Eric at the meeting, as he studied the king's powerful frame, he couldn't rid himself of the thought that it was this bald, bearded man who bedded Świętosława, and he felt Varin's hand on his back. He gritted his teeth and focused on their plans. The sea is treacherous, everyone knew that.

They sailed out the next morning. Olav's twenty ships, a mere tenth of what Eric commanded, were on the left flank. Jomsborg scouts joined them on the way. Olav couldn't make out Geivar's drakkar among their number, but his old friend recognized *Kanugård* by its golden weather vane and approached his ship.

"It's good to see you at the helm, old friend," Olav shouted.

"And you, Olav. The new king Sven has gathered his forces in Scania. Once we pass Rügen, we must take extra care."

"What of his forces?"

"My scouts have spoken of two, possibly three hundred ships. I don't know if the Danes will decide on open battle, or if Sven will wait for us in the bays. He may try to drag us onto land where we're weaker."

"Where's Sigvald?" Olav had yet to see his other brother-in-law amid the fleet.

"On the *Zealand Falcon*. He'll sail at our back, in case Sven tries to trap us in the straits and attack from behind."

Wars of the lands, wars of the seas; Olav was under no illusions that he was fighting his own battles. Once more, as it had been with Vladimir, he was the mercenary of gratitude. If at least he loved Geira, he might have convinced himself he was doing this for her. His love for Świętosława was powerful, but its strength was like a mountain avalanche. Destructive. Eric might die, and so what? What kind of person would he be if he abandoned one sister for the other?

His eyes searched the bays, his hand directed *Kanugård*, and his body didn't betray him, though his mind was feverish and burning. *My life is still not my own.*

Mieszko had commanded Olav to keep his heritage a secret: "The sole heir to the Norwegian throne—between the forces of Denmark and Sweden— might be too tempting for one of their kings. You won't lose your name sim- ply by keeping it to yourself for a while longer. Now you are Olav, Mieszko's son-in-law, which is more than enough reason for you to be one of my chiefs. Don't tempt fate, and the day when you'll be known as Olav Tryggvason will come sooner than you think."

My life is still not my own, but I can influence the lives of my people.

His eyes caught movement by the broken line of the shore.

"Ships on the left!" he shouted. "Shields on board!"

Sails appeared from behind the rocks, one after another. They seemed endless. A long line of colored points. When they were two arrow shots from each other, Olav and his companions could make out the shields.

"Thorgils of Jelling, Stenkil of Hobro." Geivar's Jomsvikings called out the names of their enemies. "Gunar of Limfiord."

"Do you see Sven's ship?" Harald's son would be desperate for a victory that would help him further secure his seat on the Danish throne. He was a formidable adversary with no ties to Duke Mieszko, who had no more daughters to marry off to establish an alliance with Denmark. The only way to keep Sven and Denmark safely contained was war. So, Mieszko had summoned his sons-in-law, and there they were—Olav, Sigvald, and Eric, all of them united, fighting for the Piast leader.

"No, not Sven's ship."

Olav continued to watch his brother-in-law, the Swedish king, as their fleets progressed. The ships under the golden boar were sailing evenly. Eric's men were nimbly placing shields on their gunwales. One might say many things about him, but it seemed that Eric knew what he was doing in a war at sea.

"Don't be afraid, King," Varin whispered. This was the title Varin used for Olav when they were out of earshot. "There'll be enough fight to go around. We'll absorb the first hit."

Olav laughed then, breathing in the wet, salty air. They needed to say no more; they missed spilling blood.

"Archers," Olav gave the command and waited for the ships to approach to avoid wasting arrows. "Now! Shields!"

He knew their enemy would do the same. The volleys passed each other in midair, and a moment after they'd released their own arrows, a hailstorm hit *Kanugård*. The crew ducked beneath their shields as the arrows rained down.

"Archers," Olav shouted and pulled the helm firmly, guiding the boat into the strongest position he could. "Fire!"

Ingvar shielded him, and he was the one to shout:

"Chief, they are driving a wedge into Eric's right wing."

Olav, protected under Ingvar's shield, ran to the other side of the ship.

Yes. A new, long snake of ships was sailing toward Eric, spitting venomous arrows as it went.

"We still outnumber them," Olav decided, returning to his place at the helm.

Geivar approached the left gunwale.

"Can you see the long ship with a horse head on its bow?" he called over the noise. "That's *Gorgeous Gunhild.*"

"She looks more like a *Bloody Whore*. She has a tatty stem as if she's been battering her whole life," Olav shouted back.

"Old Frorik from Funen is her helmsman. He'd always been in love with Gunhild, King Harald Bluetooth's sister."

"*That* Gunhild?"

"The one and only, my friend."

Olav ducked as an arrow flew by his chest. That Gunhild. The bloody widow who had sentenced his father to death. The one who had sent one hundred armed men in search of his pregnant mother.

His grip on the helm tightened as he steered the *Kanugård* toward the *Gorgeous Gunhild*. When they reached its side, Olav and most of his crew boarded the *Gunhild*, before the other ship could properly comprehend what was happening. They hadn't seen this coming; this wasn't the type of battle at sea they had prepared for. Once on board, Olav fought with a fury he really let himself feel. When he reached Frorik from Funen, the bloody ship's captain, he told him his name—Olav Tryggvason—and why he had come to kill him, but only once he was certain the enemy could never repeat it. He whispered it as he slid his sword out of the man's chest.

"Where's King Sven?" he asked Frorik's companion, the last one alive on the *Gorgeous Gunhild*.

"Not here, my lord." Frorik's veiny comrade was so old that he felt no fear in the face of death.

"Where is Sven?" Olav roared, grabbing the old man by the chain mail. "Did he run? A coward?"

The old man laughed and spat.

"Just the opposite, pale one. Redheaded Sven will plunge his Jomsborg sword into your sterns. You've lost!"

The laughter caught in his throat. He died without closing his eyes.

Sven, under the cover of his grandfather Mściwój's Obotrite ships, safely sailed out of Rügen's bay as soon as Eric's long snake of ships passed westward. His chiefs could manage the first and second collisions with the enemy without him. They had to. They had to last until he returned with backup. Jarl Haakon of Funen, Thorgil of Jelling, and Gunar of Limfiord, those he was sure of; he knew they were strong enough to defend themselves, and cunning enough to escape death. But what about Ragn of the Isles, Stenkil of Hobro, and the others? If all went well, he would know by early morning.

He set course for Jomsborg, and the *Bloody Fox* raced toward his allies. There wasn't much time. When they were near the stronghold, a drakkar with a Jomsborg wolf on its mast sailed out toward them. Sven had no reason to love the Jomsvikings, but for the first time he felt relief at the sight of the square wolf head. It was short-lived.

"Where is Jarl Sigvald?" he called out.

"He awaits you, my lord, in the sea stronghold."

"You speak to a king," Jorun, one of Sven's men, corrected him.

"All right," the helmsman of Jomsborg's ship replied calmly. "King, they call me Ulle. Sail with me."

"Something's not right," Jorun muttered, and Sven felt the same uneasiness in his own gut.

"Even so, we have no choice, friend. Without the Jomsvikings, we cannot defeat Eric. Sigvald promised to help, and he cannot deny us. At dawn, I should attack their backs with fifty ships of Jomsborg and close them in our deadly pincers."

He looked behind him. The Obotrite ships were still alongside the *Bloody Fox*. Their value in battle was marginal. They were useful for fishing, nothing more. But it had still taken much effort to get even this much from Mściwój. His grandfather was nearing his end. He had moments of clarity, but usually his thoughts meandered at the edges of the comprehensible world. Mściwój had chieftains who had insisted Sven marry Mojmira, the Obotrite leader's daughter, and reacted with anger when he'd sent her back to her home. If he'd known he would need their help so soon, Sven might have acted differently. But his father's death, which he'd known would change everything, had put into motion powers even he had not expected. Even his half sister, Tyra, had eagerly joined the opposition against him. His Denmark was a fat morsel which attracted many a hungry eye.

Sven and the *Bloody Fox* led their small fleet into the bay, nearing the iron gates of the stronghold within moments. The guards on the stone bridge called down to them:

"Ships and captains?"

"*Serpent* and Ulle. *Bloody Fox* and King Sven," the Jomsviking who had brought them called out.

The hellish sound of the chains and turnstile opening the massive gates drowned out Sven's question. When the noise stopped, Jorun repeated it, pointing at the Obotrite boats:

"What about them? We have another ten ships."

"They cannot enter the stronghold," Ulle replied calmly. "They can wait for you in Wolin's port. Nothing is lost at old Dalwin's." He laughed and added: "And the beer is better there, too."

And so the *Bloody Fox* waited alone for the guards to open the second gate, then sailed into the darkness beyond the stone bridge. As they entered, Sven studied the shore carefully. He counted the ships. Fifty. It would be enough, he thought with relief. They moored their ship to the long dock.

"It isn't good to be among the iron boys alone," Jorun muttered, placing a hand on his sword discreetly.

"It isn't good for a king to beg for help during a battle," Sven replied, then turned and walked from the ship as if he felt no fear.

A smiling Jarl Sigvald was walking toward their dock.

"Welcome to Jomsborg, new king of Denmark. We have been waiting for you with dinner, my lord, and for your companions. Come with me to the house of chiefs."

None of the other chiefs Sven knew accompanied Sigvald. Not Geivar, or Thorkel the Tall. The feeling of unease stayed with Sven. Boys waited in the entrance hall to take their weapons. Sigvald gave up his sword and knife first, the smile never leaving his face.

"Our meal has arrived today from the best of Wolin's inns. Smoked geese, boar legs baked with plums, marinated herring. And what else? Ah, eels. My wife, Astrid, personally oversaw the cooking. We don't usually have the honor of hosting a king. The last one . . ." Sigvald smiled apologetically. "That's rather a bad comparison. The last one died in our care, but that was expected by you, wasn't it, Sven?"

At the host's invitation, Sven sat down at the long table laiden with food. Sven recalled that there were no servants in Jom. A jug of mead stood by every place setting, and the guests served themselves.

"Thank you for the meal," Sven said as they began to eat. "I appreciate the show of welcome, but I didn't come here as a guest. Eric's fleet has sailed into Danish waters and even now may be fighting my men. I cannot linger."

"I am aware, King." Sigvald handed Sven a dish. "I have sent my scouts after them under Geivar's command."

"And?" Sven swallowed a piece of roasted meat. He wasn't hungry; he ate only out of politeness.

"They are following the movements of the massive Swedish fleet. Or, if you prefer, the fleet of the one known as the Massive Swede." He could only be referring to King Eric, the great bald beast of a man, and the light tone with which the Jomsviking spoke of Denmark's enemy did nothing to settle Sven's uneasiness.

"You promised me fifty war drakkars, Jarl," he said, having had enough of the wordplay. He wanted to fight his enemies, not jest behind their backs.

"They are waiting in port, King." Sigvald smiled. "Armed and ready. Did you not see them?"

"Their place is on the open waters. Let us sail before it's too late."

"It's never too late. Wine? Arabian merchants came to Wolin with cargo in the shape of molten gold. Try some, my lord."

"Jarl Sigvald, my patience is limited."

"I promised fifty ships, and I have them," the Jomsviking leader reassured him, lifting his glass. "The health of the king!"

Sven drank. The wine seemed strangely acrid.

"Where is your brother, Thorkel the Tall?" he asked the jarl. Sven knew Thorkel, and trusted him far more than he did Sigvald.

"He's not in Jom. We had a commission," Sigvald replied evasively. "As you know, King, the iron boys aren't ones to boast of what they do. They simply get it done. I can say only that Thorkel's mission has nothing to do with your business here. Oh, if you must know! He's sailed to England. Does that reassure you, King?" Sigvald had neither lowered his goblet nor taken a drink from it.

"I had assumed he would fight on my behalf," Sven said. "Where are the other house chiefs?"

"Geivar, as I already mentioned, is watching Eric's movements. There are no others. I command the full stronghold."

"Have you not named new chieftains of the other houses? Two are free, last I heard."

"There is no need. More wine?" The host reached for the jug.

Sven shook his head.

"No, thank you, that's enough. The feast is over. Let's go." Sven rose from the table, followed by Jorun and the rest of his crew.

"Forgive me, King, but I am lord here." Sigvald's smile disappeared.

"You forget that you speak to a king, Jarl," Jorun said quietly, anger clear in his voice.

"Jomsborg recognizes no kings. Harald was the first, and the last. He died in the Sacred Site," Sigvald replied, looking up at them from the bench, his goblet in hand.

The jarl was still sitting, though Sven was on his feet. The message was clear.

"Is that a threat?" Jorun asked on Sven's behalf.

"No. A fact," Sigvald answered.

Sven knew that if it came to a fight, they would lose. His twelve men against all of Jom? Besides, he hadn't come here to fight, but for aid in a war. It took all his self-control to answer Sigvald calmly. The emotions coursing through him could only worsen their position.

"Forgive me if I offended your dignity, Jarl. I am a warrior king, not a smooth-tongued courtier. You know why we're here, and surely you can understand our impatience. Please, give me the fifty drakkars as promised, I need to lead them out of Jom at once."

Sigvald looked at him with a look of surprise that Sven might have sworn was a true one, if not for the feeling of mistrust Sven felt at his core.

"You misunderstood, King," the jarl said, looking the king in his eyes. "I promised fifty longboats, and I keep my word. But there was no talk of you commanding them. The Jomsvikings will not sail under anyone else's orders. I will lead them, and you will be my guest in Jom until the war is over."

Sven's crew began to mutter behind him. Jorun reached for his knife; only when he touched an empty belt did he check himself. Sven, simmering now, felt a laugh escape his lips. He was nearly hysterical. How could this be happening?

"A guest or a hostage?" he asked. "Whose side are you on, Sigvald?"

It was the jarl's turn to bark a laugh.

"That is up to you, my lord, whether you'll feel like a guest or hostage in Jom. I give you the house of chiefs for the duration of your stay. And my men, as your royal guard. You will want for nothing, they will give you whatever you ask. Apart from women, considering our laws. And if you ask whose side I'm on, I'll draw your attention to who my wife is; I have no intention of angering her, or her family. And now, forgive me, my lord, but the drakkars await."

With that, Sigvald turned and left the hall. When the doors slammed closed, Sven collapsed onto the bench. Jorun poured him wine; it tasted even more acrid than during the meal.

"There are new loyalties in Jomsborg," Jorun observed gloomily. "Mieszko's sons-in-law have made fools of us. Eric and Sigvald."

Sven recalled now that it was in this very hall that Palnatoki, the most beloved of the old Jomsvikings and the man Sven had trusted like a father, had told him of the Piast duke's daughters.

"And who's the third?" he asked. "Who did Geira marry?"

20

POLAND

Mieszko had many reasons to celebrate, but the pain in his lower back caused him to push back the feast again, and again. A feast for which guests had already arrived. But he was unable to drag himself out of bed.

Oda came into the room almost soundlessly. He watched her for a moment from beneath half-open eyelids. She placed a jug of fresh mead and a bouquet of flowers on the table; she laid out a new towel and threw the old one into the washing basket. She walked to the perch his hawk was sleeping on and reached out a hand. It pecked her gently.

"Do you feed it, wife?"

The duchess flinched at his voice. "You're awake, my king? No, I don't feed it, how could you think that, my lord?" She approached the bed and studied him with care. "Are you still in pain?"

"It's passing," he lied. "I'll rest, then we can invite the guests."

She smiled, a look of relief on her face.

"Astrid has arrived, with a few men from Wolin," she said, stroking his unshaven cheek.

"Astrid? Tell her to come to me, I want to speak to my daughter."

"Before the feast?" A flash of displeasure crossed Oda's face. She hid it quickly, adding: "As you wish, husband," leaning down to kiss his forehead.

That's how you kiss an old man, he snorted to himself, watching her go.

"My lord." Astrid appeared moments later.

He could see at once that she brought good news. He tried to raise himself into a sitting position. He hissed in pain. Astrid knelt by the bed and helped him prop himself up.

"What's wrong, my lord?" she asked, her eyebrows drawn together with concern.

"They say that old age doesn't hurt." He forced a smile. "So this is probably something else."

"Will you let me examine you?"

"What else do you want from me? Isn't it enough that Oda is putting some monastic creams on me, which take away pain as quickly as they steal my clarity of thought . . ."

Astrid was watching him so intently that he burst out laughing.

"Everything's all right with my head, daughter."

"I never thought otherwise, but I know there are herbs which ease pain at the price of reason."

"You were going to stop with herbs," he protested sharply. "That's good for forest women, but not for a duke's daughter. It didn't help your mother, either."

"You never talk about her," she said quietly, shyly.

"But the older I get, the more frequently I think of her," Mieszko said, his voice unexpectedly light. "Give me the mead."

She rose to fill his goblet.

"Dalwin also had me bring you some Italian wine."

"Good, we can have it during the feast. There is much to celebrate, daughter." He took a gulp of mead and asked her to pour some for herself. "Let's drink to my greatest success. I'm a fisherman who has cast his net and the bait. And Empress Theophanu has taken it and helped me catch a beautiful, fat fish."

"Father." Astrid's eyes betrayed her unease. "I don't understand."

He laughed.

"You're not the only one. I think that not even Theophanu knows how it was that with her blessing and the help of Saxon soldiers, who she so loyally sent to me, I took Upper Silesia, Lesser Poland with Kraków, and now Bolesław has almost finished adding Moravia to our lands."

He lifted his goblet and took a sip.

He could drink to that for weeks. A victory on the battlefield was always dizzying. The heart beats so loudly it drowns out the shouts. Senses of sight and hearing are sharpened, the body shivers as though one were finishing inside a woman. But it was nothing compared to a diplomatic triumph.

The Ottonian empire: Theophanu and her entourage. The arrogant Saxon lords, who never tired of showing him he was lesser, a barbarian they must tolerate in their bright marble palatiums. They were surprised that, while they focused on their small wars, he, without asking anyone's advice, much less permission, had accepted God's word and baptism in running water, of his own free will.

They didn't look to the east, as if the civilized world ended at the Oder, and the band of thick dark forests indicated only wild men living beyond. They didn't see him for a long time; and one day, an Arabian merchant enlightened them to the existence of Mieszko, the ruler of lands between the Vistula and Oder rivers. The lord and leader of three thousand well-equipped heavy-armed soldiers, and ten thousand light-armed cavalrymen. The duke whose men even the Saxons had to admit were a force to be reckoned with. And now, after years of warring and maneuvering, he had proven to both them and himself that he was not only a master of the battlefield, but also of courtly intrigues.

He drank the goblet's contents. Time passed so quickly. Thirty years of ruling had gone by as if it had been merely a week. His father's death, and the torch he used to light the funeral pyre. And his brothers' deaths, Czcibor's and Dobronieg's. His hawk had still been a chick then. It was funny, but he'd had an eagle chick first, and decided he wouldn't let it die, he'd tame it and teach it to hunt. But his eagle . . . what had happened to it? And why not an eagle but a hawk? Oh, yes. Czcibor had said that an eagle cannot be tamed. No, it hadn't been Czcibor. Someone else. Or when Dobrawa had come to Poznań. Her procession seemed endless, and she . . .

"The feast that Duchess Oda mentioned is to celebrate the victories in Silesia and Moravia?" Astrid smiled at him with her mother's eyes. She'd been a remarkable woman . . . but what was her name? . . . and when had it been? . . .

"Pour me some more, child." He offered her the goblet. "What are you asking about?" His daughter's face was beginning to swim before his eyes, as if streaks of rain were smudging her image.

"About the feast, my lord."

No, it wasn't rain that smudged her face. It was the mead . . .

"Damn it!" He threw the goblet down onto the floor.

Astrid leapt up.

"What is it, Father?"

"Did you drink this mead?"

"No." She shook her head and sniffed at the contents of her goblet. "But . . . you're right, there's something wrong with it. Maybe it fermented for too long?"

"Help me get up," he decided.

Astrid offered him an arm. She was surprisingly strong, this quiet daughter of his. She pulled him up, and though he hissed in pain, once he was upright she didn't let him fall back onto the bed. He was embarrassed about his weakness in front of his daughter, but even more humiliated at his ignorance;

that he had drunk and drunk of the mead, not realizing it was to blame for his mixed-up thoughts. Astrid led him to a basin of water in the corner of the chamber.

"Pour some over my head," he ordered. "Quickly."

Astrid did as he asked, and poured out most of a full jug. The cold water covered his face, and streamed down his chest and back and along his spine.

"You're good at this," he told her.

"I've helped my husband more than once." She laughed. "The sound of the horn carries well over water. The Jomsvikings have often blown it, calling their chief, when Sigvald was finishing his dinner with me in Wolin and many drinks in."

"Another jug," he asked. "Just over my head."

After she had poured another, Mieszko shook himself. Cool needles stung him even under closed eyelids. A stream flowed from his beard.

"I didn't drink much," he said, when she wiped his face. "Only what I had since you came in."

"Don't worry, my lord. It's badly fermented mead, nothing more." She smiled kindly at him.

She only calls me *Father* on special occasions, he realized. And he answered the question she had asked him earlier.

"Yes, a feast to celebrate the great victories. Lesser Poland, Silesia, Slovakia, and Moravia. There is much to be happy about. And now, tell me what you've come with, because I can see in your eyes you have news that cannot wait."

"The Danish forces have been vanquished. Eric's army reached as far as Hedeby, and took control of the port. Sven's chiefs scattered and disappeared without trace. Sven himself is my husband's hostage in Jomsborg."

For a moment, Mieszko wondered whether his mind was playing tricks on him. No, he was sober. But he wanted to hear it again.

"Say that again, Astrid," he asked her.

"Yes. Yes, Father," she said, using the most initimate title before she could stop herself. He had seemed so vulnerable only a moment ago, so unlike the fearsome duke she'd known for most of her life. "Sven is a hostage in Jomsborg. Eric and the Swedes have scattered Sven's armies and taken Hedeby from the Danes. You were right, then, you know . . ." She was flustered again. Neither of them liked to recall that conversation. "Do you remember what you said? 'Even if Sven inherits an expansive Denmark, he will end up in a country as small as a fishing village.' Father, you were right. You gave each of your children a task, and we have all fulfilled them."

Mieszko no longer felt the pain in his lower back. He pushed himself from the bench and grabbed Astrid's face between his hands. He kissed her fore-head. She flinched in surprise.

"Where are my sons-in-law now?"

"Eric is celebrating in Hedeby. He is collecting the payment owed to a victor. Olav is keeping an eye on Eric. Sigvald is guarding Sven in Jom."

He threw back his head and began to laugh wholeheartedly.

"And your brother Bolesław is occupying Moravia. They say that a man should have many sons, but I say that there can never be enough daugh-ters. Women multiply happiness, while sons-in-law are the strength of their father-in-law, and I don't need to worry about how to divide my lands be-tween them because they themselves are adding to my victories. Astrid, you will sit on my right during the feast."

"But Duchess Oda—" she began.

"Damn Oda, her creams, her medicines, and everything else. You chased the pain away. When will you give me a grandson?" he asked, his joy making him blunt. In that moment, nothing in the world seemed more special to him than be able to watch his family and his country grow as one.

"I don't know," she said and added, meeting his eyes, "'Jarl of Jomsvikings' isn't a hereditary title. And, if we're being honest, Sigvald wouldn't make a good father. And perhaps I shouldn't be a mother. I'm sorry, my lord."

"You're talking to your father," he answered gently. This woman before him was a special one, a daughter he had often neglected. Her mother before her had been special, too. Her smile, her power, her visions of the future that she'd helped him make a reality . . .

"I'm sorry, Father," Astrid said.

"I won't deny the sense in what you say, if we are being honest," Mieszko said, smiling sadly and easing himself down to the bed again. He grabbed her hand. "But I want you to know how much I want Geira to give birth to a healthy child."

"You want to spread heirs, Father." Astrid understood the duke— her father—well. "A grandson on the Swedish throne, a grandson on the Norwegian throne . . . if you had another daughter, you'd marry her to Sven, wouldn't you?"

So clever, he thought, but he neither denied nor confirmed her words. Instead, he asked a father's favor:

"Go to Geira. She could use a sister's care while her husband is far away at war. And now, it's our time. We must both change, because Oda won't let us into the feast in such a state."

*   *   *

Astrid left Poznań fearing for her father. Since she could remember, the powerful ramparts of the borough had made her feel as if everything they surrounded was safe. Today was different. She looked up at the sky-high barricades and saw only the shadows they cast within.

No sun can reach here, she thought, and fear blossomed in her breast.

There was no one she could trust at Poznań's court, no one she could ask to keep an eye on Mieszko discreetly. If only Bolesław had been there! But he and all his men were fighting in far-off Moravia, and his new wife was making a home for them in the empty borough in Kraków. Astrid sent messengers to Wolin and Jom relaying that she was going to Gdańsk to her sister instead of heading home. She also sent word of Mieszko's order to Sigvald, to demand a ransom from Sven for his freedom.

"We can't hold the Danish king indefinitely," her father had decided. "But we can ensure that he never sits on a throne as powerful as Harald Bluetooth's. We can embarrass him in the eyes of his subjects, forcing them to pay for his freedom. We can demand so high a ransom that he will lose all honor in their eyes."

"Why not order him killed?" she asked.

"Because you don't kill kings, my child," he replied, and the words sank into her mind like a spell.

What if I send a trusted man to Bolesław? she thought. And then she berated herself: *What will I tell him? That I suspect Oda is poisoning Mieszko? We've talked of nothing else since the day she became his wife. It's the center of our cruel jokes about her. How many times have I told Świętosława not to jest like that? But this time, it's not a joke,* she told herself. *I saw it, I smelled the mead laced with henbane.*

The more afraid she was, the faster she traveled. But the dark thoughts followed, and she couldn't escape them. What if Oda was acting in good faith? Father doesn't want to admit to any weakness, and Oda might not want to show him she knows how much he suffers. She prefers to add the medicine to his mead rather than to force him to see that this is the beginning of the end. What drives her? Love, pity, or . . . ?

The intensity of her worries translated into her riding. She arrived in Gdańsk within six days, and there she found Geira over an empty cradle.

"Sister, what are you doing?" she exclaimed, in lieu of a greeting.

Geira stood up. Her fair, straight hair, once heavy and thick, was now in gray tangles. Fear shone in her eyes.

"Astrid? Is it really you?" she whispered through cracked lips. "Oh!

You've come to . . . What's happening with Olav? Is something wrong with him? No! . . ." She shook her head. "No, he can't be, he mustn't be . . ."

"Everything is all right. Olav is alive and unharmed," Astrid said quickly, seeing her sister's distress. "I've come to see you, sister."

She couldn't tell her the truth: "I've come to ensure your birth goes smoothly." She recalled Geira at their last meeting in Wolin. Cheerful, bubbling. Her older sister had never been like that before. Then she had miscarried on their way home. Word had it that she suffered the loss badly, but now she was pregnant again. The rise of her belly was clear beneath her dress.

"To see me? Really, to see me? Because you wanted to?" Geira's eyes were wide in disbelief.

"Yes, sister." Astrid summoned a happy sigh, though she felt anything but. "Are you going to make me stand in the doorway, or will you invite me to dine with you?"

The evening that followed was a pleasant one, full of laughter and memories. Astrid dug out the happiest ones she could recall, recounting them joyfully with her sister.

"Remember how Świętosława unthreaded the entire pattern on Father's banners?"

"Oh, yes! All that was left on the material was a dark shadow of it, and she convinced his squad in the morning they'd drunk poisoned mead and lost their eyesight."

"And Borzymir the flag bearer, trying to avoid admitting that he'd been drinking all night, announced that the banner was as it had always been and he'd carry it. One hundred armed men rode out against the Veleti with an unraveled banner."

"Or when Świętosława smeared honey onto Oda's stirrups and she was swarmed by wasps when she rode out?"

"Oh, Astrid." Tears of laughter streamed down Geira's cheeks. "Everything that's happy goes back to our littlest one." She wiped her eyes with the back of her hand, her expression suddenly serious. "And for me, everything connected to her ends badly."

"I don't understand," Astrid said untruthfully.

"She stole my husband."

Unable to keep feigning igonorance, Astrid decided to feign fatigue instead. "I'm very tired after my journey, sister, and you, as I hear it, are, too. Don't be angry, but I will retire to my room now."

"I'm not mad, sister. And I know what I'm saying."

I also know, but I don't want to listen to this, Astrid thought, panic flooding through her.

"Olav doesn't love me. He loves her," Geira said.

"What are you saying, sister . . ." Astrid murmured, pretending to be drunker than she was.

"It's the truth," Geira insisted. "He sleeps with me, but dreams of her. He caught a pair of lynxes for her, did you know? And he brought me back berries, as if I were a child."

"I saw you together . . . his feelings for you run deep . . ." she lied, horrified that only so recently she had envied her sister for having Olav in her life, even if she didn't have his heart.

Geira covered her belly with her arms and began to sob.

"He's smothered here . . . It isn't a life for him, I know that. But when I think he might leave, I know I'd prefer to die . . ."

"Geira, Geira!" Astrid enclosed her sister in her arms and truly embraced her for the first time since her arrival. "When should your child be born?"

"It's not time yet, at least another two moons," Geira sniffed.

"I'll stay with you until then. Would you like that?"

They went for long walks. They breathed in the salty sea air. Astrid kept an eye on what her sister was eating and drinking, and ensured Geira didn't go riding. Together, they awaited Olav's return. They prepared the house. The child's cradle. Astrid had no talent for the needle, but she stubbornly sewed caftans from white canvas. When her sister rested, she snuck out to the fields. She collected nettles, marigolds, baskets of chamomile and scented sage. She cooked oak bark carefully in the evenings.

She told herself: *Enough of this. The herbs speak to you, use them! Help your sister achieve both her dream and Mieszko's, so that his heir might be born here, in Gdańsk's borough. Their son.*

Yes, the thoughts still came, that if Geira had not been there, Mieszko still would not have allowed Olav to leave Poland's shores alone, and then she . . . but she sobered herself up whenever these thoughts appeared, imagining that someone had poured cold water over her head, as she had done for her father before the feast.

It's not for me to weave the threads of life, she told herself. *It's not for me to tangle, tie, or weave them.*

She allowed the herbs to give her their power, but she still didn't allow herself any visions or dreams. She ordered the servants to burn a fire in her chambers at night. Waking, she looked at the light, and the clearest of dreams would vanish. She didn't remember anything, not even a crumb was left in her mind's eye. *Only what might be useful for poor Geira,* she told herself day and night. *I'm doing this only for her.*

But it wasn't true. She secretly imagined successfully bringing this child into the world, returning to Poznań and sharing the news with her father, then staying to help care for him, whether the Old Hawk wanted her to or not. She'd summon Bolesław and tell him: "Brother, come back!" and together they'd stand guard over the great duke's final days. Let his death be like his life, victorious and honorable. All of these things were more important than guarding Sigvald in Jomsborg, bedding a man who she had nothing but contempt for, knowing, as she did, all of his darkest secrets.

"Mistress Astrid! My lady . . . it's begun!"

The servant's voice woke her unexpectedly, and she didn't have the clarity of mind to look at the fire when her eyes first opened. She looked instead into the darkness that enveloped the chamber.

"What's going on?"

"Lady Geira's labor has begun . . . she's calling for you, my lady . . ."

Astrid collected her herbs with a single sweep of her arm and, her bare feet pounding on the stone floor, she ran to her sister.

"Geira, no! It's too soon! You can't!"

Geira was sweating, her face as pale as a sheet. She was breathing heavily. Blood seeped out between her legs. Astrid quickly gave her a brew from yarrow and knotweed to stop the bleeding, and poppyseed for sleep. Sleep came, but it didn't stop the birth. The child came out from between her sister's thighs in waves. Astrid was dreaming with her eyes open, the dream she couldn't forget. She was a bird in her dream. A gray heron which flew between the clouds into the golden light in the heavens. The light didn't come from the sun, it turned out to be the cloak of a golden goddess, hanging down from the great throne in Sessrumnir, Freya's palace in the beautiful land of Folkvanger.

Golden Freya, Astrid groaned in her dream. *My mother wore a brooch with the goddess's image. The women of the north gave her gifts for a happy birth.*

That most beautiful goddess and the gods' lover appeared in Astrid's mind, comfortably spread on a sculpted throne, watching her from between golden eyelashes.

"I like you," she said, and her smile seemed to be mocking Astrid. "But I don't like her." She pointed a golden finger at the bleeding Geira in labor. "A goose cannot hatch an eagle egg, do you understand, heron?"

"I do," she said, "but I wish to help her, Beautiful One!"

"Then help." The golden-eyed goddess smiled indulgently. "You know how . . ."

A gust of wind blew Astrid from Freya's bright Sessrumnir and back into Geira's dark bedchamber.

She landed at her sister's bedside, though she'd never left it. She held a tiny, bloody baby's head in her hands, the body of which was still inside her sister, as if it were fighting against being born.

"You know how," the goddess's voice echoed in her skull.

Geira opened her eyes; she was still conscious.

"His seed burned me," she whispered with difficulty. "It was too strong. I couldn't hold it . . . I couldn't bear it, though I loved him so much, more than life itself . . . I'm leaving, sister . . ." She touched Astrid's shoulder and looked into her eyes. "I'm afraid, Astrid, because there is only darkness around me . . ."

"Come back," Astrid whispered, though she knew it was fruitless.

A goose, an eagle, an egg. The little eagle's head was still in her hands. She pulled gently. With a final spasm of life, Geira pushed the child into her sister's arms. Thick, dark blood followed.

"A boy! My lord father, it's a grandson," Astrid exclaimed, but the happiness didn't last long.

The child was like a chick thrown from its nest too soon. Its eyes, lips, and fists were closed. It hung on the rope of the umbilical cord as if from a gallows.

"Sister, oh sister," Astrid sobbed, holding the child close. But Geira was still, and there was no reply. Both mother and child were beyond her reach now.

Astrid didn't allow the gray servants to be called, the women who take care of the dead. No one else could help Geira in her final journey. She ordered the servants to boil water. They carried in basin after basin. Astrid washed her sister. Her beautiful, pale hair. Her eyes, which had taken in the world around her with such wonder. Her heavy breasts, filled with milk her son would never consume. Astrid gave the final ministrations as a beloved sister, wanting to repent for every small cruel envy of the past. But as much as she resisted the thought, she knew the beginning of a new life waited for her in this ritual of death. *"You know how,"* Freya had said, the night she had brought them death. *Did I know?* Astrid asked herself, searching for the answer in

Geira's dead body. In the blue bruises that blossomed on her buttocks and back. In the increasingly stern expression on her face. *What do I know of life and death? I have dreams which I chased off years ago, and which returned this night. But they are only dreams, visions, nothing more. What good can dreams do?* Words heard long ago crept out of her memory like larvae: "a strand of hair for good fortune in love," "the womb for smooth skin," "the fingernails of the dead for an abscess," "the tongue of a newborn for . . ." She chased them away. Charms. The whispers of old ones. *"Take the child's genitals at least!"* a voice in her head laughed. Astrid flinched. How could she be thinking this? Why were these thoughts filling her head at such a moment? *"It's you,"* a hiss sounded in her mind. *"It's you."*

Geira had been afraid of death, she saw darkness around her, and part of that darkness remains even now, Astrid thought. *I need to finish what I started.*

She took the clothes they had made for the child from a chest. Dressing the small, stiff body wasn't difficult. Geira's face changed from moment to moment. Her cheeks looked hollow, her small straight nose resembled a bird's beak. Astrid struggled to get the funeral dress on her sister. She couldn't get her stiff shoulders inside the sleeves. It was too much, and she knelt on the bed helplessly.

"I should have summoned the gray servants," Astrid said, too exhausted for tears, and she felt more alone than she had in a long time.

But when she looked at her sister's pale blue body, she gathered herself. She wouldn't give in. She fetched scissors and cut the dress. She fitted it around Geira, then sewed it back together once it was in place. She plaited Geira's hair and hung ear cuffs on her ears. The rings fit onto her fingers with difficulty. When she finished, she called the serving girls to clean the room.

"Oh, my lady looks so beautiful, as if she were asleep," the one who entered first cried.

That's not true, Astrid thought. *It's the illusion of jewels and a dress. The woman in this bed was beautiful when she was alive, but now she's gone into a darkness that she feared. It's horrible, to know one's final feeling is fear.*

21

POLAND

Olav learned of Geira's death only when he reached the shore, and even then, the news was delayed. He was surprised, later, by how quickly life went back to normal, as if to cover up the fact of death as quickly as possible. Life in the port went on. Fishermen mended their nets after the morning catch. Women bought fish, bartered over them, argued. Children shouted as they rolled an old, battered barrel along the bank. A dog barked. They moored *Kanugård* and threw the cargo out onto the dock. Leather sleeping bags, blankets, weapons. Plunder, of course. Within minutes, the dock was full of onlookers.

"They're back," the words traveled from lips to lips. "They're back."

"Has mine returned?" a voice shouted. "Can you see him? Is he there? Is he all right?"

"Master Olav is back," someone else called, and silence fell over them all. Dead silence.

"The one who burns ships," the children murmured.

He swept his tangled, greasy hair from his face and peered into the crowd. It wasn't Geira who was waiting for him, it was Astrid.

It occurred to him that he liked Sigvald's wife far more than his own. Dark-haired, not as bold as Świętosława, the mistress of his desire, but similarly regal. Geira was merely stubborn. He regretted this harsh thought within moments, though.

"Your wife and son are dead," Astrid told him, in the middle of the dock, in the middle of the crowd. "We buried them a month ago. We couldn't wait any longer, I'm sorry."

She was looking at him with pity, and he, though he understood what she'd said, responded with an empty, absent stare.

"Geira and . . . ?"

"Your son. She died in childbirth. The baby didn't survive."

When he'd sailed out to war with Sven, Geira had cried like a madwoman. "She begged me not to leave her alone," he told Astrid that evening.

His voice was hollow. They sat by the fire in Geira's chambers. An empty cradle stood in the corner. Geira's bed, its straw mattress and bed linen peeled off, haunted them with its freshly cleaned frame. He hadn't felt bliss in this bed, though his wife had done everything she could to give it to him. Yes, her body might have been scented and warm, but he'd never felt anything other than gratitude for her help in finding his mother. Looking at her, he had endlessly compared her to Świętosława. He had never betrayed himself with so much as a word, but he was afraid that his eyes had revealed the truth.

"Not to leave her alone," he repeated.

"Stop," Astrid said, exhaustion heavy in her voice. "It's not your fault."

"It is, Astrid. I wanted to leave her." The truth spilled from him. "Our life here was draining, in a way I can't explain. Like I was losing myself. More and more each time the tide went out and I was not sailing with it. Geira was like . . . an anchor. She held me in place."

"It wasn't Geira who kept you here, but Mieszko. He is the one who put us into the positions we're in," she said. She picked up her glass. "Let's drink."

He looked over at his sister-in-law. "Have you not had too much already?"

"Why?" she snorted. "Because I'm speaking openly? I love my father, but that's no reason to lie. I know what I said, and I won't take it back. Świętosława loved you, you loved her . . ."

"Stop it!" he hissed. "We're in my wife's bedchamber."

"Geira is dead and all that's around her now is cold darkness. She can't hear or see us, and even if she can, then at least after death she deserves some candor. Besides, she knew that you and our sister . . . she told me."

Astrid reached for the jug. Olav took it gently from her hand and poured, but only a little. He set the jug back down out of her reach.

"You weren't de-stined to be to-ge-ther," she murmured and took a sip. "A goose cannot hatch an eagle's egg." She lifted her goblet as if making a toast, then banged it on the table. With unexpected violence, she threw the cup against the wall and covered her face with her arms. The dark liquid stained the floor like blood. "And yet I still pity her, Olav. She may not have been an eagle, but she was my sister, and I feel so much sorrow . . . a goose in the dark. The darkness that terrifies me . . ."

Olav knew he should embrace a sobbing woman, but he didn't. He had vowed that he would never again embrace any woman out of pity.

Astrid rocked back and forth, covering her face. He'd heard the whispers. That she steered Jarl Sigvald into whatever direction she wanted. That her mother, Urdis, was a fortune-teller who'd seen a great future for the young Mieszko, along with her own daughter and her own death. Then, she died in childbirth—at least, that's what the stories told by the eldest in Jom claimed.

My wife also died in childbirth, Olav thought bitterly. *It's all stories.*

He drank. He should feel something for his son, anything, but he felt nothing. Not even the empty cradle could bring out any emotion to choke him. In Hedeby, when they'd conquered the Danish port, Eric had held a feast for the victors. A hundred drunk Vikings had raised toasts in the great painted hall known as the Bright Horizon. He'd been among them, pacing like a wild lynx. The one he had tracked for Świętosława. Instead of the lone beast he'd been expecting, he'd found a female with two large cubs. He didn't intend to kill them, but the mother had launched at him with claws outstretched. Olav carried the scratches on his left breast to this day. He hadn't had a chance to get his knife before the great cat was on him, saliva dripping from white fangs. Olav had clutched its throat. The pair rolled in an embrace, like wild lovers. He saw only the golden-green eyes, beautiful and untamed, like the eyes of the bold one he dreamed of. He'd strangled the cat. He was stronger. Then, he'd captured the two young ones and closed them in a wicker cage. Świętosława had survived a stormy journey to Uppsala, so if the lynxes were worthy of her, they would also make it.

Toasts chased down toasts in the Bright Horizon. "For Sigrid Storråda, our king's lady. Proud and beautiful, with two lynxes on a leash," a hairless giant with a scarred face roared. Eric's men answered him with shouts and drank to her health. The king himself spoke of his wife: "Golden-haired like Freya, beautiful like Freya, brave like Freya." He wasn't much of a word-smith, the bald Swedish giant, but Świętosława made him think of Freya, same as his men. Olav couldn't rid himself of the image of those great arms holding her, touching her, passing her a goblet.

There was no choice for Olav that evening. He couldn't sit there sober and listen to these cheers, picturing the bold one with the Swedish king; he needed to get drunk, and quickly, or leave. In the end, Olav stayed, refilling and refilling his goblet. Varin didn't leave his side. He was like a shadow, and if Olav so much as reached to touch his knife, Varin's fingers entwined themselves around his hand. The pressure sobered him every time.

"It's the darkness that terrifies me, that surrounded her in her moment of death," Astrid repeated, and Olav shook himself free of the memories.

"Let's drink, sister," he said, though a moment earlier he'd said she'd had too much.

"'I'm afraid, sister,' she whispered to me with her last breath, and her darkness haunts me." Astrid lifted her face. "I wanted to brighten it, but I didn't know how."

"Why did you not use your power, the one they say your mother passed on to you?" Olav asked. "Why do you fear it?" He reached out a hand and caressed her hair, the color of molten amber.

Astrid shook Olav's hand from her head. The presence of the man of her dreams so close unsettled her, even if they were simply mourning Geira's death together. Mourning? Or drinking to it? Many words had been spoken, but not a single tear was shed. They'd been honest with each other, at least, until he tried to get her to speak of herself.

He's honest—a voice whispered inside her. The same one whose knees went weak at the sight of him, who was ready to reverently touch every strand of his long, white hair. To kneel before him and whisper . . .

Whatever was lurking at the tip of her tongue wasn't worthy of articulating in her dead sister's bedchamber.

"I'm not afraid," she replied. "I'm just not sure yet if this power is real. I can feel it, but I can't use it. I didn't know how to help Geira," she admitted.

"There is no cure for unrequited love," Olav replied, watching her with eyes as bright as a winter sky.

Be silent! The part of her that was madly in love squealed inside her head.

But instead she heard herself asking, "Do you really want me to cast bones for the future?" She had never done this before. Like Olav, she knew the stories of her mother, of her visions, and of her death.

"I do, Astrid."

His eyes shone with the light of northern ice, before which there was no resistance. Once more, she felt pity for Geira. If his eyes could sting like this, she could only imagine how his seed must have burned.

She picked up Olav's goblet, having flung hers away earlier, and downed the contents in a single swallow. Then she reached to her belt and untied the pouch with the rune-marked bones.

"Ask," she commanded, tightening her fist over them.

"Where did Geira go to?"

One of the bones pulsed with heat against her skin. She drew it from the pile and tossed it on the table before them.

"Into an endless night."

"How can the darkness be dispelled?" Olav asked. His light hair covered his face.

The bones stuck together and she threw out two.

"Word and water. Wisdom and strength."

"Where will I find them?"

"West," she said, looking at the next bone she'd cast.

"How will I know they're real?"

"A bare rock and a dog," she choked out.

"What will happen when I accept them?" His eyes pierced her with a blue glow.

"The throne will be yours," she said.

"And she?"

She cast a final bone. She lowered her head.

"Speak!" he ordered like a king.

"Wyrd," she murmured with difficulty. "A hollow bone. The fate one creates for oneself."

She collapsed on the bench. The runes were howling their wild song at her. Olav pulled her up.

"Repeat that, sister."

"You'll make your own fate the moment you accept Christ," she said, while the girl inside her pleaded, "Kiss me, kiss me!"

Olav seemed to hear them both. He kissed her forehead and caressed her hair, blind to the fact that his touch felt like a burning seal. Astrid's head fell gently onto the cast bones.

She heard Olav's next words as if through a fog:

"There's no stone in the water, the anchor which kept me at this dock. I'm sailing to make my fate." To a bare rock, a dog, and a throne.

22

⚛

SWEDEN

Świętosława's lord husband came home from his trip to break Denmark apart in the glory of victory, leaving his men in charge of the previously Danish country. Eric had led the forces which conquered it, after all; it was only right that he would take charge of the country once their endeavor proved triumphant. "Eric the Victorious! Eric Segersåll!" his men shouted. Świętosława said nothing as her husband drank to his own success. Without pause all through autumn and winter, as if he could never be sated. But when the spring came, the king sobered up, and together they set out for Sigtuna. Eric, Świętosława, young Olof, the lynxes, Dusza, and the rest of the court, with Wilkomir and Great Ulf, who, by some miracle, instead of killing each other, managed to share their duties of protecting the queen.

When Ulf had been away fighting with Eric, Wilkomir and his squad guarded her, and Świętosława hadn't let them waste any time. She ordered each of them to take a Swedish wife and learn the language. They all obeyed her, except for Wilkomir. "The lord duke ordered me to protect you. Nothing was said of wives." Her brother's obstinate comrade took a lover, Helga, who was soon pregnant. They had a son he named after himself, Wilczan.

Helga was lovely, and their son, Wilczan, was obedient, while Wilkomir was as stubborn as a mule. However, he was the first to learn the northern tongue, though he was better at watching and listening than he was at speaking.

She realized this when they arrived in Sigtuna. While the manor was being constructed, they lived in Jarl Asgrim's home. Eric was busy with day-to-day business, accepting visits from the nobles and judging disputes. He spent an inordinate amount of time with merchants from Birka, a settlement famous for its trade with ships from foreign lands that also stopped in Wolin.

She and Olof spent their days sailing a boat in the bay and walking along a particular bank, through birch woods which reminded her so much of home. Sometimes, they took Helga and little Wilczan with them. She would let the lynxes roam free in the forest, allowing them to hunt. She had named them Zgrzyt and Wrzask, meaning "grind" and "scream" in her tongue, and which she knew sounded terrifying when spoken, even to those who didn't know the translation. Every time she unclasped the leashes from their collars, she felt the cold weight of fear settle in her belly until they returned. But they always did.

During their stay, Jarl Asgrim gifted her son two small, stocky, saddled ponies that resembled overgrown foals. It was time for Olof to learn to ride, Świętosława thought, and she decided Wilkomir should teach him.

"Not today, my lady," he told her when she announced her intentions. "I haven't had a chance to test those horses. I don't know if they are suitable for a child."

"Olof will be six soon. Bolesław was already riding at his age."

"I understand, my lady, but listen to what I'm saying. I haven't checked those horses, and I don't know them."

"They are meek, fluffy ponies. You might as well check if honey is sweet." She laughed at the look of suspicion on Wilkomir's face. "Jarl Asgrim, would you put your son onto one of these ponies?"

"Without a moment's hesitation, my lady," Asgrim replied. "They are gentle and patient."

"Then I'm taking them into the field." Świętosława, ignoring Wilkomir's thunderous expression, took Olof's hand and set out.

Wilkomir followed, soon catching up with the queen and her son. When they reached the pasture away from the manor, he once again spoke.

"My lady, wait."

"I will teach my son myself if you refuse to follow my command."

"I am not refusing." He took the reins from her hand and turned to the child: "Olof, tell me, which horse do you like more?"

"This one." Her son pointed to the horse that had the prettier saddle without hesitation. The red-dyed leather, studded with silver, was undeniably eye-catching.

"Then allow me to ride him first, and you can hold my sword in the meantime," Wilkomir said, and, not waiting for Świętosława's consent, gave the child his weapon and mounted the pony. He didn't get far; the pony bucked as soon as it felt a rider on its back, and Wilkomir fell onto the grass. It was a funny sight, and Olof began to laugh, but Świętosława did not. Wilkomir got up and ran after the pony to catch it. Świętosława quieted her son's laughter before he'd returned.

"Give Wilkomir back his sword and go into the field with Dusza." She didn't want Olof witnessing this conversation.

"What was that?" she asked Wilkomir, who was unbuckling the girth.

"'Gentle and patient,'" he repeated Asgrim's words. He ran his hand under the saddle and pulled out a thorny twig. He handed it to her. "It didn't bother the animal until a rider's weight pressed the thorns into its back."

Only now did Świętosława feel the full force of the fear that had been growing in her stomach since the moment Wilkomir had fallen from the pony.

"How did they know I'd want to try out the gift straightaway?"

He cast her a sidelong glance.

"My lady, anyone who knows you at all knows you want everything at once," he replied reluctantly.

"Why would Asgrim want to kill my son?" she whispered.

"Perhaps not kill, but hurt or maim. And it might not have been Asgrim."

"It was a gift from him."

"Which is why it's so easy to blame him. Everyone at court will have heard him: 'Asgrim said that the pony was gentle.'"

She studied the man who had sailed all the way from Poland to protect her.

"And you? How did you know something was wrong?"

He looked in her eyes.

"I don't have an answer for you, my lady. I just did what I was meant to do."

"What would you advise me to do?"

"Allow me to do my job. And next time, listen to me."

"You're a gift as valuable as you are challenging." She laughed. "You know I have trouble following others' advice."

"I'm not a gift, my lady."

She knew he hated it when she called him that. He jumped into the saddle again. This time, the pony walked calmly. He rode for a short distance, then dismounted and gave her the reins.

"You can teach Olof to ride on it. It's a good horse for the boy to start with. Let's not tell anyone about what happened. Whoever has tried to hurt the boy will try again."

She nodded soberly, then called out to Dusza and her son to return.

She watched Wilkomir lift Olof into the saddle. How he taught him to sit up straight, to press his thighs into the horse's flanks. She turned away from them; she didn't want them to see her tears. They fell down her cheeks unbidden when, looking at her child, she saw herself. Her father and mother had watched over her and Bolesław, surrounded them with guards and hosts of trusted servants, to prevent something like this from happening to either of them. Something that proved someone in their immediate circle wanted to see her son injured or dead. She felt fear for her child, but she was a queen, and she wasn't allowed to be scared.

The next few days brought no clarity. Life followed its calm, unvarying rhythm. Jarl Asgrim was a generous host. Even if the presence of the royal court in his house upset the order of things and ruined his larder, he behaved as if it was all the greatest joy of his life. He rejoiced at the progress the royal son made on the ponies he had given him. Olof, under Wilkomir's watchful eye, sat in the saddle more surely each day. Sometimes, little Wilczan accompanied them, and Wilkomir would put both boys onto the ponies. It seemed nothing could dampen the happy atmosphere, until Birger came to her with news a few days later.

"The merchants from Birch Island invite you to see them, my queen. They want to hold a feast in your honor, and your son Olof's."

"Birch Island. It sounds so familiar . . . there were so many birches around Lednica Lake, where I grew up . . ." She trailed off when she noticed the look on Birger's face. "Is it just me, or is something worrying you, Jarl?"

"Birka, or Birch Island, in the old days used to be the seat of kings. Today's merchants consider themselves their heirs, and carry a wounded pride in their hearts. I am suspicious of this invitation, my lady. Especially since they invite you to celebrate the harvest with them, knowing that Eric will be making sacrifices in Sigtuna or Uppsala and so cannot join you."

"Jarl, are you seeing threats even in banquet invitations now?" Świętosława laughed, already taken with the idea of a journey to the legendary Birka. She had heard tales of the island's riches and beauty and was looking forward to seeing them for herself.

"My lady . . ." Wilkomir's voice behind her was cool. "If memory serves, the merchants from Birka were guests of your husband and Jarl Asgrim here in Sigtuna when the ponies were gifted to Olof."

"What do ponies have to do with it?" Jarl Birger asked. Świętosława and Wilkomir had told no one about the incident with the saddle and thorns.

Świętosława nodded to Wilkomir that the jarl could be trusted, and Wilkomir explained what had happened.

"Why didn't you tell me, Queen?" Birger didn't try to hide his indignation. "You can't hide things like this from me! The king must be told . . . I suspect there's more behind this than you realize."

"No," Świętosława interrupted. "The king will not be told. And you will tell me what more may lie behind the attempt on my son's life. Now."

The lynxes raised their heads.

Does Birger know that my cats can smell fear? she wondered. *I'm not afraid, so it isn't my fear they have caught the scent of.*

"My lady," he began slowly, as if choosing his words carefully. "You'll recall that . . . I told you once that you shouldn't deny the king your presence in his bed."

"And I do not," she said curtly.

"I know, of course, my queen—but I would never have dared to give you such advice if I hadn't known that my lord . . ."

Zgrzyt growled at her feet. Birger ignored it.

"I was afraid for your position at court, Sigrid, because King Eric has previously fathered children out of wedlock."

"Well, yes," she said, as if this made no impression on her. "And how old are they?"

"The girls are nearly grown, my lady, and the boys are a few years older than your son."

"You didn't mention this at my father's court in Poznań," she observed coldly.

"Eric didn't make any of those women his queen. Only you, my lady."

She said nothing. Zgrzyt got up and walked over to Birger lazily. He sniffed the man's knees, then rubbed his head on them.

"What does it matter now, Jarl?" she asked once the silence following Birger's revelation had stretched on for as long as she could bear.

"The boys I mentioned are twins. The sons of a woman called Thordis, the only daughter of the wealthiest merchant in Birka."

"I see," she said. "I suspect Thordis also has many brothers who would happily reach for their weapons to fight for their nephews' inheritance?"

She remembered how confident she had felt the day Olof was born. How she'd believed that from that day on, nothing would threaten her position. How she and Eric had celebrated Styrbjorn's defeat together, the only potential contender to the throne—or so she'd believed.

"Does my husband have any other sons, apart from Thordis's twins? Bastards?" she used the insult, though it brought her no relief.

"Not that I know of, my lady. But there is something else you should know."

This time, Wrzask woke up, and put his head in her lap. *Yes, now I'm afraid,* she thought, sinking her fingers into the lynx's warm fur.

"Speak, Birger."

"The merchants in Birka didn't like the idea of a new manor being built in Sigtuna. They fear the loss of profits if trade moves here, since the king now lives in Sigtuna."

"I see. And Queen Sigrid, the foreign Christian queen, will be held responsible. They think they will lose profits from trade because of me, as well as any chance of Eric acknowledging Thordis's sons as his heirs. Do you know what I think, Jarl? I think I should confirm their worst fears."

She patted the lynx's head. Wrzask caught her fingers in his teeth lightly. She grabbed the lynx's jaw firmly. He growled, but didn't bite the hand that fed and caressed him.

"Do you see, my friend?" she said cheerfully. "Placing your hand in the mouth of the beast is safer than waiting for an attack. Tell the merchants from Birka that the queen will celebrate the harvest in the new manor in Sigtuna, with her king. And that I invite them to join us. Along with the, I suppose beautiful, Thordis and her sons. I wish them to come and pay homage to little Olof. And add that traditional gifts are welcome, but we don't need any more horses."

She rose and pulled on the leash. The lynxes set off in front of her. Zgrzyt and Wrzask were in the mood for a hunt.

"You did the right thing, my lady," Wilkomir said to her when she had let them off the leash in the woods. "I wouldn't have been able to guarantee your safety on the island."

"I was touched, the first time I heard about Birka," she confided in him. "I thought of Ostrów Lednicki. The womb of the Piast dynasty, hidden on water. Our nest, connected to land only by the bridges. But, as it turns out, I was mistaken."

"If the merchants refuse the queen's invitation, they will reveal themselves as enemies. And if they come, they will be forced to bend the knee to your son in front of witnesses. Unless they choose open warfare with Eric, but that will, once and for all, take any chances for Thordis's sons off the table."

"I don't want to give those pups anything, Wilkomir," she said. "I don't yet know what makes the better weapon here: generosity or ruthlessness. But I will be thinking on it."

The lynxes returned, one after the other. The first carried a hare in its jaws, the second a marten. They placed their catches at her feet and sat down, licking blood off their muzzles. Zgrzyt and Wrzask. Her new people found the names impossible to pronounce, thus ensuring no one could try to tame them apart from her. She distinguished them by their shapes. The markings

on their sides were different. And their eyes. Wrzask's were like boiling molten gold, and Zgrzyt saw the world through melted spring green. She stroked
their heads. She picked up the hare and marten and sniffed both. They smelt
of fresh blood, fur, and the sickening scent of fear. She returned the catches to
her beautiful hunters. Streaks of warm blood stayed on her fingers.

"They belong to you," she said, and the lynxes busied themselves with
ripping their prey apart.

She turned back to Wilkomir. "I don't know what else to do, but I'm
reassured knowing you and Great Ulf guard me. Two wolves and two lynxes.
Wrzask and Zgrzyt." She tried not to think of her husband's words in his bedchamber, *A man must die when he's in full strength. It's none of your concern, Sigrid.*
Or of Eric's bastard sons, and their mother, and all those who would see her
son thrown from his first horse.

She raised her hand to her lips and licked the blood from her fingers.

23

SWEDEN

Świętosława had fallen in love with Sigtuna and, when it was finally ready, with their new royal manor which sat on a hill overlooking Mälaren Bay.

Gracing the entrance were imposing doors that wood-carvers had been working on since spring. Thanks to their chisels and hammers, an entire world had come alive in the heavy wood. A majestic ash had been carved, Odin's sacred tree, Yggdrasil, but no corpses hung from its branches, as they did at the grave near Uppsala's temple. Instead, Yggdrasil pulsed with life, providing shelter for deer, a goat, a squirrel, a falcon, and even snakes. She promised herself that she might ask someone, perhaps Thora, Jarl Birger's wife, to tell her the story of the ash with its three great roots.

There was still a grove nearby where the locals made sacrifices to their gods, but it was far enough away that she didn't see it when she looked out her window, and she didn't have to pass by it on her way to the chapel.

The chapel Eric had promised her before his journey to Denmark wasn't part of the manor, as in Poznań's palatium, but a small separate building. It didn't stand out by being particularly pretty, there was no comparison with the cathedral in Poznań, but it was hers. It was Świętosława's chapel. And if it was small? Well, Jarl Birger and herself were probably the only people who would pray there anyway. She had waited for it for so long that the mere thought of crossing its threshold brought her joy.

When the chapel's construction was nearly complete, she received even more joyous news—there would also be a monk, to tend to the chapel and tend her own Christian soul. Eric had brought one back from Denmark, as one of his many gifts for his wife. Jewels, materials, furs, and a monk called Ion. Except that the jewels and furs suffered little throughout the journey, while Ion was seriously ill and recovered only a month later, after the chapel had been completed. Świętosława knew after their first meeting that this monk was a gift as valuable as he was strange. A carefully shaven head and smooth cheeks which hadn't lost their chubbiness even after his illness. Lively eyes that blinked often. A tattered but clean habit. He introduced himself as a Benedictine, and when she asked him to tell her about himself, he began to speak without pausing for a breath.

"I was in Italy at Saint Apollinaris of Ravenna, my queen, in a monastery as big as a mountain, with a port nearby, miracles, my queen, miracles, three lambs on the church's ceiling, John, Peter, and Jacob, ah, the happiest days of my life when ordo et pax, and why, why was I tempted? I left as the fourth with Romuald, the Venetian doge Peter Orseolo, and abbott Guarin—four is the apostolic number—we traveled to the south of France, to Saint-Michel de Cuxa, huge mountains, my queen, the Pyrenees, and it wasn't that bad there, hours and psalms and a monastic lifestyle, but that's where Orseolo went mad in the woods and set up a hermitage. And Romuald and Guarin went with him, and so I had to follow. But, my queen, I'm a man of labor and prayer, ora et labora, yes, yes, God, but not roots. Roots, my queen, distanced me from God, and the seclusion of the hermitage was the final Roman nail in the Savior's cross, knock, knock . . ."

"Father Ion, what did you do in Denmark?" she interrupted this frenzied stream of words.

"I ran away, my queen. From Romuald's horrible anger. He and Orseolo don't accept any weakness in a man. They didn't understand that I can worship God with a goblet of wine and smoked ham. Baked ham, too. Whereas they could only do it with roots and water. And it doesn't stand for me when all I had were roots . . ."

"From what I know of monks, it doesn't have to, Ion." Świętosława wondered if Ion was one of the mad monks she'd heard about in Poznań, or if his insanity had nothing to do with his vocation.

He looked embarrassed, but only a little.

"It doesn't have to, but it can. The Lord values self-denial highly, and we don't accept cripples into monasteries. My queen understands that by a cripple, I mean a man whose privates refuse obedience."

"Jarl Birger, what do you think of Father Ion?" she asked, studying the monk critically. Even his clean hands now seemed suspect to her.

"It's not for me to judge a clergyman, my lady," Birger replied uncertainly.

"Do you really think he's traveled so far? That he's actually visited all the places he speaks of?"

Birger raised his eyebrows, but didn't have time to respond before the monk began talking again.

"I've been elsewhere too, which I haven't had the chance to tell my lady about. But I will openly admit that I've never met a queen who leads two lynxes on a leash. I am quite afraid of them. Though, as I understand it, if Lady Sigrid is a Christian queen, then her monstrous cats won't throw themselves onto a clergyman?"

"Ion, if you can convince my lynxes that you're an authentic priest, then you have nothing to fear."

"No, no, my lady." He waved his arms as if trying to drive something away. "Just don't ask me to speak to wild beasts. It was another reason for which I had to leave the hermitage. Howling wolves would approach our flimsy shelter at night, because my brothers would pray to the Lord for challenges which they could face to prove their faith. And what can I do about it if my faith is strong enough that it doesn't need to be challenged to prove itself? No, punish me, cruel queen, but don't ask me to speak to beasts. Besides, I never said I was a priest. I am a mere monk, a Benedictine."

"Are you saying that you can't say mass in the chapel my husband has built me?" Anger was rising in her at this chattering man in a clean habit.

"Of course not, my lady." He bowed. "I have not been ordained. Monastic vows are something else entirely."

"And the sacraments? Can you absolve me, can you give me the Body of Christ?"

"No, my lady, but I can accept it." He jutted out his chin proudly.

"From whom, Ion? There is no one with Holy Orders in my husband's country, has that not reached you yet? We are on pagan soil that belongs to Odin, Thor, and their Freya." She was furious, because she realized now that the gift Eric had brought her was a useless one.

A hint of unease graced the monk's smooth features.

"Then I'm afraid that your chapel is as blessed as a shack on a ship. It stands on unhallowed ground, and, I gather, it hasn't been consecrated by a bishop."

"Where do you suggest I find a bishop in a country where the king sacrifices prisoners to his gods once every nine years?"

"Prisoners?" he asked her uncertainly.

The lynxes, asleep at her feet and unmoved by the shouting until now, chose this moment to raise their heads and cock their ears, which were decorated with brushes of hair at their tips. They could sense Ion's fear.

"Yes," she replied. "But don't be afraid, monk. You are not a prisoner here. For the time being. And the last ritual took place at Uppsala in the year I arrived, so there's two more years until the next."

"Two years." He blinked, and something occurred to him, because he

pointed a finger upward and shouted cheerfully: "My lady, the goddess
Freya, whom the people here worship just like the Danes do, and I spent
some time among them, count among their traditions one where she has
the right to half of all plunder brought back from wars. When the winged
Valkyrie steal the souls of the best warriors from the battlefield, half find
themselves in Odin's Valhalla, and the other half in Freya's palace, known
as . . . known as . . . Sessrumnir, that's what it's called. The Place of Many
Seats. So, if your husband is like Odin, then you, my lady, are like Freya . . .
my point is, when the time comes, let Ion find himself among your host, stepping after you, step, step . . ."

She burst out laughing.

"I'll tell you, monk, what I already know of you. You're a glutton who
cannot fast, a drunkard, you chatter endlessly, and you're a stinking coward.
My lynxes can sense your fear."

"God loves his children," Ion replied, entirely unfazed. "He sent his beloved Son to earth to stop them from knowing fear."

"My husband wanted to give me some pleasure by bringing you to me.
You have turned out to be useless, but I can't yet say if you are worthless. I
give you two years to prove your worth to me."

"Only two years?" Ion looked worried. "Wine, my lady, tastes better the
older it grows . . ."

"But you aren't wine, although you might end up being consumed in
much the same manner. You're not a brave soldier, either, to be collected by
the Valkyries. And I'm not Freya, Ion. I don't take prisoners. You'll return
when I send for you."

The new manor was bright and clean and smelled of fresh wood. Two
thrones stood on the platform in the grand hall. These were the only pieces
in the entire house which weren't newly built. "My grandfather and grandmother rested their hands here," Eric said with pride, pointing to where the
dark wood had been smoothed by their fingers. Between the royal thrones,
Świętosława ordered a third, with a seat as high as theirs, though a smaller
back. A place for Olof.

Fresh skins were laid on the benches for guests, wreaths of rowan berries
decorated the tables alongside baskets of rosy and golden apples. Her own
bedchamber was crowned with a present from her lord husband—a new bed,
lavishly wide and welcoming. A place of comfort and respite for his queen.
What his bedchamber looked like, she would find out that evening.

First, a feast awaited them, celebrating the end of the harvest and the beginning of new mead, a celebration not unlike those held for the shearing of the first sheep of the year, or as thanks for a bountiful harvest. A large vat had been prepared, into which she and Eric were to pour the traditional jug to begin the new mead celebration. Also prepared were Wilkomir and Ulf, who never let their eyes off her. The merchants of Birka had accepted the queen's invitation.

"I wasn't expecting them," Eric muttered when he'd heard that Thordis and her sons, as well as her brothers and father, were to participte in the feast. He said nothing more.

Świętosława had chests full of wondrous clothes and loved this time of year, the beginning of autumn, when the cool air allowed her to wear as many as three layers. Tonight, a royal purple dress, flowing freely to the floor, highlighted the line of her shoulders. She put another dress over it, green, tight, and sleeveless, held together by gilded brooches in the shape of animal heads. The goldsmith had intended them to be wolf heads, but Świętosława pictured her lynxes as she donned the gilded ornaments. A servant attached a cloak to these same brooches, more of a coverlet really, that made her figure look ethereal. She allowed Dusza to do her hair; no one could rival her skill in braiding. She created wreaths, crowns, and endless spirals from her curls, leaving some plaits free so that they fell onto her back in gleaming golden strands. For this occasion, Świętosława asked Dusza to pin back her hair with a band she'd brought with her from Poznań, a magnificent piece decorated with thirty of the most beautiful temple rings.

"My lady, you look like a queen," her servants exclaimed.

"That's because I am one." She shrugged, and the cloak moved proudly.

But today, I must prove it yet again, she thought, and wondered, *To whom? Thordis, who has two sons with the king while I only have one? Or the powerful merchants from Birka who stand behind her? Or maybe Eric himself? Jarl Birger? Who?*

The feeling of ease and contentment that had been growing within her was gone. In Uppsala, every feast was accompanied by toasts to her, glasses raised to Queen Sigrid Storråda, but this was her first feast in Sigtuna. Had she awoken some dark power by demanding a new home away from the horrific mounds? By wanting to escape the shadows of the sacrificial grove, had she turned the old gods against her?

"Bring Ion to me," she told a servant. She was meant to be welcoming guests at Eric's side any moment now, but she needed to see the monk. "And tell him to hurry."

He appeared swiftly. "The queen looks like Freya today," he said, openly looking her up and down.

"Ion. Are you here to attend your queen, or would you like to spend time with Wrzask and Zgrzyt instead?" He was still terrified by her lynxes, and Świętosława knew this.

"I did not mean to disappoint you, my lady, I just wanted to give words to what my eyes perceived." He bowed humbly, the top of his smooth-shaven head gleaming.

The sound of horns welcoming guests reached them from the yard outside. Great Ulf shifted on his feet nervously. The servants cast glances at the entrance.

"Tell me, monk, does Christ still retain his power here, on unconsecrated ground?"

"If we had all night to talk, I'd start by saying that God is omnipotent, then tell you the visions I'd been recounted by hermit priests. But I know that my queen is in a hurry, therefore I will confine my answer. I don't think that the Savior's power has reached this country. But through your baptism, you are a vessel which carries His Light in the dark night. Don't be afraid."

"Thank you, Ion," she said, moving to the front of her procession. It was time to face the dark night.

"At your service, my queen," she heard as she stepped over the threshold.

Even if she had angered the local gods, she told herself, she could not be frightened by a power she didn't believe in.

She and Eric sat on the raised platform. Their dark-haired boy took his place between them. "When I was young, I had locks of hair just like his," her lord husband would often say with pride in his voice. The king and queen had already poured the jug of mead into the great tub, and now the lords were approaching one by one, adding the mead they'd brought as a gift.

"The drink of bards was created from Kvasir's blood mixed with mead," Thorvald, Eric's Icelandic bard, was calling out. "Let the mead we'll be tasting tonight have the same power and heavenly taste; and we will drink it to the glory of the gods for the entire year."

After the mead was poured into the tub, the guests would approach the platform. They introduced their families to the royal couple and presented their gifts. Świętosława looked over the hall between the introductions, searching for one woman and her sons among the gathered crowd.

And then they were before her. "Rognvald Ulfsson, a merchant from Great Birka," it was announced. "His sons, Erling and Bjarne, and Thordis, his daughter."

Świętosława watched them, taking the woman's measure. *Where are Eric's pups? Where is the royal litter?*

Thordis was older than Świętosława, perhaps thirty. Tall, slender, fair-haired, and irritatingly like Geira. She wore a misleadingly humble dress; from afar, it was the color of ash, but up close the grayness glittered with silver woven in with the silk threads. She had a necklace between her brooches which was worth, at a glance, as much as a decent ship. Every bead was solid silver, decorated with such delicate granulations that it seemed only the ancient dwarves of legend could have created it. The ensemble must have weighed as much as a Saxon sword. Thordis kept her back straight. One who can afford to carry a ship between her breasts must be able to maintain a good posture.

What will happen when she bows? Świętosława wondered. *Will she groan under the weight of that silver as she straightens?*

"Rognvald, was it you that I received an invitation from?" Świętosława asked, forcing her voice to sound light and girlish.

"Yes, my queen," her tall, stout guest replied.

"And where did you get the idea that the queen will visit her subject before he comes to bow to her?"

"From hospitality, my lady," he replied, meeting her eye. "Do not think I intended to offend you, my queen. Every time I came to Sigtuna, you were too busy for me to pay you homage."

It's enough that you gave my son a present hidden under the saddle, she thought.

"I have heard you have two beautiful grandsons, Rognvald. Why do I not see them with you? Did they not accept Queen Sigrid's invitation? I am anxious to meet them."

"I don't doubt it, my lady," Rognvald replied, a tone of defiance creeping into his voice. "They have been kept away by illness."

"How old are they?"

"Ten, my serene lady," Rognvald replied proudly.

"Ten? So, they aren't children, but young warriors. Are they of poor health?" she asked. "That doesn't bode well for their futures, does it, my king?" she looked at Eric over the confused Olof's head.

Her husband's face was the color of whitened stone.

"No, my queen," he said loudly.

"King Eric the Victorious," she said, just as loudly. "Ask Lady Thordis about her sons' absence on the day on which you give your ring to so many boys, as a sign of loyalty between ruler and subject."

"I ask it," he announced with a voice made of bronze.

"They fell ill, my king," Thordis said quietly.

"That's a bad omen," Świętosława judged, and silence fell in the hall. "A warrior who sickens on the day of his trial, a day when the decision between his king's and leader's victory or failure is made. As a mother, I understand your pain, Thordis. Ill sons, deadly sick, I assume, since they were unable to accompany you. And you, who have come. You chose to show your ruler that instead of staying with your children on what might be their final journey . . . a surprising choice, but my heart bows to you for it."

Thordis's cheeks reddened.

Yes, I've slapped her, Świętosława thought, and raised her head. It was then that the Icelandic bard shouted,

"Queen Sigrid! Proud in her words. Unyielding in upholding the law. The lady of our swords and thoughts."

A hundred of her and her husband's warriors joined in, chanting:

"Sigrid Storråda! Sigrid the Proud! Our bold lady!"

"Queen," Rognvald, Thordis's father, interrupted the chants. "The merchants of Birch Island have a gift for you, and humbly ask you to accept it."

If it's Thordis's necklace, I'll take it blindly, she thought.

Rognvald opened a small chest and, after her nod, took a step toward the royal thrones. Zgrzyt sniffed his foot. It was indeed a necklace, placed on a bedding of blue grass. Fourteen huge silver beads, and between them seven discs of mountain crystal encased in silver nets.

Christ in the Holy Trinity! She gasped. *It looks like it must be worth the world!*

"Anyone who wants to give a queen a jewel must do so through her husband's hands," she said, hoping her desire didn't color her voice.

Bjarne and Erling exchanged glances. Rognvald and Thordis both flinched. But a hundred of Eric's warriors were watching. Eric lifted the necklace from the chest, and as he did, the crystals caught the firelight in the hall and reflected it back in bright, warm shards, like the sun on a field of ice.

"My lady, accept this gift," Eric said, clasping it on her neck.

"Thank you, husband," she whispered when she felt the weight of the necklace on her breast. "And those who have given me such an expensive present through your hands."

She lifted her arms so that the crystals glittered, encouraging her husband's men to chant once more, yelling themselves hoarse:

"Queen Sigrid Storråda!"

And then, quietly and innocently, she beckoned Thordis and her father closer, saying:

"I also have a gift for you. It's a replacement, as I return in silver what I received without the gilding."

She nodded at Wilkomir, and he handed Thordis a twig with six sharp thorns, attached to a silver gripper and chain.

"Thank you, Your Highness," Thordis replied with white lips.

The lynxes at Świętosława's feet raised their heads. Wrzask purred, Zgrzyt bared his fangs.

"Enjoy yourselves, our dear guests. A royal feast awaits you. Fish, game, cheese, fruit, barley beer, and old mead. Let's drink it today in the name of the new mead. To the glory of the sweet words it will bring us. Bard, start your song."

In Uppsala, Great Ulf would accompany Świętosława to the king's bed-chamber, then return to the feast until she summoned him again. This night, Ulf kept watch at the door, and Wilkomir walked among the guests. When Świętosława entered his rooms, Eric was lying with his hands behind his head, staring silently upward. He didn't speak as she approached. The bed-chamber was submerged in half darkness.

"My lord?" she asked, sitting on the edge of the great bed. "Would you prefer sleep instead of your wife's company?"

"Why didn't you tell me that someone wanted to have Olof thrown off his horse?" He rose from the bed and began to pace.

"Why didn't you tell me that there was someone who might have reason to desire it?" she replied calmly, her eyes following his movements.

"Power is a tasty morsel, Sigrid. There is always someone who wants some."

"You've put out fresh meat and are surprised that wolves are appearing?" She laughed sharply. "You could have not had bastards. In our wedding vows, you promised that our children will be your only heirs." Her eyes rested now on the sword that adorned the wall over his bed, the one she had given him on their wedding day. Duke Mieszko's sword made of lightning steel, said to have fallen from the sky.

"And nothing will change that." He stopped pacing and crossed his arms over his chest.

"Truly?"

"I promise you."

"You can promise me whatever you want, but that cannot change the intent of others."

"No one supports them or their cause."

"What will tomorrow bring, Eric? You don't know any more than I do," she replied softly. "Today, you're a victorious king, haloed with glory. It's the best time to make bold decisions. Remove them from Olof's way."

"I won't kill children, Sigrid," he said after a long moment.

It would be best if they could just disappear, she thought.

"Maybe I could send them somewhere?" he mused aloud. "Somewhere far away . . ."

"That's a bad idea, husband. By sending them to nowhere, you always send them somewhere. It's better to keep an eye on the boys, find something to occupy them here, so they don't feel rejected, merely intended for a different purpose than ruling. If you were a Christian king, you'd send them to a monastery, educate them, and set them on a spiritual path. If they had the privilege of being named bishops, they'd rule over people's souls."

"I'm not a Christian king, Sigrid," he replied and sat down heavily next to her.

She was furious with him, but she suddenly felt sorry for him, too. Up close, he wasn't Eric the Victorious. He was Eric the Tired. Silver streaks had appeared in his thick, dark beard. Puffy eyes revealed that he wasn't sleeping well and was drinking too much. She knew about the second, but not the first. Sitting in the great hall, he always seemed powerful and straight-backed. Now, he was slouching, breathing heavily and irregularly.

God Almighty, I wanted to be a widow queen, but not now, not when powers that can push Olof off the throne are emerging from the darkness, she thought with fear, and immediately reprimanded herself for it. *You're a queen, and you cannot be afraid. Didn't the Empress Theophanu face the rebellious Reich lords? She survived her husband's death and her child's abduction, she lost everything, but she never bent. She won back both her son and her power.*

"Eric," she said, placing an arm around her lord husband's shoulders. Still broad, even when he slouched. "Give those boys some lands. Show them that you have something for them. And send away their uncles, because support might rally to them. Rognvald is too old, he can count the ships docking in Birka until the end of his days."

Eric pulled at his beard and sighed.

"I will send Erling and Bjarne to Denmark, my cautious wife. I will make them my viceroys. They will keep an eye on royal business in our conquered country."

"Viceroys? You're too generous, Eric. Make them responsible for collecting taxes from the Danes. It's a respectable function." She laughed, tilting her head and counting on her fingers: "The Danes won't love Bjarne and Erling if they will be forced to pay tribute to them. So, we are in no danger of the sons of Birka allying with the defeated. And you will have a reason to keep an eye on Bjarne and Erling. But the function? It's honorable. Everyone knows that a tax collector is a ruler's trusted man."

Eric placed a heavy hand on her head and caressed her hair. She nearly drew back in surprise. She would have expected anything from her lord husband, but not this simple, affectionate gesture. No one had stroked her head since Dobrawa's death.

She crawled past him to the head of the bed and slipped beneath the covers. "Come here, my husband." She patted the spot next to her. "Lay down beside me."

"I was going to take a closer look at Danish matters anyway," he said after joining her in the bed. "A conquered country is easily lost when you don't pay attention to it. The Danes don't love us, or the ruler who abandoned them to us. Sven took the last men loyal to him and sailed to plunder England." Eric turned over and hissed as if his shoulder caused him pain. "Danes are good at that. They've been invading Anglo-Saxon lands for years." He laughed hoarsely. "They treat it like open chests with silver. Apparently, Sven is one of the four leaders of a fleet which has been attacking the islanders like a swarm of wasps for the past year. Jostein is the second, Guthmund the third, both battle-scarred pirates. And the fourth is Olav Tryggvason."

Świętosława froze.

"Tryggvason?" she repeated, afraid her racing heart would give her away.

"They say he's the surviving son of King Tryggve, the last of the Ynglings. But who can tell how much truth there is to that? There were times when a miraculously found king appeared every year. And the widow Gunhild sent each one to cold goddess Hel."

Świętosława's hands were trembling. She hid them under the pillow. No one knew of her feelings for Olav, or his for her—she had not spoken of them since the day Father had sent them both to marry other people. But she struggled to hide the emotions roiling inside her now.

"Eric, it's impossible for Olav Tryggvason to be in England. He's my half sister Geira's husband, and Mieszko's viceroy on the Baltic shore in Pomorze. And likely the commander of my father's armies by now."

Eric yawned and rubbed his beard. The dry crunching sound sent shivers down her spine.

"I fought with your brother-in-law at my side. Tall, white-haired . . . almost as if it were gray?" he said after a moment. "We fought Sven together beyond Rügen and we reached Hedeby side by side. Yes, his name was Olav, but I don't remember him being Olav Tryggvason."

"I know who my sister's husband is." Her heart beat faster at the memory of that silver-white hair.

I haven't forgiven either Father or her, she thought with a vengeance.

"There are always those who want power, wife. Maybe the one who is fighting in England doesn't know that the real Tryggvason is Duke Mieszko's son-in-law? He'll have a surprise waiting for him when he decides to reach for the throne. Send messengers to your father, have them try to find out if someone in England is impersonating your brother-in-law. And let's not speak anymore, Sigrid, this day has exhausted me." He reached out his arms and brought her close.

She leaned into his embrace, unresistant and flustered, but for a very different reason than that which her lord husband suspected. Prepared to make love, but not with him. The last thing she wanted at that moment was the touch of his hands. She couldn't rise and leave, though. Eric lay on top of her, murmuring something, stifling her with his weight. His wet kiss on her earlobe felt like a burn. She lay there stiffly, wishing she could disappear, to melt like a handful of snow thrown into a warm bed. But after a few moments, it was over. Her husband lay back at her side and was soon snoring. Świętosława slipped from the bed and allowed Great Ulf to walk her back to her bedchamber. She called the lynxes to her. Wrzask jumped into her bed nimbly. She clutched his fur until dawn arrived.

24

POLAND

Mieszko, returning to Gniezno with Oda and his two younger sons, felt such a sharp pain in his chest that everything around him went dark. He managed to stay on his horse until the stabbing sensation eased, and soon announced that he had decided to stay for a few days in Ostrów Lednicki.

"I want to spend some time with just you and the boys, away from the noise of court," he lied.

He couldn't admit his weakness to Oda. Not after she'd been so happy that she cured him of his last illness.

"And besides," he added, "Bishop Unger hasn't seen our island yet."

The dark-eyed Unger nodded to him gravely. When they reached the shore, he still felt the pain in his chest and summoned the bishop with a wave of his hand.

"Look, Father," the duke said. "Here is my dynasty's nest, hidden on Lednica Lake. We bring our wives here to bear children. And if the country were being consumed by fires or war, it's here we would bring what is most dear to our hearts."

"Why?" Unger asked.

"Bridges, bishop. The East Bridge, which we will cross in a moment, is shorter, the length of a grown man's two hundred and fifty steps. But the West Bridge, which you can't see, is more than twice as long."

"Dear God," Unger admitted with admiration. "I haven't seen bridges like this anywhere in the empire."

"And you won't." Mieszko reddened with pride. "We built the bridges in winter, on a frozen lake, driving oaks into the bottom of the lake. Twenty- and thirty-year-old ones are the most resilient. Well, forty-year-old ones are also good. Ha! It's the same with men as it is with oaks, isn't it, Oda?" he asked hoarsely.

"My dear duke, you look good at any age." She smiled at him, adjusting her cloak.

"The borough and ramparts were built on the island in my father's time, but I built these bridges. And a stone palatium worthy of my lady." He smiled at Oda and rode ahead of them onto the bridge.

The hawk took off from his shoulder and, like a scout, flew toward the island. The sound of his mount's hooves on the wooden bridge was the sound of home to Mieszko, as well as the sound of victory; a sound that reminded him of the strength of the empire he'd built.

"If we are ever threatened by an enemy," he said, turning to Unger and Oda, "this is where I would bring you and the children, my lady. And if the enemy surrounded the edges of the lake, I would throw a torch onto the East and West Bridges and burn them, cutting off the world from what is dearest to me. Did you hear that, my sons?"

"Yes, Father," the older, Mieszko, agreed.

The younger, Lambert, paled and nodded his bright head.

"Don't scare him, husband," Oda pleaded.

They rode onto the bank. Servants were mending boats next to the bridge, by the old shack. He looked at the docks and remembered the winter night years ago. The ice hole in the frozen lake, where he and Bolesław had jumped into the water, when he had given his firstborn son a squad of his own.

How many years have passed since then? Lambert hadn't been born yet, but little Świętopełk had still been alive, and today he is no longer with us, he thought sadly. *Eight. Eight years,* he counted, and felt a tightness in his chest again. *I'm afraid of what I want to do, that's where the pain comes from. Be careful, Mieszko,* he told himself. *And be strong.*

"God bless the food we eat thanks to His grace," the bishop said when they were seated for dinner that evening, and they began to eat.

"Are you feeling all right?" Oda looked at the duke's untouched plate with a watchful eye. "Aren't you hungry, lord husband?"

"No," he replied shortly.

"Maybe some mead?" Oda suggested, and nodded to a serving girl.

He took a sip out of politeness. Mead hadn't agreed with him recently. Instead of clarity of thought, it brought confusion, and today, more than anything, Mieszko wanted to be sober and reasonable. He felt the hawk's weight heavily on his shoulder, and summoned a servant to move the bird onto a perch.

"It's time for my will," he said.

His wife paled and dropped her goblet. Mead flowed over the table. His sons looked at him with fear as well.

"Don't be scared." He laughed. "I'm not dying yet. I'm only saying I need to think about what should happen to the country once I'm gone."

The bishop said nothing. He was glancing discreetly between the duke and Oda.

"Husband," the duchess said, recoverimg her wits swiftly, "I hope that writing a will isn't premature. I do agree, though, that things cannot be left to chance. You're the duke of a grand country, and you have not one, but three sons, and that means that you must be farsighted and cautious . . ."

"Silence, woman." He shrugged. "I know what I must be."

I should be firm, he thought, looking at his sons' pale, scared faces. *And do something that no one before me has ever done. But none before me had been a Christian duke, no one had faced a choice like this. Damn it!* He swore to himself, and at that same instant one of the torches burning at the top of the hall went out.

"What's that?" Oda said with surprise, and paled. "A draft?"

The devil doesn't sleep, Mieszko thought, watching a column of smoke rise from the torch. He wiped beads of sweat from his forehead. *Or perhaps it's a sign that I'm taking the wrong path? That I'm lost?*

The servants exchanged the torch, and the new one burned with a bright, cheerful glow.

"Father John, read us the Bible, please," Oda nodded at the chaplain.

Sometimes the nun in her rears her head, Mieszko thought fondly. *When we dine, she must hear readings. She's given me so much joy in these past ten years, so much bliss. It's hard to believe that if it hadn't been for my war with the empire, she'd be a nun until this day. Or an abbess.*

Father John was reading in monotone:

"Some time later God tested Abraham . . . 'Take your son, your only son, whom you love—Isaac—and go to the region of Moriah. Sacrifice him there as a burnt offering on a mountain I will show you.'"

Mieszko felt cold.

It's a sign, he thought. *It's a sign that I'm doing the right thing. Only my firstborn son is capable of making a new, great dukedom from the lands he won in the south. These two are little boys, children still . . . they can't do it, they must be protected. Oda is right, we must protect them . . . Yes, that's right. The eldest should inherit from his father, and the younger ones can conquer their own lands. They are little children, while he's an eagle, a predator who's already caught Upper Silesia and the great Moravia. He's strong . . .*

"Bishop Unger." Mieszko stopped the avalanche of his own thoughts. "Do you have ink and parchment with you?"

"I do, my duke." Unger's dark eyebrows were drawn tightly together.

"Do you want to write your testament today?" Oda asked, her fear apparent in her voice. "Now?"

"No. I will go and rest now. I'll send for you when I am ready."

He stood up heavily. Witosz helped him walk to his bedchamber and lie down.

"Where's my hawk?" Mieszko asked.

"Here." Witosz gestured toward the sculpted bedframe. "At your feet."

"Ah. I didn't see it. It shouldn't sit there like a crow over a corpse. I'm not dying yet, I'm still thinking. Go now, old friend. I want to take a nap. But cover me with something, it's cold in here . . ."

He fell asleep as soon as Witosz left the bedchamber. He dreamed that he was old Abraham, climbing Mount Moriah with difficulty. *I must do it,* he kept telling himself, tripping over stones, *for the good of the family, the country. He'll understand, he's as much a hunter as I am. He doesn't have to inherit a nest, because he can make his own, a larger one, and rule the whole country from it . . .* He, Mieszko-Abraham, fell to his knees in his dream and sobbed when he reached the mountaintop. From this height, he would have seen far-off lands if his vision hadn't been blurred by tears. *What should God say now?* he thought as if in a fever, and sobbed. He remembered those words, he knew them, though they didn't come to him in the dream. Instead he, Mieszko-Abraham, heard the hiss of a snake, the laughter of a girl, and the tempting scent of fruit. "The sin has been conceived." Rocks fell on him suddenly, a massive one pressing down on his chest. Abraham died in his dream, but Mieszko gasped for breath with dwindling strength and woke himself up.

"Ah," he groaned, clutching his heart.

The hawk was perched on his chest. The duke sat up heavily, pushing the bird off.

"You scared me, you knave," he reprimanded the bird, but not harshly. "Because of you I had a nightmare. What was it?" He brushed sweat from his forehead. "I think I was climbing. A tree?" He blinked. Suddenly, he realized his face was wet not from sweat, but tears. "I'm an old man," he said to himself, then called Witosz. "Only old men cry for no reason. Friend, tell Oda and the bishop to come to me. And tell Unger to bring ink and parchment with him."

25

❧

ENGLAND

Olav often dreamed of the night he and Astrid had spent in Poland after Geira's death, and the words she'd uttered over the bones she'd cast. Word and water, she'd said. Wisdom and strength, west of Poland. She'd seen a bare rock and a dog and, eventually, finally, his throne. His birthright as the last of the Ynglings, the last of the Norwegian kings.

And so, he and his troops had gone west, to plunder England and fill their coffers while he earned the gold and men needed to fight for his crown. That winter, they gathered on the Isle of Wight. Olav took over the entire northern shore of the island, along with the other chiefs of the sea bandits, known as Odin's Sword.

Separated from the southern shores of England only by the Solent, it was the perfect base ahead of their spring campaign. Jostein and Guthmund, two chiefs who had been working England's shores for a long time, welcomed Olav and his crews happily, and soon after, Sven joined the sea bandits too. He'd freed himself from his imprisonment at the Jomsviking stronghold, but he could not return to Denmark, which was now ruled by Eric and the Swedes. And so, Olav and Sven, who had only recently faced each other in war, unexpectedly found themselves on the same side.

They controlled the strait from four large camps so carefully that even the splash of a big fish would not go unnoticed. In the south, east, and west of the island they stationed sentry garrisons, and they had nothing else to do but mend their ships, clean their weapons, heat up mead in cauldrons suspended over fires, and entertain themselves with local girls.

At first, the chiefs planned to make their housing in the ruins of the Roman keep on the hill, but Olav and Sven refused, preferring to remain with their crews. Guthmund and Jostein had no choice but to follow in their footsteps.

When the warm weather came, the bandits claimed victory after victory in their summer campaigns. They had plundered Folkestone first, following Jostein and Guthmund's advice, then Sandwich and Ipswich. When they reached Maldon, they leveled Earl Byrthnoth's army as a storm destroys a fishing boat. Olav led the attack, and his faithful Varin killed the earl. Since then, he had been known as Varin the Ealdorman Slayer, rather than Painted Fangs.

They celebrated for three days and three nights after their victory, then set out along the entire length of Kentish shores, at Sven's request, attacking settlement after settlement relentlessly. Barely a month had passed before King Ethelred's messenger arrived, waving a white flag and suggesting a ransom.

The four chiefs negotiated with the representatives of the king and the local archbishop. They began at one thousand pounds of silver. Jostein had had enough at three thousand. Sven got bored at five. Guthmund at seven. Olav was still talking, counting on the archbishop's representatives rather than the king's men, and eventually he forced Archbishop Sigeric himself to attend the peace talks with the "Norman hungry for knowledge," as the archbishop soon called Olav. Tryggvason allowed the bishop to say his piece, listening to his stories about God with interest, a God who punishes the evil and rewards the good. He asked to hear about the evil ones. He asked about Lucifer, hell, and other spirits the bishop referred to as unclean. He was intrigued by the devil's names; he repeated each one after Sigeric, pronouncing with pleasure the one which seemed to swell on his tongue: "Beelzebub." "Devil, Ruler of Hellish Fires, Snake!" Sigeric shouted. "Snake?" Olav asked, surprised, and said: "I'm the last Yngling. The king whose sigil is a snake." He negotiated ten thousand pounds of solid silver in return for ending their invasion. They were paid immediately.

The chiefs of Odin's Sword then stood on the shores, the four of them, looking at the packhorses walking from land toward the docks, the never-ending line of heavily stepping animals. Each one carried a hundred pounds of silver, straight to their ships.

"A hundred times a hundred." Jostein smacked his lips, brushing beautiful but impossibly filthy dark locks from his forehead. "And I wanted to stop at three." He handed Sven a horn filled with mead.

"I gave up at five," Sven admitted. "I thought, *I prefer to fight than count,* but I take it back. I prefer to count." He drank, and the mead flowed down his beard. He passed the horn to Guthmund, who drank and burped.

"I counted to seven," he said, "because I don't know any higher numbers. And now I look at seven times seven and again, seven times seven, and still I see more horses carrying our loot. Tryggvason, you're the youngest of us all, but your hair is as white as an old man's, or like the one from the drunken bard's songs. We should call you Silver Ole, that's what."

Olav took the horn and finished it.

"Do you know what I think, chiefs of the sea bandits?" he asked.

"Not the bandits, chief." Guthmund burped again. "We're Sword Odin." He pounded his chest with pride.

"Odin's Sword, you boar," Sven corrected him. "Let Silver Ole speak. Though I think I know what the bishop vanquisher will say."

"Archbishop," Olav corrected him kindly. "I think that if they could pay ten thousand up front, they can afford much more."

Sven laughed so hard it felt as if his belly would burst. Jostein and Guthmund joined him. Olav passed the horn to back to Sven and stepped away to empty his bladder.

"Hey, Silver Ole!" Jostein called after him. "Wait, I need a piss, too."

"Me too," Guthmund burped.

"Meeee!" Sven sang. "Let's piss here."

"No," Olav protested. "I will not piss on the river of silver which is flowing toward our ships."

The ships were now on the shore and shipwrights stood around them, mending holes that looked like battle wounds. And the warriors lay by the fires on sheepskins and drank their hard-earned silver. Even if they drank themselves into a stupor, they wouldn't go through half of what they got. Olav asked his men if they wanted to take their shares and go back to their wives. They didn't. The vision of multiplied silver, as if it were a grain thrown on the ground for the harvest, excited them. And the island women fulfilled their desire for love. Warm and willing, not unlike their wives if they wanted them to be. Olav himself had no one to go back to.

The one he loved and desired was Eric Segersäll's wife. The queen called Sigrid Storråda. Residing behind a wall of her husband's shields. And the woman he'd married lay in the cold ground, along with the son he'd fathered. A clear sign that if he sowed anything, it was death.

That's why the Isle of Wight, known as the Island of Misty Visions, was perfect for him. He didn't drink his large, chief's share of the silver. It stood, enclosed in a chest, and waited for the right time. Silver to silver. It wasn't a seed that could grow in the ground and offer a branch to destructive hail. And not seed he'd leave inside a woman, waiting to see if it led to a daughter, son, or dead fetus. It was cold, hard silver which would grow when spring came, the time for battles. And autumn, when he'd collect his bloody harvest.

He'd sow seeds with his sword for as long as it took to grow a silver field in his tent. And then he'd take it all onto his ships and sail to Lade, where the lords of the north dwelt, Norwegian jarls who held the power he had a rightful claim to due to his birth and blood. There, he'd cut them down and sit on the throne of the Ynglings even if it meant having a bouquet of their heads at his feet.

The flaps of his tent moved aside and Varin the Ealdorman Slayer looked in.

"King, Chief Sven is here to see you," he announced, and his dark eyes gleamed like two narrow lines painted on with dry blood.

"Ask *King* Sven to come in," he said with emphasis. No matter the titles that the others bore, Varin would refer only to Olav as king.

"Olav, I've brought wine. It's thick and red, like blood." Sven's step revealed that he'd already drunk some.

"Come in," Olav said, discreetly signaling to Varin that he should keep his wits about him. Sven had a sword and long Saxon dagger at his belt. The rules of royal feasts did not apply in this camp. They walked around armed, from dawn till dusk, until they collapsed in a drunken stupor.

"Do you like wine?" Sven's long red hair danced in the air when he placed the jug on the bench. The Dane had stopped trimming his beard even before their victory in Maldon, plaiting it instead into two braids, which now stuck out like a fork.

"Sven Forkbeard." Olav laughed and took out a cup, tugging one of the horns of his comrade's beard. "Sit, Sven. I prefer mead, since you ask. Wine doesn't agree with me."

He'd had it at Vladimir and Allogia's feasts, and at his wedding to Geira. It tasted of debts and forced gratitude, a taste he loathed.

"So you won't drink with me?" Sven asked truculently.

"I will," Olav replied, "but I'll join you with my mead." He pulled his jug closer.

"Which of my men did you kill at Rügen?" Sven asked, taking a gulp and beginning the conversation that had been hanging between them since they'd met on Kentish shores.

"Frorik on *Gorgeous Gunhild*," Olav replied. "Forgive me, it was a matter of honor."

"Why?"

"Do you not know who Gunhild was?"

"My aunt. That swine Harald's sister." He bared teeth that shone. "My father's."

Olav was too sober to call her a sow.

"Do you know what she did to my father?"

"Gave him a quick death? It would be like her." Sven laughed. "Do you know that they call her 'Demon Gunhild'?"

"Only a demon would send men after a pregnant woman. She hunted me afterward."

"All right, Olav." Sven leaned over the bench and poured himself more wine. "Screw the demons who led us here. We have our own problems, don't we? A few things that cannot be taken back." Lifting his cup, Sven met his eye. "I remember, every day, that you were the chief of the fleet which defeated my ships at Rügen's shores. One of the ones who forced me to run from my kingdom and leave the throne I had waited for, for so many years."

Anger burned in Sven's irises. He breathed heavily. His lips trembled, like a wolf about to bare his fangs in a snarl.

"Stop," Olav replied. "Your misfortunes are not my fault. I was one of the chiefs of Eric's great fleet, you know how many ships I commanded. I fought in Mieszko's name, and you happened to be my father-in-law's enemy, that's all."

Sven laughed unexpectedly. He could burst out with a laughter as violent as fire.

"Silver Ole. Screw all this. We've left them behind and sailed here to claim solid silver. We earned it with our swords in Maldon."

"Don't lie, Sven. Not to me. You'll earn your share and return to win back your throne from Eric in Denmark," Olav said.

"And you, Silver Ole, you'll take your share and sail to kill Jarl Haakon, for the Norwegian crown," Sven growled.

"Haakon, who your father considered to be his viceroy. Old Harald, whom you hate even in death, enslaved my country. Your people and that false leader Haakon made Norway into a Danish province. And his sweet sister, widow Gunhild, helped him. What, my red-haired friend? What am I supposed to think about on aimless winter days? That by plundering England side by side, we are raising funds for a war we will fight against each other when each of us attains his goal?"

They both drank, finishing what was in their cups. This confession had reached the gnarled roots of their conflicting desires.

Wine calmed Sven down. Mead lulled Olav. They clinked cups, and droplets of the liquids splashed together. Olav looked at the wine which stained his mead with crimson. Sven watched the golden puddle on the surface of his wine's redness.

They both remained silent for a long time, until Sven spoke in a mocking voice:

"Enemies yesterday, allies today. Tomorrow we shall be enemies once more. It's a rather weak conviction to have when entering an alliance." He stroked the stiff braids of his beard and laughed. "Unless we sweeten it with all of England's silver."

"That's what I'm aiming for. Another two or three well-planned campaigns, spring to autumn. Three well-aimed thrusts of Odin's Sword under the leadership of the four chieftains . . ."

"Wouldn't it be easier if it were two?" Sven cocked his head and watched Olav, studying his reaction.

"No. Jostein and Guthmund's forces are larger than ours. You know that the ten thousand pounds of silver has not come from nowhere. If we were all fighting separately, we'd have nought but a couple of ships of plunder. I suspect that the English will mobilize their forces before spring, that's why I want to support the growth of Odin's Sword, not its destruction. Let's send recruiters. To Norway, Scania, the Danish islands, anywhere we might find men. Not mercenaries, but men hungry for adventure . . ."

"Like us," Sven interjected.

"Yes, like us." Olav managed a smile. "England is not my goal, Sven. It's merely a method by which I will reach my goal, and I don't intend to spend any more time here than I must. I want to earn my money quickly, then set my sails for the true prize."

"In this, we agree." Sven reached out an arm for his jug; he poured the liquid out slowly, watching it flow. "Although I'm of the opinion that England is a cow that could be milked forever. But . . ." The wine was finished, and Sven waited until the final droplets fell into his goblet before putting it back down. "If we work so well together here, why not continue? Maybe once we are finished with England, we can move against the Swede together and take away his title of 'Eric Segersäll'?"

To plunder, rape, and burn? Will you come to Sweden? Świętosława spoke in his memory from years ago. *Yes, if you'll agree,* he'd told her. Now he felt his shoulders and neck stiffen, as if he were turning to stone. Even his jaws set; he had to shake himself to answer Sven.

"And then you'll sail to Lade with me and we will kill Jarl Haakon together?" He banged his goblet on the table. "Let's make a pact, Sven. Let's earn as much as we need side by side, to win back our thrones, then let's stay out of each other's way. The north is big enough for us both."

"For us both? Agreed. But there is still the third, Eric Segersäll." Sven poured mead into Olav's goblet and handed it to him with a smile. "Let's drink again, Silver Ole. And don't be angry, friend, but drunk or sober, I will try to convince you to join forces with mine against the bald one."

He's not the third one for me, Olav thought, his eyes on Sven's. *He's the other one. The one who got the woman who should be mine.* Olav knew he shouldn't say another word. If he opened his mouth, he wouldn't be able to control what came out of it.

They clinked cups, and Olav drank a sip. The mead now tasted like the one in his memory, the one in the hunting lodge seven years ago. When Świętosława's eyes had gleamed green and gold when he told her: *I'll defeat your husband and ask for the queen dowager's hand in marriage. Would that suit you?* It was still what he wanted.

He walked Sven out of the tent. The fires in the camp were burning out; the time for sleep was drawing near on the Island of Misty Visions. Weak moonlight reflected off the waters. The rich and defenseless England lay on the other side. Olav took a deep breath, the air a mixture of the cold scent of the ocean, moist earth, and fire smoke. He knew that this was the smell of the camp on the Isle of Wight, but what did that matter? He could only smell one thing: Świętosława from beyond the seas.

26

POLAND

Astrid freed herself from Sigvald's arms and sat up on the bed, sweeping back her hair. She could hear his even breathing; he should be asleep. She was shaky, she wanted to gather her thoughts and prepare for her journey. The tone of Bolesław's summons left her in no doubt; Mieszko wasn't well, and they didn't know if he had months or days left. But before she left Wolin, she had to have Sigvald's word that Jomsborg would remain loyal, even after the duke's death. She felt faint at the mere thought that her husband might betray them. No, anything but that. The work to which she had dedicated her life at Mieszko's bidding could not fall apart.

"As . . ." Sigvald whispered. "Don't run away, wife. We've only just begun."

"I'm getting some water. Do you want some mead?"

"No." Her husband laughed, sounding as if he hadn't been fast asleep moments earlier. "I will drink only what the enchantress does when I'm in her presence. Give me water."

"I'm not an enchantress. I hate it when you talk like that." She passed him a cup and sat on the bed's edge.

Sigvald raised himself into a sitting position. His long dark hair streamed over his chest. He didn't hide his nakedness; quite the opposite. He always gave the impression of someone who was just as comfortable without clothes as he was in them.

"Would you prefer for me to call you a witch instead?" he asked teasingly.

"No."

"So what should I call the woman who healed a dozen dying Jomsvikings? Twelve men over whose injuries swarms of flies were already circling?" His eyes shone oddly in the gloom. "I won't forget the sight of their wounds, and the stinking green pus . . ."

"Stop it. It was the venom from poisoned Finnish arrows."

"But what to call such a woman?" He touched her shoulder.

"Call me what you will." She shook his hand off. "Sigvald, I need to get ready to leave, you know that."

"You leave in the morning, and right now it's a beautiful dark night." He grabbed her shoulders and pulled her into bed. "Come here, Astrid. I need to make the most of having you here before I lose you."

"You won't lose me," she said, and once again felt cold fear squeezing her throat. "Where did you get that idea?" She rolled from her back onto her front and looked in his eyes. "Do you mean to leave me? Me, and the alliance?"

He kissed her lips and smiled, studying her face as if trying to read the thoughts behind it.

"No," he replied slowly, touching her lips with his fingers. "No. For so long as you're loyal to me, Jomsborg and I will be loyal to you, to your father, and your brother after him."

He leaned close as he said this, and she felt his breath on her face. She didn't know how to feign love. She couldn't offer words she knew to be untrue.

"I am loyal to you, Sig," she said, and reached for him.

He responded by pulling her tightly to him, pressing his lips to hers in a kiss that had the flavor of a bite. She felt a wave of desire hit her belly like a storm. They clutched one another as if they hadn't made love for years, though it wasn't even the first time that night. No, she wouldn't lie to him by professing her love; she didn't love him. But he did awaken a wild, animal craving in her. A burning desire for fulfilment, that quickly turned to disgust after. Toward herself, for letting him wake the beast in her again. And toward him, Sigvald, a man she could never respect, because she knew his dark secret. The secret of Hjorunga Bay, eight years ago, when he, Jarl Sigvald, had been the first to call for his forces to retreat. And she knew that not all the iron boys had heeded their jarl's command. That there had been some, like young Vagn, who said no, and fought Haakon's forces. Yes, she knew the stories of his cowardice. The fear which caused him to run from the sea battle with Jarl Haakon. Sigvald had veiled this fear with stories of dark powers that supposedly fought for their enemies. She couldn't love a coward, but she had to live with him, and what's more, she was often afraid of him. She saw the evidence of his cruelty, the unpredictable changes in his moods, and his bravado. Who was he really? The coward who had run from a fight, or the hero who had imprisoned King Sven in Jom and forced a ransom to be paid for him? Whoever he was, all these thoughts were pushed out of her head by lust, like the wind which blows clouds out of its way. The beast in Astrid did not think, it desired the long-haired man with his catlike movements, who took her with the passion of a predator tearing into its prey, never closing his eyes, who seemed to revel in even the bloody scratches she was leaving on his back.

"As!" he hissed as he climaxed.

"Sig!" she replied, falling back onto the bed.

Her heart beat in her chest in a violent rhythm, and her vision darkened. She gulped in air quickly, and let it out slowly. Two, three, four . . . she slowly felt more like herself. The beast had fled into the night.

"Ah, my beautiful As," Sigvald murmured lazily. "I never doubt your loyalty when we're in bed. Why do I fear for it so when you leave?"

Because you're a coward? she thought without opening her eyes.

"I don't know," she replied quietly. "Maybe you are judging me by your own standards, Sig?" She tried to make her voice sound affectionate. "Maybe you want to break the alliance?"

He lay on his side, propped up on an arm. A chain with the silver wolf head of Jom glistened on his chest. He was eyeing her as if he wanted her again.

"No, Astrid. I've known many women, and none have pleased me as much as you. If a feast of many different dishes awaits me every night, I'd be a fool to look elsewhere." He stretched a hand toward her and slid it along a strand of her hair, to her breast. He squeezed her nipple. It hurt. "You have my word that I will not look for another, but you have a promise of your own, just as important: if I find out that you grace another with your touch, then our duty to each other will end. I will be loyal to your family only for so long as you remain loyal to me."

"I have never betrayed you."

"Then pass on what I've said to your father and brother." He smiled and kissed her lips.

She didn't flinch, though she tasted something bitter.

The yard of Poznań's palatium was busy. Carts filed in and out, the servants rushing their tasks as if they were expecting guests. Laundry was hung to dry in the sunny part of the yard; snowy white sheets and heavy tablecloths for the duke's table. Sturdy housewives, the rulers of Mieszko's kitchens, commanded all movement like chieftains at war. At their orders, barrels were rolled toward the kitchens, baskets of vegetables carried in; cages of ducks and chickens, and nets full of fish, were brought. Hay-filled baskets of eggs and Hungarian wine. Since Bolesław had conquered Silesia, Lesser Poland, and then Slovakia and Moravia, a wealthy trade route had opened and goods from the south traveled to Poznań along a well-guarded road, including Bolesław's favorite sweet Hungarian wine.

Either he likes the beverage, or he drinks it when he misses the dead, Astrid thought, handing her horse over to a stable boy. *She was a strange one, Karolda. An outsider that none of us really knew.*

"Run, Pecheneg. I'll catch you anyway, coward!" The air was pierced by a wild shriek.

The cries of housewives jumping out of the way followed swiftly:

"Mary, Mother of Christ, the young Piasts!"

"Purest of Ladies, save us, a civil war again!"

"Lord deliver us from another Piast reunion!"

Two boys chased each other across the yard. The elder was Bolesław and Karolda's son, dark-haired and stocky. His name was Bezprym. He was chasing Mieszko and Oda's youngest son, the chubby-cheeked blond five-year-old Lambert. The younger kicked up mud as he ran, screaming back to Bezprym:

"You're the wild one! Black Hungarian! I don't want to be a pecheneg again. I want to be a margrave."

"Shitgrave, that's what you can be." Bezprym aimed an old apple at him; his aim was true.

Lambert burst into furious tears, but he searched for a stone he might use to regain his honor. A third boy jumped out from behind the stables, the eldest of them all, nine-year-old Mieszko, Oda and Father's first son, named after his father. He crossed his arms over his chest and made a menacing face as he said:

"Silence now! The lord duke Mieszko speaks!"

The boy lifted his chin so high that he didn't see the chicken pecking at his feet, and the association Astrid's mind made between it and father's hawk was so comical that she burst out laughing.

Bezprym retrieved a slingshot from his belt at lightning speed, took aim, and hit Mieszko's knee with a pebble. The chicken ran away, losing feathers as it clucked throatily.

"I defeated you," he shouted happily. "And now, hand it over, you'll pay homage to me. On your knees! And the fat pecheneg, too. Homage to Bezprym! And I'll add a tribute to that, too. Lambert, you'll give me the honey cakes from dinner, and you . . ."

He didn't get a chance to finish, because Oda's servants caught up with them and separated the children. The housewives who had hidden away at the sight of the Piast battle returned to their tasks.

Astrid noticed Unger's tall silhouette in the distance: the new bishop. She nodded to him, and he raised a hand and held it in the air. He had once greeted her with the sign of the cross, not knowing she hadn't been baptized. Now he knew, so he let his hand drop and returned her bow. She walked into the palatium, and though she wanted to run straight to Father's chambers, she turned her steps toward the main hall first. She heard a child's singing, so sweet that emotion clutched at her throat. And then a voice:

"Astrid, it's so good that you've arrived. Girls, welcome your aunt, the great Astrid of Wolin."

Four-year-old Bogumiła and three-year-old Regelinda, both dressed in wide blue dresses, both fair-haired and chubby, with flower wreaths of rue, lilies, and chamomile, bowed politely. Astrid bowed lower, saying:

"Good day, my little princesses."

"May peace be with you, Astrid," they said almost in unison.

Emnilda, Bolesław's wife, embraced her like a sister.

"And where's your son?" Astrid asked.

The girls lifted fingers to their lips and pointed. Little Mieszko, their two-year-old brother, was sleeping on a bearskin, his arms wrapped around two of Bolesław's big dogs.

"How long ago did you arrive?" Astrid asked, lifting Regelinda into her lap.

"My lord husband has been here for two weeks, the children and I joined him three days ago. The journey from Kraków took a week. Do you know how hectic it is when you drag a procession of wet nurses with you?"

I don't, Astrid thought, and suddenly felt sad as she looked at this little herd.

"Did you send a messenger to Sigtuna? Does Świętosława know?"

"She does. Bolz says that if he knows his sister at all, she'll come."

Emnilda called Bolesław "Bolz," the word Saxons used for an arrowhead. She couldn't have chosen a better nickname. She also called him, out of respect for Mieszko, "her duke," that is, the duke's son. Since the two wed, Bolesław had stopped surrounding himself with mistresses. And who could be surprised at that, the woman was pure light and joy. She gave him a new child every year and seemed to only grow more beautiful. Astrid's thoughts were unbiddenly drawn to her sister Geira, who had so longed for a life and a love like this.

"I think that Bolz is mistaken, because how could it be?" Emnilda continued with a worried voice, caressing Bogumiła's pale hair with slender fingers.

"How is Świętosława meant to come here from the distant Sigtuna across the great ocean? She has a child there, a son. Will she come with such a young boy? I'm worried. He needn't have worried his sister by sending her that message . . ."

"Her little boy is older than Bezprym, who defeated two of Oda's sons just moments ago, and demanded they pay him homage," Astrid laughed.

"That also worries me." Emnilda gazed at her with blue eyes. "Those children are constantly fighting."

"Sons are like pups that must grow into hunting dogs." Astrid shrugged and pinched Regelinda's cheek affectionately. "Not like sweet little girls who sing in silver voices, isn't that right?"

"Yes, Aunt," Regelinda agreed seriously. "Lord Father says that daughters are the joy of fathers."

You don't know the cost of being your father's joy yet—she thought of Mieszko and finally brought herself to ask after him.

"There are better and worse days. Sometimes he doesn't recognize us, he calls Bolz Czcibor, his brother, and me . . ." She was flustered. ". . . he calls me the names of many women. But he always recognizes his duchess, and becomes different with her around. You know . . ."

"Submissive?"

"Obedient. It irritates Bolz. Please, go and see for yourself. Talk to your brother; he's been waiting for you."

The last few years had hardened Bolesław; he'd spent them almost entirely in the saddle, on a never-ending mission of conquest. He had filled out and grown his beard, which he kept neatly trimmed, unlike the chestnut locks which reached his shoulders. Brother and sister embraced.

"How do you make such beautiful children?" she asked, kissing his rough cheek. "And when, since you're always off fighting?"

"Do you want to send Sigvald for a lesson? Bishop Unger has set up a school by the cathedral, but I don't know if he'll reveal the secrets of an bedchamber. How is your husband? Will Jomsborg remain loyal to the dukedom?"

"Give me a personal guard to ensure that the only guarantee of the alliance isn't killed by bandits," she said. "The roads from here to Jom are dangerous."

"They are?" her brother asked, anger in his voice. "The devil take them!

I'll order the castellans be chained up, their bloody job is to ensure the safety of all the travelers."

"Wait, wait, don't rush to that end. I have arrived in good health." She held her arms out as if for proof. "But the roads could be made safer, that's all I meant. Now tell me, how is Mieszko?"

"Like you said. The Saxon bitch is feeding him something. Poison." He walked across the chamber with long steps, fuming, the very picture of fury.

"I never said she was poisoning him," Astrid protested. "I said, she gives him mead mixed with henbane—it alleviates pain, but also grants visions, hallucinations, sometimes mixes up the mind."

"So, she's poisoning him." He heard only what he wanted to hear. "Do you know what I think?" he said, pausing midstride. "Theophanu's death was the last straw for the Old Hawk. He hated the empress. He allied with her, since he'd decided it was ultimately in his favor to do so, but he hated her, and she him. Father never forgave her that, even though the empress acknowledged our rights to the south and sent us her troops, she kept Bishop Unger under lock and key in Germany, not granting Father his full Christian rights. So, although she upheld the terms of their alliance, she made sure to also bare her claws. It doesn't matter to you, pagan," he said, brightening up, "but for the dukedom, the loss of a bishop was grave indeed. Father and Theophanu met at the Hoftag in Quedlinburg last year, and she gave him the title 'dux Slavonicus' to anger the Czechs, treating the Old Hawk as the most important of the Slavic leaders. They smiled at each other, drank together, exchanged compliments. But on our way back, he spoke so venomously of her . . ."

Bolesław began to pace again. His thoughts seemed to come easier when he was moving. Possibly because, since the day Mieszko had granted him his first squad, he had never allowed himself to be still, constantly working to expand the Piast legacy.

"His rivalry with Theophanu gave him strength," Bolesław continued. "When the news came two months ago that she'd died in Nijmegen, he broke down. He remembered her as she was in Quedlinburg, blooming, commanding, the picture of health."

"The ruler of the world," Astrid muttered, understanding how personally Mieszko would have felt the empress's death. *No one is immortal* would have taken on a more real and brutal meaning. *Not even rulers.*

"What about the younger children? Has he indicated his will?"

Bolesław snorted. His dislike of Father and Oda's sons was unchanged.

There were many ways Mieszko's will might cause them trouble, but she asked calmly:

"Has he given Mieszko and Lambert lands?"

"He's planning something. Sometimes he says this, sometimes that, when Oda is with us he looks only to her . . . damn it, he must make up his mind, because I have no intention of coming to terms with his wife."

"Calm down, Bolz." She used Emnilda's name for him intentionally, like a charm for peace. It worked. He breathed out, pulled at his hair, rearranged the leather caftan.

"Can we go to him?" she asked.

"Yes. He's waiting for you. And the bold one."

"Does he believe that Świętosława will come?"

At that very moment they heard the horns from the yard, welcoming guests. Astrid assumed it must be more of Mieszko's commanders, but then she recognized the Piast signal. The horns were welcoming family. Bolesław clapped her shoulder, his anger from moments ago forgotten. He pulled her by the hand, and they raced to greet the guests. As if time had turned back and they were children again, much like the ones she'd seen fighting by the stables earlier.

"Here she is," he exclaimed as they bounded in front of the palatium.

Astrid held her breath and whispered, "It's either our bold one, or it's a Viking invasion . . ."

A procession of at least two hundred men rode into the yard. Bald or long-haired, bearded one and all. Many with faces marked by dark scars. Imprisoned in chain mail and helmets, with wolf skins on their backs. Powerful, so that the horses they rode resembled ponies in comparison. They all bore the same shields at their saddles—with the golden boar of Eric's dynasty and the god Frey, to whom Świętosława's husband traced back his lineage. The boar shone with golden thread on the flag they bore before them. Two bearded men at the head of the procession blew into horns resting on their chests; a short blast first, then a longer one, deep from their guts, as if the signal was never going to end.

"The queen of Sweden, wife of Eric Segersäll, Lady Sigrid Storråda," they announced in unison in the quiet that followed. "And Jarl Birger, the royal deputy."

"Jesus of Nazareth, Mother of God," one of the housewives groaned.

The bearded riders moved their horses aside, and from behind their wide backs appeared Birger and Świętosława. Astrid recognized her sister only because she'd been announced. Her youngest sibling had grown. Who could be surprised, she'd left home a girl, but this wasn't just about newly gained height or an aging of features. A queen looked down on them from her horse's back. Her hair, the shade of the brightest amber, was piled on top of her head in spirals, her braids woven with expensive chains. A necklace gleamed between the two brooches which held her dresses, the color of green moss, ocean waters, and fresh grain. A light cloak lined with marten fur was draped over her back. One of her bearded men dismounted and, catching her around the waist as if she were a child, swept her off the saddle and onto solid ground.

"It's inappropriate." She heard Oda's cold voice behind her. So, the lady duchess had decided to make an appearance.

Bolesław's dogs chose that moment to bark and throw themselves along Świętosława's procession. And she, instead of royal greetings, shouted:

"Bolek, call off your dogs. Wrzask and Zgrzyt, heel. Ulf, give me the leash."

Bolesław whistled at his dogs. They ran to him, whining and nipping at the air as they went.

"Better tie them up, brother," their sister called out cheerfully. "Cats on a rope."

Two lynxes stalked out from between the horses of her people.

"Wildcats!" little Lambert called out.

"*Wildcats!*" Bezprym mocked him. "They're lynxes, you chubby fool."

The "rope" was a double leash which had been clasped to the collars of both large cats. It was decorated with silver, fit for many a duchess to wear as a necklace.

Bolesław tied up his dogs and handed them over to Duszan. Only now did Astrid realize that Dusza wasn't with her sister. No woman was. Świętosława had arrived with a procession composed solely of men. Who had done her hair and dressed her? Leading the two lynxes on the leash, Świętosława stepped forward, and Bolesław walked toward her. They looked one another up and down for a moment, then fell into each other's arms. When at last they broke free, Świętosława cast a happy eye over the crowd gathered to greet her, and squealed like a child.

"Astrid!"

She threw her arms around her sister's neck. Astrid almost burst into tears, holding the sister she hadn't seen in too many years.

"Wrzask, smell and remember. This is my sister. Understand? Zgrzyt. Smell. You know what I want. And this is my brother. Brother and sister are like you. Lynx and lynx," she explained to the animals with a straight face.

"Duchess Oda," she said then, in a voice clearly used to giving orders, as she noticed the tall silhouette in the crowd and held a hand out toward her.

Oda stood frozen in place. The last time the two had seen each other was under very different circumstances. Which one should bow to the other today? They emerged from the situation smoothly—they both bowed slightly, as if by accident. Jarl Birger, following Świętosława, bowed to the duchess and kissed her hand, saving Oda the need for niceties, while Astrid looked around the crowd curiously, as did her sister, taking the measure of everyone who had come out to greet her.

"Jaksa? Zarad? Bjornar? Oh, finally, you look like men and not pimply young lads. It's so nice to see you. And those children? Come on, boys, introduce yourselves."

They stepped out in order of age, but Bezprym, unable to keep his eyes off the cats on a leash, pushed forward in front of Mieszko as the first. He bowed his head stiffly and introduced himself:

"Bezprym, my lady."

She reached a hand to him and lifted his chin up gently, studying him. The boy kept his eyes downcast.

"Mmm . . ." she said. "You have wild eyes. That's good, did you know?"

He looked at her with poorly hidden gratitude. Raised without a mother, with constantly changing wet nurses at Bolesław's order, he was mistrustful, and Astrid knew it.

"They call me the Black Hungarian," he grumbled.

"And they call me 'Golden Freya.' Which do you prefer?" she asked, not letting go of his chin.

"Black Hungarian," he said gloomily.

"That's excellent, so they call you what you'd prefer to be called. People call my son 'Skinny Ole,' do you know why?"

"Because he's skinny?" Bezprym suggested.

"You guessed right. People like to call us as they see us. They're foolish, aren't they? Because why vocalize something anyone can see? They call Olof 'Skinny,' and he'll be their king one day. Maybe, once you're a ruler, they'll call you Bezprym the Black, and who cares?"

"Me first!" Mieszko, Oda's older son, pushed his way in front of Bezprym.

"And who are you?" She let Bezprym go and studied the other boy.

"Mieszko. Don't you remember me?"

"No."

"Because I was only little when you sailed beyond the sea." He straightened up proudly. He was a handsome, belligerent boy. "But I'll be a ruler first, before Bezprym the Black becomes one."

"Why?" Świętosława asked. "Perhaps it'll be this sweet chubby one?" She pointed at Lambert. "Come here, little one." She motioned at him to come closer, ignoring Mieszko.

Lambert shook his head and took a step back.

"Are you afraid of my lynxes?" she asked. "And you're right to be. They can sense human fear, and become naughty when they do. Wrzask likes to nip at people's calves. Zgrzyt goes straight for the throat. So, if you want to greet your auntie, Lambert, you have to stop being scared."

Lambert took another step back, and his cheeks trembled.

"I won't be able to greet you, Auntie . . ." he moaned. "I think I'm going to wee . . ."

"Lambert," Oda's voice cut through the air. "Stop that immediately."

The little one burst into tears and ran, not to the duchess, but to hide behind one of the nurses.

"Lambert!" Oda shouted. "Come here."

"Let it be, my lady." Świętosława waved a hand. "He's only a child. One of many."

At that moment, Emnilda emerged from the palatium with the other Mieszko in her arms, Bolesław's two-year-old son, and a girl on either side.

"My God, who's this beauty?" Świętosława exclaimed. "And such pretty things beside her. Another boy . . . your children are multiplying."

"Sister." Bolesław walked over to Emnilda. "Meet my wife, daughters, and youngest son."

Świętosława wrapped the leash around her wrist twice in a barely discernible movement, to lengthen the distance between the lynxes and small children. Emnilda bowed deeply to her.

"My lady."

Świętosława pulled her up from her bow.

"Lady Emnilda, mother of my nieces and nephew, I so wanted to meet the woman who has tamed my brother." She studied her unashamedly. "No, they weren't wrong, all those who said such wonderful things about you. Girls, what are your names?" She leaned down to them.

"Regelinda and Bogumiła," the elder introduced them both, pointing with a finger to indicate which was which.

"Zgrzyt, Wrzask," she summoned her cats. "Sniff the girls. They're sisters. Like lynx and lynx. And your brother?" She straightened. "What's his name?"

"Mieszko," they said in unison.

"I love that name. The lynxes will now sniff little Mieszko and all will be well . . ."

"They didn't sniff me," Mieszko the elder reminded her.

"They did, you just didn't notice, little brother," she said, in a voice that sent shivers down the spines of everyone within earshot.

Astrid caught Oda's furious glance, but before she had time to savor it, a tall and slender figure emerged from the shadows.

"Sister," Bolesław spoke up, "meet the dukedom's new bishop. Unger, this is Queen Świętosława."

The moment that followed engraved itself deeply into Astrid's heart. The same sister who had just divided the family into good and bad fell humbly to her knees in front of the dry bishop, the old abbott of Memleben Abbey.

"Welcome home, daughter," Unger said, lifting her up.

"Welcome home, Father," Świętosława replied.

27

⚛

POLAND

Bolesław led Świętosława to their father's chambers, holding her hand, as if time had turned back ten years. As if they were children again, summoned by the Hawk. Except that he was twenty-five and she was two years younger, and the Hawk was a dying duke.

"Ole stayed with Dusza, which is as if he'd stayed with me, except that he'll be the only one doing the talking and storytelling," Świętosława explained. "And with Wilkomir, since my son is now being raised by men. Wilkomir's lover, Helga, is a remarkable woman, and when I have nights free of Eric, I like to drink with her more than with Thora, Birger's wife. Thora brought Olof into the world, but our age separates us. The rest of the squad you sent me is married, with children, only Wilkomir is so stubborn, he gave Helga a child but refuses to marry. Do you know what he called the boy? Wilczan. Arrogant, don't you think? And Great Ulf, that's the bald one with a missing tooth, with the scarred face, I ordered him to be prepared for anything. If they're needed for longer, I'll leave them behind, under the condition that Ulf and Birger return with me, and Jomsborg provides us with an escort. But if you need them, brother, you can count on one hundred men who cannot be bought."

He squeezed her small, warm fingers and kissed her cheek.

"Thank you, sister. I'm not lacking troops, but 'one hundred men who cannot be bought' might be the deciding factor in the next few days."

He was afraid of what might come next. He had seen Oda's nervous movements, her secret meetings with Przybywoj, a Prague nobleman who, though he'd been loyal for years, could summon Czech troops, which were ever the enemy, any day.

Świętosława continued.

"Just don't count on the lynxes. Wrzask and Zgrzyt are my children, they return to Sigtuna with me. Emnilda is as beautiful as the dawn. If you're disloyal to her, I'll be the first to cast a stone at you. And Unger? Jesus Christ, what a man. Black eyes, pale face. My knees buckled, brother . . ."

"For the first time ever?" he teased.

"Mmm."

"How are you coping in the country in the north?" he asked, serious.

"Well," she replied, "though you cannot imagine what the long northern night feels like, or what life without the Eucharist is. I'll give you a hint: one is like the other."

"They say your husband adores you."

"Of course he does." She shrugged. "Don't think for a minute that it's that simple, though. He's a proud old Viking. When he sails to war, he must win and hang up corpses for his gods, because his name is Segersäll, which means Victorious. And then, when he begins to drink in autumn, he doesn't stop until spring. Do you know what Viking drinking is? Axes and knives fly over the benches until the long night ends. And when he draws his sword, I freeze in fear because that time has come again. They call it the 'hot bed,' but it's like any other bed, though perhaps it has more polar bear fur to cover it. Thank the Almighty that he sired Olof and that our son is a strong, if skinny, boy. Apart from that, I have rebellions at home and in the conquered Denmark to manage, and Eric's bastards from before my time. The rest is, as you say, adoration. You should hear the 'Song of the Mighty,' brother. The Psalms speak of God, while the 'Song of the Mighty' preaches on how to be a northern ruler. I'll send you a bard as a present."

They reached their destination.

"Bjornar, take the leash, Wrzask and Zgrzyt shouldn't be there," Świętosława said.

"Father isn't how you remember him," Bolesław warned as the guards opened the metal-fitted doors to Mieszko's chamber.

Mieszko was fighting Count Wichman. And Margrave Hodo. He anticipated the movements of their armies as if he were a cat that could see in the dark. He gave orders, and moved around the troops by Zehden. He hit against fog as he caught the breaths of the dead. Wichman was once again dying in his arms, whispering about forgiveness and giving him his sword. And then the Veleti roused themselves with wild songs. A beauty surged in front of them, with a net through which water fell. A god with three heads nodded from their flags. They all fell into darkness. The darkness of death, that ruthless lady. And his bishop Jordan was pouring the Warta's waters over him, and the river, sacred because of the baptism, flowed through the whole country with God's grace.

"Father," Bolesław summoned him from the darkness.

"Is that you?" he asked. "My son?"

His eyes were failing him, so he'd recognize people by their voices, or by their smell. Sometimes by the colors which surrounded the figures bending over his bed.

"It's me, Father. I brought a guest. Do you recognize her?"

He strained his eyes.

"Dobrawa?" he asked, pointing at the brightness pulsating at his shoulder.

"No, Father." Bolesław's voice was severe. "Try again."

The brightness didn't wait for his response. She fell onto his bed and whispered:

"It's me . . ."

"Bold one! Daughter . . ." A feeling like the sweetest mead spread through his head. "From so far away? Why?"

"You ask that?" she replied with a sob. "The hawk launches itself for a final flight."

"Yes. I want to leave you," he acknowledged truthfully. Their hands entwined as they held each other. He saw the furious green in her eyes. Her firm grip calmed him. He hesitated. Stopped. "I'll try," he whispered, and admitted: "I was waiting for you."

"And so I've come. Astrid has too; she'll help you pass."

The hallowed silhouette of his older daughter shimmered beyond Bolesław and Świętosława's backs. It was good that she'd come. He felt surer in her presence. He squeezed the fingers of the younger one, whispering:

"Wait. Before I go to God, I must tell you something. Do you remember that night by the Warta?"

"We do," daughter and son murmured in the darkness.

"You are my north." He pointed to her. "You, my son, are the south. Now it's time you spread your wings to the east." He touched his son. "And west." He touched his daughter. "Bolesław, you're like me . . . you know how to create. Build a new nest. Do you hear what I'm telling you? In the south, ah . . . I see a crown in a deathly smudge. Brightness. You'll lift the dukedom into a sacred kingdom. My hunter, be wary . . ." The words came with difficulty, he fought for breath with each one, as if he was ripping them out of himself.

It's strange, he thought, *that a man has his entire life to hold important conversations, but he leaves them until his last moment, as if he didn't know that every word would cost thrice as much.*

"Remember, there are no boundaries . . . the horizon moves every time you reach what you thought would be the end, but . . ." He had to rest again. Calm his breath. "Eagle, you will only be able to conquer when you have peace at home. That's the most important thing . . . Don't allow the country to be divided. I leave much for the chicks, but you rule over them, or use your beak to put them back in their place. And you, my daughter queen, protect the north as you go west. Don't be afraid. It's fire that carries victory. Ice carries love and fame shorter than a song. Astrid," he summoned his daughter from behind them. "You bring them both peace. You're like the priestess of silence."

He felt his words ending. He'd told them everything they needed to know.

"Father," Astrid called from the darkness. "Tell me of my mother."

Oh, yes . . . I owe her that much.

"Urdis . . ." He summoned her beautiful figure from his memories. "Urdis was unhappy because your Freya gave her a gift beyond her strength. She saw my future in the bones she cast: great victories, an enormous country, and a crown after death. But she paid for her gift with her life, Astrid. She sent you to protect the country, and she died in my arms. Now do you understand why I always asked so much of you, daughter?" Tears danced beneath his eyelids. "Urdis was as special to me as . . . I felt so much sorrow for her . . . I would rather she had not had her gift, but had lived . . ."

The hawk screeched hollowly in the dark. Mieszko shivered.

"Father," Świętosława's voice cut through the air. "Your bird has eyes of fire."

"Bloodshot?" Astrid asked, her face vanishing in mist.

"Yes, bloodshot," his younger daughter replied.

And he knew his time had come.

Świętosława had never seen an old hawk before. A bird like this wouldn't stand a chance out in the wild. Too weak to hunt or protect a nest with chicks. Yes, nature would condemn it to death, but this was Mieszko's hawk. It had no enemies, no predator stalked it, it didn't have to hunt to eat. This wasn't how she remembered it. It was smaller, it had shrunk. Its feathers, once sleek and smooth, were now matted and stood on end. Gray spots appeared on its bright yellow talons. And that eye. Once, it had been a piercing, bright gold. Now it was a fiery, burning red. But still proud.

She sat by her father, who had closed his eyes for a moment, and she looked at his pointy beard, white as a bone, and she wondered if she'd done the right thing by coming. She could have sent Bolesław the troops he needed, and stayed in Sigtuna. She would have remembered Mieszko how he used to be. The lord father, chieftain, duke. The man whose hand she now held was fragile.

No, she told herself. *His body may be frail, but his spirit still burns. His words may come with difficulty, but what he says is still great. He's just as he's always been. Setting us tasks yet again. Ordering us around. Pushing the horizon further and further.*

The doors of the chamber opened to reveal Duchess Oda. A few lords stood behind her, nine-year-old Mieszko and chubby Lambert at her side. *Yes, they are also his children,* she sighed reluctantly. *They want to say goodbye, as we all do.* But she didn't stand up from next to her father's bed, she didn't make any space for them. *They can approach from the other side if they like.*

"Duke?" Oda asked in a quiet, meek voice.

He opened his eyes and recognized her instantly.

"Wife?"

"Yes, it's me. I brought your sons, Mieszko and Lambert." She was trying to control the shaking in her voice.

"What have you done to my hawk?" He pointed a bony finger at her. "Speak!"

"I haven't done anything to it, husband," Oda replied softly, as if she were speaking to a child.

"You poisoned it. It has a red eye. You poisoned the hawk."

Oda paled.

"Husband, the irises of old birds' eyes change color," she explained quietly. "Your hawk has seen many years . . ."

"Yes, my duke," a commander behind her added. "It's true. I have hawks for hunting and every one of them . . ."

"Who speaks?" Mieszko asked, shaking his head, unsure, like a bird.

"Przybywoj, my lord." The man bowed, though father couldn't see it.

"Did you feed it?" He returned to the matter at hand angrily.

"I did, husband," Oda admitted.

Mieszko simmered with helpless fury.

"You know I allow no one to feed it, only me, just me . . ."

Oda knelt on the other side of the bed. She grasped Mieszko's other hand. Świętosława didn't let go of the one she held.

"Husband, it would have starved to death. Yes, I have fed it, because you haven't left your bed in weeks."

Mieszko panted and realized that the duchess was right. She sighed with relief and kissed his hand.

Perhaps she's not as cruel as I thought? Świętosława wondered, watching the affection with which Oda treated Mieszko.

"I brought your sons, Mieszko and Lambert," the duchess said, touching her cheek to her husband's hand. "I want you to give them your blessing."

He nodded. Oda looked across the bed at Świętosława, as if asking whether she'd make room for the boys, but Świętosława didn't answer her gaze, and she didn't move.

The duchess sighed sadly, stood up, and called for her sons.

"Come here, to Father. Come as close as you can."

I wonder if little Lambert will be afraid, Świętosława thought. Lifting her head, she saw that there were more people in the room than before. Apart from the ones who had come with Oda, other lords had entered, ones whose names and faces she couldn't recall. Astrid had retreated into the depths of the room, but Bolesław had done the opposite, stepping forward and standing at the foot of Mieszko's bed, opposite his father.

Mieszko made the sign of the cross over each of the boys, and each one leaned down to kiss their father's hand.

"Lord Father," Bolesław said gravely, "this is a good time for you to announce your decision regarding the division of power and the country after your death."

"Leave it alone, Bolesław," Oda spoke gently. "Let's not interrupt the duke's final moments with such matters. Everything is clear."

"No," Bolesław interrupted her. "This needs to be settled. As the first-born, I want to give my brothers lands, and I want Father to choose them."

"Your father has already done that," Oda continued in the same calm and polite manner. "Bishop Unger has a document which contains everything."

What the hell is going on here? Świętosława thought, simultaneously feeling Mieszko's grip on her fingers tightening.

"Father? Do you wish to say something?" she asked quickly.

He nodded.

"Silence," she hissed at the gathering.

"Bolesław . . ." Father whispered, quietly but clearly, "is my heir, because he is like me. A strong predator. Oh, son," he groaned, "sometimes you must trample on convention . . ." He swallowed. "I have told you everything . . . everything . . . and now, my time has come. The light calls me to me . . . Dobrawa," Father laughed, "have you come for me?"

Świętosława felt a fist tighten around her heart, because she knew that this was it. A low singing reached her from the entrance. She turned around, without letting go of Father's hand. The crowd stepped aside, giving Unger space, and the priests who accompanied him, carrying large, fat candles and humming a psalm. They surrounded the bed in a bright glow. Unger stood on Bolesław's left at the foot of the bed and lifted his arm to give his blessing.

"A moment please, Bishop," her brother interrupted, and drew his sword. Oda shouted:

"No!"

The look he gave her silenced her instantly, and he walked over to father, laying the sword at his side.

"Duke Mieszko was a leader and a warrior. He must die like a chief, with sword in hand," he announced to the room.

Mieszko's fingers wrapped around the hilt.

"Yes, he was a great chief," Unger said in a voice that sent shivers down Świętosława's spine. "But, most importantly, he was the one who opened the doors to Christ. I give you my blessing, Duke, for this last journey. May the Lord's angels lead you in a procession armed with God's Word. And may they guide you to our Lord. Amen."

As he spoke, he made the sign of the cross over Mieszko. Father died with his eyes and mouth wide open, as if he had a final word he had wanted to say. The priests never stopped humming their psalm, wanting it to guide him on the other side of life.

Oda started to cry. She was covered in tears and choked on her sobs. She threw herself on the body, which was still warm, though already beginning to cool. Świętosława felt it under her fingers all too well. She didn't let go of Father's hand. One held the sword, the other her hand. There was little left for Oda.

The duchess lay across Mieszko's body while the psalm lasted. When it ended, she got to her feet quickly and, without wiping away her tears, said:

"Now we can go to the audience hall and read out the great duke's final will."

Bolesław knew that there was a document that had recently been created, in his absence and under Oda's watchful eye. Unger had told him about this, but he was pledged to secrecy and he didn't reveal any of the details. He added only that he would take the announcement of its contents on himself, and cautioned: "Prince, don't call it a will. It's only a document, please remember that."

This did nothing to settle Bolesław's nerves, which was why he had insisted so strongly on father deciding what lands his half brothers were to have. The duchess's influence over Mieszko during the last year had been so strong that he couldn't rely on his father's common sense. Now, walking to the main hall, he felt shaky. He hadn't lost a single word that Mieszko had uttered that day. *"You're like me. A strong predator." "Sometimes you must trample on convention." "I leave much for the chicks, but you rule over them or use your beak to put them back in their place."* He was afraid he would have to fulfill this bloody will.

At first, when he stepped over the threshold to the hall, he felt as if he'd gone back in time. Everything was as it used to be, the purple-red silks hanging from the ceiling, a row of court guards in silver chain mail lining the walls, and the great golden cross on the main wall, with St. Peter's sword mounted underneath it. An archaic cleaver. That's when Mieszko's empty throne on the raised platform stung his eyes. Like an open grave. Oda's throne beside it. His fingers made their way to the empty sheath at his side. His sword remained in Father's cold hands.

"We can sit together," the duchess said in a tone intended to convey her goodwill.

He stood by the platform, turned around, and spoke first to Oda:

"Forgive me, but I will decide what we do now."

Then he announced to the room:

"The great duke has died, but the dukedom remains. Even as we mourn and worship his memory, we will rejoice through our tears, because just as God promised Father eternal life, so his work on this earth hasn't yet ended. I'll accept oaths of fealty from you today."

"The will," Oda said coldly, meeting his eyes.

Far more people were gathered in the hall than could possibly have fit in Mieszko's chamber. Emnilda with their children and Bezprym. Astrid. Świętosława, who had reclaimed the lynxes from Bjornar on her way from Father's chamber, and now kept them close to her side. Black-eyed Bishop Unger, the priests. Lords from almost every land. Other nobles stood behind Oda, alongside Mieszko and Lambert. Zarad and Jaksa guarded the door. Bjornar was undoubtedly doing what he'd been ordered to outside. *Let it be done,* he thought, and said:

"Please, read the document." He remembered everything Unger had told him.

The bishop picked a priest, and he began to read in Latin. Bolesław caught individual words. *Dagome iudex*—Dagobert? The name father used when he was confirmed? *Craccoa, Oddere.* His heart beat faster. Kraków. He had conquered it himself. Damn it . . .

"Translate it, please," he ordered.

"I'll do that," Unger said, taking the parchment. "This document says that the duke, under his rarely used name Dagobert, and Duchess Oda, and their sons Mieszko and Lambert, give into the pope's care in Rome the dukedom, the lands between Szczecin and Pomorze, the lands of the Prussians, Rus in the east, Kraków in the south, Ołomuniec and the River Oder in the west."

"What does this mean?" Bolesław had never exerted so much self-control. "The duchess said this was a testament, but I hear nothing about his last will."

Unger's black eyes revealed nothing.

"The duchess used the wrong word. It's not a testament, it's a document. And it means exactly what I said, my lord. It gives the country into papal care," he replied loudly.

"And it delineates the borders of my sons' country," Oda added melodically.

The lords murmured.

"No, my lady," Unger replied firmly, his expression unmoving. "It only gives the majority of the dukedom into the pope's spiritual, not military, care."

"But he who hands over power has power," Oda announced triumphantly. "The document clearly speaks of the duke, me, and our two sons. Not a word about Bolesław."

He was about to speak, but the bishop shook his head.

"Prince Bolesław wasn't in Ostrów Lednicki, my lady, so he couldn't subscribe to this devout intention. Allow me to remind you, my lady, that the prince was at the time conquering the lands which are missing from this document: Małopolska, Moravia, Slovakia . . ."

The lords were nodding in agreement around them.

Oda took two steps toward Unger, her eyes narrowed.

"We were both in his bedchamber," she hissed. "Don't tell me, Bishop, that you don't understand that my husband's final wish was for our sons, Mieszko and Lambert, to take power in the lands named in this document. Bolesław can have the rest."

A dangerous roar went around the chamber. Bolesław silenced it with a single gesture.

"I leave much for the chicks, but you rule over them" and *"My hunter, be wary"*— Father's last words echoed in his skull. He thundered:

"Don't provoke me, Duchess, to be impolite to you in front of the court. 'Bolesław can have the rest' is the most offending thing an heir could hear.

Because this is where the Piast throne is. We are from here. From Poznań, Gniezno, Giecz. The 'rest' that you speak of, we conquered it. Or, to be accurate, I did. And I don't have anything against the fact that my lord father, you, and your sons gave my land," he said these words slowly, with emphasis, "into the care of the Holy Father. A country which has been baptized for barely thirty years could use some additional prayers in its name. But don't try to tell me, and those gathered here, while Mieszko's body is still warm, that my lord father wanted to disinherit his firstborn son, the one he had been raising as an heir for years." His voice grew louder as he spoke, and the last words echoed in a shout.

"Heir! Heir! Heir!" The hall rang with the chant.

Oda paled, but showed no humility. She collected herself, took Lambert and Mieszko's hands, and raised them.

"These are also heirs. If you insist on the importance of your father's testament, then what will you give your brothers?"

"It's not a will, my lady," Unger spoke loudly, handing the parchment to her. "It's a spiritual gift. The word 'testament' doesn't appear once, you can see for yourself, you were a nun in the abbey in Kalbe, were you not, so you learned Latin, I suppose?"

She reddened.

"God and the witnesses gathered here heard me ask Father until his last breath to indicate which lands he leaves my brothers. He didn't do it, so I must decide myself."

"He did." She threw herself at him, ready to forgo civility, it seemed. But she stopped midstep as Świętosława's lynxes growled.

Lambert burst into loud tears.

"He did," Oda repeated. "My sons' lands are named in the document. Did you not hear your brothers' tears in the moment of death?" she called out, lifting their arms.

"No, my lady, I disagree. There is nothing of the sort here." Unger used his authority to back Mieszko's firstborn son again.

Bolesław spoke clearly. "This is my will: I give Pomorze, from Kołobrzeg to Gdańsk, to Mieszko. Lambert will have the Kalisz region and Łęczyca, and he should prepare to take the spiritual path. Bishop Unger will raise him so that he might become a bishop, once he has been sufficiently educated. You, as the dowager duchess, can rule his lands as regent."

"You must be joking." Oda laughed.

"That's dishonorable, it's not enough," two nobles who supported Oda joined in, but no one else did.

"You want to remove Lambert from your path, is that it? You've separated their lands from each other so they cannot unite? And you have given me, though I am a duchess, no more than Łęczyca?" she exclaimed.

"My father made you a duchess, you were a marchioness before, and a nun. The road is clear, Lady Oda. If you don't agree with my will, I won't stop you, you can go back where you came from." He paused, for a moment, to calm his voice. And he added, levelly: "But without your sons. They stay. Lambert will begin his education immediately, and Mieszko will leave for Gdańsk. As the eldest, I'm taking over care for my brothers."

"No! No, I don't agree to this. And I name you all witnesses to how Bolesław has dishonored Mieszko's will in the moment of his death. Mieszko wanted his eldest son to rule over the conquests in the south. Silesia, Małopolska, Moravia, and Slovakia. And the younger were to get what he had written down for them. Bolesław is harming a widow and children . . ."

He walked over to her and placed his hands on her shoulders. He could see every twitch of her eyelid. Every tiny wrinkle on her still-beautiful face. Every muscle pulsating in anger.

"What harm?" he asked, and his fingers squeezed tight on her shoulders. Yes, this was a threat. She pretended not to feel it. She stared into his eyes defiantly. "I gave you and my brothers land. You will want for nothing."

"I want to stay in Poznań," she began to negotiate. And let go of her sons' hands.

"No. I don't need to live under one roof with my father's widow."

"Ostrów Lednicki, then."

"You won't bear any more children, and Ostrów is the Piast nest. Our chicks hatch there. And yours . . . they will either obey me, or I will do what the eldest eagle chick does."

"What's that?" she asked, and finally he sensed her fear.

"Peck them apart," he said, quietly that only she could hear him, and tightened his grip on her shoulders so that she hissed in pain. He added loudly: "My father was a hawk, I will be an eagle."

"I won't give up my sons to you!" she shouted, pushing his hands off her shoulders. "They're mine."

He walked over to Mieszko and Lambert in two big steps, and put an arm around each boy.

"You're mistaken, my lady. Sons belong to the dynasty." Lambert stood calmly, but nine-year-old Mieszko was shaking under Bolesław's arm. *Like me when I was afraid that Father was leading his firstborn to the pyre,* he thought, and for a moment he felt sorry for the boy. But this wasn't the time for sentiment.

"Don't allow the country to be divided. I leave much for the chicks, but you rule over them," he heard Mieszko inside his head. He continued:

"Daughters belong to fathers, then to their husbands. Widows don't belong to anyone and are reliant on the heirs' graciousness."

"Disgrace," one of Oda's guard stated, and reached for his sword. "This isn't how you treat a widow."

Bolesław didn't even have to nod. Jaksa knew what to expect and what he should do. They disarmed the guard and escorted him out of the hall.

"Does anyone else think that Mieszko's widow is being harmed?"

No one spoke. Bolesław stepped onto the platform and sat down on his father's throne. He had waited for this moment for years, but now he barely even felt it happening. Because he knew it wasn't over yet. The most important was still ahead of him. Oda stood with her children, facing away from him. She was the only one to do so.

Bishop Unger called out:

"No sin was intended when the duke's document was created, I'm sure we will all agree to that. It's time for oaths of fealty, pledged in front of God."

Bishop Unger stood by Bolesław's throne, under St. Peter's sword hanging on the wall, and the golden cross, clearly indicating who was to stand guard over the honesty of the words which were about to be spoken.

"Duchess."

Oda seemed to be fighting herself. She flinched and grabbed her sons' hands again. And then, without turning, she walked out of the hall, taking them with her. Lambert turned around for a moment, Mieszko did not.

As the gathered lords pledged their fealty to Bolesław one by one, Unger whispered with a stony expression:

"Mieszko was the one who said that when you're defending the dynasty's nest, the last step of defense is to cut off both bridges with a single stroke."

28

THE BALTIC SEA

Świętosława leaned against the gunwale of the *Wave Queen*. Eric had ordered the ship built because they'd planned for the royal couple to travel to Roskilde and Hedeby, to present themselves to their Danish subjects and bring peace to the conquered province. But plans changed, her king was smothering unrest caused by attacks from the east, and she had sailed to her father. The *Wave Queen*'s first journey was thus the journey to accompany Mieszko's last. There was enough space on the wide deck for her one hundred men who could not be bought, who were coming back to Sigtuna with her. Bolesław had managed without them, sending Oda and her boys to the Saxon border.

It had been easier than she'd anticipated, she thought, looking at the rainbow mist that had appeared as if by magic as the sun shone on the water breaking against the *Wave Queen*'s gunwale. Oda had found refuge at the court of one of her distant relatives, but despite her best hopes, none of the Saxon nobles stepped up to support her in her cause. Apparently, she had been counting on Empress Adelaide, the second wife of Otto I, as Oda had been to Mieszko. She had counted on the solidarity of second wives, but all she'd received was cool disdain. Oda was suddenly reminded that she'd walked into the marriage bed straight from an abbey, that she had placed secular service above the godly kind. Nonsense! Even Świętosława, who had hated Oda for as long as she could remember, wasn't so blinded by anger to think that it had been Oda's decision to make at the time, rather it had been Margrave Ditrich's, Oda's father. The old one was dead, his political influences lay dead with him, and Oda was now punished for it.

Duchess Icicle, as Świętosława sometimes still thought of her, was a Saxon schemer; she had tried to cheat with the document, hoping that Mieszko's lack of clarity of mind and Bolesław's long absence from court would result in her having greater influence among the nobles. But she had been wrong on every count. By giving herself into papal care, she had angered the empire, which in return refused to help her and her sons. Bolesław had won fame and the respect of the lords; he'd fought with them in the battles for their new southern territories, and all of them had gained incredible riches alongside her brother's victories. Oda had sorely unestimated the respect that had been hard-fought and well-earned by Mieszko's first son, the Eagle, as they now called him.

A seagull cawed overhead. It flashed snowy-white wings between air and water, and caught a fish in its talons.

I learned two lessons from Oda, Świętosława thought, watching the seagull with its prey. *The first was about how to control a husband. I used that one, disregarding the pain. And the other, of how easily you can lose everything if you place too much on one side of the scales. I'd be a fool not to learn from her mistakes. Dear God, I wanted to be a widow queen once,* she thought. *"Widows don't belong to anyone and are reliant on the heirs' graciousness."* Theophanu . . . noblemen and their troops had rallied behind that widow. Oh, when Bolesław had told her that the empress had died, she'd stomped like a child, shouting: "No, I don't agree, Theophanu can't be dead!" It had been almost beyond belief that the woman who had finally achieved everything had given in to death like . . . like an ordinary person, like . . .

Świętosława shook herself and walked to the stern. Wrzask and Zgrzyt slept in a cage under her tent, stretched out between the two sides of the ship. She had to close them in, since they grew unsettled at sea. They didn't want to eat, and would growl sadly. It was better they slept.

What if Oda spoke the truth? she thought. *Had father really wanted to place his younger sons within the Piast inheritance, and make Bolesław the ruler of the conquered lands in the south?* After all, he'd said: "Sometimes you must trample on convention" and "Bolesław, you're like me. You know how to create. Build a new nest. In the south." It was difficult to understand the words of the dying. No. She pushed this thought away firmly, that Mieszko might have wanted to disinherit his first-born. Nonsense.

She paused for a moment beside the men playing hnefatafl. A great royal battle was playing out on the board; round white and red stones indicated military movements. It took her no more than a glance to see that the stones of the white army were smothering the red, because though the whites had lost more soldiers, their tactics were superior.

The sun beat down mercilessly, and only the wind over the waves cooled the air. Great Ulf was dozing, shirtless, stretched out on a sheepskin. She stood over him. How old was this ugly man? His body looked like Eric's. Hard, tanned skin with a network of old scars. No longer young, but still strong and large. When Mieszko had given her away, he'd looked the same, and now he'd just died. She leaned over the sleeping Ulf and covered him with a shirt. A moment more and the sun would burn his skin like meat on a spit.

She returned to the bow of the *Wave Queen*. The view seemed endless under the clear summer sky. *"Remember, there are no boundaries . . . the horizon moves every time you reach what you thought would be the end."*

She unplaited her braids, one by one, and let her hair fly loose in the wind. Droplets of salty water splashed onto her face. The strands of hair untangled with no help from her, as if the air was brushing them for her. She closed her eyes. She lifted her arms to her head, touching the long strands floating in the breeze. She laced her fingers over her forehead and moved her hands over her head, to the back of her neck. She touched the birthmark she found there. A round mark, she could barely feel it. She had no idea she'd had it until Dusza had shown her the mark on Olof's skull. Dusza had laughed with her mouth and taking her hand, showed her that Świętosława bore the same mark. Świętosława had asked Astrid, who'd been preparing Mieszko for his funeral with the gray servants, to check if father had one too. Yes. Bolesław, Bezprym, tiny Mieszko, and the two sweet girls. She hadn't had time to check her half brothers' heads. They'd left before it had occurred to her. Damn it! Regret would change nothing, but yes, she felt sorry for those boys. Timing was not on their side.

She shook her head free of these thoughts. She felt wetness on her face: no, those weren't tears. Wet ocean wind. But what if the tables had been reversed? If Oda and her two sons had been victorious in this battle, chasing Bolesław away? Would she really be giving in to sentiment then, feeling sorry for those boys? No. She opened her eyes, knowing she preferred the truth to even the sweetest lies.

"My lady?"

She turned violently. The voice had spoken right next to her ear. Much too close.

Jarl Birger stepped back and offered an apologetic smile.

"I didn't mean to intrude."

Then what are you doing here? she thought angrily, but she assured him instead that he was not. She was a queen who still carried Oda's lesson behind her eyelids.

He took a place beside her. They stood in silence, looking at the waves, which changed from green to navy. Then she felt his gaze on her.

"Why are you looking at me?" she asked.

"Your hair is down."

"I wanted to feel free for a moment."

"I know. You carry a heavy load, and your visit to Poznań must have given you much to think about. A widow queen must have her allies, as strong as those of her dying husband."

She didn't answer. She wanted him to continue.

"Duchess Oda made a mistake women are frequently guilty of. She overestimated the power of a court, and underestimated comrades in arms. She thought too much of the value of blood, counting on the fact that two sons would be equal to a firstborn. But how do you measure such value when the firstborn are twins?" He, like her, was considering Thordis's sons, Eric's bastards.

"If I had another son apart from Olof, I'd do what Bolesław came up with. I'd make him a bishop. Spiritual and secular power in one dynasty," she replied, not looking at him.

"Even if you had another three, Eric would never agree to it. It's a good idea for a Christian country, but not for us."

"'For us' sounds ridiculous coming from your lips, Birger. The two of us wish for a Christian kingdom, after all."

He touched her hand, which was resting on the gunwale.

"Queen Świętosława . . ." He pronounced her name so carefully and with such worship that she was too surprised to withdraw her hand. "Everything you dream of is always close by. I carry the same great plans in my heart, and I want to fulfill them beside you. I was a chief at every one of Eric's wars, the army listens to me as it does to him. Give me a sign if that is what you want."

She stiffened. She should strike him now, and punish him for the insult. Bloody hell. Eric was alive, and Birger was talking about what would be after his death. But Oda's lesson was too fresh, etched into her heart too deeply. She slipped her hand from under his and squeezed his fingers, choosing her words so that they meant everything and nothing all at once.

"It's good that you're thinking about the future, Jarl. The Almighty God looks down on all our actions. The one whose name we both worship in prayer."

He returned the pressure on her fingers with rather too much enthusiasm. She wanted him to walk away, to leave her alone with her now doubly turbulent thoughts. As if on command, the wind hit the sail, which billowed dangerously, causing the *Wave Queen* to lean to one side.

Birger wrenched his hand from hers and looked upward. The sky still seemed to be clear, but a mist was approaching from the west.

"A storm rarely comes from a clear sky," he said, meeting her eyes. "More often it's from clouds which are not yet visible to our eyes. Have you spoken to your husband about the oath he made seven years ago, my lady?" Świętosława had not, though she knew perfectly well what Birger was referring to. *A man must die when he's in full strength,* Eric had said, and *My sacrifices aren't yours.* But they would be hers. Hers and Olof's. And she wasn't prepared to face them yet.

Birger's eyes never left hers.

"Time is as merciless as Odin, my queen."

29

⚭

ENGLAND

Sven needed a woman after every fight. For the Danish heir, the euphoria from a victory, fury caused by defeat, pain of lost comrades, happiness at the loot gained, gratitude that death had once again missed him, all this fermented in him like beer in a brewery, leading to only one thing: he wanted to make love and drink. In the English camps, there was plenty of opportunity to do both. They hadn't taken any women by force, they hadn't had to. The women offered their bodies in return for protection, or rather, to prevent attack. The peasants wanted to pay for their villages, the sweet merchant daughters for towns, the ealdorman daughters for entire provinces. But Sven hated having his hands tied, so he never accepted these offers. He found himself women independently, agreeing on a price. He was as good as his word, and paid with silver.

Olav Tryggvason's idea to recruit new people had been a success. A hundred new men had greeted them after their first winter on the Isle of Wight. Jarl Haakon's arrogant subjects from Norway, Icelandic bandits exiled for escaping the Althing's rulings, fishermen from Scania, who didn't care whether they caught fish or plundered English villages in times of poor crops. Those who suffered most because of the great bald Swede Eric's taxes on the small Danish islands. Sven's old subjects met him uncertainly, not voicing what they were all thinking: that Sven had lost the battle for their lands, that they held him responsible for the horrendous conditions in which they lived today. According to the agreement he'd made with Olav, each chieftain incorporated any men from their own lands into their crews. Even the deep scowls of his islanders' began to fade after the first victorious battles, and after the second plunder they loudly called for "King Sven" at the feasts.

"Yes, sweet Mary. I want to be King Sven," he whispered into the red-haired beauty's ear. He had picked her out of the crowd by her fiery hair.

"Are you fiery only on your head?" he'd asked, and she'd boldly replied,

"Between the legs, too. If you're not afraid, my lord, you can check for yourself. But don't blame me if you get burned."

But he didn't burn himself, and Mary didn't disappoint. So, he'd been checking for the past six months, and he still hadn't had enough. Perhaps because it had been six months of battle? Or perhaps because her hair was redder than his own.

"You're my king already . . ." Mary purred in his ear, rolling to her side. She liked it when he took her from the side. She was flexible, writhing in his arms like a fish lifted out from water.

"I've been a king since birth," he said, squeezing her white breast, "but I won't be content until I take my place in the great hall in Roskilde, and until my nobles pay homage to me."

"Do I not give you enough?" she asked playfully. "Take me to your Denmark. I want to be your danegeld."

Danegeld. Danish forced tribute. That's the word the English used to describe the ransom King Ethelred had paid them.

No, sweet Mary. You're only the tax on the plunder, the silver won with blood, which will give me back my throne. Even if I don't get bored with you, you'd sail with me as one of many. You won't be my lady, my queen. You're lovely, but you're not the one who will sit beside me on Harald's throne.

"Where are you from?" he asked, breathing in the scent of her hair.

"Canterbury. My father is the kennel master for Archbishop Sigeric. Ah . . ." She stuck out her bum, waiting for his thrust. "Come on, hurry up."

"Who did you sleep with before me?"

"With the head stable master, with the overseer of the archbishop's servants, with the tax collector . . . oh yes, Sven!"

"Why did you replace your tax collector with me?"

"Because you chose me . . . more, more!"

"How am I different from them?" He thrust harder and harder.

"You pay me. They took for free."

"That's all?" He grabbed her red hair and pulled.

"You're a king and your cock is better than theirs. Oh, Sven! You pay and you win against them . . . it's better to be a king and captain's mistress than a tax collector's, even if the king is a barbarian."

Jostein and Guthmund, the other two chieftains in the four who called themselves Odin's Sword, had separated from them and gone to hunt themselves. Sven had laughed, since he had proposed exactly this to Olav six months ago, and Olav had said no. They'd been saved only by their new crews, rallied at Olav's suggestion, so they didn't feel the loss as sharply.

But Silver Ole worried him. They'd fought side by side so many times now, ship by ship, shoulder to shoulder. Olav was strange. Ruthless. He didn't break eye contact when they argued. He didn't change the topic when Sven reached for his sword. And he didn't hesitate for a heartbeat when he killed. Even when the son of an English ealdorman was removing his helmet, dropping to his knees and giving up his riches and family. Olav killed even when his prey looked in his eyes. He'd say "Die!" and cut them down, cold as steel.

That first year, the two of them had joined Jostein and Guthmund, creating the army known as Odin's Sword, and had claimed ten thousand pounds of danegeld after successful attacks. When the other two chiefs had sailed away with their men, Sven had suggested they rename their troops Odin's Breath, and Olav agreed. The Breath fought against a fleet the English had been putting together all winter, led by Earl Elfric, and skirmish after skirmish, battle after battle, the Breath pushed the English forces back toward London, until they disintegrated into dust. It was a dual success: they smashed the forces gathered by the English with such difficulty, destroying their heavy and hard-to-control battleships, and, most importantly, they sowed the seeds of fear.

King Ethelred spent all of winter preparing London to defend itself from the "wild invaders," sure that the following spring would lead Odin's Breath to the Thames. And the two chiefs took their forces to the Isle of Wight for a winter rest, then went where they weren't expected to go in their third spring: to the undefended Northumbria. They plundered the northern shores until the end of summer, and eventually finished their looting with an effective attack on the giant castle—Bamburgh—which fell after a week of brutal fighting. Sven and Olav captured plunder so great that they had to take the local ships they hadn't destroyed to transport it all.

Now, they celebrated their victory in the great halls of Bamburgh: he and Olav, the chiefs of the victorious fleet, rode up the stone steps on horseback and into the audience hall, holding torches in their hands, and seeing them, their men shouted:

"Two kings!"

The crowd picked up the phrase and they chanted under the roof of the ancient British stronghold.

"Two kings! Two kings!"

The hall was enormous, with a damaged east wall where a fire had begun during the storming of the castle. A hole now opened out onto the North Sea like a great window. That's why the benches and tables were arranged by the opposite west wall. They rode up to them on horseback, and Jorun, his friend, called out,

"The Army of the Two Kings is a good name for those who conquered this castle as Odin's Breath."

"If it will tempt King Ethelred from the bear's lair he's hidden himself in, then why not?" Olav responded, jumping down from the saddle.

"And if King Ethelred pisses himself from fear, thinking it's a third army after the Sword and Odin's Breath?" Sven replied, laughing at the idea.

"So let him change his pants before he comes to negotiate the danegeld," Jorun said, passing him a horn with beer.

After that, they drank and celebrated their victory, toast following toast, and deer roasted on large spits arranged over fires on the stone floor.

"We can spend the winter here and not go back to the Isle of Wight," Olav said, before Sven had had a chance to suggest the same thing.

They frequently had the same ideas when it came to strategy; they complemented each other, as brothers might. They argued about details, and the anger between them could spark as quickly as if someone had put a torch to dry leaves. But they avoided the issue which truly divided them: Norway, and which one of them would eventually sit on its throne. They'd been avoiding it for two years, since their conversation on the Isle of Wight. Sven wondered if Olav had already thought of the plan he was about to propose.

"Jorun, weren't you the one to say that you found barrels of wine in the basement of the castle?"

"My king has the hearing of a deer where wine is concerned," his comrade praised.

"And is my friend Jorun a true one or false?" Sven eyed him critically.

Jorun had hair the color of grain on the day of harvest. If he didn't wash for a while, it stuck to his head like a well-oiled helmet. But all it took was a bath for yellow hay to fly around his head once more, and he wore a leather headband to keep it from falling in his eyes. He had pale blue eyes, slightly hidden behind bushy white eyebrows, and, according to the women, the most beautiful smile of the whole army. None had said this of Varin, Olav's companion. The moment he opened his mouth to reveal his sharpened, painted fangs, they were afraid. Varin and Jorun were their respective kings' deputies, and none could rival them where drinking was concerned; and besides, they were connected by the same blemish which hung over Sven and Olav's horizon like a dark stormcloud. Now, when Sven teased Jorun about the wine, Varin spoke up:

"No one can insult Jorun when Varin is present, not even the chief. Will two barrels be enough for tonight? That's all we've dragged up from the basement, because there's a hellish number of stairs." He heaved a barrel from under the table as he spoke and placed it in front of Sven.

Jorun opened it, poured the bloody beverage into a jug, and set it in front of Sven.

"Do you intend to introduce Jomsviking traditions here?" Sven laughed falsely. "Must I serve myself during a feast?"

"That wouldn't be the worst thing, King," Jorun admitted. "Varin and I want to play mannjafndr tonight."

"Varin, what about my mead?" Olav asked his deputy, who bared his painted fangs and placed a jug before him.

"I leave you, my king."

Olav didn't drink wine, he preferred mead. He said that wine brought back unhappy associations for him, and Sven could only guess he meant his youth at Vladimir's court. The rumor among the crews was that one of the prince's wives had been madly in love with Olav and hadn't wanted to let him out of Rus. But there were many strange stories circulating about Olav's past. About how he'd been separated from his mother during their escape from Norway when their ship had been attacked by headhunters. He had supposedly found his mother years later, when he'd married the beautiful Geira, only because she was the widow of the most infamous trader in live cargo, and that he'd ripped his mother's location from his wife before killing her. They also spoke of how he'd pursued his vendetta against the slave traders to its bloody conclusion, eating their hearts raw.

Sven didn't pay much attention to these tales, knowing that there were similarly unbelievable stories attributed to him. He had heard one in which he'd personally sucked out the blood from his father's chest, and raped his sister Tyra in front of the dying man. He also knew the one in which he was the child of Harald and his sister, the widow Gunhild, rather than the sweet Tove, Mściwój's daughter. Complete nonsense, but he preferred Olav not to hear these particular ones, since rumor had it he reacted with a sword at the mere mention of Gunhild's name.

Whatever might be said about them, they had just conquered Castle Bamburgh hand in hand, the ancient British stronghold, and they celebrated in the largest hall, which offered a view onto the North Sea through a burned wall. And this was the time he wanted to share his plan with Olav, his plan to extend their partnership for as long as possible before they fought over Norway.

"Winter in these walls? Sounds all right. I can summon my redheaded Mary to warm my winter bed. But let's talk of spring, Olav."

The white-haired man's pale eyes gleamed and he opened his mouth. Sven silenced him with a wave of his hand.

"I'm speaking first. I want to surprise King Ethelred come spring, and, sailing south swiftly, attack London. The cowardly king won't be expecting us after an attack on the northeast shores, and the Londoners, bored with waiting for us for all of last year, won't have time to properly gather their forces to face us."

Olav choked on his mead as he laughed.

"Are you sure that Tove was loyal to Harald?" he said. "Or perhaps she met a lord called Tryggve somewhere on the Baltic waters? And the noble heir of the Ynglings, before marrying my mother, sired you, Sven?"

"Were you thinking the same thing?" Sven laughed. "Then perhaps your honored mother Astrid wandered somewhere under that stallion Harald's cock and they sired you somewhere on the waters between the kingdoms, hmm? Maybe the legend that you were born on water has some truth to it? Maybe your successes in swimming competitions, Olav, come from that song?"

The young Tryggvason was a master at a game called sund—wrestling in water, during which two bold men dived, found each other in the maelstrom, and fought until one asked for mercy. He could swim without breathing like a bloody fish, deep and long. He hadn't lost a single game, and last summer the store of daredevils willing to jump into the depths with him had run dry.

"That's enough," Olav said, looking suddenly serious. "Don't mix our blood into it, because yours will flow. We had the same thought, yes, but it was the only reasonable one. Not proof of anything other than that we both have sharp wits as well as sharp swords."

"You began this bidding war," Sven reminded him with a laugh. "No one likes my dead father. Even you'd prefer to take me into your family than come into mine. And it is good," Sven said, watching the waves through the crumbling wall and feeling content for the moment. "We have the same plans. We hit London in spring, and leave with pure silver once more. Our danegeld. What happens next, Silver Ole?"

"I go to Trondelag," Olav replied firmly. "We will part ways, my red-haired friend. A pity."

"Do you remember? I told you I won't stop trying to convince you to join forces with me against Eric the Victorious."

"He's not my enemy."

"Really?"

"Jarl Haakon in Norway, the lord of Lade, is my enemy."

"So what do you say to the freshest news? Your Haakon's sons, afraid of the Yngling heir, have gone to Eric for help."

"What?"

"You heard me," Sven lied smoothly and drained his goblet. The wine warmed him and allowed the semblance of truth to arise from words misspoken. "They're afraid of you," Sven continued. "They are afraid of the rightful heir who will return surrounded by the shine of danegeld. The winner of silver. They are asking Eric the Victorious, before the time is right, to help them keep their power."

"You lie," Olav hissed, furious.

"Jorun, summon the ones who sailed from Sigtuna. Have them tell you how it is. Jorun?" He looked around for his deputy.

Jorun and Varin paid no heed to their kings. Surrounded by a circle of merry comrades, they faced each other, horns in hand, and played mannjafndr—the game of comparisons.

"My king swims like a fish from the depths," Varin called out hoarsely. "He can outlast any man in the water. Yours is barely a water duck next to him."

"Fish from depths!" the men gathered round them chanted rhythmically. "Wa-ter duck!"

"And my king," Jorun raised him, spreading his arms wide, "leaps from ship to ship like a nimble deer. Your king-fish is barely a frog next to him."

"Nimble deer! Bare-ly a frog!" the viewers of the game echoed, laughing, while Jorun and Varin finished their drinks. Others poured them more, and the game continued.

Sven laughed.

"A nimble deer and a fish from the depths must search for men from Sigtuna alone. Our deputies have kept their word."

"They promised to get drunk playing mannjafndr, and they're doing well. What a shame it's at our cost. Two kings without thrones, lands, wives, fathers . . . the list of similarities is long, and they've only gotten as far as swimming and jumping." Olav grimaced.

"Don't be so serious." Sven clapped him on the shoulder. "For so long as they aren't comparing the contents of our chests and the length of our cocks, let them do what they want. Haki!" His eyes fell on one of his best sailors by the vat of beer. "Haki, where's that boy from Sigtuna? Bring him to us."

"My dear king," Varin roared in the meantime, "has hair like pure silver, while yours like common bronze."

"Sil-ver! Bronze!"

"No, no, no," Jorun responded. "That can be described better. My king has a flaming head, yours frozen in ice."

Their companions were getting drunker than the players, the chants now muddling the phrases:

"Fla-ming ice! Flam-ing ice!"

Even Olav burst out with laughter upon hearing this. Haki brought a slender, pale-haired boy to them, who looked no older than seventeen.

"This is him. Gauti from Sigtuna," Haki introduced the boy. "Is that all, my lord?" he asked, his eyes on the game and the drinks he was missing.

"Go." Sven waved a hand. "But if our deputies try to compare our swords, call us. I'd be curious to see if there'll be rhymes."

"Gauti, when were you in Sigtuna?" Olav asked him.

He's in a hurry, Sven thought. *He doesn't want to waste a single moment.*

"In spring this year, my lord."

"What did you do there?"

"I come from lands near Mälaren. I went to King Eric and Queen Sigrid to ask for their blessing."

"For what?"

"I had a disagreement with my brothers about land after my father's death."

"You lost?"

"That's why I'm here." Gauti smiled crookedly. "I'm searching for luck and riches, like everyone else."

I don't know if I can give you luck, Gauti, Sven thought, looking at the young man. *But riches? Why not.*

"Is it true that you met the young jarls of Lade in Sigtuna?" Olav continued his questions.

"Yes, my lord. There were two men called Eric and Sven, the sons of Jarl Haakon, who rules now in Norway. They came to King Eric in Sigtuna. Eric Haakonsson said he was seeking help from his great namesake, Eric the Victorious."

"Oh, the Haakons have a way with words." Sven laughed. "The other son should sail to me then I suppose? 'King Sven, I'm also called Sven, so you should help me.'"

"I don't know, chief." Gauti spread his arms. "It's not for me to guess at the business of great lords."

"What else did Haakon's sons say?" Olav asked, bringing them back to the original question.

"That bad things are happening in their country. That Jarl Haakon is losing his influence with the noblemen because he cannot control his desire."

"Don't tell me that the Sognefiord boys haven't told you the same thing," Sven mocked. "You have three crews with those goods."

The people of Sogn were thought of as born pirates, and many had joined Olav's crew during their years of English raids.

"They talk, they talk," Olav replied evasively. "But they had no idea about the young jarls' visit to Sigtuna. Do you know King Eric's answer to Haakon's sons' plea?"

"No, my lord. The king invited them to court, and said they were to be his guests. And then, when the council met, he didn't grant me rights to my brothers' lands, so I sailed away without waiting to see what happened next."

"Thank you, Gauti. Go, enjoy yourself. Or no, wait a moment. Did you see Queen Sigrid?" Olav asked.

"I saw her, my lord. She sat on a tall chair at the king's side, with two lynxes beside her. She leads them on a leash."

"You said nothing about lynxes to me." Sven snorted.

"Because my king didn't ask."

Olav began to laugh.

"What does she call them? What are their names?"

"Oh, my lord, I won't repeat them, because it's in the queen's tongue. Two bloody words that sound as if someone ran a knife over a rusty sheet of metal."

When Gauti left them, Sven poured himself more wine. It was going to his head faster than mead, and it wasn't as sweet. But he'd taken it with Bamburgh, which was enough for him to enjoy the taste. Young Gauti had said just enough to avoid lying: the young jarls had been to see Eric, that much was true. Not everyone had to know that it wasn't help against Olav that they sought, but against their own father. There was as much bad blood between them and old Haakon as there had been between Sven and his own father. He kept the most important news from Sigtuna to himself. He had informers there who were far better than Gauti. High up in court, ones who knew the king and queen's secrets, and when the time came, would know whose side to stand on.

"How did you know about the lynxes?"

"They were a gift from me," Olav replied, then added, "And my wife, Geira. They were sisters."

"I remember. But back to the matter at hand. And? Do you still think there isn't enough reason for us to join forces against the Swedish king?"

"Firstly, there is no certainty that Eric will support the young jarls. And secondly: it is them, Haakon's sons, and not King Eric, that I would consider my next enemies. When I overthrow their father from his throne, they are the ones who will fight me for power."

He has it all sorted out, Sven judged as he drank. *And he won't let himself be tricked. Or he has even better informers in his country than I do. But I need him if I'm to defeat Eric. Silver is one thing, but the Old Boar's fleet is strong. If I lose to him a second time, I will never get Denmark back.*

". . . is longer . . ." he heard from Jorun and Varin's direction.

"What? Already? Have they started comparing our sheathed swords?" He came back to the present, asking Olav.

"No, they're talking about hair." Olav grabbed his shoulder suddenly and brought his face close. "Sven, each one of us has his own road. Let's take what we can in the new year, then both sail to claim our inheritance. We have equal chances, to start with"—Olav smiled a hard smile—"because we split our plunder in half. And what we do next? Gods only know. I want to get drunk today. Pour mead over this old castle. Bamburgh."

"Chase me, then. My wine is stronger, and I've had more than you."

Olav finished what was in his cup with one gulp and poured himself more mead.

"My mead is sweeter."

"Wine is redder. Blood's better after wine."

"Desire is stronger after mead."

"Joooooruuuun!" Varin roared from the depths of the stone hall. "The kings are playing mannjafndr themselves."

Sven stood up. He felt how wonderfully the wine of the Bamburgh heirs swayed him. As if he had a deck under his feet, and what could be more beautiful than a cruise? Their drunk comrades turned away from Varin and Jorun and staggered toward them.

"The fight of kings! The fight of kings!" they roared, approaching Sven and Olav.

"I don't rhyme. And I won't swim with you," Sven voiced his reservations.

"I won't compare. And I'm not jumping between ships with you," Olav retaliated.

"Fi-ight! Fi-ight!" a hundred drunk warriors chanted, men who had been with them as Odin's Sword, Odin's Breath, and now the Two Kings.

They leaned against each other, foreheads touching.

"They've challenged us," Olav whispered. "We have to show them what chieftains are capable of."

"Let's drink," Sven decided. "Since we both want to get drunk . . ."

"A barrel of mead against a barrel of wine," Olav shouted.

"Two long horns," Sven demanded. "Who falls over first, loses."

"Who wins, drinks more. Where is my bard Omold?"

The bard looked as if he'd been playing this drinking game since the morning, but hearing Olav's summons he shook it off and stood up.

"What song does my master want to listen to?"

"The 'Song of the Mighty,'" Olav roared, preparing for their competition. "Peel out drunken verses from Odin's wisdom."

"I'm ready," the bard announced.

"Pour." Sven offered his horn.

When both their vessels were full, the bard began:

You don't have a worse provender
than a full barrel of mead . . .

"That's why mead will be the better one," Olav exclaimed, and began to drink.

"Wine will win," Sven replied, moistening his lips with it.

Not as good as they say,
is mead for generations of men,
because he has less, the more he drinks,
of man's common sense.

They drank at the same pace, and held out their horns for more simultaneously. They gulped this down, too.

Lazily does the "crane of poor memories" fly over drunks,
stealing men's souls.
The feathers of this bird have bound me . . .

The second horn was drained as quickly as the first. Everyone knew that the shorter the pauses, the better. Olav swayed at the third, but he didn't give in.

I was drunk, as drunk as a bull
in the wise man Fjalar's house . . .

The bard was doing all he could. Odin himself was warning them against drinking through his lips, but they were finishing their fourth horns, egged on by the comrades gathered around them. Sven felt as though he was about to be sick.

Beer is best when
a guest claims back his common sense . . .

He placed the horn under the barrel for the fifth time, but he could feel the liquid spilling down his sleeve instead of falling into the vessel. He couldn't hold it straight. The stone castle floors danced before his eyes, and a storm began raging under his feet. Falling, he grabbed Olav, who was collapsing, same as him. They landed at the same time.

Don't hold on to your goblet, drink with caution,
speak wisely or hold your tongue . . .

"I'll kill you, Omold . . . with caution? Drink with caution?" Olav gurgled. "Now you tell me?"

"Two kings! Two kings!" their companions roared overhead.

"Lost! Won!"

"Sven and Olav, always equal," the bard recited. "They win together and lose together."

"Sail with me to Sig-Sig-Sigtuna," Sven fought the hiccups. "We'll de-defeat Eric and con-con-conquer the queen!" His eyes closed of their own volition.

He felt arms dragging him upward.

"Jorun?" he whispered, opening his eyes.

No. It was Olav. Where did his strength come from? He brought his face close to Sven's. He was just as drunk.

"You take the kingdom," he hissed, as if the Yngling snake had come alive inside of him. "I'll take the queen. You sail for Sigtuna. I'll go for Sigrid."

Olav didn't have strength for more. He let go and they both collapsed on the stone floor again. It rose and spiraled along with his body. Sven held Olav by the shoulders. Olav held on to him. If they let go now, the castle would fall, and they'd land in the maelstrom of a sea at its feet. Sven couldn't remember if he'd had five or six horns, but he felt as if an eternal hammering was beginning inside his head.

. . . drink with caution . . .
. . . speak wisely or hold your tongue . . .

30

⚛

ENGLAND

Olav guided his boat, keeping a sharp eye on the water for any rocks. It was a low tide, and the pale blue waters around the Isles of Scilly, just off the coast of Cornwall in the Atlantic Ocean, were swarming with rocky traps. Olav and his men rode a small, modest boat, the kind used here by fishermen and oyster catchers. He was accompanied by three men from *Kanugård*'s original crew: Omold the bard, Ingvar, and Rafn.

The rest of the ships of the Two Kings had been divided into small troops in the bays on the southern shore of England, waiting for the right moment. Olav had left Varin in charge, since his painted fangs demanded respect from even the most defiant crews. The main chief of the Two Kings, until Olav's return to England's mainland, was Sven.

It was the first full moon of spring. They'd planned London's attack for early autumn, and until then Olav intended to lull Ethelred's alertness with a series of small attacks on Ireland, the Isle of Man, and Cornwall. They wanted to create the impression of chaos, as if the attacks were led by small, dispersed groups.

"King." Rafn pointed toward the shore. "I see two ports."

Olav had already seen them.

"Omold, what was the message again?" he asked.

"'The eastern shore of Scilla. Turn south when you see two ports. There is a third behind a line of rocks by the shore. A broken dock clinging to stone ramparts.'" The bard recited from memory.

The wind died down, and their small sail hung limply from the mast. They picked up their oars, heading south.

Olav had been waiting on the Isle of Wight for three trusted men to arrive from Sogn. Instead, a salt merchant came, with the message that Olav's men had been taken in by a medicine man on Scilla, after common robbers had nearly killed them. Of course, it crossed Olav's mind that this might be a trap. But the information from the Sogn men was so valuable that he took the risk without a moment's hesitation. He ordered Varin to keep the merchant's ship, cargo, and crew hostage until he returned, as protection. A small consolation, but better than nothing. If someone was casting a net for him, perhaps they'd be willing to trade for salt?

"A line of rocks along the shore." Omold pointed at what they'd just seen. Apart from having an excellent memory, the bard liked to repeat with words what the eyes were already aware of.

"The most foolish place for a harbor," Ingvar observed, wiping sweat from his forehead.

"Unless you're not wanting guests who arrive unannounced," Rafn replied.

Olav raised his head and saw a white dog on one of the rocks by the shore. He was sure he'd seen it before, or had he only imagined it? *A bare rock and a dog . . .*

"From the boat!" he called out, and his men put down their oars and jumped out.

"To shoulders on two," he ordered, and they pulled the boat onto the soft pale sand.

"A broken dock clinging to stone ramparts," Omold recited, pointing at the rotting planks of wood which barely hung on to the rocks. "Well, it looks like we found them."

The dog had disappeared without so much as a single bark, leaving Olav to wonder whether it had really been there in the first place.

"Rafn, stay with the boat. Ingvar and the bard will come with me," Olav decided, climbing the rocky shore.

Placing a foot on lichen-encrusted stone, he remembered his vision from so many years ago, after consuming the mushrooms. He, Bolesław, and Świętosława at the hunting lodge by Poznań. That's where he remembered the dog from. But in that vision, the animal had led him to a gate guarding a strange building, and now the dog had disappeared, leaving the island seemingly deserted.

"There's a path here." The bard pointed at a narrow, well-trodden track leading upward. Olav had already begun to follow it.

He didn't feel fear, mostly just curiosity. They climbed to the top. In the distance was a small house with a narrow pillar of smoke. Omold, thankfully, didn't feel the need to tell them about this. The waters looked impossibly blue from above. A furious blue that Olav had never seen anywhere else. And then his eyes fell on a pile of stones, a short way from the path. He turned to take a closer look, and froze.

"A circle of stones," the bard said from behind him. "Unfinished. Strange, isn't it?"

"If we're searching for a medicine man, it's not that strange," Ingvar responded. "Healers do many things. I knew one in Rus who chewed sand. Everyone wondered why he was doing it. Nobody knew the answer, but there wasn't a single sick man who regretted having him take care of them in a fever."

They returned to the path and approached the hut in silence. Dogs barked, small and fluffy, so they couldn't have been the pups of the white one from the harbor. A stocky, armed man exited the hut, followed by another who looked identical to the first. Both were looking against the sun, and they shaded their eyes, looking at Olav, before exclaiming:

"The one whose . . ."

". . . name we cannot . . ."

". . . speak . . ."

". . . has arrived. Our . . ."

". . . king and . . ."

". . . master."

And then they each fell to one knee, though Olav noticed that they managed to drag a board underneath their knees before falling. The yard was muddy.

"Who are you?" Olav asked.

"Brothers," they replied in unison.

"I can see that you're twins."

"That too, but . . ."

". . . we are the brothers of . . ."

"Halvard."

"He's Bersi." One of them pointed at the other.

"And he's Duri." The other did the same as the first.

Olav had never seen either of them, but he'd come here searching for Halvard.

"How is he?" He was worried about his scout's fate. He didn't relish the thought of conversing further with the strange twins who divided every sentence into two.

"He's alive," Duri replied.

"But he doesn't rise," Bersi filled in.

The one whose name we cannot speak, he thought. *So, my command to keep my identity a secret has become a name in itself. That's all right. It won't be long now, not long.*

"These are my companions." He introduced them. "Ingvar and Omold the bard. Lead us to Halvard."

The twins rose and nimbly turned the board they used to kneel on so that Olav might walk across it to the hut. It was dim inside, despite the small fire, and a quiet voice reached them from the gloom:

"God Almighty and sweet Mary, Mother of Christ, my king has come to me and I cannot rise . . ."

"Lie still, Halvard." Olav had recognized the wounded man. "What's wrong?"

"A spear thrust to my calf, another in my thigh, they both caused my collapse. And the axe blow under my shoulder blade stole my breath and, believe me, King, I waited for the beautiful Valkyries, I was sure they were flying for me. But then I remembered that Odin's virgins take only warriors from the battlefield, I'd never heard of what awaits a drunken man from Sogn after a brawl at an inn. And this injustice saddened me so much that I decided to live. Bersi and Duri were also sad, sad and furious, and twins in anger are truly unpredictable. They destroyed my attackers with their axes, or so they say. But they took pity on the innkeeper, because our mother and uncle raised us to be good men, and what fault was it of the innkeeper's? It paid off, he put us on a boat and we came here, and the medicine man did miracles. I cannot stand, but I'm alive. The medicine man says I'll get out of it, because he sees the future."

As do I. I've seen this harbor and the dog before I came here, Olav thought.

"Is the healer here?"

"No, my king. But he'll come at dusk. He'll be here for certain."

"During the day he goes . . ." one of the twins began shyly.

". . . to collect rocks . . ." the other added, and then they spoke in turns again.

". . . herbs and . . ."

". . . his thoughts."

"Do they always do that?" Olav asked Halvard.

"Yes, my lord. That's just how they were born, doing everything together. They went to have their fortunes read by the healer together, too, but he separated them and told them he could only speak to each one alone. They didn't agree to it."

Olav looked at them more carefully. He didn't think he'd be able to tell one from the other. Dark-eyed, dark-haired. They could be twenty, or twenty-five, though their stocky figures made them look rather more intimidating.

They had chests as wide as bears under their caftans. They braided their beards, but these didn't stick out like Sven's. Ring after ring shone on their short, fat fingers.

"Is the boar your family's sign?" Olav observed aloud more than asked. Freya's boar, Golden Bristles. Food, drink, a sword ready to fight in both battlefield and bed. He gritted his teeth. Eric, Świętosława's husband, was the Golden Boar. Damn it.

"Yes, King," Halvard replied, and the twins' eyes gleamed as if he'd given them the highest praise.

"What news of my country?" Olav asked. This was the reason he had come to this harbor seeking his scout. "Did you meet with Skjalgsson in my name?"

Erling Skjalgsson, since his father's recent death, was the head of a family which controlled two counties in southern Norway, Rogaland and Hordaland. A good and old family, whose times of greatness had come under the last king accepted by all of Norway, Haakon Haraldsson, also known as Haakon the Good. This family had been essentially removed from power by Jarl Haakon, though.

Olav had spent not just tens, but hundreds of sleepless nights coming up with the best strategy to win back power, and he knew that everything must begin in the south, where his father, Tryggve, had once ruled. Their family nest was Viken, and he knew that Viken would accept him with open arms. His mother lived there now, with her new husband, Lodin, and their children. If Olav wanted to ensure safe passage for himself to the north, he would need the support of Erling Skjalgsson, a crucial step to taking back the throne.

"Yes, my lord," Halvard replied. "Erling supports your plans. He is the heir of a proud family, and the memory of this is very much alive. Haakon the Good . . ." He cleared his throat meaningfully.

I know, Olav thought. Erling's great-aunt had been the king's lover and Haakon the Good's mother. Anyone who had once felt part of the royal family would always crave a return to grace.

"Is he married?" Olav asked, a plan beginning to form in the corners of his mind.

"No, my lord," Halvard replied.

"And what of Lade?" Olav asked, abruptly changing the subject.

That's where the heart of the country beat, around Trondheimfiord's bay. That was where Jarl Haakon had his settlement, and that was where he called his council, which all the lords of the north attended.

"Lade will fight, my lord," Halvard said bluntly. "But the Lade jarls are weary of Haakon's rule. It's beginning to feel like a thorn in their side . . ."

"Attack and . . ."

". . . kill the old one," Bersi and Duri said.

"Preferably with a stranger's hands," Halvard filled in.

"And Jarl Haakon's sons, Eric and Sven?" The two men Sven Forkbeard's scout said had come to Sweden seeking help from Eric the Victorious.

"They don't command the same respect their father does, because Haakon has embarrassed them in front of others more than once."

He thought about this as he kept talking to Halvard. He'd spent too much time with Sven Forkbeard to be unaware of how great and furious the power of an abandoned son could be. But there were two of them, so their anger would be halved. Kill the old one? No, he wouldn't go as far as murder. Not after what had happened to his family.

Hundreds of sleepless nights, or had it been thousands? He'd left his country in his mother's womb. His entire life revolved around his return. What was seething inside him so? He'd wondered about this endlessly. What was driving him? Royal blood? Or ordinary human ambition? Or perhaps the memory of hurt and the desire for revenge?

He didn't hear the door of the hut open, though he saw the sunlight streaming through it. Dust particles whirled in the patch of light. The man in the doorway was so small that he seemed a child at first; it was a moment before Olav recognized the figure as an old man bent over.

"My savior," Halvard said, respectfully.

"Come with me." The old man motioned to Olav with a gnarled finger.

Tryggvason rose and gave Ingvar and the bard a signal to stay behind as he followed the healer out of the hut.

The old man led him to a forest, which turned out to be a garden of stone circles and spirals, some of them only one stone high, others stacked higher, like castle towers half built and left unfinished. To Olav, it seemed as if the stones grew from the green moss. They might have been there for hundreds of years. Like the vibrant blue waters which washed Scilla's shores, the moss in this forest was an impossibly bright green. The old man walked slowly, leaning on a gnarled staff. He paused at certain circles, as if he wasn't sure whether they'd reached their destination yet. And then he'd continue, swinging his skinny dry neck from side to side. Olav followed.

Dusk had fallen by the time they reached a stone wall, muting the forest's bright hues. In the last of the day's light, Olav saw another stone structure, this one as tall as a man and much wider than the rest. Using the staff to touch its walls, the old man led Olav to a small open space behind the rocks. A flat round stone lay in the center.

"Sit," his guide commanded, and banged his staff on the boulder as if Olav hadn't understood his meaning.

Tryggvason stepped onto it and sat down, his feet curled beneath him. He lifted his head. A great silver moon was ascending over the stone wall and the forest around him.

The man stood in front of Olav, leaning on the staff with both hands, his gaze boring into him. He nodded, as if to say, "good." They remained like this until the moon had covered a third of its journey. There was a moment when Olav thought the old man had gone, and that a white dog was running along the wall toward them. When he blinked the man was before him as he had been. *A trick of the light,* Olav told himself, *and the result of not moving for so long.* That's when the old man spoke:

"They call you 'Silver Ole.' They call me 'Hundrr.'"

Hundrr. Hound.

"Why have you brought me here, Hundrr?" he asked.

The old man cocked his head, first one way, then the other. He sucked his lips.

"You need a hound, heir of kings," he finally murmured.

"Will you give it to me?"

Hundrr chuckled hollowly, and his mockery echoed off the rocks so that it seemed that many people were laughing at him.

"The hound is within you, little Ole. Wake it up. No, no, not now, no need, boy. Not here. Later, later."

The old man took a few small steps toward him, still moving his lips. He suddenly lifted his staff, as quickly as a young man. He moved as if he wanted to strike the moon, and the disc in the sky seemed to jump as if it were feeling the old man's touch.

"Well, well," he squawked somberly. "The first full moon. It's the time of death, and the resurrection of the new god, Ole. Christ, the son of the Almighty God. Has anyone seen such wonders as a single God in a Trinity?" He chuckled, then fell silent. "Blessed are those who didn't see but believed, do you understand, Ole? This God doesn't need to give signs. He gives them anyway, but he doesn't have to. He's the Lord of the Word. Anyone who hasn't seen but has believed His words will be redeemed. Do you know what redemption is? You know nothing, Ole, I'll tell you quickly. It's the gift of life after death, more interesting than the one here, today. The miracle of the light which disperses darkness. No terrible goddess of hell, or Odin's

feast in Valhalla, where the Three-eyed keeps the heroes to give them up
to be slaughtered in the great war. No, no. It's life for life's sake, when man
and God join into one. Who understands this shall be redeemed, and who
doesn't is condemned to darkness. The path to the house of the Lord is neither straight nor wide. It is a stony and steep road on which everyone who
doubts will twist an ankle, falling into the abyss." He chuckled again. "An
abyss for all eternity. Only the chosen ones set out down this road, and He
chose you, boy."

"Baptism?" he asked, remembering Astrid reading the runes.

"Yes, yes. But not at my hands. I'm so old that I can remember every one
of Odin and Thor's adventures in this world. I only read the future, which
hangs between the worlds like a spiderweb in the winds of a long dawn."

"Are you a seer?" Olav recalled the words the priest at Poznań's palatium
had sung.

"No." The old man looked offended by the question. "My name is
Hundrr. If you want something from the old gods, you can ask for it today."
He pierced the air above his head with the staff. "The moon hangs above
you, silver boy. If you want something, ask for it. The runes will sing their old
song for you one last time."

Olav didn't hesitate.

"The woman I love. The throne I want to regain. The kingdom I wish to
rebuild."

The old man searched the pouch of blue-gray leather at his belt. He
blinked eyelids with no eyelashes and whispered, concerned:

"Three questions, and three thorns in reply, Silver Ole."

"I don't understand," he said, feeling as if the moon's shine was a blanket
of frost falling over him.

"Longing, desire, dissatisfaction, my boy." Hundrr sighed. "The terribly
ancient curse. The old gods cast it on you, though they say this curse will
bring you great fame."

Owls called to one another, hooting in the depths of the forest.

"Yes, yes." Hundrr nodded his head. "The old gods are giving you a
miserable gift. Your hope lies in the new. Perhaps He will want to change it?
You've been marked, that's certain. I've seen your arrival a hundred times in
my dreams. But have you been chosen? Let the new God tell you."

When morning came, in the dark hour after the moon had set and before
the sunrise, Olav reached the boat Rafn was guarding, with Ingvar and the

bard. Rafn was fast asleep, curled into a ball under a cloak. Before Omold had a chance to yell to his friend, they heard the crow of a rooster from the old man's hut. Once, twice, thrice, startling Rafn awake.

"No," he shouted, "I'm not . . ."

"It's just us, friend," the bard reassured him.

"I had a horrible dream." Rafn shook himself. "Forgive me, King. I was dreaming that you'd been crowned with thorns."

Rafn gazed at him, rubbing his sleepy eyes. He couldn't tear his eyes away from Olav.

Three thorns, Tryggvason recalled the old healer's words.

The tide was high as they pushed the small boat out, jumping over its sides as they left the shore. The restless swish of water against its sides seemed to Olav the sweetest sound.

"Bersi and Duri are two good men," Ingvar said, speaking of the strange twins they'd met on the island. He grabbed the oars. "It would be good to have them in our crews. And Halvard, too, if he recovers," he added, looking at Olav.

Dawn had risen. The pink smudge hovered over the dark water, like an unhealed wound on a neck. The ocean's slit throat.

So, the southern lord Erling would help; his family's connection to Olav's family, though forged in the past, carried his loyalty even today. And though Lade's jarls would fight for Jarl Haakon, their hearts wouldn't be in it. And if Halvard's information was reliable, Haakon's sons, Eric and Sven, wouldn't have enough of a following to be a threat to Olav, if Jarl Haakon had humiliated them enough. These rumors suggested Olav had a fighting chance. And a chance was all he needed.

"East," Olav said, and looked over his shoulder at the island's high shores.

His small crew all turned their heads, as if following his command. A great white dog stood on a rock by the bank.

"An empty shore," Omold the bard sang quietly, searching for the right tone. "An empty, rocky shore bade the men goodbye."

Olav asked them afterward, and all three denied it. None of the others had seen a white dog on Scilla, not once.

31

⚔

ENGLAND

Sven summoned the bard every time he sailed into the wide currents of the Thames, telling him to recount the legend of the Romans who had come here to conquer the British Isles from the far south hundreds of years earlier. He didn't like the city, which was squeezed behind a stone fortification. He, a man of the seas, couldn't imagine how one might willingly be enclosed by a wall, though that didn't mean he didn't want to conquer it. Sven didn't believe in the power of ramparts or walls. Harald Bluetooth, his father, had put much effort into renewing and strengthening old ramparts intended to protect Denmark from the Slavs, Saxons, and eventually, the empire. What use was it, though? All it took was Emperor Otto gathering an army large enough, and he broke through the ramparts with ease. The upkeep of such fortifications cost more than it gave, yet people still believed that they could protect themselves behind them.

This autumn, he and Olav, leading the Two Kings, wanted to prove that the walls of London could hide no treasures from them. They headed a fleet of ninety-four ships. Three thousand battle-scarred men, experienced in fighting on the English shores of Northumbria, through Kent, Cornwall, as far as Ireland and the Isle of Man. Three thousand sea robbers divided into eager and obedient crews. These weren't bloodthirsty men, but men who hungered for English silver.

Ethelred's subjects did their best to stop the Two Kings' arrival, sinking the wrecks of ships in the Thames, as if these could act as barriers to the invading fleet. Sven and Olav's sailors avoided them as if they were but twigs in a wide river. And then, at Sven's command, all the drakkars raised their sails and, one after another, like a never-ending sea snake, they approached the city. He could almost smell the fear from beyond London's walls, and he breathed it in as though it was the most beautiful scent in the world.

They tried first to attack from the river and its banks, but they quickly abandoned that approach; you can't vanquish a wall with an axe. They returned to their ships.

On the other side of the Thames lay Southwark, a city market where the defenders had raised a provisional fort that guarded the entrance to the bridge. It was this great stone wall which was the main line of defense for the city. There were guard towers along it, and the defenders hid behind their wall and fired hailstorms of arrows at the invaders every time they approached.

The Two Kings tried to conquer the Southwark stronghold to open a way onto the bridge for themselves. They gave up after the fifth unsuccessful attack.

"We're losing too many men," Sven announced as their forces regained their strength on deck, a safe distance from the bridge. "We're opening ourselves up to their arrows, and even if we can eventually hack away at the stronghold, there will be a mere handful of us left. Who will conquer the city then?"

"And who will take pleasure in the looted treasure?" Olav agreed.

"Let's burn it." Jorun pointed at the huts decorating the city walls. "It's weak wood and straw. The houses of the poor, workshops, henhouses, pigstys all stand empty. The people hid themselves behind the walls, and these buildings continue all along the ramparts. If we set fire to them at the same time, the defenders won't be able to put all the fires out, and they will spread to the walls."

"London in a ring of fire," Olav smiled. "I like this plan."

They positioned some of the ships away from the shore so the people on the walls wouldn't guess what they were planning. Crews armed with barrels of tar went on land under the cover of night. They needed time to surround the city and prepare it, until it was a torch ready to be lit. Sven and Olav watched everything from the deck of the *Bloody Fox*, while Jorun led the operation. The first flames appeared long before dawn, followed by more and more of them.

"And so the lightning and thunder came, and a great earthquake, and the enormous city fell into three pieces," Olav said, looking at the fire surrounding London.

"What?" Sven bellowed. "What are you saying?"

"Nothing." Olav shook his head, then suddenly grabbed Sven's arm, pointing at the sails, which lurched in that moment, making the mast groan.

"The wind will spread the fire," Sven said, "but . . ."

"This wind might bring rain with it."

They weren't wrong. After a few strong gusts, the fire started by their men leapt upward, lively and quick, trapping nearly the full length of the ramparts within a ring of flames. But right after the fortunate winds, rain poured from the sky. Fat, sharply angled droplets. Streams of water from the heavens. The flames faded, smothered by the rain; the sun came out and revealed the burnt cinders around the walls. Cinders which could not be set on fire a second time.

That was the moment they knew they wouldn't conquer London. Sven sent ten men to clear the shipwrecks from the Thames so they could make a quick retreat.

"Summer has passed," Olav said to him that evening, when they met on board *Kanugård*. "But the beautiful autumn continues. Let's not waste it."

"Kent and Essex?" Sven asked with a smile.

"And Hampshire, and Sussex," Olav added. "Perfect for ninety crews. I don't think we've wasted our time. We didn't set fire to London, we haven't conquered the city, but we've sown fear in its dwellers. Fear grows faster than grain."

"Let us collect the harvest swiftly." Sven raised a toast. "The wine from Bamburgh is running out."

The crews and helmsmen were ready. They hoisted their sails after midnight, by the weak, but bright enough, moonlight. There was still movement on the Thames before dawn, though the crews moved as quietly as possible. Sven on the *Bloody Fox* sailed last. He didn't want the Londoners to see them leave. He wanted them to see an empty river in the morning. He sensed this would bring them euphoria, after which fear would return faster than a heartbeat. The sight of an enemy's retreating backs is encouraging, but its disappearance creates uncertainty. When the *Bloody Fox* entered a bend in the river, Sven turned around and looked at London as it disappeared from view behind a hill.

"I'll return, and I will cross those walls," he told Jorun.

He raised an arm and made a gesture as if he were catching the city in a fist. And then he laughed, as the wind blew from the side and tangled his long red hair.

They divided into four groups and attacked Essex and Kent almost simultaneously, areas also known as the Saxon shores, defended by a band of small fortresses. Next, they sailed on Sussex and Hampshire. Their plan of attack was the same every time: appear unexpectedly, sow terror, shout that they were taking no prisoners, set fire to the straw-roofed huts to create

fire and dark smoke quickly. It was enough that as the tales of their conquests spread, the people began to offer gifts the moment they saw the Two
Kings' sails. Sometimes, there was a hard lord who preferred to fight and
die rather than pay, but these were few and far between. The Two Kings
always ensured that a few witnesses escaped safely to "warn the king." As
if that king hadn't seen their long sea snake on the waters of the Thames
for himself.

"Why do they think that we kill for the sake of it? They're making monsters of us, beasts in human skins," Jorun complained one day, arranging
their plunder.

They camped in Hampshire, in one of their conquered villages, moving
into the huts to regain their strength after a month of hard fighting. Jorun
was tearing silver decorations from books and separating chalices for mass
from ordinary cups. He scratched blood off one of them with his fingernail.
Sven's only response was laughter. His red-haired Mary had remained on the
Isle of Wight, so he found solace in the fair-haired Alice with freckled cheeks.

"So, little Alice, tell me, why do you make monsters of us?" He pinched
her chin and kissed her.

"That's what the priests say, my lord. That you're the punishment that has
befallen us for the sins of the entire country. That you're the devil's bastards,
hellish fire. That you howl like demons, sowing death and destruction. I don't
know why they see beasts in you," she lied, looking in his eyes. "Perhaps it's
because you are?"

"Wrong answer," he said. "Do I look like a beast to you?"

"No, my lord. Not you."

"And Jorun, my friend?"

"Not him, either. But the one who walks with the other king, the one
whose teeth are . . ." She shook herself and made the sign of the cross.

"Varin is my comrade," Jorun warned Alice. "He's a great warrior and a
gentle man."

"Does a gentle man paint and file his teeth? Why does he do it if not to
drink human blood?" She rose from Sven's lap. "Gentle people farm the
land, breed sheep, bake bread; they don't attack others."

"You see, Alice, if we hadn't invaded you, others would have done it,"
Sven explained. "That's what the world is; gentle men breed sheep, and
brave men want to eat them. If your king were a good ruler, he wouldn't let
us eat your sheep."

"They call him Ethelred the Helpless," she sniffed. "He abandoned us . . .
Who'll protect us?"

"Don't cry, girl. I've conquered you and now I will guard you. You're a sheep I will watch over, and I won't let any wolves come near you."

"You don't look like a sheepdog."

"And you don't look like a sheep." Sven was tiring of this conversation. "Go, bring us something to eat."

When she walked out, Jorun said, "Don't be angry with her, Sven. She does resemble a sheep. She's as foolish as one, and she baas like . . ."

They heard a terrified scream from outside the hut then, and Varin entered.

"Why does that pretty girl scream like that?" he asked. "I smiled at her, and she . . ."

"She sees a beast in you," Jorun replied. "I'll explain tonight, friend."

"I don't know if we'll have time for that." Varin nodded. "King Olav sends me, asking that you set off for his camp in Southampton immediately. Archbishop Sigeric is on his way. The English want to negotiate danegeld."

32

SWEDEN

Świętosława was struggling for breath. She was running through the snow, alongside a stretcher that two men carried. The body lying on it was Thora's, Jarl Birger's wife. *Sweet Thora,* Świętosława thought, a sob in her throat. *Sweet, kind Thora. Who welcomed me warmly when I was but a young foreign queen. Who brought my son safely into the world.* Świętosława looked at the drowned woman's face again. *Can it really be her?* Świętosława allowed herself for a moment to imagine that the swollen face was not her friend's but a stranger's. Another poor soul that had been taken from the earth, water now dripping from her hair, cloak, and dress, leaving melted marks on the snow.

"She fell into an ice hole," one of Birger's men told her. His sadness at these words was clear. *Sweet Thora,* she cried again inside. "The water is freezing; Mistress Thora would have passed quickly."

In the torchlight, Thora looked as if she were fast asleep. Terribly pale and sleeping.

"Does the jarl know yet?" Świętosława asked, raising her head and pulling her fur cloak tighter around herself.

But her question was answered when she looked ahead, toward the manor. Birger had just stepped outside. He was watching the procession and their torches approach.

Oh, God! she thought. *Heaven help him.*

They placed the stretcher at the jarl's feet. A crowd began to gather, and Świętosława saw Ion's chubby face amid the throng.

"Our mistress . . ." one of the servants who had carried the stretcher began, but seemed to struggle for words. "The fishermen had made an ice hole by the old bridge. They were the ones to find Lady Thora."

Birger nodded, but didn't seem to be processing what had happened. He knelt by his wife. He touched her wet hair. His expression was as still as her dead face.

"Birger," Świętosława said quietly. "Perhaps you'd like Ion to pray for her?"

"My wife wasn't Christian," he replied hollowly, and rose to his feet.

"Perhaps you'd like Ion to pray for you?"

He blinked. Świętosława could see that none of this was reaching him. She nodded and gave the orders to the servants herself. Birger needed to be alone right now. Helga, Wilkomir's lover, appeared at her side, sobbing.

"I don't believe it, don't believe it . . . we laughed together . . ."

It was true, barely a few days earlier the three of them had sat by the fire, sipping beer and mead, exchanging stories and laughing until tears streamed down their faces.

"What was she doing by the old bridge?" Helga was shaking her head. "Why had she gone there?"

Świętosława put an arm around Helga's shoulder, and they entered the manor together. Servants were rushing about nervously, back and forth, tracking in snowy mud. Świętosława could hear the impatient growls of her cats from her rooms. She sat Helga by the fire and went to feed them.

"Do you know, Dusza," she said as she gave meat to Wrzask, "Birger is acting as if he'd been struck by lightning. It's a good thing he wasn't the one to find her, who knows if he wouldn't have jumped into the water after her. Zgrzyt, wait. You're bigger and fatter, your brother eats first. What was Thora doing at the harbor at night? Strange, isn't it?"

But a moment after she finished speaking, Birger walked into her bedchamber. He was pale. He pulled off his gloves, looking around.

"Dusza, bring mead for the jarl," she ordered. "Sit down, friend."

Zgrzyt caught her fingers lightly, demanding meat. She gave it to him and walked to her guest.

"I'm sorry, so sorry," she said.

"I know why Thora had gone to the harbor," he said, so low Świętosława almost did not hear. "I'll tell you, my lady, though it brings me no glory. My wife had a lover. She would sneak out to see him. Do you understand, my queen?"

"No," Świętosława denied it. "That's not true."

"I wish that were the case."

Dusza returned and handed Birger a cup of mead. The jarl took the cup, looking at Świętosława with sad, red eyes.

"I never caught her in the act, but I knew. She'd been leaving more frequently in the last few days, and because the night is still long it's easier to hide . . ."

"Stop. Thora wasn't sneaking about having trysts." Świętosława raised her voice. "She was going to see a certain woman who lives on the western shores of the bay. She's a famous soothsayer and a good healer. She gave your wife hope that she might bear a child."

They'd spoken about it that evening by the fire. She, Helga, and Thora. Mulled beer with mead and laughter. So much laughter.

Birger shook his head.

"No, Sigrid. Thora didn't tell you the truth. She accused me of infertility, and if she was searching for a way to get pregnant, it was in the arms of another." He drank his mead in a single gulp and stood, his expression full of so much pain that she shivered.

Wrzask and Zgrzyt pushed their heads against her, rubbing themselves on her legs.

"That's what took her," he said bitterly. "She was running to her lover . . . Only why did she step on the ice? God . . ." He gathered himself. "I'll give her a funeral as a wife deserves. Let this damning secret remain between us, Sigrid. I just wanted you to know."

He bade her goodbye and left. Zgrzyt was purring so loudly that the sound might have woken a dead man. She flinched at this thought. Its purr wouldn't bring back Thora.

"Where's my son?" she asked Dusza.

Her friend displayed an open palm against which she tapped her fingers.

"Ah, yes. With Eric. Dress warmly, then. Let's go."

Świętosława needed Helga because she didn't know how to reach the healer's house alone. She had only heard about her from Thora. Wilkomir asked no questions, or at least not as many as he usually did. He only shook his head as he ordered the dogs to be harnessed to the sleigh. The three of them sat down. Helga and Dusza pressed tightly on either side of her. Once they had passed the last houses of Sigtuna, she let the lynxes off their leashes. They were faster than the sleigh led by twelve men on horseback holding torches. Winter was ending, and the sun appeared briefly at midday, but though the deepest frost was melting, high snows still covered the roads and paths. Branches stuck by the roadsides indicated the path between mounds of snow.

I know this won't bring Thora back her life, Świętosława thought, saying nothing to Helga and Dusza, *but perhaps it will ease Birger's pain? So he won't spend the rest of his days feeling so betrayed and alone?*

Świętosława wanted to speak to this healer that Thora visited for advice. She could clear the dead from suspicion.

And if she doesn't? Świętosława thought. *What if I'm the one who knows nothing about Thora's life?*

She hid her face in her fur and closed her eyes. The sleepless night stretched out sleepy talons toward her. She dreamt of a flaming sail flying straight at her. Even as she dreamt, she knew this wasn't the first time she was having this dream.

"Sigrid?" Helga shook her shoulder gently. "My lady, wake up. We're here."

"Where are my lynxes?" she asked, stepping down from the sleigh. The dogs were panting, tired after the long journey.

"They're probably hunting." Wilkomir shrugged and reassured her: "They'll come back. They always come back."

She looked around. The hut they were standing in front of was small; if it hadn't been for the thin stream of smoke, it could pass for a long snowy mound. Helga pushed the door first.

"Is anyone here?" she asked, entering cautiously.

The room was dim.

"Who asks?" a squawking voice replied from within.

"Queen Sigrid Storråda," Helga said.

"And I'm sweet Freya," the old woman gurgled with laughter. "Or Gerda, the beautiful giantess."

Świętosława stepped in front of Helga.

"I am Sigrid," she introduced herself, and looked at the woman closely.

She was so small that she might have been a dwarf, or so old that age had sucked her body inward. If Świętosława hadn't known that she was a woman, she wouldn't have been able to tell. Strands of white hair stuck to her naked skull in oily clumps. She had large, ridged ears, and you could barely discern her irises in her eye sockets. Stiff hairs grew on her withdrawn, trembling chin.

"Indeed," the old woman replied, cocking her head. "Help me stand."

Helga walked over and offered her a hand. The woman was half lying on something that might have been a small bed or large chair.

She dragged her feet along the floor. She was wearing a dress of thick gray wool, so long that Świętosława was afraid the old woman would step on the hem, tripping and falling. She stretched out a shaking hand, pointing at something in the corner of the room.

"Give me my cloak," she said eventually.

Helga helped her get dressed, then the old woman shuffled over to a small table, and, quite nimbly, climbed onto the chair that stood there. She ran her shaking hands over the table's surface as if trying to wipe it clean of crumbs.

"Yes . . ." She lifted her head. "Sit down, Queen, opposite me."

Świętosława sat. The woman looked at her, holding her gaze, and whispered:

"Have them leave. Only you. And tell them to silence those dogs, or I'll say nothing. At my age, you have hearing like . . . What do you call that bird that has hearing like mine?" She put a finger in her mouth and began to suck on it.

Świętosława gave Helga and Dusza a sign to do as the old woman said. When they were alone, she spoke:

"I've come to ask about Thora. Do you remember Thora, Birger's wife?"

"Is she pregnant?" The old woman's head swayed.

"No, she drowned."

"Well"—this time she nodded her head, back and forth—"the bones didn't lie. The land of the wet death came for her."

"Her husband thinks she was betraying him with another."

"His thoughts do not belong to me. He can wonder what he wants." She puffed out loose cheeks.

"But . . ."

"I won't talk of the dead or to them. I won't touch seidr—I won't look into the past. And you should stay away from it, too. Who once dips their fingers in seidr will never clean them. Black magic is for witches. I heal and see the future, but I do not deal in black magic. I say what I see, I heal what I can, that's all. Do you want me to look forward for you? Into the years that will come?"

"I do," Świętosława said quickly, certainly, before she could frighten herself out of it. "Do it."

"Reach out your hands, bold lady, and touch me," the old woman demanded.

Their fingers joined. The old woman placed her hands on hers, and Świętosława shivered. The thick, worn nails moved as if the old woman were lightly scratching her. Until suddenly, she dug her hands into Świętosława's, and Świętosława felt as if the old woman was sucking the life from her. She ripped her hands free. The old woman chuckled.

"Yes, yes. The bold lady wants to rule fate herself. Why did you stop my beautiful visions? Each one of your sons will be a king, but the youngest will give you the most love, I'll tell you that much. Each death will bring you a crown, that's how one's born a ruler, eh?"

"Will I know love at a man's side?" she asked.

The old woman cocked her head.

"I didn't see."

She looked at her with eyelashless eyes for a long moment. Świętosława said nothing. She felt unsettled under the old woman's gaze.

"I'll throw bones for this love," she said eventually, and retrieved a box of polished wood from under the table. "Bones enclosed in bones." She laughed and, not looking at them, pulled one out. The smile froze on her toothless lips. She grimaced and said reluctantly: "Thurisaz, it means thorn."

"What does a thorn have to do with love?"

"All that's the worst." The toothless gums seemed to chew over these words. "Rape and force. Lust and dissatisfaction. Desire which cannot be fulfilled. Even worse than one thorn are three thrown simultaneously."

"There was a branch with six thorns under my son's saddle, placed there by the merchants of Birka," she said thoughtfully.

"Pff." The old woman's lips twisted. "That was a branch with thorns, it's not what I speak of. Beware, bold lady, of three thorns thrown out together."

On their ride back to Sigtuna, the healer's words rang in Świętosława's head; she could still feel the clawed grip on her hands. Świętosława regretted asking the woman to look into her future. Even more so, that she'd asked about love. Though the vision of more sons warmed her heart.

On arriving in Sigtuna, they found a sad feast was underway, with Jarl Birger the host.

Eric and Olof hadn't returned; her lord husband had taken their son for a winter hunt of reindeer.

"He's nine years old, Sigrid. He's almost grown," Eric had said, prepared to argue with his wife, but she'd be the last to stand in the way of a man's upbringing. In her husband's country, there was no tradition of ceremonial haircutting of six-year-olds, but that was roughly the age at which they passed into their fathers' care. She could still remember Bolesław's hair-cutting. Świętosława had been four, sweet Dobrawa had been alive, and Mieszko had been in full health following his defeat of Margrave Hodo at Cedynia. That time, her father had been the one to humiliate the empire. Her brother's dark-gold curls were thrown on the fire, to the joy of those subjects who could not yet appreciate the depths of faith. And then father had led Bolesław to the chapel by the palatium, where old Bishop Jordan had given her brother his first taste of the Eucharist. The feast for the nobles under purple-red tents in the manor's yard, and a feast for her father's squads on tables around the palatium. And a feast for everyone else who had come to Poznań for the prince's first celebration on the green fields by Warta. A few weeks later, Bolesław, accompanied by a procession of armed men, left for Magdenburg to become a blood hostage for Emperor Otto. He returned half a year later, when the emperor died, and the Reich lords had their own issues to manage. He'd brought Jaksa back with him. The wild Redarian pup. Oh, she missed that skinny, never-smiling boy. And Bjornar, the redhead. Dark-eyed Zarad, whom she'd kissed when she was seven. And her brother. Bolesław, Bolz. Tumultous and strong. Dear God, and Lord Mieszko! Father . . . she missed them all, the men who had never let her down.

She shook herself free of the memories. Wilkomir and Great Ulf could not be faulted. And Eric, her lord husband? He'd let her down by having had bastards before she'd become his lady and wife. Was that such a great fault? No, if it didn't affect her son and Eric's heir. Jarl Birger. She could rely on him, too, and now, drowning in grief, he'd need her. She changed quickly; the cloak and bottom of her dress were wet with snow. The lynxes had sated their hunger by hunting on the journey, so she didn't need to feed them.

"Dusza, do you want to go to the feast?" she asked, looking at her servant's tired face.

Dusza shook her head. Świętosława kissed her cheek, pink from the outdoors.

"Go to sleep, then."

The lynxes meowed, stretching. Zgrzyt began to circle, as always when trying to settle down to rest. It made her laugh. She stroked first one, then the other on their great heads. She pulled at the black clumps of hair growing from their ears.

"The lynxes are off duty, too. They don't have to come to the feast with their mistress."

Wrzask arched his back, then stretched his paws out, adorned with beautiful black claws. He meowed and lay down.

"Good night, my loves," Świętosława whispered, and left for the feast.

"Queen Sigrid." Jarl Birger stood up when he saw her. "We're drinking the goblet of memories."

"I'll join you. Thora was my friend." She sat down and motioned to Birger to settle near her. She noticed now that he'd slipped off the silver rings which had held his long beard in place.

"In the past, the goblet of memories would have been filled with horse blood and passed around over a fire," he told her glumly. "Do you know, my lady, what happens to blood that's heated by a flame?"

"I do," she said, cutting him off. "These aren't those times, thank the Lord. Although I'm sorry that your Thora's soul will travel to the goddess Hel rather than bright paradise."

"She made her choice," he said firmly, and took a long gulp of his mead. "I asked her so many times to turn herself toward the Good News. It didn't help, like chopping a log with a blunt axe."

"That's a horrible comparison," she chided. *His grief is making him careless with his words,* she thought. "Even if she was a pagan, she was a good woman, and she deserves respect."

"As you wish, my lady," he replied, and lifted his goblet again.

"I don't believe in her betrayal, Birger. I went to see that healer. She confirmed that Thora had been coming to her for herbs to help her conceive. Believe me, it was an unfortunate accident, friend."

He gave her a long look. She forgave him. It was still the day his wife had died.

"Rognvald Ulfsson is sending ships to England," he said, leaning toward her.

Rognvald, the powerful merchant of Birka—Thordis's father, grandfather to Eric's bastard sons. Her enemy. To England? Her heart beat faster. *That's where Olav is,* she thought.

"Is he?"

"Undoubtedly, he's searching for means to reach out to Sven, the Danish king we banished," Birger finished.

"What for?" she asked, her hopes cooling at the mention of the Danish heir rather than the Norwegian.

"To collude, my lady. Sven has made himself a wealthy man from his attacks on England, like none of our chieftains has in times of peace. Denmark itself is dissatisfied with the tribute they must pay us."

"Rognvald's sons are the tax collectors, don't forget that, Birger." She smiled.

"And his grandsons are the king's sons, my lady," he replied firmly. "For you to feel safe . . ."

"I sent them away, you know that. My lord husband has given them lands in the northermost part of the country."

"What will that change once the king dies?" He moved nearer to her, and she could smell the mead on his breath.

"The king is alive," she said, so firmly that had her voice been steel, it would have pierced him through. She pushed away the fear she felt every time she thought of the promise Eric had made to Odin, which Birger's words now summoned to her mind.

"You haven't talked to him. You know nothing." He nodded sadly.

"Tell me, then," she demanded.

"I cannot, my lady. But . . . know that I only want what's best for you. I feel responsible for you, ever since the day that Eric sent me south across the blue-gray, storm-ridden Baltic Sea. The bastards should vanish once and for all," he finished firmly. "Those girls, too, his daughters. They've already planned husbands for them, and it wasn't our good king who did it, but their mothers and grandfathers, bitter about your position."

She felt a cold tightness in her chest. She lifted her head, drawing in a deep breath. She spotted Ion in the distance, looking at her from across the hall.

"Young, beautiful maids. A good match for any brave, energetic, and ambitious man," Birger was saying without looking at her, his gaze locked sightlessly in front of him. "They will give birth to sons swiftly, and they will tell them from childhood how they are the heirs of royal blood."

"What do you advise?" she asked, pronouncing every syllable.

"We have an evening with the chalice of memories, my lady. What can a widower possibly advise on such a cold, deadly night?"

33

ENGLAND

Olav remembered every moment of the last six months, since the day he had met the old man Hundrr, as clearly as if it had all happened just the day before. Scents, colors, voices, the creak of the rigging, the wind's howls, the splash of water against *Kanugård*'s gunwales, the tap of shoes on the stone floor—all these accompanied his memories in vivid detail.

The archbishop of Canterbury, Sigeric, the same one they'd negotiated with three years earlier as Odin's Sword, came to Olav's camp in Southampton in the company of Earl Ethelweard, also known as the lord of the western lands.

"Why doesn't King Ethelred want to meet us in person?" Sven didn't bother to hide his annoyance from the king's men. "It's impolite. We made so much effort to go to see him in London."

Olav adored Sven in moments like these. His red-haired friend looked like a boy who hadn't gotten the toy he wanted. Sigeric might remember that Sven liked such games, but the earl let himself be tricked time after time.

"It isn't in King Ethelred's habits to meet with invaders, you must understand, my lord."

"I came to England to meet the king." Sven puckered his lips. "What else must I do to make Ethelred understand?"

"My lord . . ." Ethelweard began to explain.

Sven banged a fist on the table and roared:

"I'm trying as best as I can! I went to Bamburgh, Essex, the four fortresses of Kent, in Hampshire. I went to Cornwall and London, what else does your king want?"

"For you to sail back home, my lord," the earl whispered.

"No. I always get what I want," Sven hissed into his face. "I want to meet your king, and I will do so."

The earl let out a breath and wiped his forehead. Olav still hadn't said a word. He leaned back in his chair, as if he were separating himself from the negotiatons. The archbishop stepped in.

"King Sven, King Olav, we managed to reach a compromise in the past. Let's try to do the same tonight and find a way to satisfy both sides."

"Remind me, Archbishop," Olav spoke now, "where did we end?"

"I don't understand." Sigeric looked confused for a moment.

Olav and Sven were looking at him, though, so he refreshed his memories swiftly.

"Ten thousand pounds of silver." He nodded, and immediately added: "But then, there were four chieftains, and now we have two."

"Do you wish it were otherwise?" Olav asked.

"No . . ." Sigeric suddenly regretted his own argument. "No, no."

"I need to tell you something, Archbishop. I always start where I left off," Olav said coolly. "I wouldn't want to waste your time or ours. If you don't have your king's permission for an adequate beginning to these negotiations, let's end them now. Do you agree, King Sven?"

"Yes." The redhead rose immediately. "We'll sail to our castle in Bamburgh, and have a careful look at the western lands on the way. I'd like to see once more the remains of Hadrian's wall."

"No!" Earl Ethelweard couldn't help but fall into the trap Sven had laid. "We have . . . that is, the archbishop has . . ."

Sigeric gave him a deadly stare, but it was too late. They reached an agreement at midnight.

"Sixteen thousand pounds of silver!" Sven yelled once Ethelred's messengers left Southampton, and the two of them made their way to the stony shores, taking in the cool night air. "Promise me, Tryggvason, that we'll stand here and watch the never-ending line of horses carrying our silver on their backs. Our plunder."

"We'll stand, watch, and rejoice. And drink. And wonder how to protect such a fortune. You know that now we will be the best mark, right? The hulls of our ships, heavy with silver."

"I love worrying about this." Sven clapped him on the shoulder. "Ah, I could worry like this every year."

"Silver doesn't age, but we do," Olav replied, looking into his friend's eyes. "It's time we parted ways. It's good to conquer a kingdom when you're still young and beautiful."

"And rich, like us!"

Sven refused to be serious in this moment, and Olav sensed there was a reason for this. Sven wanted him to be the one to say he remembered the end of their drunken competition in Bamburgh. He was provoking him, never mentioning what they'd told each other, simultaneously protecting himself in case Olav didn't remember. But it wasn't true. They could both recall it, Olav knew that very well.

"I'll tell you something, as a gift," Sven said as they walked back to the camp. "I'll tell you what happened to the widow Gunhild."

Olav nearly choked. The cool ocean air no longer felt refreshing, and the dark night that had fallen around them no longer seemed peaceful.

"Tell me," he said.

"They drowned her in a swamp, as if she were a witch. Those who drown in wetlands don't go to the kingdom of the dead. They took her life, her memory, her glory. A great queen, and she died like . . ."

"Like she deserved. Thank you, Sven." He embraced him, and held on. "Why are you only telling me this now?"

Sven narrowed his eyes and, of course, began to laugh. He was predictable in his unpredictability. Olav didn't want to talk to him any longer; he knew that whatever they said now wouldn't matter. Sven had tried to convince him to join forces, to create an alliance beyond the one they had built on England's shores. But to no avail. Their time together was done. Their roads were dividing, and neither would promise the other that they wouldn't meet again on opposing sides. And if that happened, a different Olav would face Sven. Tryggvason had discovered that the real reason he had come to England was more than just silver.

Olav had known from the start it had to be Sivrit, no one else. He didn't want Sigeric, the archbishop of Canterbury, or any other fat, arrogant chaplain like the ones he'd met surrounding King Ethelred. He trusted only Sivrit.

Just as, years ago, Sivrit, my mother's brother, brought me out from slavery, he thought, *so will Bishop Sivrit bring me out of the darkness.*

Earlier that night, as they negotiated the value of the danegeld in Southampton, when Sigeric bartered for every one hundred pounds, a short, thin, bald man had walked into the room, wearing a gray habit. He carried a cross in his hand and anger in his eyes.

"Babylon," he said, in a voice that made the archbishop fall silent. "Babylon fell and became the nest of demons and unclean spirits. The wine of his impetuosity in the anarchy he caused fed nations. And the kings of

the earth allowed for anarchy alongside Babylon, and the merchants grew
wealthy on its greed. Dishonor, Archbishop Sigeric. Dishonor. This is how
you sell your country."

"That's not true, monk," the archbishop snapped. "I'm buying our freedom. Yours and mine, and our king's and the small ones we have been
charged to protect."

"I don't believe in freedom purchased with silver," the newcomer said.
"Imprisonment is better next to it, with a clear conscience."

"Oh, yes?" Sigeric said obstinately. "Go ahead then, be my guest. Go to
these barbarians as their prisoner."

And that's when the newcomer turned his pale eyes on them. He had a
face as unpolished as a slab of unplaned wood. A narrow nose that looked
like a mere bone covered with skin, it would make any other face look stubborn, but not his. His eyes slipped over Sven and paused on Olav.

"These aren't barbarians, Archbishop," he said slowly, his eyes never leaving Olav's. "These are people. You make them into beasts in your sermons,
but they are the same as us. Only much stronger. Goodbye." He turned and,
leaving, paused by Sigeric for a moment. "Negotiate!" he said harshly.

It could have sounded mocking, but I heard an order, Olav thought. And he said:
"Until next time, monk."

"Until next time," he replied, and left.

They then returned to their negotiations, and soon ended on the sixteen
thousand pounds of silver. And when, after a few weeks, the danegeld was
counted, divided, and loaded onto the ships, Earl Ethelweard came to Olav
with an invitation.

"King Ethelred wants to meet you, kind Olav. But only you."

"What changed your master's mind?"

"Sivrit. The mad monk who interrupted our talks," the earl replied. "The
king listens to him."

"And the archbishop of Canterbury?"

"Well . . ." The earl spread his arms. "If you consider the archbishop the
head of the English Church, then Sivrit is its soul."

Thankfully, Ethelred didn't invite Olav to London, as he would have had
to decline. He knew that he could not allow himself to be led into any stronghold, behind any wall, but he demanded hostages nevertheless before he set
out to meet the king on the wide green fields near Andover.

A great royal tent waited for him, set up on a hill, surrounded by Ethelred's
guards. Before Olav ascended on horseback, Earl Ethelweard greeted him,
asking him and his companions to surrender their weapons. Olav unbuckled

his sword without a word; he had agreed to the terms of the meeting when he took the hostages. Varin, though, as he handed the earl his sword, hissed and bared his fangs. Ethelweard moved back. Apart from Varin, Olav had Omold the bard with him, and ten others, only men from the original crew of *Kanugård*. He wished that Geivar were also with him, but he was a chieftain of Jom now. This day was an incredible milestone in their journey, the one he and Geivar had begun together when they freed themselves from the clutches of Allogia and Prince Vladimir. Olav didn't agree to walk up the hill on foot; he wasn't defeated, he was a victorious guest. He rode on horseback.

King Ethelred was a disappointment, though. Olav had expected to see an old man, broken by joint pain, or a drunkard with a fat belly and circles under his eyes. But he was met by a barely thirty-year-old man with pretty, curling hair, lined in places with gray.

"King Olav," he said cheerfully. "So those who called you the most beautiful barbarian to invade England weren't lying."

"Did you ask the girls?" Olav laughed.

"No. My chieftains and advisers. They said you had pale eyes and hair like the silver you've gained from us. They said you're tall and broad-shouldered. Nimble and clever like—"

"A young snake," Varin interjected. "The symbol of the Yngling dynasty."

"Yes, yes, I know. I've asked here and there," Ethelred said evasively, leading Olav to the table laid out under the tent. "Please, sit, you're my guests. Cupbearer, wine."

Olav didn't like wine, so he asked for water. The king acted as if there was nothing strange about this.

"Water for my guest. So, you're an Yngling heir, Olav. You and I sitting at one table sees history turn a full circle."

"What do you mean?"

"Our ancestors. Your grandfather, Haakon known as the Good, and mine, Athelstan. Do you know their story?"

"My mother told me, but I'll listen to the one you'll tell."

"Haakon was the youngest son of the Norwegian ruler, Harald Fairhaired."

The youngest and from a mistress, Olav added in his mind. *And Fairhaired was the first to unify the country with a firm hand.*

"Harald Fairhaired had a good future planned for his son," the king continued, "but he was afraid that his own brother would murder Haakon before his son reached adulthood, so he sent him to England."

He was right to fear this. This elder brother is Eric the Bloodaxe and the husband of the widow Gunhild, the reason for my family's murders—Olav was not cheered by the knowledge that the witch had died in a swamp. He'd have preferred to have found and killed her himself, with the majesty of the law.

"So young Haakon Haraldsson came to England and became King Athelstan's ward. He was baptized here, fifty or sixty years ago. And when his time came, he returned to Norway, defeated his uncle Eric the Bloodaxe, and ruled the country justly and well."

"Under the watchful eyes of the jarls of Lade," Olav reminded sharply. "The good king made a deal with his subjects, according to which he didn't stop them from worshipping the old gods, and they let him worship Christ. Allowing the jarls power was the price of this alliance, that's why Haakon is remembered as good, but also as weak."

Ethelred was taken aback, as if his sword had been knocked out of his hand in the heat of a battle.

"You misjudged me, King," Olav continued. "It's not in my nature to make alliances, but to subdue others. Thanks, at least partly, to your silver." He smiled as he finished.

"I'd give you twice as much for an oath that you never again set foot on my shores," the king said.

"I don't want oaths or more silver. Baptize me," Olav said.

The king's open mouth revealed what Olav had known; this request wholly disrupted the plan the king had come into their conversation with.

Olav was no fool, he knew what the king had intended. He knew Ethelred planned to squirm and writhe until he'd eventually ask Olav to accept God's Word and cease the invasions. The king would do it to improve his standing among his noblemen, so he might brag that, yes, he had given much treasure, but he had also gained a "lamb for the Lord's sheepfold."

Since his conversation with the old healer on Scilla, who'd spoken of three thorns and a curse from the old gods, Olav hadn't wasted a day. He attacked abbeys, but he ordered the books to be hidden in chests. He took monks prisoner, ordering them to tell him everything they knew in the evenings. He had an excellent memory, and when Sivrit had entered the danegeld negotiations, mentioning Babylon, he knew that the monk had been referring to the fall of the overflowing Babylon and the creation of a New Jerusalem. Apocalypse. The Revelation of John the Apostle. He knew it. He knew about Mary, Mother of God, the Immaculate Conception, the Spirit in the form of a dove, the burning bush, the slabs of stone with their ten commandments, John the Baptist, and Christ, who would baptize with fire. And he wished for them all so badly that he didn't want to wait for the king to tell his smooth stories. He wanted holy water. Immediately. He had waited long enough in the Lord's front rooms.

Ethelred gathered himself. "We must wait for the bishop to arrive."

"Let's agree on something, King. You can be my godfather, like Athelstan was to Haakon the Good. A bishop can be there for the ritual, whichever one you want. But Sivrit will be the one to baptize me. And it's up to you to make him a missionary bishop. If you don't agree to these terms, we are both wasting our time."

"I agree," Ethelred said, and added: "This will take time. The monk, though pious and close to my heart, hasn't been ordained as a priest."

"The best time for a baptism is the first spring full moon, so you have time, King. But not a day longer, for the day after my baptism I will sail away, with Sivrit beside me on *Kanugård*. You decide where I sail. To Lade, to defeat Jarl Haakon, or to London and Bamburgh. Thank you for the water I have drunk and the conversation in which you've reminded me of my family's history."

Olav didn't see Sivrit until the day of his baptism. He didn't need to, he had an excellent memory, and in it was the image of a thin bony man who didn't judge, but also knew no compromise. His bald, shiny head and hairless chin, divided in two by a line as straight as a knife cut. His nose, the narrow bone covered with skin. Thin lips and pale eyes; the light which streamed from them when he lifted his eyelids.

Olav walked to meet the waters of baptism alone, without weapons or the company of soldiers. A white dog accompanied him from the harbor, so silently that Olav couldn't be sure if it was truly there or a mere figment of his imagination. Dry, pale-green lichen covered the rock beneath his feet. Olav breathed in the scent of the sea and aromatic smoke. He found the stone archway of the gate. That's where he unbuckled his belt and threw down his weapons. He pulled off his shoes, threw aside his cloak, and let down his white hair. Finally, he faced the dark entrance to the stone building. The freed monks awaited him, those he had imprisoned when conquering the abbeys. He'd given them back their freedom to mark the occasion of his baptism. They reached out for his clothes, and he walked inside naked. He felt the coolness of old stones under his feet, the soft moss which lined their edges, and he heard the rustle of water.

"Are you ready, Olav?" Sivrit asked, waiting for him in the torchlit chamber inside.

"Yes."

"Do you deny the devil?"

"Yes."

"Do you want to be God's child?"

"I do."

"Do you surrender to the baptismal waters, the waters of a new life?"

"I'm a sailor. Water is my element. I want to enter the Kingdom through it, and sail with the Word in my sails."

"Then step into the water, in the name of the Father, the Son, and the Holy Spirit."

"Amen," Olav replied, walking into the holy water.

"From this day forth, you're God's child," Sivrit said. "Serve Him, and He will give you a new life."

Olav's new life howled like a torch thrown onto dry wood. Fire danced in the water, turning it to a boiling surge in which the iceberg melted. Mountains which revealed a cross from beneath their rocks. Two lynxes jumping to the throats of the unfaithful. A message burned into skin like a brand. A snake that slithered into a throat, following fire. His knees buckled.

"Lord, I am not worthy . . ." he whispered.

"You're not," Sivrit said harshly, but as if to reassure him, he added, "No one is. And yet he still sacrificed himself for us."

"But only say the word and my soul shall be healed . . ."

Blood flowed from his knees when he stood. Sivrit leaned down and plucked out three thorns.

"Our Lord was given a crown of thorns," he said. "King Olav, this is a sign that He has chosen you."

34

SWEDEN

Świętosława wrapped her arms around Eric's thick neck. Her lord husband had laughed and drunk, praising their son's cunning and agility at the feast. "They call him Skinny Ole because Olof isn't as strong as other boys his age," he told her in private. "But he's superior to them in brains and courage. That's a good sign. You can work in the training yard to increase your muscles. You get your mind from your parents. And one must be born with courage. Our son has it." They were in her husband's bedchamber now, and Świętosława welcomed the silence after the noise of the welcome feast. Eric threw off his shirt. He stood before her, tired and naked. His eyes asked her for love, and she very much wanted to give it to him. For the first time, she didn't want to act like Oda, she didn't want to conquer, force her will on him, or negotiate. The time of his absence, and Birger's sharp words, *You haven't talked to him. You know nothing,* had been difficult to bear. She needed this moment with her husband; she needed to know what it was Eric had promised his gods. Did that mean she was once again stepping into the bed to glean information?

She kissed his thick lips. She ran her fingers along his hard chin, hidden under the waves of his flowing beard. She placed her small hands on his cheeks and caressed him gently with her thumbs.

"Come, husband," she whispered. "I want love."

Something shone in his eyes, but it couldn't have been a tear. They made love in long, heavy thrusts, which gave her pleasure, not pain. In the arch of Eric's eyebrows as he leaned over her body. In her sigh when he massaged her breast in his large hand. *He remembers,* she thought, as Eric nipped her lip at the end of their kiss. *And he remembered this . . .* she thought, when he began to kiss her ear. He remembered what brought her pleasure sometimes, and to realize this meant more to her than anything else they had shared.

"Sigrid," he purred into her ear as he kissed it. "You're my love . . ."

"And you're my joy, my lord," she replied. "We have so many years to bring each other pleasure . . . Ah!"

Her hips lifted to meet her husband's next thrust.

"We don't have years, my lady," he panted, looking in her eyes. He was so close she felt he might swallow her whole. "But we have days . . ."

"What are you saying?" she whispered, finding strength to arch under his weight.

"We have days . . ."

She didn't hear what he said next, as her body was wracked with shivers she couldn't control, and didn't want to. She felt like Wrzask or Zgrzyt when they tore their prey apart. She felt something warm and red behind her eyes. Blood? Ah . . .

Eric arched above her and made a sound like a wild animal. Like a wolf. His face, seen from below, was terrible, like the image of a beast in an attack of pleasure.

"We have the whole world," she said, pulling him close as her body continued to shiver.

"No, my love. We have but days," he said, collapsing onto his back beside her. "The One-Eyed Lord will take the rest."

He was breathing heavily, and Świętosława couldn't gather her thoughts. She felt shaky still, but she had heard what he'd said.

"What have you done?" she whispered, rolling onto her front.

"I paid for our victory. For your and Olof's peace," he said, lying on his back and staring into the smoke hole through which a stream of gray rose from the fire.

"Who have you sacrificed to your god?" she asked, placing a hand on his chest. "I know that you made a bloody sacrifice. Tell me who it was? Styrbjorn, your nephew? Or an important prisoner from your war with Sven?"

"I'm not a coward, my lady. I won't hide behind someone else's life. I gave myself."

She stiffened.

"In return for defeating Styrbjorn, I promised myself, in nine years time. I knew that that would be enough to raise our son and strengthen his and your positions at court." He stretched out an arm and clenched his fingers to make a fist. And then he straightened it, looking at it for a moment. He let his hand fall with a heavy sigh. "I didn't know then that I would fall in love. I liked you from our first meeting on the waters of Mälaren, but it's normal for a man to like a beautiful young woman. But then, year by year, day by day . . . sometimes I despised my weakness for you. An old warrior, and I melted in your hands like snow . . . I regret every day we won't spend together, every night doubly so, but . . . I don't regret any moment we have lived." He reached out and pulled her to him.

Her initial reaction was fury. She shrugged him off and began to beat his chest.

"You think only of yourself! This is—this is horrid . . ." She flung the words like they were stones, and hoped they landed on him as painfully. "Die, what could be easier? You're leaving me! Styrbjorn is dead, but your mistresses and children prey on me from every corner . . . ah!"

"They are mere shadows that vanish when the sun comes up again," he said, stroking her head.

She lay down on his chest then and cried. As the anger faded, her courage returned. She mounted Eric and began to make love to him again, whispering:

"This is what you want to leave? This is what you want to give up?"

"Stop." He kissed her. "Stop . . ."

"No. You stop scaring me with death. Change your mind. You're a king. Give Odin someone else."

He laughed and gave himself up to love.

"Don't you have prisoners?" Świętosława asked, after they had finished for the second time. "Then move your arse to war and get some. Maybe that's what you need? Another victorious war?"

"Maybe," he admitted eventually, as dawn rose. "I go to Uppsala the day after tomorrow, messengers from Denmark await me there."

"Yes." She clung to the thread he offered. "Let's board the *Wave Queen* and sail to Roskilde together. We should have done it long ago, let's do it now. You can settle the unrest among the Danish commoners with your sword and feel the blood course through your veins again."

"I feel it already, my lady." He kissed her and fell asleep.

She too gave in to sleep, and when she awoke, Eric wasn't beside her. She could hear his voice from the hall, how he laughed with his chieftains and roared at the servants to bring more meat, because he was as hungry as a wolf. She stretched out in his bed. Yes, this was good. The fears of the night had evaporated. As she rose and dressed, she thought that Eric might be a king, but he was also a simple, ordinary man. A bed, good food, mead, and the vision of victory.

Świętosława didn't want to go to Uppsala with him. She hadn't had a bright manor built in Sigtuna only to return to the darkness of the old house.

"Take Olof," she advised him. "Let him learn how to rule beside his father."

"That's good advice." He nodded.

It wasn't long before they were ready to leave.

She bid them goodbye in the bright light of the early spring sun. Olof had switched from ponies to full-sized horses a long time ago. He seemed too big on horseback. *How fast he's grown*, she thought as she watched him ride away.

When they were gone, she summoned Wilkomir:

"The lynxes want to hunt. Zgrzyt, Wrzask!" she called, and her cats understood they were about to give chase.

Świętosława wanted to forget this long and dark winter that was finally ending, to lose it in the horse's canter. Thora's death. The old healer's strange visions. Birger and his ominous advice. The image of Odin's sacrifice, which Eric had scared her with a mere two nights before. She knew that now, with each day growing longer, things would only get better. That it was the darkness of winter which brought out the worst instincts in people, and now brightness and warmth were coming. Ion had promised her that they'd meet in the chapel in the king's absence, the chapel he usually spoke of as being no more sacred than a boathouse.

"But, as the Holy Scriptures say, the place where two people meet in my name, there am I also, my lady. So, let us meet in your hut in God's name, and at least I can read you the Bible which our good king has stolen from the church in Roskilde." The servants she had brought with her from Poznań ten years ago, though they now dressed like local women and had adapted to most of the local traditions, still prepared painted eggs at Easter, and she knew they were already coloring this year's batch with melted wax. She promised herself she'd make at least one, and give it to Eric. She laughed. Her husband ate only raw eggs.

She felt flushed after the ride. Wrzask appeared first with the hare he had caught. Then came Zgrzyt, with two young foxes. They returned at a walk, they didn't need to fly anymore. She had outrun her dark thoughts and left them behind. But as they approached, she noticed Birger in the yard. The jarl was obviously waiting for her, and his expression betrayed the importance of the news he bore. She gave her horse to a stable boy, attached the leashes to her lynxes, and called out to him cheerfully:

"Wait for me, Jarl, I'll take the cats inside and come out to you."

Ion was pacing in the hall, and his usually self-satisfied face was unsettled.

"My lady . . . I must tell you something . . ." He almost caught her sleeve as she walked past.

"Speak."

"Not here. Privately. It's important."

"Jarl Birger is waiting for me. I'll speak to him first." She gave the leash to Dusza and walked back toward the exit.

Ion crept behind her.

"My lady . . ."

"Either speak now, or wait, monk," she threw over her shoulder.

"I'll wait, my lady."

The usual hubbub met her in the yard. A pig with bound legs, led under the axe, was squealing.

"My queen . . ." Birger appeared beside her so suddenly that she flinched. "Did I startle you?"

"No. The squeal of that animal . . . Can't they do it somewhere else?"

He called out loudly, ordering the servants to leave. The animal was led behind the manor, to which it reacted with an even more terrified bleat.

"I will be meeting Ion to read the Holy Scriptures," she told the jarl. "Would you like to join us? It's Easter." She nudged him with her shoulder, laughing, trying to lighten the somber mood he carried with him.

"Yes, but I'm afraid I have more pressing matters, my lady. There is less and less time—"

"Stop!" she interrupted him angrily. "I spoke with my husband. He promised to deal with the matter differently than planned." The details of that night and the discussion between king and queen were not the jarl's business.

He nodded, as if agreeing, then whispered,

"The girls won't cause us any more trouble. I've done what was necessary."

The frightened wail of the dying pig reached them from behind the house. She began to feel sick.

"I don't know what you mean, Jarl," she whispered.

"Yes, you do, my lady," he replied. "But you're right, not everything needs to be spoken aloud. I only wanted you to know that you can depend upon me unquestionably."

Her mouth was dry. She wanted to say something, but for the first time in her life her voice refused to obey her. In the same moment, dogs barked and a procession appeared in the yard.

"Olof?" she couldn't believe her eyes. Her son had left for Uppsala with his father at dawn to meet the Danish messengers.

She ran toward them.

"Where's the king? Why have you returned?"

"My lord father has sent me back to you. We received news on the way that the messengers hadn't arrived as expected, and my lord father ordered me to come back."

It wasn't true. The messengers were already in Uppsala, she'd heard Eric and Birger discussing their arrival the day before. Her heart beat so hard she was sure it would break her chest apart.

"And the king? Where did the king go?"

"To Uppsala, lady mother."

Her son's dark eyes were honest. Olof told her what he knew, having no idea what was truly happening.

"It's begun," Birger said in her ear, and she felt cold.

"Why didn't he take you with him?" She grabbed Olof's horse by the reins.

"He said he wanted to carry out a ritual in Odin's great temple and that you'd prefer for me not to be there."

"Great Ulf!" she screamed so suddenly that Olof's horse whinnied in fear. "Wilkomir! Gather a squad. We are going to Uppsala, to the king. My son comes with us. A horse!"

She turned around and saw Birger's solemn face.

"It has begun, my lady," he repeated.

"Stay in Sigtuna, Jarl. I charge you with care for the manor."

He went down on one knee in front of her and kissed her hand.

"I won't let you down, my queen."

They had to make one short stop on the way to avoid exhausting their horses. Olof was unsettled, and he ran over to her as soon as they dismounted by a stream.

"Mother, why are we going? What's happening?"

"You're all grown-up, my son . . ." She didn't want to hurt him with careless words. What was happening? Even she wasn't sure. Had Eric told Olof the truth and sent him away so the boy wouldn't participate in the ritual, or . . .

"Your lord father promised me something," she said. "We're going to see if he keeps his word. I know that if he sees us both, it will be important to him, and he will be . . . more likely not to break his promise."

They entered Uppsala after dark. Her mare was exhausted from the mad ride, but Świętosława couldn't slow down. Instead, when she saw the torches burning along the path between the mounds, she urged her mount forward.

"More, more, my little one, my fast one," she drove her.

"Who goes there?" A guard on horseback barred her way.

"Queen Sigrid. Out of my way! Where is my husband?"

"In the temple, my lady." The guard rode away at the last moment, when it became clear she had no intention of slowing.

God Almighty! I have never crossed the threshold of this house, and now . . . She was already riding between the mounds. She looked to the left. There wasn't a single sacrifice hanging from the branches of the great tree, but crows were gathering in bleak expectation. She felt a cramp in her belly, as if her stomach wanted to lurch out of her. The lights of the old manor appeared in the distance. She took a sharp right, to the temple. She glanced over her shoulder. Her riders were right behind her, as was Olof. *He manages so well in the saddle,* she thought, *as if this mattered right now.*

A great fire had been lit in front of the temple. A large crowd had gathered around it. Women, men, some children. They looked at her mistrustfully. She stopped and dismounted.

A man walked out to meet her, who she recognized as the temple's guardian. They'd seen each other when she'd still lived here, once or twice. After that, he'd stayed out of her sight.

"My lady, what brings you to us?" he asked. "Would you like to abandon your Christ and cross over to our gods?"

"No," she replied curtly. "Where's my husband?"

"In the temple."

"I want to see him."

"You cannot."

"You speak to the queen!" she shouted angrily. "Ulf, stop this man. Wilkomir, come with Olof and me."

"It's not a good idea," Ulf said quietly. "You cannot enter the temple during a ritual."

"I have to do this," she whispered back, and said loudly: "This is Olof, Eric's son. And I am Queen Sigrid Storråda, your lady. I'm going to meet my husband in Odin's temple."

"You have to swear, my lady," the guard spoke, "that you won't interrupt the ritual. Otherwise, you might die."

"Don't threaten the queen," Wilkomir growled loudly, and whispered to her what Ulf had already observed, "My lady, this is a bad idea."

"I don't have a better one," she whispered back. And, louder, she added: "I won't interrupt your rituals."

"Do you swear it?"

"I do," she said, and pulled Olof with her.

People stepped out of their way reluctantly. She saw unfriendly faces.

Glum men and women who wanted to tell her: "This isn't your place." She walked faster, pushing them aside. She was afraid of every moment lost. When she was close, she heard singing from within the temple. No, not singing. Someone was reciting the 'Song of the Mighty' loudly, but it wasn't her husband's Icelandic bard. There were fewer people directly in front of the temple. She was almost running, pulling Olof by his hand. He asked no questions, but his palm was sweaty. She had maybe twenty steps left when the temple doors were thrown open and the most beautiful old man she'd ever seen stepped out. Tall, powerful, broad-backed, with long white hair that flowed down his shoulders. His gray beard looked like silk. He was dressed in a wide gray cloak, with the hood thrown over his shoulders.

Who is he? Why have I never seen him before? she wondered, quickly followed by another thought: *Someone so beautiful and majestic couldn't possibly . . .*

"My lord," she exclaimed. "I'm Queen Sigrid . . ."

"I know who you are," the man replied calmly, raising an arm and turning to the waiting crowd. "Your king Eric has made his sacrifice! May this bring him eternal glory. The king who keeps his word is the gods' favorite in life as he is in death."

A thorn pierced her heart. The bloody thorn from the old woman's runes. Her knees buckled. She wanted to enter the temple, but the old man stood in her way. He reached out to her and grabbed both her and Olof's hands. His touch muted her pain for a moment. He raised their arms and proclaimed:

"Here is the dowager queen and her son, King Olof, his father Eric's heir. Bow to them."

At first, the crowd muttered angrily, but the old man's strength was too great, and, one by one, they bent their knees. A thought crossed her blank mind: *Olof, don't cry. You cannot show weakness.*

"The queen dowager! King Olof!"

One of Ulf's men was the first to shout out, and others joined in, directing the crowd's chants. When they fell silent, she spoke as loudly as she could:

"We will give my husband a wonderful funeral. One worthy of a king and chieftain. One of which Odin would approve." The words passed through her throat more easily than she would have thought. "We'll burn a pyre here, among the kings' mounds, and here his ashes shall rest. And we will drink the goblet of memories for him. Because there has never been a better ruler of this country than my husband."

She paused as the crowd shouted their joy at her words, and then continued:

"My son Olof is his father's only heir. Until he reaches manhood, I will stand by him and help him rule. You will be as safe and happy under his reign as you have been under Eric. And now, let me see my king."

The old man led them inside. Flames danced in the round fireplace, piercing the darkness inside. Huge statues of Odin, Thor, and Frey lined the walls. Eric lay on a stone slab in front of Odin's wooden likeness. She leaned over him. His chest had been slashed by a single knife thrust.

"Why isn't he bleeding?" she asked.

"I collected his blood." The old man pointed at a dish standing to one side.

That's when Świętosława realized that, apart from the great white-haired old man, no one else was in the temple.

I took my husband's murderer for the most beautiful old man my eyes had ever seen, she thought, disgusted with herself. She stared at Eric's still expression and blamed first him and then herself, in turn. She felt nothing.

"My lady?" The old man reached out a hand to her.

"Is this the hand which dealt him the blow?" she asked.

"The sacrificer makes and accepts sacrifices. He is merely a tool between the world of gods and men."

She grabbed his hand. His tool. And she suddenly felt at a loss about what to do next.

"Don't be afraid, my queen. I will guide you."

35

SWEDEN

Świętosława and Olof took up residence in the old royal manor house, behind Odin's sacrificial grove in the shadow of the mounds.

"This is where you were born, son." She showed him the old bedchamber and bed.

Olof sat on the edge of the bed. For a moment he sat silently, looking down at his hands, then he asked, "Why did Father do that?"

"Because he was an old stubborn Viking." There was no anger in her voice, only exhaustion. "When he went to war with his nephew, he swore he would give his life to Odin if he won. And he kept his word. He always kept it. He promised my father he'd defeat Sven, and he chased him out of Denmark. That's just who he was."

"Did you know about it?"

"I should have guessed," she replied honestly. "But I didn't. Only that night . . . I thought I convinced him to change his mind."

Preparations for the funeral and the great feast began the next morning. She sent men with invitations to all of Eric's chieftains. To the merchants of Birka, too. To proud Rognvald Ulfsson and his daughter Thordis. One shouldn't avoid one's enemies. She missed Jarl Birger and his advice, but the old man was with her. His name was Bork. Except she couldn't tell him everything that weighed on her, and she didn't know how to ask about it either.

After two days, one of Birger's trusted servants arrived from Sigtuna and said that his master had given him a private message he was to share with the queen. Świętosława was sitting with Bork while he explained the funeral ritual to her, step by step.

"We'll finish talking about the funeral," she told the messenger, "then I'll speak with you."

"But, my queen, this is about the funeral," the servant insisted. "And it cannot wait."

"Speak, then," she ordered.

He glanced at Bork uncertainly.

"If it's about the funeral, then speak," she urged him.

"My master asks if the queen has decided on a funeral according to the old traditions."

"Yes, I have already announced it to the people."

God, she thought, *my father had enough strength to put an end to these old bloody rites, and I'll have to place my lord husband on a funeral pyre.*

"Jarl Birger agrees." His servant nodded. "He would like to pass on that King Eric deserves the full ceremony, like the rulers of old."

"I know that," she said, hearing the growl in her mouth.

The servant pretended to be oblivious to her impatience.

"Jarl Birger would like to advise you with regards to the woman."

"I don't understand." She looked at Bork. His old, gentle face was impassive. "Explain it to me, my lord."

"The jarl means . . ." the servant began, but Bork interrupted him.

"The queen asked for my opinion." He had a quiet but emphatic voice. That night, when he'd stood with her and Olof in front of the temple, he hadn't shouted, but the crowds had heard them. "Bold lady," he began. He addressed her the same way the old woman in the forest had done. She didn't stop him. "It's an old tradition that the king, apart from his beloved horses, dogs, and hunting falcons, is accompanied by a mistress. To take care of him in his journey to Valhalla."

"I don't know any of my husband's mistresses," she said defiantly.

"Thordis from Birka," Birger's servant hissed.

So, this is the jarl's plan? He wants to send Thordis into the flames with Eric? If it weren't for the fact that it is barbarian and insolent, I'd have thought it a perfect solution.

"No," she said loudly. "I don't agree. Thordis is a noblewoman. She was my husband's mistress before my time. She has two sons with him, and I will not allow such cruelty."

"Rightly so, my lady," Bork said.

"Jarl Birger only implied that this was the only known mistress of King Eric," his man deftly suggested.

"That's not true. There are two other women, I don't know their names, but he conceived daughters with them."

"Alfdis and Holmfrid, my lady," Bork said, and she realized the old man perhaps knew more of her husband than she did.

"Unfortunately, they are already dead," the servant said impassively.

The girls won't cause us any more trouble. I've done what was necessary. She recalled what Birger had said to her in the yard, moments before her departure. *Christ, how could I have forgotten? He killed those girls, but does that also mean he killed their mothers? I should speak with him, he's acting like a madman. He cannot do this.*

"So a slave must be taken," Bork said. "Young and beautiful so as not to shame the king."

"Is that necessary? Did Eric's father also take someone's innocent life with him?" she asked, already knowing the answer.

Bork nodded. She felt incredibly drained once more.

I'm doing this for Olof and for myself. To ensure our subjects don't turn on us. Once I have strengthened our position on the throne, I'll invite a bishop to Sigtuna and baptize this bloody country.

The gray-bearded man looked at her sharply then, and she realized she shouldn't allow herself such thoughts in his presence. Clearly, the powers his gods had given him stretched to understanding words unspoken.

"Does your master have anything else to tell me?" she asked the servant.

"Yes. I've brought Dusza and both lynxes with me. Jarl Birger said you likely needed their company, my lady. And your servants have packed chests with clothes and jewels."

She felt such gratitude for Birger in that moment that if he'd been there, she would have forgiven his cruel plan for Thordis and embraced him.

"The jarl also wants you to know he is fighting a fever and is doing all he can to arrive in time for the funeral. But should he fail, he will send appropriate replacements and parting gifts."

"What fever is this? Is he in danger?" Noting the way her chest tightened, she realized that although he might be unpredictable in his cruelty, she couldn't lose him. She needed him now more than ever.

"Fever, just a fever. Even a strong man succumbs to something so ordinary. He asked you not to worry about anything, my lady."

The pyre was arranged beyond the last of the royal mounds. *This is where he will burn, and where his own mound will rise.* A sharp spring wind pulled at their cloaks as the procession walked toward the place from which her husband would make his final journey. Dragging his boat up here had taken much effort, and the soft muddy ground was full of wounds left by the logs used to transport the boat. It wasn't the *Golden Boar,* that was too big to drag from the harbor, but it was a good and beautiful dragon boat.

She walked with her lynxes on a leash and with Olof at her side, but she made sure she didn't take her son's hand.

"They'll be watching us, son, to see if you are strong enough to take your father's place, and if I can rise to the challenge. That's why we cannot cry, or show any weakness. Do you understand me?"

"I understand, Mother," he replied.

He seemed to have collapsed in on himself since the day Eric died, withdrawing inward. She understood what he was feeling as no one else did; she'd been even younger when she lost sweet Dobrawa. And that's why she knew that the slightest expression of a mother's sentiments could bring him to tears. For his own good, she wasn't affectionate toward him.

Gray-bearded Bork led the procession. She and Olof followed him, then Wilkomir, Ulf, and her entire guard. Her husband's chieftains and their squads. The chieftains' wives with their children. The lords of the lands, among them Rognvald of Birka and Thordis, his daughter. Her twin sons hadn't come, and perhaps that was better; they lived in the far north now and were busy bickering with the Finns. And then followed another hundred people she didn't know.

They surrounded the boat. She saw horses, dogs, and falcons held on the side by servants. A small fire burned nearby, ready to light the torch that would send her husband on his final journey. She shivered. Where was the girl Bork had chosen?

The gray-bearded man stepped forward and asked:

"Who will lead the king's servants to the boat?"

Świętosława knew it was meant to be a woman known as the Shadow Hunter. Bork told her the woman was so old that she'd participated in the funerals of both Eric's father and grandfather.

"I," a squawking voice answered.

Świętosława recognized the sound. She turned. The old woman she'd met after Thora Birger's death stepped through the crowds. Świętosława felt bile rising in her throat. *The woman had said she didn't touch magic. That she heals or tells fortunes, nothing more, damn her. She lied to me!*

The old woman was wearing a cloak of bird feathers. Some were so old they looked moldy. The woman walked by Świętosława, not gracing her with a single glance, as if they'd never met before. But it must have been her. Almost bald, a bare skull with grayish, wispy strands stuck to it. Deep-set eyes. A jutting chin with clumps of hair.

She was helped onto the bridge constructed next to the boat's gangplank. On the ground nearby was a man with a wooden bat. The healer lifted her arms and howled:

"The king's dogs will walk beside him in an endless hunt!"

The servants led the dogs. The animals barked, resisting being led up the gangplank. The man with the bat hit them so quickly that they had no time to realize what awaited them. One by one they fell to the ground, stunned. The servants picked them up and carried them onto the boat.

"He will ride his horses to Valhalla," the old woman called out, and the horses were led over.

The great chestnut stallion and black mare neighed and twisted their heads away from the boat. The old woman's servant stunned them skilfully, and they were dragged into the boat along the gangplank, where one slit of a knife opened their throats.

"Falcons!" she screamed. "The swift falcons will hunt with the king."

The birds had their necks twisted and they were placed at the king's feet on the boat.

Świętosława stared at her husband's body. His face was hidden behind a parade helmet. Only his long dark beard emerged from under it. *The same one that touched my naked breasts so recently,* Świętosława thought.

He'd been dressed in a rich, purple-red caftan, the best chain mail, and an ornately decorated cloak, fastened by a brooch shaped like the head of a boar. And tall boots of well-oiled leather, the kind he wore when he ran into the water before jumping onto a ship. The sword he had defeated Styrbjorn and Sven with was clasped in his hand. He also had a long knife at his belt.

This isn't my husband. It is only a body that the soul has abandoned, she thought, though she knew that Eric didn't believe in the soul, but in the spirit of a man which leaves his body to sit beside Odin in his great golden hall, waiting for Ragnarök, the battle at the end of days.

"His mistress will make his journey more pleasant," the old woman squawked, and everyone saw her look toward Świętosława.

The girl was brought. She couldn't have been older than sixteen. She was gorgeous in her youth, with blue eyes and fair braids. She was wearing a necklace that she had probably never seen before this day. The girl's wrists were decorated with silver bracelets, simple but still too expensive for a slave or servant.

Had she ever given us our goblets during a feast? Or had she only cleaned pots in the kitchen? Bork said she had volunteered. Had Eric really bedded her?

She was drunk, and two other servants led her, supporting her under her arms. Her fingers traveled up to touch the necklace every now and again. The lynxes growled when she swayed too close to them.

Świętosława knew that they could smell the girl's fear.

"What's your name, girl?" Świętosława asked, ignoring the old woman's snort.

"Bolla," she muttered absently. "They call me Bolla, my lady."

"Who told you to accompany the king?" she asked.

"No one, my lady . . . I did . . . it's a great honor to go to Valhalla . . ."

"Were you the lord's mistress?"

"I always wanted to be . . ." she whispered provocatively. "And now I will be the one to go with him, not you, bold lady . . ."

The servants dragged her over to the old woman, who gave the girl a cup of mead.

"Bolla!" Świętosława shouted. "Repeat her name so that they may hear it in Valhalla before her arrival."

Bolla drank greedily, the mead flowing down her chin. Świętosława felt her fear; the lynxes growled, pulling at the leash. If there was a way of turning the girl around . . . but she was already taking a swaying step onto the gunwale. Everyone was looking at her; this was her day. She never had, and never would again, know a moment such as this. Świętosława's soul howled for Bolla more than for Eric. He had made a conscious decision. Bolla had done so in a surge of some foolish euphoria.

"Our lord's mistress . . ." the old woman began, but Świętosława interrupted her, calling:

"Bolla!"

"Bolla, the lord's mistress, goes with him," the old woman finished furiously, and her servant approached the girl from behind, cutting her throat.

She fell, and she was dragged to lie at Eric's feet. Beside the falcons and dogs. Świętosława stepped forward.

"Mother," her son whispered. "You gave her her name, that's enough."

Świętosława sobered instantly. Olof. How smart he was. She squeezed his fingers secretly. He pulled his hand away.

"Odin summons the bravest men to feast with him in Valhalla," the old woman howled. "But they must sail there on waves of flames. Who will raise the sea of fire under the ship, King Eric asks?"

"His son!" Świętosława called out, and gently pushed Olof. "His only son."

She saw Thordis and Rognvald's thunderous looks from across the pyre, but she didn't look away. They had come here without the boys. That was her luck, and their mistake.

Oh, Thordis, she thought, *you look at me with such hatred, and you have no idea that if it wasn't for me, you'd be the one lying at my husband's feet with your throat cut.*

Olof stepped forward. He was composed, his pale face showing neither fear nor disgust. He reached out an arm holding a torch and dipped it into the fire. Then he placed it under the pyre by the ship. The dry wood caught quickly. Olof waited for the kindling under his father's ship to burn evenly, and only then threw the torch onto the deck.

"Let King Eric sail on his final journey and not worry about his kingdom," her son shouted. "No enemy threatens our lands, because his wife and son guard them. Father, sail. You gave me life, and now I will make the most of it. Burn and sail!"

The chieftains chanted, the people shouted, and the wood burned brightly. And with it left Eric the Victorious, her husband. The arm which held the sword burned as brightly as his loins. His beard was probably the first thing to turn to ashes. That beard which had tickled her breast. She clenched her fists tightly in anger.

Oh, husband, she thought. *If you hadn't been so stubborn, you'd have turned back from this road and we'd be sitting by the fire in Sigtuna today, drinking mead from one cup. And we would have met in paradise after death. But no, you chose your gods, like a man who puts his comrades' company and the goblet above his wife. You bet on them and you gave away the chance to save your soul. That is why we won't meet after death. We will never meet again, unless dreams give you to me.*

Heat radiated from the burning boat, but no one stepped back so as not to offend the dead. Suddenly, the spar cracked and collapsed in a shower of sparks. The old woman's servant picked her up and carried her from the gangplank at the last moment. If it wasn't for him, she would have been severely burned. At that moment, Świętosława felt a burning sensation on her hand. A drop of molten amber was melting into her skin.

Eric! she thought angrily. *You burned me. You were a good husband, though as stubborn as the devil. I regret that you're dead, but I agree with you on one thing; I don't regret a single moment we spent together. I forgive you the fur of the polar bear on which you took me that first night. Maybe what I felt for you wasn't love, but what I feel now is loss. Eric, you left me!*

36

SWEDEN

Świętosława discovered that funeral feasts were a horrific tradition. They lasted for as long as it took for every guest to feel sated. Countless barrels of beer and mead were emptied and replaced. Exhausted servants, barely still standing, placing bowls of food on the tables day by day, and Świętosława looking in the face of each one of them, wanting to see Bolla. The cruelty of a ritual which takes away a woman's right to live simply because her master died repelled her. *"Where are their wives' mounds?"* she'd asked Mieszko years ago, when he'd taken her and Bolesław to see their ancestors' burial mounds. *"They went to the pyre with their husbands,"* Father had replied, and she'd been angry at him then, while today she paid homage to him for breaking this murderous cycle.

She sat on a tall chair in Uppsala, her son and Bork beside her, and the lynxes at her feet. A hundred of her husband's chieftains drank in the great hall, day after day, for ten days. Thordis and her father left after the first feast.

"It's not an insult," Bork explained.

She nodded. Even if they'd been drinking her mead and sharing her plate, she wouldn't have been able to trust them.

"Distrust is only caution taken a step further," Bork said, and she was grateful to him for those words.

When she asked, he told her about Yggdrasil, the great ash carved into the doors in Sigtuna. She had planned to ask Thora about this tree, but she hadn't made the time, and now . . . *It's always the ones we don't expect who die,* she thought. The wound from the molten amber was healing slowly.

Finally, after twelve days, the endless feasts at which she was expected to drink, remember her husband, and take care of her guests came to an end. And when the last of them had left her court in Uppsala, she realized she had only survived this nightmare because of Bork's company. The gray-bearded man's presence at her side had done far more, though: he'd shown her people that he supported her. And if he did, so did Odin. The one who plunged the knife into her husband's chest was the first one to take her hand and declare, "This is your queen and your young king!"

Unknown are the plans of gods, she thought, bidding Odin's sacrifice goodbye, and she rode out from between the mounds with relief. She recalled Birger's words from years before: *"Picture green hills when you look at them, and don't think about the fact that they hide the burned remains of rulers."* She would never again be able to imagine something so innocent as she rode past. Eric's mound was still being made, but when autumn arrived, she would search for her bearded husband's face in the last cairn.

Świętosława had ridden from Sigtuna in spring and had missed the time of Easter, painted eggs, and the reading of the Holy Scriptures. She returned in the height of summer, and the first thing she felt as she rode into the yard to the sound of welcoming horns was that she was home. The lynxes shared her view. They began by chasing the dogs, then the chickens, while Wrzask attempted to bite a large muddy piglet. Her servants ran out of the house with happy squeals, not remembering for a moment that they were greeting a widowed queen, and fell silent and bowed. Helga welcomed Wilkomir back with blushing cheeks. Gerda, one of the manor warden's daughters, turned bright red at the sight of Great Ulf's scarred face. *Yes,* Świętosława thought, *we're home.*

"My lady," the housewife greeted her. "We're having a feast for you tonight."

Please, no, not a feast, she thought, jumping off her horse. But she laughed aloud and said:

"Yes, let's have a feast. Wilkomir, catch the lynxes. Or don't, let them hunt something for tonight. My appetite is back."

She had barely walked into the house when Ion appeared at her side.

"You haven't read the Scriptures to me, monk," she called to him. "We'll have to make up for that. I need to scrub away the vision of death and Odin's heavy rituals."

"I need to speak with you, my lady," he said, glancing nervously around them. "You've probably forgotten about it . . . I have to tell you something before . . ."

At that very moment, horns sounded once again in welcome from the yard. Świętosława laughed. "Ion, Ion, it seems as if we are never meant to have this conversation . . . I need to welcome our guests."

"My lady!" A clammy hand grabbed her arm. "Find a moment for me when we can be alone. And please, beware of Birger, because the jarl . . ."

"Queen Sigrid," Birger entered the hall, pulling off his leather gloves.

Ion retreated at lightning speed.

"My lady, I ran straight from the road to greet you and . . ." He stood before her, seeming embarrassed. As if he was momentarily at a loss for words.

"It happened," she said. "At first, I regretted not listening to you and speaking to my husband earlier, but there, in Uppsala, I understood it wouldn't have changed anything. My pleas made no difference. I spoke at length with Bork . . . Have you ever thought, Jarl, that Odin's sacrifice of hanging upside down on a tree for nine days and nine nights resembles Christ's sacrifice?"

"Yes, my lady," he replied, absently. "I have thought of that often. And I hope that we can speak of it more than once." His gray eyes were restless. "We have so much to talk about, my lady."

"I invite you to tonight's feast. We can drink a goblet of memories to Eric, though I must admit, I've drunk so many of them that at the mere thought of mead my head and stomach pain me." She laughed. "But the people here, in Sigtuna, deserve to remember the king. Then we can talk."

"Sigrid Storråda! Sigrid Storråda!" her people chanted when she stepped onto the platform to make a toast.

Yes, Sigtuna was her court, these were her people. She didn't need Bork's strength and somberness here to win the people's favor. Every one of those gathered before her in the hall tonight was her subject. Hers and Olof's.

"The young king! The young king! Olof Ericsson!"

Enough days had passed since the death that they could smile and enjoy themselves now.

"I'll serve you, my lady." Birger offered to fill her goblet.

"I don't want mead, I had plenty in Uppsala. I would like some water."

"As you wish, Queen." He summoned a serving girl and took a jug of water from her. "And our young king? What will he drink?"

"Mead," Olof said, and blushed as he looked at his mother.

Birger filled his goblet, and she leaned toward him to say with a smile:

"Train your head, son. You've had your first lesson in Uppsala. The king must be able to drink more than all his noblemen."

He nodded to her, still somewhat embarrassed, but also partly entertained. She thought that she must find some time to spend alone with him, and soon. Everything that had just happened would leave its mark on his young life.

"It's the night of fires soon," Birger said when the feast gained color. "Midsummer Night."

"Oh, Birger! I'm beginning to doubt your baptism." She hit his arm playfully. "Tomorrow is Pentecost."

"Pentecost," Ion gurgled, swaying in between them. "The fiftieth day after the Lord's Resurrection. Uuuu . . ." He spread out his arms like a child pretending to be a bird, and he howled as he spun in a circle: "And suddenlyyyy there was heard a ruuuuustle from the heaveeeens! Tongues of fiiiiiire appeared and rested on eeeevery one of theeeem!"

"Be careful," Olof said, as one of Ion's outstretched arms knocked the goblet out of his hand.

"Ion." Świętosława laughed. "You're drunk."

"These people aren't drunk, as you might suppose, because it is nearing only the third hour of the day." Ion chuckled. "But the prophecy of the prophet Joel is being fulfilled: I will pour the Holy Spirit onto your body in the last days, and your sons and daughters will prophesize." He placed a finger at the jarl's head as he spoke.

"Have you gone mad, monk?" Birger growled.

"No, my lord. My queen wanted me to read the Scriptures to her, so I am reading the letters arranged in my head. The Acts of the Apostles, my sweet lady."

"Drowning in mead, monk. Bring the king a new goblet, and perhaps he will forgive you."

Ion jumped from the platform clumsily, encouraging the laughter of the guests, but he returned a moment later with a jug and stood next to Olof.

"I'll be your cupbearer. Our good lady, do you know that Theophanu had three cupbearers, and each one had to taste the wine before it was given to the empress? Ah, what a worthy tradition . . . how much a humble Benedictine would like to be the king's cupbearer . . ."

"You drunkard." Świętosława was laughing so hard her whole body shook. "Tell me more about Theophanu."

"The empress brought the fork to the Saxon court, and that was why the Reich hated her. The fork, that is, tiny silver pitchforks used to stab a piece of meat and place it in her mouth without touching it with her fingers. And, of course, she made a chosen servant try every single dish."

"Was she afraid of poison?" Birger asked.

"Yes, my lord. But nobody ever attempted to poison her. And I, a humble Benedictine, would give much to be able to try those delicate pâtés and roasts, even if it meant risking my life."

"Glutton." Świętosława clicked her fingers at a serving girl who walked by them with a full bowl.

"Yes, God's glutton, my lady." Ion grimaced comically. "I will eat a bloody sausage and this thigh so crunchily roasted and I will praise our good Lord . . ."

"Fool." Birger shrugged.

"Be my cupbearer, Ion," Olof said with a smile. "If it makes you happy . . ."

"That depends on what we drink, my lord," Ion sighed. "If you allow me, I dragged a jug of mead with me, which I have prayed over. The Litany of God's Generosity. Wait for me, King, I'm coming . . ."

Ion, intentionally or not, had begun a wild, drunken game in which every guest tried his neighbors' drinks, to their left and their right. Świętosława felt a swell of happiness watching this lighthearted revelry. *Laughter and hope best honor my great husband's memory,* she thought, *not fire and sacrifice.* The goblet beside her sat empty; she was content to drink in the pleasure she saw on her subjects' faces. Until the moment Birger spoke to her in a whisper:

"The boys won't threaten you, either. I went north and took care of everything. One drowned in the river, the other fell during a careless rock climb."

"What are you talking about?" she asked almost inaudibly. She felt as if her blood had frozen in her veins.

"About the bastards, the twins, my lady. Thordis and her father mean nothing without those children spawned by Eric. And now there are no children between you and the throne." His voice grew gentle, sounding almost affectionate. "I told you that you could rely on me, my lady."

Ion's words from before the feast echoed in her head. *Beware of Birger.* She didn't move her head. She sat, still as a statue, wondering what she should do next.

"I did you a favor, my lady," he whispered. "I was the only one willing to do it, no one else."

"I never told you to kill," she said. "Those children were innocent."

"You don't have to give a command. That's the queen's right, to have her unspoken thoughts come to life."

"Ion," she called. "Can the king's cupbearer fill the queen's goblet?"

"With pleasure, my lady." He shuffled over to her, sweaty and clumsy. "In Cana in Galilee our sweet Lord changed an entire tub of water into wine, so I, your humble servant . . ."

"Thorvald, I'd like the 'Song of the Mighty,' from the first to the last verse. Loud and clear," she called to the Icelandic bard, the one who had won a prize for his song about the victory on Fyrisvellir's fields.

All the exits must be seen,
must be studied, before you enter . . .

The guests began to stamp, banging spoons on the table as they joined in:

Must be studied, before you enter . . .

An indescribable noise filled the hall, the bard's voice leading it skilfully.

Because you never know where, at a feast
your enemies have taken a seat!

Ion walked to her side, the opposite one to Birger.

"Here is sweet mead for our sweet lady," he kept saying.

"Speak quickly," she whispered.

"The mead he wanted to give Olof was poisoned. He killed the bastards and his own wife. He is clearing a path for himself to you and the crown."

"My good monk," she exclaimed loudly, though she felt herself shaking. "If this mead isn't strong enough, I'll have to throw you to my lynxes for safekeeping."

"Is my husband's bedchamber as he left it?" she asked quietly.

"It is."

The guests' laughter drowned out their conversation.

"Let's drink! Let's drink to the great days that have been, and the great days that will come. The queen asks you for a toast of loyalty!" she called out, rising from her throne and interrupting the song.

Jarl Birger rose also. She whispered to him without turning.

"Meet me in Eric's bedchamber in a moment. I want to thank you for your thoughtfulness."

Birger's eyes shone with a steely light, and his mouth parted, as if for a kiss.

Common sense is needed by one who travels far.
Everything seems easier at home.

She had to drink two goblets. The first one calmed her thoughts, the second stopped her arms from shaking. Then, she slipped away as if heeding a call of nature. Dusza followed, and together they ran to the king's empty bedchamber. When Świętosława first entered, she nearly choked. No candles were lit, so the room was in complete darkness, and she felt as if she could still smell their last night together, their night of love. But this was not the time for sentiment. She'd drunk enough goblets of memory. She glanced at the wall over the headboard, and gave Dusza a knife she had slipped up her sleeve as she left the feast.

"Hide under the bed," she told her, and heard growls. The lynxes. They had followed them.

"Zgrzyt, Wrzask," she ordered. "Hide with Dusza."

The bedchamber's door creaked. A stream of light fell through the crack, and noise from the hall erupted inward.

Fire is needed by the one who comes from afar.
Guest, sit by the hearth.
Sit! Sit! Sit!

"You've come." Świętosława feigned affection. "Close the door. No one should see you here."

The jarl did as she instructed. She heard him walk toward her in the dark.

"Birger, tell me what you've done for me," she said aloud, and to herself: *confess your sins.*

He placed a hand on her shoulder.

"I removed every child Eric had out of wedlock from your way. The two daughters, their mothers, just in case, and the boys, his sons. I regret that you didn't allow Thordis to join him on the pyre, but I understand that you were afraid of the risks . . ."

I'm afraid of nothing but you, she thought.

"What else?" she asked, making sure that her voice remained soft.

"Well, my lady . . ." Birger's whisper was close, and heated. "We've both been widowed, we are free . . . I, as the first of Eric's chieftains, control his army . . . I will be a good husband, and I will love you as no man ever has . . ."

"Oh, yes," she moaned. "So why wait? Undress, let's go to bed. Let this be our pre-marriage arrangement. We're both experienced, are we not? You stood opposite me at the altar, standing in for my husband."

Birger threw off his belt and caftan, struggled with his boots and trousers. She heard his quickened breathing. So long as the lynxes don't growl, she thought fearfully; but they had accompanied her on her nightly visits to Eric and had never been moved by them.

"Tell me that you planned all this so carefully in Poznań," she whispered. "That you were only waiting for the right moment . . ."

"Yes, my love." He straightened, and stood before her completely naked.

She knew he couldn't see her face in the dark, and it gave her courage. He'd have seen nothing but disgust.

"Lie down. I want to show you what a queen's gratitude looks like," she said, pushing him lightly onto the bed.

She saw only the smudge of his body in the thin stream of light which fell through the smoke hole. He lay down and reached out his arms for her. She threw off her cloak, climbed onto the bed, and stood over him.

She took a step forward. Birger grabbed her ankles. His hands glided upward, to her calves. She knew that this was the moment, that she couldn't hesitate for a second more. She reached for the wedding present she had given Eric, pulling it from the wall over the bed. Mieszko's sword, thundered steel. And she pushed it into Birger's chest with all her strength. He howled, and Wrzask and Zgrzyt leaped out from under the bed with snarls. She still held the sword's hilt. Birger pulled her legs out from under her and she collapsed on top of him, leaning her whole weight on the sword. It drove in deeper. Blood sputtered from the jarl's mouth. He was dying. The lynxes were sniffing at him, their fur standing on end.

"You were the only friend I had in this country. The only Christian," she choked the words out. "And you were the first to betray me, Jarl Birger. Burn in hell."

Zgrzyt licked the liquid draining from the jarl's chest and shook his head. Świętosława climbed from the bed.

"Dusza," she summoned the one who had been with her since childhood. "Tear my dress on my chest." The sound of ripping fabric rang in the darkness.

Then for a moment, no longer than a heartbeat, they looked into each other's eyes. She and Dusza. Then Świętosława pushed open the bedchamber door and let the lynxes lead the way. Thorvald was no longer reciting, he was howling:

It's the fool who thinks he'll live forever
when he avoids the battle . . .

The heat of the fires washed over her, along with the stink of beer, mead, and boar fat. She could still smell Birger's blood. She stood in the doorway to the hall, in a ripped dress, with Mieszko's sword in her hand, and called out:

"You feast, and in the meantime Birger wanted to use your queen!" Her voice struggled to be heard over the racket around her.

"I was drunk, drunk as a bull," Great Ulf was shouting his favorite line.

Olof saw her first. He leaped from his chair. The bard fell silent. Świętosława walked toward them, slowly.

"On the night of the king's remembering. In his bedchamber, he tried to force himself on me. Jarl Birger . . ."

They were all rising from their seats in a drunken haze. Helga tried to wake Wilkomir, who had fallen asleep on the table. Great Ulf rushed toward her, tripping over sleeping men. Some of them ran to Eric's bedchamber, ripping belts with weapons from the walls as they went. Others came to stand near her. They looked at her ripped dress. At her naked breasts, visible between the torn silks. At the blood and the sword.

They chopped Birger's body into pieces, taking out their anger and drunken guilt on his corpse. Olof tried to control the chaos. Ion draped his cloak over the queen. She walked onto the platform, her nakedness covered but still holding the sword, blade pointing at the ground.

"Bard, silence the people," she called out.

Thorvald tried to make himself heard over the feverish, drunken clamor, but his efforts were unsuccessful. Could anyone control a hundred drunk Vikings? The only thing the bard managed was to shout out:

"Our lady! Sigrid Storråda!"

They picked up this call, turning it into a chant, as they had many a night as she had walked through the hall to her husband's bed.

"Bold lady! Bold lady! Bold lady!"

She knew that the fire could start anew at any moment. The people hadn't put down their weapons, they were holding on to them, soiled by the body they'd destroyed. She was afraid. In this moment, she felt a fear like she had never known. A frenzied but paralyzing feeling, like all was crashing down around her at once. But she was a queen; she could not be afraid. She lifted the sword and shouted:

"I will defend you as I defended myself. And you? Will you defend me?"

They stopped chanting, they fell silent. They approached her, one by one. And they kissed the sword that dripped with blood. Looking at them that night, she thought that some of these people saw their daughter in her, and some saw a woman who they lusted for. And that was exactly why they would stand between her and any man who wanted to claim her.

37

❀

Świętosława sat in the small chapel with Ion. There was nothing there except for a wooden cross on the wall. Eric had brought a silver crucifix back from Denmark with him, but she'd refused to accept it when she learned of how he came into its possession.

"You're right, monk. It's just a boathouse." She nodded sadly.

She came to pray here in the sorrow she felt after Birger's murder. If the people would love her for her ruthlessness, she couldn't let them see the shame and guilt she truly felt.

"Will God forgive me, monk?"

"I am just as guilty as you. I should have followed you to Uppsala, and told you of my suspicions."

"Why didn't you?"

He shrugged. He didn't look particularly sorry.

"I suspected that Birger killed his wife. I had just seen him walking to the bridge that night. Was it proof? No. A mere suspicion. And you know what Jesus said: Let him who is without sin cast the first stone. So, I didn't cast one."

"What is your sin, Ion?"

He sniffed and made a mill with his fingers.

"I thought Birger was like me. I slip out during the night sometimes, too. I throw off my habit, change, and search for happiness in the tavern. A man's weakness."

She sighed. Why had she ever thought that the world was any different?

"When did you see through Birger's plans?" she asked. "Once he'd killed the girls?"

"No. Only when he suggested that Thordis go on the pyre. And when he went north instead of to the funeral in Uppsala. He spoke to me before his departure, and asked me if I can marry people. I told him: 'Jarl, I cannot, but if you want to marry some beauty then do what you did in the past. Buy her from her father and prepare a beautiful morning gift.' The tone of his answer made it clear he was thinking of a great celebration and great lady. And there are no great Christian ladies here other than you." Ion sniffed, but didn't use his sleeve. He took out a handkerchief and blew his nose loudly. "And when he returned and said he'd killed those boys, everything fell into place in my head. But until the feast, I never suspected he would try to get rid of Olof, too. I thought that he'd try to marry you and rule as regent. You know, my lady"—childish indignation crept into his voice—"I had never suspected him of something so monstrous."

"Nor had I. I'd thought that, as a Christian, he was above the cruel laws . . ."

"We were both wrong. Oh, he was as much of a Christian as I am a hermit."

"And the mead?" Świętosława persisted.

"I don't know if it had been poisoned, and if so, I don't know what with. But it was a jug that Birger brought with him to the feast, and he poured out a goblet only for Olof."

"I asked for water." She felt guilty again.

"And he poured some for both you and himself. When I saw that, I preferred to act like a drunken fool than to risk Olof's life."

"Thank you, Ion." She grabbed his pale hand. "Thank you."

He flushed, and withdrew his hand from hers.

"If it comes to it, let's split the blame for Birger's death in half on Judgment Day. I'll say: the queen held the sword, but I was the one who told her where to bury it. Oh, my lady! In the worst case, we will burn in hell together."

"That's not much consolation," she muttered. "I want to go to heaven, to meet my mother, father . . ."

"Don't expect Eric to be there." He wagged a finger at her. "But Olof needs a proper baptism, he's family, after all. He'll speak for you to St. Peter and then, my lady, you can speak for me. The boy knows we did it for him."

"I didn't tell him."

"No?" Ion looked embarrassed. "Why not?"

"Because I don't want him to be afraid that someone wants to kill him."

"Oh, no, my lady. That's not the way to raise a son. He must know, not so that he's afraid, but so that he understands that being a king comes with risks. And he should be grateful that we saved his life."

"You don't know much about raising children, monk, so spare me the advice."

"None?" he asked offended.

"Oh, stop it. Don't let me send you away next time you have something to say that cannot wait."

"If the queen didn't constantly threaten me with the lynxes then perhaps I'd have been bolder. Let me say this, now that the blood-drinkers aren't with us: Birger may have been the first, but he wasn't the last."

Świętosława shifted.

"What do you mean?"

"Suitors, my lady. The queen dowager is a tasty morsel. You can be sure that there will be plenty of them in Sigtuna soon. Each one thinking he is worthy of your kingdom and your hand. Oh, many will call themselves 'king,' even if their 'kingdoms' are nothing more than five stones covered in gulls' shit. You'll have to choose someone. If it wasn't blasphemy, I'd say: 'Pity that Birger isn't with us, he always has good advice.'"

"Stop." She leaped up from the bench. "We're . . ."

"In a boathouse." He smiled. "You see, my lady, everything is relative. This is a chapel in terms of intentions, but its value isn't great when it stands on unconsecrated ground. The same will happen with your suitors: the one who praises his strengths the loudest will likely possess the fewest. The key is patience, because, for so long as you have enough of that, you can separate the grain from the weeds."

"Patience?" she asked, moving toward the door. "And where do you suggest I find that?"

Ion had not been wrong. Sigtuna was soon teeming with suitors. They arrived one after another. Stuf from Scania was a young man who had only dark hairs on his upper lip instead of a beard. Osvald from Blekinge was a thin man with a cataract on his left eye. Kolfinn from Dalarna could have been three times her age. She greeted them all politely, and sent them on their way also, she thought, politely. Although Great Ulf undoubtedly offended Kolfinn when he asked, at the end of the audience: "Do you want me to walk you out, Granddad?"

"Ah, Dusza," she groaned one evening. "Are things with me really so bad that old men, invalids, and children all ask for my hand? Dusza, hold me, please. I feel I'm going mad!"

The affectionate gesture Dusza offered at her plea only amplified her longing for love. She was free, and she could marry whomever she wanted, but the one she desired was somewhere in England, someplace far away, out of her reach.

"Should I send him a message that I've been widowed?" she whispered into Dusza's shoulder.

No, she answered herself. *If someone like that youngster Stuf from Scania heard about Eric's death, and a granddad like Kolfinn from Dalarna, then why wouldn't Olav have learned of it? If I still mean anything to him, he'll find out. And if not . . .*

A night after such a confession was sleepless. Świętosława tossed and turned like one with a fever. Dusza gave her a hot drink of mead and lime, but it only increased her restlessness. When Eric had been alive, she'd smothered every thought of Olav. Then, in naming her son "Olof," she repeated his name, over and over again, as if he'd been beside her. When she received the lynxes from him, she hid her sighs in their fur. These last few months had made her forget him almost entirely. At first, there had been the raw pain of Eric's death, lined with uncertainty concerning their fate on the throne. Then, the nightmarish episode with Birger, who, though he allowed himself to go too far, had helped her solidify her position with his cruelty. Nobody connected the deaths of the girls and boys with her name, and no one stepped forward to challenge Olof's right to the throne.

She allowed herself to think of Olav only now, as a line of suitors began to creep toward her. A procession of horrid creatures, while somewhere out there was the one she loved, beautiful and strong.

Wrzask leaped into her bed first and, purring, moved his nose toward her. The lynx's green eyes were pulsing. Zgrzyt, larger than his brother, rested his head on her belly. His golden eyes seemed to widen and shrink. She clung to their fur. She cried into it. She should be happy. Wasn't this what she'd wanted? To be a dowager queen, her own mistress. A queen shouldn't remain a woman, with a woman's heart, she thought.

"Vissivald of Rus and Harald of Oppland." Yet more guests were brought into the hall.

At least these are neither too old nor too young, Świętosława thought, tired after another sleepless night.

"Do you both hope to be my husbands?" she asked them, forcing cheeriness.

"No, Queen," the one from Rus replied. "We met on our journey to you and decided we would arrive together. Perhaps you will want to compare our strength in a fight or wrestling match, or you'll order us to play mannjafndr to see who is better."

"Or you'll have us play hnefatafl and we will work this out in a fight of pawns."

"Or I will have you dance and recite something." She waved a hand, bored. "Vissivald, is your name not Wsiewołod?"

"That's what they say in Rus," he confirmed.

"You don't want to say that you rule the Kiev dukedom?" Keeping a straight face was costing her everything.

"Not in its entirety, but it is enormous. I am a son of Knyaz Valdemar."

"Prince Vladimir," she corrected him, and sighed. "My God, which son? Because I can recall at least fifteen, though don't expect me to know each of their names. And I remember the prince having five wives, though, as the merchants tell it, since he's married the imperial Greek daughter he has been baptized and has just one wife. Which son, Wsiewołod, are you?"

The guest reddened. He was a good-looking man, though too portly for her tastes. He had long hair the color of dark chestnut, and an evenly trimmed beard. He was dressed richly, but brightly. Red leather shoes seemed a step too far, though. And who needed three belts?

"I'm a son out of wedlock," he said. "My mother didn't become one of the prince's wives, and then, as you so rightly pointed out, Queen, my father took no other wives after his wedding to the empress's daughter."

"Did he give up his concubines too?" she laughed. "You see, Wsiewołod, your father has quite a few sons he has acknowledged. He probably has twice as many bastards, and each one will feel he has a right to the throne."

"Rus is large," Wsiewołod replied.

"Then try your luck there," she advised him, and turned to the other of her suitors. "And you, Harald? Where do your lands lie?"

"They border Trondelag in the north," the short, dark-haired man with a common brute's face declared. He was trying to sweeten his appearance with an intricate and thick silver chain hanging on his chest.

"So your lands border with Jarl Haakon's of Lade, is that right?" She remembered the Norwegian jarl's sons well, young men named Eric and Sven, who had asked for her husband's help in their conflict with their father. And she remembered that this jarl was Olav's main opposition in his reach for the throne.

"Yes, beautiful lady, though it's no longer Haakon's land as the old jarl is dead."

She felt a tingling in the tips of her fingers. Wrzask growled. *Quiet, cat!* She patted his head.

"He's dead, you say? What from?"

"A slave butchered him, my lady. It was a dishonorable end to a great chieftain."

Does Olav know? she thought feverishly. *Is he sailing to claim his throne? Or have Haakon's sons already taken his place?*

"That is not a tempting vision, Harald," she replied calmly. "To become the wife of a man in whose country slaves murder great lords."

"It wasn't in my lands," Harald responded sharply. "It was in Lade."

"Close enough," Świętosława decided. "You are ruler over only one piece of land, but I am a queen. Why do you think you're worthy of my hand?"

"You're beautiful, my lady," he said.

"You were meant to speak of your assets, yet you talk of mine."

Those gathered in the hall snickered. Great Ulf was the loudest.

"Beautiful women shouldn't be alone," the suitor, thrown off his track, stuttered. "I could ensure your safety."

"But I am not worried about that, Harald. As I understand it"—she turned to her men—"my guests have more to offer than they have shown us here today. They must be guided by modesty, or other hidden motivations, because the proposals I have heard in this hall now sound more like a jest. You give us your hand and your kingdom, but we won't give you anything in return. That is not how marriages are arranged. And by the way, Wsiewołod, your father, the prince of Rus, Vladimir, asked for my hand in marriage over a decade ago. He didn't receive it. And when King Eric asked, he offered a great alliance against Denmark in return, and he kept his word. Wsiewołod and Harald, if you want to offer me anything else, you have until tomorrow. Ulf, show our guests to their quarters. I bid you good day."

Świętosława dismissed them and retired to her room for the afternoon. *Does Olav know that Haakon is dead?* This question was the thought in her mind. And, did he know that Eric was dead? Wilkomir came to her in the evening.

"My lady, your suitors are getting very drunk and speaking badly of you."

"They are drinking my wine and cursing me?" Świętosława's anger was quick to rise.

"You humiliated them," Wilkomir replied calmly.

"And what was I supposed to do? Praise them? Give one of them my hand? You can see for yourself this is nothing but mockery."

"Just give the order and Great Ulf will happily show them their way home with his sword."

"It's time to end this line of suitors. We receive scum from half the world . . ." She sighed. "No more. I will announce tomorrow that I do not intend to marry again."

"You have that right." He nodded. "Just in case, I'll increase the number of guards."

"Make sure the drunkards don't wander around Sigtuna. Tell them to stay in the guesthouse. I don't want any fights."

But the command had come too late; before she had finished speaking to Wilkomir, they heard shouts from the yard. Ulf bounded into her bedchamber, his face twisted in distress as she had never seen before.

"They kidnapped Olof, my lady!"

"What?"

"The boy went to heed the call of nature, they must have been waiting behind the manor. They dragged him to the guesthouse. I'll kill them! I'll kill them!"

"Jesus Christ! They kidnapped my son in my own home? Tell them that if a single hair on the boy's head is harmed, neither will leave Sigtuna alive."

"I'll kill them!"

"Calm down!" Wilkomir shouted at him. "They are holding the boy. We must act with caution."

"Yes," Świętosława replied. "Wilkomir, go to them. Tell them that they should all be in the house I gave them. I will go to them shortly."

She went, clutching the leash in her hand, and Great Ulf and his men surrounded her. Wilkomir's men surrounded the guesthouse. There was an angry crowd of locals in the yard.

"It's preposterous," she announced as she walked into the hall. "Where is King Olof?"

Wsiewołod was holding the boy by his shoulder.

"Here," he growled.

"Give me my son back," she said, counting the people as she looked around. There were no more than thirty.

"You must apologize to us first, my lady. For the embarrassment you've caused us."

"A woman should not belittle a man, even if she is a queen," Harald added, stepping forward.

She was seething. She could let her lynxes off their leash. She could give the order to Wilkomir. But they still had Olof. Her child. And suddenly, the maelstrom in her soul subsided, as if someone had thrown a block of ice into the pot.

"I understand that you expect the kind of apology that women usually offer to men?" She laughed.

"Yes." Wsiewołod's eyes gleamed greedily. He even licked his lips.

"Yes, my lady." Harald still looked like a hound, tensed before he pounced.

"And do men go to the bathhouse in your countries before they invite women into their beds?"

"Are you saying we're dirty?" Wsiewołod shook Olof.

"No," she said with a smile. "But I'd like for you to freshen up before your night with the queen. Wilkomir? Are the fires in the bathhouse burning?"

"Like every night, my lady."

"Very well. Let us not delay any longer. Take my suitors to the bathhouse. Their men can spend the night here, drinking Queen Sigrid's health. My son comes back to me. Olof . . ." She reached out a hand.

Wsiewołod was already letting go of the boy, but Harald stopped him, placing his hand on Olof's head.

"How do we know this isn't a trap?" he asked suspiciously.

She laughed melodically.

"I really don't understand my suitors. They are angry if I point out their weaknesses. But when I invite them to the bathhouse, they are afraid."

Harald pulled Olof's hair, then pushed him toward her.

"Do not accuse us of cowardice, my lady. We've had enough of your games. This is to be a proper apology."

She saw Harald shake Olof's hair from his fingers. She reached out a hand and grabbed her son, giving him the leash with the lynxes.

"Oh, I assure you, it will be. Harald and Wsiewołod. You promised me today a game of comparisons, wrestling, and one at being king. I will happily play them all when you come out of the bathhouse. I will wait for you, so don't test my patience. Ulf, walk the men out."

She left with Olof without turning around.

"Have they hurt you, son?" she asked him quietly.

"No," he replied with annoyance, rubbing his head in the spot where Harald had pulled his hair. "They embarrassed me."

"And they insulted me. I will not forgive them, because if I show them mercy, more like them will venture here," she replied firmly. "Go inside with Wrzask and Zgrzyt, and no matter what, don't come back out."

"Mother . . . you won't go with them, will you?"

"No, son. I will only escort them and ensure the bathhouse is warm enough."

She stood in the yard, watching Ulf lead Wsiewołod and Harald into

the bathhouse at the back of the manor. She watched Wilkomir lead all his
men out of the guesthouse where the suitors' men were settled. She watched
servants with jugs of mead enter. She counted them. One, two, three . . . six.
And she counted to six as they filed back out. That's when she nodded to
Wilkomir, saying:

"Bar the door."

When the doors had been closed from the outside, she called out to her
people and servants standing outside:

"Women will carry water, men wood."

Then she walked to the bathhouse beside the guesthouse. Great Ulf and
his men surrounded the small wooden building. Steam poured from the
smoke hole.

"Close the door," she told him. "And set fire to it from outside. Let them
bathe in flames."

No one questioned her. In a matter of moments, both buildings were on
fire. Shouts erupted from them. The servants with buckets of water waited,
silent, ensuring the fire didn't spread to any of the other buildings.

"They broke the laws of hospitality by abducting my son. They will not
know any more hospitality from me," she called out.

"Bold lady." Great Ulf touched her shoulder and pointed at the people
surrounding them. "Look at them. They're proud that their queen didn't
allow anyone to mock her. You need not explain yourself to anyone."

She looked around. It wasn't a drunken crowd, like on the night of Birger's
death. A crowd that didn't know what they were doing. These were people
who decided to punish the sinners as consciously as she did.

She took Wilkomir and Ulf to one side.

"From this day onward, you divide your duties. You, Ulf, stay with me.
And you, Wilkomir, don't leave Olof for a single moment. My son has become the victim of an attack for a second time, it cannot happen again. And
one more thing: if we are ever faced with any kind of danger and you are
forced to choose who to protect, you must always choose Olof. Do you understand? That's an order. He is the heir to the throne."

No shouts had been heard for a few moments now. The bathhouse collapsed first, followed shortly by the guesthouse. The servants poured water
over the cinders and began to clean up after the ghastly fire without a word.
She had turned to leave when Ion approached her.

"I have heard of burning fields," he laughed. "But to separate the grain
from weeds by fire, that is new to me. You're bringing in novel traditions,
my lady. Do you think your subjects might give you a new name? Sigrid

Storråda. Bold Lady. Now it's time for you to be the Fiery One. Or 'The one who greets her suitors with flames.'"

"Stop. This doesn't entertain me," she snarled.

She could still smell the fire.

"You had no choice once again, my lady." He patted her arm. "But now you might finally be able to make up your own mind regarding your future marriage. You won't stop people from talking. They'll spread stories. You've sent a clear message out into the world."

I hope that he hears it, too, she thought.

"You've shown everyone that you will not tolerate mediocre proposals. It won't be long now before, and your Ion can promise you this, a real royal suitor appears. If I had the prophet's gift, I'd say your king is already sailing to you."

PART III

A STORM FROM A CLEAR SKY

❧

The Second Crown
995–997

38

∞

NORWAY

Summer glinted on the water in the reflected light of a sated sun. The golden glow swayed on the waves. A new moon soaked the dusk with darkness, like a cloak thrown over a flaming fire. The cold new moon complicated sailors' plans, mocking the helmsmen keeping a lookout after dark. The new moon which brought about sudden changes of the wind, dark clouds appearing as if from nowhere, or from beyond the horizon. As if the future would be decided beyond its limits. The wind rocked the ships until they lost their rhythm.

Olav had left most of his fleet in Viken, under his mother's husband Lodin's protection. He set out modestly on his journey, taking only three boats. He wanted to slip through the Øresund Strait unnoticed, and that wasn't easy on its narrow waters. Older sailors said Øresund was like a too-tight trouser leg. He had no choice but to squeeze through it.

This route took them too near Roskilde for Olav's liking, where Harald Bluetooth had resided in his great manor. Olav's scouts assured him that Sven was busy building alliances in Jelling, the seat of power he'd built himself while his father was still alive; but if the shore guards spotted his boats Olav would be facing trouble enough. They sailed through the narrowest part at night, with the wind in their favor; *Kanugård* sliding over the waves.

"My king commands even the winds. He's his own weather vane," Varin joked when, at dawn, they finally escaped the claws of the Danish straits and reached the open waters of the Baltic.

"Don't mock," Olav said. "The ocean doesn't like bragging, and neither do I. The weather vane will return to the mast once we're farther north and in safer waters."

He'd had it removed for their journey, because its golden plates proudly reflected the sun, attracting attention, which was exactly what he was trying to avoid. If luck truly was still with him, they'd arrive before the autumn storms and in seven, at most eight days he'd sail into Mälaren Bay.

He left Varin by the helm, and walked to the starboard side. The water glimmered with shades of green and steel. He had sailed here four years ago, on his way back from attacking Denmark, alongside his brothers-in-law and at the request of the great Piast duke.

Afterward, he'd taken a sharp course south, stopping at Jomsborg. Astrid had been waiting for him in port, with the news of Geira's death. He flinched at the memory. Was it only four years ago? It seemed to him that his life with Geira was an eternity away. He didn't want to remember. That time was darkness. He thought instead of the spring full moon and the stone circles on the island of Scilla. Of the old man who chewed on his words. *Longing, desire, dissatisfaction, my boy. The terribly ancient curse. The old gods cast it on you, though they say this curse will bring you great fame. Your hope lies in the new. Perhaps He will want to change it? You've been marked, that's certain. I've seen your arrival a hundred times in my dreams. But have you been chosen? Let the new God tell you.* Christ's answer, given through the freezing waters of baptism, still pulsed with light inside of him, as if the silver full moon never ended. Sometimes, though, it was covered by thick clouds.

I am surrounded by blind men, he thought, breathing in the humid, salty air and looking at the gray line of land in the distance. *Blind men who I must return sight to. Even if I must lift their eyelids with the point of a knife. I have promised God, and I will keep my word, as He did.*

His first steps in his homeland had been different than he'd expected. He'd had too much time to imagine it over all those years of longing. In his dreams, the ground shook under his feet when he stepped ashore, but the rocks of Viken did not differ much from the countless others at which he had anchored in the past. The moss was green, like everywhere else, not bright like in Scilla. Maybe the wealth of dark lilac flowers matched what he'd remembered from his mother's stories. She was sweet and affectionate. She had looked at him with pride when Omold the bard spoke of the conquest of England. She wiped away her tears in secret. "I see your father in you, Olav," she'd said. "And much, much more, if his memory will forgive me for saying. You've already gained more fame than he ever had with your conquests in England."

"I didn't do it for fame, Mother. Only for the silver and men who will follow me."

Lodin, his mother's husband, was a cautious man. His dark hair was peppered with gray, but his back was still straight. "Is it true that you've been baptized?" he asked.

"It's true," Olav replied. His mother paled, and he saw the nervous finger movements which she quickly hid inside the sleeve of her dress. Lodin settled for gritting his teeth.

"And your men?" he asked after a long pause.

"All of them. Every single one. Who doesn't want baptism chooses death."

Lodin peered at Olav from under bushy eyebrows, and he called for the servants to fill his goblet more often than usual that night.

Olav allowed himself many days in Viken, getting to know his family. First, his older sisters, who had stayed in Norway under the care of relatives when his mother escaped east with him in her belly. One had her name, Astrid, the other was called Ingebjorg. He looked in their eyes and searched for his father, but they both resembled his mother. Then, the two younger girls, Lodin's daughters, his half sisters, Ingireda and Ingigerda. And the boy, Torkil. If he'd met them without knowing who they were, he thought, he wouldn't have felt anything, as if they shared no blood. Even his mother . . . the one he had missed for so many years in Rus. The one he'd searched for so stubbornly that he allowed Mieszko to push him into Geira's arms to pay for finding her. His mother also seemed different to him than before. Sweet and affectionate, but a stranger. Their first meeting eight years ago had passion in it. They had showered each other with embraces, memories, tears of joy. A mother and son, reunited after years, like survivors of a shipwreck after weeks of wandering on uncharted waters, finally seeing a stretch of land.

Now, he looked at them and felt only pity, for their eyes were blind to the Lord's truth. They cared about poor harvests, worried about cattle, feared lest there not be enough fish in the next catch. "Yes, yes." His mother nodded. "You're King Tryggve's son, it's no strange thing that you're consumed by kingly matters." He sensed the fear which underlay those words. By saying "You've already gained more fame than your father," she seemed to add silently: "And that's enough, son, enough now." Lodin's love had cured Astrid of her desire for revenge. His affections and the children he gave her healed the old wounds. His mother rejoiced that her son had returned, but she'd have preferred to see him build a great house on a hill, sitting in the hall with his wife, rather than preparing to fight for his throne. He bit his tongue and said nothing, but he looked at her, knowing she would see old Tryggve in his eyes.

He saw the dirt, the dark layer smothering the souls of them all, stuffing their ears and covering their eyes. Until, one day, his mother couldn't take it anymore, and she began to cry. "Your father had a hard stare," she sobbed, "but you, son, have hardened steel in your eyes." And so, his family gave in, bending their knees to the Lord. He allowed Sivrit to baptize them, and when they cleansed their souls, he could love them once more. And he entrusted them with his plan.

He had been working on it for years, changing and adapting it as he listened to news of Norway during sleepless nights on the Isle of Wight or in the stone walls of Bamburgh. No, he wasn't surprised that he had been offered betrayal right from the start. He had expected it, like Judas's kiss, and offered his cheek.

He'd still been in England when Jarl Haakon sent messengers to him. They were supposed to tempt Olav with the promise that when the old jarl died, the people would wait for him. But he had kept men in Norway for two years. He called them his sleeping guards, and they were only meant to listen, watch, and wait for a sign. And he had the scout Halvard and the strange twins, who divided each sentence into two. He knew that old Haakon was alive and was trying to trap him.

He'd sailed straight to Norway anyway, with *Kanugård*'s golden weather vane announcing his arrival, and with thirty ships, his part of the army once known as the Two Kings. This show of strength had been enough for the old jarl to flee back to land from the ship in which he had been awaiting Olav, leaving one of his sons behind him to face Olav on the water. This young one wasn't either of the two who had searched for help from Eric in Sweden long ago.

"The last of the young ones leaped in to feed the eels, my arrow in his arse," Ingvar concluded, though Omold the bard desperately wanted to add a rhyme to it. The jarl's fleet was divided into those who turned and fled after their master, and those who surrendered to Olav. Bishop Sivrit taught them the truth of faith swiftly; the ones who understood stayed with him, the others went under the axe. Rafn became the executioner, the same Rafn who had thrown slaver corpses overboard from the *Wolverine*.

All the men from the old crew, the one he'd left Rus with, were baptized first. "We are connected by too much, King," Varin said, "to be divided by a god." Each one, after years of plundering England, was rich enough to sail wherever he wanted and live on the silver in his chest until the end of his days. But none of them wanted a separate fate. "Where you go, we'll follow," they said, not bothering with explanations. Those who'd seen English churches and castles, who'd tasted wine from ornamental chalices, who'd accepted danegeld bought with blood, would be no good in a yard at home, keeping servants in their place. They accepted the baptism as if it had been another challenge; as if spreading the Word which comes from the One God was the next land they could conquer.

When they had scattered Jarl Haakon's small troop, they didn't go on land. They stopped at the anchor point, with the open sea behind them and the bay at their bows. Whoever wanted to talk to Olav had to come to *Kanugård*. He sent squads in search of the jarl, but not because he wanted him found, only to ensure that Haakon had to keep fleeing and hiding. So the jarl's subjects could see him as the prey he was, shaken by a deadly fear. After a week, perhaps a bit later, a stocky, dark-haired man appeared. A slave known as Kark. In a dirty leather bag, he brought Jarl Haakon's head. "This is for you, my lord," he said, throwing the gift at Olav's feet. The bruises on the jarl's bloody face and the uneven marks on his neck told the story.

"Who was he to you?" Olav asked Kark. "My master," Kark replied, and rubbed his wrists absentmindedly, where he had likely been bound by a rope in the past.

"What do you want in return?" Olav asked. The man shuffled from foot to foot, cocked his head, and said, shyly: "A reward of some sort . . ." Olav summoned Rafn, who removed the cloth covering the bloodstained tree stump they had on board for executions, and for his deadly gift, Kark lost his head. "It's a terrible crime for a servant to kill his master," Olav said. "Who has betrayed once will do so again." He sent Haakon's head to his family for a proper burial.

The news spread across Norway, and though Olav had nothing to do with the jarl's death, it cast a shadow over the beginning of his road to the throne. Some said: "Let Olav Tryggvason rule over us." Others called: "We want the young jarls to return, Eric and Sven, Haakon's sons." For both sides, though, baptism caused the biggest problem. They held on to the old gods as a child does to their mother's breast.

He was the blood of the kings they'd forgotten during the jarl's twenty-year rule. He was the hero songs had been composed for. The conquerer of English silver. A Yngling. And yet, the cross on his breast made him a stranger to them.

He had the strength of thirty boats behind him, rich with danegeld, and crews experienced in battle, but it wasn't enough to take the whole country. "I'll cut off any head you order, King," Rafn said, cleaning the axe after the execution of Kark, "but who will you rule when I'm done?"

The two chieftains invading England, Olav and Sven, had returned home at just the right time. The death of King Eric Segersäll of Sweden, Świętosława's husband, and the death of Jarl Haakon of Norway, helped them both. Eric's death left the road clear for Sven to take back Denmark. Sven's people would accept him as a savior, because Eric had been a conquerer. *Me, though I am one of them, they fear, because I bring a foreign religion.*

He wanted to laugh, but it was bitter laughter. He remembered Sven in Castle Bamburgh getting him drunk and trying to convince him to face Eric at his side. Eric was dead, Sven's problem had solved itself, and the lucky man, Olav's redheaded comrade, the second chieftain, was taking back his power in his homeland with no trouble at all.

Olav remembered the debates he'd had with himself about how to defeat Haakon without destroying the country. He'd spent months thinking about this on the Isle of Wight, and it turned out that Haakon simply disappeared from his path. However, then his subjects stepped into it, saying: "You, Olav, we accept, but not your god."

"The path to the house of the Lord is neither straight nor wide. It is a stony and steep road on which everyone who doubts will twist an ankle, falling into the abyss."

But they didn't know the prophecies like he did. Their Haakon, the jarl they'd loved, had taken power as Denmark's viceroy. He, Olav Tryggvason, would give his homeland a triple gift: independence, the unity of lands, and baptism. He'd walk up the stony, steep path, but he wouldn't fall into the abyss. A new time was coming. Two deaths threatened the balance of the three northern kingdoms. The word of a single woman could bring the balance back.

"My lord," Varin called, "a cloud as dark as lead and as large as a whale is approaching."

Olav turned around violently a mere moment before the first gust of the wild wind hit him. He had time to breathe in the smell of the impending storm. The rigging creaked. Tryggvason spread his arms wide and his cloak caught the air like a sail. He laughed wholeheartedly.

"Thy will be done. I will sail to the bold one through a storm."

39

❧

SWEDEN

Świętosława rode across the heathland covering the hillside. Zgrzyt's golden back flickered between small bushes. Wrzask was already at the top, sitting and stretching his head upward as if he'd caught the scent of something. Her cats didn't have to hunt to survive, which is why they did it with double the passion whenever she let them off their leash. She'd been afraid, when they were younger, that captivity would dull their hunting instincts. She'd been wrong, while Wilkomir had been proven right when he said that being a predator wasn't a choice; it was a calling.

The slender, green-eyed Wrzask and muscular, golden-eyed Zgrzyt were the most beautiful creatures she knew. She loved the low growls they made without even opening their jaws, a sound that stopped anyone hearing it for the first time dead in their tracks until Świętosława gave the lynxes the sign that all was well.

They slept at her feet when she saw jarls and commoners alike. They went with her when she ventured outside the manor's boundaries to see her lands. They were indifferent to most people, they allowed only the closest to pet them: Olof, Dusza, Great Ulf, Wilkomir and his son, Wilczan. Świętosława was under the impression that they liked little Wilczan more than anyone. The boy had thankfully inherited his mother Helga's looks, rather than the permanently grimacing features of his father, though he certainly had his father's alertness. Was he her son's best friend? Rulers don't have friends, but Olof was still a boy, so yes, it seemed that he preferred Wilczan's company over that of her chieftains' and jarls' sons.

Zgrzyt suddenly crouched down low, his belly to the ground. Świętosława stopped her mare to avoid startling his prey. Three, four long steps and a leap. The lynx had something in its jaws. She moved toward him. The rabbit was still alive, but frozen, motionless, feeling Zgrzyt's long fangs on the back of its neck. This moment, she thought, looking at the predator and its prey, this moment before the inevitable death: What is it? Is it still life, or death's first breath? She shivered.

"It's only an animal," she whispered. "A cowardly rabbit."

She rode to the top of the hill. Wrzask stretched in greeting, and after a moment, Zgrzyt joined them. He lay down and licked the blood from his muzzle. The last sign of the rabbit. Świętosława looked down on the vast green fields that spread inland. Beyond them, the horizon was a distinct dark line of the forest, dividing itself from the sky.

"My kingdom," she said, and immediately thought of her father. *Remember, there are no boundaries . . . the horizon moves every time you reach what you thought would be the end . . .*

She didn't want to push the boundaries. This was enough. The unease which had accompanied her since Jarl Birger's death had evaporated along with the wisps of smoke that rose from the bathhouse cinders, where she'd burned Wsiewołod and Harald, the last of her suitors. The servants had removed every trace of that evening from the yard, down to the last burnt splinter. For the time being, no one mentioned anything to her about marrying again. The dowager queen Sigrid Storråda sat firmly in her saddle. At least in this real one, on her mare's back. She sighed and called her lynxes.

"Wrzask! Zgrzyt! We're going back!"

Zgrzyt arched his back and reluctantly followed her. Wrzask trotted off in front, lifting his short tail that ended with black hairs. She leaned backward to maintain her balance on the ride downhill. The mare was stepping carefully, but suddenly Świętosława felt the need to go faster. There was no one beside her to tell her no, no one to warn her, as if she were a child, that the horse might break its leg. She squeezed her calves to the mare's sides, and it snorted. She did it again, harder this time. Thorhalla sped up, hesitantly, but after the first few steps her confidence grew. Świętosława squeezed her calves again. And that's when the mare stretched out her neck and launched forward, neighing.

"Yes!" Świętosława exclaimed. "Yes, my beautiful Thorhalla. Let's do something foolish. Nobody can see us. Nobody can stop us."

She laughed. She laughed wholeheartedly, and Thorhalla gained speed with every step. *God!* Świętosława thought. *I'm the daughter of a great duke. The dowager queen. I was Eric Segersäll's wife. I'm the mother of his son. And I still only do what I must, what I should . . .*

The mare leapt over a flat stone with a long jump, instead of going around it. Świętosława's buttocks slammed against the saddle as they landed. She laughed loudly again. They were at the bottom already, but Thorhalla couldn't stop her mad dash, and she ran toward the shore. Wilkomir barred her way.

"My lady!" he shouted. "What are you doing? The mare could have broken her legs, she could have thrown you off!"

Wrzask and Zgrzyt, running in an arc around them, were coming back, panting.

Świętosława stopped Thorhalla and patted her neck. Wilkomir rode over to her. His features seemed more twisted than usual. She looked into his face defiantly.

"I've always done just what I should have, my whole life," she said, fighting for breath. "Today, I wanted to do something for no reason at all." She noticed that Wilkomir was looking at her with surprise. "Something I wanted to."

The deep sound of the horn from the harbor interrupted her. Then a second, and third.

"Guests?" she asked.

He responded with raised eyebrows, and without a word, they moved toward the port. Eleven of Wilkomir's men joined them. *Oh, yes,* she thought bitterly. *And I thought I'd gone for a ride by myself.*

She clutched the mare's neck out of sheer helpless frustration. The mare neighed and tossed her head.

Three ships. The scream of seagulls. A golden weather vane gleamed on one mast. She breathed in the salty wind and clenched her fists so tightly that she momentarily lost feeling in her hands. She recognized him before his *Kanugård* had reached port. He walked across the deck. Tall, fair-haired, with a face tanned from the wind. He had on a worn leather caftan stained with salt and long-dried blood. The world was shrinking like a tunnel between them. *"You've sent a clear message out into the world. If I had the prophet's gift, I'd say your king is already sailing to you."* It wasn't a dream, she howled inside. *This cannot be merely a dream.*

"My lady," a surprised Wilkomir said. "It's Olav Tryggvason. What is he doing here?"

His crew was mooring the ship, and Olav, not waiting for them, jumped onto the wooden planks of the deck and walked toward her. Thorhalla neighed.

"Świętosława," he said.

"Olav," she replied, unable to choke out another word.

Five, ten, twelve steps and he was beside her mare, lifting his head. He reached out a hand. She took it and jumped down. They faced each other. Him and her. Her heart beat evenly. It was real, not a dream. But if she didn't do something immediately she'd wake up somewhere she didn't want to be.

"Wilkomir," she said, turning to the captain of her guard, "is the sailors' house empty?"

"Yes, my lady." He lifted his eyebrows in the same way he had before.

Had he understood yet?

"Then that is where I will ride to talk with my guest. Your task is to ensure that no one interrupts us, even if it takes a long time." She looked straight in his eyes and, to reassure him, added: "I promise the mare won't break any legs."

He understood, and replied with a bow:

"I will carry out your orders."

Olav's hands were rough, hot, as if there was a hidden heat in his fingertips. He held her face like a goblet that he drank from. They couldn't, wouldn't, tear their lips from each other. They pulled apart for a moment, both as dizzy as if drunk on mead. They undressed without a word. They faced each other, naked, and she felt the heat which emanated from him. In the hut's dimness she saw only the pale outline of his body. She reached out for him, and he fell into her arms. He pressed her to him so hard that she couldn't breathe. Only his scent, salty, sharp, moist. She was drunk on his scent. Olav wrapped his arms around her and lifted her. No, he lay her down, but against the smooth wood of the wall. He thrust into her. She moaned. But then she didn't so much as breathe, because it was enough that she felt his sword in her sheath and that was that. She belonged to him as she did to nobody else. Her hips moved of their own volition, finding the rhythm like a ship and a wave, a horse and its rider, the sail and the wind. It could have lasted an eternity, it could have been a few moments, she didn't know, she wasn't counting. She didn't even know if Olav was inside her, or she inside him.

She remembered only, or she thought she did, that she saw Olav lift her into his arms and lay her down on the sailor's cot. He covered her with a coarse blanket. Then she felt warmth and panting.

"Wrzask? Zgrzyt?" she asked, touching the fur.

She was consumed by a wave of heat.

"No," Olav said, lifting a wet face from between her legs. "It's me."

"Ah . . ." She gave herself to him, letting go of his white hair.

Olav waited for his audience with Queen Sigrid. He had spent the night in her husband's bedchamber, which he'd been given for the duration of his stay. He wondered if this was the bed in which Eric and Świętosława had lain together. He shook off the image. He kept pushing away the thought of anyone else having had her before him. Not after what they'd experienced in the sailors' hut. But it was the truth. She'd been Eric Segersäll's wife, and she'd borne him a son. That could not be erased. Was that a certainty? The cruel thought lit up in his mind.

A sword hung over the bed. He touched the blade. Someone must have sharpend it recently. And cleaned it.

A servant walked into the bedchamber.

"My lord." He bowed. "I have brought you your meal."

"I'm not hungry. I want to speak with the queen," he replied impatiently.

Świętosława had left him in the sailor's hut and returned to Sigtuna alone, saying: "Come to my court as an official guest. We'll speak there." He was completely helpless, drunk on the night they'd had together. He agreed, and then, once he'd sobered up, he was angry. He'd have preferred to speak with her alone, without anyone else present. She and him. But yes, Świętosława was a queen, and he couldn't expect her to behave like an ordinary woman.

"My lady will see you as soon as she's finished speaking with her advisers. That's what she ordered me to tell you."

He sent the servant away. He waited. *Ordered,* he thought, and he didn't like the tone. That night, she'd given herself to him with no conditions, no orders. Everything had gone well, like a dream. Their ships had sailed through the storm without any mishaps. When he'd seen her in port, he was lost for words. The fact that she'd found herself in the same place as him couldn't be an accident, it was a sign. And the lust which took them both as soon as they closed the door. The love they lost themselves in, as if every moment could be the last. He could still feel himself entering her, joining with her. How he wanted to, once more . . . He broke into a cold sweat and leapt up. There was a small jug of water in the corner. He emptied it over his head. The lust didn't disappear, but his common sense returned.

"God, forgive me," he groaned. "I want her more than you. I'd have been prepared to forget what I had come here for, and only because I want her so."

The bedchamber doors opened and the servant from earlier stood in them. He cast a surprised glance over Olav.

"The queen asks you to join her for the feast," he said.

"I'll come after I change," Olav snarled, his long hair dripping. "Leave."

He didn't rush. Not because he wanted to get back at her for making him wait, but to calm his thoughts. He pulled on dry clothing and reached for his gift from Bishop Sivrit to ensure he didn't lose his mind to his emotions. My bishop, he thought, and pictured his pale, ruthless features. He donned the chain with the golden cross and walked out of the airless bedchamber.

There was a racket in the great hall. Fifty, maybe sixty people were sitting at the tables. He noticed his own, Varin, Rafn, and Omold the bard. He nodded to them as he walked toward the platform. Świętosława sat on a tall chair, with a slender, dark-haired boy beside her, her son, he guessed. A chubby monk sat next to them, with restless eyes and smoothly shaven head. Also a great, bald warrior with a scarred face, and Wilkomir, who had ensured their night had been undisturbed. He noticed the familiar face of the girl-shadow behind the queen's chair. What was her name? Dusza. Dusza gave him a radiant smile.

Świętosława, who had met him yesterday in a plain riding outfit, was wearing a rich green dress today and a necklace of crystals enclosed in silver. Her hair was braided in delicate plaits, reminding him of how it had tickled his bare belly, golden and loose. All he had to do was think of that night and he felt naked, heated, ready for her again. He touched the cross on his chest, pushing his lust away. The lynxes lazily lifted their heads from where they lay at Świętosława's feet. What had she called them last night? He couldn't repeat the names. The cats approached him like their mistress's front guard and sniffed his hands. The smaller one licked his fingers. Olav shivered.

"My lady." He bowed his head to her and asked in greeting, "What's it like to love a live animal?"

Something shone in her eyes, but she put it out quickly, and replied with a smile.

"As you can see, I no longer wear a lynx fur. That which lives always comes before the dead."

"What did you name them, Queen?"

"Don't you remember?" She cocked her head flirtatiously.

"I remember," he answered, his eyes not leaving hers, "but I cannot repeat it."

"In that you don't differ from any of us," the monk spoke up. "The queen gave the beasts names which come straight from hell."

"Wrzask and Zgrzyt," Świętosława said. They still hadn't broken eye contact. "Do you remember what these words mean in my mother tongue?"

"First, there's the shout to the skies, and then the sense that something had gone wrong," he replied in her language. This wasn't their literal translation, but his words clearly meant something between the two of them.

Świętosława didn't blush, but she narrowed her eyes. She stood up and shouted to her people:

"Our guest tonight is the final heir of the Yngling kings, famous for his English conquests, Olav Tryggvason. I give the feast tonight to honor him. Mead! Let us rejoice."

A hubbub followed as the servants carried in steaming bowls and trays, taking their rounds with jugs of mead, girls glancing at him and blushing. Świętosława invited him onto the platform, telling the monk to make space for him. The man moved over reluctantly. Before Olav sat down, she stopped him and grabbed the boy's hand.

"Son, meet my childhood friend, King Olav."

The boy looked at him darkly.

"I'm Olof, King Eric's son," he said.

He could kiss the tips of her fingers for naming the child as she had. But it wasn't his child.

"And I'm Olav, King Tryggve's son," he replied, meeting the boy's eyes.

"Your father wasn't the king of all of Norway, he was only the ruler of Viken, the south of your country." The boy pursed his lips.

Olav wanted to grab the pup around the throat and squeeze.

"But I will rule a whole country," Olav said, and took his seat next to the queen.

"When?" she asked quietly.

"As soon as possible," he replied.

"Mead?" Her voice sounded just as soft as it had the previous night. He felt heat between his legs.

"No, my lady."

"Wine, then? You probably drank wine in the English castles, Olav?"

"I won it, but I didn't drink it."

They talked in half whispers so that only the boy and the monk could hear them. They didn't turn to each other, looking instead straight ahead at the guests.

"Why?"

"The plunder wasn't my goal, only a method of reaching it."

"What is your goal, then?"

You. Your womb. Your kisses. Stomach, thighs, breasts with their sharp dark nipples. He touched the silver cross.

"Have you been baptized?" she asked with surprise.

"Yes, my lady. I have known the mercy of redemption." Only now did he turn toward her, and they met each other's eyes.

"My husband, Olof's father, gave his life to Odin," she said.

He wasn't sure, but he thought he heard admiration in her voice.

"So he died in the dark, like my wife and your sister, Geira," he replied firmly.

"In the dark . . ." she echoed him. "How did it happen?"

Did it matter? She lived in the darkness and left in the darkness, he wanted to answer, but unexpectedly, he told the truth:

"She died giving birth to my son. The birth began too early."

"Were you happy with her?"

"No," he answered.

"Were you with any other women?" she asked quickly.

"Only the last one," he replied just as swiftly, and felt a wave of heat as he heard his own words.

They were silent for a moment, until the monk spoke:

"So you were baptized in England, my lord. It's wonderful news. What do your people think of it?"

"The same as yours, monk," he answered calmly.

My people would like nothing better than to spit on my cross and drain the holy water from my body.

The man blushed, and Świętosława snorted. Olav didn't understand.

"My lady? Have you given up your faith, living here?"

"No. I realized I will not baptize this country. My son will be the one to do that."

This surprised him. "Why not you?"

Hoots and joyful shouts resounded among the guests. The servants, sagging under the weight of great trays, carried whole roasted piglets in. The first plate was placed on the table in front of Świętosława, and the others on tables for the guests. The queen raised a goblet of mead and shouted, "Let's feast!"

They responded as if following an order:

"Queen Sigrid Storråda! Storråda!"

That's what he'd called her when the three of them had tasted the mushrooms. He, she, and Bolesław. What had he seen in his vision? His baptism. Who had held him up? She had. Ages ago.

She smiled to her people and drank, and the bard began a song about a beautiful goddess. In his version, two lynxes pulled Freya's sleigh, rather than the white cats from the legends. By the time he realized this, the guests were already chanting:

"Bold lady! Two lynxes!"

Without turning to him, she answered the question he'd asked earlier:

"You can see for yourself. I came here as a Christian, and they see a pagan goddess, and that's the only Sigrid they love. I'm under no illusions, Olav. If I ordered them to give up the old gods, they'd give up on me. But my son will be in a different position. They've known him since he was a child, he's the heir of their beloved Eric. He will do it." She turned toward him suddenly. "What is the purpose of your visit?"

Your lips. Your hand. Your army.

He didn't reply. He looked at her. Ten years had changed Świętosława. Then, she'd been the unruly girl who had stolen his heart. Now, she was a queen who could claim his soul if he'd only let her.

"I want to marry you."

40

⚘

Bolesław was returning to camp from his fights with the Veleti.

For Bolesław, the participation of his men in the war against the Veleti was the price they paid for peace, an obligation to the emperor. A dull obligation, though, because if he'd been given command, he'd have defeated the Veleti within a year. He got the impression that the Veleti, though troublesome, were really just a show for the Reich lords.

In front of the emperor, the margraves and counts made it sound as if this annual battle was a fight for everything. And in return for their continued fighting on this front, the emperor considered them to be productive for the empire and gave them a free hand to do what they wanted in other matters.

This year could change that, though, as Otto III had decided to come and face the Veleti himself, not as the six-year-old to whom Mieszko had given a camel, but as a fifteen-year-old, almost a man, and in any case, an independent ruler. This was an unusual and spectacular gesture by the heir to the throne. But in the next year, along with reaching an adult age, Otto's imperial coronation would take place in Rome. Bolesław suspected that by taking part in this battle, Otto was hoping to prove himself publicly before his coronation.

And so, all the lords and counts made sure they were accounted for in the camp over the Elbe River. That night a great feast was held in Otto's royal tent, at tables covered with golden-threaded material, where all the dukes, bishops, margraves, and army chieftains gathered.

The margraves were talking comfortably as they waited for Otto. Bolesław sat beside Sobiesław, who was from an old Czech family that Bolesław's Czech in-laws felt threatened by. Sobiesław had been a useful ally to Bolesław in his fight against the Czechs for Lesser Poland, though, when he was taking over Silesia. As a show of gratitude, Bolesław had invited Sobiesław to this gathering, and it would be his first time meeting the imperial leader.

Soon they heard the trumpets, which meant that Otto III, who would soon become the emperor of half the world, was about to grace them with his presence. The fifteen-year-old, golden-haired Otto took his place on the platform.

"Alone?" Sobiesław whispered into Bolesław's ear, surprised that the ruler wasn't sitting with his nobles.

"Byzantian traditions," the duke explained quietly. "The future emperor is already suggesting he is a demigod."

"I don't know if he's a god, but he's as pretty as a flower," Sobiesław whispered with admiration.

So long as he's braver than one. The duke sighed inwardly. Otto's love of study and religion was common knowledge, but what could be the surprise in that? The boy had been crowned when he was three, surrounded by the wisest men in the world, raised to be a ruler since birth. Bolesław hadn't seen him since that time with the camel. That Otto had been a boy who had almost collapsed under the weight of the crown. Before them today was a slender young man with alabaster skin. They were introduced to him one by one.

"Bolislaus Dux Sclavorum," the herald announced him, and when Bolesław lifted his head, their eyes met.

"You've changed, Duke," Otto said.

"So have you, King," Bolesław replied. "How is the camel?"

"Dead. My noble mother said that it was out of homesickness."

If it died while Theophanu was still alive, then it didn't last long, Bolesław realized as he did the math.

"I have no doubts that the empress knew what she was talking about," he said loudly. "Next time I'll make you a gift of a more resilient animal."

"Your father, Duke Miesico, was never apart from his hawk, if I recall."

"And he took it with him to his grave. The bird didn't survive Lord Mieszko's death. Have you ever seen, King, the fiery eye of a hawk before it dies?"

Otto's eyes pulsed with light. *This boy has something strange about him,* Bolesław thought.

"And you, Bolislaus? Did you tame a wild bird when you took the throne?" he asked.

"No, King. I don't want to tame wild things; that feels to me like taking away their will to live. But since you ask, I do feel a comradery with the taloned creatures, much like my father. My symbol is the eagle."

"Really?" Otto asked with interest. "The eagle is also the imperial bird. We have much in common, Bolislaus."

I'm not sure about that, Bolesław thought, but he kept it to himself.

When the long presentations of the guests ended, the prayers began. Bolesław mumbled the Latin words, bored. He could only thank God silently that he had Bishop Unger in Poznań. The bony holy man represented a very different kind of religious leader. His prayers resembled military orders more than flowery psalms. Once the prayers were said, the servants poured wine, and bowls of food were brought out from the camp kitchens.

When the feast finally ended, Bolesław invited Sobiesław to his tent.

"We achieved nothing, as usual," he said when they walked in.

Duszan, without asking, handed them horns with mead. Bolesław's dogs gathered at his feet. He patted their big heads fondly.

They had barely taken a sip before the dogs began to bark. Bjornar burst into the tent.

"Duke!" he shouted. "There's been a fire!"

"Where?" Bolesław asked, spilling mead as he jumped up.

"Oh, no, sit down," Bjornar panted. "I didn't mean to cause alarm. The fire wasn't here."

"Make up your mind, redhead."

"Forgive me, my lord. I exhausted two horses on my way from Jom. I have news from Sigtuna."

"Tell me," Bolesław said. One of his dogs whimpered.

"King Eric Segersäll is dead. Suitors have begun to visit your sister. The dowager queen is a tasty morsel . . ."

"That's my sister, a queen, you speak of."

"No, my lord! I mean, you can hit me if you'd like, but I'm not insulting the bold lady. I'm only relaying news . . ."

"Oh, all right." Bolesław fell back onto the bench and gestured toward the seat opposite. "Carry on."

Bjornar sat down and shook himself. Then he frowned.

"What?" Bolesław snapped.

"Nothing." Bjornar reddened. "Nothing. The suitors . . . kings of small nations . . . You know what the north is like. Five rocks and one calls himself 'king.' She sent them all away. Then . . . only don't be angry, . . . I'm only relaying news, I'm only the messenger, my lord . . ."

"Speak!" Bolesław was losing patience with the squirming man in front of them.

"Harald of Oppland and Vissivald of Rus went to see her—that is,

Wsiewołod. Prince Vladimir's bastard son. And they insulted your sister . . . so, she sent them up in smoke . . ."

"What?" Bolesław didn't understand.

"She burned them?" Sobiesław asked.

"Yes, yes. In a bathhouse," Bjornar explained, as if that was somehow an extenuating circumstance.

"Jesus Christ. That's murder. Świętosława has stained her hands with blood," Bolesław said.

"Perhaps that's how it should be seen under our laws, but in Sigtuna, it's been interpreted as a . . ." Bjornar hesitated. "An honor? Duty? Her right? In any case, a song about Sigrid Storråda burning suitors was brought to Jom . . . but that's not what I came to tell you, my lord. Wilkomir, who you made your sister's adviser, is asking who she should marry. He sends word that Olav Tryggvason has come to see her in person."

Olav, Bolesław thought, and he saw the hunting lodge. The three of them. Mushrooms and mead. Yes. Joining his sister's Sweden and Olav's Norway would be like a hammer to Sven's Denmark. Yes, yes, an excellent idea.

"And the queen wants to know if she should marry him?" Bolesław felt himself sobering, despite the mead he'd consumed. "Is that what my sister asks?"

"No, my lord. The queen sent no questions, only Wilkomir."

Bolesław hadn't expected his sister to ask for advice. He remembered her childhood fascination with the widowed empress, Theophanu, who ruled independently. Lifting his horn, he drank to her and the Yngling in her bed, for the joining of two countries. Mieszko had shown Świętosława the north and the west in his vision.

"I'd like to meet your sister," Sobiesław said. "What a shame that I'm only the duke of Libice. If I was the ruler of all of Bohemia, I'd ask you for her hand and we'd be connected by family ties."

"A beautiful thought, but as you can see, too late. Świętosława has sown her grain in the north, and that's where she will be picking the harvest."

41

❈

SWEDEN

Świętosława looked into his pale eyes. They were transparent, like water shot through with sunlight. She didn't hear the noise of the feast, the laughter, or the toasts. She heard only Olav.

"I want to marry you," he said.

Christ, she groaned silently, *it's come true.*

She felt Dusza's hand on her back. Her loyal friend, her shadow. Her fingers dug into Świętosława's back, as if Olav had proposed to her. Only Dusza knew how badly she'd wanted this moment. *I want to marry you, I want to marry you*—his words echoed in her head. She responded calmly, though.

"You're not the only one. My advisers tell me I should accept the proposal of the prince of Rus, Vladimir."

"He's an old man," Olav said aggressively. "And he has many wives."

"No, he hasn't offered himself," she said with a smile, "but his son, Jarosław."

Olav burst out laughing.

"Jarisleif? I know him, he's a kid," he said, and she heard not just anger in his voice, but disdain.

"He's seventeen," she replied, burning with contrariness. "Or almost seventeen."

"When I last saw him, he was five and attached to his mother's skirts. He ran to her the moment she called. Światopołk, his older brother, was stronger and harder."

"Are you suggesting I should marry Światopołk?" she smiled. "Or do you just dislike children?"

He gave her a look that chased away all flirtatiousness.

Vestar and Toki, brothers-in-law who were joined by a friendship as strong as their mutual jealousy of each other's lands, were beginning a loud game of comparisons at the table farthest away from them. The guests were turning toward them, laughing, as each feast with the brothers' participation had to end with a game. Better this than the times in which they reached for their knives.

Sigrid Proud, Sigrid Ruthless,
to whose bright home
suitors doggedly come,
from the rocky borders along a swampy path . . .

"That's enough, Thorvald," she silenced the bard, afraid she was going to hear the verses about the bloody bathhouse. "Give us another song."

She moistened her lips with her goblet. Last night had left its mark on her, one she hadn't expected. She still felt Olav inside her, every kiss, the touch of his rough hands, the scent of his skin and hair. In the morning, when she'd returned to Sigtuna with Wilkomir, she wouldn't let the servants prepare a bath. She was afraid it would wash off the rest of that night along with the deep scent of the two of them. Now, during the feast, she could feel the heat emanating from him. If he touched her, she'd drop her goblet. But she was a queen, and though she'd allowed herself something the previous night, something she had craved for years, today she had to think like a queen.

"I'll marry Tryggvason," she had announced to her advisers that morning.

"Has he asked?" Ulf questioned.

"No, but that's what he's come for."

"He hasn't regained power in his country yet. He's not a king," Wilkomir said.

"He will be," she'd replied.

"What about your son?" Ion had asked, studying her carefully, as if he knew what had happened that night. "What guarantee do you have, my lady, that a new, young, and, I expect, virile husband won't do something to push Olof away from the throne? Kings are no different than animals, my lady. Each male wants his own young."

She could have told Ion that if she wasn't carrying Olav's child after last night, she'd be more than happy to jump back into bed to make it happen. But she bit her tongue and sobered up. Advisers were not confidants.

"I want you to be my wife, Świętosława," Olav repeated.

The shy sound of two flutes came from nearby. Girls wanted to dance. Below the platform, a roasted pig was being torn apart. Someone was greedily reaching out to take its head. The piglet was grabbed too violently, and its ears fell off. Laughter.

"I understand what you ask for," she replied quietly. The words came with difficulty. "But I don't know if you understand what you're asking for. I'm a queen, and I rule in the name of my son. There is a place for a husband in this arrangement, but I don't know if for a king. Where would we live?"

"I will set up a new royal court in Trondheimfiord," he answered.

"Oh, yes. You invite me to a kingdom that you haven't yet won." The words felt heavy. "My son cannot leave Sweden, otherwise the merchants will claim power."

"Your son will stay here," Olav replied. "You will sail with me to Norway as my wife and queen. My fleet awaits in Viken. When we join forces, conquering the country will be a mere formality."

"When we join forces . . ." she repeated after him.

That morning Wilkomir had said, "Olav needs a marriage with you because that will help him demonstrate strength to his people. And I suspect he also needs our ships and armies."

"Isn't that obvious?" she'd asked them all in the morning. "Isn't Tryggvason a better choice than any one of these . . ."

Ion finished for her. "Men burned alive? Ah, my lady, those were minnows. Our queen deserves a whale."

"You marry a whale, monk," she threw out angrily.

And that's when Great Ulf announced: "This is a good match, my lady, but the devil is in the details."

And Wilkomir asked: "Who would your brother see beside you? Shouldn't Bolesław have a say?"

She had been furious at that. "Bolesław backed Olav a long time ago, but the decision is mine. Not his."

Now, she said calmly, "Olav, I'm tired today. We'll discuss matters between us tomorrow."

"Do you want to sleep, Świętosława?" he asked quietly, and she shivered at his voice. "Do you want company?"

Yes! she wanted to shout. *Come to bed, undress, lay me on your breast. I want to feel you inside me again, I want to melt under your fingers, howl with delight.*

"No, Olav. I want to be alone," she replied, and walked away without looking at him.

Olav tossed and turned in bed. This night was even worse than the previous day, steeped as it had been in waiting. He couldn't sleep. He kept imagining that the sword hung over the bed was about to fall and cut off his head. He couldn't take it any longer, and, when morning wasn't far off, he got up and walked out of Eric's bedchamber, heading toward her rooms. Great Ulf barred his way.

"What are you searching for, my lord?" he asked. "Water, mead? Everything is here." He pointed at the remnants of the feast which lay scattered on the tables.

Olav grabbed a goblet and drank. The mead tasted bitter. Ulf stretched, and then, as if by accident, placed his hand on the hilt of his sword and stood in front of the queen's door.

"Sleep well, my lord." He yawned. "Tomorrow's a new day."

Sleep finally came at the end of the night, and his dreams tired him even more. In them, he was fighting. Without a weapon, fighting a female lynx, feeling her breath on his face, her growls. Fangs dripping with saliva. The cat was lighter than him, but he still couldn't free himself from her muscular paws. Her two pups were playing under the ferns on the side. Wrzask and Zgrzyt. He could pronounce their names in his dream. He rolled the lynx over onto her front, found himself on top of her, and suddenly felt lust far stronger than fear. He dug his fingers into her spotted fur and wanted to mount her. To copulate with her. He ripped himself free from the dream covered in sweat, disgusted by the fantasy. He rolled across the bed and grabbed his groin. He was breathing hard. He heard a sound which resembled a throaty meow. A soft head nudged his hand. Was that her? Was he still dreaming? No. It was a lynx. One of them.

He sat up. The cat jumped onto the bed, looking in his eyes.

"Wrzask or Zgrzyt?" he asked.

Green eyes. Wrzask. *"First, there's the shout to the skies, and then the sense that something had gone wrong."*

The lynx he'd caught years ago and given to the bold one had grown into a predator. *What is it like, to love a live animal?* He didn't need to ask Zgrzyt what had gone wrong. He touched the cross around his neck. It was wet with sweat. The lynx stretched out its neck, wanting to lick the salty metal.

Olav shooed it away. The lynx leaped down to the floor and began to circle, sniffing the bed.

The path to the house of the Lord is neither straight nor wide. It is a stony and steep road on which everyone who doubts will twist an ankle, falling into the abyss, the old man, Hundrr, chuckled in his memory, *an abyss for all eternity. Only the chosen ones set out down this road, and he chose you, boy.*

Zgrzyt was pulling at something under the bed. He let out a long growl and pulled out a dirty piece of material, tormenting until it was torn into pieces. In the flickering light of the oil lamp, Olav saw old, brown blood on the snatches of cloth. *Dear God, what happened in this bed?* he wondered, and felt a wave of sorrow for Świętosława. He hadn't asked, even once, what her marriage to Eric had meant to her. Receiving her husband's bedchamber for his guest room, all he'd thought of were *his* feelings, his own fits of jealousy and madness.

Longing, desire, dissatisfaction, my boy, Hundrr squawked in his head again.

Olav dressed and walked outside. The smudge of light on the eastern skies promised the impending dawn. The stable boy woke up as Olav led one of his horses from its stall.

"I'll return before noon," he told the guard at the gate.

No one dared stop him.

When he reached the shore of the bay, darkness had been chased away, but the sun hadn't yet risen. A pale glow indicated dawn would soon be victorious. He undressed and walked into Mälaren's cold waters. He swam until he lost his footing. Then he took a deep breath, and dived.

When he emerged from the water, he was shaking; he'd put his body to the test once again, as he had in the Dnieper waters. He'd forced it to swim without breath, to conquer the challenge posed to him by his own lungs. And he'd been victorious. It was only a body. It must give way to the soul.

That day, she decided to speak to him before the feast, and Olav knew that this gave him a chance. She invited him for a ride, one on one. He waited for her in the yard by the stables, watching her son and Wilczan, Wilkomir's son, throw javelins at a shield hanging on a pole. Eric's boy was determined, practicing technique, not strength. When he noticed Tryggvason was watching, though, he tried to show off. Unfortunately, he missed four out of five throws.

"You're tensing your shoulder too much," Olav said.

The boy looked at him darkly.

"Don't think about who might be watching," he advised. "Focus only on your target."

The boy, without dropping his arm with the javelin, twisted toward him and changed his grip on the shaft so that the head was aimed at Olav's chest. His eyes were narrowed into slits and sweat gleamed on his upper lip.

"Is this better?" he asked. "I'm thinking only of my target now."

Olav saw the boy's determination begin to change into fury. He tried to find something of Świętosława in his face. He couldn't. This pup is a stranger's litter, he thought.

"Aiming at an unarmed opponent isn't a worthy thing to do for a man," he said calmly.

The kid reddened.

"Oh." Świętosława's voice sounded behind him. "I see that my son has chosen you as his target. Olof, focus on your training, leave the guest to me."

She walked between the two of them, holding her lynxes on a double leash. She smiled at her son and added:

"Besides, the king is your namesake, that's an obligation."

"For whom?" they both asked.

She laughed.

"Both of you." She kissed her son's forehead and, placing her hand on the javelin, pushed firmly so it pointed at the ground. "Shall we?" she asked Tryggvason.

The stable boy brought her horse, and little Wilczan helped the queen mount. Olof still stood motionless, with the javelin aimed toward the ground. When Olav was in his saddle, he saw the boy boring a hole in the earth with the tip. As they rode through the gate, he wondered what was worse. Not having a father, like him, and arranging his entire life to win back his inheritance? Or having it, and living always with the pressure of matching a victorious parent?

When they rode into the fields of heather around Sigtuna, he noticed the armed men accompanying them, in front of and behind them. He looked at Świętosława. She was wearing a simple woolen dress the color of autumn leaves. She had a cloak lined with fox fur over her shoulders, and a hood, since the clouds hinted at rain. She shrugged.

"I've gotten used to it," she said, motioning toward the guards.

"Are you still the mistress of your own fate?" he asked.

She stopped her mare and looked at him with golden-green eyes.

"I'm the servant of the kingdom." As she spoke, she unclipped the leashes and the lynxes bounded away, always ready for a hunt. "But I remain the mistress of my own heart. And you, Olav?"

"Baptism has made me Christ's servant," he replied. "He rules my heart and soul. I swore I would make my country Christian."

"A beautiful goal," she said, and turned away from him, setting off again. He urged his horse to catch up to hers. They rode side by side. Her silence seemed ominous to him. A seagull sobbed loudly on a nearby rock. The lynxes were tearing apart her young. Feathers spiraled in the air.

"What do you say to my proposal, Świętosława?"

"I've been waiting for it, Olav," she replied quietly, looking straight ahead. "I've been waiting for you. The old Świętosława would have dropped everything . . . Do you know, I looked for you, every day I spent on the *Haughty Giantess*. I dreamed that you'd stand up to my father, leave Geira, and catch up to the *Haughty Giantess* with your people. You'd defeat Jarl Birger and the crew, and kidnap me. I imagined that we lived on some island, just you and me. But those were merely the fantasies of a young girl. And then you'd return to me every time my lord husband . . . I squeezed my eyes shut, clenched my fists, and pretended it was you . . . but now I have a ten-year-old son who needs years before he's ready to rule by himself. Until that happens, I cannot leave him. I have enemies in this country, as does any ruler. They'd leap at the chance and I'd have you, my girlish dream, while my son lost his kingdom. So, if you're asking if you're still the master of my heart, the answer is yes. And what's more, since last night you're also the master of my desires."

Olav felt his entire body contract, as if the swim in the cold water at dawn hadn't happened, as if he were not the master of his own body. All it took was hearing those words from her mouth, and desire came over him in a wave so strong that he could have taken her there and then, on the heather, never mind the guards. He breathed in and realized Świętosława was still speaking.

". . . but all the reasons which I've mentioned before mean that I can't say yes to your proposal. That doesn't mean I'm renouncing you, Olav."

She stopped her horse, and he did the same. They turned to face each other. She had sad, glassy eyes. She looked like an old woman in that moment. *Longing, desire, dissatisfaction, my boy.*

"Give me time, Olav. Four or five years. That's enough for the nobles to acknowledge my son as old enough to rule independently. Once the council declares him a king, I'll come to you and we can exchange marriage vows."

"I need you now, Świętosława," he said firmly.

She threw the hood off her head. Her golden hair gleamed in the sun. She was herself again. She whispered heatedly:

"So what are we waiting for? Let's go to the boathouse by the port, wherever, somewhere no one can see us, and let's share our love for one another."

He collected himself.

"We can't just ride the waves of lust," he replied, although he was keeping his own at bay with difficulty.

She frowned, and her cheeks blushed crimson.

"You said you wanted me now," she said haughtily.

"When I return to my country with a wife, a Christian queen, the task the Lord has given me . . ."

"Say it! Say it as it is. You don't want me, you want my armies. You need support to win back your throne."

"I desire you and I need your armies, that's true," he replied. "Does the vision of our joined kingdoms not tempt you? A country twice as big? A kingdom we can give to God?"

"You speak of God more than you do of me," she snorted.

"Because He comes first," he replied. "A man cannot come before God."

"Then my proposal should suit you." She lifted her head high. "First, win back your throne and baptize your country. You'll fulfill your mission, and then my time will come."

She whistled and, without waiting for a reply, urged her horse forward. He saw Zgrzyt and Wrzask run toward her and the guards riding at a canter, enclosing their queen in an unbreachable circle of spears, swords, and shields.

Świętosława, riding into the yard of the manor house in Sigtuna, was resentful and angry. She hid her face in her hood, not wanting Wilkomir to see her emotions. He was right, damn him! Olav wanted only her strength, authority, and armies. He had asked "Will you marry me?" but he hadn't said "I love you." Damn him!

Will I know love at a man's side? she'd asked the old crone, picturing those lashless eyes and the squawking voice. *I didn't see.*

Dusza waited for her in the yard, questions in her eyes. Świętosława pulled her by the hand into her bedchamber and as Dusza helped her change, she was finally able to voice her anger aloud.

"I won't be a pawn in their games. First Duke Mieszko. And now Olav? . . . I waited for him . . . I soiled my hands with Birger's death, burned the suitors . . . Everything was for him . . ."

Dusza squeezed her fingers on Świętosława's shoulders and lifted her face. She cocked her head and shook it, saying no.

"All right, I admit," Świętosława gave in. "Birger and the suitors . . . that was for me."

Dusza agreed, nodding her head.

"He speaks of God all the time," Świętosława complained. "Not of me."

Dusza went to the old chest in the corner of the room. She rummaged inside and dug out a small worn cross. She gave it to Świętosława, who sighed as she took it in her hand.

"Dobrawa's cross," she said. "Mother rubbed it when she prayed for Father to truly open himself up to God . . . Oh, stop it," she exclaimed, when Dusza folded her arms over her breast as if she were cradling a child. "You have too good a memory!"

Dusza turned her so that Świętosława's gaze was directed at Eric's flag hanging on the wall. She pushed her toward the golden boar. She pushed her against the wall.

"Enough." Świętosława wished to stop the stream of memories. "Yes, I know. I prayed that Eric might want to be baptized. And after his death, I got Olav, who thinks only of baptism. But does the Lord have to give in extremes?"

Dusza spread out her arms. What do they know.

"It's not that simple, Dusza. There is still my son."

The girl nodded.

"Dusza, hold me," Świętosława groaned. "Hold me before I lose my mind."

But as her arms surrounded the queen, they heard someone knocking. Dusza embraced her mistress briefly and let go. She went to open the door.

Świętosława saw the priest's straight back and long beard first. Bork was waiting for her in the hall.

"Bold lady," he greeted her with a bow. "I bring news."

"Be my guest, whether it is good or bad." She invited him onto the platform.

"Rognvald Ulfsson is meeting with people," Bork said.

"Ulfsson?"

"The merchant from Birka, father of Mistress Thordis," the old man reminded her.

Eric's old lover, she added in her mind what Bork left out. She remembered how angry they had looked across the king's pyre, and how quickly they had left the funeral feast.

"Mead," she called out to a servant girl.

Wrzask and Zgrzyt lay down at her feet. Bork accepted a goblet. He drank a little.

"Rognvald accuses you of his grandsons' deaths."

"How dare he!" She was shaken.

"By the right of a grandfather who has lost all hopes for heirs." The old man turned toward her, twisting his entire body like someone with stiff shoulders. His gray eyes were sad. "He doesn't claim that you did it alone, he is not a fool. He knows that the boys died when you were in Uppsala, surrounded by people. He's suggesting that you might have given the command, though."

Curse Birger's name, she groaned inwardly.

"Quite the opposite," she said calmly, meeting his eyes. "I gave an order. And when I found out it had been broken, I punished the one responsible."

"Who was it?" Bork asked without averting his gaze.

"You know who it was. The same man who . . .

". . . suggested Thordis go onto the pyre."

"Yes. Birger. He had many sins to atone for."

"What is a sin?" Odin's priest asked.

"A wrongdoing against God's and people's laws," she replied.

"For breaking the law, a man should face judgment." Bork sounded strict. "If you'd done that, nobody would dare accuse you, bold lady."

"It is up to the ruler to decide on how to punish the guilty."

"But the verdict should be public," Bork argued. "How did you punish him?"

Only now did she realize that Bork didn't know. How was it that the news hadn't left this hall? No servant talked, none of the guests . . . The burning of the suitors was already the stuff of songs, but Birger's dismemberment was veiled with silence. Gratitude toward her people flooded through her; to all of them, from the cook and kennel master to the chieftains and their wives.

"Do you want to hear my confession?" she asked Bork.

"What's a confession?"

"Owning up to one's sins."

He nodded. She told him what had happened that night. He drank the contents of his goblet and placed it on the table.

"I see no sins here. I see the bold lady who defended her rights and dignity. I said the same thing to Rognvald."

"What?" she was taken aback.

"That you saved his only daughter from the honor of the pyre, so you couldn't be behind his grandsons' deaths. The right of revenge is not his. He'll believe it, but that doesn't mean he won't stop stirring the pot that you're in, bold lady. Some people cannot make peace with loss, and they are prepared to start a civil war, or worse, let foreigners in."

She recalled what Birger had said the night after his wife's funeral: "Rognvald Ulfsson is sending ships to England." She felt cold, as if someone had placed steel at her breast. Zgrzyt got up and nudged her hand with a cold nose.

"Foreigners?"

Bork turned away sharply. He lifted his face and began to study the smoke which left the hall through the smoke hole. He moved his head as if he was sniffing the air. He closed his eyes, opened them, blinked.

"Someone is approaching, bold lady," he said, with something akin to fear. "A husband is nearing, who is led by a bright, powerful hamingia."

"Hamingia?"

"Power. The spirit that leads a man." Bork was still looking in the smoke as if he could see the hamingia he spoke of.

"Is this the foreigner you mentioned?" she asked with unease. "The foreigner that Ulfsson wants to send for me?"

"No, bold lady. This is not the one that the merchant of Birka has in mind. But the man who approaches is stranger to me than . . ."

At that moment, both lynxes leaped toward the entrance to the hall. Świętosława shouted:

"Zgrzyt! Wrzask! To me!"

But the cats didn't heed her. She rose to go after them, afraid they might hurt someone. Bork grabbed her hand and held her in place.

"Stay with me," he whispered, and she heard terror in his voice.

She froze. Wrzask ran back into the hall, snorting. Olav Tryggvason was following him, his hand on Zgrzyt's head. She felt a heat rush over her. Olav took his gloved hand off the lynx's head as if he wanted to greet her, and only now noticed the gray-bearded priest. He drew back his hand and frowned. Bork didn't let go of her. The great, gray-bearded man, who had taken her husband's life to offer it to Odin, was afraid.

"Świętosława," Olav said. "I wanted to finish our conversation."

"That's him," Bork whispered.

Olav studied the old man carefully. He must have heard his whisper. Zgrzyt was pulling Tryggvason's glove affectionately, as if he wanted to play.

"I can see that you're otherwise engaged," Olav said slowly.

"Yes," she replied. "I will meet with you later."

He took a few steps toward them, his eyes still on Bork.

"Are these your advisers, Świętosława?" he asked. "The ones you discuss our issues with? The ones who advise you to reject my proposal?"

A threat colored his voice. Zgrzyt was still nipping at his hand, but Olav didn't seem to feel it. Wrzask walked over to her and Bork and growled once, a second time.

"I saw his hamingia," the priest whispered.

"Answer me, Świętosława," Olav insisted. "Is this the man pulling you away from me?"

If she said yes, Olav would reach for steel, she was sure of it. Zgrzyt pulled on Olav's glove with his teeth. Tryggvason ripped it back from the lynx's mouth without taking his eyes from Bork.

"Who have you become, Świętosława?" He finally looked at her.

She saw surprise and anger in his eyes. He walked toward her and Bork with a soft step until he was an arm's length away. She could smell the scent of his skin when he spoke again.

"Do you place Odin's priest above the Almighty's message? Do you choose his advice? Are you prepared to leave me for someone like this?"

"Silence," she ordered. "You don't understand, Olav, and you're breaking the laws of hospitality. Bork is under my roof and you aren't to insult him, as that is an insult to me. Be silent before it's too late."

Olav's eyes narrowed like a snake's. For a heartbeat, she was sure she heard a hiss. He sucked in air. She felt the fury and wounded pride which emanated from him. He lifted a hand, holding the glove as if he wanted to hit one of them. Bork let go of her hand and grabbed Olav's glove. Zgrzyt leaped up and tore it from their grasp.

"Enough!" Świętosława shouted.

Great Ulf barged into the hall with his sword drawn. She stopped him with a gesture, saying:

"This conversation is over."

Not this. Not more bloodshed. She saw the silent Dusza take hold of the lynxes' collars, quiet and transparent as a specter. Olav cooled. The anger seeped from his features. They were standing so close that she could see the movement of every muscle. The white of his hair. The shadow of a beard on his well-defined jaw. The clear outline of his lips. The light reflected in his irises.

"My lady," he said, coldly and calmly, as if nothing had just occurred. "Apart from English gold and silver, I've brought you a pair of falcons. The

Danish, my country's invaders, used to call Norway 'Falcon Island,' because they took their tribute from them in the shape of these birds. That's over now. There will be no more tributes, because the rightful king has returned. The falcons are reliable and trained. Do you know how they hunt, my lady? In pairs. The female and the male set out for the hunt together. One of them chases the prey, the other catches it and finishes the task. They are so swift that one cannot tell whether it's the female or male who delivers the deadly blow. Does it matter, if they form a couple? No. These have been trained not just to hunt. They can find me anywhere. We can meet at the estuary of the Göta älv, the river where the three kingdoms meet. If you want to give an answer to my proposal, send a falcon, and I will come."

God, she groaned silently, *don't take him away from me. Olav, don't leave, I beg you.*

She lifted her head high and said:

"If I have an answer for you, I'll send a falcon."

She didn't move. Didn't reach out. Didn't touch him. That night shone in his eyes. They clung to each other, their gazes locked in a final violent act of love. He turned away from her slowly. She didn't close her eyes when his broad back disappeared through the door.

42

THE BALTIC SEA

Sven was sailing on his first journey on the *Wind Hunter*.

"Let's see how much you're worth," he'd said, patting the gunwale as he stepped on board.

Now he watched the *Hunter's* enormous sail billowing in the wind. A great fleet swayed on the water behind him, as far as the eye could see. A hundred ships had sailed east with their king.

After returning from England, the *Bloody Fox*, as Jorun pointed out, was good only to serve as firewood, but Sven firmly forbade this. Everything he'd ever achieved had been on the deck of the *Fox*, and the old ship was like a brother to him. He ordered it renewed, no matter what the cost. When he was a gray-bearded old man, he'd have himself burned on its deck. Gray-bearded King Sven: he smiled at the thought.

Eric Segersäll's death was an unexpected gift from fate, so much so that he hardly dared to believe it at first. He didn't have much time to think through strategies; the news that the great Swede had died reached him as he was packing up his treasures on the Isle of Wight. He'd left so quickly that he wasn't able to send for the sweet redheaded Mary so she might sail away with them. Ah, well, he sighed. When he was being honest with himself, he hadn't truly considered bringing her. Mary had been a fine companion for a chieftain of the Two Kings, but not for the king of Denmark.

When Sven had landed on Danish shores, Gunar, an old comrade, waited for him. He'd received Sven with great celebration, shouting: "The rightful king has returned!" But Sven had lived through too many exiles, escapes, and betrayals to trust so easily. How had his country changed during his absence? Gunar had proven himself loyal in the past, but who would he be loyal to today?

While Sven drank with his host at the welcome feast, Jorun and a handful of scouts had mixed in with the crowd. They spent the evening getting guests drunk, asking questions, and, when morning came, Jorun had come to Sven, still sober, and whispered:

"Gunar was loyal to you. Thorgils of Jelling also. Jarl Stenkil of Hobro, Ragn of the Isles, Uddorm of Viborg . . . those are the names of old and loyal friends. The names of your enemies are Vigmar, the merchant of Ribe, and his brother, Bishop Oddinkarr. Vigmar supported Eric's viceroys. Bishop Oddinkarr sides with the Saxons, but you can't accuse him of treason because he has the archbishop of Bremen behind him, and that will give you trouble from the imperial army."

What Jorun said matched what Gunar had relayed. Over the following day, old allies came to him, rejoicing in the ruler's return, paying him homage. Sven drank, celebrated, gave expensive gifts, accepted oaths of fealty, and immediately demanded proof of these. He'd ordered Thorgils of Jelling to imprison all of Eric's men. The viceroys, tax collectors, and allies. He didn't allow them to be killed, he wanted them alive. He commanded Uddorm to bring his half sister Tyra to him. She had plotted against him more than once, but harming her would lose him support from the people. He could invite her to his court, though, and keep her near and under careful watch.

"Sooner or later, Tyra will lead you to your remaining enemies," Thorgils told him. It was valuable advice.

He hadn't lingered long at Gunar's welcoming house, and as he sailed to Roskilde, he felt as if they had stepped back in time. To that winter night when he'd hurried to kill his father, to claim his power. The *Fox*'s sails had been filled with wind and anger in equal measure. Now, he returned home as a victor, the one who had defeated not just his own father, but also the English king on his own land. The manor in Roskilde was just as he'd left it years before, when, after Harald's lengthy funeral rites, he'd left to face Eric. He touched the beautiful sculpted oak columns. The likenesses of Odin's two crows stared at him from above. Huginn and Muninn, the omniscient birds.

What future awaits me? he asked himself, crossing the threshold.

He took power in Roskilde easily. He held a feast, hosted allies, and accepted oaths of fealty. Melkorka, the old housewife of the manor house, brought him a small girl with flaming hair.

"Her mother named her Gyda," she made an introduction for the child standing silently next to her, whose eyes darted nervously from the floor to Sven's face and back again. "And she said: when the king returns, give him back his daughter. She didn't last long enough to see you, my lord, she died of the fever last winter."

"What was her name?" Sven asked, recalling more than one woman he'd bedded during those years he'd spent in Roskilde.

"Runa, my lord. A fair-haired beauty, the daughter of Hauk of Trelleborg."

"What about this Hauk? Why doesn't the mother's family raise their granddaughter?"

Melkorka puffed out her cheeks, and the girl hunched her shoulders.

"They chased beautiful Runa away, my lord. A daughter with a belly and no husband." The housewife spread out her arms helplessly.

He took a good look at the little one. He didn't know much about children, so he couldn't judge how old Gyda was. Six or eight? She was slender, blue-eyed and as red-haired as he was.

"Melkorka, do you swear that this is my daughter?"

The old woman huffed. "Her mother was a good girl until a young red-bearded king arrived to lead her astray."

Sven acknowledged Gyda as his child in front of the entire country. And he gave her to Melkorka to raise. The days passed quickly; Sven had years of absence to make up for in his kingdom. But his most pressing concern was Black Ottar, the exile from Lejre.

Before his grandfather Gorm had united the country under his reign, the lords of Lejre had been mighty. Gorm chased them off the island and forced them to bend the knee, and Sven's father, Harald Bluetooth, accepted oaths of fealty from them. But these past few years without a king were enough for the exiles' old ambitions to be resurrected. Black Ottar was an old man, but he had sons. And a wife, Arnora, whose family had held power in old legendary clans. Sven knew he must deal with Black Ottar and his family, because tolerating these dissenters and their ancient ambitions was dangerous. Though he knew that making them disappear was equally risky. So, he decided he would use one enemy to defeat another.

He summoned Vigmar of Ribe to Roskilde, and his brother, Bishop Oddinkarr. He accused them of rebelling against the rightful king, an accusation equal to that of treason, and then, mercifully, he gave them an opportunity to make up for their sins: he ordered them to kill Black Ottar and his sons. Oddinkarr writhed, flinched, called on Christian mercy, but Sven had touched a nerve with the bishop: the Lejre family was the oldest refuge of Odin's cult.

"Arnora, too?" Vigmar of Ribe asked.

"No," Sven said. "She's too old to have more children. She will live at my court until the end of her days, as a warning to those who might consider rebelling. Maybe I'll have her shown to the public in Roskilde's church?" He laughed, and noticed the terror in the bishop's eyes.

"King," a pale Oddinkarr whispered, "that wouldn't be appropriate. The church is not the place . . ."

Sven interrupted him angrily:

"Don't instruct me, priest. I know what a church is, and I know that many a sin was committed within it. I was baptized in childhood, never asked for an opinion. I warn you: do not build a nation within a nation here. I know about your secret dealings with the Saxons, and with the archbishop of Bremen."

Oddinkarr opened his mouth, but before he could protest, Sven grabbed his shirt and hissed, "Silence, and I will let you keep your diocese in Ribe."

He let the bishop go just as violently as he'd taken hold of him, and he turned to Vigmar, pointing a finger at him.

"Don't speak, and do as I say: Black Ottar and his sons. And I want the old crone brought here."

He didn't trust the bishop or his brother, but after three days their servants brought Arnora and three heads on a cart lined with wolf fur. That's when Sven decided he had the country under control. He stretched, and went to the shores to investigate the progress being made on his new fleet. The thump of axes sounded amid piles of fresh wood shavings. He praised the wood-carver for the slender bow of the *Wind Hunter*. He noted the restoration of the *Bloody Fox* underway. He was content. He summoned his chieftains to the biggest feast he'd thrown since his return. The servants, under Melkorka's instructions, carried bowls of steaming food onto the tables: smoked herring, dishes of salted codfish and cream, roasted pigs and bloody sausages. Skuli the Icelandic bard, who he'd adopted during his invasion of England, began to recite in a strong, hoarse voice:

The wise king orders battle worms to slink away to the sheath,
The powerful snake of war . . .

He interrupted him with a toast:

"My friends, who have awaited me in my homeland. And you, comrades, who fought beside me, shield by shield, in England. Now we are all united again, and Denmark has its king. But this isn't the time to go for our winter rest. We have a new challenge and a new fight in front of us. I haven't forgotten how King Eric treacherously invaded my country, and I haven't forgiven him. Eric is dead, but he has left behind a son, and I want my vengeance. Eric conquered Denmark. Now, I will conquer Sweden. Bard, encourage us. Friends, drink to another journey."

The snake of the clash of swords knows how to find a trail of blood!
The worm moves along heavy paths of thought toward the warm river of
 death . . .

The taste of wine which flowed that night in Roskilde, the sound of Skuli's bloody verses, the shouts of joy from the chieftains, their desire for revenge awakened . . . he could still hear it all as he stood, now, on the *Wind Hunter*'s deck, and sailed on its first journey. East. He stood on the bows and reveled in the salty air whipping around him. He let his red hair down. He spread out his arms and shouted:

"Queen Sigrid Storråda, a king is coming for you!"

SWEDEN

Świętosława went hunting with the falcons.

"His gift should be useful for something," she said firmly.

Wilkomir cast her a sidelong glance and handed her a glove.

"No," she said, hesitantly. "You take the falcons. I . . . don't know if I want to tame them."

"I understand," he said, and they set off.

Barely a week had passed since Olav's departure, but it seemed to her as if it had been a year. She had summoned the merchant of Birka, Rognvald Ulfsson, whose plotting Bork had warned her of, but he had refused to come to the queen. Jarl Asgrim was under no illusions: "Rognvald is leaning toward outright rebellion. You should quell him, my queen."

Quell him, but how? Should I send Great Ulf to the Birch Isle? she wondered gloomily as she followed Wilkomir to hunt. *It's nonsense. The island doesn't need walls to become Rognvald's stronghold, and he knows that. I should have summoned his sons from Denmark, Erling and Bjarne, before King Sven took back the country. If I had those two in hand, I could call their father to heel.*

They passed through the alder forest beyond which a field stretched, then the swamps began. Wilkomir stopped.

"We'll hunt here, my lady."

His men were taking the pair of falcons from their cage. They sat on Wilkomir's glove, their feathers standing on end.

"Aren't you taking off their hoods?" she asked.

"In a moment. Let them calm down. The falcon is sensitive, easily riled."

Like me, when I saw Olav in the harbor, she thought. She felt sick. Memory chased memory.

"Let the lynxes off the leash, my lady. They'll scare the water birds from the reeds. Falcons hunt only in the air."

She unclipped the leash. Wrzask and Zgryzt stretched, and trotted off, disappearing in the tall grass.

"Do you remember my father and his hunts with the hawk?" she asked hollowly, to draw her own attention toward anything other than the Norwegian king.

"I remember everything," he said. "The night before Yule when your father gave your brother half his squad. And that you came there voluntarily, dressed as Dusza. And you faced down Duchess Oda."

He removed the falcons' hoods delicately. The birds shook their heads at the same time. The female was larger than the male and towered over him on Wilkomir's arm. The birds had black, shining eyes with no pupils. They cocked their heads, as if trying to see into each other's souls.

"Do you wish Mieszko hadn't sent you north, Wilkomir?"

"No," he replied. "I don't."

The sound of rustling wings reached them from the bushes where the lynxes prowled. The falcons stretched their necks. A gaggle of wild geese flew above the field. The falcons launched themselves off the glove with powerful talons. They quickly gained speed, flying in circles and, rising higher, almost immediately separated.

"I can't tell which is which anymore," Świętosława shouted, shielding her eyes with her hand.

"Nor can I," Wilkomir replied. "Look, one of them is attacking."

The bird had risen above the geese and was diving toward them now. In a split second, faster than the blink of an eye, it hit its target. The goose desperately beat its wings, but began to fall. Then, with a lightning fast, long glide just above ground, the second falcon slid and caught the goose.

They are so swift that no one can tell whether it's the female or male who delivers the deadly blow. Does it matter, if they form a couple? Olav, in her memory, looked in her eyes, then slowly turned and walked away. She felt as if someone had just landed a blow to her stomach. She hunched over, clinging to her mare's neck. Thorhalla responded by neighing quietly.

How long would Olav pain her? Would this feeling dry with time, like blood on a skinned knee? Would it be covered with a layer of thick skin, untouchable?

"If you want to give me an answer to my proposal, send a falcon," he'd said before he left. Wrzask appeared from the grass, followed by Zgrzyt. The bloody streaks on their muzzles told of their successful hunt. Predator cats, predator birds, all had their hunts today. She was the one left with empty hands. If he'd at least confessed his love for her, instead of asking for her hand and armies. Uniting their kingdoms was more important to him than uniting lovers. And the cheek with which he'd behaved under her own roof. Damn him!

Wilkomir was summoning the falcons.

"My lady . . . Świętosława . . . I'll say this to you now, while no one can hear us, and I'll never repeat it. You will not hold your throne alone. You will be forced to marry someone who can defend your and Olof's inheritance. You know that the game of royals is not without its losses. Your father would say that no alliance tasted of mead. The better the agreement, the bitterer the taste. Tryggvason wouldn't be a bad choice, even if he cost you some pride."

The falcons landed on his arm, one after the other. Świętosława digested his words. Did he know what she truly felt, that Tryggvason had stolen her heart? Did he want to embolden her? Help her make up her mind? Wilkomir wasn't a child; she'd ordered him to guard the boathouse when she locked herself in with Olav.

"Give me the glove," she replied. "I want to tame a falcon."

"The male or female?" he asked.

"I don't care." She reached out. "They form a pair, anyway."

The mare shook her head a few times, as if irritated by the bird's presence. Świętosława tried to ride evenly. The falcon didn't weigh much, but the presence of the hunter of the skies, whose deadly skill she'd just witnessed, made her feel shy. A live creature, she thought, which takes away life.

The hunt was meant to calm her, to prepare her for her conversation with Rognvald Ulfsson. Instead, it sent her thoughts reeling. *He wouldn't be a bad choice?* she repeated after Wilkomir. Since Olav's departure, she kept catching bits of sentences echoing in her mind. The alder wood gave way to heathland. She should call the lynxes before they reached the road. How? She couldn't shout, it risked startling the falcon trustingly perched on her

forearm. They rode uphill slowly. Wilkomir stopped his horse; without turning around, he waited for her to join him. They saw yellow-green fields, peppered with heather, from the flat, wide hilltop. In the distance, they could see
the smoke rising from Sigtuna's houses. The stony, windy path along which
a few people were riding. A week ago, she thought, we rode down this hill
and we heard the horns in the harbor. And then the salt on his skin . . . she
didn't think any longer. She pulled the leather hood off the falcon. She lifted
her arm up.

"Find Olav," she commanded.

The bird launched itself from her arm and into the air. It screeched
sharply.

"Find him," she repeated.

The falcon beat its wings, and headed west. Wilkomir turned sharply,
frowning. She didn't return his gaze. The riders below had caught her attention, because Great Ulf was leading them. Wilkomir had also recognized
him.

"Ride down slowly," he cautioned.

She led Thorhalla carefully, and they met on the road.

"My lady. A foreign fleet is headed our way. It passed Gotland just yesterday. Scouts counted nearly fifty warships."

"Who?" she asked.

"King Sven."

Thorhalla neighed, as if she knew what Great Ulf had said. Świętosława
made up her mind on the spot.

"I will sail out to meet him."

"What?" Ulf asked, not understanding her initially, and shaking his head
when he did. "No, my queen. It will be a fight. Sven will want to take his
revenge for Eric's conquests in his homeland . . ."

"I will sail to meet him to avoid bloodshed," she announced calmly.

"Świętosława is right," Wilkomir said, surprising them all. "If anyone can
prevent bloodshed, it's a queen sailing out to meet a foreign king. But we must
hurry, before they reach Mälaren Bay."

Two days later, dressed in purple-red dresses, with the rich necklace of crystals on her neck, and a cloak lined with ermine fur, she stood on the deck of
the *Wave Queen* as it approached Sven's fleet with its sails billowing.

". . . eight . . . ten . . . twelve . . ." Asgrim counted.

Tense silence reigned over the deck. It wasn't fifty ships, as the scouts had said. It was one hundred. Over one hundred. She'd need at least four weeks to match that. At the moment, there were barely twenty with her.

I am paying for my father and Eric's war, she thought. *For humiliating Sven all those years ago. They're both dead, and if I don't come up with something, Olof and I will die, too. Christ, I sent Tryggvason a falcon. Olav is probably heading toward Göta älv's estuary right now. If the falcon could speak, and ask him for help in my name . . . Nonsense. I didn't help him, and the falcon is just a bird.*

The enemy fleet approached, arranged like an arrowhead with one ship in the lead, the royal one, she suspected. On seeing her ships spread out in a line, the invaders did the same.

"Give the command to sound the horn—to welcome our guests, not to start a war," she told Great Ulf.

Both sets of ships stopped. They were close enough now that they could make out individual people on each other's decks.

"Which one is Sven?" she asked, walking to the bow.

"The tall redhead," Great Ulf said.

"Will he accept my invitation to come onto my ship?"

"He would be a fool if he did."

"Welcome him in my name," she said, rearranging her cloak.

Great Ulf had a powerful voice.

"Queen Sigrid Storråda welcomes King Sven onto her waters," he roared.

"King Sven is honored that the great lady has sailed out to meet him," a fair-haired man next to Sven replied.

"What brings you here?" Ulf shouted.

Sven's men began to beat their shields with their swords in reply. The terrible, rhythmic sound of steel carried toward them over the water. Świętosława's heart raced.

"Suggest a meeting, in the middle," she said quickly. "Him and me, six oarsmen each, no weapons."

The Danes agreed, and two small boats were soon lowered onto the water. Wilkomir wanted to climb down first, but she stopped him.

"No, my friend. You stay here. If anything happens to me, you will look out for Olof. Jarl Asgrim and Great Ulf will come with me."

Wilkomir grimaced as he always did, and nodded. Asgrim helped her climb down. She almost lost her balance when the small boat swayed under her feet. The even movements of the oars, the slap of water; they were approaching each other quickly. A seagull called overhead. The boats stopped side by side, and then she recognized him.

Years ago, his red beard had been shorter, and it hadn't been plaited into two braids. But that hair . . . still long and restless like the flames. Silver circles decorated his wrists, and he had a triple belt on his hips. Yes, today, he looked like the god Thor.

"Queen," he said.

She replied:

"Tilgiv mig! Hold oje pa hvem du rorer! Nej, du skal holde oje!"

Those had been the first words she'd learned in the tongue of Vikings. Ten years ago, in Wolin. A stranger and Astrid had shouted at each other on the dock after the man had collided with them. Świętosława hadn't known then what they meant, but today she repeated them with full understanding. "Be careful who you stumble into."

He looked at her for a moment, frowning.

"Don't you remember our first meeting? You weren't a king, nor I a queen, but we've stumbled into each other before, Sven."

He laughed.

"That's what I'd call a good beginning. My lady, I am honored to meet you a second time."

"I would have been content with the first."

"If your husband hadn't rushed into my waters, perhaps I would agree. But, as I'm sure you understand, things have gone too far. Vengeance, a debt of honor."

"My husband is dead," she announced, lifting her chin high.

If he wasn't, you'd never have dared, she thought furiously.

"That's why I need to settle the score with you," he said, and anger gleamed in his blue eyes.

Over one hundred warships against my twenty. A grim outcome was certain.

"What do you suggest, King Sven?"

"Well, my lady, since you ask . . . You have no husband, and I could use a wife . . ."

Christ help me, she thought, forcing her expression to remain neutral. *Anything but this.*

"I suggest a good, amiable solution," Sven continued.

"I have a son, an heir to the throne," she said firmly.

"Good," Sven praised. "That's proof that you're fertile."

"And you?" she replied quickly, trying to stop herself from slapping his face.

"I have a daughter, if you need proof of my manhood, my lady, before we meet in the bedchamber." He laughed, as if surprised by his own forwardness. "I will take care of your son. I can bring your unsettled nobles under control, and persuade them to be loyal to . . . what's his name? Oh, yes, Olof."

How does he know about them? she thought. *Maybe he's just guessing?*

"And?" Sven asked, cocking his head. The smile didn't leave his face. "Do you think we have something to talk about? Or would you prefer for us to part in anger and . . ."

"There is always time for anger if we run out of goodwill," she said calmly. "Accept my invitation to Sigtuna, King. And leave your ships here. Let's exchange hostages to prove our good intentions."

"I will happily see the famous royal court. But forgive me, my lady, I will not accept an invitation to the bathhouse. I have heard songs about how hot the baths are in the home of Sigrid Storråda."

She laughed for the first time.

"Oh, King! Those are ordinary suitors, and you, from what I hear, have not come to ask for my hand."

"You're right," he agreed. "I will not ask."

43

⚭

Olav rode south to the estuary of Göta älv, where he'd told Świętosława he'd meet her; she would be heading there from Sigtuna, traveling west. The falcon had found him, though it arrived half-dead. When had she sent the bird? When would she arrive at their prearranged meeting place? He left without delay, but he was aware that the bird and the meeting he'd suggested, it was all at least a little strange. If it hadn't been for the emotions which ruled him . . . He regretted it now. He had been sure that she wouldn't reply, that her wounded pride would win. Something had gone wrong and it was hard to say which one of them was to blame. That's why the falcon had surprised him; when it had arrived, he didn't pause to wonder for a second, he left Varin in command and his armies continuing from Viken to Agder, while he turned back and made for the estuary. The squad his mother's husband, Lodin, had given him accompanied him.

They rode along the path by the shore; they hurried, and didn't spare their horses, though when night found them they were forced to stop. The night was dark, moonless and cloudy. They expected autumn rains. They went deeper into the forest, unharnessed the horses, and allowed them to graze. His half brother Torkil organized the night watches and advised them not to light fires.

"If I'm counting correctly, we've crossed into the borderlands," Torkil said, making himself a bed from branches and his cloak. "This area has been the bridge between Sweden, Norway, and Denmark for years. My father told me that in the old times, kings would come here and share their plunder from bloody wars. They negotiated peace, marrying their daughters and sons. They exchanged hostages, struck alliances. Sleep, Olav. If all goes well, we will be at Göta älv's estuary by tomorrow night."

Despite his half brother's advice, Olav didn't sleep well. He lay awake, remembering his time in Sigtuna. Odin's gray-bearded priest in whose defense Świętosława had stood. Her anger. And she'd confessed her love for him! Why couldn't she have acted as a woman should, and leave matters of the kingdom to him?

He laughed humorlessly at his own thoughts, trying to imagine anyone telling the bold one how she should act. He was foolish not to have expected this of her. His heart had been stolen by a lion, not a lamb.

He got up. There was no point tossing restlessly anymore. The mist was beginning to rise, and a cloudy dawn was coming. He nodded to the watchmen and went for a walk. To loosen his joints, stiff from the cold night. Eventually, he came to a clearing with several big flat rocks. He sat down on one.

The sun pierced the clouds and, rising between the trees, painted the damp morning air in gold. He heard a cracking branch to one side. An animal returning to its burrow after a night's hunt? A forest always echoed with sounds familiar only to itself; it was a silent forest that was dangerous. He rubbed his hand over the rock, which was already warming in the sunshine, and some of the moss coating stuck to his fingers. He shook his hand, flinging the bits of dirt and grass away, then looked back down at the rock. He froze. Then he was scrambling up and tearing the moss piece by piece from its surface.

Images were carved into the flat stone. Long ships appeared as the vegetation was scraped away, sailing side by side in the stone, drawn with men holding spears on their decks. There were silhouettes of reindeer, deer, and great sea fish. A lone dog. People hunting animals. People fighting each other. Dead people, falling to the depths of the seas. Olav felt sweat break out on his forehead. Someone had carved the histories of battles, victories, defeats, deaths, and births into these rocks. And then his gaze fell onto the highest point, where he'd been sitting moments before. Two great figures, a long-haired woman and a man opposite her. Reaching out to each other like lovers. There was a silver layer of lichen above them.

He jumped toward them and rubbed the rock clean, his heart hammering. A man, or an old priest, or perhaps an old god, with a great axe in his hand. It was leaning over the pair of lovers, in the midst of delivering a powerful, deadly blow. The stone had immortalized this moment. The lovers would forever reach out to each other longingly, while their murderer would endlessly be about to strike, until the day that time crumbled the rocks. Olav was breathing quickly, shallowly. He understood. The lovers wouldn't meet, because fate wasn't in their favor. That's when he heard quiet footsteps. He turned around sharply. A dog. A great white dog.

"Are you a vision?" he asked in a whisper.

The dog barked and jumped onto the carved rock. Olav walked over carefully, reaching out a hand. The dog sniffed it, whining briefly, then lay down on the rock, at the feet of the carved lovers.

SWEDEN

Świętosława sat on her tall chair in Sigtuna's hall. Dusza had braided her hair, placing a silver band among the plaits. Her son sat to her left. Then Wilkomir, Jarl Asgrim, Ion. To her right, at some distance, sat Sven, with Jorun and Jarl Stenkil beside him. She called his men by their names, she'd learned them all, even those who sat at the tables farthest away.

Thorvald, the Icelandic bard, was reciting a poem about the queen.

Sigrid Proud, Sigrid Ruthless,
to whose bright home
suitors doggedly come,
from the rocky borders along a swampy path . . .

Before the feast, she'd ordered the servants to go through their crockery. "Don't use anything that Eric brought back from Denmark. Goblets, jugs, bowls . . . hide everything. We can't let the guests be given food in their own dishes."

She lifted a goblet and smiled at Sven.

"To a satisfying conclusion of our talks."

He responded with a smile, and drank. At sea, in the sunlight, he had seemed younger than he did now in the flickering firelight. She had already figured out that his smiles meant nothing, that he could serve threats with a cheerful expression. His eyes were the thing that couldn't lie. *Could he really do it?* she wondered. *Could he really drink my mead, eat food under my roof, and still start a war?*

Those who came at the wrong time
Were reprimanded by our merciful lady.
The flames washed their soiled hands
The fire cleansed their . . .

"Ah, if only that could be repeated," she whispered to Wilkomir in their mother tongue.

He maintained a stony expression, nodded, and looked at the men sitting at the tables. Her eyes followed his. Sven's men were looking from the bard to her, open-mouthed. Her people were greedily looking at the flames of the fireplace.

No, my loyal ones, my loved ones, she thought. *We gave them your sons as hostages. No more burning those who "came at the wrong time."*

Thank God that Thorvald remembered to leave out the flowery verse which described the burning bathouse, the heat of the flames, the smoke rising from the cinders, the arrogance of the punished suitors, and the screams with which they bid the bold lady goodbye. He moved on to lighter verses, leaving the violent details for other celebrations in a smaller circle.

Sigrid Storråda flies in a golden sleigh
Pulled by two wild cats.

"Oh, my lady," Sven spoke cheerfully. "There are stories that you have tamed lynxes. Could we see them?"

"If you'd like, my lord."

She nodded to Dusza; the girl returned after a moment, leading the lynxes. She bowed to Świętosława and handed over the leash.

"They aren't tame," Świętosława said. "I beg you, my king, and let Master Jorun and Jarl Stenkil be my witnesses, do not touch them. I have guaranteed your personal safety, my lord, and I would not like to break my word."

Sven's eyes gleamed; she could see he was fighting himself, wanting to touch the cats. Wrzask growled warningly. She pulled on the leash, and the lynxes lay down at her feet.

"Then, in the port in Wolin, you were wearing a lynx fur," he said.

So, he remembers our meeting after all, she thought.

"I don't wear that fur since I've had live lynxes," she replied.

A lighting clad in speckles leaps
wherever its mistress commands.

"Must we listen to the entire poem?" Sven asked.

It's not just the one. I ordered Thorvald to add another hundred verses so that Ulf's men might have time to summon the crews from the northern parts of the country, she thought. Out loud, she said:

"Don't you like poetry, my lord? Perhaps more mead will help you appreciate it?"

"I'm a king, a warrior, and conquerer, which means I cannot live without bards who will make rhymes about my feats," he replied, and his blue eyes shone coldly. "Let's return to affairs of state, my lady, and then we might have more time for poetry. I will ask you a question. Do you want war?"

"No."

"Then we can keep talking. Firstly, please accept this gift from me." He handed her something in an open palm.

"It's a silver coin," she said, taking it.

She brought the denar close to her eyes and read: ZVEN REX DENER. Sven King of Denmark.

"I ordered a few thousand to be minted. Take it, it's a gift."

"I'd prefer to see one that said Olof King of Swedes."

He laughed aloud.

"You fight for your son. But you don't have to, I don't intend to harm him. As proof of my good intentions, please accept another gift from me. Jorun, bring them."

Jorun's hair was as wild as a bale of hay. He looked like someone who would stop at nothing in battle, but his pale eyes were good-humored. He returned after a long moment, leading two men with ropes around their wrists. They were dirty and miserable, and at first she didn't recognize them. Wilkomir had to remind her who they were.

"Erling and Bjarne, the sons of Rognvald of Birka."

I told Eric to send them to Denmark as tax collectors, she thought quickly. *If they are in Sven's hands, then he might know from them that Rognvald has been rebelling.*

"You're welcome, Queen Sigrid. They're yours. You can do with them what you wish." Sven's blue eyes flashed.

"Firstly, feed them and send them to the bathhouse," she said.

Uncontrollable laughter spread around the hall.

"For them to wash," she added loudly. "We will need them alive. And guard them."

She turned to Sven. "I appreciate your gifts. What are your terms?"

"You will be my wife and I will take you to Roskilde. In return, I will give up my plans to invade Sweden, and your son will remain here, in Sigtuna, and he'll rule the country in his own name. In case of trouble from the proud merchants of Birka, or other nobles, I'll serve him with my armies and help . . ."

You'll take regency over Olof. Yes, you'll help keep his opposition in check, but in return you gain influence in his kingdom. They'll be able to call him a "Danish viceroy." It's unacceptable, she thought, translating his words into facts. *And, what's worse, by taking me to bed, you'll disgrace Eric's memory. You'll wash away his greatness and undo*

the defeat you received at his hands . . . Christ, and I thought Olav Tryggvason's terms
were beneath me . . .

She interrupted Sven.

"My lord, is it true what they say, that you still worship the old gods, even though Emperor Otto himself baptized you?"

He took out a chain from under his decorated caftan and waved it toward her with a smile. A small silver cross hung on it, and Mjolnir, Thor's hammer.

"I know how to marry the old with the new, my lady."

"My first husband, Eric Segersäll, was a pagan. Have you heard the stories of how he ended his life? If you know those which feature Odin, a knife, and a temple, then let's accept that you know the truth, my lord. When he burned on the funeral pyre, I swore to myself that if I married again, it would have to be a Christian union. What do you say to that, Sven?"

He pulled on Mjolnir, ripped it off the chain, and handed it to her.

"Lay it down as a gift to Thor in Uppsala. The old gods have apparently heard your prayers."

She took the silver decoration with a small laugh, shaking her head.

"I don't lay down gifts for the old gods. Back to the matter at hand. We will be married by a priest, and if God blesses us with children, they will be baptized."

"Will the bishop of Ribe satisfy you?" He bared his teeth. "His name is Oddinkarr. I know, it sounds suspiciously Odin-like, but I assure you, he has been ordained in Bremen. Or, if you'd prefer, I'll have a bishop brought over from England. To be honest, that would suit me, as the aforementioned Oddinkarr is rather too friendly with the Saxons."

"An English bishop is fine." She nodded. "But Ion, my monk, comes with me."

"The fat man with cheeks as red as an apple? Do you like stocky men?" Sven asked, patting his flat stomach.

"A monk is not a man," she announced.

"I disagree," Ion interrupted. "The queen knows that I worship the Lord in every moment of my life . . ."

"No more maids, Ion," she cut off firmly. "You may have been unpunished here, but there you'll be under the eye of the Church."

"They don't have to be maids," Ion groaned. "They can be married women . . ."

"Zgrzyt," she whispered, and the lynx rose. "Ion," she pointed.

Zgrzyt growled and snapped his teeth lazily. He most certainly did not want to bother with Ion, but the monk fell quiet.

"You mentioned a daughter, King Sven," she returned to their conversation. "Does her mother also live at court? Do you have other children out of wedlock?"

"And you, my lady?" he cocked his head.

"No. Olof is my only son."

"And does your heart not beat faster for anyone else?" he persisted, studying her with interest.

"The heart of a queen beats only for her kingdom," she said.

A mere two weeks earlier, Olav had sat where Sven did now.

I was proud and foolish, she thought. *Now, as punishment, I must negotiate for myself, knowing that if I fail, my fate will be ruined, as will my son's and my country's. Olav didn't threaten me, he only wanted what seemed then too much.*

"You give excellent replies, my lady. I will be honored to have such a wife."

"Not so quickly, my lord. We haven't finished yet. Let's talk about my son . . ."

"The only one for now," he interrupted and winked, licking his lips with the tip of his tongue.

Maybe Great Ulf's men will arrive in time? she thought. *Maybe they can get the ships?*

"I cannot speak about children I do not have," she replied. "I want Olof to retain his independence. I did not speak in jest when I mentioned his denar. Give him a minter who will prepare coins with my son's name on them, and a sign to name him the only king of Sweden."

"Sigtuna," Sven corrected.

"Fine. Sigtuna and Sweden. Olof King of Swedes, that's what his name shall be from now on."

She leaned to her left and squeezed her son's hand. It was cold, but sweaty. She smiled to Olof, and Sven laughed again. Laughter must be an answer to what angers him as well as that which he finds entertaining, she thought.

"Olof King of Swedes," Sven replied, and rose. "Olof, come here, let me embrace you. I will be your stepfather."

Świętosława stopped her son in his seat and turned to the king.

"You can embrace at our wedding. We haven't finished . . ."

Sven nimbly turned to her, grabbed her shoulders, lifted her, and whispered straight into her face.

"The bold lady allows herself too much. Choose your words carefully, girl, because instead of you I'll marry Thordis of Birka, and then neither you nor Olof will be of any use to me."

She froze as she heard this, knowing he meant what he said, her mind suddenly overrun by the image of herself and her son falling, struggling for breath, trapped beneath the ice. She imagined them dripping and cold, as Thora had been when they'd pulled her from the river. At the same moment, she heard the lynxes growl throatily, and she felt the leash go taut. Without thinking, she leaned in toward Sven's lips and kissed him. He was surprised, she could tell, but then responded quickly. He released her shoulders from their iron grip and embraced her. Wrzask and Zgrzyt calmed beside her. Joyful cheers sounded in the hall:

"Queen Sigrid Storråda and King Sven!"

"Sigrid and Sven!"

The redbeard grew passionate. He kissed her as if he were fighting a battle, and his hands moved from her shoulders toward her breasts. That's when she bit him. He jerked back and lifted a hand to his lips; there was a drop of blood on his finger. Świętosława grabbed his hand and laughed.

"And this is our first night together. The first blood has flowed."

And she licked it off, pulling his fingertips to her mouth.

44

SWEDEN

Sven had fallen in love with her. That wasn't wise. He'd come to conquer and defile her, but there it was. *It'll pass,* he reassured himself. *It'll pass after the wedding, one doesn't love a wife, after all.*

He planned to leave Sigtuna as soon as possible. He wasn't a fool, he knew that Sigrid might be playing for time and gathering armies in her country. Besides, that wasn't the only reason he wanted to hurry. Olav Tryggvason was the second. He'd received a message that the Yngling had been in Sigtuna before him, and apparently, he and the queen had parted in anger. But he knew the stubbornness of the "second chieftain," and he suspected Olav wouldn't give up so easily. Yes, they were going head to head, as if fate had decided to lead them in tandem. Like Sigrid's two lynxes on a leash, he thought, then pushed the image away angrily. *She got those lynxes from him, and I am not on her leash.*

The two deaths Sven and Olav had needed, Eric the Victorious's in Sweden and Jarl Haakon's in Norway, had come at the same time. If Olav had joined with Sigrid, their united countries would be more powerful than his Denmark. But Tryggvason, according to Sven's information, hadn't come here with a fleet or threatened the queen with war. And he didn't have a crown to offer her, because he hadn't won it yet. *Who has a crown has the queen,* he laughed to himself. *I wasn't first, but I still beat him to it. I can't wait for the wedding night, when I take to my bed the woman of both my old enemy and the new. Maybe I should call myself Sven the Victorious?*

He watched carefully who his new wife was taking with her to Denmark. Without mincing her words, she bartered for everything, for every man or woman.

"Dusza is my shadow, she never leaves my side." She was adamant that the silent servant was coming with her.

"So I'll be taking both of you to bed?" he mocked.

"Perhaps let Jorun join us then," she retorted with a smile.

He blushed. Even his boldest lovers had never suggested such a thing. He hoped she couldn't see the color in his cheeks.

"Great Ulf and Wilkomir with their men."

"You've got to be joking, my lady. It is tradition that a wife brings her maids with her to her husband's home. I have been surprised by many things in Sigtuna, but I hadn't expected your procession of servants to consist of warriors with scarred faces."

"I prefer men marked by scars than those with smooth cheeks," she said, narrowing her eyes.

He undid his belt and grabbed his caftan as if he were about to take it off.

"Do you want to see my scars?" he asked.

Instead of blushing, she shrugged.

"If you like to undress in front of the servants." She motioned at the girls laying the table for the feast.

Damn it, he cursed in his head, letting go of his caftan. *I'm not taking a virgin. And I'm letting her provoke me as if I were a pup.*

"Great Ulf can come, but not Wilkomir," he decided. He preferred one of Eric's old chieftains to be beside her, one who would not be loved in Roskilde.

"Fine. Instead of the father I'll take the son. Wilczan for Wilkomir."

"Is he like his father?"

"Quite the opposite, and he's practically still a child."

"Why do you want a little boy? I assure you, I'll give you one of our own quickly."

"Don't brag." She stuck out her tongue as if she were a defiant child herself. "I'm taking Wilczan."

She didn't let Sven kiss her, though the sight of her tongue drew him to her immediately. The hellish lynxes were beside her already, though.

"The cats stay," he said, teasing her just to see her anger. Since he'd arrived, he'd discovered that he liked sharp women. The ones he'd taken to bed and paid in the past were often sweet and docile.

"Fine, the cats stay. But the lynxes come with me. Let's talk of the dowries."

"I prefer morgengold," he teased again. "I can't wait to give you the morning gift."

"But you'll have to."

He waved a hand.

"I don't need your dowry. I'm rich."

"But I want to receive one from you, a bride price, like a real wife." She smiled sweetly. "Otherwise, someone might argue our marriage could be annulled."

Finally, after two days of bartering, he managed to load everything and everyone that Sigrid wanted to take. In the end, she even ordered a cage with the falcons to be brought on the *Wind Hunter*'s deck. The bird she had sent to Olav had returned; every time she looked at the falcons, the pair of them together, it pained her, but it would have pained her more to leave them behind. She bid her son goodbye, and her chieftains, jarls, and servants. The great, gray-bearded priest of Odin even walked her to the harbor. Sven's Christian fiancée, who had so vehemently argued for a church wedding, somehow didn't mind the blessing of a pagan sacrifice. When they pushed off, she looked behind her only once. He urged the crews to hurry so that they left Mälaren Bay for the open waters as quickly as possible. They had the wind, which he took as a good sign. When they met the rest of his fleet, they exchanged the hostages each side had held during the negotiations, and Sven's ships sailed west.

"We're going home, my lady," he shouted to her. "What was your ship called?"

"*Wave Queen.*"

"*Wind Hunter* will replace her from now on. Look behind you, my lady, and see what your future husband is building his might on." He took her by the shoulders and delicately spun her around, showing her his ships. "That's the *Fiery Cub*, with twenty-four benches. And these three brotherly ships are the *Night Thorn*, the *West Thorn*, and the *Long Thorn*. Fast, sharp, and reliable for boarding . . ."

"Three thorns?" she asked, paling.

"Yes! Three *Thorns*. Behind them are *Loki's Spear*, *Golden Helmet* . . ."

He felt Sigrid slide to the deck.

Olof rode Thorhalla along the shore. His mother had left him her mare. "It's a sensitive and brave animal," she'd said when giving it to him. He felt his eyes fill with tears again at the thought. He turned around. Wilkomir was riding quite a distance behind him. *That's good,* Olof thought. *I don't want him to see me crying.*

Olof understood what had happened; he wasn't a child, he was ten. But everything inside him rebelled against the tide of events. First, his father's death, and then everything that happened at the speed of an avalanche. Everyone referred to him as "Eric's heir, the young king," but nobody valued him. None of the string of nightmarish suitors who wanted to marry his mother came close to filling his father's shoes, but they dared to come to his court and pat him condescendingly on the shoulder. He sat at his mother's side at the feasts thrown for them, and felt disgust at the thought that one of these old men twisted with arthritic joints, youngsters, or fat ones with chain mail that barely covered their bellies would take his lord father's place. He wasn't a fool, he knew that each of them dreamed of taking away the crown from a little boy, the crown that was his by right of birth. The two who had kidnapped him and threatened him with a knife . . . what sort of candidates for fathers were they? It was a good thing that Mother burned them, too, though that horrific night still awoke a monstrous fear in him.

The memory of the drunken feast at which she'd killed Birger was even worse. He woke in the middle of the night sometimes, seeing her in her bloody dress, holding a sword as she walked through the hall. He knew that she'd had to do it, that the treacherous jarl had tried to force himself on her, but even so, when he dreamed of her with the sword and the blood, he felt angry at her. Worst of all, though, had been the last few days, with King Olav and King Sven's arrivals. White- and red-haired. He was afraid of them. The others, fat and old, were unthreatening uncles, well, maybe apart from the ones who pulled out his hair and placed a knife at his throat. But these two . . . he'd eavesdropped, and heard almost every word that had been uttered during the feasts. "Your son will stay here" or "I don't intend to harm him." As if he were nothing more than an animal, a horse you can give away at a market.

He felt awful, knowing they talked about him while sitting beside him, but they didn't care about him. And then, even worse then that in the end: Mother had stolen Wilczan from him. The only friend he'd had. He could forgive her for leaving him and sailing off with Sven, but he would never forgive her for taking Wilczan.

They reached the lake's banks. Thorhalla stopped of her own accord. Wilkomir was right beside him. Olof cautiously wiped his nose on his sleeve.

"What now?" he asked Wilkomir, careful to make sure his voice didn't break.

"Have you ever gone fishing?"

"Fish?" Olof seemed surprised. "A king eats fish, but he doesn't have to catch them."

"He doesn't have to," Wilkomir agreed. "But it's worth knowing how the fish on his table have been caught. I'll show you."

"If you want." Olof shrugged and dismounted.

Wilkomir took a pouch from the horse's back, threw it over his shoulder. "Come on," he called.

Olof shuffled after him. A long dock was hidden in the reeds. The rotten planks shifted under their feet.

"This is barely held together." He grimaced.

"Mm," Wilkomir confirmed. "An accurate observation."

"Someone should fix it."

"Who?"

Olof shrugged.

"I don't know. Someone."

"Sit down and hold this," Wilkomir said, taking a hazel fishing rod from behind his back. "Do you miss your mother?" he asked, taking the pouch off his shoulder.

Olof didn't reply, too busy fighting off tears.

"I miss my son," Wilkomir spoke after a moment. "But I know this is better for him."

"Better? Mother stole him from me!" Olof shouted. "And from you, and Helga. Wilczan didn't want to go with her."

"You're right. He didn't want to leave you, or his family. But he knows that the queen has given him a great chance." As he said this, he placed a tip of a different wood onto the hazel rod. Olof smelled fresh juniper.

"What chance?" he grumbled angrily.

"He'll grow up at her court in Roskilde. He'll meet the most important people in Denmark. In the future, when you're both adults, Wilczan might be useful to you."

"I don't understand." He watched Wilkomir place a line made of horse-hair onto the rod.

"King Sven has assured your safety, but he won't live forever. Wilczan, raised at his court, will learn more of the Danes than anyone, and when the time after Sven comes, you will have a loyal friend there."

Olof, though he could see the logic now, still felt angry.

"So why didn't Mother explain this to me, instead of simply taking Wilczan as if he belonged to her and not to me?" he snorted.

Wilkomir threw the line. A bait with a feather floated on the water.

"What, was she supposed to tell you this in front of Sven? Olof, you're under my protection, but that doesn't mean I'll lie to you and protect you for your whole life. You want to be a king? Then learn!"

"What?" Olof mocked. "Catching fish?"

"No," Wilkomir snarled. "How to use a fishing rod."

The feather jumped on the water and Wilkomir pulled on the rod. A small silver fish gleamed at the end of the line.

"Do you know what this is?" he asked.

Olof only shrugged.

"In the country your mother and I come from, we call it a smelt. Here, you call it a nors."

"Mm," Olof confirmed, and leaned closer to examine the fish.

"Do you like it?"

"It's small. We eat fish this big at feasts." Olof spread out his arms to show Wilkomir what a fish for the royal table should look like.

Wilkomir threw the smelt back in the water and put the rod down. He rummaged in his pouch and brought out an iron instrument that looked like a small pitchfork. He showed it to Olof and said:

"This is a fishgig. We use it to catch bigger fish."

He then busied himself by attaching the fishgig to a stick. He didn't look at Olof, he was absorbed in his work, but he wouldn't stop talking.

"The kingdom belongs to you by right of inheritance, but that doesn't mean you'll be a good king. And if you're a bad one, the council will remove you from power, or someone else, stronger, wiser, and more cunning, will take it away from you. Your mother also had to learn this, because nobody is born a king, even if they are a king's child." Wilkomir finished attaching the fishgig and aimed it as you would a spear. "Do you know how many attempts there have already been on your life?"

Olof felt his mouth go dry.

"I know . . . those two . . . Wsiewołod and Harald . . ."

"And Birger, who wanted to poison you, and Rognvald of Birka, who wanted to maim you. Should I continue?" Saying this, Wilkomir was walking up and down the dock, staring into the water. Suddenly, he lifted his head and added, in a completely different tone: "Big, predator fish like to hunt in the reeds by the shore. Where the small fish feel safe."

Wilkomir's eyes flashed strangely and Olof felt uneasy. Was he speaking of fish or of him? Meanwhile, Wilkomir chose a spot and placed the fishgig lightly in the water; gazing into the depths, he went still. He continued speaking, but in a quieter voice:

"Your mother did everything she could to protect you and the country. Do you think she wants to be Sven's wife? Nonsense. She wanted to marry someone else, but the queen . . ."

Wilkomir thrust the fishgig into the water.

"The queen's heart belongs to the kingdom," Olof repeated what he'd heard his mother say during the feast with Sven. He'd been offended by these words at the time, because she hadn't mentioned him, but now he understood that she was thinking of something else.

"Yes. Learn that from her."

"Did you catch anything?" Olof asked, interested.

"No, but I'll keep trying," Wilkomir replied, and stilled once more with the tip of the fishgig covered by water.

Olof thought about what he'd just heard. He watched Wilkomir, who looked like a spearman ready to pounce. After a moment, he buried the fishgig in the water with such force that it seemed he wanted to pierce the lake bed. And he withdrew it carefully, with difficulty. A great fish thrashed on the iron pitchfork.

"Oh my . . ." Olof said.

"It's a pike. My Helga calls it a gädda. A beautiful predator."

He slid the fish off and placed it on the dock. He took off the iron fork from the handle and said:

"A ruler who thinks only of himself lives comfortably until the day he loses everything, never even knowing how it happened. The one who denies himself in favor of the life of his family and country is loved."

Olof stood up, dusted his trousers, and looked at the greenish lake waters.

"Is the love of your subjects enough when faced with someone who wants to defeat you?" he asked.

"No," Wilkomir replied calmly. "But without it, you won't stand a chance."

Olof folded his hands over his breast, as his father had once done. He lifted his head high and looked around. He recalled that he must straighten his back, for a king doesn't slouch. He walked toward the horses with a confident step. When he reached them, he turned around, surprised; Wilkomir wasn't with him. Olof walked back to the dock. Wilczan's father was cleaning the pike, throwing its insides into the lake. The seagulls squawked, chasing each other to reach them.

"What do you want to carry, Olof? The fish or the rod?"

"The rod," the boy replied, hesitantly, and leaned down to pick it up.

And when they walked back together, he asked Wilkomir:

"Perhaps to start off with, I should have that dock repaired?"

"Yes. That's a good idea, King Olof."

45

DENMARK

The moment they'd sailed into Roskilde, Świętosława already felt like someone planning an escape. She'd stared at banks, memorizing the islands and
shallows.

"Do you like my country?" Sven asked, standing beside her.

"Country?" she responded with a question. "I like this fjord."

"It's the way to my home." Pride colored his voice.

"Soon, it won't be just yours"—she tried to make her voice sound light
and teasing—"but ours."

He leaned to her ear and whispered:

"If you hadn't denied me in Sigtuna, I'd already be calling it ours."

*I was afraid you'd act treacherously or without dignity. That you'd dishonor me, take
me to bed like spoils of war, and then you'd brag that you'd had the queen but didn't intend
to follow through with your agreement. Then my people would have to defend my soiled
honor, and we'd have had a slaughter. I don't trust you, Sven.*

But she was in his hands. Before leaving Sigtuna, she'd left orders with
Wilkomir. She didn't establish a regent, to avoid weakening Olof, but Jarl
Asgrim was made the viceroy of the kingdom. He was responsible for the
loyalty of the other parts of the country. He was meant to keep ships at the
ready in case something went awry here in Roskilde. And Wilkomir, as soon
as Sven's ships with her on board disappeared from view, was told to send
messengers to Bolesław. "Tell my brother to have Dalwin of Wolin send merchants to Roskilde. I will send a message through them. I received a big dowry
from my new husband, it will be enough to pay the Jomsvikings. If the king of
Danes turns out to be traitorous, I will pay for his death with his own silver."

The church in Roskilde was small, wooden, and under the name of the Holy
Trinity. Ion summed this up quietly: "Believe me, my queen, many of Sven's

subjects still believe that the Holy Trinity means Odin, Thor, and Tyr." The monk was probably correct, but at that moment that didn't matter to her. All that mattered was that Wulfric, the English priest who married them, knew who he was praying to and for what. Sven was in a hurry; he had decided they would go to the church for the ceremony as soon as they were off the *Wind Hunter*. Dusza did her hair and dressed her in a tent set up between the ship's gunwales. "I know why he's in such a hurry," Świętosława said to Dusza as Dusza wound braided plaits into crowns on her head. "He's afraid of my brother's anger. Ah, I would happily accept Bolesław's anger, if only my dear brother had enough ships to help me push Sven back."

There was no one who spoke against the match; Wulfric went through the ceremony quickly and joined them in the eyes of the Almighty until death parted them. Thank God, he didn't ask either of them to swear on mutual love, because she couldn't have coped with the blasphemous oath. Wulfric asked them only to promise mutual loyalty until death parted them. She looked at the carved wooden cross. And the dove that stood in for the Spirit. She thought: *Has the falcon found Olav? Is Tryggvason looking for me at Göta älv's estuary in vain? Is he cursing me?*

Sven, tall, red-bearded, and proud, kept turning his head to glance at her. He didn't smile, and she had no idea what he was thinking.

They walked out of the church as man and wife, king and queen. The sun blinded her for a moment, after the dim indoors. Then she saw the crowd. Great Ulf was standing on one side with eleven of his men, little Wilczan with them, and Dusza with the lynxes on a leash, and three maidservants from Sigtuna. A handful compared to the crowd of her new lord husband's people. Order was kept by a line of warriors from Sven's personal squad, all dressed the same. She could see that the iron blades of their axes were decorated with silver, one metal blending into the other, delicately ornamented. Was it still a weapon, or a mere decoration? She wondered. Between the axemen, she recognized individual faces she knew from Sven's time in Sigtuna: fair-haired Jorun, Jarl Stenkil, the bard called Skuli. The rest of them were strangers. Quite a few richly dressed women looked at her curiously. Children squeezed themselves between the adults to see her.

I didn't want to be here, I didn't want to meet any of you, I didn't want to be Sven's wife. But from now on, I'm your queen, she thought, and smiled to everyone, greeting them with a wave of her hand. Wrzask and Zgrzyt tried to free themselves from Dusza, so she took the leash from her, turning to Sven.

"Let's go, then."

"Where to?" he asked mockingly.

"Home."

He took her arm to guide her. The manor in Roskilde made little impact on her, from the outside. It was large and beautiful, but as dark as the one in Uppsala, where she had felt so stifled and alone. Solid sculpted columns by the entrance, with two wooden crows on their tips. Had the falcon found Olav? Was he waiting? Was . . . ?

"Is that your mother?" she asked, looking at a richly dressed old woman in the group of people standing in front of the manor's entrance.

"Not at all." Anger shook Sven's voice. "That's Arnora, the wife of one of my enemies."

"Have you invited these enemies as well?"

"I am not in a habit of inviting corpses to dine with me."

Świętosława nodded to Arnora, and studied her carefully. This woman looked like a queen of old. Pride, worship, pain, and anger were written in every wrinkle on her face. She didn't return the greeting.

"Meet Melkorka." Sven summoned another woman. "She is the house-wife in charge of Roksilde's manor house."

Keys clanged at Melkorka's belt. She held her head high, with dignity. She had hefty breasts and hips, while her chapped red hands revealed that even if she chased the other servants to work, she didn't do any less than them. She had a decorated dress-apron, but her hair, pulled back in a tight knot, indicated she preferred efficiency over elegance.

"And my daughter, Gyda." Her lord husband summoned a slender, red-haired girl.

"How old are you, pretty one?" Świętosława asked.

"Ten," she replied very quietly.

"You look like the king, like two peas in a pod."

"Does that mean I'm pretty, too?" Sven joked. "Come on, you can meet the rest during the feast. Let's not test Melkorka's patience. Have the pigs been roasted, hmm?"

"They'll be too dry," Melkorka said matter-of-factly, "if we force them to hang on the spit for a moment longer. I made them well, like King Harald used to like them, so if they're burned or dry out, it's not my fault."

"And if King Sven prefers dry ones, not like King Harald?" Sven asked.

The woman blushed, glancing at Świętosława's slender figure.

Together, the king and queen walked inside. The great hall wasn't any smaller than the one in Sigtuna, perhaps even a bit longer. The torchlight crawled along the carvings decorating the walls. She stared at them as they walked toward the royal seats. One mythical creature caught the next. A wolf, stretching out long paws decorated with claws, reached out toward an eagle that covered itself with wings turned inside out. The ornament of the creatures chasing one another had no beginning or end, because one beast transformed into the other. Dark and predatory, it fascinated her with its beauty. The platform was laid with animal skins, covered with a purple-red material threaded with silver. *He probably tore it off the wall of some English castle,* she thought, stepping onto it carefully. Wrzask and Zgrzyt had no scruples and lay down contentedly on the patterned material.

"Sit, my lady." Sven indicated her seat. "I want you to meet my friends, and for them to enjoy you. Melkorka and her pigs will have to be patient, as it won't do to leave the most important people in Denmark waiting."

A balding, wiry man with dark eyes stood before them.

"This is Jarl Thorgils of Jelling," Sven introduced him. "To give you an idea of how much I trust him, know that I left my country in his care while I sailed for you."

He's looking at me as if he wanted to bite me, she thought.

"And this brave man is Haakon of Funen, my lady."

A short, broad-shouldered, bearded man. A scar under his left eye— she memorized the face along with the name, smiling to all she was introduced to.

"Finally, meet Gunar of Limfiord. He, Thorgils, and Haakon are my friends of old, when we defeated the Saxons and claimed back Hedeby."

Gray hair, stubborn lips, but cheerful eyes. She nodded at Gunar of Limfiord.

Then came Ragn of the Isles, who had birdlike features, the chubby Uddorm of Viborg, the handsome Gjotgar of Scania. She already knew Stenkil of Hobro; he'd been in Sigtuna with Sven. And Skuli. Who was this Skuli? Oh, yes, Sven's bard who hadn't recited anything at her court, listening instead to the songs of Thorvald, Eric's bard.

"And now, wife, meet the lord of Ribe, Vigmar." Contrariness echoed in Sven's voice. *This is an opponent,* she thought.

"Where is Ribe?" she asked Vigmar.

"On the western shores of Jutland," the man replied, bowing his head to her.

"Close to the Saxon border," Sven added. "Why has your older brother, the reverend Bishop Oddinkarr, not accepted my invitation?"

"His health hasn't been the best, my lord," Vigmar replied stiffly. "He's asked me to convey to you and the new lady that he rejoices in your union."

"Has he sent a gift to make up for his absence?" Sven asked impudently.

Świętosława studied Vigmar and her lord husband with curiosity. She would have been happy to meet the bishop to find out something more about their conflict. The lord of Ribe looked rather disgruntled at having to participate in the celebrations. *Will my husband's enemies be my friends?* she wondered.

Arnora sat at the back of the hall, in the corner. Świętosława's eyes kept being drawn to her. A silver-haired woman with her head held high, the woman seemed completely removed from the celebration around her.

Is she clad in chains under that rich cloak? she wondered, but she knew from Sven's earlier reaction that she shouldn't ask about it. Not now.

The hall was full to the brim. Women, wives and chieftains' daughters; Wulfric with some priests; and groups of men with determined faces whose names she hadn't yet learned. Her own people were seated around the hall, dispersed, and she saw Dusza taking care of little Wilczan. *What's my son Olof doing now?* Her chest tightened at the thought.

Jorun, her husband's constant companion, stood at the foot of the platform and, lifting a large decorated horn, shouted to the gathering:

"Here we see that all the gods, the old and the new ones . . . new one," he corrected himself swiftly, "favor our king. After the infamous and victorious invasion of England, he's returned home happily, giving us and the country riches. And now the king has given us a queen, the famous Sigrid Storråda. Let's greet her warmly under our roof."

She exchanged a swift glance with Ulf. He didn't like this toast, either.

"To the king!" the guests replied to Jorun.

"To the king!"

She felt her cheeks burn. They didn't want to drink a toast to her. *They looked at her as Eric's wife, not Sven's. As if she were no more than the spoils of wars, and not their lady. Damn it! It's as if he's dragged me here in chains.*

Jorun handed Sven the great horn, and he drank from it and stood up.

"I'm honored the queen Sigrid has accepted my proposal. It's a sign that the times of war are becoming times of peace, and we all love peace! If you're bored with it, if home hearths bore you, I will lead you west or north. Let's give England a chance to rebuild itself after my last visit, and to fill her coffers . . ."

They were finally cheerful, interrupting Sven with loud laughter.

". . . the time will also come to move northward. Norway is forgetting about our old hold over her . . ."

The guests were hitting the table in glee. She felt bile rise to her throat. *So, this is how it will be, lord husband? You conquered England side by side with Tryggvason, and now you dream of defeating Olav?*

". . . my father's sister, the famous Lady Gunhild, was the queen of

Norway," Sven continued, "but since she was exiled, Denmark has lost its Norwegian fiefdom . . ."

Is he speaking of the widow Gunhild? she wondered feverishly. *The one who was behind Olav's father's death? The one who chased after his pregnant mother? Who preyed on the last heir of the Norwegian kings? Where is he going with this?*

"There is an honorable old tradition, according to which a woman changes her name when she comes to her husband's country after the wedding. I want to ask my new bride to accept the name of the Lechitic Gunhild, to remember the Danish Gunhild. In this way, we will celebrate my famous aunt as well as my new queen's homeland."

Her heart was beating quickly and unevenly. Stenkil, Thorgils, Ragn of the Isles, and Uddorm were the first to take up the chant:

"Gunhild! Gunhild!"

Over my dead body, she thought as she listened to them. Sven turned to her with a horrid, mocking smirk.

"What do you say, my lady?"

She stood up. Wrzask and Zgrzyt immediately followed suit, standing either side of her.

"Husband, lords of Denmark. Gunhild is a beautiful name," she called out in a singsong voice, and fell silent as she looked at them all. "But you mentioned, my king, that Queen Gunhild had been exiled. And I, since I've met you and since you've shown me your country on our journey here, would not want to have to leave sweet Denmark for all the riches in the world. These dark-green waters, charming rocky isles, gentle slopes of the fjords. Why, at the same moment that you've shown me such a wonderful and welcoming country, would you want to give me the name of an exiled queen?"

The silence she heard in the hall encouraged her to continue.

"I met your brave men today. Thorgils of Jelling, Uddorm of Viborg, Ragn of the Isles, Haakon of Funen, Gjotgar of Scania . . ." She nodded at each of them. "And I had the honor of hosting the noble Stenkil of Hobro in my home in Sigtuna. I suspect that your loyal comrades fought against my previous husband years ago, King Eric. Do you think it doesn't matter to them, my sweet Sven, that now at your side sits Sigrid Storråda, their old enemy's wife? My new friends, will your hearts not be happy to hear this name? It is, after all, the best proof of your victory."

They were nodding. Yes. She wielded their own weapon against them. Would she win? She turned to Sven. He looked concerned. She smiled radiantly at him.

"But it is your right, husband. If you wish it, you can call me Gunhild."

"Gunhild," he reached for her, "welcome to Denmark."

Have I lost? she thought angrily. *May the devil take you, Sven. A name is just a dress. It can be discarded at any moment.*

"Gunhild Lechitic!" Jorun shouted. "Our queen! Long live the queen!"

"Gunhild!"

"Sigrid!"

"The queen!"

She held on to the mixed shouts greedily. Sven had chosen, but his people were hesitant. She could not openly disobey him. Not now.

Sitting down next to him, she caught his eye. The redbeard was satisfied. She had no intention to give him more reasons for satisfaction by being angry.

"Don't let Melkorka wait any longer," she said. "I'm hungry."

He gave the sign and trestles were quickly brought onto the platform. A fair-haired servant covered it with golden-threaded fabric, and another, redheaded like Sven, laid the crockery. Świętosława's attention was caught by two goblets of green glass, given by the servants almost worshipfully.

"An ice cup," Sven said proudly. "A great rarity."

"A beautiful thing," she agreed, lifting it against the light. "We had many at my father's court, and carafes, too. From green and, far rarer, blue glass. Arabian merchants brought them for my father."

Sven's eyes narrowed. It made her happy, and without letting her expression change, she added:

"Yes, glass is very precious. We have a palace chapel in Poznań where my parents are buried. An entire wall of the chapel is made of glass bricks. It has a beautiful hue, you know? Like Baltic amber. What will we drink from your glass goblets?"

"Wine," he shouted.

"Your country surprises me more with every passing moment. Do you have vineyards?"

"No. But your husband knows how to get wine," he snarled.

He's volatile, she thought, as the fair-haired servant poured her wine.

"What's your name, maid?" she asked the girl.

"Vali," she replied, quite confidently.

"Thank you, Vali. That's enough."

She took a sip. The wine was sweet and strong.

Should I get drunk to handle my wedding night with redhaired Sven better? Or should I remain alert and sober?

She had two daggers with her. One in the top of her shoe, and the other, a small one, hidden on her back, under an ornamental belt of hard leather she'd put on under her dress, just over her shirt. She and Dusza had devised it as she was being dressed for the wedding. She had managed Sven well enough in Sigtuna, but here, he was at home. She must still be prepared for anything.

"Tell me about your mother, Sven," she asked when they'd brought out the food.

Melkorka's pig looked appetizing, though the meat was already cold. She helped herself to a portion out of politeness, but she only nibbled at some bread. It was fresh and crunchy.

"Beautiful, sweet Tove," Sven said with his mouth full. "She was a Slav like you, my lady."

"Mściwój's daughter, the Obotrite ruler." She remembered her conversations with Mieszko. "What was she like?"

"A mother is a saint to her son," he said, washing the meat down with wine.

Świętosława caught Melkorka's uneasy glance. She bit into the roast immediately. Cold, burned, full of fat, and so tough that she could barely swallow it. The guests seemed to have no difficulty, though. They stuffed themselves as much as they could.

"Like a wife is to a husband," she responded to his comment about Tove.

He drank from his goblet as if it were mead rather than wine; he placed it on the table, wiped his mouth with the back of his hand, and laughed.

"You jest, Sigrid. If that were the case, we'd marry our mothers."

Pig, she thought, but she noted what he'd called her with satisfaction. She didn't comment. Let him get it wrong as often as possible. She took a sip of wine. Could it be that he knew about her and Olav? Was that why he wanted to name her Gunhild? Impossible, how could he know? It was more likely that he wanted to send Tryggvason a warning, to threaten him, or at least rattle him with the memory of the bloody widow. At the thought of Sven starting a war with Olav, she felt sick. She reached for her wine. She didn't have to think about everything right now.

The feast flowed lazily. Skuli, Sven's bard, was killing them with a poem about his king, in which Sven, as a brave warrior, was referred to as the "feeder of carrion," "Thor's flame," or "the destroyer of wolves' hunger," and his sword was compared to vipers. Świętosława missed Thorvald's verses, or anything other than this arrogance.

"Do you know the 'Song of the Mighty,' Skuli, bard with the silver voice?" she called out. "I'll give you a ring if you can recite it for me."

"The whole thing, my lady?" he asked, his eyes flashing.

"Yes, the whole thing, Skuli." She laughed. "So long as my husband has nothing against that."

"Me? Of course not." Sven took the goblet from his lips. "I'm surprised that my lady, a Christan, wants to hear Odin's verses."

"Wulfric." She turned to the monk. "Are you, a priest, offended by it?"

"Of course not, my queen, what's wrong with poetry? Besides, adversae res admonent religionem."

Adversae, adversae, she repeated. *I heard this before. Where? When? Father John! That's what the good priest had been muttering with a sigh when he left the lesson he'd spent trying to teach Bolesław and his friends the catechism. "Adversity reminds men of religion," yes!*

"I agree with you, Wulfric," she exclaimed cheerfully. "So, Skuli? Will you accept my challenge?"

"'Song of the Mighty' for Queen Sigrid," the monk Ion shouted.

"Gunhild," Sven corrected him.

"Attendite a falsis prophetis," the chubby monk muttered.

"What are you saying, priest?" the king asked sharply.

Wulfric refrained from laughing and answered for Ion:

"The pious Benedictine is quoting the Holy Scriptures, King. I will be happy to help you familiarize yourself with them."

"Later." Sven swatted Wulfric away as if he were a fly. "Today is my wedding day. Wine!"

Attendite a falsis prophetis . . . Does that mean "beware of false prophets"? Świętosława tried to remember. In a matter of moments, she felt as if she were back at the feasts in Poznań. Duchess Oda knew some Latin, and had tried to show it off in front of Father John and his chaplains at every opportunity. She'd been moderately successful, and thanks to that Świętosława and Bolesław had grown somewhat familiar with the sound of the Church language. *Could I include Wulfric among my allies? Give me him, at least.*

Skuli began the long poem. For the first three verses, silence reigned in the hall, then he had to move closer to the platform as her husband's men grew bored with Odin's story and returned to talk brought on by beer, mead, and wine.

"Husband? Aren't you drinking more wine?" she asked, noticing that he pushed away fair-haired Vali when she approached him with a jug.

He smiled at her cheekily.

"And you, my lady?" He motioned at her goblet, which was still half full. "I have washed down all these celebratory rites. Wulfric, the long sermon in the church, the oaths to God or this and that. I'll be ready to go to bed before Skuli is finished with the poem. What, my beauty? Did you think I'd get drunk on my wedding night? Not likely!"

May you rot in hell, she groaned inwardly.

"Excellent. The next goblet will be shared," she said, and turned away so she didn't have to look at him.

She pretended to listen to the bard, but the only thing she heard was the terrified beat of her heart. She remembered the rabbit Zgrzyt had once caught. The animal had been alive, but it had frozen in fear when it was captured by the lynx. She sipped at her wine, and she was the rabbit held between those jaws. *No!* She interrupted the vision of fear, and pulled on the leash. Wrzask and Zgrzyt moved toward her. She placed her hands on their heads, and closed her eyes.

Skuli was making his voice heard over the noise of the feast with difficulty:

Flame begets flame until it burns out.
Fire starts another fire . . .

She recalled Eric's bard's songs about Brunhild, the Valkyrie clad in armor and surrounded by a circle of flames. She imagined armor growing out of her skin, invisible to the human eye.

"What do you think, wife?" Sven's voice reached her.

"About what? I'm sorry, the guests are celebrating too loudly, I didn't hear."

"I said that we should send Duke Bolesław the happy news of our marriage."

"Do you think my brother will be happy?" she asked coldly.

"If we are speaking honestly," he replied with that arrogant smirk, "then I think Bolesław will be furious."

"You're farsighted, husband."

"Your first marriage was aimed at me . . ."

"Don't flatter yourself," she interrupted, jutting out her chin. "It was about your father."

He burst out laughing.

"I am discovering the joys of conversation at your side. I hope to have a taste of other enjoyable things tonight."

"This changes nothing with regards to my brother, if we return to the matter at hand."

"And his fury will change nothing regarding our union. As they say: that ship has sailed. But I don't care for my brother-in-law's anger . . ."

Brother-in-law? Bolesław would hit you if he'd heard that. "I'd want you for a brother-in-law," he'd said to Olav that night, before they had swallowed the mushrooms.

". . . you know him, tell me then, wife, what would satisfy him? I want to send him a gift."

"He'd be content if you sent back his sister, untouched." She smiled innocently at him. "But it's hard for me to say what might sweeten the bitter news of our marriage . . . Is the minter you left in Sigtuna the only one you brought back from England?"

"Would you like to send your brother a minter? I see that my queen likes to give fishing rods rather than fish as presents. You impress me, wife."

"Let's come back to it in the bedchamber. And if you'd like to soothe Duke Bolesław's anger, prepare a minter for him."

Fatten the horse at home, the dog in your neighbor's yard . . .

Skuli the bard was losing his voice.
Sven stretched widely in his chair, his bones cracking.

Give no faith to a girl's words,
or those spoken by your wife.
Because women's hearts are made on a turning wheel,
Unsteadiness beats in their breasts . . .

"That's the end of the song," he shouted, so loudly that the noise in the hall quieted in an instant. "Your king is ready to fulfill his marital obligations."

"The bedding ceremony!" the fair-haired Jorun exclaimed.

"Bed-ding!" the guests chanted.

Jesus protect me! Świętosława gritted her teeth. She flexed her muscles to feel the knife under the belt on her back.

"Shhh. . . ." they hissed from below.

An old man who hadn't been introduced to her rose from his seat. A decrepit old man covered with silver.

"This is the first beeedding," he screeched, "since Kiiiing Ha-ha-ha . . ." He began to cough terribly, but everyone waited for him to finish. "Harald and Queen Toooove! Looooong liiiiiive the Helling dynasty! . . ."

"Skjoldungs!"

"Long live! Long live! Long live!" they roared in unison.

Great Ulf rose from his seat and walked toward her. Dusza too. The women exchanged glances. Dusza's eyes showed compassion, Świętosława's the fire which protected the Valkyrie Brunhild. Świętosława handed Dusza the leash. Wrzask and Zgrzyt stretched, rising from the purple-red material. Zgrzyt growled as he walked off the platform.

"Who will accompany the king to the bedchamber?" Jorun called out.

"His warriors!" the hall answered, and moved toward him. A dozen or so men pushed each other out of the way to have the honor of carrying Sven. They lifted him onto their shoulders and walked down with him.

"The king is throwing off his belt!" one of them shouted, and they pulled off the triple belt from Sven's hips.

"He doesn't need his shoes in bed!" they pulled off his long leather boots.

The women at the feast were chuckling, taking the discarded clothing as the men carried him toward his bedchamber.

"Who will carry the queen?" Jorun asked once the procession with the redbeard disappeared from view.

"I will!" Great Ulf replied in a loud voice, and, not waiting for anyone to fight him for the privilege, he picked her up.

"We will, we will, we will!" Sven's jarls from the highest table called out and moved toward them.

"Adversae res admonent religionem . . ." Wulfric called to her weakly.

Adversity teaches piety? That's what was meant to comfort her? She sat on Ulf's shoulders as if she were in the embrace of a high chair. Thorgils of Jelling reached them first. His dark eyes gleamed, and the redness in his cheeks revealed how much he'd had to drink.

"Does the queen need her shoes?" he called and looked at her.

"No, Jarl of Jelling," she replied in a sweet voice, and took them off herself. "Take my shoes and guard them. The queen will come for them in the morning."

"Yes," he murmured, clutching the shoes to his chest.

"Does the queen need her cloak?" the drunk Ragn of the Isles howled.

"No, my jarl of all small and great islands. The queen gives you her cloak with the same plea: take care of it until morning." As she spoke, she took the cloak off her shoulders and handed it to Ragn.

"Dre . . . Dre . . ." Gunar choked. He stared at her, barely conscious.

She motioned to Ulf, who set her on the table.

"Do you want my dress, Jarl of Limfiord? The jarl of many ports? The most loyal of the loyal?" she asked.

"Yeee . . . I want . . ."

"Vali!" Świętosława shouted. "Beautiful girl, come here with a knife and help your queen get undressed."

The fair-haired girl ran over.

"Don't you have a knife?" Świętosława asked with concern. "Never mind. Thorgils of Jelling, come back with my shoes. Vali, search inside them. Are you surprised?" she asked the people who surrounded her in a circle. "In the country I come from, every woman carries a dagger in her boot. Those are our traditions."

And the other one is hidden on your back when you walk into the marriage bed, she thought, gritting her teeth.

Vali took out the dagger and held it up.

"Gunar of Limfiord wants to take my dress off, but Sigrid Storråda's dresses must be removed with a knife. Vali, do as Jarl Gunar has asked."

Świętosława lifted her arms and the girl cut through the seams of the dress.

I'm wearing armor that is invisible to the human eye, Świętosława repeated as the thick silks pooled at her feet. She was left standing in a thin, translucent shirt held by a leather belt. She lifted her head up proudly and twirled.

"Does anyone else want to take something off me?" she shouted teasingly.

"Yes," Vigmar's completely drunk voice answered her. "I'd like to rip that shirt off you, my lady, but I daren't do so."

"Rightly so, since you aren't first among my husband's men. To the bedchamber, to the marriage battle, bear me, Wolf," she ordered, and Ulf quickly picked her up again.

"Queen Sigrid Storråda! Stor-rå-da!" the ones who had undressed her shouted. "Sigrid! Storråda!"

The victory was naked and bitter, but it tasted real enough.

Ulf placed her on the stone floor of the bedchamber. She felt the cold beneath her feet and shivered.

Sven, with a goblet in his hand, naked from the waist up, exclaimed:

"My lady! So, you've come to fulfill your marital duty."

"Yes, husband. I humbly ask you to accept me into your bedchamber."

She heard Ion's whisper from behind her:

"What God has joined together let no man put asunder."

And the bard's inspired voice:

"Let us now do everything with a brave heart that we have bragged about with a full cup."

The redbeard stroked his naked belly with the hand which wasn't holding a goblet.

"Come in, Gunhild," he said, cocking his head.

"Sigrid Storråda," his chieftains panted, staring at her nakedness under the spiderweb thinness of her shirt.

I'm clad in a Valkyrie's armor, she told herself, gritting her teeth and raising her arms.

"Sigrid! Storråda!" they chanted even louder.

Sven shouted furiously:

"Get out! I will be with my lady one on one!"

"Storråda," they whispered in unison, giving her courage.

46

⚜

NORWAY

Olav had no doubts, since the moment he saw the axe hanging over the pair of lovers in the rock, that he had been sent a message from his new God to turn from his chosen path. He didn't go to the place of kings' meetings of the past at Göta älv's estuary. He sent a messenger to Sigtuna to warn Świętosława: "If God allows it, we'll meet again." And he hurried northward with his troops, stopping only to let the horses rest. The white dog he'd encountered at the rock hadn't been a vision this time. It chased after them.

He met with his mother and Lodin in Viken, but only for the short time it took to prepare the ships, and not a day longer.

"Your men under Varin's command have carried out your orders," Lodin told him. "They are going from settlement to settlement, calling all those free to come to Gula for the council. It seems you had the right idea: the people are eager to finally see you, to know you and find out whether you truly are as great as the legends that speak of you."

"Remind me, what's the wealthiest of those men called?"

"Olm, King."

"Olm," Olav repeated the name of the man who must be the first to realize the legends were true. "Lodin, prepare your family for the journey. My sisters, Ingebjorg and Astrid, and your daughters, Ingireda and Ingigerda. Your son, Torkil, is an agile young man, let him be responsible for your safety on the road. I expect my mother to accompany you. Come to Gula. There is no need to rush, the council will be held in spring. I want to see you all there, as my family."

"What do you plan to do until then?" Lodin asked uneasily.

"I will sail to the entrance of Hafrsfiord with my fleet," Olav replied, looking in his stepfather's eyes. "I will remind everyone how Harald Fairhaired, my great-grandfather, began his reign."

Lodin stroked his smooth chin and gave a small nod.

"If you've thought this through, Olav, then all I'll say is that you don't lack courage. To face the people of the western counties and say: here, over one hundred years ago, my ancestor destroyed yours—"

"It could be understood differently, Lodin," Olav interrupted. "Accept my reign, because I want to unify the country."

"Do you know what the result was of that 'unification of the country'? Fleeing and exiles. Fairhaired allowed no place in the country for those who thought differently than he did."

Olav shrugged.

"Don't be naïve, Lodin. There can be no strong rule without the putting down of opponents."

His mother's husband retreated. "Perhaps you're right. Our country was only ever unified under Fairhaired. Only at what price?"

"My cause is right. And I have something my great-grandfather didn't. I have the true faith."

Lodin sighed heavily. If he had any doubts, he had hidden them since Bishop Sivrit had baptized him and the rest of the family. Just before Olav left, when he was already in the saddle, Lodin approached him, humbly took his stirrup, and whispered:

"I beg you, for your mother's sake, the woman we both love. Don't force those who refuse to accept the faith to flee the country, as your great-grandfather forced those who disagreed with him. King Olav, you yourself have been an exile, and your faith is based on mercy . . ."

"My faith?" Olav repeated after Lodin. "Or ours?"

Olav said nothing more, setting off toward the docks. The white dog didn't leave him for a moment.

The warm ocean currents meant that even in winter, the southwestern shores of Norway were rarely covered in snow. Olav ordered thirty ships be arranged in a line, with their sails up, so as to be visible from land. People soon gathered on the rocks, looking at them, unsettled. Eventually, in the afternoon, a small boat approached them with a piece of white fabric mounted on the mast.

"Who are you and what do you want from us?" the helmsman asked.

"Who asks?" Olav shouted back.

"Lord Erling Skjalgsson of Sol, to whom most of these lands belong."

"Tell your master that Olav Tryggvason, the rightful heir, has returned home."

"In that case, my lord invites King Olav to his court," the helmsman called out.

"No, King Olav invites his master to the council in Gula."

"So you will not attack us?" the messenger asked.

"Tell your lord that my intentions are peaceful."

The helmsman spoke with two older men sitting with him in the boat for a moment. They clearly weren't sure how to proceed.

"I want to celebrate the memory of my great-grandfather, Harald Fairhaired, and the place where he defeated the unsubmissive."

Olav arrived in Gula long before the council. He had some of the ships come into the docks, and he left the other half at the anchor point. They looked excellent, like an army, identically dressed, because, once they had taken down their sails, they each raised a flag with a silver snake on a purple-red background. The Yngling snake. He'd asked his mother and sisters to make the banners before he'd sailed to Świętosława. He returned from Sigtuna without his beloved, but the women who loved him unconditionally had done as he'd asked. Thirty snakes fluttered on the masts of the ships at Sognefiord's entrance. Olav set up a large camp around Gula and joined his forces with Varin's, which had come by land from the south.

Varin only had to look at Olav to know what had happened on his journey, but Omold the bard couldn't refrain from adding:

"And so it happened. Our king has come without Queen Storråda. But he has brought a dog."

The pale-eyed and cool Bishop Sivrit summarized it rather differently:

"That was the will of the Lord."

Olav met with his "sleeping guards" privately, the men he'd stationed in the country for the time he'd been in England. There wasn't a day that messengers from one of the local lords didn't come to ask if it was truly him, inviting him to their masters' houses. He declined these invitations the same way he'd declined Erling of Sol's, saying, "I invite everyone to the council."

"They say that Sognefiord is the most beautiful place in Norway," Varin said. "My mother's mother was apparently from Sogn."

"Let's take a boat and see how much truth there is in that, friend," Olav suggested.

The dog jumped on board first. They left the bard on shore, so they wouldn't have to hear him speaking grandly of all he saw and could simply take in the view as it was. The boat had three sets of oars, and was boarded by Lodver, Ingvar, Orm, Eyvind, Rafn, Varin, and Olav. A delicate, early spring breeze pushed it along. Varin stood by the helm with the dog beside him.

"This dog is strange, my king. I haven't heard it bark yet."

"It barked once," Olav replied. "In greeting. It isn't strange, it's extraordinary. I feel as if I've known it its whole life."

"The hound's within you, little Ole. Wake it up."

"What now, King?" Rafn, who the people now called God's Axe, asked. "Will we fight or be baptized?"

"Rafn was bored without you, chief." Ingvar spat into the water. "He sharpened his blade every day."

"He could shave with it," Orm added.

"He should," Lodver interjected. "If he could see how poor his overgrown mug looks."

"Each one of you is to shave and dress well before we walk into the council. I want them to look at you and say, 'Olav's men look honorable.'"

"Will women be there?" Lodver couldn't help but ask.

"Not at the council, but in the inns and camps of the lords of the western lands, yes. But I warn you, you're to behave in such a way as to bring me no shame."

"That means how?" Rafn asked.

"I want the people to be afraid of you, while also wanting to be like you."

For a moment, there was no sound other than the even splash of oars in water. Olav watched the huge mountains, wet from the spring sun. High on the mountain passes a phenomenal white snow lay, but the bushes on the sunny sides had already begun to turn green. They sailed over emerald waters. Varin sighed longingly.

"Oh, to have some land here. Build a house, bring a woman under its roof . . ."

"Not just yet, friend, not just yet," Olav interrupted the dream, though he had just been thinking himself that he'd love to show all this beauty to a certain woman. "We have a long road ahead of us. The council at Gula comes first, in a few days. Then we must face Frostating in Trøndelag,

Jarl Haakon's old place. When both gatherings accept me, when I convince the people to accept the faith throughout the entire country, then we can rest."

"Hmm," Orm said to the helmsman. "The woman you bring under your roof will be old by then."

"That doesn't matter," Varin replied, though the longing could still be heard in his voice. "I swore my oaths to the king, not the woman."

A large island soon came into sight to their right. The dog lifted its head, sniffing. It turned to Olav, looking at him, and then back to the island.

"Is the dog speaking to you, King?" Varin asked, surprised.

"Head toward the island," Olav said.

When the boat began to move toward the shore, the dog wagged its tail.

"It speaks!"

They came to a small dock hidden between two rocks. The white dog leapt quietly onto the shore and ran into the bushes.

"What in the devil's name . . . ?" Orm snarled.

"Don't call on evil," Olav reprimanded him. "It wants to lead us somewhere."

"Six grown men, conquerers of English gold, listening to a dog," Orm, who stayed to keep watch over the boat, said to himself with resignation.

Olav followed the direction the dog had gone. It wasn't long before he heard it barking. He couldn't believe his ears. Until now, the dog really had only made a sound once.

"Vigi," someone shouted. "Where've you been?"

"My lord . . ." Varin touched Olav's shoulder. "The dog may have led us into a trap. I told you it was strange."

They peered carefully between the trees. They saw a poorly dressed peasant in a large field, with a staff in his hand and a herd of sheep searching for the first spring grass. The dog was prancing around them, as if it had been a sheepdog all its life, and the man was talking to it. "Tell me, Vigi? Where have you been for so long?"

Olav clapped Varin on the shoulder and laughed.

"It's brought us to its home."

They emerged from the bushes, but Varin kept his hand on the hilt of his knife.

"My good man," Olav called to the peasant. "Is this your dog?"

The man hunched in and crossed himself when he saw them. This piqued

Tryggvason's curiosity even more. He made the sign of the cross and shouted as he approached, "Don't be afraid, we come in peace. And, as you can see, we believe in the Only God, as you do."

"My lord." The pale man bowed. "Forgive me, but I'd sooner believe that flowers will bloom in the dead of winter than that a wealthy man who greets me with the sign of the cross comes to my island in peace. Are you a vision?" The man waved a hand in front of his own eyes. "No . . . you're not."

The dog ran back toward Olav and rubbed itself against his legs.

"Is it your dog?" Tryggvason asked again.

"Mine, my lord. It disappeared in autumn and only just returned, as if it knew it was high time to let the sheep out to graze. It's a strange dog, and this wasn't the first time it had disappeared . . ."

Olav and Varin exchanged glances.

"Are you real, my lord?" the man asked again, staring at the silver cross on Olav's neck.

"Touch me," Olav suggested, "and see for yourself."

The peasant reached out a trembling hand and lightly touched Olav's chest. He pulled back quickly and crossed himself again, this time with relief.

"Praise the Lord!"

"This dog brought us here," Olav said.

"I said, it's a strange animal," the man nodded.

"But I met it very far from here. In the south of the country."

"Vigi, you vagabond!" The man tugged fondly at the dog's ears.

"You call him Vigi, is that right?"

When Olav said its name, the dog leapt up and caught the gold band on Olav's wrist in his teeth, pulling gently.

"Would you be willing to give me your dog?" he asked, taking off the bracelet. "I will pay you."

The peasant flushed when he saw the gold Olav held out to him.

"My lord, I am not worthy . . ." he whispered. "That's gold . . . it's too much . . ."

"I think Vigi is worth it," Olav replied, knowing that he'd pay even more to ensure he didn't have to separate from the white dog. *The hound's within you, little Ole.*

"I . . . I . . ." the surprised man stuttered.

Vigi took the gold bracelet between his teeth and handed it to the man, as if it were conducting the transaction.

When they returned to the boat, Orm was waiting. "And?"

Varin filled him in. "The dog's name is Vigi, and it cost as much as a good ship, although before it became worth as much as treasure itself, it had been a simple sheepdog."

"That's not true," Olav disagreed, stroking the white head. "The old owner said it had always been an extraordinary dog."

Olav found Halvard and his twin brothers, Bersi and Duri, waiting for him when he returned to camp. He hadn't seen them since Halvard had been injured on the small island, where the old man had taken Olav through a field of stone spirals and spoken to him of the gods.

"Ah, King!" They knelt in front of him. "Our dreams have come true. You have come to our land."

"Because we are . . ."

". . . from here. We were. . . .

". . . born here . . ."

". . . and we want to. . . ."

". . . by you, King . . ."

". . . be baptized! . . ."

Yes, this worked well for him. To baptize the locals and encourage others to accept the faith. But they had to wait for the council.

"My bishop will prepare you for the sacrament," he said, ordering them to stand.

"We have already . . ."

". . . been preparing somewhat . . ." the twins said, pointing at the large crosses on their chests.

". . . trophy . . ."

"These are large crosses, to hang on the wall. You wear smaller ones on your neck," he said, muffling his laughter.

The stocky twins, almost in synchrony, put their hands under their caftans and pulled out a small cross each.

"Like these?" they asked in unison.

"Like these. I'll be your godfather," he promised them, and before he could stop them, they'd both leaned down and kissed his hand.

"Halvard," he called to the eldest brother. "I want to speak to you privately."

"It's an honor, King."

"I need a good hideout in Sogn. Not for myself," he added, since Halvard's face indicated he was ready to surrender his house immediately, "but for the silver."

"I understand." He nodded. "We have plenty of those here. You know yourself, my lord, what Sogn is known for. It's beautiful, but poor. Our people have for years . . ."

Harald Fairhaired made it better, Olav thought. *But when his time came, your people once again had to struggle with ordinary sea robbery. Attacks on merchants, forcing tolls and ransoms, straightforward piracy. Mercenaries from Sogn have had a bad reputation for years.* But that's exactly the kind of people he needed to safely hide part of the English silver.

"These crosses . . ." he asked Halvard after a moment. "Where did you get them from?"

"Ah, Scania, King." Halvard took the cross between two fingers and examined it. "But they look like English work. Anyone who could sailed to King Sven's wedding, and one of the merchants left a few chests in a badly guarded house, so we made the most of it, if I can express it in a roundabout way."

"Sven's wedding?" Olav repeated. "King of Denmark?"

"And Queen Sigrid's from Sweden. A great thing."

Olav felt as if someone had buried a dagger in his back.

"When?" he asked, barely containing the tremor in his voice.

"In autumn. Apparently, the king and queen were chased by a storm all the way from Sigtuna to Roskilde. So they say, but we didn't stumble across any storms."

I was the one who sailed to her in a storm!

Vigi touched his hand with a moist nose. Ah, white dog. Olav pushed it away. You dragged me away from my journey to Göta älv's estuary. She'd sent me a falcon!

"King?" Halvard asked, concerned. "Are you all right?"

They stood alone, in the shadows on the edge of the camp, far away from burning fires.

"Do you have mead?" Olav asked hoarsely. "I need a drink."

"I do, my lord. Maybe you'd like to sit?" He took off his cloak and threw it over a rock.

Olav sat down and took a long swallow from the pouch Halvard passed him.

"What do you know of this wedding? Tell me."

"Well, only what people said. How much truth and how much fancy there is in that . . ."

"Tell me," he commanded. "Everything you heard."

"Sven arrived . . . some say with two hundred ships, some a hundred. The queen sailed out to meet him, but she only had a few ships. Apparently, she offered him her hand herself, and he agreed."

The night in Bamburgh's stronghold. The drunken fight with Sven. *You take the kingdom, I'll take the queen. You sail for Sigtuna, I'll go for Sigrid.* Yes, he'd said that, completely drunk. Then they both pretended those words had never been spoken. Bloody Sven! He waited for the right moment and he took her. One hundred ships. He'd threatened her.

"And the young king?"

"He stayed in Sweden, and is called Olof King of Swedes. I don't know anything else."

47

Olav Tryggvason invited Bishop Sivrit to his tent that night. Varin was with them, but no one else.

"This isn't a personal matter, my lord," Sivrit said of recent events. "Even if King Sven had known about your feelings for this lady, and even if he received a message that you'd been to see her first."

"And I think," Varin said darkly, "that it's exactly the opposite. Sven has always competed with King Olav. My lord! Why didn't you threaten Queen Sigrid? You should have taken her by force!"

"This marriage has destroyed the balance." Sivrit didn't raise his voice, nevertheless it seemed as if every sentence sliced through Olav. "Denmark and Sweden are stronger than the lone Norway."

"You both speak the truth, though neither of you hit the bull's eye," Olav finally spoke. "Sven did, though. He's hurt my pride, and now he waits for me to respond with something equally hot-tempered and personal. Perhaps he expects me to halt my march for the crown, turn around, and start a war with him. I think that is the main reason for his blow: to stop me from uniting the country. I won't meet his expectations. I won't turn around, because now I have no choice. You spoke truly, Bishop: two countries are stronger than one. But one can still stand up to two if it's strong enough."

"King Ethelred could aid you, Olav. It's in his interests to weaken Sven," the bishop said.

"I won't accept foreign help, Sivrit."

"As I thought." The priest nodded. "Pray that God helps you, then."

Olav prayed until he finally fell asleep, exhausted, and it wasn't God he dreamed of, but her. Naked, burning with love, shouting in bliss. *It has been done,* he thought, pouring cold water over his head. *You are at my enemy's side, whether by choice or not.*

* * *

The day was crisp and clear; the spring sun shone, the birds called to each other in the air. The council square was full of people. The wealthiest men of these parts had come with their squads and chieftains: Olm and his brother, Thorleif the Wise. Their relative, Erling Skjalgsson of Sol. They parted when Olav walked between them, with Varin in front, carrying the purple-red banner with the Yngling snake. Bishop Sivrit walked on his right, his mother, Astrid, on his left. Lodin, his four sisters, and his half brother followed. Then, *Kanugård*'s crew.

"My name is Olav Tryggvason," he said when he stood in the center. "You may still remember my mother, Astrid. Some of you may have helped her escape from the widow Gunhild's executioners years ago. If you didn't side with her, I don't blame you. The widow's reign, and those of her sons, were a dark time of civil war. I have come back to you, the rightful heir, and I bring you gifts: a united kingdom, and the Good Word. You can accept both, or reject both."

"The Yngling's return is a good word," Thorleif the Wise said thoughtfully. "But we've heard other news that worries us. They say you've been baptized, my lord, and that you intend to force us to abandon the faith of our fathers."

"I don't want to force you to do anything, I want you to give it up voluntarily. Like those who are with me, and all of Viken, my father's family land, which has been baptized."

A murmur of discontent passed through the crowd.

"If any one of you has something against Christ, let him speak now," he called out, and looked to the bishop. Sivrit nodded, as if to say "I'm ready."

A powerfully built man stepped forward from among Olm's men.

"Christ and his mother called Mary," he began in a confident voice, and then stopped, as if he'd choked. He moved his lips, reddened, and snorted. Someone gave him a horn filled with mead. The man drank it and began coughing properly. He waved a hand and moved back to his place. The crowd murmured, surprised. Another man stepped forward, this one much older than the first.

"I'll speak. We would like to accept you, King, because although your great-grandfather's reign was strict, it was fair. We didn't pay a tribute to the Danes, and our country was united from the southern shores to the northern lights. Riches and fame were with us. But your great-grandfather shared our faith, and Christ is . . ."

The old man moved his lips, but no sound came out. Someone in the crowd burst out laughing. Embarrassed, the man moved back to the place he'd stepped out of.

Olav cast a secret glance at Sivrit. The bishop's pale cheeks were now red. His eyes were shining, as if he had a fever. "I'll be beside you when you face the people," he'd said the previous night. "And God will be with us both. Your opponents will be lost for words, they won't be able to slander Him. The Almighty knows how to give compelling signs."

"Is there anything else you'd like to say?" Olav asked.

"Was that some sort of magic, King?" Olm asked defiantly.

"No. The God I bring you views magic and charms with contempt."

"How is it possible that a great warrior like you, my lord," Olm continued, "prefers to believe a god who was killed than in warrior gods like Odin and Thor? They say your god died on a cross."

"Don't pay heed to nonsense, Olm, you're too wise a man for that," Olav replied cheerfully. "Christ didn't die, but He allowed himself to be crucified as a sacrifice to save humanity. His godliness isn't in His death, but in His resurrection. Christ promises to raise us from the dead, too, when the Day of Judgment arrives."

"Ragnarök?" someone asked curiously.

"No, brother," Olav replied. "Ragnarök is the end of the world of the old gods. It's supposedly the battle that is meant to be fought. The battle in which both men and gods shall die. The final destruction. But the Day of Judgment that Christ will call us to is a moment of truth in which He will weigh our good and our bad deeds, and decide whether we should be rewarded or punished. Each of us has a choice. If we follow the path of His teachings, then He will sit us on his right side on the Day of Judgment, and give us eternal life rather than the darkness of extermination."

"It isn't honorable to abandon our ancestors' faith," a gray-haired, red-cheeked man replied with conviction.

"Who was your father?" Olav asked.

"A good sailor."

"And he never made a mistake, not once in his life?"

"There are no perfect people," the other answered evasively.

"Exactly. Our ancestors may have been wrong, because they hadn't heard of Christ's teachings. We must be wiser."

"You speak wisely, Olav Tryggvason," Olm told him. "And everyone here has seen that whenever someone in your presence attempts to speak against the god you want to give us, they lose their voice. You say it is not magic. I'm a simple man, and I think it is magic. Are there any men among us that you have converted successfully?"

Bersi and Duri, the twin brothers, and Halvard stepped forward confidently.

"Us," they said. "We want to be baptized."

"Hrafn's nephews," a whisper traveled through the gathering. "Impossible . . ."

"The waters of baptism are not mead that you can drink, though I assure you that its acceptance is equally sweet." Olav invited them to his procession with a single gesture.

Olm, clearly shaken, asked for a break. He conducted a stormy conversation with his relatives.

"They're yours," Sivrit whispered to Olav.

Olm gave a sign after a moment that they had finished.

"My lord, what choice do you give us?"

"The most important choice of all. Life or death," Olav answered without a smile.

"That's not a choice," Olm protested.

"Why not?"

"Becauuse nobody wants to choose death."

"Then choosing life, you choose it twice over. An honorable life here on earth, and an even greater one after death."

"You conquer us with your persuasiveness without even drawing your sword." Olm spread his arms. "But before we accept this immortal life that you promise, allow us to enjoy our earthly one. We will accept you as our king, and your faith, too, but you need to give us proof of your good faith, and invite us into your royal family."

"They're yours." This time it was Varin who whispered.

"You have sisters, my lord," Olm continued. "Marry them to our sons and we will be connected by blood."

And the most important one of you has no wife yet. You're mine, he thought, and said:

"One son may marry one of my sisters, as I have only four, and I have told you already I want to unite the entire country. Each one will be married in the lands of one council: Gula, Frosta, Eidsiva, and Borg. This is how I will unite Norway through family. Introduce me to my future brother-in-law."

This time, he heard murmuring behind his back. One of the girls sobbed quietly. Young Erling of Sol stepped forward. The sleeping guards had made accurate guesses, Olav thought. Waiting with our sails billowing at Erling's gates has borne its fruit. He turned to his sisters. He saw that Ingebjorg was pale and her eyes were red from tears, and the youngest, Ingigerda, was making eyes at Erling. *Forgive me, sister, but it's not for royalty to marry for love.* He imagined his bold one standing among them for a moment—his love, his queen. But it was not to be.

"Astrid, come here." He reached out to the eldest. "Meet Erling, the son of Skjalge of Sol. Here is your husband."

The spring council in Gula ended, and he had six months before the next one in Lade. The wedding celebrations and the western lords' baptisms took an entire month. The news of his reign was spreading fast; he decided to travel inland, east, and seek support there before winter came to the nest of the northern lords.

"The sister Astrid has stayed with her husband, and likely you will soon have a nephew, King." Omold the bard caught up with him. "Gula council has accepted your sovereignty, and there was no work for Rafn's axe. All has gone well. Maybe God's Axe won't be needed again after all, King?"

Rafn, riding in front of them, looked around and touched the polished blade on his back. Olav left them and rode up to his mother. She looked at him darkly.

"Thank you for accepting my invitation," he told her. Earlier, his mother had insisted she would stay in Sol with Astrid and her son-in-law.

The hood had slipped from her head; fair hair, with occasional strands of silver, flew in the wind.

"I didn't do it for you, son, but for my daughters, and your sisters," she said sharply. "Astrid and Ingebjorg were small children when I had to leave them to my brothers and escape from Gunhild with you in my belly. They grew up without me. Each day, two small girls climbed the hill behind the settlement and watched the east road, waiting for their mother and brother to return." She swept her hair from her face. A vertical line cut along her forehead. "When Lodin bought me out of slavery and married me, I found my daughters. I swore that I would never leave them again. I told them about you, how brave you were when the headhunters found us. Ingebjorg and Astrid cried at that story, and I hugged them and said: one day our little Ole will return. When mine and Lodin's children were born, your sisters helped me take care of the little ones. They'd tell their sisters: When our brother Olav returns . . . And finally, our dreams and prayers came true. You came. A wonderful strong warrior, the son-in-law to the great duke of

Poland. You were like a young god to them, they adored you. But since you sailed to England, everything changed. You returned a ruler. You say us but you think I."

"The kingdom requires sacrifice," he replied to Astrid, looking at the blue mountains rising in the distance.

"But I'm not speaking of the kingdom," she interrupted him. "I'm speaking of our family. And do you know what I think? We've had to sacrifice enough already. I don't want any more. I lost Tryggve, my husband and your father, and the most beautiful years of my youth. Now, I want a good, ordinary life for each of my children."

His mother wrapped the head scarf around herself more tightly; she looked at him with a plea in her eyes.

"Ingebjorg has someone in Viken. Don't force her to marry."

"A king's sisters cannot marry just anyone," he replied as calmly as he could. "Their marriage could mean war or peace. Ingebjorg . . ."

"We've all accepted your faith," his mother interjected impatiently. "Do you know why? Because it promises us a life together after death. Not separately, where our beloved men go to Valhalla to do the same thing they did on earth, to wage war and to fight. Christ says that in the heavens, we will be together for all eternity. But today I can see that if we argue here, on earth, then that eternity together will be unbearable."

"I don't want to argue with you," he said gently. "I only want . . ."

"You want us to do your bidding," she finished.

She shook her head and moved away from him, and for the remainder of the journey she avoided him.

Two brothers ruled the lands east of the shore, Hyrning and Thorgeir. Their welcome to the king was a rebellion against him. Olav sent his troops ahead with the message, "Life or death." They chose to fight; it was short, bloody, and convincing. When he asked them a second time what they preferred, life or death, they asked to be baptized. They swore oaths of fealty to their Lord in the heavens and their king on earth. Olav gave them his half sisters to wed, Ingireda and Ingigerda. Ingebjorg remained unmarried and stopped hiding her red eyes under a hood drawn low over her face.

When they set off for Lade in autumn, his mother came to him and asked:

"Can Ingebjorg and I return home?"

"I haven't finished asserting my rule, Mother."

"You've conquered the south. The west and east have also bowed before you. Your father was only the ruler of Viken . . ."

She isn't proud of me, he thought. *She wishes I were like him.*

"Exactly. Tryggve was only the ruler of Viken, one part of a separated country. Don't you understand that the world has changed? That the weak have no chance today? I bring three inseparable gifts to this country: independence, unity, and faith. None of them can exist alone."

Astrid narrowed her eyes, and he watched a network of wrinkles spread around them like a spiderweb.

"I only understand that it's never enough for you," she said.

Where is the woman who yelled at me in my dreams to never forget who I am?

"We go to Lade tomorrow. That's where the country's true heart beats. If you're tired of the journey, Mother, have a wagon prepared for you."

His spies had warned him. Jarl Haakon, murdered by his slave half a year before, had not been forgotten in Lade. His sons, Eric and Sven, had fled from the country before Olav's triumphant pilgrimage, but the families who'd thrived under the old, proud jarl did not hide their opposition to the return of Tryggve's son.

"They're not used to a strong royal ruler," Bishop Sivrit said, as they sailed north on *Kanugård*. "They will probably not give in as easily as the others. No one likes to lose influence."

"My father-in-law, Duke Mieszko, told me once how he introduced the faith in his country," Olav replied, recalling the duke's proud figure, a hawk on his shoulder. "He didn't make any arrangements with the priests of the old gods, he never gave them a choice. He simply killed them, one by one, discreetly. None of his subjects saw the deaths, or even the corpses. It was as if they'd disappeared, making space for Christ. In reality, the duke was behind their disappearance, and he said it was better to kill those few men in order to stop the bloodshed which would have followed an open rebellion."

"Did King Ethelred tell you the story of your King Haakon?" the bishop asked.

"The good, educated king that was a Christian and made deals with a pagan people? Yes, but that story doesn't end well. For some reason, good kings meet bad ends, usually while they're still young."

"There was a priest of Odin in a temple in Lade in King Haakon's day who had a vision. He saw in it that the time of the White Christ was coming, and that the old gods had agreed to leave in peace."

"Really?" Olav said with surprise. "What happened then?"

"He announced this vision, making the Christian king happy. But not the northern lords. The priest was found dead, with a slit throat. I don't need to tell you that a legend was created about the old gods' revenge." It seemed as if Sivrit was smiling, though no muscle moved on his face. "In that way, years of King Haakon's good work were wasted. Your father-in-law wasn't wrong. Some matters are best dealt with in silence, without letting everyone have a voice."

Yes, Mieszko was right, but his nobles had been unquestionably loyal to him. And I'm faced with the disobedient in Lade, and likely his troops, too.

"It's better to sacrifice a few than to allow a war in which hundreds will perish." Sivrit nodded.

"Has the minter prepared a design?" Olav changed the subject.

"Yes, my lord. He's promised that the denar will be ready in Lade."

They waited for him in a council square that had been cleared of snow. Eight jarls, and behind each of them, their troops and men. The northern lords, dressed in polar bear and wolf skins. The nobles whose families had benefited for generations from the trade of walrus fangs, whale and seal skins, furs of mammals, and the feathers of wild ducks. Many of those gathered looked as if the blood of the mythical giants flowed in their veins. Olav walked among them and said what he had at the three council meetings before this one:

"My name is Olav Tryggvason. I am your king, the last heir of the Ynglings."

Styrkar, Asbjorn Selsbane, Orm, Maldor, Kar, Halldor, Karlshofud, and Hoskuld all stepped forward separately to give him their names and families. None bowed. Finally, the ninth man stepped forward and said:

"I'm Skegge, and I carry out the rites in Odin's temple."

Olav replied:

"Meet Sivrit, my bishop."

The council looked at Sivrit curiously, though they didn't hide their distaste. Sivrit, in a simple dark cloak, with a cleanly shaven head and pale, ruthless eyes, returned their stares.

"We're curious to hear what you have to offer us, King," Skegge said defiantly.

"A king's peace," Olav replied.

"We've heard that you bring it using a sword. You force people to accept your god," Maldor spoke angrily.

"That's not true. Baptism can only be accepted voluntarily."

They began to mutter. Names of those who had fallen under Rafn's axe were mentioned. Olav silenced them with a hand gesture.

"It is a king's duty to pass judgment, to reward the good and punish evil.

That is what I do. It is the privilege of a king to feast with his chieftains. Tomorrow, Yule begins, so allow me to invite you to a feast. I want you to eat and drink with me, there will be time to discuss important things over a cup of mead. I will try to convince you, you'll try to convince me, and we will reach a compromise. I've rented a small inn near Lade, because I swore I would not walk into Jarl Haakon's house until your council names me their king. I invite you, lords of the north, to a feast."

The inn truly wasn't large, it could fit twenty people at most, and its asset was a large stock of mead, arranged in huge barrels along the walls. Olav paid up front for them all. Because of the limited room, he invited only the northern lords inside, and had fires lit outside for their people, with spits arranged over them all on which young boars and rams were roasted. Beer and mead stood near the fires in large vats. Olav raised a toast in the yard first, with everyone.

"To good fortune!"

"To good fortune!" they replied, in a hurry to get to the food and drink.

Styrkar, Asbjorn Selsbane, Orm, Maldor, Kar, Halldor, Karlshofud, and Hoskuld walked inside, where tables sagging under the weight of food awaited them. A silver denar with the phrase ONLAF REX NOR waited by each seat.

"King Olav knows how to make a generous gesture," Asbjorn muttered, taking off his bear fur and hanging his belt up on a peg. "Is this a gift?" He looked at the denar longingly.

"Yes." Olav nodded. "It's a gift."

I cut off the minter's hand because he spelled my name wrong on the stamp, he thought with distaste.

At first, Olav ordered the door be left open so that the lords could watch their men enjoy themselves, but as the evening wore on, the noise and laughter from the fires were so loud that they couldn't talk properly indoors. Maldor himself closed the door, though even then they could hear the drunken shouts. The guests drank mead, goblet after goblet, but they said nothing. They stared at Olav greedily.

"Why has Skegge not come with you?" Olav asked. The priest of Odin was not among those feasting and drinking in the inn.

"He's sharpening Thor's axe before the king's visit." Asbjorn chuckled, examining the denar.

Styrkar picked a piece of meat out from between his teeth and smiled lopsidedly.

"Skegge is waiting for us in Odin's temple, my lord. He said that if we reach an agreement with you, we should bring you to him and he'll put horse blood on you, as old traditions demand."

"Then, we will all acknowledge you as our king." Orm bared his teeth.

"I see," Olav replied, then nodded to Omold to fill his guests' goblets again.

They drank with satisfaction.

"Then you've already decided what the conclusion of our talks will be," Olav observed. "Well." He spread out his arms. "All that's left is for me to get properly drunk, then, otherwise I won't be able to stomach that horse blood."

The northern lords laughed in unison. He gritted his teeth.

"Varin," he called out. "Get some more barrels; your king is going to drink."

"Pour us some, berserker," Asbjorn called out, but then his smile froze on his lips.

Olav's men, armed to the teeth, leapt from the barrels. The ones who had scaled Bamburgh's walls with him. Omold stood behind Asbjorn, the bard as skillful with a blade as he was with a song; Rafn God's Axe was behind Maldor, Eyvind behind Orm, Ingvar behind Kar, and Thorolf behind Styrkar. Each of the northern lords had a knife at his neck.

"It was foolish of you," Olav said coldly, "deciding the conclusion of negotiations before they've even begun. I'll be merciful, though, and I will let you choose."

"Between what?" Asbjorn, held by the bard, choked out.

"Death or baptism," Olav replied cheerfully. "I've already told you that one must accept baptism voluntarily."

"That's not a choice!" Kar roared, reddening in Ingvar's embrace.

"Why not?" Olav asked, surprised. "You've watched death many times, each one of you has dealt it out in war. You know what it is. And baptism? Why are you afraid of it if it's the gate to life after death?"

"King," Varin called. "Do you want me to open the door? Do you want the men of the northern lords to see them make their choice?"

"No," Maldor snarled. "I've already chosen. You've convinced me, King, that your god is strong, if he's pushed you to such lengths."

"Let him go, Rafn," Olav said. "I want him to swear his oath to me without a knife at his throat."

"Let me go, too," Styrkar added calmly. "I've chosen what I want. Nobody will be forcing me."

One by one, they agreed to his terms. That's when Varin opened the door and called to those celebrating to come and be witnesses to the oaths of fealty. The eight northern lords knelt before Olav and place their swords at his feet.

"Let us rejoice," Olav shouted. "And let's go tell Skegge the good news. He's been waiting for us in the temple for too long."

Those who had been feasting outside joined them, cheerful, tipsy, completely unaware of what had happened before the oaths of fealty they witnessed had been given. Olav knew that this was the most difficult part of the night. His men were watching, and troops under Lodin's command should already be waiting around the temple in the shadows. So long as his mother's husband didn't fail. Today would be the day he'd find out how much Lodin's loyalty was worth.

Skegge, tall and proud, stepped out to meet them.

"Have you brought your chosen one?" Skegge asked.

"Yes," Maldor said, and Olav heard his voice shake.

"I want to find out whether the gods you serve are stronger than Christ," Olav called out loudly enough for everyone to hear him.

"Then leave your weapons here and step into the temple." Skegge's eyes gleamed.

Olav unbuckled his belt and gave it to Varin. His friend held his hand for a moment and whispered:

"I believe in you, Olav the almighty."

Tryggvason stepped over the threshold, guided by the priest. Skegge closed the door behind them. Olav's eyes needed a moment to adjust to the darkness inside. Then, he saw the statues. A great iron axe lay over the wooden Thor's knees. *Let it be true that it's sharp.* Skegge leaned over the rack by the fire and stirred the contents of the pot which hung over the flames. The odor of horse blood permeated the small space. Then, suddenly, Olav sprang toward Thor's statue, grabbed the great axe it held, and, before Skegge could shout out, struck the warrior god's chest with it. The wood broke in two, cracking under the blade, falling to the ground.

"How dare you?" Skegge exclaimed and, jumping away from the fire, spilled the boiling blood.

Olav ran to him, grabbing him by his caftan.

"So, priest. Your Thor has fallen," he hissed into his face. "What will you tell your people now? That the Thunder Lord was a wooden puppet? Why hasn't he hit me with lightning if he has power?"

"How dare you?" Skegge repeated.

"Man is stronger than the gods you boil blood for." He pushed him toward the solid wooden bench in front of Odin's statue. "If you believe in what you tell the people, I give you the most honorable death."

Skegge tried to get up and hide under the bench, but Tryggvason pulled him out from under it and threw him on top. He swung the axe, cleaving the priest's chest. Blood splattered from the wound and onto Olav's face. Skegge had no time to shout, he died with his mouth open. Olav cut down the statues of one-eyed Odin and old Tyr, and then, hammer in hand, moved toward the doors, where a great golden ring hung. The famous gift from Jarl Haakon for a victorious battle against the Jomsvikings, he recalled, and took it off. He weighed it in his hand as he pushed the door open.

The crowd who had followed him to the temple still waited outside. The eight northern lords stared at him, at the axe by his leg and the blood on his face. Behind them were the people of Lade. His people. He lifted the ring he'd taken from the door and threw it onto a stump of wood. He hit it with the axe. The ring split.

I knew it, he thought.

The ones who stood closest had also now noticed the fake gold. The gold plating had crumbled off the iron ring.

"Jarl Haakon gave your gods a false sacrifice, but that doesn't matter. None of the old gods has survived a meeting with mine," he said calmly, and threw the ritual axe behind him. "Tonight, it has been done. Odin has accepted a sacrifice from his last priest. Give me water, for I want to wash."

Bishop Sivrit walked through the crowd and, for the second time in their lives, poured water over Olav.

The people of Lade walked over to the temple doors in dark silence, looking inside to see the broken statues. Then, Rafn God's Axe began to hack away at the doors and walls of the temple. The fire inside grew until the flames roared high into the sky.

48

❈

POLAND

Sigvald pulled himself away from Astrid's warm back. His wife slept on her side, her arms crossed tightly over her breasts. Usually, when they finished making love, she rose and dressed, not allowing him what he most longed for, for them to cool off from their lovemaking together. Sometimes, though, she fell asleep, like tonight, but even in her sleep she'd wrap herself in the armor of her own arms. This marked the differences between them. He'd want to lay her on his chest, stroke her hair of the strange amber hue, and talk lazily. But today, he was the one who had to get up, dress, and go to the docks. Geivar's scouts had conveyed that someone was waiting for him in Jom. He kissed his wife's bare shoulder and walked out quietly.

It was windy in Wolin's port, and snow fell from the winter sky. He banged his fist three times on the wall of the house of sailors and, after a moment, the men who had been waiting inside for him ran out.

"It's good to sit by the fire in weather like this," Ulle sighed, pushing off from the dock.

"Drink mulled beer or warm a hand under the skirts of some nice maid," his brother Kalle agreed, grabbing an oar.

Sigvald laughed and wrapped himself tighter in the cloak of sealskin. It wasn't far from Wolin to Jom, but there was time enough to get cold before they passed through the great iron gates.

Geivar appeared in the harbor; the cold, probing eyes of the chief of the house of scouts looked out at Sigvald from under a hood.

"He said his name was Gretter, but he could be giving a false name," Geivar said straightaway. "He claims that he's come from Roskilde, though I know his ship belongs to a rich merchant from the west of Denmark, Vigmar. And Vigmar—"

"I know," Sigvald interrupted him. Vigmar was a nobleman who had opposed Sven during King Eric's invasion, and he never hid his Swedish preferences during his absence in the country. "Where is he waiting?"

"In the house of chieftains. It was too crowded in the Sacred Site for a private conversation tonight."

"Let's go then; it's cold."

Now that Sigvald's sister-in-law, Świętosława, had married King Sven, Duke Bolesław had him pay extra heed to any news of Denmark. Once every few months, Sigvald sent a ship that officially belonged to Wolin's merchants, but with half the men comprised of Geivar's warriors in disguise.

Two young boys were standing guard outside the house of warriors, some of the newest recruits. Cold, red faces indicated they hadn't yet grown used to winters in the stronghold, but as soon as they recognized who was walking toward them, they straightened and stood proudly.

Geivar and Sigvald entered, and a short, slender man with a birdlike face waited for them by the fire.

"The jarl of Jom's stronghold, Lord Sigvald, and the chieftain of the house of scouts, Lord Geivar," Frosti introduced them.

"Gretter of Ribe," the guest introduced himself.

He spoke the truth, Sigvald thought, mentally praising Geivar's scouts.

"You said you've come from Roskilde."

"It's true. I've been visiting Princess Tyra."

"In whose name do you speak?" Sigvald took his seat at the main table and reached for a jug. He tipped it and swallowed. He grimaced.

"Frosti, bring some mulled beer from the kitchen," he called out.

Gretter of Ribe looked around and visibly relaxed when he saw Frosti walk out.

"Thank you, my lord, for sending the servants away," he said with relief. "I cannot speak in front of witnesses. The message I have to convey is intended for your ears only."

"There are no servants in Jom," Sigvald told him coldly. "And Geivar here is a chieftain of one of the houses. Don't think I will send a chief away."

The guest looked even more embarrassed, but he clearly forced himself to ignore the feeling and lifted his head, trying to speak with confidence:

"As you wish, Jarl. You rule here."

"Indeed. Tell me your news."

"I don't know if you've heard that since Sven's return from England, his half sister Tyra suffers many humiliations from him."

She deserves it, the traitor, Sigvald thought. She was plotting against her brother, prepared to let Saxons into their country. Sigvald, since he'd imprisoned Sven in Jom, had developed something of a sympathetic feeling toward the man. And besides, he hated anyone who plotted behind their family's backs. He glanced at Geivar. The scout's face, as always, revealed nothing.

"Speak on," he encouraged the guest.

"King Sven has forced his sister to live in Roskilde—"

"That is indeed terrible," Sigvald interrupted him. "Forcing a princess to live at court."

"That's not the point, Jarl." Gretter's eyes were too restless. "In reality, Sven keeps his sister . . ."

He fell silent suddenly when Frosti walked into the chamber with a great jug of steaming beer under his cloak. The red-faced boy from the house of hosts placed the jug in front of Sigvald and added three cups to it. Sigvald poured some for himself, then Geivar reached for the jug. The scent of beer heated with mead filled the room.

"Help yourself, guest," Sigvald invited Gretter. "I told you, we have no servants here."

Frosti disappeared discreetly into the front room.

"He's imprisoning her," Gretter finished in a whisper. "Armed guards stand in front of her room. When the princess wants to leave to go to church, they follow her there, too."

"That's the fate of valuable ladies," Sigvald concluded, taking a sip of beer. "Good. Frosti!" he called out loudly. "Tell the kitchens it's good."

"Yes, my lord," the host shouted back.

Gretter was confused. Geivar took over the game now; so far, the only time he'd moved throughout the entire conversation had been when he was pouring himself beer.

"What do you need for your lady?" he asked, barely opening his mouth.

"Princess Tyra is searching for allies."

I don't doubt it, Sigvald thought. *And you know we've humiliated Sven once already.*

"The Jomsvikings don't meddle in kings' business," Geivar repeated their motto.

"But they are the most effective weapon in decisive battles between them," Gretter stuttered, surprisingly bravely. "My lady wishes to marry and . . ."

"I'm already married," Sigvald joked. "But Geivar, perhaps?"

"I know, my lord, that's why I'm here." Gretter wouldn't be that easily distracted. "Your wife, the noble lady Astrid, is the sister of the great duke Bolesław . . ."

"He's also got a wife," Geivar added in his horrible, emotionless voice.

"My lady has no noble protectors in her country. Ones who would have influence among other rulers, equal to her in station. If Duke Bolesław agreed to help her and represent her, in the greatest secrecy, of course . . ."

I wonder who the Danish princess wants to marry, or if she's counting on Bolesław to find her a husband? Either way, doesn't mean I can't pull more information out of this Gretter.

"Why hasn't your master come to us in person?" Geivar asked coldly.

"My master? Who do you mean, chief?" Gretter's restless eyes suddenly widened.

Aha, Sigvald noted.

Geivar, completely by chance, of course, chose this moment to bare his painted fangs.

"I serve the princess . . ."

"And she's availed herself of Bishop Oddinkarr of Ribe's care in the past," Geivar finished.

"Care is a broad term. Tyra is a Christian, so is it surprising she feels an affinity with spiritual men?"

"How will your bishop benefit from the princess's marriage?" Sigvald asked, though he knew the answer already.

"Did she not have enough connections in Bremen to find an adequate husband?" Geivar joined in.

"Or has the Saxon bishop denied you help because he's afraid of Sven's vengeance?"

"Yes," the messenger gave in with a heavy sigh. "King Sven is now powerful enough that the Saxons do not wish to get involved. And great Duke Bolesław will be beyond all suspicion, since his beloved sister has married Sven and born him a son."

"So long as Duke Bolesław remains interested in playing this game." Sigvald shrugged carelessly.

He knew very well that his brother-in-law was searching for a way to take revenge on Sven for marrying Świętosława without his agreement. He could picture Bolesław's expression when he brought this excellent piece of news to him. Let the snow fall all night. Tomorrow, they'd harness the sleigh and go to Poznań. He and Astrid. In the cool of the sleigh, his cold wife would cling to him under the fur.

"We can try to engage in this discreet game," he said aloud. "So long as Princess Tyra, or Bishop Oddinkarr, can afford to pay silver for the services of the Jomsvikings."

DENMARK

Sven sat by the fire and cleaned his weapons lazily. Peace reigned in the great hall in Roskilde. Absolute peace. The silence was so complete that he imagined he could hear the snow falling. Before the Yule, blizzards had chased snowstorms, and more than once the servants would wake to find they couldn't open the manor's doors because of the snow piled outside; only when the stable men came were the inhabitants freed from snow's fetters. After the celebrations, the winds died down and calm reigned in nature once more. The snow kept falling, but the thick flakes fell slowly, covering Roskilde almost reluctantly, increasing the feeling of blissful laziness.

His queen sat on the other side of the open fire, on a low wide bench with a comfortable back, wearing an ordinary housedress of thick wool, with no decorations save for one simple silver cross on her breast. She'd tucked her legs under her, leaning her head back until her long loose hair fell over the bench's back. Her wordless servant was kneeling there, delicately and affectionately brushing her mistress's hair with a bone comb. The golden strands, lit up by the shine from the fireplace, seemed to glow. The queen had her eyes closed as if she were asleep. But no, she wasn't sleeping. She held their son in her arms at her breast, Harald Svensson. She was feeding him, stroking the child's cheek with a finger.

Sven lifted the sword from his knees and examined it against the light. Karli the Dwarf had forged it, the best blacksmith in Jelling, the same one who had once altered the silver cross to make Thor's hammer out of it. The steel reflected the flames with a glow. He placed the sword between his legs, leaning it against a knee, and continued to polish it. The queen sighed. He raised his eyes.

Dusza sat frozen with the comb in her hand, looking at her mistress. His wife, without opening her eyes, let her lips part and arranged Harald more comfortably on her breast. The servant returned to combing her hair. Sven, without ceasing to clean his sword, couldn't tear his eyes from the queen. She was a woman of many faces to him, as well as many names. He liked to stubbornly call her Gunhild in front of the whole court; he liked how angry it made her, hearing that name, but he didn't protest when his people called out "Sigrid Storråda" at the sight of their queen. He himself whispered it to her in moments of rapture in the bedchamber. In the morning, he pretended that he didn't remember this. It wasn't true, though, he remembered well enough. Sigrid Storråda was the one he'd taken from Sigtuna, his old enemy's wife whom he had taken to erase the memory of Eric's invasion. Sigrid Storråda was Olav's hidden desire, the dream Sven had taken away from his old comrade and now enemy forever.

The bold one drew Sven to her with her never-ending stubbornness, independence, and impudence; she was the lady of two kingdoms, and she acted as if she wore two crowns at once. That was what truly drove him into a frenzy, and excited him at the same time. He'd only truly felt like a king with her at his side, drinking in the worship, desire, and fear of his chieftains, who glanced at his queen cautiously.

When she gave him a son, less than a year after the wedding, he thought he'd go mad with joy. When she was giving birth, she screamed so loudly that all of Roskilde must have heard. He had to surround the manor with a circle of his personal axemen because a crowd had gathered, sure there was trouble brewing inside. Wulfric, with an army of English chaplains, lay in the shape of a cross in the church and prayed, convinced that his queen was dying. Her two lynxes growled furiously, biting the bars of their cage; the boy she'd brought with her from Sigtuna, Wilczan, had to take the cats for a long walk into the forest because otherwise they'd have broken free and mauled the women helping with the birth. He himself, hearing her scream, thought he'd go mad. But in the middle of the night, the noise stopped, and Melkorka came to the great hall and announced: "You have a son. Big, healthy, and red-haired." Then, out of joy, he had learned to speak her real name, Świętosława—Sventoslava, as the Polish name would be pronounced. He whispered it to her when she slept, exhausted after the labor, thanking her for his firstborn. When she awoke, he called her "Gunhild."

"Ah . . ." she sighed quietly, stretching.

Sven was still polishing his sword with long strokes. He felt himself breathing heavily. His hands were sweaty, and he wiped them on his thigh. The queen turned, sighing softly as if drifting to sleep, trying to push her son from her breast. Sven's breathing quickened again. He couldn't take it anymore. He put the sword down quietly and stood up. Dusza looked up at him. He lifted a finger to his mouth and walked over to them soundlessly. He gestured to the servant to take the child and leave. She nodded. When she was rising from her knees, he took the comb from her hand and knelt where she'd been a moment before. He brought his face close to the queen's hair, breathing her in. Dusza gently took the boy from his mother's arms and left.

Sven swallowed as he looked at his wife's wet breast. He touched its tip. The queen sighed softly as she had a moment ago.

"Sventoslava . . ." he whispered to her golden hair. "Sventoslava . . ."
And, strand by strand, he ran the comb through it.

Astrid hated being asked when she would bear a child. She wanted to say: Why don't you ask Sigvald? She knew why, though. The Jomsviking chieftain made people feel shy. Well, not many knew him as well as she did.

Their journey to Poznań made her happy; a pleasant change after a bloody boring winter. Although, of course, once there, she had to answer the hated question countless times. The only person who didn't ask was her brother's wife, Duchess Emnilda.

They were sitting in the warm hall, she and Sigvald, Emnilda with Bolesław, red-haired Bjornar, Jaksa, and dark-haired, laughing Zarad. Their gathering might almost be a family one, if it wasn't for the presence of Bishop Unger.

"Princess Tyra . . ." Bolesław repeated thoughtfully once Sigvald had summarized his conversation with the Danish messenger.

"The archdiocese in Bremen has a predatory attitude toward the North Churches. Denmark and the bishop of Ribe are still under its rule if we follow the Church's hierarchy. King Sven has brought many priests from England, in this way indicating that he wants to make his churches independent. That's why Bremen doesn't want to engage in a conflict with Sven, because they're doing what they can to keep the Danish king in their, let us say, arms," Unger said.

"The Empire is influencing the neighboring priests of both sides." Bolesław grimaced. "Through Otto's power and the Church organization which answers to it."

"That's only true of the archbishops who truly are discretionary to the emperor."

"Do you remember, Bishop, how it was with you?"

The duke had a talent for getting carried away with his emotions in a matter of moments. Astrid had thought that Bolesław would grow out of it one day, but no; her brother had forged this into another weapon which he wielded with no small skill. He rose from his chair and was already pacing around the hall, throwing out words like arrows. His two dogs got up from their bed and followed their master like a pack.

"You were ordained as a bishop right after our pious Jordan's death, but Theophanu, wanting to get back at my father, kept you in Memleben." His eyes gleamed in anger, and he snatched a stick out of a dog's mouth.

"I don't deny that. For eight years."

"For eight years, the Church in my country had no shepherd. There was no one to ordain new priests, consecrate new churches. The empress weaved her web like a spider. And the pope, not the emperor, should have been your superior." Her brother threw the stick he had taken from the dog furiously into the fire.

For a moment, it seemed as if he was waiting for the dog to follow.

"In theory," Unger replied calmly. "May she rest in peace."

Bolesław circled the bishop's chair, then turned around.

"Anger dictates vengeance, but that's sweetest when prepared cold."

He sat back down as he said this. He was calm, as if this outburst had never happened. Astrid and Emnilda exchanged glances. Her sister-in-law's delicately raised eyebrows indicated amusement.

"Mead?" she asked shrewdly.

"Mead," the duke confirmed.

Emnilda could give the servants commands without a word. Astrid watched her with admiration. A goblet and a previously invisible servant arrived at the duke's side.

"Sven took Świętosława by force," Bolesław announced, and Astrid thought for a moment that another wave of anger would follow. But no, her brother maintained an unexpected calm. "He put her in a situation in which she could not refuse him, and of course, I am furious at him for that, but I also admire him. To put it bluntly, I'd have done the same if I were him."

Emnilda coughed and observed politely:

"I'm still here."

"And you'll be here forever, because I don't intend to spend a single day without you." Bolesław leaned over and kissed her hand.

"The duke speaks of brutal politics, my lady," Unger explained. "Not matters of the heart."

"Nevertheless," Bolesław continued, "Sven has made my plans void. I saw Olav Tryggvason at my sister's side, and, from joining his country with Świętosława's, a counterbalance to Sven."

"I will be bold enough to point out that the Danish brother-in-law is still much stronger than the never realized Norwegian one. And simultaneously, instead of having to fetter Sven, you no longer have to fear him. For so long as your sister is his wife, it's unlikely he'd step out against you," Unger said.

"Sven still has influence among the Obotrites, and they keep joining with the Veleti and then breaking that alliance continuously," Jaksa, silent until now, pointed out. "You could, Duke, try to pressure him, as your brother-in-law, to stop encouraging the Slavs to rebel."

Astrid glanced at her brother. He should reprimand Jaksa for telling him what he should do. He didn't. He only said, calmly:

"Tyra should marry Olav Tryggvason."

Astrid felt the blood rush to her head.

"Why?" She couldn't stop the question or pretend the others hadn't heard the note of panic in her voice.

She fell silent then, catching the glance her husband gave her. She blushed. Damn it. So many years, and she still reacted at the sound of his name like a virgin at the sight of her lover.

You're a fool, she thought, making fists with her hands and digging her nails into her palms with all her strength. The blush should be gone by now.

"Because," Bolesław said, putting down his goblet, "Sven will be furious. It will be as accurate a blow as his leap for Świętosława. The Danish princess at Olav's side will balance the scales that were unbalanced when Sven kidnapped my sister."

I wouldn't want to be in your skin, brother, when the bold one finds out who's behind the marriage of the man she loves, Astrid thought, then realized she was thinking, just as she had been all her life, of her sister first, and then of herself.

"Tyra is a Christian, so is Olav." Unger nodded. "Although I've heard that people already call the Yngling a 'beast with a cross in his hand.'"

And then her husband asked for permission to speak.

"The Jomsvikings do not meddle in kings' business," Sigvald recited his motto. "They stand to one side. But sometimes, things are clearer from the side than they are when you face them head-on."

"Then speak bluntly," Bolesław snarled.

Her brother's anger was always unexpected. Sigvald didn't seem cowed by the outburst, but he did speak quickly and without the smile behind which he usually masked his concerns.

"Tyra at Olav's side could become a reason for war. Sven will find a way. He'll say that the marriage was unlawful, or come up with something else. By giving her hand to Tryggvason, you're giving Sven a reason to attack Olav."

The duke laughed and drank. Emnilda, by some secret method known only to herself, guessed her husband's goblet was empty, and summoned the servant to fill it. Astrid watched all this as if she weren't a part of the meeting at all. She felt as if she were floating, up by the stone ceiling of the palatium, watching them all from above. She even saw herself, pale, pushed against the back of the chair, with a hand covering her mouth. Sigvald kept repeating the same words: "a reason for war, a reason for war, a reason for war." She felt the salty, metallic taste of blood in her mouth and thought she saw a red, bloody river flowing across the middle of the table.

"Astrid?" Emnilda's voice brought her back to reality. "Are you unwell?"

She shook herself. It wasn't blood that flowed on the flat surface, but mead from the goblet she'd overturned. The servants were already beside her, cleaning up the mead, handing her a fresh goblet.

"Maybe my sister is expecting a child?" Bolesław asked happily, looking at her.

Child, rape, intrigue, war . . . it's all the same to them, she thought bitterly.

"You'll have to ask Sigvald about that," she told her brother sharply.

Bolesław did turn to her husband then, but it was to ask a different question.

"You say, Jarl, that it would be a reason for war? Then I hope that none of the Jomsviking swords have rusted."

"No, my lord." Her husband smiled. "Our weapons have never been more ready."

49

⋈

DENMARK

Świętosława weaned Harald when it was still winter. Melkorka found her a wet nurse.

"Her name is Heidi, Queen," she introduced the girl. "But everyone calls her Goat."

Indeed, the reason for the nickname was apparent. Goat Heidi had large breasts, carefully covered by a wool shawl, and her pale, almost white hair was plaited at the top of her head in two braids which stood on end like horns. Harald was already sucking on her nipple greedily, so there was no fear he might not accept the wet nurse's milk.

"Is my lady preparing for a second child?" Melkorka asked.

Sven was growing increasingly persistent with his demands for her presence in his bedchamber, but the real reason she wanted a wet nurse was her son's endless hunger.

"Harald is my second child, Melkorka," she replied, thinking longingly of Olof.

"I'm sorry." The housewife bowed clumsily. "I'd forgotten." Her red fingers fidgeted with her apron nervously.

"It's all right. Is your back in pain? Perhaps you should rest?"

"There is nothing wrong with me, my lady, nothing wrong at all. I can work and carry out my duties." She blushed, and her hair, pulled into a too-tight bun, seemed completely white. But Melkorka was the type of person who was more content when working than when at rest. Though unfortunately, when it came to her duties in the kitchen, she was quite inept.

"Of course," Świętosława dismissed her. "Thank you for bringing a wet nurse."

After Olof was born, she'd learned all the shades of a child's shouts and cries. Olof screamed the house down, which made Eric happy, because he saw courage in the noise his son made. But there were no shades of nuance to Harald's cries; he only ever wanted to be fed. If he wasn't eating, he was crying. Women at court said one could never overfeed a baby, and little Harald must have been born with similar views. He ate, and ate, and ate.

"Now it's your worry, Heidi," she told the wet nurse.

The girl laughed cheerfully.

"Ah, what haven't I fed! Though this is the first time I have a royal son at my breast. Oooh, he sucks like a blacksmith's son. He has pincers in his mouth. I'll manage, your majesty."

The first thing Świętosława had done when Dusza had handed her the red little body was to see whether he had the mark on his skull. He did. She kissed him there, on his "Piast mark."

I'm like a bitch sniffing its litter to tell apart my own from a changeling, she thought later. The little one had a head covered with pale red fuzz, which made Sven just as happy as did the fact that it was a boy.

"You gave me a son," he laughed, lifting him above his head.

"I'm not giving you anyone," she replied indignantly. "He's as much mine as he is yours."

Their marriage still resembled a battle. Sven provoked her, and she irritated him. When one of them wanted to bury the hatchet, the other decided to attack. They could fight about everything, and making peace was an uphill battle; what they achieved was more of a cease-fire. There were also days when they were simply in each other's way. She learned quickly that to get anything from him, she had to ask for something other than what she wanted. Or pretend she didn't care about it. Endless games. Sometimes, during feasts, Sven and Jorun would talk about the English invasion of the Two Kings. During those times, she could listen to stories about Olav with no repercussions and, if they were drunk enough, she could even ask questions. She just had to be careful not to let her emotions show. She realized quickly that Sven had spies in Norway. He met them outside of the manor, so she couldn't find out their names or faces, but he spoke of the news they brought at feasts with his noblemen. Since Heidi was taking over Harald's feeding, Świętosława could begin attending them once more.

"Should I serve yet?" Melkorka asked, her cheeks flushed. "I prepared the wild geese that the king brought back."

"Yes, bring them out. I love roasted geese."

"I boiled them, Your Grace."

"That's all right, too. I think I wanted them boiled." Świętosława smiled to the cook and walked out of the kitchen to the great hall.

She heard the clank of iron in the dark passageway. Chains? She looked around. Arnora. The regal old woman. *My enemy's wife*, Sven had said. Świętosława walked over to her.

"Are you coming to the feast, Arnora?" she asked, a rare feeling of shyness coming over her as she spoke.

The woman turned to her so haughtily, it seemed that she was the mistress here.

"I am, Queen," she replied.

Świętosława had watched her from afar more than once. The old woman always sat in the corner of the hall, and never responded to her nods of greeting.

"Will you take my arm?" Świętosława suggested, seeing the chain that connected to the ones on her legs drag.

Arnora didn't deign to answer. She shuffled her feet, though she held her back straight. She finished her step and paused. Świętosława lost herself in the network of wrinkles and lines on her face. Arnora's eyes shone with a pale, intense blue hue.

"That's how I imagined you," she said, after a moment of staring at Świętosława.

"Why do you say that? You've seen me at every feast."

"Ah, youth," she said, something akin to amusement in her voice. "I don't see people from afar, but mere shadows."

"That's why you never answered my greetings?" Świętosława asked, feeling suddenly relieved. She didn't know why, but on hearing that this woman had not been scorning her, Świętosława felt a warm twist of joy in her stomach.

"Do you like to play hnefatafl?" the old woman asked. "Do you like to lose?"

"No one likes losing," Świętosława replied, and felt awkward once again.

Arnora continued to stare; there was no intrusiveness in her eyes, but Świętosława still felt as if the woman could see past her carefully constructed exterior.

"Who chooses to play must be prepared for any result. And rulers must always be playing."

"Why are you telling me this?"

"If you'd like to have a game with me, you know where to find me. Come, and bring your lynxes. I'd like to touch them. Your quiet servant can come with you, too. But I don't want that oaf in my hermitage."

"Great Ulf is my guard."

"It's not him I speak of, but the fat monk. Go now, Thorn Queen. Your husband summons you to the feast."

"Thorn Queen?" Świętosława repeated, her heart thudding in her chest.

"I told you that I see well up close," Arnora laughed. The chains clanged, and she continued her laborious journey. "Only don't get lost when you come looking for me. There is more than one hermitage in this manor."

Her conversation with Arnora had thrown Świętosława off-balance. When she walked into the torchlit hall, she wasn't herself.

"Gunhild, how good it is to see you." Sven rose from the platform and moved toward her. "Will you drink with me from the long horn?"

Jorun handed him the horn as he passed. It was indeed longer than most. He gave it to her and whispered straight into her ear:

"I'd like you to stroke my horn tonight."

She blushed. Yes, she wasn't herself. She took a big gulp and regained her strength.

"All right, so long as Jorun won't be putting yours in my mouth."

Now Sven blushed, and so did his friend. She took her husband's arm and let him guide her to her seat.

"We have guests from the north with us today," he said, motioning toward a few men standing off to one side. "They stopped at Lade on their way to Iceland, and they bring interesting news."

She nodded to them, and they bowed back. *Are they Sven's spies?* she wondered. *He's never met with them in Roskilde. Or are they simply merchants or sailors, adventure hunters?*

"Dusza, the lynxes," she called out, to draw attention away from her interest in the guests. "My cats are so tame that they are meowing for the feast to begin. They have had enough of feeding our son."

"Your lynxes are tame?" Ragn of the Isles asked indignantly. "They almost took off my hand yesterday."

"Then you must have reached for something I commanded them to guard."

The guests laughed, and Ragn quickly hid his face in a cup. No, she wouldn't reveal his secret. Ragn of the Isles, since her wedding night, seemed to suffer from a peculiar need to touch her cloak. Wrzask had indeed scared him a little when he'd tried to take the garment she'd thrown on a bench.

"Let's drink to my son and his beautiful mother," Sven exclaimed.

"More than once," Stenkil called out.

"I hope," the red-bearded king smiled, "it will be more than once. Let my queen give me many sons."

Melkorka's kitchen procession brought in the bowls. Świętosława was hungry. Her appetite left her for a moment when she spotted Arnora walking into the hall. A band of boar fangs rested on her long, silver-white hair. *I didn't see it in the dark, or did she go back to her hermitage to put on that strange crown?*

Fair-haired Vali placed a bowl in front of Świętosława.

"Specially from Melkorka, since the queen loves wild geese," she smiled prettily.

Not like this, Świętosława groaned inwardly, looking at the gray, over-cooked meat in a wreath of wilted onions.

The cook stood in the doorway and watched her tensely. Sven leaned over to her and said quietly, "Wash it down and you'll manage. Red wine can save even Melkorka's cooking."

She did as he suggested, but still felt as if she were eating rawhide.

"Should I send her to the country?" Sven asked.

"No, please don't. I'll think of something," she replied, chewing the stringy meat. She nodded to Melkorka to indicate her satisfaction, and smiled to Sven. "Have you any more wine left?"

When the cook disappeared into the kitchen, Świętosława discreetly threw the goose under the table. Zgrzyt made short work of it.

". . . since he baptized the northern lords in Lade, Jarl Haakon's old settlement, they call him the 'beast with the cross,'" one of the newcomers was saying.

Sven turned to her and said quietly, "Olav has always had a tendency toward cruelty."

But he wasn't the one to threaten me, she replied silently. *You were.*

"He burned Odin's temple, after he'd chopped its last priest to pieces inside . . ." the traveler continued.

"I told you," Sven muttered. "He's a monster."

"So how did you survive three years of conquering side by side?"

"I'm not afraid of the beast." He shrugged, not hearing the mockery in her voice.

"I understand that Christianity is spreading in his country like wildfire," she said to their guests.

Sven understood the joke and laughed. The newcomers exchanged uneasy glances.

"Queen Sigrid Storråda has had some experiences with fire," Skuli the bard explained. Seeing they were still confused, he waved a hand. "I'll explain once we're a few more drinks in."

"One could say," the guest continued, "that Olav has baptized most of the country. Everywhere he's been, the noblemen have accepted him. Though he undoubtedly faces some troubles . . ."

"I'll say," the second of the men offered, "that whoever sees him bends the knee."

I know something about that, she thought, and realized she'd have to be more on her guard than usual this evening. She couldn't let her heart rule her thoughts in front of her husband and these men.

"Speak more clearly," Sven ordered.

"Hamingia, my king. The powerful spirit which comes before him . . ."

"You speak like an enchanter," Świętosława said with a disdainful laugh. She must have been convincing enough, because Sven laughed as well.

The spirit that comes before him, Bork had said—the priest of Odin who had first killed her husband, then protected her and their son. He had warned her in Sigtuna a moment before everything had ended.

"Forgive me, my lady." The traveler wasn't embarrassed by the king and queen's apparent skepticism. "It's difficult to describe it otherwise. He walks among a crowd of armed noblemen, his enemies, he says a few words, and those who claimed they'd never bow to him before he arrived, fall to their knees."

"What does he say?" Sven asked, saving her the trouble.

"He says, 'I am your king. The Yngling heir. I have come to give you baptism and faith in the lord Christ, and to take the crown. My name is Olav Tryggvason.'"

I can picture it so clearly, she thought. *His pale, translucent eyes, his almost white hair swept backward . . .*

". . . and they shout, 'No, we have our gods, we don't need kings.' That's when he replies, without even raising his voice, 'I'm already your king.'"

"We saw it with our own eyes," the last of the travelers joined in. "That's what happened."

"A servant girl in an inn we later stayed at summed it up most accurately. The woman had seen Olav from behind, from afar, and said, 'Even from behind he looks like a king.'"

"Nonsense," Sven said, angrily banging his goblet on the table. "Women's nonsense."

You're wrong, husband. The servant is right.

"But the truth is . . ." the one who had spoken first continued. "The truth is that in the far north, in the country of northern lights and the isles, he has powerful enemies. Those are the regions that the king's influence doesn't reach. The places that require weeks on a sleigh to reach, where the sun never sets in summer or rises in the winter. The country ruled by jarls who make sacrifices to Odin, wealthy men who own the largest herds of reindeer . . ."

"The time for the north is coming, though," one of the others interrupted. "No one believes that reindeer lords can stop a ruler like Olav Tryggvason."

"That's enough stories for one night," Sven said, cutting off the litany of Olav's praises. "Enjoy yourself as my guests. Skuli, take care of the travelers."

The bard understood at once that he was to get them drunk away from the king. He pulled them to a table in the far corner of the hall.

Sven gave a sign to his jarls to sit closer.

"His strength is growing," Thorgils of Jelling observed, tapping a nail against his cup.

"If he only has the reindeer lords left to convince, then one might say all of Norway is already his," Haakon of Funen added somberly, taking a gulp of mead. "There are few lords that far north, and their ties with the country have always been weak."

"In your father's time," Gunar of Limfiord began carefully, "those from the farthest north didn't pay tribute either. They lived in the wilderness, and when Harald sent his tax collectors, only three out of the twelve returned. They said later that the rest had been lost in canyons of ice, and they never found those famous reindeer lords at all, or any other living soul."

"They spoke of impossible things." Ragn of the Isles spat.

Świętosława looked at him sharply, and he realized he hadn't behaved as he should. He smeared his saliva with his boot, embarrassed.

"I don't give a shit about the reindeer lords," Sven roared. "I care that Olav's power is growing. He did what he set out to do, the bloody second king."

"It's a bad thing that Tryggvason ever left England," Thorgils of Jelling said, his words cold and calculated.

Sven clenched his fists over the arms of his chair, glaring at the chieftain from Jelling.

"You weren't there, so be silent," he replied.

Jorun moved closer to Thorgils and said, "You have a small imagination, Jarl of Jelling, if you think that Olav could have been killed without beginning a war. The army known as the Two Kings did not appear from thin air. King Ethelred would have been ecstatic if we'd started fighting among ourselves and killed one another, doing exactly what his armies had failed to do."

"Forgive me, King." Thorgils lowered his head, but his humility was obviously feigned. "I merely made an observation. I had no intention of criticizing any of your men, or suggest that Olav might have been removed after you took the danegeld . . . at sea, for instance . . . or an accidental death . . . a fall from a rock . . ."

"Thorgils." Świętosława's voice sounded sharp and clear. "My husband is a man of honor. I am certain that he'd never commit such a crime."

Christ, I want to believe that, she thought.

Sven placed his hand on hers. It was cold. He squeezed lightly.

"The queen is right. I'd much prefer to defeat Olav in an open battle than in an unworthy game."

Why do you want to defeat him at all? she wondered feverishly, and shuddered under Sven's cold touch. *Leave him in peace, in peace.*

"There are wars which are waged either at sea or on land," Uddorm of Viborg, silent until now, spoke. "And there are those which never begin if you adequately plan the little battles in the bedchamber."

His heavyset face revealed a man who enjoyed the pleasures of life.

"Our beloved queen and brave king are the best example of that. Let's face the truth head-on. If you hadn't fallen in love so explosively and hadn't tied the marriage knot, we'd have had a war, destruction, and death. Corpses at sea, burned ships, orphans crying for their fathers. And now? We rejoice in the blossoming of two kingdoms. Our merchants sail safely, multiplying the treasures in their royal chests." His moist lips stretched in a smile.

Sven squeezed her hand again, pulling it toward him. She took a deep breath and tried with all her might to summon a smile. From the point of view of the kingdoms, Uddorm was correct. So why did that victory still taste so bitter?

Sven kissed her hand, and his lips were cold. Or maybe her hand, where he so delicately placed his lips, was burning hot.

"Uddorm, Uddorm," Sven said cheerfully. "We all know that you're called the 'father of Jutland.' You've placed your daughters and sons, nephews, nieces, and the rest of the Uddorm family in every house in Jutland."

"I won't deny it, my king." Uddorm smiled. "That's how, when the grain is destroyed by the rains in the north, my servants can still brew beer from the south. You have a sister, King. Think about where you'd like to settle her. Or rather, where you'd like for her to reproduce."

"Tyra?" she and Sven asked in unison.

Świętosława had only seen this woman her husband called a traitor a handful of times. She had beautiful, dark red hair and much grace in her movements. She seemed shy and withdrawn, though she could simply be governed by fear. All Świętosława knew about her was that Sven held her as a prisoner for her previous sins against him, though the one time they exchanged a few words, Tyra had said that other than her freedom, she lacked for nothing.

"Tyra," Uddorm repeated. "The royal sister. Wouldn't her hand in marriage be an assurance of peace?"

"Oh, of course." Sven snorted. "If I wanted that. But as it happens, my friend, I don't want peace with Olav, I want war. I want Norway to be Danish, as it has been in the past. That's my plan, and I don't need Tyra to fulfill it. Let her sit in her chamber and wait for me to find her a husband."

"If the king dreams of war," the previously reprimanded Thorgils said, "then I'd like to suggest an appropriate husband for Tyra."

This wasn't the first time she noticed that Thorgils had the dangerous charm of a snake, carefully hidden under much better manners than those of most of her husband's companions.

"Jarl Haakon's sons, Eric and Sven. The offspring of Tryggvason's greatest enemy. They escaped Norway when Olav arrived, and our scouts tell us they've been searching for luck in the wide world. Why shouldn't they find it here? Let's reward one of them with a marriage to your sweet sister, and this way, Olav's enemies gain the strength and legitimacy of your great country, my king. Then, once we push Tryggvason off the throne, we can place the old jarl's heir on the throne, bringing back peace."

"Taking the Yngling from both sides?" Świętosława could hear in her husband's voice how much he liked Thorgils's plan. "Which one of these two young men is better, Gunhild?"

She didn't react.

"Queen? Remember them? After all, you met both at court in Sigtuna."

"King Eric Segersäll received many guests," she replied stiffly. "I don't recall these two."

"Then we must rely on what our scouts say." Sven laughed. "And they seem to favor Jarl Eric."

"Why do this?" she couldn't stop herself from asking. "Don't you pity your sister? Do you want to condemn her to disregard at the side of someone who used to have power, but never had any rights to it? His father was a confirmed pagan, the son is probably the same. Your sister has been baptized."

"But my dear wife"—an indulgent note colored Sven's voice—"I'm not thinking of marrying Tyra. Apart from a half sister, I also have a daughter out of wedlock. Gyda will be perfect for the young jarl."

"But she's just a child," she protested.

"Don't exaggerate." Sven waved a hand. "She's slight, but those younger than her have been married off when the need arose. Besides, who do you feel sorry for, Gunhild?" he asked, trying to provoke her. "Gyda, or rather . . ." He let the statement hang in the air.

Me and Olav, my lord husband, she thought vengefully.

"Did your father ask for your opinion when you were wed?" Sven continued.

"Duke Mieszko referred to me as his most precious daughter," she replied coldly. "And let's not speak tonight of how much my hand was worth, in this beautiful hall in Roskilde, because your people remember that price to this day." She pulled the leash. "Forgive me, but I prefer the company of tamed predators than beasts plotting over mead."

"We'll meet in the bedchamber, my lady," Sven called after her.

"Good luck," she replied without turning around. "Wrzask and Zgrzyt will be guarding the door, my lord."

50

⚛

DENMARK

Świętosława didn't sleep at all that night, and that's how she knew for certain that Sven had never come to her door. As she walked through the great hall the next morning, she carefully avoided the remnants of the previous night's feast. Some slept where they'd fallen. She woke Wilczan, and the boy got up silently. They walked out of the manor and toward the small wooden church. She saw Ion leaving one of the huts on her way.

"My lady without her beasts." He yawned happily when he saw her. "For a walk? This early?"

"Ion." A sleepy woman came out of the hut. "You forgot this." She placed a basket outside the door and disappeared inside, slamming it.

The monk lifted the basket.

"Not for a walk, to church, you heathen," she reprimanded. "I understand you're coming with me?"

"Oh, if the queen commands it," he muttered reluctantly and rubbed his eyes. "The beast is here, after all."

She turned around. A sleepy Ulf was running toward her from the manor. She smiled at him.

"I don't miss mass," Ion explained himself, "because I lost faith—don't think badly of me, my lady—but because I don't like to hear that Wulfric saying it. It doesn't suit me at all."

"You didn't like the roots at Romuald's hermitage," she snorted. "And the boathouse in Sigtuna. You're a picky monk."

"I never said otherwise." He straightened and shook the basket. "I don't go to Gudna for gossip, but suppers and breakfasts. I cannot stand Melkorka's cooking. It gets stuck in my throat."

Świętosława smiled. "And what's in the basket?"

He took off the cloth covering it and rummaged inside.

"Eggs, dried fish, pancake-like things . . . Oh, these are good. With honey and dried berries."

"Give me one, I'm forever going hungry here as well. Ulf, Wilczan, do you want one?" She turned to those behind her.

Ulf shook his head. She followed his gaze and stopped walking.

"Why are there guards outside the church?"

The small wooden building was surrounded by four axemen, Sven's guards. Ulf walked toward them, while Ion pulled her arm as if he was afraid.

"Let's go back," he whispered.

"Don't jest. This is my home, I'm not turning back."

Instead, she quickened her pace, and the guards at the church's doors straightened as she approached.

"What are you doing here?"

"Guarding, my lady."

"The church?"

"No, my lady. Princess Tyra. It's the king's command."

"Oh, yes. Which one of you has been baptized?"

They glanced uneasily at each other.

"We all have."

"Good, then two of you stay outside here to ensure Princess Tyra doesn't break down the door or escape through the chimney, and two of you come to mass with me. You can guard her while you pray. What are you staring at?"

"At you, my lady," the youngest blurted, and immediately blushed. "Well . . . before now I've only seen the queen from afar . . ."

"Now you can accompany her to mass, then." She took his arm. "The axe stays here."

It was dim inside, the darkness dispelled only by a few flames of tallow candles. When Świętosława, Ion, Wilczan, Ulf, and two axemen walked in, Tyra turned around, and rose swiftly from her knees. Wulfric, who had been giving the sermon, fell silent. Świętosława knelt beside Tyra and, placing a hand on her shoulder, said:

"Don't be afraid. Let's pray together. Priest, I brought you the faithful, continue."

The church was small. During her wedding and Harald's baptism, only their closest guests had squeezed inside. Ion was wrong, Wulfric led mass excellently. When it was time for the Eucharist, Świętosława rose and turned to the axemen.

"Are you ready to accept the body of Christ?"

They looked at her uncertainly. As she'd thought, this was probably the first time they were in church since the day they'd been baptized. It was even worse with Wilczan and Ulf, neither had ever been baptized. And Ion? She knew as well as he did that Gudna gave him more than a basket of fruit. He lowered his eyes humbly.

"My lady?" Wulfric walked over to her with a chalice and white bread.

"I am not worthy of taking part in the Lord's feast," she announced, and knelt with her head lowered.

How could she confess, if she sinned anew each day? *I don't love the husband I made my vows to, I must feign love.*

"Ite, missa est," Wulfric ended the mass.

"Stay, my lady," Świętosława whispered to Tyra, and turned to the group that had come with her.

"What's your name, axeman?"

"Kalle."

"And you?"

"Hauk." The boy was staring at her.

"I'll take responsibility for your religious education, Hauk and Kalle. From now on, I will bring you to mass once a week, and Father Wulfric will introduce you to the sacrament of penance."

"Yes, my lady," they whispered.

"Ulf, Wilczan, Ion will start teaching you the basics of faith. Beginning today, Ion." She wagged a finger at him just as he started to open his mouth to protest against the task. "And now, leave the church. I want to say a litany with Princess Tyra. You'll wait for us outside. You too, Father Wulfric."

When the doors closed behind them, Świętosława placed a hand on Tyra's.

"I want you to know that I am not your enemy," she said. "Sven likely will not let us be friends publicly, but if I can offer you even a small friendship, here or in other moments away from prying eyes, then know you can count on me, Tyra."

Tyra's eyes shone.

"Don't cry," Świętosława said. "Or do, if it helps you."

Tears streamed down the princess's face like a river swollen once the winter frosts are gone.

"I'm afraid of him . . ." she sobbed. "He's unpredictable . . . Do you know what he did in Jelling years ago?"

Świętosława put an arm around her, not because she wanted to, but because she knew that's what you should do when a sister cried.

"He burned a church," Tyra choked out. "Sigrid, he ordered a black-smith to recast the chalice into Thor's hammer, the one he wore around his neck . . . He ordered a triple belt be made from the Bible binding . . . Sweet Jesus . . ."

"Shh . . . not so loud, Tyra, shh . . . He doesn't wear Thor's hammer on his neck anymore. He gave it to me, and I threw it into the Baltic. It's all right now. Calm down. Sven won't hurt you, you're too precious to him. He'll hold you in a room until he finds a husband good enough for you . . . of course, don't take that literally. Good for Sven doesn't mean good for you, sister, but you probably know that?"

Tyra was still crying.

". . . and he had gloves made, covered in metal plates . . . Holy Mother of God! That night when he burned the church, all of them were with him. Uddorm, Ragn, Haakon, Stenkil, and Thorgils of Jelling . . . My lady, how could Thorgils allow a church to be burned? God . . . And I was there . . . he had invited me there to try and convince me to help him remove Father from his throne . . . He's ruthless, my lady . . . How do you live with him?"

"Tyra, calm down." Świętosława pulled back and wiped the princess's tears with her sleeve.

"My lady, my lady . . ." Tyra kept sobbing. "Don't trust them, they're all pagans . . . liars . . . they pretend in front of you that they've given up on the old gods, but they drink horse blood over the fire . . ."

"That's enough. Thank you for sharing with me what you know, but calm is needed now, because now you must face those outside. Even a litany must end at some point. How can I help you?" She shook her. "How can I help you?"

"Help me escape."

"No. That would be a betrayal of the king."

"So you condemn me to death?" Tyra's eyes brimmed with tears again.

"Stop crying, and don't try to manipulate my emotions," Świętosława scolded impatiently. "You're the king's sister. Behave like one."

"But . . ." Tyra shook her head as if she didn't understand.

"There is no 'but.' Do you want to be treated like a princess? Then stop crying. A tavern whore has more strength than you, when she smiles and goes to bed with a rogue, only to stab him in the back in the morning. Take hold of yourself. Either you play the game, or they will play you, there's no other way."

Do you like to lose? Arnora, the chained queen, had asked her before the feast. *No one likes losing,* Świętosława had replied.

"And now wait a moment, until it doesn't look like you've been crying, and then we'll leave." Świętosława stroked Tyra's dark red hair gently. "Right now, you look like my little Harald does when you take the breast away from him for too long. Courage, girl!"

51

⊗

NORWAY

Sigvald gave the order to start rowing as they neared Agdenes. The Jomsvikings were entering treacherous waters, where sudden winds could shatter boats that had seemed safely moored in the bay against the surrounding rocks.

Sailors unfamiliar with these waters, like himself, never sailed into the dangerous Trondheimfiord unless they absolutely had to. Usually they moored in Agdenes and switched to horses to reach Lade quickly.

This treacherous water journey was doubly fraught for Sigvald. To reach Lade, he had to sail past Hjorunga Bay. The place where he'd lost his honor twelve years ago. Where he'd been defeated. Had sailed away from the battle. Had felt death's breath on his face.

Until this day, he'd buried the memory of the hailing clouds that had appeared as if by dark magic in the summer skies, in mead and Astrid's warm body. It had been a scorching hot day, and the opposing fleets had spread out to face each other. Ship to ship. Bow to bow. He played hnefatafl and knew the dark rule, that the team of the king's defenders won more often than that of the, often larger, team of the invaders. He hadn't cared then. Jarl Haakon wasn't a king, and the Danish king Harald had paid the Jomsvikings with pure silver for this war. The tables would be turned. The rules of the game reversed. The Jomsvikings were a squad of the king's mercenary invaders. Jark Haakon had been a defender without a crown. But he had won, though it hadn't been a clean victory.

The jarl had harnessed dark powers to aid him. This wasn't something Sigvald could say aloud, but he had seen the fog and hail that had surrounded the Jomsvikings as soon as the battle had begun, and he knew in his gut that it was the work of some unnatural force.

They were experienced warriors, the iron boys of Jom, and they'd taken Harald's silver for this job, so they battled on despite the fog. But berserkers leapt at them from its milky depths, warrior beasts who tore their enemies apart with their bare hands. With his men falling around him, Sigvald had seen the black spirits of war gliding above, and he had shouted "Retreat!" because he had committed his iron boys to fight living men, not evil incarnate. *Retreat!* . . . That call weighed heavily on him to this day, as he had been the only one to see the power in that storm of hail. He knew those who hadn't been in Hjorunga Bay that day whispered *coward*, but none of the Jomsvikings ever called him that, the ones whose lives were saved by his call to retreat. Only Sigvald knew how much courage that command had taken; he had given the order, taken the infamy on himself, and never shared it with anyone.

Now, Tryggvason welcomed him in Nidaros, which lay on the other side of the river from Lade. The settlement Olav had begun building with the church, to wash away the memory of the pagan jarls of Lade, and Odin's burned temple.

"King Olav." The Jomsviking chieftain bowed to Tryggvason. "Jarl Sigvald of Jomsborg has the honor of bowing before you."

When he raised his head, Sigvald had to narrow his eyes. There was a gold-plated cross hanging behind the king, and the torchlight reflected off it in such a way that, for a moment, it was blinding.

"Sigvald," Olav said. "If it hadn't been for Geira's death, we'd still be brothers-in-law."

"My wife, Astrid, has never stopped mourning her sister," Sigvald lied.

"Is that so?" the king asked. "I thought we'd mourned the darkness of her passing in Gdańsk. But I do not know the souls of women. Perhaps they do things hidden from our eyes."

"That is their charm." Sigvald laughed, and moved to discuss the reason he had come all this way. "Duke Bolesław sends me."

"So we have a reunion of the almost-brothers-in-law," Olav joked.

Sigvald looked at Olav, not understanding the jest, but then recalled Bolesław had been the one to say that Olav and the widowed Świętosława should form an alliance. Making the two of them brothers-in-law once more. Had Tryggvason known of those plans?

"Bolesław offers you a chance to take revenge on Sven."

"Get to the point, Jarl."

"Marriage to Princess Tyra, Sven's sister."

Silence fell. A great white dog paced beside Olav's throne. The severe-looking bishop at his side looked deep in thought.

"Sven knows nothing of this?" Olav asked.

"No. The princess is imprisoned by him, and she seeks contact with you through trusted men, my lord."

"Why does a sister plot against her brother?" the bishop asked coolly.

"Because he, as I've mentioned, is holding her captive. And furthermore, Lady Tyra is a Christian, and is searching for a Christian husband. Your fame in this regard has crossed borders, King."

He's as alert as a hungry wolf, Sigvald thought, *and as cautious as a satisfied snake.*

Once more, silence fell. Sigvald couldn't rid himself of the feeling that the king and bishop were holding a wordless conversation before him somehow. The white dog never took its eyes from him.

"How is Astrid?" Olav asked eventually.

What do you care? Sigvald wanted to shout, but replied as court's manners dictated.

"Well, King. My beloved wife has a role to play in this task."

"What role?" the king asked, too quickly for Sigvald's liking.

"She'll have to get Tyra out of Roskilde."

"Why can't you do it?" Olav asked, accusation in his voice.

"Because I held Sven in Jom when you and Eric conquered Denmark," Sigvald replied, allowing his frustration with these questions to show. "The king's men would recognize me even in the dead of night."

"Ensure that Astrid is safe, Jarl of Jom. Women like your wife need to be taken care of. They are a bright light in the filthy world of warriors that we live in."

Yes, Sigvald agreed wholeheartedly. And pictured himself gouging out this new king's eyes.

"And how is Świętosława coping with Sven?" the fair-haired king asked.

"My wife's sister copes well with everything she does," Sigvald replied. "She has given the king a son who they've called Harald. The old king's name, the one who died in my arms in Jomsborg. They say she is expecting again, so Roskilde will probably be celebrating another heir to the Skjoldung of Jelling dynasty any day now."

"Enough," Olav interrupted him, lifting an arm. "The weather is beautiful, let's take a walk to the harbor. I'll show you the fleet my shipwrights are building, and you can tell me about Tyra."

The king mounted his slender horse, a pure white, magnificent-looking creature.

"A gift from my bishop, Sivrit." Tryggvason smiled, noting Sigvald's stare.

"An English horse." Sigvald nodded with admiration, and thought angrily: *White horse, white dog, white king, White Christ. He and his bishop know how to seduce the commoners. And the procession of armed men with silver crosses on their chests. It makes an impression.*

And so it was that the people they passed on their way to the harbor bowed low to Olav, and made the sign of the cross when they saw their ruler. Sigvald forgot himself for a moment, and imagined it was him they bowed to.

Why am I any less than Olav? he thought. Even the great Mieszko valued me more than this exile. He gave him only Geira, the widow of a slaver from Bornholm, while I got Astrid, Dalwin's granddaughter. The daughter he shared every thought with, the one he trusted and respected. Olav began as a slave. I wonder if he has a slave mark burned into his skin? What would these commoners say if they saw the mark of disgrace?

They reached the fjord. The shipwrights were attaching the planks of the cover to a beautifully curved frame.

"Remind me, King, what was that ship with the golden weather vane called?" he asked.

"*Kanugård.* It's deserved its winter sleep."

"*Kiev!* Ah, yes, I remember, you received it as a gift from Duchess Allogia."

He knew his comment touched a nerve when Olav said no more about the gift.

"This one will be called *Crane,*" the king replied.

"It's a beautiful vessel. Enormous. Thirty benches, if I'm not mistaken."

"Yes. Sixty rowers."

"It's hot today. I'd like to swim. Is there a bay somewhere nearby?"

"Let's go." Olav latched onto the idea, and his dog led the way, as if it knew where they were headed.

They rode down the tall rocks to the bay hidden between the stones. They led the horses to the shadows of a grove. Olav's men took hold of their reins. Sigvald was first to take off his caftan, then his shirt.

"I heard that you test your men by having them jump from oar to oar," Olav said, undressing.

"Yes. I have no ship here, so I cannot demonstrate my favorite game, but if you want, we can wrestle," Sigvald suggested.

"If you'd like," Olav replied, without a shadow of a smile, and passed his caftan to one of his people.

Sigvald looked at him carefully. There was no mark on his chest. Perhaps it was on his back?

They ran into the cold water, and Sigvald dived, wet his hair, and jumped upward, shaking himself like a dog.

"Too cold?" Olav asked.

"It's perfect. Shall we begin?" He turned a full circle in the water, checking to see if Olav's men were watching. They stood on the shore with their arms crossed. He felt uneasy for a moment. Was he wise to suggest coming here and swimming? He was alone. He'd left his Jomsvikings in Nidaros. Olav had twelve armed men with him; if they wanted, they could . . . he pushed the thoughts away. He was Bolesław's messenger, they couldn't do anything to him.

Olav gave a sign and dived. Sigvald did the same, opening his eyes underwater. He saw Olav's silhouette swimming deeper into the bay and followed. He typically needed four, at most five strokes to catch a man underwater. This time, he neared Olav only after twelve. When he finally caught his leg, Tryggvason twisted around, grabbing Sigvald around the waist, pulling him deeper. The jarl knew this maneuver and knew how to free himself with a powerful kick. He was out of air then, and stretched his arms upward, rising until his head was above the water. When he surfaced, Olav's men shouted:

"Sigvald!"

He took a breath and looked around. Olav didn't appear. In that instant, he felt something tug his leg. Tryggvason was pulling him into the depths. Sigvald freed himself again with a kick, and moved to attack, but Olav was faster, swimming behind him and grabbing him around the throat. Sigvald couldn't free himself from the iron grip, he couldn't even lessen it. He thrashed and choked. Finally, he lifted an arm, signaling for a break. Olav released him immediately. Sigvald swam up and breathed again. He started to cough, but he still heard the shout from the shore.

"Who?"

"Sigvald again."

He couldn't stop coughing, and he turned in a circle once more. Olav hadn't surfaced. What the hell was going on? Hadn't he run out of air yet?

Sigvald dived quickly. For a moment, he felt dizzy, unable to spot the king in the depths. Then he saw him. Olav was swimming from below, from the bottom of the bay, with his arms outstretched like an arrow shot from a bow. Sigvald dodged Tryggvason's attack at the last minute. He sped upward, fleeing, and though it wasn't his intention, he surfaced.

"Who?"

"Sigvald, for the third time."

"The king has won!"

Sigvald slapped the water furiously. He had intended to humiliate Olav; there was no better player than him in Jom.

"Tryggvason, come out, you've won," he shouted angrily and looked around. Olav didn't surface. For a moment, the wonderful thought floated through Sigvald's mind: he had drowned. Then he saw that the people on the bank were stretching out their arms, pointing into the distance.

"There! There's our king!"

Sigvald turned to look where they were pointing and spotted Olav, far out in the bay. Sigvald didn't wait for him, he swam to the shore and got out.

"Don't worry, Jarl of Jom," a fair-haired bard said to him. "No one has ever beaten our king, and those who know how he swims never play with him. You were very brave to suggest wrestling Olav in the water."

Sigvald hissed as he wrung water out of his hair. "If you'd like," that's what Tryggvason had said when he suggested the game. *I let myself be tricked like a child.*

"Our king swims like a fish." Another nodded his head and stretched, yawning.

Sigvald saw that this man had painted fangs.

"What do they call you, berserker?" he asked, gritting his teeth.

"Varin, Jarl."

It's not him, Sigvald inwardly sighed with relief. That one was called Gerhard the Lizard, and his image had haunted Sigvald since the battle in Hjorunga Bay. The bald berserker who walked along the ship's gunwale with a bare chest in the middle of the battle, tearing his iron boys apart with his hands. This wasn't him.

"Have you been with Olav long?" Sigvald asked, calming his breath.

"From the beginning. We sailed the Dnieper together. I remember the king when I was a boy, he scared us, experienced sailors, when he leapt into the billows." Varin's eyes gleamed. "Here comes our king."

He walked past Sigvald as if they hadn't been in the middle of a conversation and ran to Olav. The chieftain ignored the insult and walked over to join them.

"Congratulations, King. I've never wrestled such an opponent before." He offered his hand.

Olav smiled and returned the gesture. He took the chain with the cross from Varin and put it back on his chest.

"Tell me, Jarl, how will we get my fiancée out of Roskilde?" he asked, wringing water from his hair.

"I sent your old friend, Geivar, who is the chieftain of the house of scouts in Jom, for me. He sailed to Roskilde under the guise of a merchant, and is meant to find a safe way to bring Tyra out from under her brother's guards' gaze. It won't be easy, but the Jomsvikings like a challenge."

"I should sail to claim my wife myself, but I know that that would ruin the grand scheme Bolesław has planned. Sven also knows many of my men; we fought in England together."

"Strange are the twists of fate." Sigvald smiled. "First I kidnapped Sven, and now I'm to kidnap his sister."

"He kidnapped the woman I wanted to marry," Olav said, anger appearing beneath the veneer of calm he wore. Sigvald finally saw the fair-haired man could be provoked.

"That's why Duke Bolesław knew you'd like the plan."

"And she?" Olav asked. "What does the woman Bolesław sees as my wife look like?"

"I haven't met her, my lord. They say she's tall, slender, and not as red-haired as Sven." He laughed wholeheartedly and pointed at his nose. "They also say she resembles me like a sister."

"Then we are endlessly turning in a circle of sisters," Olav said, reaching to take his shirt from the bard.

Yes. There it was. Sigvald saw a clear blue-black mark on Olav's shoulder blade. Like the imprint of a chicken's foot. Tryggvason pulled his shirt over his head and stepped into his trousers. Sigvald glanced at the king's men. Had they seen the slave's mark? It was impossible that they would have missed it. They'd been with him for so many years. But there wasn't a shadow of anger in any of their faces.

Olav was buckling his belt, joking with his men. Playing with the dog.

You were a slave, you bear the mark, and today you're a beloved king, served by them. Strange are the twists of fate, and who knows how many times it will still surprise us, Sigvald thought.

"King, there remains the matter of Tyra's dowry," he said, returning to their conversation as they mounted their horses. "And something for her. Because, as we are both aware, the matter is rather delicate, and we can't give Sven any reason to contest or annul the marriage. Duke Bolesław has had an idea."

"Tell me," Olav said.

"It's said you have English minters, do you not?"

52

DENMARK

Sven didn't hold it against his queen that she didn't attend the wedding of little Gyda and Eric, Jarl Haakon's son; he wished she were there, of course, but his pregnant wife's health was more important to him. She was in her second pregnancy, so she was his Sventoslava again. Harald was strong and healthy, taking his first steps, and, according to Melkorka, the second child would come any day. He had no doubts that it would also be a son. Heidi Goat, Harald's wet nurse, said:

"I can feel it in my breasts, I know that another greedy prince is coming. It's to be a boy, you'll see. The lady looks as beautiful as a sunrise and her stomach sticks out so. That means it'll be a boy."

He'd catch himself listening to the women, he, bloody Sven. He'd catch himself staring at Sventoslava, as he found himself calling her in his mind, all night like some foolish, lovestruck youngster. If only his sweet wife didn't insist on being involved in state affairs, if only she didn't always have a contradictory opinion, they'd get along wonderfully.

He pretended not to know that she was meeting with his sister, Tyra.

"We participate in mass together." She'd stamped her foot when he pointed it out. "And you, taking Thor's hammer off your neck, promised that . . ."

"All right." He waved a hand. "Leave it be. Going to church twice a year is enough for me."

"It's not enough," she announced. "Eric was a confirmed pagan, and yet he built me a chapel in Sigtuna. You, as a Christian king, should be funding churches. You can afford it."

"How many?" He grimaced.

"The more the better. At least one for every borough."

"I'm asking how much money you want."

"Am I a builder that I should know how much that costs? I'm your queen, and I'm telling you, one in Scania, one in Funen, a third in the north of Jutland, so there's more than just your enemy, the bishop Oddinkarr, in Ribe there, and our one in Roskilde needs to be enlarged. It's embarrassing. Barely larger than a boathouse."

"You'll ruin me. Why do we need so many churches? Who will go to them?"

"The faithful. We need more priests from England. I talked to Wulfric, he'd take the mission on himself."

"What mission?" He was rather taken aback by her passion.

"First, in bringing the priests over, and then converting the country to Christianity. Why do you stare so, husband? Would you prefer for the Saxons to come here to face the Danish pagans? Emperor Otto hungers to chase the pagans from Europe, look at what he's doing in Połabie. Duke Bolesław, my brother, sent Bishop Adalbert to Prussia to take God's word to their people, while you sit in Roskilde, feast with your jarls, and drink away your best years."

He had reprimanded her for this speech, they'd argued, and she didn't speak to him for days, informing him through Wilczan that if he wanted to talk to her, he should come to mass.

He went, though it was early in the morning. At first he thought he must still be drunk; he'd stayed up late the previous night, and since he couldn't spend the night with her—when she was angry she left her lynxes outside her door—he sat and drank. Then, when he was closer to the church, he thought he was still dreaming. Only once he was almost there did he rub his eyes and realize that what he saw was very much real.

Twelve of his axemen knelt outside the church. There was quite a crowd around them, there was no way to get inside, there were so many people packed together he had to push through. His wife was right in front of the altar; beside her was Gjotgar, the young jarl from Scania, and his sister, Tyra. He barely managed to make his way over to them.

When mass had finally ended, Tyra left the church without a word, surrounded by the axemen, who had risen from their knees. His wife turned to him with a smile.

"Jarl Gjotgar says that he'd be happy to contribute to the construction of a church in Scania, if King Sven cannot afford it."

"You're too late, Jarl," he grumbled. "I've already given the order. And the silver."

Gjotgar was younger than him. Tall, clean-shaven, with a lithe figure.

"Excellent," his wife announced. "Let it be in Lund. Lund in Scania. Let's go, then."

He thought that if financing a few churches would end the fights in their family life, it was a good price to pay. He hadn't known then that his wife intended to drag that much money from him continuously.

"A Christian king," she explained, "rewards his subjects when they're baptized. He gives them gifts."

"And yet, it's been the Christian kings of England giving me gifts until now," he said.

"Acknowledge the difference between a ransom and a gift, husband. They paid you because they saw a wild Viking in you, a barbarian."

"I'm not wild," he snorted.

"Then prove that to the world," she said firmly, and began to tell him what he should spend his silver on.

He gave in, since she was pregnant. No, that wasn't true, he gave in because he heard what the merchants coming from Norway were saying. "Olav Tryggvason, the Christian king." He wouldn't let the rest of the world think any less of him than they did of the other chieftain.

Year by year, he grew more convinced that Tryggvason was mocking him. Claiming power in Norway, calling himself king, it was all a challenge issued to Sven. As if that Silver Ole from years ago was saying, "And what will you do about it, my red-haired friend?" Sven felt that he should do something, but only a conquest would suffice, and his chieftains wouldn't agree to that.

"We remember the Jomsvikings' defeat at Hjorunga," they said. "And we remember that it was your father who sent them, and many of our boys sailed with them. Barely anyone returned." He wouldn't sail if the chieftains didn't give him their men; for now, Thorgils of Jellings's cunning strategy would have to be enough—surrounding Olav. He married Gyda to young Eric, sent them both to Scania, and planned his next move.

"King," Jorun interrupted his thoughts. "The merchants from York have arrived."

"Fat Edwin?" Sven guessed. Edwin knew his weakness for English weapons and he came to Roskilde twice a year.

"No. A new one. His name is Morcar, and his men call him Frog."

"What?"

"A nickname, one that our lady would say is an 'as you can see' one. His face is . . . froglike, I suppose."

They went to the port. They recognized the merchant as they approached, his bulging eyes, wide lips, flat nose. Morcar Frog.

"Why hasn't Edwin come?" Sven asked, when Frog had bowed and introduced himself.

"I hope, King, that when you see my cargo, you'll cease being interested by Edwin's offerings. There are many of us in York, and Edwin doesn't have the best blacksmiths working for him. Those masters work for Morcar Frog."

"Show me," Sven ordered.

The merchant first ordered a beautiful carved chair to be carried over for the king. When Sven was sitting comfortably, they offered him wine, and his men began to carry in the chests.

He was supposed to refrain from drinking, he'd promised himself not to make any purchases when drunk, but the wine was good, and Jorun stood behind him, watching his back and counting every sip.

They knew by the time they looked at the daggers that Frog hadn't lied. The blades were perfectly balanced, and so many hilts to choose from! From antlers and bone, decorated with silver.

It'll be expensive, Sven thought, *but worth it.*

"What do you think, Jorun?"

His friend leaned down and whispered into his ear:

"Don't drink anymore. Judge it sober."

"I'm asking if it's worth it." Sven handed him a knife.

Jorun took it.

"It fits as if it had been made for my hand," he praised, and threw it at the lid of a chest that hadn't yet been opened.

The knife turned beautifully in the air and sank into the wood as easily as if it were butter.

Jorun and the king both nodded, and the knife was placed into the empty chest that the thoughtful Frog had placed at their feet.

Then there were swords, which they spent the longest time choosing; they also spent much time with the axes, because Morcar had a few different kinds of blade. Straight, bearded axes, to be attached to a long handle, and simple ones meant for swinging, forged from extraordinarily good steel. He also had huge ones, meant to be used with two hands, with wedges to be bent and driven into the handles, creating a blade that wouldn't fall off no matter how violent the battle. There were silver cleavers decorated with an intricate English pattern, with ornaments at the base of the handle. And a treasure he was sure his lady wife would like: a murderous, wide blade with a cross carved into it. He had his axemen summoned so that they could choose for themselves. They all pointed at the cross axe.

Night began to fall, so the merchant of York ordered torches to be lit. Sven stretched.

"We'll finish tomorrow, I don't intend to buy in the dark. Value what I've chosen."

Morcar tapped a finger against a wax tablet on which he'd been making marks as Sven made his choices.

"Thirty pounds," he announced.

Sven grimaced. He didn't like this part. But he couldn't murder the merchants because then none would come to his harbors. Besides, that's not what a Christian king would do.

"Are you sure you're not mistaken?" Jorun asked Frog. "Thirty pounds is a mass of silver!"

"No, friend." Morcar's expression seemed to convey concern at the prospect of earning so much. "Thirty pounds. Though perhaps there might be another solution . . ." He scratched himself behind a large, sticking-out ear with the stylus and smacked his lips horribly.

"Speak," Jorun rushed him, knowing Sven hated sounds like that.

"Edwin has recently brought back from Roskilde a denar of silver with the writing ZVEN REX DENER on it. He bragged about it terribly, and that angered me. If I could be paid in such denars, I'd lower the price."

"You're a fool, though you have excellent blades and steel," Sven reprimanded him. "Those aren't for making purchases, they are the king's stamp. Edwin received one from me as a gift."

Morcar Frog counted.

"If King Sven gives me a jug of these denars as a gift, then I would give him everything he chose for free," he declared, smacking his lips again.

"Silence him or there'll be murder," Sven said, disgusted.

"Stop making that sound," Jorun told him.

"I beg for forgiveness." Frog bowed clumsily. "When I count, I smack my lips without thinking. I won't now, I've finished counting. I ask for the king to consider my proposal overnight. We can also throw the jug of denars on scales and see how they match up to the thirty pounds. I assure you that my proposal is fair."

Sven glanced into the chest before they left. Beautiful blades. And that cross.

In the evening, he went to see his wife, and he bumped into Melkorka as she left the queen's chambers. The two lynxes lay by the door.

"The king has no reason to go there," the cook said. "The lady will be giving birth any day."

"You've been saying that for a week," he said angrily.

"If the king knows more about giving birth," the old one snorted, "then why doesn't he do it himself? I don't stick my nose into matters of war."

"Bring me my dinner," he snapped, and regretted it immediately. She had given him burned grits the previous night, saying she had no time for cooking because she was busy with her mistress.

"Vali cooks from now on," she announced, satisfied. "My lady has said she needs me with the children. I'll be looking after Harald, and the new child, too. It's far more important than the kitchens."

When fair-haired Vali brought him dinner, quite a few people came to the hall, lured by the scent of roasted meat. Great Ulf, his wife's guardian, and little Wilczan ate, shouting:

"As good as it was in Sigtuna."

Sven, for the first time in a long time, ate until he was sated. And he didn't drink much. When Melkorka slipped across the hall, glancing into the almost empty bowls, he told her:

"I'm so glad you'll be looking after our sons."

"What if the second is a daughter?" She winked at him almost wantonly, showing a gap where her front tooth had been.

Jorun joined the king at his table, a roasted goose leg in his hand.

"We have four jugs of svens left. One weighs as much as fifteen pounds, so we're saving half the money. Considering that every merchant always asks for more, we still gain at least a quarter."

"It's worth it. The minter can make more svens later. Why are you holding on to that leg? Are you afraid someone might steal it from you?"

"Not someone, King, but you." Jorun bared his teeth and stuck the goose leg into his mouth.

They went to the harbor again in the morning. It was trade day, and there was raucous activity in all of Roskilde. Merchants dragged carts with goods, their servants setting up stalls. It was even busier in the port, as boat after boat of fishermen arrived with their catches. Morcar Frog brightened when he saw them.

"So early? Has the king had the chance to consider the suggestion of a humble merchant of York?"

"I know only impudent ones from York, confident and greedy for silver," Sven greeted him. "I have a jug of denars for you, don't worry. Jorun, show Master Frog that we're making his dreams come true. But Morcar Frog should add something for it to truly be a fair trade. Something pretty.

Christ, don't smack your lips, man! Count silently, because nothing disgusts me more than that and snoring."

"And rot," Jorun reminded him, sitting down comfortably. "Rot disgusts the king, so if you have anything rotting, don't show him."

"I'm coming," Frog said, and walked onto his ship, where he shrilly ordered his servants to carry their chests. He returned momentarily.

"Should the chest with the weapons you chose last night be delivered to the royal manor?"

"Yes."

It was so large and heavy that four men had to carry it. A girl ran down the ramp to the ship, curtsied to Sven, and ran on, toward the stalls of the craftsmen.

"My daughter," Morcar Frog said to her back, which was vanishing into the crowd.

"So pretty?" Jorun was surprised.

"I'm also surprised, and have been every day for the last seventeen years."

"She's only seventeen? She looks older." Sven had the irritating feeling he'd seen her somewhere before. Was it possible he'd slept with her in England?

"My wife says it's my daughter," the merchant continued. "And that she's so pretty because she takes after her. Maybe, the girl is as much of a miser as I am, but she doesn't speak. Not a sound. I taught her to count on a tablet, so she counts, but she doesn't speak, so don't take offense that she didn't greet you. But yes: if she takes after my wife in her looks, then she should take after me in her talk. So, I ask, how is it that she took the looks but not the voice?"

"You, Frog, had better not ask," Sven advised him with some pity. "Think about what would have happened if she had your looks and your wife's tongue?"

"Oh, that I didn't think about, King Sven. How good it is to talk to an intelligent man. And how sad that I must leave today. Will we finish by noon?"

Sven laughed, and waved a hand to encourage the merchant to get to the point.

"So what will I show you today? Please, Kris, bring me the chest worth half the kingdom. Accessories. Silver- and gold-plated brooches, English work. Eagles in flight, eagles catching prey, falcons and a bear, a fish and an eagle . . ."

The men Morcar had sent to carry the weapons had returned. They carried the chest onto the ship. Sven kept an eye out for the merchant's daughter, because he was still convinced he knew her. But he'd never slept with a girl who didn't speak at all, or at least, not that he remembered. The girl however, didn't appear. When he heard the tolling of the bell, which he had bought at the queen's request, and which his axemen rang every day at midday to praise the Lord, Sven finished picking out jewels. Morcar had graciously added them without extra charge. He took the jug of denars and carefully carried it onto his ship. He returned with a jug of wine to celebrate the successful trade, but at the same moment, Heidi, his son's wet nurse, rushed over, out of breath and panting. "My lord! My lady! My lord!"

Sven leaped up.

"Has something happened?"

"My lord . . . my lord . . ." The Goat tried to catch her breath.

"Speak or I'll kill you!"

"A son!" she exclaimed. "You have a son!"

53

❧

DENMARK

Świętosława's labor had been easy. Her water broke in the late morning. Wrzask whined, Zgrzyt stared at her with golden eyes and licked the puddle she stood in.

"Dusza, go fetch Melkorka, tell her it's begun."

When Dusza disappeared, she laughed. "Tell her . . ." She felt no pain, the contractions weren't starting. She walked slowly around the bed. Melkorka soon appeared with Goat at her side.

"Prince Harald is playing with Hildigun. The king is in the port buying weapons. It's empty in the manor. You can shout as much as you need, my lady," Melkorka informed her.

"I don't want to," a surprised Świętosława replied, watching as Goat skilfully set out the basin with water, the canvas towels, compresses, and a knife. When she looked at the knife, it began.

"Dusza," she whispered, once the first contraction had passed. "Find the Damascene knife I bought in Wolin years ago. I want it to be that knife. I always did, but Olof and Harald were both so difficult, I lost my head."

"Will you lie down, my lady?" Melkorka asked.

"Not yet. I'll be lying plenty yet."

"Wine or mead?"

"Wine. Tyra was meant to pray for a happy birth this morning. Wait!" She didn't take the wine from Melkorka because another contraction caught her. She grabbed the back of a chair, leaned over, breathed. The wave of pain receded. "Give me a drink."

The gulp of wine spread over her body warmly.

"A boy or girl," Goat squeaked. "I just can't wait. What would you prefer, my lady?"

"I have two sons, two kings," Świętosława whispered, because another contraction was coming. "I'd like a daughter, auuu . . ."

"I've fed a dozen boys and only one girl," Goat bragged. "So if you ask me, I'd prefer a daughter, too."

"My lady." There was fear in Melkorka's voice. "I worry that you aren't shouting. Forgive me for saying, but with Harald you screamed the house down. Are the contractions not too weak? The waters have broken, you have to give birth quickly or the child will be smothered."

"Weak? No. They're strong, but they don't hurt like the others . . ."

"A friend told me that her aunt also had many children like our lady," Goat interjected, gesturing wildly, "and then with one child she had painless contractions. She just stood there and gave birth and kept chatting away with my friend, but wait . . . no . . . with her mother, because they were sisters, and she had a dead baby. With no pain."

Dusza hissed, but Goat didn't realize what she'd said. Only once Melkorka tapped her forehead and made a face did Heidi see how inappropriate her story had been. She blushed, but after barely a few moments her need to fill the silence won.

"Another friend, from this village near Lejre, gave birth in her sleep. She just didn't feel a thing, didn't know she was in labor. She woke in the morning and her child, it was a son I think, was already sucking on her breast."

"You must be drunk," Melkorka scolded her. "What nonsense is this?"

Świętosława groaned, because she finally felt the pain of a contraction, as if the child had slammed its head into her pubic bone.

"Lie down, my lady, it's time," Melkorka ordered.

"Give me more wine, I'll stand for a while longer."

She drank a sip, then one more, but another contraction caused the goblet to fall from her hand. She thought she heard the clang of chains. Zgrzyt raised his head and pricked his ears.

"Dusza, open the door. Arnora is coming to us," Świętosława ordered.

The lynx walked to the door as if on command.

"No, don't let her in here," Melkorka protested. "She'll bring you bad luck, bad fate."

"I don't believe in superstitions. Give me more wine."

Świętosława stood, leaning against the chair, her side to the door. She had to turn her head to see Arnora.

"Come in," she said, seeing the woman pause in the door. "I'm inviting you. I'm in labor."

Dusza offered Arnora an arm and led her to a bench. The old woman sat, and the golden-eyed Zgrzyt lay down at her feet. Wrzask paced around Świętosława.

"If you know any interesting stories, tell us, because Heidi says whatever comes to mind. Melkorka, give her wine."

"The tales of my family are beautiful and sad," Arnora said. "One of my ancestors, disregarding the vows he gave his wife, fell in love with an ocean enchantress with whom he sired a monster . . ."

"Holy Mary," Melkorka groaned.

"Ah . . ." Świętosława took a breath to survive the contraction.

"You're right." Arnora nodded her silver head. "The story of Grendel isn't the most appropriate for a time of birth. The son you are having . . ."

"We wanted a daughter," Goat squeaked accusingly, and fell silent.

". . . has been sired from a knot . . ."

"Wine!" Świętosława shouted.

It was true. One night, they'd argued again, but at least Sven hadn't called her Gunhild, so she, to let out her anger, was tying knots in a silken kerchief. Then he asked if she'd come to him, and she agreed. Great Ulf and Jorun walked her to her husband's bedchamber. He asked if she'd give him the kerchief. He sat on the edge of the bed and, one by one, undid the knots she'd made during the feast. "If we could do the same with our problems . . ." she said. "You know, Sigrid," he replied, "when you get so angry with me, I desire you even more, but I'd like to receive just an ordinary love from you one day. Men have different fantasies. Mine is simply love." And they'd both thrown off their clothes, went to bed, and had simply made love. She wasn't taking her anger out on him, and he wasn't defeating Eric by claiming her. She'd stayed with him until morning; they fell asleep together, a thing they never did. She woke up, covered by his long red hair. Then, he helped her tie her dress, and they had breakfast together, laughing over little things. She briefly entertained the thought that she could grow to like him. But by the time evening came, they'd argued, about one thing or another, until sparks flew again, and she wouldn't let him touch her. Then, it turned out she was pregnant, and the lynxes began to guard her door.

"You give birth as the queens of old did," Arnora said. "In the past, women didn't give birth lying down. They had children standing up, or crouching, or sitting on a royal chair." She took a sip of wine and caressed the lynx's head. "It's uncomfortable on the chair," she grimaced. "It's better to stand. Well, finally it's begun. Bold lady, hold on. And one of you, on the ground to catch the child."

She was right. It began. Contraction followed contraction.

"Dusza, cut open my shirt," she asked.

"You'll be naked!" Goat said indignantly. "Ah, but there are just women here, and those boy lynxes . . ."

They all started to laugh, as if Goat's comment was the best joke in the world.

Świętosława was groaning and laughing at the same time. Melkorka lay on her back between her legs, reaching out her hands and chuckling until she cried. Arnora sipped her wine.

"I can see the head," Melkorka said. "Push, Queen, push!"

Świętosława dug her fingers into the wood. And she closed her eyes, because it was better like that. An image of her sister Astrid, who she hadn't seen for so long, came to her. It felt like a good omen.

"It's coming out! Push!"

"Conceived from a knot," Arnora called out. "Come to us."

"Push!"

"Son of the queen, come to us!"

"Push!"

"King of the north, come now!"

"Push!"

"He's flying!" Goat squeaked. "Like a bird!"

"A king is born."

"A boy, healthy and red-haired," Melkorka announced from between her legs. "Dusza, help me, because I can't get up. That's the first time I've received a child on my back."

Dusza knelt next to her and lifted up the child as much as the umbilical cord allowed.

"Turn it upside down," Arnora ordered, when Melkorka was struggling to rise. "Pat his back so he coughs it up."

Wrzask whimpered. The child made a quiet sound. Olof had screamed from the first moment. Harald had shouted as much as he could. But this one only mewled.

"Dusza, hold the child, and the queen can have the afterbirth." Arnora took over without rising from the bench.

She was right, the afterbirth splashed out onto the floor.

"Give him to me," Świętosława ordered.

"Lie down first, in case you get dizzy."

Goat offered an arm and helped her to the bed.

"Maybe the next one will be a daughter, hmm?" She sighed sadly. "Unless our queen plans to have an entire troop."

"My knife," Świętosława said, once she felt the softness of the bed under her back.

Dusza lay the child on her chest, along with the cooling placenta. Świętosława cut through the cord and hugged the child tightly. He found his way to her breast himself, and began to suck.

"How quiet," she said. "How quiet."

"A war dog doesn't bark," Arnora said, and clinked her goblet against the bench.

Goat ran off to find the king, Dusza and Melkorka began to clean the bedchamber, and Świętosława closed her eyes, holding the child close. She woke when Sven entered. Arnora was no longer there.

"A son? Really, a son?"

"See for yourself." She smiled sleepily. "The boy conceived from a knot."

"Then let's name him Cnut. From the old tongue, meaning knot, and may he tie us and our kingdoms together as tightly. May I?" he asked, reaching out for him.

"Take him," she said. "He's the queen's son, but yours, too."

She saw people crowding the doorway. Jorun, Gjotgar, Haakon, Stenkil, Great Ulf, little Wilczan, others.

The shouts of the axemen reached them from the depths of the manor.

"The queen's son! The queen's son! The queen's son!"

Sven took the child carefully and lifted him high, saying:

"This is my son, Cnut!"

And Cnut urinated on him, tensing.

Melkorka burst out laughing, Dusza too, and the rest followed suit. And Sven himself. Sven laughed so hard that tears streamed down his cheeks. Świętosława had no strength left to laugh. Little Cnut fell asleep in the air, held by his father. The chanting didn't wake him.

"The queen's son! The queen's son! The queen's son!"

Sven handed her the child back carefully, whispering:

"Rest now. I'll come back later."

At the same moment, they heard noise from within the manor. Shouts and the clamor of running soldiers. Sven grimaced.

"Quiet! My wife and son . . ."

"King!" someone from the hall shouted. "Princess Tyra has disappeared. She's gone!"

Author's Note

In Poland, Mieszko and his son, Bolesław the Brave, the first king of Poland, are very well known; they even appear on bank notes. Kids are taught about them. But nowhere in the textbooks is it mentioned that Mieszko had a daughter. When I stumbled across a mention of her in a historical source, I was surprised to learn that her history is so amazing. She is mentioned in a few serious medieval chronicles, however none of them covers her entire, rich life. They describe only moments of her life, as a wife, mother, widow, banished or returning queen.

When I folded these into a sequence of events, a remarkable, strong character was revealed, a woman whose life was full of astonishing plot twists and who defeated adversity to win in the finale. She flashed through the chronicles unnoticed; not one of the chroniclers wrote down her name. For them, her husbands, father, brother, and sons were more important. For them, those were the true warriors and rulers. The truth is different—she, Świetosława, was the one who unites the stories of them all. It was her life. Stories of the men were just a part of it, they were just episodes in her great, epic story.

With this book, I wanted to change the way of looking at that part of Polish, Scandinavian, and English history between 985 and 1017. Events in the history of several kingdoms which previously seemed to be unrelated get their guiding thread—Świetosława, the causative axis of events. Writing this novel, I wanted also to return her what the chroniclers took from her—her name.

Next year, the continuation of *The Widow Queen*, a novel under the title of *The Last Crown* comes out. New players, and a new dimension to the story. I invite you to join me on a journey from Roskilde to the lands of northern lights. From Poznań through all Bolesław's great wars. From Prague to Kiev. From Gniezno, across the mysterious Kałdus. And to England, because perhaps you know who "the queen's son" will grow up to be?

But don't think you know everything about the Bold One.

Now, it's time for *The Last Crown*.

CROWNS
HOUSES
KINGDOMS

Family Tree Key

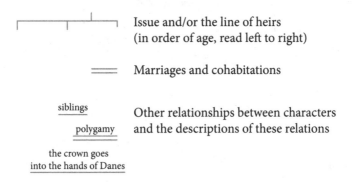

Issue and/or the line of heirs
(in order of age, read left to right)

Marriages and cohabitations

siblings

polygamy

Other relationships between characters
and the descriptions of these relations

the crown goes
into the hands of Danes

The descriptions of historical figures follow the order of
appearance on the family trees, top to bottom and left to right

POLAND

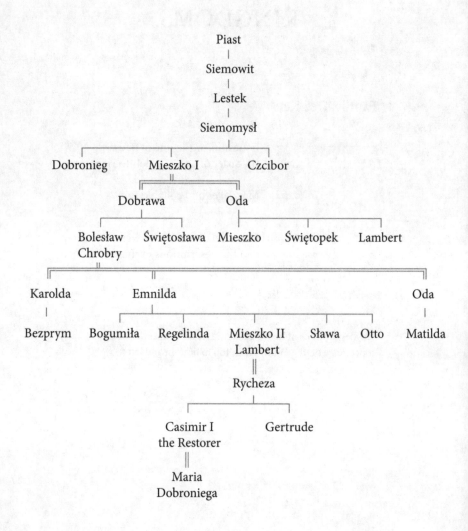

Piast
|
Siemowit
|
Lestek
|
Siemomysł

Dobronieg — Mieszko I — Czcibor

Dobrawa — Oda

Bolesław Chrobry — Świętosława — Mieszko — Świętopek — Lambert

Karolda — Emnilda — Oda

Bezprym — Bogumiła — Regelinda — Mieszko II Lambert — Sława — Otto — Matilda

Mieszko II Lambert — Rycheza

Casimir I the Restorer — Gertrude

Casimir I the Restorer — Maria Dobroniega

POLAND

PIAST   the legendery founder of the Piast dynasty

SIEMOWIT   Piast duke (9th century)

LESTEK   Piast duke (9th century)

SIEMOMYSŁ   Piast duke (until approx. 950)

DOBRONIEG   older brother of Mieszko I, died in battle against Geron and Wichman

MIESZKO I   Duke of Poland (960–992), the first baptized Polish ruler

CZCIBOR   younger brother of Mieszko I, he fought at Mieszko's side near Cedynia and against Wichman

DOBRAWA   first wife of Mieszko I, a princess from the Přemyslid dynasty

ODA   second wife of Mieszko I, daughter of margrave Ditrich from the Northern March

BOLESŁAW CHROBRY   Duke of Poland (992–1025), first king of Poland (1025), Duke of Bohemia (1003-1004) (modern Czech Republic)

ŚWIĘTOSŁAWA   known in the north as Sigrid Storråda or Sigrid the Haughty (in Denmark she was sometimes also known as Gunhild), Queen of Sweden, Denmark, Norway, and England

MIESZKO   exiled from Poland by Bolesław Chrobry after his father's death

ŚWIĘTOPEŁK   died in childhood

LAMBERT   exiled from Poland by Bolesław Chrobry after his father's death

KAROLDA   second wife of Bolesław Chrobry, from Hungary (also known as Judith)

EMNILDA   third wife of Bolesław Chrobry; a Slavic princess

ODA   fourth wife of Bolesław Chrobry, a marchioness of Meissen

BEZPRYM   Duke of Poland (1031–1034)

BOGUMIŁA   a Polish princess (the name has been chosen by the author for one of Bolesław Chrobry's unnamed daughters)

REGELINDA   a marchioness of Meissen

MIESZKO II LAMBERT   King of Poland (1025–1031)

SŁAWA   a Polish princess (the name has been chosen by the author for one of Bolesław Chrobry's unnamed daughters)

OTTO   a regional duke

MATILDA   a Polish princess

RYCHEZA   wife of Mieszko II Lambert, daughter of a prince-elector of the Electoral Palatinate, granddaughter of Otto II, niece of Otto III

CASIMIR I THE RESTORER   Duke of Poland (1034–1058)

GERTRUDE   wife of Iziaslav I, Prince of Kiev

MARIA DOBRONIEGA   wife of Casimir I the Restorer, a Kiev princess and Duchess of Poland

SWEDEN

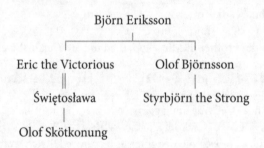

Björn Eriksson
     |

Eric the Victorious   Olof Björnsson
    || |
Świętosława   Styrbjörn the Strong
    |

Olof Skötkonung

BJÖRN ERIKSSON   King of Sweden (882–932)

ERIC THE VICTORIOUS (SEGERSÄLL)   King of Sweden alongside his brother Olof (970–95), after Olof's death he won the battle for the throne against his nephew Styrbjörn

OLOF BJÖRNSSON   King of Sweden alongside his brother Eric (970–995)

ŚWIĘTOSŁAWA   known in the north as Sigrid Storråda or Sigrid the Haughty (in Denmark she was sometimes also known as Gunhild), Queen of Sweden, Denmark, Norway, and England

STYRBJÖRN THE STRONG   a contender for the Swedish throne following his father's death, defeated by Eric at Fyrisvellir

OLOF SKÖTKONUNG   King of Sweden (995–1022), the first baptized Swedish ruler

DENMARK

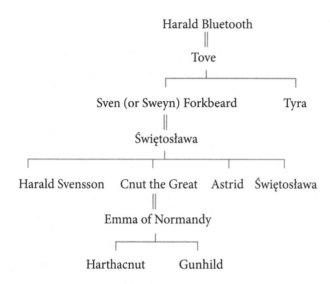

Harald Bluetooth
‖
Tove
├─────────────────────┬─────────────────────┤
Sven (or Sweyn) Forkbeard   Tyra
‖
Świętosława
├──────────────┬──────────────┬──────────────┤
Harald Svensson   Cnut the Great   Astrid   Świętosława
‖
Emma of Normandy
├──────────────┤
Harthacnut   Gunhild

HARALD BLUETOOTH King of Denmark (958–987) and Norway (974–985), the first baptized Danish ruler

TOVE a Slavic princess and Queen of Denmark, daughter of the Obotrite leader

SVEN (OR SWEYN) FORKBEARD King of Denmark (987–1014), England (1013–1014), and Norway (987–995 and 1000–1014)

TYRA Queen of Norway

ŚWIĘTOSŁAWA known in the north as Sigrid Storråda or Sigrid the Haughty (in Denmark she was sometimes also known as Gunhild), Queen of Sweden, Denmark, Norway, and England

HARALD SVENSSON regent of Denmark (1013), later King of Denmark (1014–1018)

CNUT THE GREAT King of England (1016–1035), Denmark (1018–1035), and Norway (1028–1035)

ASTRID a Danish princess

ŚWIĘTOSŁAWA a Danish princess

EMMA OF NORMANDY Queen of England, earlier wife of Ethelred the Unready

HARTHACNUT King of Denmark (1035–1042) and England (1040–1042)

GUNHILD Queen of Germany

NORWAY

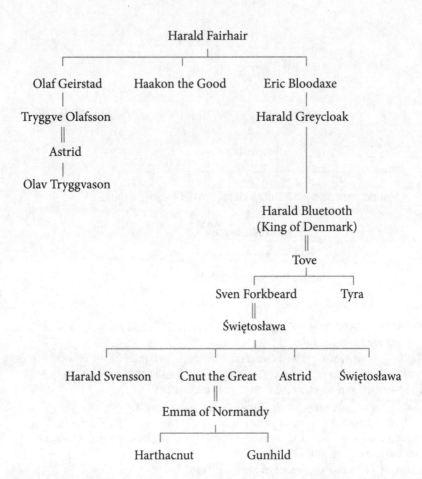

Harald Fairhair

Olaf Geirstad   Haakon the Good   Eric Bloodaxe

Tryggve Olafsson   Harald Greycloak
‖
Astrid

Olav Tryggvason

Harald Bluetooth
(King of Denmark)
‖
Tove

Sven Forkbeard   Tyra
‖
Świętosława

Harald Svensson   Cnut the Great   Astrid   Świętosława
‖
Emma of Normandy

Harthacnut   Gunhild

NORWAY

HARALD FAIRHAIR   King of Norway (872–930), he united the country and abdicated the throne to his son

OLAF GEIRSTAD   King od Vingulmark and Vestfold

Haakon the Good   King of Norway (934–960/961), son of Harald Fairhair out of wedlock, he grew up at English court and took the throne after Eric was overthrown

ERIC BLOODAXE   King of Norway (930–934) and Northumbria (947–954), his cruelty forced the nobility to bring back the son of Harald Fairhair, Haakon, from England to replace Eric

TRYGGVE OLAFSSON   King of Viken

HARALD GREYCLOAK   King of Norway (961–976)

ASTRID   Queen of Viken

OLAV TRYGGVASON   son of the King of Viken born after his father's death, King of Norway (995–1000)

HARALD BLUETOOTH   King of Denmark (958–987) and Norway (974–985), the first baptized Danish ruler. His vassal, jarl Haakon Sigurdsson, ruled Norway in his stead

TOVE   a Slavic princess and Queen of Denmark, daughter of the Obotrite leader

SVEN (OR SWEYN) FORKBEARD   King of Denmark (987–1014), England (1013–1014), and Norway (987–995 and 1000–1014)

TYRA   Queen of Norway

ŚWIĘTOSŁAWA   known in the north as Sigrid Storråda or Sigrid the Haughty (in Denmark she was sometimes also known as Gunhild), Queen of Sweden, Denmark, Norway, and England

HARALD SVENSSON   regent of Denmark (1013), later King of Denmark (1014–1018)

CNUT THE GREAT   King of England (1016–1035), Denmark (1018–1035), and Norway (1028–1035)

ASTRID   a Danish princess

ŚWIĘTOSŁAWA   a Danish princess

EMMA OF NORMANDY   Queen of England, earlier wife of Ethelred the Unready

HARTHACNUT   King of Denmark (1035–1042) and England (1040–1042)

GUNHILD   Queen of Germany

RUSSIA

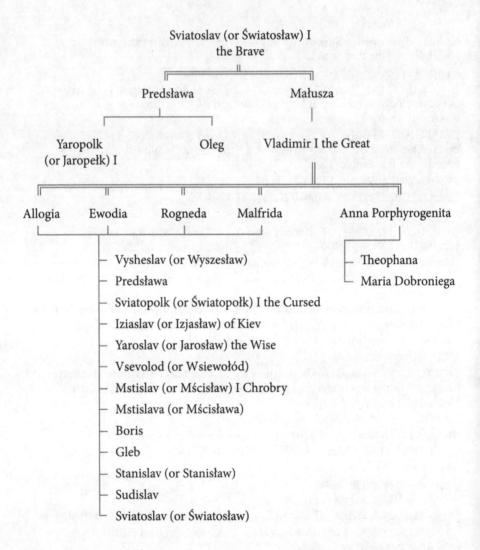

Sviatoslav (or Światosław) I
the Brave

Predsława   Małusza

Yaropolk   Oleg   Vladimir I the Great
(or Jaropełk) I

Allogia   Ewodia   Rogneda   Malfrida   Anna Porphyrogenita

- Vysheslav (or Wyszesław)   - Theophana
- Predsława   - Maria Dobroniega
- Sviatopolk (or Światopołk) I the Cursed
- Iziaslav (or Izjasław) of Kiev
- Yaroslav (or Jarosław) the Wise
- Vsevolod (or Wsiewołód)
- Mstislav (or Mścisław) I Chrobry
- Mstislava (or Mścisława)
- Boris
- Gleb
- Stanislav (or Stanisław)
- Sudislav
- Sviatoslav (or Światosław)

RUSSIA

SVIATOSLAV (OR ŚWIATOSŁAW) I THE BRAVE   Grand Prince of Kiev (945–972)

PREDSŁAWA   wife of Sviatoslav I

MAŁUSZA   concubine of Sviatoslav I

YAROPOLK (OR JAROPEŁK) I   Grand Prince of Kiev (972–978)

Oleg   ruler of the Drevlyans (969–977)

VLADIMIR I THE GREAT   Prince of Novgorod (969–977 and 979–988), Grand Prince of Kiev (978–1015), younger brother of Yaropolk

ALLOGIA   wife of Vladimir I the Great

EWODIA   wife of Vladimir I the Great

ROGNEDA   wife of Vladimir I the Great, a princess of Polotsk

MALFRIDA   wife of Vladimir I the Great

ANNA PORPHYROGENITA   wife of Vladimir I the Great, daughter of Byzantine Emperor Romanos II

VYSHESLAV (OR WYSZESŁAW)   Prince of Novgorod (988–1010)

Predsława   concubine of Bolesław Chrobry

SVIATOPOLK (OR ŚWIATOPOŁK) I THE CURSED   Prince of Turov, Grand Prince of Kiev

IZIASLAV (OR IZJASŁAW) OF KIEV   Prince of Polotsk (989–1001)

YAROSLAV (OR JAROSŁAW) THE WISE   Prince of Rostów, Grand Prince of Kiev (1016–1054, with breaks)

VSEVOLOD (OR WSIEWOŁÓD)   Prince of Volynskyi

MSTISLAV (OR MŚCISŁAW) I CHROBRY   Prince of Tmutarakan (988–1036) and Chernigov (1026–1036)

MSTISLAVA (OR MŚCISŁAWA)   Princess of Kiev, at Bolesław Chrobry's court from 1018

BORIS   the first saint of Kiev Rus' along with his brother Gleb

GLEB   the first saint of Kiev Rus' along with his brother Boris

STANISLAV (OR STANISŁAW)   Prince of Smoleńsk (988–1015)

SUDISLAV (OR SUDZISŁAW)   Prince of Pskov

SVIATOSLAV (OR ŚWIATOSŁAW)   Prince of Drevlians

THEOPHANA   wife of Novgorod posadnik Ostromir

MARIA DOBRONIEGA   wife of Casimir I the Restorer, a Kiev princess and Duchess of Poland

HOLY ROMAN EMPIRE

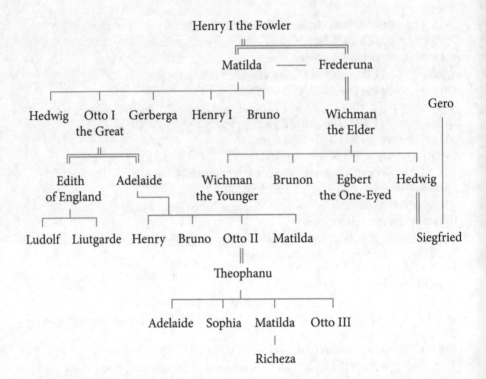

Henry I the Fowler

Matilda ——— Frederuna

Hedwig   Otto I   Gerberga   Henry I   Bruno   Wichman   Gero
          the Great   the Elder

Edith   Adelaide   Wichman   Brunon   Egbert   Hedwig
of England   the Younger   the One-Eyed

Ludolf   Liutgarde   Henry   Bruno   Otto II   Matilda   Siegfried

Theophanu

Adelaide   Sophia   Matilda   Otto III

Richeza

HOLY ROMAN EMPIRE

HENRY I THE FOWLER   Duke of Saxony (912–936), King of Germany (919–936)

MATILDA   second wife of Henry the Fowler, a saint

FREDERUNA   sister of Queen Mathilda

HEDWIG   Duchess consort of the Franks

OTTO I THE GREAT   Duke of Saxony (936–961), King of Germany (936–973) and Emperor (962–973)

GERBERGA   Duchess of Lorraine

HENRY I   Duke of Bavaria

BRUNO THE GREAT   Archbishop of Cologne, a saint

WICHMAN THE ELDER   a rebellious count from the Billung dynasty, married to Matilda

EDITH OF ENGLAND   wife of Otto I

ADELAIDE   a princess of Burgundy, second wife of Otto I

WICHMAN THE YOUNGER   a count of the Billung dynasty, he invaded the lands of Mieszko I on Geron's orders

BRUNON   bishop of Verden

EGBERT THE ONE-EYED   count of Hastfalagau

HEDWIG   wife of Siegfried, son of Margrave Geron

LUDOLF   Duke of Swabia

LIUTGARDE   Duchess of Lorraine

HENRY   died in childhood

BRUNO   died in childhood

OTTO II   King of Germany (973–983), Emperor (980–983)

MATILDA   Abbess of Quendlinburg

GERO   Margrave of the Eastern march (937–965)

THEOPHANU   a byzantine princess, regent for Otto III

SIEGFRIED   son of Margrave Geron, died in battle

ADELAIDE   Abbess in, among other places, Quendlinburg

SOPHIA   Abbes of Gandersheim and Essen

MATILDA   Countess Palatine of Lotharyngia

OTTO III   King of Germany (983–1002), Emperor (996–1002)

RICHEZA   mother of Casimir I the Restorer, daughter of Count Palatine of Lotharingia, granddaughter of Otto II, niece to Otto III

ENGLAND

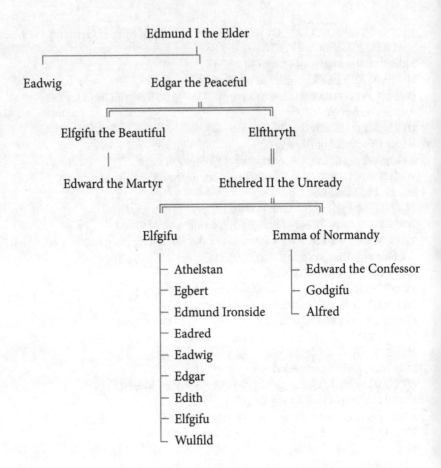

Edmund I the Elder

Eadwig   Edgar the Peaceful

Elfgifu the Beautiful   Elfthryth

Edward the Martyr   Ethelred II the Unready

Elfgifu   Emma of Normandy

- Athelstan
- Egbert
- Edmund Ironside
- Eadred
- Eadwig
- Edgar
- Edith
- Elfgifu
- Wulfild

- Edward the Confessor
- Godgifu
- Alfred

ENGLAND

EDMUND I THE ELDER   King of England (939–946)

EADWIG   King of England (955–959)

Edgar the Peaceful   King of England (959–975), Eadwig's younger brother

ELFGIFU THE BEAUTIFUL   first wife of Edgar the Peaceful, known also as the Just

ELFTHRYTH   second wife of Edgar the Peaceful, first crowned Queen of England

EDWARD THE MARTYR   King of England (975–978), a martyr and a saint

ETHELRED II THE UNREADY   King of England (978–1013 and 1014–1016)

ELFGIFU   Queen of England, daughter of the Earl of Northumbria

EMMA OF NORMANDY   Queen of England, later wife of Cnut the Great

ATHELSTAN   prince of England

EDWARD THE CONFESSOR   King of England (1042–1066)

EGBERT   prince of England

GODGIFU   Countess of Vexin, later Boulogne

EDMUND IRONSIDE   King of England (1016)

ALFRED   prince of England

EADRED   prince of England

EADWIG   prince of England

EDGAR   prince of England

ELFGIFU   Countess of Northumberland

WULFILD   Countess of East Anglia

Acknowledgments

The acknowledgments are the most pleasant chapter in any novel. They are a sign that the work has ended, and I can return to those who have helped me, not to badger them with further questions, but to honor their contributions.

The Widow Queen would not exist without Andrzej Zysk's conviction that Świętosława's story might interest American readers. And, of course, it would not have been possible if Andrzej hadn't met Lindsey Hall. Lindsey's commitment, coupled with her incredible enthusiasm, have allowed Świętosława to sail across the ocean as *The Widow Queen*, even though during her lifetime she only crossed the seas. And finally, Maya Zakrzewska-Pim; her sensitivity and imagination guided Świętosława's story across the language barrier.

While working, I always rely on the expertise of historians. Thank you to Professor of Archeology Przemysław Urbańczyk, who shares my passion for the Piast dynasty. Thank you to Doctor Jakub Morawiec, an investigator of the Scandinavian Middle Ages and a master of Icelandic sagas. I am also grateful to the excellent Polish medievalists Tomasz Jasiński and Tomasz Jurek, as well as the experts in old kitchens, hunting, riding, fashion, sailing, building, and weaponry. This book would not have been so complete without you.

Finally, I would like to thank my husband, Darek, and our daughters—Julia and Kalina. We have been on so many journeys together with Świętosława, Olav, Sven, and Eric, that the novel's heroes have become part of our family and our lives. Thank you for accepting their presence under our roof.